Here is what others are saying about
Lee and Miller's Liaden Universe novels

"I envy everyone who will have the opportunity of reading these stories for the first time.

Over a decade ago I had the privilege of reading *Agent of Change* for the first time. As I began the story I soon realized that this book marked the debut of an exceptionally talented pair of authors, and the introduction to a fascinating universe.

All too seldom an extraordinary book comes along, where the characters are so vivid that they linger in the mind long after the book is closed. And yet here we have not one marvellous book but three, each of which has its own special magic.

In *Agent of Change* you meet Val Con and Miri, each of whom is trying desperately to survive against overwhelming odds. An accidental meeting leads to an unlikely partnership, which soon becomes their only chance for survival.

In *Conflict of Honors* you meet Priscilla Delacroix y Mendoza, a woman who has been betrayed first by her own people, and then by her captain and shipmates. In desperation she accepts a berth on a Liaden freighter captained by Shan yos'Galan. There she finds friendship and learns to live up to her potential, and to confront the demons of her past.

When *Carpe Diem* begins, Val Con and Miri have been stranded on a backwater planet. With no rescue in sight, they try to blend in with the native culture and learn what it means to be life partners. Meanwhile, Shan, Priscilla and Edger are leading the search for Val Con, not realizing that their search will bring them into direct conflict with the deadly enemies who are plotting Val Con and Miri's deaths, and the destruction of Clan Korval.

These stories have it all. Adventure, intrigue, romance. Loyal friendships and hidden treachery. The authors deftly weave plot elements that stretch across the known universe, while still remaining focused on the characters who drive the action. Ultimately this is a story about extraordinary people (both human and alien) who find in friendship, loyalty, and love the strength to face overwhelming challenges.

You will want to buy two copies, one to keep and one to share with your friends."—Patricia Bray, author of Regency romances, whose work includes *An Unlikely Alliance* and *The Irish Earl.*

"I have always loved the Liaden series and think it deserves to take its rightful place among the worldbuilding triumphs of SF literature. If SF were a meritocracy, Steve and Sharon would be living in a solid gold castle twelve miles high."—Rosemary Edghill, author of *Shadow of Albion*

"The Liaden series is a delight, with people and events that surprise and captivate at every turn. Lee and Miller have taken standard space adventure fare, added a touch of romance, and turned the whole into powerful stories that are at once sly comedies of manners, exciting adventures, complex spy thrillers, and compelling tales of human drama. Best of all, they've done it in literate yet comfortably transparent prose that brings their alien worlds, societies, and people vividly to life in the reader's entranced imagination. I could not put them down, and now like any fan I am impatiently awaiting more."—Melisa Michaels, author of *Cold Iron* and *Sister to the Rain*

"The plot threads are intricately interwoven, but in due time, they all come together in a very satisfying crash-bang finale, complete with music and clinch. The plotting is careful and well-balanced. ...the great excellence lies in the relationships."—*Analog*

"The book is full of action, exotic characters, plenty of plot, and even a touch of romance. The world building is outstanding."
—*Booklist*

"Ambitiously creating a complex emotional environment, Mr. Miller and Ms. Lee pique our curiosity with an equally complicated plot development."—*Romantic Times*

"Hurray for the Liaden Universe, where women can be tough, men can be tender, and turtles can be, well, Turtles. Though not always human, Miller and Lee's characters are genuine, their conflicts are believable, and their adventures are utterly breathtaking."—Maureen Tan, author of *Run Jane Run*

"Val Con and Miri are the most romantic couple in SF!"—Susan Krinard, author of *Touch of the Wolf*

"The Liaden books have it all—action, adventure, romance, wit, and a story that keeps getting better. Sharon Lee and Steve Miller deserve the many accolades they've received for this great series. It's the kind of epic science fantasy that I love, and that this field needs more of—and will get, because Lee and Miller are now writing the rest of the series. Read it now!"—Kate Elliott, author of *King's Dragon* and the *Crown of Stars* series

Partners in Necessity

by

Sharon Lee and Steve Miller

Meisha Merlin Publishing, Inc.
Atlanta, GA

Conflict of Honors Copyright © 1988 by Steve Miller and Sharon Lee

Agent of Change Copyright © 1988 by Steve Miller and Sharon Lee

Carpe Diem Copyright © 1989 by Steve Miller and Sharon Lee
Partners in Necessity Copyright © 2000 by Sharon Lee and Steve Miller

This book is printed on an acid-free and buffered paper that meets the NISO standard ANSI/NISO Z39.48-1992, Permanence of Paper for Publications and Documents in Libraries and Archives.

PARTNERS IN NECESSITY

Published by Meisha Merlin Publishing, Inc.
PO Box 7
Decatur, GA   30031

Editing & interior layout by Stephen Pagel
Copyediting & proofreading by Teddi Stransky
Cover art by Michael Herring
Cover design by Neil Seltzer

ISBN: Soft cover 1-59222-118-1
ISBN 13: 978-1-59222-118-9

http://www.MeishaMerlin.com

Second MM Publishing edition, first printing: September 2006

Printed in Canada
0 9 8 7 6 5 4 3 2 1

TABLE OF CONTENTS

AN INTRODUCTION TO
PARTNERS IN NECESSITY

Conflict of Honors is the first one of the Liaden series that I read. And immediately asked my editor, Shelly Shapiro, at Del Rey if there were any more. She sent me *Agent of Change,* and *Carpe Diem* when that saw print. I badgered her for more of the same by Steve Miller and Sharon Lee. They became a trilogy on my 'comfort' shelf: the books I *have* to have because I liked them so much and have to reread them frequently. These have been reread so often the covers are cracking. (By the way, I have two sets in case *someone* might have the audacity to abscond with one.)

I don't have many books in the 'comfort' category: (*Kim* and *Islandia* have top priority.) And I don't know why this trilogy is so satisfying to reread. It just is! If I'm depressed, the adventures of Val Con and Miri cheer me up and I can snarl out frustration against the devious Department that had taken Val's music from him and turned him into 'other'. I can delight in Shan's philanthropy and cheer that Priscilla has found him at last despite her exile. I won't spoil your delight in these adventures by mentioning more of the delights in store for a new reader. Let it suffice that they *are* my 'comfort books'.

Therefore, when I finally found out where I could badger Steve and Sharon to continue writing about the Liaden worlds, I did so. To my delight, I discovered my search is not in vain. The authors kindly sent me *Plan B* by email, which I printed out and devoured. (I also wondered about an absence of a scene that I very much wanted to see written out...a writer does this from time to time, *knows* that there should be a scene written.) I was sent the scenes, which had been deleted, in the misguided notion that the book was too long. *Nothing* about the Liadens, Val Con, Miri, Shan and Priscilla, Gordon, Nova, Mr. dea'Gauss, Clan Korval, the Edger and his Clan of knife making 'turtles'—the whole gang of them—could be too long. In fact, there still isn't quite enough to satisfy this devoted reader.

Considering the state of my copies, I was delighted to learn that the astute Meisha Merlin Publishing Company was bringing out *Partners in Necessity*, an omnibus of my special 'comfort' books. I highly recommend that you start with this volume and then go on to *Plan B* and whatever other delights Steve Miller and Sharon Lee have in store for us in the Liaden Universe.

Anne McCaffrey
Dragonhold-Underhill 1999

Partners in Necessity

by

Sharon Lee and Steve Miller

CONFLICT OF HONORS

MAIDENSTAIRS PLAZA
LOCAL YEAR 1002
STANDARD 1375

Eight Chants past Midsong: twilight.

In the plaza around Maidenstairs a crowd began to gather: men and women in brightly colored work clothes; here and there the sapphire or silver flutter of Circle robes.

The last echo of Eighthchant faded from the blank walls of Circle House, and the crowd quieted expectantly.

In a thin pass-street halfway down the plaza, a slim figure stirred. She adjusted the cord of the bag over her shoulder, but her eyes were fixed on Maidenstairs, where two of the Inmost Circle stood.

The shorter of the two raised her arms, calling for silence. The crowd held its breath, while across the plaza a dust devil swirled to life. The watcher in the by-street shivered, hunching closer to the wall.

"We are gathered," cried the larger of the two upon the stairs, "to commend to the Mother the spirit of our sister, our daughter, our friend. For there is gone from us this day the one called Moonhawk." He raised his arms as the other lowered hers to intone the second part of the ritual.

"Do not grieve, for Moonhawk is gathered into the care of She who is Mother of us all, who will instruct and make her ready for her next stay among us. Rejoice, indeed, and be made glad by the fortune of our sister Moonhawk, called so soon to the Mother's side."

The crowd spoke a faint "Ollee," and the shorter Witch continued, her voice taking on the mesmerizing quality appropriate to the speaking of strong magic.

"Gone to the Mother, to learn and to grow, Moonhawk walks among us no more. For the span of a full lifetime shall she sit at the feet of the Mother, absorbing the glory, seen by us no more. In this Wheel-turn none shall see Moonhawk again. She is gone. So mote it be."

"So mote it be," echoed the larger speaker.

"So mote it be," the crowd cried, full-voiced and on familiar ground.

The slim watcher said nothing at all, though she ducked a little farther back into the byway. The dust devil found her there and made momentary sport of her newly shorn hair before going in search of other amusements.

A tall woman at the edge of the crowd made a sharp movement, quickly arrested. The watcher leaned forward, lips shaping a word: *Mother.* She dropped back, the word unspoken.

It was useless. Moonhawk was dead, by order of she who was Moonhawk's mother during this turn of the Wheel. The funeral pyre of her possessions had been ignited at Midsong while the mother looked on with icy face and sand-dry eyes. The watcher had been there, too. She had cried—perhaps enough for the mother, as well. But there were no tears now.

In the bag over her shoulder were such belongings as she had been able to bring away from her cell in the Maidens' wing of Circle House. The clothes she wore were bought in a secondhand store near the river: a dark, soft shirt with too-long sleeves that chafed nipples unused to confinement; skintight leggings, also dark, except for the light patch at the right knee; and outworlder boots with worn heels. The earrings were her own, set in place years ago by old hands trembling with pride of her. The seven silver bracelets in the pack were not hers. In the shirt's sleeve pocket was a single coin: a Terran tenbit.

The two of the Inmost Circle left the stairs; the crowd fragmented and grew louder. The watcher quietly faded down the skinny by-street, trying to form some less desperate plan for the future.

Moonhawk is dead. So mote it be.

At the end of the by-street the watcher turned left, toward a distant reddish glow.

You might, she thought to herself diffidently, go to the Silent Sisters at Caleitha. They won't ask your name, or where you're from, or why you've come. You can stay with them, never speaking, never leaving the Sisterhouse, never touching another human being...

"I'd rather be dead!" she snapped at the night, at herself—and began to laugh.

The sound was horrible in her ears: jagged, unnatural. She knotted her fingers in the ridiculous mop of curls, yanking until tears came to replace the awful laughter. Then she continued on her way, the rosy glow ever brighter before her.

SHIPYEAR 32
TRIPDAY 148
SECOND SHIFT
10.30 HOURS

"Liadens! Gods-benighted, smooth-faced lying sons and daughters of *curs!*"

A crumpled wad of clothing was thrown toward the gapemouthed duffel with more passion than accuracy. From her station by the cot, Priscilla fielded it and gently dropped it in the bag. This act failed to draw Shelly's usual comments about Priscilla's wasted speed and talent.

"Miserable, stinking half bit of a ship!" Shelly continued at the top of her range, which was considerable. "One shift on, one shift off; Terrans to the back, *please,* and mind your words when you're speaking to a Liaden! Fines for this, fines for that...no damn shore leave, no damn privacy, nothing to do but work your shift, sleep your shift, work your shift...*hell!*"

She shoved the last of her clothing ruthlessly into the duffel, slammed a box of booktapes on top, and sealed the carryall with a violence that made Priscilla wince.

"First mate's a crook; second mate's a rounder...here!" She slapped a thick buff envelope into Priscilla's hand.

The younger woman blinked. "What's this?"

"Copy of my contract and the buy-out fee—in cantra, as specified. Think I'm gonna let either the first or the second get their paws on it? Cleaned me out good and proper, it has. But no savings and no job is better than one more port o' call on this tub, and that I'll swear to!" She paused and leaned toward the other woman, punctuating her points with stabs of a long forefinger. "You give that envelope to the Trader, girl-o, and let 'im know I'm gone. You got the sense I think you got, you'll hand in your own with it."

Priscilla shook her head. "I don't have the buy-out, Shelly."

"But you'd go if you did, eh?" The big woman sighed. "Well, you're forewarned, at least. Can you last 'til the run's over, girl?"

"It's only another six months, Standard." She touched the other woman's arm. "I'll be fine."

"Hmmph." Shelly shouldered her bag and took the two strides necessary to get her from cot to door. In the hall, she turned again. "Take care of yourself, then, girl-o. Sorry we didn't meet in better times."

"Take care, Shelly," Priscilla responded. It seemed that she was hovering on the edge of something else, but the other woman had turned and was stomping off, shoulders rounded and head bent in mute protest of the short ceiling.

Priscilla turned in the opposite direction—toward the Trader's room—her own head slightly bent. She was not tall as Terrans went, and the ceiling was a good three inches above her curls; there just seemed something about *Daxflan* that demanded bowed heads.

Nonsense, she told herself firmly, rounding the corner by the shuttlebay.

But it wasn't nonsense. All that Shelly had said was true—and more. To be Terran was to be a second-class citizen on *Daxflan,* with quarters beyond the cargo holds and meals served half-cold in a cafeteria rigged out of what had once been a storage pod. The Trader didn't speak Terran at all, though the captain had a few words, and issued his orders in abrupt Trade unburdened with such niceties as "please" and "thank you."

Priscilla sighed. She had served with Liadens on other trade ships, though never on a Liaden ship. She wondered if conditions were the same on all of them. Her thoughts went back to Shelly, who had sworn she would never serve on another Liaden ship; though Shelly had done okay until the Healer had left two ports ago, to be replaced by a simple robotic medkit. That move had been called temporary. "More Liaden lies!" she had said. "They're liars. *All* liars!"

The first mate was a crook and the second a rounder—whatever, Priscilla amended, a rounder was. Liaden and Terran, respectively, and as alike as if the same mother had borne them.

Perhaps, Priscilla thought, the Trader only hired a certain type of person to serve him. She wondered what that said about Priscilla Mendoza, so eager for a berth as cargo master that she had not stopped first to look about her. Yet she *had* been eager. In a mere ten years she had gone from Food Service Technician—which meant little more than scullery maid—to General Crew, and then into cargo handling. Among her goals was a pilot's certificate, though certainly there was no hope for furthering *that* aim while on *Daxflan.*

The Trader's room was locked; no voice bade her enter when she laid her hand against the plate. So, then. She shook her head as the 1100 bell rang. She would be short of sleep *this* shift.

The captain, she decided, would do as well. She continued down the hall toward the bridge, then paused, hearing voices to her right—a man's, raised in outrage; a woman's, soothing.

Priscilla turned her steps in that direction, Shelly's envelope heavy in her hand.

The door to the Liaden lounge was open. Heedless, Sav Rid Olanek flung the paper at his cousin, Captain Chelsa yo'Vaade.

"Denied!" he cried, the High Tongue crackling with rage. "They dare! When all my life I have left this finger free to bear only the ring of a Master of Trade!" He waved gem-laden fingers also at Chelsa, who blinked, automatically cataloging Line-gem, school-gems, Clan-gem among the glittering array of others less important to Sav Rid's melant'i.

"They say you might reapply, cousin," she offered hesitantly. "You need only wait a Standard."

"Bah!" Sav Rid cried, as she might have known he would. "Reapply? *That* for their reapplication!" He snatched the letter back and rent it twice before flinging the pieces away. "They think me unworthy? They shall be schooled. We shall show them, *Daxflan* and I, how it is a *true* master of the craft goes about his business!" He turned then, eyes catching on the shadow at the door.

"You, there!" he snapped in Trade, crossing the room in four of his short strides. "What is it, Mendoza?"

Priscilla bowed, offering the envelope. "I did not wish to disturb you, sir," she replied in Trade, "but Shelly van Whitkin bade me give you this."

"So." He tore the envelope open, glanced at the paper with no great interest, and fingered the coin idly before slipping it into his belt.

One cantra, Priscilla saw, her stomach sinking. A sum so far beyond her resources that it was absurd to consider following Shelly's example. She might, she supposed, jump ship, but the thought of the dishonor attached to such an action cramped her stomach further.

"You may go, Mendoza," the Trader told her, and she bowed again before turning away. As she stepped into the hallway, she heard him address another comment in High Liaden to Captain yo'Vaade, something about having made a cantra and lost a big mouth to feed.

SHIPYEAR 32
TRIPDAY 151
FIRST SHIFT
1.30 HOURS

Daxflan was two days out of Alcyone, and dinner looked terrible. Cargo Master Mendoza meekly accepted her tray and carried it into the crowded, steamy Terran mess hall. Peripheral vision showed Second Mate Dagmar Collier waving to her from a table near the door. Face averted, Priscilla moved to a newly vacated corner table. Self-preservation would not allow her to sit with her back to the noisy room, but the temptation was strong.

She frowned at the greasy soup and put her spoon down, then picked up the chipped plastic mug. Grinning, she sipped the tepid coffeetoot, recalling that Shelly had never sat down to a meal on *Daxflan* without indulging in a rant, the salient point of which was always the economic infeasibility of a tradeship serving 'toot instead of the real bean.

It had been Shelly's belief that serving 'toot to the Terrans was another deliberate snipe from the Trader. However, Priscilla had overheard Liaden crew members complaining that the beverage called tea aboard *Daxflan* had never seen Solcintra. Shelly had only a spacer's handful of Liaden, High or Low, and had just shaken her head at Priscilla's theory that perhaps *none* of the crew was treated very well.

Resolutely, the cargo master put the 'toot from her and picked up her spoon. Horrible as it looked, the soup was dinner and she would get no better; the alternative was the sodden breadroll and the sticky lump of cheese she knew from experience to be inedible to the point of nausea. It would have to be the soup.

Taking a gelid spoonful, Priscilla found her mind turning, as it had these last two shifts, back to the containers they had taken on at Alcyone Prime. Sealed cargo. Nothing unusual in that; she had the manifests listing the items the sealed hold contained, their weights and distributions. All according to book. And yet there was something...

With a scrape and a *thump!* the second mate was with her. Priscilla jumped, splashing greasy soup on her sleeve. Clamping her teeth, she patiently daubed at the spot, avoiding Dagmar's eyes. The second grinned and leaned back in the chair, flinging her legs out before her.

"Scare you, Prissy?"

Priscilla's slim shoulders stiffened. Dagmar's grin widened.

"I was thinking." There was no emotion in the cargo master's soft, level voice.

"That's our Prissy," Dagmar said indulgently. "Always thinking." She leaned across the tiny table and touched the back of a slender hand, delighting in the slight withdrawal. "What about after dinner, though? What say I bring along something to keep you from thinking, and we have fun?"

"I'm sorry," Priscilla said, hoping she sounded like it, "but the distribution charts are behind. I'm going to have to spend some of this off-shift getting caught up."

Dagmar shook her head, secretly pleased at Prissy's seemingly endless supply of excuses. The game had run three months now. Dagmar considered the quarry worthy of an extended pursuit. It might be easier if the girl weren't so serious about her work—and so popular with the crew. The younger woman wasn't much on getting high or sleeping around. But Dagmar knew that Priscilla would have to relax and reveal a weak point one day—and when she finally did catch Prissy out, the spoils would be that much sweeter.

"That's all right," she said consolingly. "You work as hard as you want. Good to see that in a new hire. And at the end of the run—if you do *real* good—I'll give you a reward." She narrowed her eyes a bit, looking for signs of distress on the other woman's face. She detected none and played her ace.

"A reward," she repeated, and reached across the table to take one cool, slim hand in hers. "How 'bout...at the end of the run you and me go off—just us two—and have a Hundred Hours together? Huh? A hundred hours of loving and cuddling and fancy food and drink. Don't that sound nice?"

It did, Priscilla admitted to herself. Present company excluded.

She withdrew her hand carefully. "You're very generous," she murmured, "but I'm not—"

The second recaptured her hand. "Think it over. Got plenty of time." She squeezed the hand until she heard knuckles crack and then released it. "Nice, long fingers. You ought to wear rings." She smiled again, tipping her own hand so that light glittered sullenly across the dirty gems worn three deep on each fat finger. "I'll buy you a ring," she finished softly, "after our Hundred Hours."

Priscilla drew a deep breath, trying to drown a sudden, flaring urge to mayhem. She stood.

"Going so soon?"

The cargo master nodded. "Those calculations are going to take awhile." She fled the mess hall.

A *ring!* Holy Mother! Priscilla became aware that she was breathing hard, nearly running down the lowering corridor. She slowed, willed her hands to unclench at her side, and continued with outward serenity toward her quarters.

Inwardly she still raged. Day after day of the second's pursuit was bad enough, though at least *she* could be put off with excuses, but only this past shift had First Mate Pimm tel'Jadis come to her in the master's cubicle, and the less thought of *that* encounter the better.

Caught between the two of them, powerful as they were, with neither the Trader nor the captain willing to take the part of a Terran against a Liaden, or of one Terran against another...Priscilla slapped the palmplate and thumbed the light switch to HIGH before entering her tiny cabin.

The room was empty.

Of course, she jeered at herself, stepping in and locking the door. She leaned her head against the door frame and closed her eyes briefly. Stress, poor food, little sleep—she was getting nervous, fanciful. Surely the first mate would not secret himself in her cabin and wait to surprise her.

Not yet.

"*Damn!*" she said violently. She moved to the cramped 'fresher cubicle. Stripping off her clothes, she shoved them into the cleanbot and twisted the dial to SUPERCLEAN. More carefully, she removed the silver and opal drops from her ears and put them on the shelf under the short mirror. Then she dialed the unit temp to HOT, the intensity to NEEDLE, and stepped under the deluge.

SHIPYEAR 32
TRIPDAY 152
THIRD SHIFT
19.45 HOURS

Priscilla rubbed dry eyes and sat back, frowning at the screen. She was right. At first, she had mistrusted her equations and so rechecked everything a second time, and a third. There was no doubt. She wondered what she was going to do now. Contraband drugs were certainly nothing she wanted to be involved with—and as cargo master, she had signed for them!

Shaking her head, she leaned over the keyboard again.

First, she told herself, you're going to seal this data under the cargo master's "Confidential" code. Then you're going to take a cold needle shower and hope it'll make up for a sleepless night— you're on duty in an hour! She rose and stretched.

She would make no decisions until she had had at least a shift's sleep. It was important not to make a mistake.

"The following personnel," blared the speaker over the door, "will report to Shuttlebay Two at 20.00 hours: Second Mate Dagmar Collier, Pilot Bern dea'Maan, Cargo Master Priscilla Mendoza, Cargo-hand Tailly Zeld, Cargo-hand Nik Laz Galradin."

"What?" Priscilla demanded, spinning to stare at the speaker. Bay 2 at 20.00 hours? That was less than ten minutes from now!

She spun back to the desk and cleared the screen, then spun again to rake her gaze around the closet-sized room, tallying her meager possessions. There was nothing she would need on Jankalim here. Smoothing her hands over her hair, she left the room.

It was only as she was striding toward Bay 2 that it occurred to her to wonder why she was needed at all. Jankalim was a drop-only, the sort of thing most commonly handled by the first or second and a couple of hands.

Maybe there had been a mistake? There had been no trip worldside listed on her schedule last shift, of that she was certain. Come to think of it, it was *silly* to send the cargo master on a trip like this one. Almost as silly as sending the Trader.

She rounded the corner into the bay corridor at a spanking pace and brought herself up sharply to avoid walking over the small man just ahead.

Trader Olanek turned his head and inclined it in unsmiling recognition. "Mendoza. Punctual, as always." The words were in Trade and heavily accented.

"Thank you, sir," she said, politely shortening her stride to match his. Somehow, she had never managed to inform the Trader that she had limited fluency in his language. She glanced at his profile and shrugged mentally. The Trader's temper was legend on *Daxflan,* but he seemed to be in as amiable mood as she had ever seen him.

"Are *you* going worldside, sir?" she ventured respectfully.

"Of course I am going worldside, Mendoza. Why else should I be here?"

Priscilla ignored the irritation in his voice and plunged on. "Has there been a change in schedule, then? My last information was that Jankalim is only a drop point. If we're going to take cargo on—"

"I must therefore assume, Mendoza," the Trader cut in, clearly irritated, "that your information is not complete."

Priscilla bit her lip. It was folly to goad him further. She inclined her head and dropped back to allow him to procede her into the shuttle. Then, sighing, she slipped into the first unoccupied seat, eyelids dropping. Half an hour, ship to world. At least she would get a nap.

"Hi there, Prissy," an unwelcome voice said in her ear. "You're not asleep, are you?" A hand was placed high on her thigh.

Gritting her teeth, Priscilla opened her eyes and sat up straight.

Jankalim possessed one spaceport, situated on the easternmost tip of the southernmost continent, within a stone's throw of the planetary sea and the edge of the world's second city.

As spaceports went, this one was subaverage, Priscilla decided, watching Tailly and Nik Laz unload the few containers and pallets that represented their reason for stopping here at all. The spaceport boasted three hot-pads for in-system ships, four shuttle cradles, and a double-dozen steel warehouses. All the pads were empty, though there was a surprisingly well-kept shuttle in the end cradle.

She glanced at the corrugated metal building to her right. A lopsided sign proclaimed it to be the port master's office. Trader Olanek had disappeared within it immediately upon setdown, Dagmar trailing behind like a double-sized shadow.

As if summoned by the thought, the second appeared in the doorway, jerking her head as she crossed the yard. "Gimme a hand, willya, Prissy? Trader wants a couple boxes from that end house. Ought to be able to get 'em fine between us."

Raising her eyebrows, Priscilla looked back at burly Tailly and miniature Nik Laz, who were just setting the last pallet in place.

"Aah, give 'em a break, Prissy," Dagmar growled. "They worked plenty hard already."

Kindness was uncharacteristic of the second mate. Probably the woman wanted a little privacy to press her suit further. Trapped without a reasonable excuse, Priscilla nodded and fell into step beside her, keeping a cautious distance between them.

The lights came up as they entered the first warehouse. Dagmar turned confidently to the right; Priscilla, a few steps behind, let her lead the way. Several more turns led them to a musty-smelling hall, somewhat dimmer than the previous corridors, flanked with blank metal doors.

Priscilla wondered what the Trader could possibly want from a section of warehouse that was clearly abandoned, then she shrugged. She was cargo master. It was her job to stow what the Trader contracted for.

It just would have been nice, she stormed to herself, if the Trader had seen fit to inform his cargo master that he expected to take on goods at Jankalim.

Dagmar moved slowly down the hallway—counting doors, Priscilla thought—then stopped and slid a card into a doorslot.

The light in the frame lit, but nothing else happened. Dagmar grunted. "You're real good with computers. You try it."

The tone of voice made Priscilla uneasy. She took the card, inserted it, and was rewarded with both a light and a clicking noise from within.

Dagmar pushed at the door, then grunted again. "Damn thing's stuck. Come 'round here, Prissy—that's right. Now, I'm gonna pull back on the door an' get it started in the track. When it starts to slide, you get yourself between an' *push*, okay?"

"Okay."

Dagmar laid her hands against the door and exerted force. For a moment it looked as if the mechanism would resist. Then Priscilla saw a crack appear. She slipped her fingers into the slender opening as the crack began to widen, adding her own pressure to the enterprise. The gap widened farther. She slid her body into the opening and shoved.

As she pushed, there was a shadowy movement behind her, and she heard Dagmar say, "Can't be all that smart now, can ya, Prissy?" Then something clipped her behind the ear, and she crumpled sideways, tasting salt.

JANKALIM SPACEPORT
LOCAL YEAR 209

There was a window high in the sidewall, and that was good. The door was locked from the outside, and that was bad. Her head ached, and that, she decided, was worst of all. Neither the soreness of her face nor the pain in her shoulder came near it, though the throb of her ribs ran a close second.

Moving with extreme care, Priscilla went to the window and stood on tiptoe, craning. No way out there: the pane was solid blast-glass, and even had she the means to break it, the opening itself was too small even for her lanky frame.

Outside, the well-kept shuttle was still in its ratty cradle.

Daxflan's shuttle was gone.

Left me, she thought through the fog of dizziness and pain. And then, with a gasp that sent knifing fire down her side, the reality hit her. *Left me! Here,* with the door locked and no way out and *how* could they have left me? Surely the Trader would have missed me...or if not me—but how could they *not* have missed me! Tailly, Nik Laz, Bern...how could they have *left*...

She took a deep, deliberate breath, ignoring the pain.

"I will not," she informed the room austerely, "sanction hysterics."

Her voice came back to her from the empty walls, deep and oddly comforting. Priscilla closed her eyes and concentrated on breathing until the panic stilled.

I have to get out, she told herself, forming the thought carefully.

She surveyed her prison. Empty. Dustless. Dim. What light there was came from the window. She would have to do whatever she did before day failed.

Leaning against the wall, she went through her pockets: stylus, pad of paper, ID, strapping tape, comb, two Terran wholebits, magnetic ruler, penknife, calculator—nothing heavy enough to break a triple-thick window or strong enough to jimmy the door.

She took another look outside. The yard was as empty as the room she stood in. She settled her shoulders against the wall and considered her resources.

Stylus. Not too likely. It went back into her pocket. Likewise the paper; also comb, ID, and money.

Tape? She kept it out for the time being. Penknife? Why not? Ruler? No— Yes. Yes, wait a minute—magnets...lock...jimmy the *lock!*

She knelt at the door to get the cardslot at eye level, then peered cautiously within. It just might be possible...

Sitting back on her heels, she unrolled the ruler and tried unsuccessfully to pry the thin rectangular magnets off with her fingers. The penknife did the trick—fifteen minutes later she had four flat magnets, each with its own long tail of tape, lined up on the door next to the cardslot.

With the tip of the knife she inserted them, one at a time, thanking the Goddess that there were only four contacts within the mechanism and that no one had expected the place to be used as a jail.

The last magnet was affixed. She withdrew the knife, holding her breath...but nothing happened.

Wrong combination, she told herself, and patiently inserted the knife point again, reversing the polarity of the magnet on the extreme left.

She had worked through twelve combinations, and multicolored spots were shimmering before her eyes, when there was a soft click. Hardly daring to breathe, she looked up.

The light over the door frame was lit.

She scrambled to her feet, folding the knife automatically and dropping it into her pocket. Leaning forward, she put her hands against the panel and prepared to push—but suddenly the door slid open.

Priscilla twisted, gasping, and regained her balance before the man on the other side extended a hand to grab her.

"Hold there, now." The grip on her arm changed. "Who by hell are *you?*"

"Priscilla Mendoza—cargo master on *Daxflan.*"

"That's so, is it?" He eyed her. "Bit beyond yer territory, would say?"

"Without a doubt." She gritted her teeth against the pain and fought to keep the edge out of her voice. "There's been a—misunderstanding. I'm sure Trader Olanek will vouch for me. He was with the port master..."

"That be so," the man agreed. "Then he an' his went off. Nothin' was said about a missin' mate. Happen a Trader would notice his cargo master wasn't to hand, would say?"

She sighed. "I don't really think I'm prepared to say any such thing. Are you going to let me out of here, or aren't you?"

"Now there, mistress, don't be chivin' me. Happen you'll have a better tale for Master Farley." He stepped back, keeping a firm hold on her arm. "We'll be walking this way now."

Priscilla clamped her jaw and matched his stride firmly.

The glare of sunshine made her gasp with quadrupled pain. She was abruptly thankful for the man's bruising hold—without his support she would have fallen.

Sunlight gave way to shadow. Her captor paused and laid his hand against a plate, and a door slid open. Obedient to his tug, Priscilla stepped into an echoing cavern of a room. Four dark terminals sat at intervals on the empty counter; the ship-board suspended above displayed one row of tired amber letters, brilliant in the gloom: DUTIFUL PASSAGE SOLCINTRA LIAD.

She stopped, staring at the board. A Liaden ship, surely, but...dear Goddess, they *had* gone! They had left orbit, left the sector, without her. She had been abandoned deliberately on this quarter-bit world!

"Come along, mistress, we've not got all the day." The man jerked hard on her arm, and Priscilla went with him, blankly.

She should be angry, she knew, but the various pains and shocks seemed to cancel emotion. Her overwhelming desire was for sleep— but no. There was the port master to see, and an explanation to be made. She would need money—a job. Two Terran wholebits was hardly a fortune, no matter how backward the world.

"In here, mistress." He gave another tug. Priscilla ground her teeth against a snapped retort and obeyed.

Port Master Farley was a plump man with a dejected yellow mustache and apologetic blue eyes. He blinked at Priscilla and turned toward her captor. "Well, now, Liam. What have you here?"

The man holding her renewed his grip and straightened, giving the impression of having brought his heels smartly together. "Computer reported some tamperin' with the lock on door triple-ay, corridor seven, house one—one o' the empty sections, Master Farley."

The port master nodded.

"Went to check things out—thinkin' it'll be a malfunction, you understand." He yanked Priscilla forward. "Found this one on the *inside*. Tells the tale o' bein' Priscilla Mendoza, cargo master on *Daxflan* as just left us."

The port master blinked again. "But what were you doing in the warehouse, lass? Especially along that way—it's been empty for years."

Priscilla took a deep breath. The pain in her side was less, she noted, down to a persistent dull ache.

"Trader Olanek and Second Mate Collier came into this building to speak with you, sir," she said. "I was outside, supervising the unloading. After a time, the second mate came out and asked me to go with her to the warehouse. She said the Trader wanted something out of one of the rooms. When we arrived, she put a card in the lock and asked me to help her push the door open, since it was stuck—"

"Like as not," Liam muttered. "Damn thing hasn't been opened this tenyear."

"And then," Priscilla concluded, "she hit me over the head and left me there. When I came to, I tried to gimmick the lock with a couple magnets off my ruler."

Master Farley was staring. "Hit you over the head and left you? And you her mate? Why would she do such a thing?"

"How do *I* know?" Priscilla snapped, then dredged up a painful smile. "Look, do you mind if I sit down? My head *does* hurt."

"Surely, surely." He looked a little flustered. "Liam..."

The warehouseman loosed her with reluctance and placed the chair close to the desk before taking up a position directly behind it. She sat carefully, hands curled around the plastic armrests.

"Thank you."

"You're welcome." Master Farley sighed, drummed his fingers on the rubbed steel top of his desk, screwed his eyes shut, and opened them again. "You'll be having some ID on you, of course."

She nodded, earning a flash of pain and a renewed flurry of dots. The hand that held her identification out trembled, she noted, and she was aware of a flicker of anger.

Master Farley took the packet and fed the cards one by one into the unit beside his desk. He studied the screen carefully, sighed, and turned back to her.

"Well, your papers are in order. Cargo master for *Daxflan,* out of Chonselta City, Liad—plain as rain." He shook his head. "I'll be right out with you, lass. I can't see the why of leaving you like this. A cargo master is an important part of a trade vessel. All this about being hit on the head and left—it don't add up. And I'll tell you what else: Trader Olanek was here, and we had a very pleasant chat. But I never saw this second mate you be speaking of. Nor I never saw you."

"You don't believe me, in fact."

He waved his hands soothingly. "Now, lass. Admit it don't seem so likely."

"I *do* admit it," Priscilla told him. "I don't know why it was done any more than you do. Perhaps the second felt she had a grudge—but nothing to warrant cracking my skull." Which means the Trader ordered it, she thought suddenly, crystally. Dagmar wouldn't have mugged her and left her—not without orders. It was more in her style to try rape, if she had thought Priscilla had insulted her. And if the Trader had ordered it, that meant...

Master Farley's chair creaked as he changed position. "Well, then, lass, I'm just bound to say that done's done. There doesn't seem to be any harm you've done—is that so, Liam?"

"Yessir," the warehouseman said regretfully. "Happens that's so."

The port master nodded. "Then the wisest thing to do is give you back your ID and send you on your way." He pushed her cards across the desk.

Priscilla stared at him. "Send me on my way," she repeated blankly. "I'm *stranded.* I don't have any money. I don't know anybody here." The Trader had ordered it. Which meant that her deduction was correct: *Daxflan* had been carrying illegal drugs in enormous quantity. Never mind how he had gotten at her data, locked under her personal code. He had found it, given her credit for being able to make the deduction—and acted to remove a known danger.

"Best you go to the embassy," Master Farley was saying with apologetic kindness. "Likely they'll send you home."

Home? "No," she said, suddenly breathless. "I want to go—I must get to Arsdred." That was *Daxflan's* next port of call. And then? she asked herself, wondering at her own urgency. She shoved the question away for the present. She would take one thing at a time.

"Arsdred," she repeated firmly.

He looked doubtful. "Well, if you must, lass, you must. But I'm not the one to know how you'll go about it. You said you'd no money…"

"The ship in orbit now—*Dutiful Passage?* Is she a trader?"

He nodded, blinking in confusion.

"Good." She took a deep breath and forced her aching head to work. "Master Farley, you owe me no favors, I know. But I want to apply for work on *Dutiful Passage*. Will you help me?"

"It's not me you need to speak to about that, lass. It'll be Mr. Saunderson, who's the agent." He puffed his chest out a little. *"Dutiful Passage* stops here every three years, regular."

A ship that listed Jankalim among its regular ports of call? And a Liaden ship, too. Priscilla paused, trying to picture conditions less appealing than *Daxflan's.* Imagination failed her, and she smiled tightly at the port master.

"How do I get in touch with Mr. Saunderson?"

"His office is just in the city," Liam said from behind her. "Anyone can tell you the way."

"That's so," Master Farley agreed slowly. Then he squared his shoulders and stiffened his mustache. "You can use the comm to call him from here, if you like to."

Her smile was genuine this time, if no less painful. "Thank you so much."

"That's all right, lass. Pleased to be of help," he muttered, cheeks going pink. "Liam here will show you to the comm room." He made a show of turning back to the unit beside his desk, and Priscilla stood.

Liam looked as if he would have liked to grab her arm again, but satisfied himself with walking close behind her down the short hall to the communication room. He showed her the local screen and, after a moment's hesitation, punched up Mr. Saunderson's code. Priscilla smiled at him, and he flushed dull red.

Mr. Saunderson was old, his face a translucent network of wrinkles from which a pair of obsidian eyes glittered. He listened to her name and the statement that she had been employed until recently on *Daxflan* and heard her say that she was interested in employment on the orbiting ship.

"It is my understanding, Ms. Mendoza, that *Dutiful Passage* is fully staffed. However, if you would care to hold on for a few moments, I will ascertain whether this understanding is correct."

"Thank you, sir. I appreciate your trouble."

"Not at all. One moment, please." The elderly face was replaced with an image of an unlikely landscape, portrayed in various shades of tangerine and aqua. The picture had not been calculated to soothe raging headaches, and Priscilla closed her eyes against it.

"Ms. Mendoza?"

Priscilla snapped her eyes open, cheeks flaming.

Mr. Saunderson smiled at her. "The captain professes himself interested in an interview, Ms. Mendoza, and wonders if you would honor him by a visit." He cleared his throat with the utmost gentility. "He does indicate that *Dutiful Passage* employs a very able cargo master. He does not wish you to visit under a misapprehension, or if you cannot accept any position except that of cargo master."

Priscilla hesitated, wondering what positions the captain had in mind. But she was determined to get to Arsdred.

She looked at Mr. Saunderson, who was patiently waiting in the screen, and tried to visualize him whetting the captain's supposed appetite with a glowing description of her, bruised face and all. The vision brought forth a grin.

"You're very kind," she told the old gentleman carefully. "I am willing to accept any crewing work that might be available on *Dutiful Passage*. When and where may I visit the captain?"

"I shall send 'round Ms. Dyson, our pilot. Is twenty minutes convenient? Good. She will convey you to *Dutiful Passage*. I will inform Captain yos'Galan of your coming."

"You're very kind," she said again.

"Not at all." Mr. Saunderson smiled. "Good luck, Ms. Mendoza." He cut the connection.

Priscilla sighed and leaned back in her chair. She had twenty minutes until Pilot Dyson came to collect her. She looked at Liam. "Is there someplace where I can wash my face and hands?"

He snorted and jerked his head. "Down the hall, first door on the left. Nothin' fancy, it isn't."

"As long as it's functional." She levered herself up and went past him into the hall. He followed and leaned against the wall, arms crossed over his chest, watching as she opened the door and entered the 'fresher.

There was no shower, which was a shame. She had rather hoped for a hot deluge to ease some of the crankiness from her bruises. There was a sink, water, and soap. She would make do.

Automatically, she reached up to remove her earrings, then froze in disbelief when her fingers encountered only naked earlobes. Slowly, she went over to the tiny square of mirror on the far wall.

Reflected back at her was a creamy oval face surmounted by a tangled cloud of ebony curls, black eyes very wide under slim brows, and nostrils distended with anger. The fragile ridge of the right cheek was already purpling. There was a small hole in each perfect earlobe; the left one showed a thin line of blood, as if it was torn just a little.

How dare she? she thought furiously. My earrings, given to me on my Womanday, that were my grandmother's! How dare— Rage, sudden and shocking, drove out pain and fears. Priscilla was abruptly trembling, wishing fiercely to have Dagmar's neck between her hands.

Arsdred, she told herself, trying to still the fury. I'll have them both. Just let me get to Arsdred.

Slowly the rage became manageable; she enclosed it, as she had been taught, banked and ready for the proper moment.

Woodenly she went to the sink, turned on the cold water, bent, and began to splash her face.

SHIPYEAR 65
TRIPDAY 130
FOURTH SHIFT
18.00 HOURS

"Asleep, Mendoza?" Dyson inquired from the pilot's chair.

Priscilla opened her eyes and sat up straighter. "Just resting."

"Okay by me. End of the line in about five minutes. Word is you'll be met and escorted to the captain's office. Got it?"

"Yes. Thank you."

Dyson snorted. "Don't thank me, Mendoza; I'm just passing on the facts." She thumbed the comm, reeled off her numbers, and grunted at the acknowledgment before turning her full attention to the board.

Orbit and velocity were matched with an offhanded exactitude that earned Priscilla's silent praise even as she regretted her own uncompleted certificate.

There came assorted mechanical clankings and ringings before a final authoritative *thump*. Dyson locked the board with a sweep of her hand. "Okay, Mendoza. Roll on out."

"Okay." She unstrapped and stood. "Thanks."

"What they pay me for, Mendoza. Beat it, all right?"

Priscilla grinned. "See you around."

She went out the hatch and through the door—then stopped, blinking.

Carpet was beneath her feet; she was struck by the vaulting, the well-lit spaciousness…She was in a state reception room.

The identification was hard to refute. To her left and some twelve feet downroom was a grouping of chairs and loungers—Terran- and Liaden-sized in equal proportion. Farther on, a podium was shoved against the wall, directly beneath the mural of an enormous tree in full, green leaf. Hovering behind and a little above, nearly dwarfed by the tree it guarded, was a winged dragon, bronze and fierce, emerald eyes looking directly at her. There were words in Liaden characters beneath the roots of the tree.

Priscilla sighed slightly, recalling little Fin Ton, who had taught her Liaden in an even exchange for games of go. But his lessons had not extended to reading. Priscilla turned her head carefully to the right wall, which held what appeared to be a collage of photographs and drawings.

Obviously she was in the wrong place. She had better return to the docking pod and see if there was another door that led onto a more reasonable area—one containing her escort to the captain.

Half a second later she had abandoned that plan. Over the door by which she had entered, the atmosphere lamp glowed clear ruby, indicating vacuum in the pod beyond.

Priscilla turned. The door directly across from her, then? Or a ship's intercom? Surely, in a room as spacious as this one she could find an intercom.

That thought brought to mind all kinds of interesting questions about the room itself. Tradeships did not, in her experience, devote space to ballrooms or auditoriums. Three of *Daxflan's* holds would have fit comfortably into this area.

Priscilla put speculation from her mind. First, she had to find an intercom.

The door across from her opened, and a rather breathless small person erupted into the room. He skidded to a stop about two feet away and executed an awkward bow.

Not Liaden, she noted with relief. But—a child?

"Are you Ms. Mendoza?" he asked, then swept on without waiting for an answer. "Crelm! I'm *awful* sorry. I was supposed to be here when you came in. Cap'n's gonna *skin* me!"

She grinned at him. He was a stocky Terran boy of perhaps eleven Standards, dressed in plain slacks and shirt. There was a smear of grease on his right sleeve and another on his chin. An embroidered badge on his left shoulder bore the legend "Arbuthnot."

"I've only been here a minute," she told him. "Surely he won't skin you for that?"

The boy gave it consideration, tipping his head birdlike to one side. "Well, he still might. He *told* me to be here, didn't he? And it's rude, you gettin' off the shuttle and there being nobody to meet you." He sighed. "I really *am* sorry. I *meant* to be here."

"I accept your apology," Priscilla said formally. "Are you my escort to the captain, by any chance?"

"Oh, crelm," the boy said again, and laughed. "I'm making a rare mingle of it! An' he told me to make sure I welcomed you onboard, too!" He looked at her out of hopeful brown eyes. "Did I do that?"

"Admirably," she assured him, fighting down a rare spurt of her own laughter.

"Good," he said, relieved. He turned, waving at her to accompany him. "My name's Gordy Arbuthnot. I'm cabin boy."

"Pleased to meet you," Priscilla said gravely, trying not to stare around the wide, well-lit hallway. *This* was the ship that visited Jankalim every three years on a regular basis? The little she had seen so far would contain most of *Daxflan*. She opened her mouth to ask Gordy how many holds *Dutiful Passage* could carry, then thought better of it and asked another question instead. "What *was* that room back there? I thought I'd made a wrong turn getting off the shuttle."

"Reception room," he explained offhandedly. "For when we have visitors. Most of us just use the cargo docks when we come back on-ship."

"But I'm a guest?" She frowned. "Do you get a *lot* of visitors?"

Gordy shrugged. "Cap'n has parties sometimes. And sometimes people take passage with us—'cause we go where the liners don't, or 'cause we go there faster."

"Oh."

They entered a lift, and her guide punched a quick series of buttons. Shortly the door opened to a narrower hall, wide enough for four Liadens to walk abreast, Priscilla estimated. She smelled cinnamon, resin, and leather; she took a deep breath and held it a moment before sighing.

Gordy grinned. "Best place in the whole ship for smells. That's Number Six Hold." He pointed. "There's Cap'n's office."

Priscilla caught her breath sharply and bit her lip against a flare of pain in her head.

There's nothing to worry about, she told herself firmly. The captain wants an interview. The worst that can happen is that he has no job to offer. Time enough, when that happens, to think of another way to Arsdred.

Gordy laid his hand against the palmplate in the captain's bright red door. There was a chime, followed by a subdued "Come."

The door slid open.

Priscilla crossed the threshold on the boy's heels, then stopped and frankly stared.

Once again she was overwhelmed by spaciousness. Shelf after shelf of booktapes, bound books, and musictapes lined one wall. On another hung a tapestry worked in dark crimson, dull gold, jade, and azure, a twining geometric design at once restful and surprising. Below that was a unit bar; to one side of it was another shelf of tapes interspersed with bric-a-brac. Straight ahead, in the center of the room, two chairs faced a wooden desk supporting a computer screen and two untidy piles of hard copy. To the left of the desk was a closed door bearing a diagonal red stripe. A deep, hedonistic chair was placed at an angle to the corner, several books and a sketch pad were piled helter-skelter on the carpet nearby, while more books littered the nearer low table. The second of the set supported a chessboard. Seated on the edge of the sofa and bent over the board was a white-haired man in a dark blue shirt.

The captain was *old.* Priscilla found it somewhat easier to breathe.

Gordy Arbuthnot stepped to the table and cleared his throat. "Cap'n?" he said in Terran. "Here's Ms. Mendoza, come to see you."

"So soon? Pilot Dyson has outdone herself." The man sighed and shook his head at the chessmen. "I don't think this stupid position *has* a solution."

He rose and cane forward a few graceful paces before inclining his head. "I'm Shan yos'Galan, Ms. Mendoza."

He was tall—a giant among Liadens. Silver eyes thickly fringed with black lashes looked directly into hers. Nor was he old—the frostcolored hair had misled her. His face was that of a man near her own age.

But, Goddess, *what* a face! Big-nosed, jut-cheeked, wide-mouthed, with a broad forehead, triangular chin, and thin white brows set at a slant over the large eyes. Anything farther from the usual delicacy of Liaden features would be hard to find this side of the Yxtrang.

Recovering herself with a start, Priscilla bowed stiffly in the Terran mode. "Captain yos'Galan," she said with precision, "I'm glad to see you."

"Well, you'll be among the first," he commented, and his accent was of Terra's educated class, not of Liad at all. "Though my family professes something of the sort. Of course, they've had time to get used to me. Gordy, Ms. Mendoza wants something to drink. Also, my glass is missing—and wherever it is, it's probably empty. What do I pay you for?"

The boy grinned and moved toward the bar. Pausing, he looked back at Priscilla. "The red wine's best," he said seriously, "but I think the white's probably pretty good. And there's brandy—I'm not sure about that…"

"What do you know about it at all?" the man demanded. "Nipping my spirits while I'm not watching, Gordy? And who said the red's best? Your own trained palate?"

"*You* drink the red, Cap'n."

"Unprincipled brat. You don't offer brandy to a person who's come for a job interview. Strive for some polish."

"Yessir," Gordy said, not noticeably abashed by this rebuke. "Ms. Mendoza? There's red wine, white, canary, green, blue—I mean, misravot—and tea and coffee…"

Another alarming bubble of laughter was rising. Hysteria, thought Priscilla, and suppressed it firmly.

"White wine, please," she told the boy, and he nodded, turning to the bar.

"Come sit down," the captain invited, waving a big brown hand toward the chairs and the desk. Light glittered off the stone in his single ring—the large carved amethyst of a Master Trader.

Obediently, she followed him to the desk and sank gratefully into one of the chairs. Master Trader? This ugly, too-tall Liaden was a Master Trader? And captain, too? With an absent smile Priscilla took her drink from the cabin boy.

On *Daxflan*, Sav Rid Olanek—a mere Trader—and Captain yo'Vaade split administration of ship and crew between them. That had been the one thing about *Daxflan* that had followed the routine she knew from other ships. Captain was a full-time job, after all; Trader, somewhat more than that. Yet here was a man supposedly doing *both*. And more. There were perhaps a double-dexon—twice a dozen dozen—of Master Traders in all the galaxy.

"Gordy." His clear, rather beautiful voice held a mild note of exasperation. Priscilla brought her attention back to the present.

"Cap'n?" The boy froze in the act of handing the man his glass.

Shan yos'Galan sighed and laid a blunt forefinger on the grease-smeared sleeve. Gordy flushed and bit his lip.

"There's a matching one on your chin. Are we out of water? Or soap? Is there some atavistic or religious significance attached to going about with grease on your face? Maybe you put it there purposefully, after long thought, feeling that a little facial decoration would call Ms. Mendoza's attention to you more favorably? You hoped she would be so overcome by the artistry of the smear that she would fail to chide you for being late to meet her?"

"How did—" Gordy interrupted himself and raised his eyes to the man's face. "I'm not Liaden, Cap'n."

"I have independently noted the fact. No doubt you feel it has some bearing on the matter at hand." He took his glass and leaned back in the chair.

"Yessir."

"I'm intrigued. An explanation, please?"

"Yessir." Gordy took a breath and squared his round shoulders. "Liadens consider the face the—the *seat of character*. Because of that, Liadens don't use cosmetics on their faces, like Terrans might, to—to dress up or to make themselves more attractive." He paused. The captain raised his glass and waved at him to continue.

Gordy nodded. "Also, the face has an—*erotic*—significance to Liadens. There are certain social situations where it's okay to touch between Liadens where Terran code of behavior would forbid. But only extreme intimates—like family members—touch hand to face or face to face." He took another breath. "So it follows that Liadens would be *particularly* careful about keeping their faces clean. Terrans, whose cultures don't include a strong facial taboo, are less strict."

There was a small pause while Shan yos'Galan raised the glass to his lips. "'Taboo' is rather strong," he commented. "I think perhaps 'tradition' does nicely. Liadens love tradition, while you're dealing in generalizations, Gordy." He raised his glass again, and this time, Priscilla saw, he drank.

"As far as it goes, your grasp of the information seems sound," he continued thoughtfully. "However, I'm not sure your inferences are correct. That tends to happen when you extrapolate from general, rather than specific. In any case, I have found—again, through independent observation, not to say experience—that it *feels nicer* to be clean than it feels to be dirty. Also, I have found that I prefer looking at clean faces as opposed to dirty faces. This is, I believe, a personal preference. I may be wrong. Since I am captain of this ship, though, I think I have the rank to indulge in a few harmless eccentricities. So, for the fourth time: Gordon, I would very much prefer that you endeavor to keep your person as smear-free as possible." He raised the glass again. "The next time, I'll have to dock you. What do you think might be a reasonable sum?"

The boy looked down. He rubbed at his soiled sleeve, then looked up. "Tenbit?"

"Fair enough." The captain grinned. "I detect the makings of a gambler in you. Or a Trader. We'll want lunch in half an hour or so."

Gordy blinked. "Lunch?"

"Yes, *lunch*. Did I use the wrong word? Cheese, fruit, rolls— that sort of thing. Speak to BillyJo; I repose all faith in her ability to resolve the matter for you. Now jet."

"Yessir." And he was gone, the door sighing shut behind him.

Shan yos'Galan shook his head. "It's my fate to raise small boys." He lifted his glass. "Are you ready to be interviewed, Ms. Mendoza? Or have you changed your mind?"

Priscilla sipped her wine, then met his gaze straightly. "I'm ready to be interviewed, Captain."

"Brave heart." He extended a long arm and flipped two switches set along the desk top. "Your name, please, and planet of origin."

"My name is Priscilla Delacroix y Mendoza. I was born on Sintia. I am a Terran citizen."

"Do you honor the Goddess, then?" His face was sharp with interest. "Hold to her teaching exclusively?"

"I did," she said carefully. "After all, She's part of everyday life...But I've been on trading ships since I was sixteen. And the Goddess isn't as powerful in the galaxy as She is on Sintia."

"Since you were sixteen," he repeated, abandoning the Goddess abruptly. "What do you know?"

She raised her brows. "I know how to cook for a crew of twenty, how to wash up for a crew of thirty-three, how to decode messages, how to code messages. I can drive a jitney, calculate weight distributions, figure loading capacities. Whenever possible, I've pursued pilot training. My marksmanship rating is ninety percent accuracy at two hundred paces with a standard pellet gun. I speak Trade, Terran, Crenish, and Sintian. I understand Liaden better than I speak it. If I have to, I can shoot astrogation."

He nodded. "Your last position?"

"Cargo master on *Daxflan,* out of Chonselta City."

"And you held that post how long?"

"Four months," she said with determined serenity. "I signed on at Tulon."

"Did you?" He raised his glass to his lips. "And what brings you to apply for work on the *Passage?*"

"I don't have any choice."

The slanted brows pulled together. "Has Mr. Saunderson still got that impressment operation going? I did ask him to stop, Ms. Mendoza, I give you my word."

For the third time in an hour Priscilla felt laughter rising. She drowned it in a swallow of wine. "I'm sorry—that was rude. What I meant to say was that I've been—dismissed—from my post on *Daxflan.* Yours is the only ship in at Jankalim now, so I'm applying here."

"I see." He sipped wine. "Your dismissal sounds abrupt."

"Extremely."

He nodded again, shifted in his chair, and rested his arms on the desk top. "Ms. Mendoza, I have a copy of your record here…" He spun the computer screen around.

Priscilla frowned, her eyes traveling automatically down the lines of information. *Ladybird…As You Like It…Tyrunner…Selda…Dante… Daxflan.*

"Motherless, lying, spawn of a—" She gasped, and the rest was lost as the enormity of the thing hit her. *Ruin…*She met Shan yos'Galan's eyes. "It's a lie."

"Do you want to say so officially?" He spun the screen back. "It looks pretty bad, doesn't it? 'Suspected larceny. Jumped ship, Jankalim, Standard 1385.'" He leaned back in the chair and sipped wine, his eyes on her face. "I don't know of any reputable captain who would take on a person with a record containing that entry— even granting the overall excellence of the rest. What happened to your earrings?"

"The second mate hit me over the head," she said tonelessly, trying to conquer the shock. "They were gone when I came to."

"Odd sort of thing for a second mate to do," he commented. "But maybe there were extenuating circumstances. You disliked each other?"

"I disliked *her.* She liked me all too well." He was toying with her, drawing out the talking when there was no use in talking anymore. Priscilla tightened her grip on the wineglass, fighting to keep her face calm. On his ship, in his power...and who would miss a suspected thief who had jumped her last ship? Who would believe a suspected thief if she chose to tell outrageous lies about a Master Trader? He must have called up her record while speaking with Mr. Saunderson and seen that damning entry.

The man across from her shifted sharply. "And yet," he persisted, demanding her attention, "liking you so well, she hits you over the head and steals your earrings." He drank. "Forgive me, Ms. Mendoza, but *that* sounds even odder."

"The Trader ordered it," Priscilla said, clinging to serenity as if it were her last hope of salvation. Let him hear, Goddess, she begged silently. Let him believe the truth.

"Ah, dear Sav Rid." The expression on his face was one of mild puzzlement. "He will have his little joke, you know, Ms. Mendoza. But surely there were other avenues open to him, had he conceived a desire for your earrings. Why order the second mate to hit you over the head for them? Couldn't he merely have purchased them from you?" He snapped his fingers lightly. "He had offered a fair sum, and you refused to sell. Rendered desperate—"

"Stop it!" She snapped forward, eyes riveted on his. "Captain yos'Galan, please. It's imperative that I get to Arsdred. It's a large port—I'd hoped your ship would dock there. Any crewing duties you have—I'll work my passage to Arsdred as assistant mess cook, and you can lock me in a closet off-shift! You don't have to trust me—believe what you will. I *don't* think it's very funny to abandon someone and ruin their record, make it impossible to find—to find honorable work..." Her voice had developed a quaver. Horrified, she bit her lip and clenched her hands tightly to squeeze out the shaking. "I *must* get to Arsdred."

He broke her gaze and drank wine, then swirled the remainder in the glass. "Revenge," he told the glass softly, "is a highly appropriate desire. Among Liadens, revenge is something of an art form. There are strict rules. There are certain punishments which are not considered *proper* revenge." He glanced at her. "Death, for instance. At least, not directly from the hand of the vengeful party. Should the dishonor attending a balancing of accounts prove so vast that one has no other choice—" He shrugged. "Well." He set the glass aside and looked closely at her. "I will not have a murderer on this ship."

Priscilla stared at him. "But you *will* have a thief?"

"You said it was a lie. Or did I misunderstand? Perhaps something else was a lie?"

The shaking was worse, extending up her arms and down her legs. Did he believe her? Or the record? It was impossible to read the expression on his face.

"*Daxflan's* record—that I was stealing and then jumped ship—*that's* the lie."

"Do you want to say so officially?" he asked again.

Priscilla shook her head. "I can't prove it—how can I? '*Suspected* larceny'? His word against mine—and *he's* the Trader. 'Jumped ship'?" She produced a wan grin. "I'm not there now, am I? Though why anyone with three consecutive thoughts in her head would jump ship on a place like Jankalim, with twobits in her pocket..."

"And no earrings in her ears," he agreed. "But maybe you saw they were on to you and were frightened. Jankalim might have been your last chance for free flight—leg irons are so cumbersome. There are excuses for a bit of poor planning..." He tipped his head. "But why *did* Sav Rid order the second mate to hit you over the head, Ms. Mendoza? At your direction, I dismiss avaricious thoughts regarding your earrings."

"I can't prove it," she said again. "I *think* they were running contraband."

"Do you? What a peculiar thing to think. You told Sav Rid, and he was—quite understandably—annoyed. Thus the second mate, the warehouse..."

"I'm not *that* stupid," Priscilla muttered, and wondered why he grinned. "There was sealed cargo," she continued. "I had the manifests—I knew what was *supposed* to be there. But—something seemed wrong. I didn't know exactly what. So I got the idea of checking the piloting equations, just to prove to myself that I was imagining things."

"And you found what to be the case?"

"I found the equations were so far off that the captain had to be a reckless fool. Or she had to know exactly what she was doing." She took a breath. "So I checked the densities of the cargo."

"Did you?" He leaned forward. "Now why—no, you've had some pilot training. And I'm interrupting. Forgive me, Ms. Mendoza—you checked the densities, matched them to the captain's equations, and?"

"The captain knew what she was doing. The densities didn't match the substances that were *supposed* to be in the cargo. *Daxflan* ships mostly pharmaceuticals. I started going through the list, checking the numbers..." She shook her head. "I *think* there's Bellaquesa onboard. It's listed as Aserzerine on the manifest. Everything's all wrong for Aserzerine, though. Bellaquesa matches—but so does sugar. But why would you call sugar Aserzerine?..."

She shrugged. "It all *looked* interesting—but I can't *prove* any of it. I never *saw* the stuff. And I'll lay my last bit the data's not locked under my personal file anymore."

He nodded and leaned back in the chair again, staring blankly at the ceiling. Priscilla finished her wine and carefully put the glass aside. Now what? she wondered. She forced herself to sit loosely in the chair, hands relaxed on her knees.

Abruptly, be spun to face her. "We leave Jankalim in fourteen hours," he said slowly. "Before the two of us can discuss specifics, there are several tests required. They are rather lengthy, and, unfortunately, my presence is demanded worldside this evening. If you feel able, you may take the tests directly after lunch. The ship will extend a cabin for you to guest in, and we can speak again at Seventh Hour. Agreed?"

"Agreed."

He nodded and seemed about to speak further when the door opened to admit a clean-faced Gordy behind a wheeled cart piled high with eatables.

"In the nick of time!" Shan yos'Galan cried, flipping off the toggles. *"Now* you offer brandy, Gordy..."

SHIPYEAR 65
TRIPDAY 131
FIRST SHIFT
1.30 HOURS

Former Cargo Master Priscilla Mendoza leaned back in her chair, sipping at a mug of *real* coffee, the remains of an extremely edible meal on the table before her.

The tests had been lengthy—and rather odd. Among the standardized examinations had been random lists of words to define; questions regarding her personal tastes in books, music, sports, and art; and surveys soliciting her opinion on a surprising range of topics.

Priscilla sighed and sipped her coffee appreciatively. She was tired, her thoughts moving in hazy slow motion. Soon it would be time to look again at the map she had been given and puzzle out the route to her cabin. But having come to rest at last, with no immediate task before her, she was content to simply sit and sip, letting her eyes randomly scan the vast, nearly empty dining hall. She had gathered from the cook on duty that First Hour was not the usual time for people to be fed. He had laughed her apology aside and heaped a plate high, setting it on a tray with a steaming white mug.

"Start on that," he had told her, grinning broadly. "If you're still hungry when you're done, come on back and say so."

"Thank you," Priscilla said, blinking in confusion at the tray. It seemed to hold more food than she had seen at one time in months. The man laughed again and returned to his duties.

Her eyes were drooping closed. Odd, she thought drowsily, that I should feel so comfortable.

She sat up straight and drank the last of her coffee in a snap. After all, tomorrow's interview with the captain could end with her back on Jankalim, no better off—with the exception of a few good meals—than she had been this afternoon. So much depended on the tests, and on the captain. *Did* he believe her?

Why should he? she asked herself fiercely. She sighed and looked up.

A midsized Terran was standing across from her, coffee mug in hand, an expression of admiration on his round face.

Priscilla felt her stomach sink. Here we go again, she thought.

"Hi," the man said easily enough. "You must be the only person onboard who hasn't had a message to send this trip."

"That's because I'm not onboard," Priscilla told him, then grinned and shook her head. "No, *that* doesn't make sense. I mean that I'm only visiting..."

"Yeah?" he said interestedly, and extended a soft-palmed hand. "Rusty Morgenstern, radio tech. Pleased to meet you, Ms.—"

"Mendoza." She took the hand and shook lightly; she was agreeably surprised when he did not try to prolong the contact. "Priscilla Mendoza. Sit down?"

"Thanks." He slouched down and put his elbows on the table, fingers curled loosely about the mug. "Who're you visiting, if that's not too nosy? And how come they left you to eat by yourself?"

"I'm not explaining things too well. What I'm doing is applying for a job. I took some tests earlier, and I'm to see the captain at Seventh Hour to find out how I did." She sighed. "The whole thing seems pointless, though. Mr. Saunderson—the agent on Jankalim—said the ship's fully staffed."

"Well, that's true." He paused to swallow coffee. "What's your line?"

"I was cargo master on my last ship."

Rusty shook his head. "Got a hell of a cargo master—old Ken Rik. Forty years older'n Satan and twice as slippery. Don't play cards with him." He drank more coffee. "But that doesn't mean much. If the cap'n figures you'll work out, there's bound to be something for you to do."

Priscilla blinked at him. "I'm sorry?"

"Well, it's like—" He pointed a finger at her. "Cabin boy. You met Gordy?"

She grinned. "He met me when I came on."

"Nice kid. Point is, we've had a couple different cabin boys. One was backup astrogator. 'Nother spent more time helping Ken Rik figure distributions than she did fetchin' wine. Last guy—seemed like all he did was play chess with the cap'n. Gordy—he's teaching the cap'n—aah, what is it? Restructured Gaelic? Some damn thing—old Terran dialect. Happens to be the everyday parley where Gordy's from."

"The captain's learning Old Terran from Gordy Arbuthnot?" Priscilla picked up her cup and frowned into it. "Why?"

Rusty shrugged. "Cap'n likes to talk."

"I noticed. But—Old Terran? And an obscure dialect, at that?"

"Better ask him—I don't know. But to get back—if the tests check out okay, you're in. And you'll work." He grinned. *"Every-body works."*

"But it seems that cabin boy is filled," Priscilla pointed out.

"Cap'n'll think of something," Rusty said with decision. "More coffee?"

She smiled. "Thanks."

"No problem. How you like it? Black? Back in a sec."

He was back almost immediately, handing her a mug; he remained standing, eyeing her consideringly. Priscilla took a gingerly sip and hoped he wasn't about to say anything unfortunate.

"If you got a minute," he began as she clamped her jaw, "let's go 'round to the lounge. There's a screen there. We can call up the spec freight and you can give me lots of ideas for making money. Ought to be interesting, since you've been a cargo master and all."

Priscilla let out her breath and stood with a smile. "Okay."

"Right this way."

Matching his stride, Priscilla asked, "What's the spec freight?"

"Speculation," Rusty explained, and grinned at her blank look. "See, every crew member who wants to pledges a certain percentage each trip for speculation. Wood, say—that's what I'm interested in. Or perfume—that's pretty chancy, but Lina seems to do okay with it. Musical instruments—I don't know. Little while back we had some Grestwellin caviar—one of Gordy's finds. Sold out next port we put in." He shook his head. "That kid's gonna be one hell of a Trader. Knows what's gonna be hot next port, even if we don't know where next port *is*—here we are."

The door slid open at their approach, and Priscilla followed him over the threshold into comfortable dimness and subdued chatter. There was a card game going on in a bright corner—Rusty waved in that direction and got two or three absent responses—and a few other people were scattered about, some in conversational clusters, some alone, with books or handwork.

"There's Lina," Rusty said, and made a detour toward a single chair where a brown-haired Liaden woman was reading a bound book.

She glanced up and smiled. "Rah Stee. They let you from your cage so soon?"

"It's later than you think," he told her, waving Priscilla forward. "This is Priscilla Mendoza. She's a guest onboard this shift. Got an interview with the cap'n next. Priscilla, this is Lina Faaldom, chief librarian."

Honey-colored eyes considered her gravely. Prompted by an impulse she could not name, Priscilla did what she had never done to Sav Rid Olanek or any of the *Daxflan's* crew—she performed the bow between equals, exactly as Fin Ton had shown her. "I am happy to meet you, Lina Faaldom," she said, with a careful ear to her accent.

The woman clapped her hands. "She speaks Liaden! See, now, Rah Stee, are you not ashamed?" She stood and returned the bow gracefully. "No happier than I am to meet you, Priscilla Mendoza." She straightened and added in Terran, "Perhaps you will prevail upon this lazy Rah Stee to learn, as well."

"Nag," Rusty said without heat. "I was going to call up the spec for Priscilla. Want to kibitz?"

"I do not know. What is it—kibitz?"

"It means to look over our shoulders," Priscilla explained. "Rusty wants me to give him ideas to make money."

"Money, money. Already Rah Stee has more money than he can gamble away. Why does he need more? But yes, I would like to kibitz. Thank you."

The screen was in the corner opposite the card game. Rusty waved his hand at the lightplate and entered his code. Lina perched on the arm of his chair, and Priscilla sat on the hassock to the left, legs curled under her.

"Here we are. Contents, Hold Six: twenty kilos mahogany; ten kilos yellow pine; fifty-eight gallons Endless Lust perfume—*Endless Lust?*" Rusty turned a pained face to the woman beside him.

"It is the *smell*," Lina told him with dignity, "not the name."

"You're the expert. Four hundred bushels raw cotton; and thirty-two dozen bottles Essence of Themngo." He shook his head. "That kid better be right this time...What do you think, Priscilla?"

"Impressive," she said sincerely. "You seem to have chosen well—mostly luxury items. I'm not an expert on woods, though. Thirty kilos sounds like either too much or too little."

"It is the artists," Lina explained. "Everywhere we go, there are the artists, always looking for something new. Rah Stee starts with the wood…oh, *long* ago, when the captain's father was captain. Now, we have orders. The wood becomes a—a usual thing. We are expected."

Priscilla nodded, struck by another thought. "You've got an entire hold tied up in the crew's speculative cargo? What about capacity fees?"

"Cap'n pledges that. On condition the ship gets her share first out of any profit. The ship shares any loss, too—it's a fair deal."

"More than fair." She sipped her cooling coffee. "Your captain sounds unusual."

"He is a good captain," Lina said.

"And the *Passage* is a profitable ship," Rusty added, turning back to the screen. "Most of the wood'll go at Arsdred—the Artisan's Guild put in a big order. We might pick up a few odds and ends there—not too likely, though, since almost everybody running this sector stops there. Number Six'll be empty for a while." He glanced at Priscilla. "Can't make money that way."

"But you just said the wood's an ordered item," she pointed out. "You've got a profit, right?"

"Yeah, I guess." He brightened. "Tell you what—let's try and get our shore leaves matched for Arsdred. Then we can go scouting together. Who knows? Something might turn for the spec. Or even for the ship."

Priscilla stared at him. "I might not be onboard at Arsdred, remember?" She drank the rest of her coffee and shook her head. "Do you *all* look for the ship, too? What's the Master Trader do?"

Lina laughed.

"He trades," Rusty said, his round face serious. "*We* don't trade. But anybody might see something. Cap'n's only one person—he could miss a deal just 'cause he can't be in three places at once. So as many of the crew as can go worldside. If you see something, you hotfoot to the nearest comm and call the cap'n or Kayzin Ne'Zame—first mate. If it turns out to be a go, there's a finder's fee." He blinked at her. "What's wrong?"

"Nothing. I—the last ship I was on didn't—encourage—the crew to go worldside. And the Trader did all the trading."

"Sounds like a stupid arrangement to me," the man said flatly.

"It does not make good sense," Lina agreed slowly. "The ship is everyone's venture. We all take a share of the profit. It is only sensible to work hard for a *big* profit." She looked carefully at Priscilla. "Perhaps you were not on such a good ship before."

"Perhaps I wasn't," Priscilla said dryly, and lifted a hand to cover a sudden yawn. "I'm sorry. It's been a long day. Better be finding my room…" She uncoiled her legs and stood.

With a nod, Rusty signed off and moved out of the alcove. One of the card players looked up and waved him over. "In a sec," he called, and turned back. "Priscilla, I bet you threebits you'll be on the *Passage* at Arsdred."

"I don't have threebits to bet," she said ruefully. "But I hope you're right. It was good to meet you."

"See you later," he responded, and drifted off toward the game.

"You should excuse Rah Stee," Lina said, waving a hand at his retreating back. "You know where your room is from here?"

"I have a map," Priscilla began, fishing in her pocket.

The smaller woman laughed. "The map is good, but it will take you by all the main halls. I know the short ways. If it does not offend, I can show you. It is time I went to sleep as well."

"I don't want to put you to any trouble…"

"It is no trouble," Lina assured her. "Only let me get my book."

They turned left from the door of the lounge rather than right, as the map directed, and pursued several short zigzagging corridors before regaining the main hall. They followed this past several closed doors, one marked GYM and another POOL, before turning into a slimmer, dimmer way.

Lina left her with a smile and a slight bow at the third door on the right. "Sleep well, Priscilla Mendoza. I will look for you tomorrow."

"Sleep you well also, Lina Faaldom," Priscilla answered softly in Liaden. "Thank you for your care."

The room was a blur to her overtired mind. She located the cleanbot and pushed her clothes into the slot, hoping that the black smear on one yellow cuff would come out in the cycle.

There was a clock on the shelf over the bed; she keyed in a request for Sixth Hour and curled into the luxuriously soft cushions with a sigh as she belatedly waved a hand at the lightplate.

She was asleep before the room was dark.

SHIPYEAR 65
TRIPDAY 131
SECOND SHIFT
6.55 HOURS

"Priscilla Mendoza?"

She started, almost spilling what was left of her coffee, and blinked at the small person who had appeared suddenly before her. The woman was a Liaden of middle years, with golden skin showing deep lines about eyes and mouth, and yellow hair going gray.

Priscilla smiled. "I am sorry. I was daydreaming. How may I serve you?"

The handsome face did not relax its austere lines. "The captain's compliments, Ms. Mendoza. He requests that you come to him, if you have broken your fast." She hesitated before inclining her head ever so slightly. "I am Kayzin Ne'Zame." The first mate.

Priscilla smiled again, despite the stiffness of her face, and pushed back her chair. "I've just finished this minute. I'll go to the captain as soon as I've cleaned up my tray." She was fairly confident of the route, having studied her map throughout breakfast.

"I shall escort you," Kayzin Ne'Zame said uncompromisingly.

Fear returned. Priscilla would be sent from the ship—or she would be required to remain—it was impossible to know which was the worse possibility. Breakfast was a handful of cold rock in her stomach; she abruptly remembered the woman she had met last night and wished they had had a chance to speak further.

Priscilla laid her tray gently on the conveyer belt and turned back to the first mate. "Thank you, Kayzin Ne'Zame. I am ready now."

The captain was behind the desk, fingers busy on the keypad. A glass of wine sat to hand, and the previous day's stacks of paper had given birth to two others like themselves.

"Captain," the first mate said formally. "Here is Priscilla Mendoza, come to speak with you."

He glanced up absently. "Ms. Mendoza. Good morning. I'll be with you in just a moment. Kayzin, old friend, will you come to me in an hour?"

"Certainly, Captain." She executed a disapproving bow, but he had already returned his attention to the screen, and Priscilla did not think he saw. Frowning, the mate turned on her heel; the automatic door did its best to bang shut behind her.

Priscilla stood, fighting cold nausea. Biting her lip, she studied the man behind the desk, combating fear with observation.

It was a puzzle, she decided. He was so tall, his skin warm brown rather than golden. Like all Liaden men she had seen, his face was as fine-grained as a child's, without a hint of beard. The white hair and brows made a vivid contrast; the lean cheeks and mobile mouth were not displeasing.

Really, she thought, if you don't expect him to look Liaden, he's not ugly at all.

Certainly he was not an ill-made person. Beneath the wide-sleeved shirt his shoulders were level and broad, his back straight without being rigid. The big hands moved with graceful economy on the keypad, and Priscilla did not think they would be babysoft like Rusty Morgenstern's.

Abruptly he nodded, leaned back, and extended a long arm for his glass. The slanting brows pulled sharply together as he looked up. "Does Sav Rid have delusions of grandeur? Sit, sit. Have you eaten? Will you drink? Did you sleep well?"

Priscilla considered him. "I don't know. Thank you. Yes. No. Very. Did *you?*"

"Not too badly," he said, raising his glass. "Though Mr. Saunderson's idea of a party *is* a bit risque. We played charades. And sang rounds. The youngest Ms. Saunderson attempted to elicit my promise to wed her when she comes of age." He shook his head. "Alas, it seems clear she is more enamored of adventuring about the galaxy than she is of my elegant person, so there's a brilliant match gone begging. I have your test scores. Are you interested in discussing them now?"

Priscilla made an effort to settle her stomach firmly in place. "Yes, sir."

He ran his fingers in a quick series over the keys. "Physics, math, astrogation—yes, yes, yes. Colors red, colors blue, taste in books—yes?" He glanced up. "Prebatout. You recall the question? 'How many toes should a prebatout have?' And here is Priscilla Mendoza saying, 'As many as it feels comfortable with.' I've only known one other person to answer that particular question that way."

"Have you?' Priscilla asked, hands ice cold. "Was she a suspected thief, too?"

"Thief? No, a scout. Though, come to think of it, the two trades might have some similarities. I've never considered it in that light. I'll ask, the next time I see him…" He returned to the screen, humming to himself.

Priscilla curled her fingers carefully around the armrests, refusing to rise to the bait—if it was bait—of his last comment. Let *him* talk, since he seemed to like it so much.

He moved his shoulders, gave the keypad a final tap, and leaned back. "You don't have a pilot's license? That won't do, will it? Let me see…forty-eight crew members, counting the captain—eight of them pilots. Too few by far. You'll have to study, Ms. Mendoza. I insist on it. Every ninth shift you'll be on the bridge for lessons."

"Wait a minute." She took a breath. "You're signing me on? As a pilot?"

"As a pilot?" he repeated blandly. "No, how could I do that? You're not a pilot, are you, Ms. Mendoza? That's why you'll need to take lessons. Certification's no problem. I'm rated master, all conditions—is something wrong?"

"Forgive me," she said carefully. "I thought you were captain. And Master Trader, of course. You're a pilot, too?"

"A little of this, a little of that. The *Passage* is a family enterprise, after all. Owned and operated by Clan Korval. And piloting runs in the blood, so to speak. I got my first class when I was sixteen Standards—been ratable for a few years before that, of course. Did my first solo on this ship when I was fourteen—but rules are rules, and they clearly state that no one may be certified until sixteen Standards. But I was saying—what *was* I saying? Oh, yes. Since I'm a master pilot, there won't be any delay once you earn your certification. Are you *certain* you haven't got a license, Ms. Mendoza? Third class, perhaps?"

"I'm certain, Captain." Things were moving too fast; the torrent of words was threatening to unmoor her fragile hold on serenity. "Just what will my position be?"

"Hmm? Oh—pet librarian."

"*Pet* librarian?"

"We have a very nice pet library," he told her gravely. "Now, details. We're nearly half done with the route. I can offer you flat rate from Jankalim to Solcintra—approximately a tenth-cantra upon docking. You'd be eligible for the low-man share of any bonus the ship might earn from this point on—finder's fees and special awards are the same for everyone, based on profit of found cargo and merit, as judged by the majority of the crew." He raised his glass. "Questions?"

She had a myriad of them, but only one was forthcoming. "Why," she demanded irritably, "do you keep waving that glass around if you never drink from it?"

He grinned. "But I *do* drink from it. Sometimes. More questions?"

She sighed. "How much will the ship charge for pilot training?"

"If you fail to report for training every ninth shift, the captain will dock you twentybits. Three unexcused or unexplained absences will be grounds for immediate termination of your contract. Understand, please, Ms. Mendoza, that pilot training is an essential part of your duties while you are a member of this crew. I will not allow abandonment of that duty—the penalties are quite in earnest." He paused, his light eyes gauging her face. "You *do* understand?"

"Yes, Captain." She bit her lip. "It's that I've been charged for training on every other ship I served on—and pursued it during my free time. *Daxflan* denied me permission to continue training while I shipped on her."

"Sav Rid, Sav Rid." He shook his head. "However, this is not *Daxflan,* and her rules do not apply here. Now. Your supervisor— no. The ship will extend you credit for a Standard week's worth of clothing, to be reckoned against your share at the end of the route. Please draw what you need from general stores. Your supervisor will be Lina Faaldom, who is chief librarian."

"I met her last night—"

"Yes? She will introduce you to the residents of the pet library and acquaint you with your duties there. I don't believe the work to be arduous, so you'll be expected to take on other duties as necessary. Janice Weatherbee will be your piloting instructor. If she is called elsewhere upon occasion, I will take her place. I believe that's everything. Are the terms agreeable to you?"

"Since I was almost certain I'd be back on Jankalim this morning, yes, Captain, the terms are agreeable to me." She paused, studying his face. Sometime during the interview the fear had dissipated, leaving her limp and slowly warming. "Do you *really* need a pet librarian?"

"Well, we didn't have one," he said, spinning the screen toward her. "So I guess we do. Palmprint here, please."

Shan yos'Galan was tipped back in his chair, arms folded behind his head, eyes apparently resting on the crystalline mobile hanging in the far corner of the ceiling. The expression on his face was one of dreamy stupidity. He did not glance around at the hissing of the door; he did not even seem aware that he was no longer alone in the room.

Kayzin Ne'Zame knew better than to be deceived by appearances. She sat in the seat that Priscilla Mendoza had recently vacated, her spine two inches from the chair back, and frowned at his profile.

"You've signed her on?" she demanded in the High Tongue, each syllable icy with disapproval.

"I did say that it was my intention to sign her on," the man reminded the mobile gently and in Terran. He spun the chair lazily around, unfolded his arms, and sat up. "What is it, Kayzin?"

"She is too beautiful." The Terran words were no less cold.

"But that's not her fault, is it? People can't choose their faces, can they? If they can, I want to know why I wasn't told about it."

The older woman regarded him with something perilously close to amusement. "I am, in fact, to pity her."

"What harm can it do?"

"What harm! You ask it? Or is it the game again? Do not trouble yourself, I beg you..." She paused, visibly taking herself in hand. "And what harm is it—to the ship, to the crew, to your Clan, and to Shan yos'Galan—should Sav Rid Olanek prove clever as well as dishonorable? What harm, should this so-pitiful, so-beautiful woman prove to be a tool in his hands—a blade at your throat? What harm—"

"Kayzin..." The big hands made a soothing motion; concern for her showed in his face.

She slumped back in her chair. "Shan, it is my last trip. I prefer it to be an uneventful one."

"There's no reason for it to be otherwise, old friend. Why should Sav Rid want to plant a—what? spy? *assassin?*—on the *Passage?* He's had his coup—and a very fine laugh. There's no reason for him to go to such trouble. No reason to think of the affair at all, except to chuckle and extend the story in port taverns as proof of Shan yos'Galan's rabid foolishness." He grinned wryly. "And he's not too far off the mark, is he?"

She gestured, speechless.

"You worry too much, Kayzin—and without cause. Circumstance, synchronicity—I don't believe Sav Rid would *wish* Priscilla Mendoza here, assuming he wished her any place at all, except, perhaps, dead. I think it more likely that he acted twice as opportunity dictated. It's interesting—but not impossible—that the victims of both actions should come together."

"It is also not impossible that Olanek has grown wary—or even that he has grown greedy. What a coup for him, should he bring Korval entire to its knees..."

Shan's brows pulled together. "Do you really think he could? Not that he doesn't have the potential for being that greedy—or that reckless. Kayzin, the *Passage* proceeds as ever. For our years together and the time you spent raising me, I will attempt to keep the rest of the route as uneventful as possible. In the meantime, please try to be kind to Priscilla Mendoza." He picked up his glass and drank slowly. "And wouldn't you say it was better, Kayzin, to keep the knife—if there is a knife, of course—in our view rather than have it poised at our back?"

She smiled. "You will reward him properly?"

"Steps are being taken to bring accounts into balance," he promised, and finished his wine.

SHIPYEAR 65
TRIPDAY 135
SECOND SHIFT
9.30 HOURS

Glass in hand, Shan yos'Galan rounded the corner into the leisure section. Ahead was a slender figure, gay in raspberry tunic and celadon sash. He stretched his long legs and caught her by the intersection to the athletic hall.

"Well met, Lina."

She looked up, her smile radiant. "Shan. I'm glad to see you."

"And I'm glad to see you. As always. You're looking exceptionally lovely. Off to a party? Will you bring me with you? I promise not to brag of my exalted position. How do you find your assistant?"

She laughed. "But it is exactly of Priscilla that I wished to speak! Have you truly a moment? I know how busy it is to be captain. I hardly see you…"

"Languishing? He raised his glass, his light eyes mocking. "By all means speak to me of Priscilla. Do the residents approve? Is she impossible for you? Shall I send her to Ken Rik?"

"Oh, no, not to Ken Rik. The small ones are each delighted—Master Frodo to the point of purrs. You knew he would be." She stopped, frowning up into his face. "Shan? What is wrong with her—do you know? There is joy—one can feel it—but she denies…suppresses…I like her very well. Don't you?"

"It would be enough to lower anyone's feelings, wouldn't it, to be hit over the head and deserted with no money, a ruined record, and no friends?"

"It is more than that," Lina insisted. "She wants Healing."

"Does she?" He sipped. "Is she impossible for you?"

"Not at all. Though perhaps *you*…"

"Me?" He laughed. "I'm not a Healer, Lina; I'm the captain."

"Bah!" She banished this quibble with a tiny contemptuous hand. "As if you haven't the skill and the training!" She tipped her head, considering information of which the expression on his face was only a small portion. "Shan?"

A lifted shoulder denied her. He frowned slightly. "What—perfume—are you wearing, Lina?"

"The one we bought—Endless Lust." She chuckled. "Rah Stee objects to the name."

"As well he might." He moved back a step or two. "Very potent, isn't it? I don't recall that you reported aphrodisiac qualities."

"It has none!" She grinned. "Are you certain it is the perfume?"

"Forgive me," he murmured. "I have admired you forever, Lina, but amorous thoughts were far from me this evening. If it *isn't* aphrodisiac, it's the next best thing. Did anybody explain how it works?"

"It is the smell…" She sighed sharply, asked permission with a flicker of her hands, and slid into the Low Tongue, on the mode spoken between friends. "It is an enhancer of one's own odor. Thus, if you are attracted primarily, you will be more so when the perfume is used. Harmless, old friend, I assure you."

"I," the Captain said in Terran, "am not convinced. There are laws on certain worlds about perfumes and substances that—what *is* the official phrasing?—'take away volition and make pliable the will'? Something more or less pompous." He took a drink and drifted away yet another step. "Do me the favor of submitting what is left of your vial to Chemistry, Lina. I would so hate to break the law."

"It is harmless." She frowned. "It does *not* take away volition—no more than a Healer might, encouraging one to embrace joy…"

Shan grinned. "I believe you may be splitting hairs. *Are* you going to a party? I would like to accompany you—purely scientific, you understand. It might be very interesting to observe the effect of this perfume of yours on a roomful of unsuspecting persons."

"I," Lina said dampingly, "am going to watch a Ping-Pong match between Priscilla and Rah Stee. You may come, if you like. Though if you persist in backing away from me in that insulting manner…"

He laughed and offered an arm. "I have myself in hand now. Let us by all means inflict ourselves upon the Ping-Pong match."

Rusty was sweating and puffing with exertion, the expression on his round face one of harried doggedness.

In contrast, Priscilla was coolly serene, parrying his shots with absent smoothness, barely regarding the ball at all. Yet time after time she fractured his frenzied guard and piled up the points in her favor.

"Twenty-one," he said, his voice cracking slightly. "I don't believe it."

"No, Rah Stee, it *is* twenty-one for Priscilla," Lina said helpfully. "I counted also."

"That's what I don't believe." Rusty leaned heavily on the table, directing a sodden head shake at his opponent. "You're blowing me away! I don't get it. Half the time I don't even see the ball coming."

"That's because you have the reactions of a dead cow," Shan explained, not to be outdone in helpfulness.

The other man turned to glare at him. "Thanks a lot."

"Always of service..."

"Maybe," Priscilla offered, cutting off a scorching reply, "it's because you look for the ball. I almost never do that."

"Then how do you know where it *is?*" He ran a sleeve across his forehead and sighed hugely. "Dammit, 'Cilla, I'm good at Ping-Pong. Been playing for years!"

"But not against pilots," the captain said, sipping wine.

"What's that got to do with it?"

"A great deal, don't you think, Rusty? Your reaction time's slow; you move in a series of jerks rather than a smooth flow; you fail to apprehend where an object *will be.*" He raised his glass. "Don't feel too bad, my friend. We all have our niche to fill. After all, I could hardly fill your place in the tower, or operate the—"

"Like hell you can't," the other muttered, spinning his paddle clumsily on the table.

"I beg your pardon, Rusty?"

"Never mind." He turned suddenly and flipped the paddle to Shan, who caught it left-handed, lazily. *"You* play her."

The captain blinked. "Why?"

"You're a pilot. She's a pilot. Maybe I'll pick up some pointers." Grinning, Rusty retired from the field and flung himself into a sideline seat. "Besides, I need a break. You don't want me to keel over dead from exertion, do you?"

"Now, that would be a tragedy. So young, so handsome, so wealthy—he had all to live for...Ms. Mendoza? Are you interested in a game? Observe that you have the advantage of youth over dissipated old age."

Priscilla swallowed a laugh. Lina frowned.

"Certainly, Captain. I'll be happy to play with you. Will you offer me a handicap?"

"You should offer one to me," he said, setting his glass aside and wandering toward the table. "Remember that I'm frail, please, and easily bruised. You'll serve?"

She nodded, and the ball was even then skimming smoothly over the net...to be returned with casual force, heading toward the edge of the table, barely brushing; it was caught as it struck and sent backspinning over the net, to be returned again, barely inside her play zone, then flipped by a cunning paddle edge back into his court.

"Twenty-seven, twenty-five," Priscilla said nearly forty minutes later. She actually grinned at the man opposite. "Good game, Captain."

"Fighting for every point," he agreed, laying his paddle down and moving in the direction of his wine. "Notice, please, Rusty, that I barely won. *Have* you picked up any pointers?"

"Huh? I'm gonna retire to a home for the physically degenerate." The radio tech shook his head. "You're so fast! If I hadn't heard it hit, I'd've thought you were runnin' a scam: pretending to have a game with an invisible ball."

Priscilla drifted over to Lina's chair and sat carefully on an upholstered arm. The Liaden woman smiled up at her. "You played very well, my friend."

Friend. The word was unexceptional from Lina, yet Priscilla never heard it without a small thrill of warmth. She smiled gently. "Thank you." She moved her shoulders in response to a slight twinge. "No excuse for not sleeping tonight."

Lina shifted. "You have not been sleeping? On our ship?"

Priscilla allowed herself the luxury of another grin. "I sleep better on this ship than—than I sometimes do." She moved her shoulders again, half a shrug. "It's nothing. I get by."

"In two days we are at Scandalous," the smaller woman offered, apropos of nothing. "A drop only. Then, in three days more, we are at Arsdred. Do you like us, now that you have been here a whole week?"

"Has it been a week?" The question woke echoes of Shan yos'Galan's voice in her mind's ear, and she smiled again, almost lazily. "I like you very much. Everyone's been kind..." Except Kayzin Ne'Zame, of course. What ailed the woman? She glanced down and saw Lina's small golden hand resting on the chair arm at her knee. It looked strong and capable and curiously pleasing. With hardly a thought except that it would be comforting to do so, Priscilla laid her own hand over it—and flicked her eyes, startled, to the other woman's face.

Lina smiled at her.

Priscilla sighed; the sound seemed to come from very far away. Friend, she thought, and her fingers tightened around Lina's. She received warm pressure in return and smiled for the fourth time in five minutes. From across the room she heard the soothing murmur of voices: Rusty and the captain, speaking between themselves. She shook her head. "I must be more tired than I thought..."

"Yes? Would you like to go to bed? I will walk with you, if you like."

Priscilla looked into the face of her friend. Goddess, it would be hard to tell Lina good-bye..."I'd like you to come with me," she said softly. "That would be good."

"I think so, too," Lina said, and stood, keeping their hands linked.

Across the room, Rusty suddenly sighed. "Here I thought she liked me," he complained, "and then she goes off with Lina!"

Shan glanced around absently. "I'm afraid you were outgunned. Lina was wearing that new perfume of hers."

"Was she?" He looked up, all interest. "Damn. That stuff's gonna make us *rich.*"

They reached Priscilla's quarters and entered together when the door slid away. Just inside, Lina stopped and smiled up at her tall companion a little quizzically. Cautiously, she touched the bruise on the pale cheek. "I am sorry that they hurt you, my friend."

"It wasn't so bad..." Priscilla murmured, gazing down into her face. Slowly, with a sense of inevitable tenderness, she bent and kissed Lina on the mouth.

SHIPYEAR 65
TRIPDAY 136
THIRD SHIFT
11.30 HOURS
AROUND SCANDALOUS

Master Frodo the norbear burbled happily and ran to the port opening as fast as his bowed legs would carry him. His three companions came more slowly from their cozyplaces and followed, Tiny
uttering a small, dignified *bwrrr* of welcome.

Priscilla carefully measured out three portions and placed each
in its appointed place. Tiny, Delm Briat, and Lady Selph fell to with
a will, while Master Frodo stood by, fairly quivering with anticipation. As the last measure was placed, he extended a small clawed
hand and snagged a fold of sleeve.

"Did you think I'd forgotten you?" Priscilla asked as he
clambered into her hand. Master Frodo rubbed his head against
her fingers.

Smiling, Priscilla brought him to her shoulder. He rolled off
and sat up on hind legs, one hand clutching the curls over her ear
while with the other he solemnly accepted pieces of corn and stuffed
them into his cheek pouches.

"It's the tower for me today," Priscilla confided as Master Frodo
broke his fast. "I'm to report to Tonee sig'Ella by Twelfth Hour."

Her companion vouchsafed no direct reply, though he let her
know by the quality of his eating that Tonee sig'Ella was not a bad
sort, received everywhere by norbears of consequence.

Since Priscilla was able to verify by the sign-out that Tonee was
no infrequent visitor to the norbears' hearth, this information was
not startling. She thanked Master Frodo for his recommendation,
however, and scratched him lightly between the ears before replacing him in the tank.

He settled to the sandy soil with a little sigh and twisted his head
sideways, peering upward, one paw raised in supplication.

Priscilla grinned again. "No more for you," she said sternly,
rubbing his belly with a gentle finger. "You're getting positively fat."

Master Frodo let it be known that among norbears a certain portliness of figure was considered attractive. Priscilla might, of course, think what she would. He did not like to mention it, but *she* could use a little extra corn to advantage.

Caught in the imagined dialogue, she shook her head. "I've always been scrawny," she said, closing the hatch and sealing it.

She shook her head again. Talking to yourself like a Seer. If anybody catches you, they'll have you down in sick bay before Master Frodo can give you a reference.

But the thought failed to alarm her. Lina had in fact caught her talking to Master Frodo a shift or two back. The Liaden woman's only response had been to tug on one rounded ear and warn Priscilla not to let the norbear charm her out of extra rations.

"He is a rogue, this one," Lina had explained, laughing at the creature's antics. "And you must not be taken in. He will exploit you shamelessly."

Priscilla left the pet library by way of the side door, which gave onto the library proper. Lina was at the desk, frowning at her screen, but she glanced up with a smile. Still unused to such warm and easy friendship, Priscilla caught her breath. "Everyone's taken care of," she said, striving for serenity. "I'm going up to the tower now."

"So? Call me to Tonee's attention. We have not met often this trip." She touched the back of a slim pale hand. "Shall we share prime meal, my friend?"

"Yes." She drew breath against the pounding of her heart.

Lina smiled. "I will see you at prime, then. Be you well, Priscilla."

"Be you well, Lina."

The tower was opposite the library and up six levels, a dome in the ship's center section exactly balancing the dome of the main bridge, six levels below. Priscilla entered a lift and punched her route, then leaned back into a corner.

Pet librarian. So far, she had spent only one shift performing the duties attached to that post. Her assignment was on her cabin-screen when she awoke, always allowing her ample time to see to the needs of the creatures she cared for. And then she was sent elsewhere: to the maintenance bay to help lanky Seth with an overhaul, to the kitchen to assist garrulous BillyJo, to the holds to pore over distribution charts with sharp-tongued old Ken Rik. And, of course, to the inner bridge for piloting lessons with Janice Weatherbee, second mate and first class pilot.

Only a week, and I must have worked everywhere but the pet library, Priscilla thought. But she found she did not mind the variety of work. Rather, it seemed to ease her in some unidentified way, even as the mix of personalities exhilarated her.

People. One might find friends here. She had found at least one friend already. And since she had had no friends at all, that was a treasure past any attempt at counting.

The lift stopped, and the door slid away to reveal a bright yellow hallway. Priscilla walked to the end of it, feet soundless on the resilient floor, laid her hand upon the door, and entered.

Instruments were flickering; one console was clamoring for attention, while a screen set in the far wall flashed orange numbers: seven in series; pause; repeat.

No human occupant was apparent.

"Hello?"

"Hahlo! Yes! A moment!" There was a harried scrabbling from behind the center console. Priscilla started in that direction and almost bumped into the person coming the other way.

"You are Priscilla Mendoza, yes?"

"I'm Priscilla Mendoza," she agreed, bowing the bow between equals. "You are Tonee sig'Ella?"

"Who else? No, we have not met—you must not regard..." An abbreviated version of the courtesy was returned. She had a moment to wonder if Fin Ton would have approved before her hand was caught in a surprisingly strong grip and she was pulled toward the console.

"You are a decoder, yes? You have operated the bouncecomm and know the symbols? There is a difficulty with the in-ship, and I must have time, but the messages—you perceive? Do you but decode what arrives; encode what must be sent—I will have my time; we will not fall behind. All will be well!" the little tech finished triumphantly, pulling out the console chair.

Priscilla sat and flicked a glance at screens, transmitters, receivers. The equipment was standard; there should be no problem.

"How are we getting the messages to the proper people onboard?" she asked. "If the in-ship's out—"

"I have spoken with the captain," the other interrupted, rubbing wire-thin hands together. "The cabin boy will be dispatched to the tower and will carry messages as they are ready. It should not be long. You are familiar? You will contrive?"

"I will contrive." Priscilla made the assurance as solemn as she could, despite the rising wave of laughter. She swallowed firmly. "Lina Faaldom asked to be remembered to you. She says you haven't seen each other often this trip."

"Lina!" The gamin face lit, eyes sparkling. "I will call on her— say, to beg her forgiveness!" A quick laugh was accompanied by the lightest of touches to her shoulder. Then she was alone. On the other side of the tower, Tonee was removing the cover of the noisy console.

Priscilla shook her head and turned to the task at hand.

Gordy had just left with his third handful of messages. Priscilla heard the sound of the door cycling without assigning it importance, most of her attention captured by an unusually knotty translation.

Could it really be "desires your most religious custom?" she wondered, fingers poised over the keys. The message was directed to Master Trader, *Dutiful Passage*. It would be best to take a little time to be sure.

"What," demanded a heavily accented voice, "are you doing here?"

Priscilla glanced up, stomach sinking. Kayzin Ne'Zame stood before the console, and it was apparent she was in no mood to be pleased.

"I was assigned here," she began.

"You are not cleared for this work!" the first mate snapped. "Who assigns you?"

"My screen lists my duties at the beginning of each shift," Priscilla explained, keeping her voice even. "This shift, I was assigned to Tonee sig'Ella at Twelfth Hour."

"Who is your supervisor?" Kayzin asked awfully.

"Lina Faaldom."

"Lina Faaldom. And it is your belief that a librarian has the authority necessary to assign you to the tower as a decoder of messages?" There was no mistaking the sarcasm.

"She has apparently," Priscilla snapped, "had the authority to send me to the maintenance bay, the cargo holds, the kitchen, and hydroponics. Why should I assume this shift's assignment was different from those?"

"Has she?" There was an odd expression on the first mate's face. She turned, scanning the tower, eyes lighting on the hunched figure at the far corner. "Radio Tech!"

Tonee turned and hurried forward with a sigh. "First Mate?"

"How came this woman to you?"

The radio tech blinked. "Under orders, First Mate. She was expected. Twelfth Hour, so went the captain's word."

"The captain—"

"First Mate, she is required!" Tonee pleaded, as if suddenly perceiving where that line of questioning might lead. "She has been of utmost assistance. The in-ship is nearly repaired. Before we leave orbit, I promise it—but you must not take her now! The messages—surely you know the need!"

It was apparent from her expression that Kayzin *did* know the need. She looked from Tonee to Priscilla, rigid at the console, then inclined her head. "A question of clearance, Radio Tech. However, since you have the captain's word, there is no more to be said." With that, she turned on her heel and left the tower.

Priscilla and Tonee exchanged glances before the little tech flung both hands out in a gesture of wide amazement.

"You work well. When we leave orbit, the screens will be clear. The first mate..." There was a ripple of narrow shoulders. "Her temper is chancy, a little. Do not regard it."

With another delicate pat on the shoulder, Priscilla was left alone to conquer bewilderment and return to the matter at hand.

SHIPYEAR 65
TRIPDAY 137
FIRST SHIFT
1.30 HOURS

Priscilla whipped about—and froze. The alley behind her was full of men and women, hands ominously clenched, righteousness shining from each grim face. She fell back, forgetting the danger behind—

Until with a jerk the precious bag was torn from her grip and she was dealt such a blow between the shoulders that she fell to her knees in the alleyway.

She was up in a flash, facing Dagmar with fury. "That's mine! Give it back!"

"Yours?" the other woman sneered as Pimm tel'Jadis came laughing to her side. "That ain't the tale I heard, Prissy." She jerked open the bag and thrust her hand within, rummaging about. Then, uttering a crow of triumph, she raised high a fist in which were clutched the seven silver bangles of a Maiden-in-Circle.

The crowd shrieked.

The first rock caught Priscilla on the thigh as Dagmar brought a fist across her face.

The second rock slammed solidly into her right arm, breaking it with an audible crack.

The third took a rib, and she screamed, rolling into a ball on the filthy alley floor, trying to protect her head while the rocks struck with greater and greater force, and the crowd cried out her names: Liar! Coward! Unperson!

"Priscilla!"

She felt hands on her, and she struggled.

"Priscilla! No, denubia, you must not..." The voice was familiar, concerned.

"Lina?" She lay still, hardly daring to believe it.

"Of course, Lina. Who else?" The hands were soft on her face, her hair. "Open your eyes, denubia. Are you afraid to see me?"

"No, I..." She achieved it and beheld her friend's serious face. "I'm sorry, Lina."

"And I. Such *terror*, my friend. What was it?" The kind hands continued their caress; comfort like a healing warmth enclosed her. Priscilla sighed and shook her head.

"It was nothing. A bad dream."

"Yes?" Lina ran light fingers along Priscilla's jaw and down the slim throat, then laid her hand flat between rose-tipped breasts. "A very bad dream, I think. Your heart pounds."

"I dreamt—I dreamt I was being stoned." She shivered, drew a breath, and tried to recapture inner peace.

"Stoned?" Lina frowned. "I do not think—"

"It is the custom on my—on the world I'm from—to throw rocks at a criminal until she—until she dies."

"Qua'lechi!" The smaller woman sat up sharply and reached to trace the line of her friend's brow. "No wonder you were frightened." She tipped her head. "But this thing was not truly done to you?"

Priscilla managed a smile. "No, of course not." There, she had found the well-worn way to serenity and set her spirit feet upon it. "I'm not very brave," she told Lina softly.

As Priscilla's lashes drooped and her breathing evened, the Liaden woman frowned. Tentatively she unfurled a mental tendril, as one might with a fellow Healer, extended it along the least dangerous of the lines—and nearly cried out as Priscilla reached the place she had been seeking and firmly closed the door.

The library door slid open, and a tall, broad-shouldered person ambled to the center of the room and stood sipping from his glass, quietly regarding the figure hunched over the master terminal. It was perhaps five minutes before she sat back with a sharp sigh and spoke with the ease of long acquaintance. "Are there Healers among Terrans, old friend?"

He considered it, coming forward. "Not formally, I believe." He bent over her screen, frowning at the upside-down characters. "You want 'empath,' my precious. It's listed under 'paranormal.'"

"Paranormal!" Lina's head was up, eyes flashing.

"I didn't put it there," Shan pointed out mildly. "I only offer information. That's where it was when I searched it."

And, Lina realized, he would have done just such a search a few years ago. She smiled. "Forgive me. There was hard work done, if little accomplished. I am—edgy."

He bowed slightly. "I might offer aid."

"So you might." She smiled again and reached to touch his stark cheek. "I thank you, bed-friend and colleague. Grant me grace and offer another time."

"So I will." He drank wine. "Don't stay up all shift, please, Lina."

"Bah! And what of you! Or does the captain never sleep?" She chuckled, then sobered abruptly. "Kayzin was complaining to me that Priscilla is assigned where she has no right to be."

"I heard." Shan shook his head. "What did she want me to do? First she tells me this is her last trip and I must not ask her for decisions concerning future trips, then she takes me to *severe* task for daring to follow her instructions! I tell you, Lina, it's a hard life the captain lives!"

"Alas," she managed around a mouthful of laughter.

He grinned and raised his glass. "Search well, Master Librarian. Sleep well, too."

"Sleep well, Shan."

But he was already gone.

SHIPYEAR 65
TRIPDAY 139
THIRD SHIFT
16.00 HOURS

The *Dutiful Passage* broke orbit smoothly and proceeded down the carefully calculated normal space lane to the Jump point and passed without a quiver into hyperspace.

Priscilla ran through the last check, reaffirmed destination and time of arrival, locked the board, and leaned back, barely conquering her grin.

"Not too bad, Mendoza," Janice Weatherbee said from the copilot's seat. She glanced at the chronometer set in the board. "Quittin' time. See you 'round."

"Okay," Priscilla said absently, still watching the grayed screen. It was not the simulation screen this time—it was the prime piloting screen on the main bridge, and she had done it all. She, Priscilla Delacroix y Mendoza, had plotted the course, worked the equations, chosen the coords—done everything, out of her own knowledge and ability.

She closed her eyes against the screen, cherishing the solid wedge of belief in her own ability. For this little time, at least, it seemed not to matter that she was outcast and lawfully nameless, with no more right to call herself Mendoza than Rusty Morgenstern had.

"Sleeping, Ms. Mendoza? It's a very comfortable chair, I grant, but someone else might wish to use it."

She opened her eyes and grinned at the captain, who stood with one hip braced against the ledge and a glass of wine in his hand.

"Sorry, Captain. I was indulging in vulgar self-congratulation."

"Well, that's encouraging," he said, grinning back. "I was prepared to believe you had no faults at all. But now that you admit to gloating, I'm sure we'll get along very well together. Janice is a bit laconic, is she?"

"Maybe she's trying to make up for you," Priscilla suggested, then bit her lip in horror.

Shan yos'Galan laughed. "Could be. Could be. *Some*one should, I guess. Are you working a double shift? Even so, you're allowed an hour to eat—ship's policy. And there's really not much to do here now, is there?" He glanced vaguely at the gray screen. "Seems to be in hand. Why not take a shift or two for yourself?"

"Thank you, Captain," she said. "I will. Good shift."

"Good shift, Ms. Mendoza." He raised his glass to her.

She was to meet Lina and Rusty for prime at Seventeenth Hour. Priscilla turned left, away from the lift. There was time for a walk to stretch legs cramped by hours in the pilot's chair.

Hugging her recent accomplishment to herself, she wandered down a quarter mile of hallway, took a down-lift when the way deadended, and smiled at dour old Ken Rik when she stepped off one level below.

I feel good, she ventured, probing the thought as if it were a shattered bone. A mere quiver of pain answered, to be quickly blotted out by another warm thought.

I have a friend. The first real friend since her girlhood on Sintia. The friendship existed independently of the sudden physical relationship. She'd had bed-mates from time to random time, and it was very nice to be loved and petted and—made comfortable. And it was wholly delightful to be permitted to return that grace as best as she was able. But this was not the thing that was precious, that prompted her now to reexamine the plans she had laid out for herself.

Again she heard the sleepy voice of her friend: "Priscilla? Go back to sleep, denubia. All is well."

All is well. For the first time in many years she allowed herself to think that it could, in time, *be* well. If she remained a member of this ship, with its odd captain, and clumsy Rusty Morgenstern and Gordy and the old cargo master and Master Frodo and Lina—of course, Lina...

Perhaps if she stayed there...if she put Sav Rid Olanek and Dagmar Collier out of mind and concentrated on a future full of friendship, where all might be well...

"What are you doing here?"

The sharp voice brought her up short. She blinked at the unfamiliar hallway to which her unheeded feet had brought her, then looked back at Kayzin Ne'Zame and inclined her head. "I'm very sorry. I was thinking and lost my way. Is it restricted? I'll go away."

"Will you?" The first mate was tight-lipped with anger. "You will just walk away, is it so? I *asked* what you are doing here. I expect an answer. Now."

"I am sorry, Kayzin Ne'Zame," she said carefully. "I gave you an answer: I was walking as I thought, and lost the way."

"And you so conveniently lost the way in such a manner that you come to the main computer bank. I will have truth from you, Priscilla Mendoza. Again—what do you here?"

"I don't think that's your business," Priscilla flared. "Since you won't believe the truth, why should I keep repeating it?"

"You!" If she had been angry before, the mate was livid now. "How much does he pay you?" she demanded, her accent thicker by the second.

The Terran looked at her in blank astonishment. "One-tenth cantra, when we reach Solcintra—"

"Have done!" There was a pause while Kayzin looked her up and down. The set lines of her face did not alter; she opened her mouth to speak further, then closed it, eyes going over Priscilla's shoulder.

"Go!" she snapped. "And mind you do not lose your way to this place again. Do you hear me?"

"I hear you, Kayzin Ne'Zame," Priscilla replied evenly. She inclined her head and turned away.

Shan yos'Galan was leaning against the wall, glass of wine held negligently in one hand, arms crossed over his chest.

Priscilla took a breath. "Good shift, Captain."

"Good shift, Ms. Mendoza," he said neutrally. She walked past him and down the intersecting hallway.

He turned to Kayzin. "Correct me if I'm wrong," he said softly. "The crew is allowed access to all portions of the ship?"

"Yes, Captain."

"Yes, Captain," he repeated, his eyes holding hers effortlessly. "Priscilla Mendoza is a member of the crew, Kayzin. I can't think how you came to forget it, but please strive to bear it in mind in the future. Also, it is just possible that you owe an apology."

She drew a deep, deep breath. "Say that you trust her!"

"I trust her," he said flatly, giving her the grace due an old friend.

"You are besotted!"

"Quite sober, I assure you," he said in icy Terran. Then he switched to the High Tongue, that of lord instructing oathsworn. "I act, having given consideration to laws of necessity."

Kayzin bowed low, pride of him glowing through her mortification. There were those who said that Er Thom yos'Galan's lady had foisted a full-blooded Terran upon him as his eldest. If those could but see him, standing there, with the eyes spitting ice and the face just so! Who could behold him thus and say he was not Korval, blood and bone?

"Forgive me, Captain," she murmured. "It shall be as you have said."

"I am glad to hear it," he replied in Terran.

ARSDRED PORT CITY
LOCAL YEAR 728
MIDDAY BAZAAR

Arsdred Port roared. It pushed, yodeled, shoved, sang, shimmied, stripped gleaming naked, and swathed itself head to toe in bright colors and glittering gems. Much of the noise—and most of the color—was contributed by the people behind stalls, before store-fronts, and beside carts piled high with Goddess knew what. These were Arsdredi, dark-skinned Terrans, doe-eyed, hook-nosed, and voluble. They wore layer upon layer of gauzy, brilliant cloth and hawked their wares, sweatless, in the glare of the midday suns.

Some of the clamor, to be sure, was generated by those for whom the wares were displayed. Thronging the narrow streets were members of half a dozen races: Terrans of all description; graceful Liadens, dark-lensed Peladins, hairless Trimuvat, silent Uhlvore. Priscilla started, catching a gigantic figure out of the corner of an eye, wondering if even the Yxtrang stopped here— but it was only a towering Aus, golden-haired and full-bearded, head bent as he addressed a booming remark to the tiny woman skipping at his side.

"Firegems, pretty lady? The finest here—for you—so pale your skin, so black your hair! For *you,* beautiful lady, what else but azure? A mere twentybit—sacrificed on the altar of your beauty! Only try and see how it becomes you."

"Cloth, noble lady? Scarves? Crimson, gold, serpentine, xan-thin, indigo! Wear them about your head, twist them 'round your waist—a fair price, noble."

"Porcelains, lady? Guidebooks...Ices...Incense...Gem-stones..."

Peace.

Priscilla rounded a corner into a less traveled thoroughfare, breathing a sigh of relief. The roster had granted her leave this first day in port. Rusty and Lina had drawn time together on the third, a circumstance that brought a frown to the Liaden woman's face while Rusty shrugged. "Maybe next time."

Secretly, Priscilla was relieved. A leave-companion would have quickly discovered the state of her finances. She was pleased not to burden her friends with that particular information and perhaps be forced to endure kindhearted offers of a loan or, worse, an outright gift.

It was better this way, she thought, strolling along the hot little street. A day of rest before a trying tomorrow. For the roster's other news had been that she was to assist Cargo Master yo'Lanna with the worldside unloading next shift-worked.

She had come to the first cross street when a familiar voice intruded upon her.

"Hi, Ms. Mendoza! Is this your day, too? Want to partner?"

She turned, smiling down into Gordy Arbuthnot's round—and exquisitely clean—face. "I'm afraid I'd hold you down," she said carefully. Then she added more briskly, "You aren't here *by yourself,* are you, Gordy?"

He grimaced. "Well, sort of. Cap'n says he knows I got enough sense not to get in trouble, but that accidents happen an' my grandad'd break his nose for him if I came by one. So, we compromised." He tugged something off his belt and held it out for inspection: a portable comm.

"I've got the cap'n's direct beam-code. If I get in a scrape—even a *little* one—I'm supposed to get on the beam and *yell.*" Gordy sighed, then looked up again, trying to put a good face on it. "I guess that's not too bad, is it, Ms. Mendoza?"

"It sounds," Priscilla said truthfully, "very generous. And reasonable. A great many people, you know, would think you were only a little boy."

"Well, that's true," he agreed. "Even Ma said something like that when Grandad told her he'd got everything fixed with the cap'n, and she's usually—reasonable too. But Morgan'd been talking her ears off about how Shan wasn't *really* related to us—and Liaden, besides. I guess," Gordy concluded rather breathlessly, "that kind of thing'd be enough to make *any*body unreasonable."

"It certainly sounds like it would be," she agreed with amusement. "Is the captain related to you?"

Gordy nodded as he clipped the comm back to his belt. "Shan's ma was Grandad's sister. So we're cousins—Shan and Val Con and Nova and Anthora. Well, at least," he said scrupulously, "not Val

Con. He's a fosterling. But I call him cousin, too. And he's *Shan's* cousin, so I guess we're related, some way." He grinned at her. "Want to partner?" he asked again.

Priscilla shook her head. "I think I'd rather just roam around and get my thoughts in order, rest a little. I'm scheduled to help Ken Rik tomorrow."

Gordy laughed. "You better rest, then. Ken Rik's okay, but he likes to make people squirm. Good at it, too. Tell you what: I'm due at the shuttle Last Hour, shiptime. Let's go up together, okay, Ms. Mendoza?"

"Okay." She smiled at him. "You might as well call me Priscilla. Everybody else does."

"Cap'n doesn't," Gordy pointed out, moving off. "I will, though. See you later—Priscilla."

"See you later—Mr. Arbuthnot."

That drew another burst of laughter. Priscilla shook her head, still smiling, and turned left down the cross street, away from the voice of the bazaar.

It was a little past Nineteenth Hour, shiptime. Priscilla, feeling very well in a lazy sort of way, had quit the municipal park some moments before and was sauntering down a thin avenue that curved in the general direction of the port.

Most of the shops along this way were closed, though she passed a brightly lit window displaying an extremely ornate chess set carved of red and white woods and set with faceted stones. She paused, considering the set and comparing it to the chessmen she had seen upon the captain's board. Those pieces had been carved of ebonwood and bonebar, but very plainly—a set for a person who played the game, not for a collector of the exotic.

She continued on her way. The next window, under a sign that read TEELA'S TREASURES, was crowded with an eye-dazzling collection of objects. A carved ivory fan lay next to a tawdry firegem tiara; a gold necklace with a greenish tinge lay as if flung across a bound book of possible worth and definite age; while a cut-plastic vase hobnobbed with an eggshell porcelain bowl down on its luck.

Fascinated, Priscilla bent closer to the window, trying to puzzle out more of its contents. A carved wooden box with a broken hinge; an antique pair of eyeglasses, untinted; a—her breath caught in her throat as she spied it, balanced precariously atop a stack of mismatched flowered saucers: a blown-crystal triglant, caught by the artist in a mood of pensiveness, wings half-furled, tail wrapped neatly around its front paws. A charming piece—and hers!

Hers. And of the few things she had been able to bring with her from Sintia, it had been the most treasured. *She* had commissioned the work, paid for it with the labor of her own hands. *She* had built the velvet-lined box in which it had been lovingly displayed.

Perhaps the thief had thought the box worthless.

Priscilla stalked stiff-legged into the shop, twobits clenched in her fist. Fifteen minutes later, she came out, carefully tucking the paper-wrapped figurine in her pocket. Broke, she reminded herself, trying to call up fear.

But all she felt was warm contentment. She had the triglant. She had a berth on the *Passage.* She had a tenth-cantra waiting for her when they docked at Solcintra. It would suffice. She had a friend— perhaps even three. That was so much more than sufficient that she barely had room for the grief of leaving her other things in the hands of the proprietor of Teela's Treasures.

She took the first cross street, hurrying now toward the port. To her right, a shadow moved. She spun.

"Hello, Prissy," Dagmar said, grinning widely. She took two steps closer.

Goddess, aid me now…"Good-bye, Dagmar," she gritted through, her teeth. She made to pass on.

The bigger woman blocked her way, grin widening. "Aw, now, honey, you ain't gonna let a little thing like a headache come between us, are you? I was just following orders, Prissy. And I sure am glad to see you again."

"I'm not glad to see you. Good-bye." She turned away.

Dagmar grabbed an arm and yanked Priscilla forward, while her other hand found a breast and squeezed.

Priscilla swung with all the force in her, slamming five knuckles backhanded across the other woman's leer as she twisted, just managing to get free.

Dagmar lunged, grabbing a handful of shirt. Priscilla continued her twist. The fabric tore, and Dagmar pitched backward, scrabbling for support.

It was time to run. Priscilla dived forward.

It was easy.

Dagmar was bigger—and no doubt stronger. Certainly she was more accustomed to this kind of business than was her prey.

But she was *slow.*

Priscilla had the measure of the game now. Moving with pilot swiftness, seeing with pilot eyes, she landed an astonishing number of blows, though the ones she received were telling.

She ducked back, slammed a ringing blow toward the ears that was only partially successful, and suffered a numbing crack to her right shoulder.

Several more passes and she saw how it might be ended—quickly and to her advantage. She began the spin to get into position—

The hum warned her, and she snapped backward, rolling heavily on her right side, wishing she had had the sense to run before.

Dagmar had pulled a vibroknife.

Gordy was late.

He streaked across the municipal park, causing consternation among the local duck-analogs, and careered into Parkton Way. He passed the window containing the chessmen without a glance, though he did slow as he came abreast Teela's Treasures, out of respect for the policeman half a block ahead.

A side street presented itself, wending portward. Gordy took it—and froze in disbelief.

Before him was Priscilla Mendoza, shirt torn nearly to the shoulder, bent forward like some two-legged, beautiful, and quite deadly predator, carefully circling a larger, broader woman, who circled in her turn.

The position of the two changed sufficiently for Gordy to see the rest: The larger woman held a knife.

Gulping, he turned and ran back the way he had come.

Priscilla considered the knife dispassionately. It could be done. She was fast. Dagmar was slow. Her objective was only to dispose of the blade—*she* was no knife fighter.

Priscilla moved.

Dagmar twisted—so slooow—and Priscilla's fingers swept through hers, dislodging the evil, humming thing and sending it spinning into the shadows. The larger woman finished her twist and slammed heavily into her opponent, trying to grab and hold two slender wrists in a big hand, hugging her tight, and Priscilla could not breathe...

"Here now, here now! That'll be enough of *that* kind of carrying on!" Strong hands grabbed and pulled—and breath returned.

Priscilla sagged backward, too grateful for the boon of air to resent the hand irons so competently slapped into place. Dagmar, she saw presently, was in worse shape. She had apparently taken a stunner charge and was retching against the wall, her face already beginning to purple.

The cop finished affixing irons and turned away—and his eyebrows went up with his stunner. "All right, my boy, fun's over. Give it to me, please."

Gordy blinked, reversed the vibroknife, and held it out. The cop took it gingerly, then jerked the comm from the boy's belt and clipped it to his own.

"That's mine!"

"Then you'll get it back after the trial. Hold out your hands."

"I won't wear irons." The round chin was rigid.

"Then you'll go unconscious, over my shoulder." The cop considered him. "Might drop you, though."

Gordy looked over the man's shoulder at Priscilla. She managed a ragged smile and a nod. He held out his hands.

ARSDRED PORT MAGISTRATE'S CHAMBER
LOCAL YEAR 728
EVENING BAZAAR

The exhibits were on a table against the far left wall: a vibroknife, a portable comm, a pile of glittering shards that had once represented a triglant at rest.

The prisoners were to the right. The slender woman and the boy sat next to each other, as far away as possible from the bulky woman with the battered face. Sedatives had been administered to all, in keeping with the magistrate's order. Though there had been no renewal of hostilities, the arresting officer was keeping a sharp eye out. One never knew with outworlders.

Priscilla fought the tranquilizing haze, struggling for clear thought. They were waiting, the cop had said, for the arrival of a ranking officer from *Daxflan* and from *Dutiful Passage* so that the trial could commence.

Kayzin Ne'Zame, Priscilla thought laboriously. She dislikes me—here's a Goddess-sent opportunity for her to be rid of me altogether.

Lina. What would Lina think? Would Priscilla be allowed to speak with her, explain what had happened, before the *Passage* left orbit? She caught her breath, her mind suddenly clear of fog, aware of a nearly overmastering desire to fling herself down and sob.

Fool, she told herself harshly. You should have run.

There was a rustle of robes in the outer hallway, and Gordy shifted next to her. "Maybe that's the judge," he said drowsily, "I sure hope so. Crelm, Priscilla! Do you know how late we are? Shan's gonna *skin* me!"

Her reply was cut off by the arresting officer.

"All rise for Magistrate Kelbar!"

She stood; she started when Gordy slipped his hand into hers, and then squeezed his fingers.

"That's you, too!" the cop was telling Dagmar, who mumbled something and climbed to her feet.

Magistrate Kelbar swept into the room, an imposing figure in his sun-yellow robes of office. Out of stern brown eyes he considered the three of them before seating himself with a flourish upon his throne. He waved a hand in a languid gesture that the cop translated sharply.

"Prisoners sit!"

Dagmar grunted and slouched back onto her bench. Priscilla sat quietly, though Gordy heaved a sigh.

Let it be done quickly, Goddess, Priscilla prayed.

As if in answer to that thought, the door was opened from without, admitting a small, fair man.

Sav Rid Olanek had been called from a party, Priscilla thought: His shirt was shimmering rose silk; the pale trousers surely were velvet. Jewels glittered in his ears, on his hands, and from the buckle of his belt, and around his throat was a titanium collar worth double the pay she would never collect at Solcintra.

Recognizing a person of consequence, the magistrate snapped his fingers at the prisoners to rise and swept forward. "Good evening, gentle sir!" he said in affable Trade, extending a wide hand. "I am sorry to have had to summon you here. A small matter, I am sure, and easily settled, once your honored colleague arrives. I am Magistrate Kelbar."

He was accorded a flickering glance from bright blue eyes, and the barest possible bow. "I am Sav Rid Olanek, Trader on *Daxflan,* out of Liad," he said coldly. "I am afraid you may be too optimistic, however." He pointed at Priscilla, who returned his gaze with determined serenity. *"That* person is a desperate criminal. She is without doubt a thief. What else she may be—"

"Good evening!" a voice called in cheerful Terran, preceding its owner into the room by a heartbeat. Sav Rid Olanek bit off the rest of his sentence, and Priscilla felt Gordy shift next to her.

It was not Kayzin Ne'Zame, after all.

He wore a shirt barely less bright than his hair, and soft black trousers. His belt buckle was merely silver, its design changing from a fanciful bird to an impossible flower as Priscilla watched. An amethyst drop exactly matching the color of the gem in his master's ring hung from his right ear.

He was the most welcome sight Priscilla had ever beheld. It'll be all right now, she told herself, and didn't even wonder why she thought so.

He smiled at the magistrate and bowed easily, then came forward with hand outstretched. "I'm Shan yos'Galan, sir. Am I very late? Forgive me, please. I was at Herr Sasoni's—but perhaps I should say no more. Except that I was on the verge of concluding a very—interesting—piece of business, so it was fortunate your message reached me when it did."

The magistrate actually laughed, taking the more slender hand in his. "But this is dreadful!" he cried. "Surely you were able to procure her key for later use? I should never forgive myself, sir—"

"No matter," the captain interrupted easily. "I'm sure we'll be able to clear this matter up in a moment or two, and I'll return— what *is* the matter, by the way, sir? I—" He turned his head, eyes alighting, apparently for the first time, on his glaring colleague.

"Good evening, Sav Rid," he said politely in the Liaden High Tongue.

"You!" the other snarled.

"Well, of course, me. I couldn't very well be anyone else, could I? Has this little inconvenience put you out of temper? I'm sure we'll be shut of it in a moment. The magistrate seems very amiable, don't you think? As I just said to him—but I've forgotten, you don't speak Terran, do you? A sad pity, since so many other people do, but no doubt you have your reasons."

"I do, and they are not yours to inquire into." Trader Olanek waved his hand in their direction, though his eyes did not leave the captain. "You might wish to turn your limited understanding to the matter at hand. It may be that you have undervalued the inconvenience."

"Yes?" The silver eyes swept the three of them vaguely. "Well, I must say, your crew member—I assume she is yours—looks as if she's taken rather a tumble. In her cups, perhaps. But you're too experienced a Trader to allow a little drunken sport among the crew to spoil your whole evening."

"Gentles?" Magistrate Kelbar said in firm Trade. "If we may get on with the hearing? I am certain we would all rather be elsewhere." He resumed his seat with another flourish and waved the prisoners forward. "Will you two gentlemen please identify these persons?"

Trader Olanek pointed. "That is Dagmar Collier, second mate on *Daxflan.*"

"And, as her superior officer, you are willing to speak for her?"

After a slight hesitation, the Trader said, "Yes."

"And the two remaining," the captain said cheerily, "are mine, sir. The young gentleman is Gordon Arbuthnot, cabin boy on the *Dutiful Passage* and my kinsman—"

"You mean to say you acknowledge that connection?" The Trader's High Liaden carried outrage. "It's full Terran! Have you no sense of the honor due your Clan?"

"Well, we're *half* Terran, after all," the captain said mildly. "You knew that, didn't you, when you propositioned my sister? And he's a good lad."

"You cannot be serious."

"He is under Korval's wing." The captain's inflection shifted subtly, his voice nearly cold. "Do not mistake me."

"Pah! Korval's wing unfurls too far for health. Does the same apply to the bitch beside him?"

She stiffened, outrage erupting—

"Priscilla!" the captain snapped, and she stilled, cheeks flaming.

"You keep it on a short leash," the Trader commented. "How much do you pay it? Or does it serve for the pleasure of looking at your beautiful face?"

The captain shook his head. "On Priscilla Mendoza's home world, Sav Rid, you would have just now uttered an insult demanding your death for balance. It's fortunate, isn't it, that her knowledge of our tongue is a scholar's? But I am forgetting my manners again! You are acquainted!" The light eyes were on her. "Have you no greeting for the honored Trader?"

She stared at him. Did he really expect her— And then she smiled, recalling another of Fin Ton's lessons. Loosing Gordy's hand, she bowed low.

"Forgive me the situation, Master Trader," she said in her careful High Liaden, "and believe me all joy to see you."

"What!" Sav Rid cried, visibly shaken. "How is it possible that—"

"Gentles," the magistrate said. "I must insist that we keep to the matter at hand."

"Of course, sir." The captain was contrite. "Do forgive us. My colleague is an avid student of lineage and sought enlightenment regarding Gordon's place in the family tree. To continue, indeed. The lady with the torn shirt is Priscilla Delacroix y Mendoza. She is under personal contract to the captain of the *Dutiful Passage,* serving as librarian, pilot, and apprentice second mate." He smiled. "I'm quite happy to speak for both of them."

What was this? Pilot? Second mate in training? Priscilla tried to recall the precise phrasing of her contract, but the magistrate's voice defeated the effort.

"As all three have someone in authority to speak for them, the hearing now commences. What we know is this: Yonder knife is the property of Dagmar Collier. We have taken imprint readings and find it to be so. She does not deny it.

"It is important to note that two other sets of prints are found on the hilt, besides those of the arresting officer: those of Gordon Arbuthnot, and a faint, very blurred set which we believe to be those of Priscilla Mendoza." The magistrate paused to clear his throat importantly.

"We will hear from the arresting officer."

The cop's statement was brief and to the point. He had been hailed by Gordon Arbuthnot, who cried that there was a fight in Halvington Street. Arriving on the scene, he had found "those two persons there" in close embrace, the larger apparently engaged in squeezing the smaller breathless. The arresting officer was of the opinion that this project was near completion and so had administered a judicial stunner blast to the larger person, hand-ironed both combatants, and turned to find Gordon Arbuthnot with "that knife, there, sir," in his hand. So, in the interest of fair play, Gordy had been ironed as well, and all three brought in. The officer paused, scratched his head, and added that he had also taken from Gordon Arbuthnot a small rectangular object with a belt clip—very likely a portable comm and no harm to it. But at the time he had seen no reason to take unnecessary chances.

"Quite right," the captain said approvingly, and the cop grinned shyly.

The magistrate motioned him back. "We will now hear from Dagmar Collier."

Dagmar came forward slowly and darted a glance at Trader Olanek. He did not meet her eyes.

She made a woeful attempt to square her shoulders. Her voice when she spoke was hoarse, the words mushy. I hope I broke every tooth in her mouth, Priscilla thought.

"Prissy and me are old friends," Dagmar was telling the magistrate. "Used to serve on *Daxflan* together. It was just natural for me to go over and say 'hey' when I saw her walkin' down the street."

She shrugged. "Must've been drunk, I guess, Your Honor, 'cause she just hauled off and hit me."

There was a short pause before the magistrate asked dryly, "Is that your statement of the affair?"

Dagmar blinked. "Yessir."

"I see. We are willing to hear you again, should something else occur to you after Priscilla Mendoza speaks."

Priscilla stood forward. "Ms. Collier and I were never friends," she began hotly. "She has stolen from me and sold my things to a— a *thrift shop* on Parkton—"

The magistrate raised his hand. "That is not the issue at trial here. Please limit your remarks to the incident in Halvington Street."

Priscilla bit her lip. "I saw Ms. Collier in Halvington Street," she began again, "as I was on my way back to the port. She spoke to me. I returned the greeting and tried to pass on. Ms. Collier blocked my way and grabbed me—I *believe* she intended rape, but that may be unjust. At the time it seemed exactly what she meant, and I—" she broke off, her eyes seeking the captain's. "I lost my temper," she said wryly. He nodded, and she turned back to the magistrate.

"I tried to defend myself against what I thought was an attack. Ms. Collier continued to block my way and at some point pulled a knife. I *did* disarm her, but she grabbed me. Which is how I came to be in the absurd situation from which the officer rescued me." She sighed. "That is my statement, sir."

"Very clear, Ms. Mendoza. Thank you."

"I would like to point out," Sav Rid Olanek said abruptly, "that the animosity between these two individuals seems of long standing—"

"Exactly," the captain interrupted. "in which case, Magistrate, I venture to say that each has had ample opportunity to vent her spleen. A fine, of course, is in order, for breaking the peace. But, since it is highly unlikely that they will meet again soon..."

Magistrate Kelbar beamed at him. "I am sure you can be trusted to control the members of your crew during the rest of your time in port, sirs. My trust in your discretion prompts me not to demand that both individuals be rendered ship-bound for that period. They will, of course, be confined to the port proper. And, there *is* a fine." He coughed gently. "For engaging in fisticuffs in a public thoroughfare: one hundred bits each. Drawing a deadly weapon: two hundred fifty

bits. Possession of said weapon without Arsdred certificate of permission: six hundred bits. Resisting arrest—" He looked up and smiled,
first at Gordy, then at the captain. "I think we might dispense with
that. Transport fee: fifty bits each.

"So then, owed from Dagmar Collier, through her superior,
Sav Rid Olanek: one thousand bits. Owed from Priscilla Mendoza,
through her superior, Shan yos'Galan: one hundred fifty bits. Owed
from Gordon Arbuthnot from his superior, Shan yos'Galan: fifty
bits. You may pay cash at the teller's cage as you leave, gentles." He
arose and sailed from the room, the arresting officer in his wake.

Shan considered Olanek's set face. "One thousand bits," he
murmured in sympathetic Trade. "Will it put you out of pocket,
Sav Rid? I can extend a loan, if you like."

"Thank you, I think not!" the other snapped, jerking his head at
his crew member.

Shan sighed. "So short-tempered, Sav Rid! Not sleeping
well? I do hope you're not ill. At least we know you don't have a
guilty conscience, don't we? By the way, Ms. Mendoza seems to
have lost a very special pair of earrings. Do you know Calintak,
on Medusa? Wonderful fellow, very good-tempered. And the
things he can fit in just a *little* bit of space: built-in sensors, track-
ers—that sort of thing. If you're ever in the market for something, since you wear so *much* jewelry..."

Dagmar Collier was hovering close, eyes riveted. "Sensors?"
she asked with a kind of fascinated dread. "How small a space?"

"Oh, are you interested? He's quite dear, you know—but hardly
any space at all. An unexceptional earring, for instance, is all the
room he needs to work in. An artist—"

"Oh, have done!" Sav Rid snarled, turning on his heel. "Pay
him no mind, he's a fool. Now, come!" He was gone, Dagmar
following.

Shan shook his head and held out a hand to Gordy, who came
and slid his own into it. "Well now, children—Ms. Mendoza?"

She was at the exhibit table, picking up the shards of crystal,
one by careful one, and settling them in her palm.

"Crelm!" Gordy muttered, and went to her side. "Priscilla,
what're you doing? It's busted."

She did not look away from her task. "It's all I own, anywhere,
and I'm taking it with me." Her tone was perfectly flat, with an

absence of emotion that raised the hairs on Shan's neck. He stepped forward quickly, pulled a square of silk from his sleeve, and dropped it in front of her.

"You'll cut yourself, Priscilla. Use this."

"Thank you." Her voice was still flat, though he fancied he detected a quiver of *something*...

Hand in hand, he and Gordy waited until she had finished and tied the silk into a knot. Gordy took her hand, and, so linked, they went out to pay the cashier.

SHIPYEAR 65
TRIPDAY 143
FIRST SHIFT
2.00 HOURS

"You will do me the favor, won't you, Gordy," the captain murmured, "of neglecting to inform your mother that you've been arrested?"

"Was I?" the boy asked hazily. "I mean, I wasn't *really*. They didn't do anything to me."

The man laughed. "Arrested, I assure you. The details may vary by world, but the larger outlines remain constant: irons, hearings, magistrates, fines—not at all the kind of thing mothers enjoy hearing of, even when it's carefully explained that you were completely without blame. Which reminds me—how did your imprints come to be on that thing?"

"Priscilla was losing," Gordy explained. "And the knife was just lying there. I was trying to figure out how it worked..."

"Yes? To what end, please?"

"Well, I thought if I cut Dagmar's arm, she'd let go."

"It's a theory," the captain admitted. "Report to Pallin Kornad after breakfast, please. I see it's time you learned how to protect yourself."

"Yes, Cap'n." He paused. "Shan?"

"Yes, acushla?"

"Is it—can I tell Grandad I was arrested? I didn't do anything *wrong...*" This last was spoken, it seemed to Priscilla, with considerable doubt.

A boot heel scraped on the pavement as the man went down on one knee, eyes level with Gordy's.

"You will *absolutely* tell your grandfather," he said firmly, his big hands on the boy's round shoulders. "He will be proud of you. You acted with forethought and with honor, coming to the aid of a shipmate and a friend." He cupped a soft cheek. "You did very well, Gordy. Thank you."

"Yes." Priscilla heard her own voice from far away. "Thank you, Gordy. You saved my life."

He blinked at her over his cousin's shoulder. "I *did?*" She nodded, not sure what her face was doing. "She really was winning. I couldn't breathe. You did exactly right."

She should, she thought vaguely, find something more to say, but it was unnecessary; doubt had vanished from the young face. He grinned. "I'm a hero."

"You're an impossible monkey." The captain stood and held out his hand. "And you're well behind your time to return to the ship. Come along."

They walked a little way in silence. The drug was gaining the upper hand again, and Priscilla stumbled; she caught herself and asked over Gordy's head, "What was that about your sister?"

"Sav Rid's little joke," the captain said easily. "It amused him to propose marriage to the eldest of my sisters."

"What!" Gordy was outraged. "That—person? To *Cousin Nova?*"

"Indeed, yes. Exactly Cousin Nova. Why? Do you think Anthora might suit him better? I admit it's a thought. He so fair and she so dark...But he was more enamored of fair with fair. You can't really blame him, Gordy; it's merely a matter of taste."

"What did you do?" Gordy demanded awfully, ignoring this flow of nonsense.

The man looked down at him. "What could I do? I was from home. Besides, Nova is well able to take care of herself. Simply told the fellow she'd rather mate with a Gehatian slimegrubber and sent him about his business." He sighed. "I'm afraid he didn't take it in very good part. Well, how was she to know he had a horror of the creatures? I'm sure she would have thought of something else just as revolting to compare him with, if she'd had the least idea. Very resourceful person, Cousin Nova. The more I think on it, the more certain I am that you're right, Gordy! Anthora would certainly suit him far better! A pity he didn't see it that way and allowed himself to be enraptured by a mere pretty face. Perhaps we should suggest—"

"Pretty!" the boy choked. "Cousin Nova's *beautiful!*"

"Well," the lady's brother conceded, "she is. But I wouldn't let it weigh too heavily with you. Gordy. Sort of thing that might happen to anyone. And she's really quite clever."

They came at length to the cradles and crossed to their shuttlepad in silence. A shadow loomed at the door, bringing two fingers up in a casual salute. "Evening, Cap'n."

"Good evening, Seth. Two passengers for you. Take good care of them, please; they both seem a bit yawnsome—is that a word?"

"Bound to be," the lanky pilot returned good-humoredly. "Not going up yourself?"

"Business, Seth. Duty calls."

"He has to get her key," Gordy said helpfully.

"Brat." His cousin sighed. "Don't forget Pallin next shift, Gordy."

"No, Cap'n—at least, *yes*, Cap'n. I'll remember."

The captain laughed and began to move away, then checked himself and came back, fishing in his belt. "My terrible memory! I knew there was something else. Ms. Mendoza!"

She started. "Captain?"

He was holding out a flat rectangle, a card of some sort. She took it automatically.

"Do take care of it, Ms. Mendoza," he chided gently. "It's really not the sort of thing you want to leave lying around. Good evening." He was gone.

Priscilla frowned at the card, but the uncertain light or her sedative-fogged eyes defeated the attempt to identify it. She put it in her pocket with the knotted kerchief and followed Gordy into the shuttle.

Gordy was asleep when they docked. The snap of the board being locked jerked Priscilla out of her own doze, but even the most stringent effort she was able to make would not rouse her companion from his.

Sighing, she fumbled her webbing loose, then opened his. Her several attempts to pick him up should have roused one dead, she thought foggily, but Gordy only grumbled a few sleep syllables and tried to curl farther down into the chair. Priscilla rubbed her forehead with the back of a hand and tried to apply her mind to the problem.

"Out for the count," Seth commented from beside her. "I gotta get back down. Can you carry him, or should we call Vilt?"

Priscilla gave him what she hoped was a smile. "I can carry him. Getting him up is the problem."

"Naw. Not when somebody's that far out." He bent, grabbed an arm, heaved, turned, and offered Priscilla an armful of boy.

She took Gordy and allowed herself to be escorted to the door of the cargo dock. It slid open for her, and she stepped into the corridor, blinking a little in the directionless yellow light.

Before her she saw, with the vivid disconnection of a dream, a bronze-winged dragon hovering. No. It was a painting on the wall, a smaller reproduction of the design in the reception room. Under Korval's wing, Priscilla recalled. She shifted her burden and began the long walk to the crew's quarters.

She had made it, staggering only now and then, to the top of the corridor where Gordy had his room, when she heard quick steps behind her and an exclamation.

"Priscilla! Is that Gordon? What has—is all well, my friend?"

"Well?" She considered Lina muzzily. It took several seconds to formulate an appropriate response. "Gordy's all right. It's mostly that stupid stuff they injected us with at the police station. Makes you...makes you groggy. Half asleep, myself."

"Ah." The other woman fell in beside her. "The police station? Does the captain know?"

Priscilla nodded, then paused to regain her balance. "He came to bail us out—dear Goddess!" She stopped, arms closing convulsively around Gordy, who muttered. "Dear Goddess," she said again, though not, Lina thought, prayerfully. "One hundred fifty bits! Out of a tenth-cantra? And the clothes..." She took a hard breath and began to walk again. "Broke. No money at all."

Lina's worry increased, but she refrained from pursuing questions, merely remarking that they had reached Gordon's room and lifting his hand to lay it against the palmlock.

Priscilla laid him on the bed, pulled off his boots, straightened the blanket, and pulled it up. Lina stood by the door, watching and saying nothing.

The boy disposed comfortably, Priscilla glanced around the room, and nodded slightly, then bent and ruffled the silky hair.

"Ma?" Gordy inquired from the depths of sleep.

She started, then completed the caress. "It's only Priscilla, Gordy. Sleep well."

Lina followed her out, stretching her short legs to keep up with the pace her friend set, even half-drugged.

At the top of the hall Priscilla made to turn right. Lina caught her arm. "No, Priscilla. Your room is this way."

"Have to go to the library," she protested. "Now."

"Not now," Lina said with decision. "Now, you must rest. The library will be in place next shift."

Priscilla shook her head. "Have to see my contract."

"Your contract? Priscilla, it is—conselem—an absurdity! What good does your contract do when you must sleep? You are signed until Solcintra. You may look at your contract any time these next four months. Come to bed."

"He lied," Priscilla said flatly, a decidedly mulish look about her lovely mouth.

Lina sighed. "Who lied? And why must— The captain lied?" She stared up at her friend. "That is not much like him, denubia. Perhaps you misunderstood."

"I'm very tired," Priscilla said clearly, "of misunderstanding. I must see my contract."

"Of course you must," Lina agreed. "It would be very bad to have misunderstood the captain. Let us go to your room and access the file from there." She slipped her arm around the other's waist.

Priscilla stiffened and moved away—a very little. Lina's eyes widened, but she said nothing, only withdrew her arm. And waited.

"All right," Priscilla said presently, the mulish look much abated. "Let's do that. Thank you, Lina."

"I am happy to help," Lina said carefully as they turned left down the hall. "What happened, my friend?"

There was a long pause before the taller woman shook herself and answered, "I was attacked on the street. Gordy tried to help, and we all three got arrested. They called the captain out of a party to—to speak for us."

"Most proper," Lina said, and stopped, waiting for Priscilla to lay her palm against the lock.

It seemed for a moment that she did not recognize her own door. Then she shifted and placed her hand in the center; when the panel slid away, she entered, with Lina trailing after.

"Most proper," Priscilla repeated, standing in the middle of her cabin and staring around as if she had never seen the place before. She spun.

"It cost *one hundred fifty bits* to *speak* for me!" she cried with an unexpected but wholly gratifying flare of passion. "One hundred fifty! And I'll have earned a tenth-cantra by the time we reach Solcintra, *and* I already owe the ship for my clothes—and all my things—my things are gone…" Abruptly she sat on the bed, running violent fingers through the curly cloud of her hair.

Lina came forward, daring to lay her hand on a rigid shoulder. She frowned at the startled jerk. "I did not attack you on the street," she said severely.

Priscilla looked up, apology in her eyes. Lina smiled, lifting the tips of her fingers to a pale cheek.

"Of course I did not. I have been very well brought up." She tugged gently on an errant curl. "Of this other thing: The ship has a—*legal fund*. Since *you* were attacked, I think the fund will pay the expense of your bail. It is a thing you should speak of with the captain. Was he angry with you?"

Priscilla blinked. "I don't think so. Does he get angry?"

Lina laughed. "If he had been so, you would not be in doubt. So, then, I would not worry about my wages. It is very likely that they remain intact. Now, allow me to call your contract up." She went to the screen.

Behind her, Priscilla stood, moved unsteadily to the mirror shelf, and began to pull things from her pocket. The knotted silk she placed carefully to one side of the usual oddments. Patting her pocket to be sure it was empty, she felt a flat thickness—the card the captain had given her at the shuttlepad. She pulled it out and examined it, her breath catching.

"Lina!"

The Liaden woman was at her elbow instantly. "Yes?"

Priscilla held out the card in a hand that was not at all steady. "What is this, please?"

Lana subjected it to a brief, two-sided scrutiny and handed it back, smiling. "It is a provisional second class pilot's license in the name of Priscilla Delacroix y Mendoza. Ge'shada, my friend, you have done very well."

"I've done very well. Done well…" Priscilla stared and suddenly threw back her head, uttering a sound so shattered that no one could have called it laughter. Then she bent double, torn with sobs.

Lina put her arms about her and probed with a Healer's sure instinct, evading weakened defenses and slashing at the protected reservoir of pain.

Priscilla cried out and went to her knees. Lina held her closer, withdrawing somewhat, content for the present to have the storm rage.

After a time, the sobbing eased and she coaxed her friend to the bed. When they were lying face to face, she probed again, projecting on all possible lines.

Priscilla stirred, sodden lashes lifting, then extended a tentative finger to trace the lines of her friend's face, exhausted wonderment on her own.

"I see you, sister," she murmured. Then her hand fell away, and she slept, bathed in warm affection and comfort.

SHIPYEAR 65
TRIPDAY 143
SECOND SHIFT
6.00 HOURS

"But why can't we sell the perfume here?" Rusty demanded, staring at Lina over a suspended forkful of ice-toast.

The Liaden woman sighed. "It is—bah! I have forgotten the word. It is to *force* one to love another, a…"

"Aphrodisiac," Priscilla supplied, looking up from her own breakfast. "Aphrodisiacs are illegal on some planets. I guess Arsdred's one of them."

Rusty scowled at his plate.

"Rah Stee, do not!" Lina was laughing. "You will spoil your food! It is not so bad. We will sell at another port." She shook a slender finger in mock severity. "You believe I have given us a loss! But I claim the dice for more than one throw. You will see, my friend: the perfume will sell—and at high profit!"

Rusty looked dubious, and Lina laughed again.

"Priscilla?" a breathless young voice asked at her elbow. She turned her head to discover the cabin boy, clutching a box.

"Good morning, Gordy," she said, offering him a storm-beaten smile. "I thought you were supposed to be learning self-defense first thing this shift."

"Crelm!" he said scornfully. "I did that an hour ago!" He held out the box, plainly expecting her to take it. She did, full of wonder.

"Cap'n's compliments," he said formally. "And his apologies for sending you planetside alone." Gordy tipped his head. "He said he was a fool, Priscilla, but he can't have meant me to tell you that, do you think?"

"Very likely not," she agreed. "So we'll pretend you didn't."

"Right. Gotta jet. Morning, Lina! Rusty!"

She sat holding the box in her lap until Rusty inquired, a little impatiently, if she wasn't going to open it.

"Yes, of course," she murmured, making no move to do so. Allowing me planetside alone? A test, Goddess? she wondered.

To see if I would choose revenge, after all? It occurred to her to wonder if the captain's watch over her had been rather closer than she had supposed. She shook her head and reached for a blunt-edged jelly knife.

The sealing tape broke easily. She laid the knife aside and un-folded the flaps. The box contained several objects, each wrapped in bright gossamer paper.

Very slowly, she pulled out the first object. She unwrapped it as slowly, refusing to acknowledge what weight and shape told her until her eyes added irrefutable evidence.

The object was a rosewood comb, intricately carved with a pattern of stars and flowers, the tines satin-smooth from years of being pulled through a waist-length cascade and, more recently, a brief, unruly mop of hair.

Priscilla took a breath, laid the comb aside, and returned to the box. One by one she uncovered them: the brush and hand mirror that matched the comb, several fired-clay figurines, a thin folder of flatpix, a brass-bound kaleidoscope, four bound books, nine musictapes, and three thin silver bangles.

Priscilla held the bangles in her hand for a moment before lay-ing them with the other things. Once, there had been seven: the full complement of a Maiden-near-Wife. Four she had sold at different times, as need had dictated. They would have been worth far more as a set, sold to a collector of the occult. She never let one go without a wrench that was almost a physical illness.

She laid the bracelets carefully beside the other objects. In the bottom of the box was one more item: a small red velvet box. Frowning, she picked it up.

"What is all this?" Rusty demanded, breaking the silence that had fallen on the three of them.

"My—things," Priscilla. said hesitantly. "My personal things that were left behind on *Daxflan.*" She held out the red box. "Ex-cept this. I don't know…" She lifted the lid.

Earrings.

Not *her* earrings, which had been ornate and old. These were new, not at all ornate, just simple hoops; their plain design was de-ceptive, for the weight and sheen said platinum, and the individual who had crafted them had signed each with a proud flourish.

Priscilla looked at Lina. "They're not mine."

"Ah."

"Why?" Priscilla whispered.

Lina moved her shoulders. "He sent apologies. Perhaps he felt you were owed. You should, perhaps, ask."

"Yes…" She closed the lid carefully and put the box with the rest of the items.

Rusty picked up the kaleidoscope and peered through it. "Nice," he murmured.

"Mother, look at the time!" Priscilla cried suddenly, pushing her chair back. "I'm as bad as Gordy! And Ken Rik *will* skin me! Lina—"

"I will take care of them," her friend said, picking up the mirror and beginning to rewrap it. She looked up with a fond smile. "Go. Give Ken Rik a kiss for me."

"You do it, if you want him kissed," Priscilla retorted, and was gone.

Rusty picked up a piece of tissue and clumsily crumpled it around the kaleidoscope. "Funny sort of thing for the cap'n to do," he said thoughtfully.

Lina glanced up. "Do you think so?"

"Yah, I do." He looked at her closely before returning to the remains of his breakfast. "And don't try to bamboozle me into thinking you don't think so, either. We been on too many rounds together for that to pass."

"Well," Lina said conscientiously, "there are many reasons why he might do so."

Rusty grinned and drank the rest of his coffee. "Knew you were fuzzed," he said triumphantly, pushing back his chair. "You think of more than one, come on up to the tower and tell me what it is."

Ken Rik had done no more than glare at her rather breathless arrival. He slapped a clipboard in her hand and set her to supervising the emptying of Hold 4, adding a caustic rider to the effect that he hoped she knew enough to balance the load properly for the shuttle.

Priscilla rounded her eyes at him. "Thank you," she said in an awed whisper. "I would never have done it without a reminder. Lina said you were kind."

The old man looked at her suspiciously, saying he knew very well Lina had said no such thing. But Priscilla thought he sounded somewhat less cross.

Hold 4 contained the agricultural plants belmekit and trasveld, both stasis-held items; both on their way—so the clipboard informed her—to the warehouses of one Herr Polifant Sasoni, Offworld Bazaar, Arsdred. The last pallet came up on her board as "samples." She followed the jitney bearing it to the shuttlebay, her mind on breakfast.

Ken Rik took the clipboard, rechecked her figures, approved the weight distributions with a sniff, and waved her into the shuttle.

Automatically, Priscilla started for the copilot's place, to be sharply called to book by her companion.

"Are you a moonling?" he demanded, dropping into the co's chair himself. Priscilla stared at him until he snorted in exasperation and pointed at the board. "Come along, woman! Don't waste my time."

"You want *me* to take us down?"

"No, I want the shuttle to fly itself," Ken Rik snapped with relish. "I am told you are a pilot. You will, therefore, pilot." He folded his arms over chest and webbing, leaned back, and closed his eyes.

Priscilla webbed into the pilot's chair. Slowly at first, then with more assurance, she ran her fingers over the board, calling up rotations, distance, wind speeds, upper atmosphere. Then she chose her approach, cleared the site, and signaled ready.

They left the *Passage* in a neat tumble, skimming toward the planet in a matching arc, hit atmosphere a little later with the barest possible bump, and slid into the approach approved by Arsdred Port. The wind gave her a little trouble, but she managed to hold the craft steady, her teeth indenting her lower lip, her hand unfaltering over the board.

In a glass-smooth glide, they settled on the pad. Priscilla rechecked and locked the board, then flipped the toggles that unsealed the hatch and snapped her webbing loose.

Ken Rik was already standing. "Not too bad," he allowed grumpily, "for a first attempt."

Priscilla grinned. "Praise, indeed."

"Hmmph," Ken Rik said, and turned away.

ARSDRED OFFWORLD BAZAAR
LOCAL YEAR 728
DAWN BAZAAR

"In addition," said the fat man in the electric purple overrobe, "we have fourteen dozens of the finest quality firegems in a multitude— a double rainbow!—of colors. It is certain that the honored Trader must feel impelled to acquire so worthy an item."

Shan took a careful puff on the hookah that his host had so graciously provided for him. The smoke was narcotic—mildly to the individual across from him, rather more than that to even a large Liaden well fortified with anti-intoxicants.

"Firegems," he said, blowing a thoughtful smoke ring. "But surely the honored merchant jests. Why should I wish to purchase firegems of any quality, when all the galaxy carries them? More profitable to ship ice. Or atmosphere."

The fat man smiled with unimpaired good humor. "I see the honored Trader is a man of discrimination, with an eye for the beautiful and the rare. Now, it happens that we also have in our warehouses Tusodian silks of the first looming, elbam liqueur, essence of joberkerney, praqilly furleng, tobacco such as we now enjoy..."

The honored trader yawned and blew another ring. "Herr Minata, do, please, forgive me! When Herr Sasoni spoke of you— of your warehouses, the rarities—but I misunderstood! My command of your language falls short. A thousand apologies for having wasted your time, sir! Believe me, your most obedient..." He stood, bowed with more courtesy than abjectness, and turned to go.

"Master Trader!"

He turned back, concern apparent in his face. "Yes, Herr Minata? How may I serve you?"

The fat man dropped his eyes and toyed with a fold of his robe. "Perhaps we might speak again," he suggested delicately.

"That would be pleasant," Shan said with apparent delight. "We will have our pavilion in Ochre Square within the port, as always. Anyone will tell you the way. Please do come. I will be most happy to see you there."

He bowed again and turned away. This time the merchant let him go.

Outside, Shan took a deep breath of double-baked air and allowed himself a moment of self-congratulation. *That* fish was well netted and no mistake. Praqilly furleng—essence that was mere perfume for some, and a religious necessity for others—Tusodian silks...a vivid mind-picture of Priscilla Mendoza draped in diaphanous garnet silk presented itself for his inspection.

That will do, he told himself sternly, banishing the picture and merging with the flow of pedestrians heeding toward the Outworld Bazaar. The sample case would be down by now, and Ken Rik would surely have something choice to say if his captain were not present at the raising of the pavilion in Ochre Square.

The shipment had been taken to Herr Sasoni's warehouse and handed over to a capable-looking young man who inspected the packing and gravely counted the crates before signing the receipt and handing it back.

Returning to Ochre Square and Ken Rik, Priscilla maintained a sedate pace through the bustling pedestrian and jitney traffic, prolonging her first opportunity for quiet thought since the previous evening's encounter with Dagmar.

The second class provisional in her pocket had proved to be neither counterfeit nor imaginary. Sworn to by Master Pilot Shan yos'Galan, it had been issued and registered at the Arsdred branch of the Galactic Pilots Commission yesterday.

A pilot—even a provisional second class pilot—could always find work, she thought, steering her jitney carefully through a crowded corner. The red and yellow plastic card in her pocket represented a solid, respectable future; it represented a breathing space, if she required one when they hit Solcintra, before looking about for another berth.

She slowed as she reached another knot of traffic, then stopped as it became apparent that the driver of the jitney stuck sideways across the thoroughfare was going to be some time in righting his error. Sighing, she leaned back and ran her eyes absently along the crowded street.

What a difference from Jankalim! The air was filled with the whine of jitney motors and the deeper throbbing hum of the monotrains running on the maze of catwalks and rails that roofed the whole of the port. And, of course, voices: raised in conversation, song, argument.

Priscilla yawned and reached for the thread of her thoughts. She had not yet reviewed her contract. That was the first thing to be attended to, next off-shift. Then she would speak with the captain.

With her eyes on the bustling, bright crowds, it occurred to her that she had several things to speak with the captain about. That he should restore her belongings was a puzzle. Lina had said something about owing, but that made no sense. She was Terran; no Liaden could feel honor-bound to balance accounts with her. And if honor had not prompted him to return her things, what in Her name did a gift of earrings mean?

Priscilla sat up suddenly, eyes sharpening on the crowd, catching sight of a familiar bulky figure just turning the corner into Tourmaline Way.

Dagmar.

Her hands clenched the steering rod convulsively even as her breath hissed out between her teeth. Stop it! she ordered herself sharply. That one who has been in the service of the Goddess should feel hatred for a fellow being...

She swallowed hard and sent her thoughts back to the comfort of her friend—to meet with mockery even there. Done well, Lina?

"C'mon, honey—move that thing! Coast's clear!" Priscilla shook herself, automatically shifted into gear, and sent the jitney forward again, resolutely declining to think of anything at all.

"Took your time, did you?" Ken Rik asked, though not with the air of one who expected an answer. "Found the warehouseman amusing?"

"There was a jitney jammed across Coral Square," Priscilla said tonelessly, sliding out of the seat and offering him the clipboard.

He took the board and glanced at her sharply. Priscilla shrugged. Sharp glances, after all, were not unusual in the old cargo master.

"All right," he said after a moment. "Help me with the samples. When the captain arrives, the pavilion will be raised."

"And the captain *has* arrived, so work may proceed without interruption," concluded that gentleman, walking toward them with a grin. "Thank the gods. I was certain I was late and living in terror of a tongue-lashing, Master Ken Rik!"

"You're a bad boy, Captain," the old man said repressively.

"My expectations fulfilled! Thank you, old friend. Now—" He spun slowly on one heel, surveying the immediate neighborhood. "Wonderful, a temporary-permanent next door. We shall ignore it, secure in the knowledge of our superior taste. The southeast corner, I think, Ken Rik, and we'll have the nerligig for catching eyes. Herr Sasoni's order has been safely delivered?"

"Priscilla Mendoza has just returned from the warehouse. The trip down was unexceptional."

"Unexceptional?" Priscilla demanded. "You told me it wasn't too bad."

Ken Rik sniffed and burrowed into the depths of the sample crate.

"Carried away by exuberance," the captain explained. "It's the sort of thing that happens to Ken Rik rather often. My father had to speak to him frequently."

The subject of this palpable untruth turned his head to glare. "Are you going to help raise this pavilion or not?"

"Absolutely! Nothing could induce me to miss such an undertaking! I was only just now having the most delightful chat with Merchant Herr Minata. We could have gone on for hours, so at one did we find ourselves on all matters of importance. But no, I said to him, making my excuse, I *must* go and help raise the pavilion, for Master Ken Rik rules me with an iron hand."

A small sound escaped Priscilla, somewhere between a sneeze and a cough. The captain looked at her curiously.

"Are you well, Ms. Mendoza?"

"Perfectly, sir. Thank you." She took hold of the slippery pavilion cloth and kept her eyes lowered.

"Now," Ken Rik said, shoving a portion of fabric into the captain's hands, "we begin."

It took some time to arrange the corners to Ken Rik's satisfaction. Eventually it was accomplished; the valves were closed, and the pavilion began to inflate.

Priscilla, standing a little way back and watching the first wriggling upheaval, caught sight of a tip of bronze against the bright yellow fabric and inclined her head, as if welcoming a friend.

"Is Korval the dragon or the tree?" she wondered to no one in particular.

"Neither," the captain said. "Or both. The Tree is Jelaza Kazone, originally the cipher for Clan Torvin—Line yos'Phelium. The Dragon is Megelaar, for Clan Alkia—Line yos'Galan. Together they're Clan Korval."

She frowned a little. "Two Clans merged to make one?"

"Oh, well," he said, smiling, "they really didn't have a choice. Cantra yos'Phelium was the only member of her Clan on the colony ship—when it landed on Liad, you understand—except for her unborn child. Tor An yos'Galan was in the same fix. At least, he wasn't pregnant, so perhaps his fix was worse. She had been pilot; he'd been co. When they finally raised a world—landed the ship safely—she asked him to raise her heir, should something happen to her. He accepted it, poor child, ready to abandon Alkia to the void and become Clan Torvin. But Cantra seems to have been a fair-minded sort of person, among her other faults, so Torvin *and* Alkia ceased to be, and Clan Korval emerged." He moved his shoulders. "Family history. But you asked for it."

"Yes, I did. Your Clan was made when the ship landed on Liad?" Priscilla was still frowning; it seemed a very long time.

"A young House," he said cheerfully. "An upstart. There are some who trace their ancestry back to the Old World. Sav Rid's family, for instance—"

"Captain?" Ken Rik said from the seat of the jitney. "I'll go to Thessel's now and see if there's news. Unless you would rather go?"

"I," the captain said, "would rather get my hands dirty setting up the nerligig. By all means go to Thessel. And *do* say all those polite things she seems to find so necessary to her comfort."

Unexpectedly, Ken Rik grinned. The jitney slid easily into the flow of traffic, heading west.

The captain wandered over to the sample case, rummaged about for a few moments, and emerged with a toolbox in one hand and a dark nerligig in the other.

Dropping the toolbox, he sat on a crate before the slowly inflating pavilion and put the nerligig on his knees.

"Might as well put waiting to work," he murmured with the air of quoting someone. "Why don't you take a walk, Ms. Mendoza? There's nothing for you to do here right now."

Priscilla hesitated, nettled by this casual dismissal. But his head was bent over the mechanism, and he was to all appearances absorbed in making the necessary adjustments, so she eventually stalked away.

Ochre Square was a crowded, busy block under the shadow of the monotrain station. Over the buzz of the track, the jitney traffic kept up a perpetual whine. Priscilla considered the other Traders' displays and tents from a distance that said she was not a potential customer. Several things tempted her, and she regretted her lost money. Presumably Dagmar had kept the cash she had found in Priscilla's cabin.

Shan was still concentrating on his work when Priscilla came leisurely back toward the fully inflated pavilion with its striking dragon and tree design. It was comforting, she thought suddenly, to see him there, patiently working, the big, clever hands manipulating the tools with precision.

Frowning, she shook her head. There was no reason at all for her to be comforted by the captain's presence, yet twice now she had distinctly had that sensation. She was not altogether certain she approved of it. Irritably, she looked away.

The jitney was driverless. It was speeding, helped along by the double load gripped in its front claw. And it was on a collision course with the *Passage's* tent.

Later, Priscilla was never sure if she had run or merely flung herself across the distance that separated them. She struck the captain with brutal force and knocked him rolling from the crate, rolling herself as he twisted away, hearing sounds of destruction from too near at hand until she caught up, gasping, against the wall of the temporary-permanent.

She came to her knees, horror-filled.

He lay a little distance from her, his back against the wall, his eyes closed. If he was breathing, he was going about it very quietly.

"Captain?" she whispered. She laid her hand along his cheek.

The slanted brows contracted, and the dark lashes snapped up. "Don't do that, Priscilla."

"All right." She dropped her hand and looked at him uncertainly. "Are you hurt?"

"No," he said shortly. "I'm not hurt." He sat up and looked past her, his silver eyes enormous. Priscilla turned.

The pavilion was gone, tangled crazily about something that surged and tottered and whined like a netted wilmaby. A crowd was beginning to gather.

"Your arm please, Priscilla," said the captain, eyes still on the wreckage.

She rose and offered a hand. He accepted the aid and linked his arm in hers, his hand curved lightly about her wrist.

"Captain?" she said softly, hating to say it but certain it should be said. "I saw Dagmar earlier, on Tourmaline Way...

"She has a right to be here, Priscilla; this is the port. Ah, a policeman. How nice." He started toward that official, and, arm-linked, she went with him.

SHIPYEAR 65
TRIPDAY 143
SECOND SHIFT
10.30 HOURS

Thankfully, the library was empty. Priscilla had no wish to speak to anyone at the moment, not even Lina. She located an isolated screen by the door to the pet library and sat down, fumbling with the keys.

The interview with the policeman at the port had been interesting. Disentangled, the jitney was identified by an emaciated gentleman in cherry and white robes as belonging to his employer, one Herr Reyes. He had noticed its absence approximately twenty minutes before and had reported the disappearance to the police before undertaking a rather lengthy walk back into the city. By coincidence he had been turning into Ochre Square as the Tree and Dragon suddenly shrieked, shuddered, and folded in on itself.

A quick examination by the policeman at the site showed that the steering rod bore no imprints at all.

At that point Priscilla had opened her mouth. The captain's fingers tightened briefly on her wrist. Priscilla closed her mouth.

This happened three more times during the course of the captain's conversation with the cop and once as he was speaking with a visibly shaken Ken Rik. He then gave Priscilla into the cargo master's care and instructed him to escort her to the shuttle.

"What!" she cried. *"Why?"*

The captain returned her stare calmly. "You've had a hard shift, Priscilla. Take the rest of it off and come to me at prime. Be back as soon as you can, Ken Rik. There's a bit of cleanup to do. I'll be speaking with Merchant Reyes's clerk." He had turned away.

The screen chimed, bringing her back to the present. She fed in her request, then waited a few anxious moments until the proper file was retrieved and displayed.

SERVICE RECORD. PRISCILLA DELACROIX Y MENDOZA.

She began to scroll through it impatiently. Suddenly she hit PAUSE and went back a screen.

STANDARD 1385, TULON. TEMPORARY BERTH *DAXFLAN,* CARGO MAS-TER TRANSSHIP JANKALIM AS AGREED *DUTIFUL PASSAGE,* PILOT (PROV SEC), LIBRARIAN. NOTATION: COMMAND POTENTIAL; SECOND MATE TRAINING INSTITUTED.

She read it twice, each time going back to the beginning and scanning every line to the end. There was no mention of thievery or of jumping ship. TRANSHIPPED JANKALIM AS AGREED.

At the end of the file she paused again, staring at the certification from the registry office on VanDyk.

It was dated one Standard Week ago.

"Impossible," she told the screen.

The words persisted. She read them again and keyed in her next request.

CONTRACT SIGNED BETWEEN PRISCILLA DELACROIX Y MENDOZA, FIRST PARTY, AND SHAN YOS'GALAN AS CAPTAIN, *DUTIFUL PASSAGE,* SEC-OND PARTY. FIRST PARTY SHALL AGREE TO PERFORM DUTIES INHERENT IN THE POST OF PET LIBRARIAN AND ALSO TO UNDERTAKE PILOT TRAIN-ING ONE SHIP WATCH OF EVERY NINE, WITHOUT FAIL, AND ALSO TO UNDERTAKE ANY ADDITIONAL TRAINING OR DUTY DEEMED REASON-ABLE AND JUST BY SECOND PARTY.

Priscilla leaned back. There it was. She briefly and belatedly recalled advice given a much younger Priscilla: "I tell you what, young-ster. Don't you ever sign a Liaden's contract. I don't care how careful you read it. If he won't sign yours, let the deal go. Safer that way."

Still, there was nothing wrong with undergoing second mate's training. She would have appreciated being told, but she was sure that he had meant it for the best.

It was not until she had cleared the screen and left the library that it occurred to her to wonder why she *should* be sure of it.

SHIPYEAR 65
TRIPDAY 143
THIRD SHIFT
16.00 HOURS

Priscilla exited the lift and walked resolutely toward the captain's office. She was dressed in the yellow shirt and khaki trousers she had worn when she first walked down this hall. In her pocket was the provisional second class. The rest of her belongings were in the cabin that had been hers, the clothes neatly folded and stacked beside the scrounged plastic box. She must remember to tell the captain to offer the bracelets to a collector. The price they would bring as curios would go far toward paying her debt to the ship.

She rounded the corner by Hold 6 and nearly walked into Kayzin Ne'Zame.

The first mate recovered first and swept a surprising bow, as deep as one would accord the captain, augmented by an odd little flourish that mystified Priscilla entirely.

"We are well met, Priscilla Mendoza," she said in a light, quick voice much unlike her usual manner of speech. "I have been remiss in offering you an apology for my behavior several shifts gone by, when we spoke near the central computer." She took a breath and looked up. "Pray forgive it. I was discourteous and in error."

Priscilla blinked, collected herself immediately, and bowed in turn, though not as deeply, nor did she attempt to copy the flourish.

"Do me the honor of putting the incident from your mind, Kayzin Ne'Zame. I shall do the same."

The Liaden woman inclined her head. "You are kind. It shall be as you have said. I leave you now."

"Be well, Kayzin Ne'Zame," Priscilla murmured, laying her hand against the captain's door.

"Come!"

He was standing, hands hooked in his belt, his bright head bent over a chess problem. It was a new one, Priscilla saw, and she wondered if the other had had a solution, after all. He glanced up as the door closed and smiled. "Hello, Priscilla. Did you rest well this past shift?"

"I visited Master Frodo for a while," she said, hesitating between desk chairs and couch.

"A very restful companion. I've always found him so, at any rate. Ken Rik labels him terminally cute. But Ken Rik likes snakes. What may I give you to drink?"

"Nothing, thank you, Captain." She decided on one of the chairs before his desk, drifted over, and perched on the arm.

"Nothing?" The slanted brows drew together as he crossed the rug. "Are you angry, Priscilla? Or am *I* angry? If it's me, I assure you that I'm not. And if it's you—but surely you knew I had to send you away? It would have been unforgivable to keep you by, especially when I'd put you in so much danger already."

"You put me in danger?" She stared at him. "It's the other way around, Captain. *I* put *you* in danger. Which is why I would rather not accept a drink. I'm not stopping long." She forced herself to meet his eyes calmly. "I think it would be wisest for me to leave the *Passage* immediately."

"Do you?" He paused. "What a very odd notion of wisdom. If you were staying long enough to have a drink, Priscilla, what would you prefer? Purely hypothetical, of course." The light eyes were mocking her.

"Idle speculation, since I'm not staying that long," she said crisply. "I came only to say that—"

"It would be wisest for you to leave the *Passage* immediately," the captain interrupted, holding up his hands placatingly. "You *did* say it. I heard you. Now, Priscilla, please pay attention—this is very important. You might at least have some consideration for my feelings in the matter. I'm thirsty, and you're telling nonsense stories, which you could as easily tell while having a glass of wine with me like a civilized person." He tipped his head. "*Do* strive for some courtesy, Priscilla."

She felt laughter rising and clamped down, with limited success. A small sound woefully reminiscent of a hiccup emerged. "Red, please," she said, glaring.

"Red," he repeated, moving toward the bar. "An excellent choice, as even Gordy will tell you. Though, of course, there's nothing wrong with the white or the jade or the *blue.*" He was back and handing her a cut-crystal glass. Her fingers curved around the stem automatically. "And the red won't ruin your taste for prime—you will have time to dine with me, won't you, Priscilla? I agree that I should have first found if your schedule was clear, but it did seem rude to ask you to come to speak with me at dinnertime and then rob you of dinner."

She sipped her wine and tried again. "Captain, surely you must see that the longer I stay with you—with the *Passage*—the more danger you're in? If I'm gone, then you—"

"Priscilla, you have a woeful tendency toward single-mindedness," he interrupted, sitting on the edge of the desk and swinging a leg.

She clamped her jaw and stood. "Thank you for all you've done, Captain, but I really must be going."

"You can't do that, Priscilla; you have a contract. You're bound to this ship until Solcintra. That's four months, as the route runs. You don't have the buy-off fee, do you? I didn't think so." He raised his glass. "It looks like you're stuck, child. Might as well sit down and finish your wine."

"I'm not a child!"

"Well, I can't be expected to know that, can I, if you persist in acting like one? You really must try to curb these tastes for melodrama and resignation."

"Melodrama!" She glared at him, her fingers ominously tight about the glass. "At least I'm not high-handed and—"

"High-handed!"

"*High*-handed," she asserted with relish. "And dictatorial. And *obstinate*. As if you couldn't see why—"

"High-handed! Of all the— Priscilla, when we reach Solcintra, I engage to introduce you to my brother's Aunt Kareen. Call *me* high-handed! Before that, you'd best improve your grasp of the High Tongue—your accent's *execrable*. And another thing! How dare you profess yourself all joy to see me? Have you no sense of propriety? I hardly know you."

"Nor will you know me any better," she stated, suddenly calm. She set her glass on the edge of his desk. "Because I'm leaving. Contract or not. Sue me."

"I won't. But I will arrest you, if you force me to it." He was in front of her, his face quite serious. "Priscilla, have some sense. Don't you realize you saved my life this afternoon?"

She gaped, aware of a strong desire to take him by the shoulders and shake. "Do *you* realize it? You act like—Captain yos'Galan, if you know it, then *let me go!* Surely you see that the sooner I'm gone, the sooner you're safe! People will stop trying to kill you—"

"No, wait." A big, warm hand closed around one of hers. "Priscilla, please—a favor. Come sit down…here's your wine. Now, if you please, tell me what happened at the port today."

She sat carefully, accepted her glass, and took a sip, steadying heart rate and breathing, embracing serenity. "You know what happened, Captain. You were there."

"I was there," he agreed, back at his station on the edge of the desk. "But I'm Liaden. You're Terran. From what you've said, it seems clear we think that two different things occurred." He leaned forward, eyes intent on her face. "Tell me, Priscilla. Please?"

She took another sip and looked at him straightly. "Today someone deliberately tried to kill you by aiming a jitney at you, jamming the rod, and jumping out. By the grace of the Goddess, I was close enough to knock you out of the way." She took a breath. "I believe—though I have no proof—that Dagmar Collier made the attempt. I also believe that it was ordered by Sav Rid Olanek, striking at you because you gave me sanctuary. So, if I leave the *Passage,* show myself to be a free agent, no more attempts should be made on your life."

"There it is," he said softly, brows pulled slightly together. "Why sacrifice yourself to keep me safe, Priscilla? Assuming all of what you say is accurate, of course."

"I brought danger to you," she said patiently. "It's only just that I take it away again. It's what is honorable."

"Is it?" He raised his glass, reconsidered, and lowered it. "Then I'm afraid we have a conflict of honors. The code I was raised to says that, having been so careless as to have necessitated your saving my life, I am very much in your debt. Setting aside the fact that allowing you to go would be murder, if my assessment of Ms. Collier's character is correct, I owe you the protection of this ship— of my resources, say rather. To send you away—unprotected and unprepared—to decoy danger from me is lunacy. And also highly dishonorable. It makes far more sense, is within the limits of honor— and duty!—to stay where it is relatively safe and work to balance what is owed them!" He did drink this time, slowly, then lowered his glass and shook his head.

"The fact is, Priscilla, you don't know the rules. I grant that the admission of Ms. Collier and yourself into the game alters things somewhat, but not enough to matter. Certainly the larger points remain constant. Am I being sinister enough, or should I wrap myself in a cloak and snigger?"

"Can you snigger?" she asked with interest.

"Probably not." He grinned. "But I'll do my best if it takes that to convince you to let me have my high-handed, dictatorial, and—what was the other one?"

"Obstinate," Priscilla supplied, though she had the grace to blush.

"A fairly accurate reading of my faults. Though you omitted inquisitive and meddling. Your suspicion of Sav Rid does him less than justice, by the way. I don't think he ordered me eliminated. It's my belief Ms. Collier was acting on her own initiative. Sav Rid has his limitations, even in stupidity. And it would be extremely stupid to murder me." He drank. "Besides, I don't think I scared him that much."

She blinked. "Were you trying to—oh, the earrings?"

"The earrings. But that seems only to have frightened Ms. Collier into an indiscretion. Lamentable. Sav Rid really ought to screen his people more carefully. I saw Ms. Collier's record—idle curiosity, you understand. She had been a marine. Dishonorable discharge. Personnel complications." He tipped his head. "I said that she used to be a marine, Priscilla; please pay attention. How close did you come to killing her?"

"I didn't—" The lie choked her, and she looked down, then looked back at him. "She's so *slow*. But I misjudged the knife, so she almost killed me, not the other way around."

"An error of inexperience, I believe. I doubt it would happen again. Forgive me, Priscilla, it had seemed a good idea."

This was more than usually convoluted. She put it away for later thought. "What are the rules, Captain?"

"The rules are—" He paused and looked at her consideringly. "Whose life did you save, Priscilla?"

"Shan yos'Galan's," she said, wondering.

"Did you? Good. It makes things somewhat simpler. Now, what—oh, the rules. Wouldn't you rather have the story first? I always need something to hang the rules on, don't you? My dreadful memory. But maybe yours is better."

"It's awful," she told him seriously. "I'd better have the story."

He grinned. "Not too bad, Priscilla. With a bit of practice you should be quite convincing. More wine? No? Oh, well." He finished his glass and set it aside, lacing his fingers around a knee.

"For the sake of argument," he said pensively, "we'll say that the story begins with Clan Plemia, Sav Rid's family. A very old, most respected House. And also one that's fallen on hard times these last hundred Standards or so, which makes money…oh, not as plentiful as it once was. Fortunes rise, fortunes fall, and Plemia's case, while no doubt uncomfortable, isn't *dire*. There's every reason to expect that a bit of careful husbandry will bring them about. In time." He paused, then shrugged.

"Unfortunately, Sav Rid doesn't seem a patient man. He wishes to restore Plemia to its pinnacle *now*. I assume that he cudgeled his brain and finally hit upon the happy plan of taking a lifemate. He possesses lineage, address, a comely face, an elegant person—an extremely eligible individual in all ways. It need not be said that one of Plemia might look where he chose."

Priscilla smiled. "Which is how he happened to propose to your sister."

The captain grinned. "Well, it does make a certain amount of sense, you know. Nova's of age; she might choose whatever husband or lifemate suits her. She has lineage, address, a comely face, an elegant person—and is, incidentally, of course, quite wealthy. There was no reason why they shouldn't have been very happy with each other."

A sound escaped Priscilla, neither a hiccup nor a sneeze—a chuckle, low and obviously delighted. "But she sent him off with a flea in his ear."

"So she did. But she was sadly provoked, you know. The silly creature wouldn't take no for an answer—kept asking and asking. The final time, he paid a morning call for the sole purpose of pleading his case once more. He sighed. "We none of us have gentle tempers—very hotheaded family, the yos'Galans; and the yos'Pheliums are worse. At any rate, the morning call was the nether end of too much, and she threw him out." He looked at her earnestly. "I wouldn't have you think less of her, Priscilla. She really did try very hard to be civil."

"I'm sure she did. It's irritating when people won't believe what you tell them." Her grin faded. "But if there's a—vendetta—

it would be on Trader Olanek's side, wouldn't it, Captain? If he wanted to believe your sister had insulted him?"

"I should have warned you," the captain said, picking up his empty glass and sighing, "that it's a rather long story. Will you have some more wine? Thirsty work, talking."

"I'd have thought you'd be used to it."

"You wrong me, Priscilla; I'm often quiet. Reports are that I hardly ever talk in my sleep, for instance." He was at the bar. She turned in her chair, considering the fit of his shirt and the worked leather of his belt, the gentle bell of cloth from knee to instep. He always dressed with immaculate simplicity. She saw now that the fabrics were costly, the tailoring precise—not readymades from valet or general stores.

He turned around, brows twitching. "Yes?"

"You had said your Clan—Korval—is an upstart?" She stopped short of all she wished to ask, unsure of the polite way to do so.

He grinned and handed her a glass. "Oh, we're respected enough. After all, we trace our lines to Torvin and Alkia, and thence to the Old World. It is, of course, to be regretted that my father should have seen fit to allow Terran blood into the Clan, but there's nothing wrong with Terran blood that I know of. Does its job just as well as anyone else's blood. Purists may frown, but not many Clans can recite a lineage that doesn't include the odd Terran or two. My brother tells me that the Clutch-turtles simply call everyone 'The Clans of Men' and let it go at that. In a little while—according to *their* view of things—we'll all be one race. No Terrans. No Liadens. No half-breeds." He raised his glass. "Ready for Chapter Two?"

"Please."

"Again we start with Sav Rid, I think. Why not? He and Chelsa yo'Vaade, both of Clan Plemia. Chelsa isn't too bad a pilot but doesn't have any brains to speak of. She does what Sav Rid tells her to do. A pity.

"Also important to this story is Shan yos'Galan, who is, please remember, a fool." He paused, brows twitching. "You said, Priscilla?"

"I wanted to know how a fool became Master Trader," she repeated.

He grinned. "It's easier than you might think. And my father would settle for nothing less from me." His face became more serious. "Several people hold the opinion that Shan yos'Galan is a fool,

Priscilla. There's a certain advantage to that. Several other people believe that Shan yos'Galan is *not* a fool, if it comforts you, but Sav Rid isn't one of them.

"To continue. In the course of his trading, Sav Rid took on a quantity of mezzik-root—highly perishable, but also highly profitable, if one happens to be going to Brinix. Sav Rid was, hence the root. He, in fact, jumped out of Tulon System, pegged for Brinix. And returned just an hour or so after the *Passage* docked at Tulon Prime. I met Sav Rid at the trade bar a little time after that and heard his tale. *Daxflan* was urgently required elsewhere on business of Clan Plemia. The mezzik-root would pass its time before he had any hope of delivery. Would I be going near Brinix? Would I consider buying the shipment at a flat figure, thus helping a fellow Liaden and enriching myself?"

He shrugged. "It was an opportunity, and I took it. It does occur that one is suddenly called away on Clan business and must dispose of cargo as it's possible. I knew nothing of the honored Trader except that he had annoyed my sister—easy enough to do. She's seldom completely in charity with *me,* for instance. The price was paid, the load transferred. Other business completed, the *Passage* jumped out-system, pegged for Brinix—which was found to be under medical quarantine and expected to remain so for the next local year, far past the time when the mezzik-root would have started to deteriorate." He paused to drink.

"The tower manager was polite—and astonished. *Daxflan,* under Captain yo'Vaade, had been in orbit not many days since and had promised to deliver news of the quarantine to Tulon."

Priscilla took a breath. "How much did you lose?"

"Forty cantra. But I did enhance and improve my reputation as a most wonderful fool, which must be counted a gain." He shook his head.

"By the time we got back into Tulon, the story was all over the trade bar. The report had been delivered two minutes after the *Passage* jumped out. *Daxflan* was gone, having hired a new cargo master."

"All that for—balance—for being insulted by your sister?" Priscilla was frowning.

"Now there," the captain said, "I'm not at all certain. Nova is old enough to mind her own honor. If Sav Rid had a quarrel with her reading of his character, then his satisfaction lies with her. He might have assumed that I forbade the match, as Head of Line, you see. I didn't, and probably wouldn't have, if she'd set her heart on him. It never came to me at all; I learn everything after the fact, and in pieces—which, come to think of it, is the only way you learn anything from him—from Val Con, who was kind enough to show Sav Rid the door on the occasion of his morning call." The movement of his shoulders was not quite a shrug.

"For whatever reason, a debt is owed—has been owing. Sav Rid's belief that I am too foolish to be considered an able—" He stopped, brows contracting. "Here's a thing that doesn't happen often," he murmured. "Forgive me, Priscilla; my Terran seems to be lacking. Can it be *debt-partner?*" He sipped wine, considering the carpet with absent intensity.

"Say debt-partner," he decided after a moment. "It makes less nonsense than the other possibilities."

Priscilla shifted in her chair. "This happened at Tulon?"

He glanced up. "Yes. At the beginning of our run."

"And you still owe him for—dear Goddess—forty cantra?" The amount of the loss was staggering.

"Forty cantra's the least of it. I owe him a lesson to treat me with courtesy and respect, not to mention honesty." He sipped, eyes on her face. "These things take time and planning, Priscilla."

"So it was lucky that I came here asking for a job," she said, making the connections rapidly. "I could be a very useful weapon."

"Now, Priscilla, for Spacesake, don't get into hyper again!" He was in front of her, hands spread-fingered and soothing. "I'd have given you a job if Sav Rid were my best friend! Only a lunatic would turn down someone of your potential." He grinned at her. "Foolish, yes. Crazed, no. And it's not a question of giving. You're earning your pay."

"Am I?" she demanded, refusing to give in to her desire to be mollified. "And when will I start training as second mate?"

"You've started," he told her, lowering his hands slowly. "Ken Rik thinks very well of you. So does Tonee. And Lina. And Seth, Vilobar, Gordy, BillyJo, Vilt, Rusty, and Master Frodo. If you keep on at this rate, you'll have the expertise by Solcintra. You already have the ability. Are you angry, Priscilla? Don't you want to learn the job?"

"Of course I want to learn it," she said irritably. "I just would have appreciated being told instead of finding out by accident."

"High-handed," he said mournfully. "I'll try to curb it, but don't expect miracles. I've been this way a long time."

"You're not much older than I am," she told him severely. "How did you manage that trick with my record—dated last week! And no mention of theft or jumping ship."

"Oh." He drifted back to the desk, hoisted himself up, and recaptured his glass. "More high-handedness, I'm afraid, Priscilla. Please try to bear with me." He drank. "I contacted the captain of *Dante* for a more specific recommendation, took every word as truth, and pin-beamed your updated record to VanDyk with a notation that it superseded all previously dated information."

He grinned at her. "Sav Rid had ruined your record within the sector; but he's tight-fisted, and the courier bounce to VanDyk will take months. Just imagine his unhappiness when he finds his report of your nefarious activities returned to him marked 'Superseded by Data Attached.' Do you think he'll file an official complaint? And risk a hearing into the specifics of your so-called crimes? Will he insist that his very negative report be inserted next to all those glowing ones?" He raised his glass in salute. "I think not."

"You pin-beamed...Captain, do you know how expensive pin-beaming is?"

"No. Tell me." The silver eyes were laughing at her.

She frowned, rediscovered her glass, and took a healthy swallow.

"Don't worry about it, Priscilla We've got a pin-beam on board—Rusty's favorite toy. One of the services the *Passage* offers the more backward of our ports is the use of the pin-beam. For a fee, of course. I'm well paid, by contemplating the expression on Sav Rid's face when he reads 'Data Attached'— Dinner at long last!" he interrupted himself as the door chimed.

Gordy grinned from behind the serving table. "I'm on time," he pointed out with considerable pride. He parked the table and came around to Priscilla. "Now you're a hero, too."

"No," she said with decision. "I'm *not* a hero, Gordy."

He tipped his head, clearly puzzled, and turned to the captain. "Shan? Isn't she?"

"She just said she wasn't, didn't she, Gordy? People have a right to define who they are, don't they? If Priscilla doesn't want to be a hero right now, she doesn't have to be. It's probable that she's hungry. Very difficult to be heroic when you're hungry."

The boy laughed and went to the table to begin unfolding leaves, and releasing odors. Priscilla suddenly realized that she was very hungry.

"Ken Rik said to tell you the nerligig works fine," he said over his shoulder.

The captain stared at him. "It does? He tried it on all settings?"

Gordy nodded. "The case is pretty dented, he said, but since it's for attention getting, that doesn't matter." He paused to glance at his cousin. "He really did say that."

"Of course he did. Ken Rik doesn't believe in curbing his tongue for anyone. I'd be seriously concerned for his health if he started now. Besides, he met me when I was younger than you are, and twice as clumsy. No doubt that makes it occasionally hard to proffer the appropriate respect. What about the tent? Has he gotten a new sample case together? And he'll—no, never mind; I'll wander over and speak with him later. Is prime ready yet?"

"Whist, now, Johnny Galen," Gordy murmured in an exaggerated accent.

The captain laughed and drank wine. "Intolerable puppy. I bear that from your grandfather. But I'm bigger than you are. Please try to keep it in mind."

"Bully," Gordy said, settling plates amid an amazing amount of clatter.

"High-handed," the captain corrected, and grinned at Priscilla, who dropped her eyes.

Gordy stepped back. "Ready. Should I stay?"

The captain glanced at him in surprise. "Did I ask you to dinner, Gordon? Forgive me, the invitation slipped my mind. I seem to recall a report that you've fallen behind in your studies, a circumstance your grandfather, my uncle, would not forgive me. We're due for a review, aren't we? At breakfast."

Gordy swallowed visibly. "Yessir."

"That bad?" He raised his glass. "Well, better see what you can catch up on beforehand. And mind you're in bed at a reasonable hour. I won't need you anymore."

"Yessir," Gordy said again, looking so comically crestfallen that Priscilla had to forcefully swallow the rising laughter. "G'night, Cap'n. G'night, Priscilla."

"Good night, Gordy," she said, smiling at him warmly.

"Good night, Gordy." The captain reached over to the boy and ruffled his hair lightly. *"Do* sleep well."

The boy smiled up at him, made an awkward bow, and departed, the door hissing closed behind him.

"Now, then, Priscilla, if you'll pull up the chairs, I'll serve us. I hope you're as hungry as I am."

A little time later, the edge of hunger blunted, she leaned back and considered the top of his head and the thick, well-cut hair gleaming in the room's soft light.

"Johnny Galen?" she wondered.

He glanced up, smiling. "It's my Uncle Richard's fancy that Liadens are the 'little people' of Old Terra's legends. Thus, Arthur Galen, Johnny, Nora, and Annie Galen. And their foster brother, the king of Elfland."

"Oh, no!" A chuckle escaped, but she didn't notice.

"Oh. yes," he assured her. "Complete with 'my Liege' and 'your Highness.' Pretty comical, actually. My father finally did manage to put a stop to it, but I think he had to resort to threats."

"But he let himself be called Arthur, and you Johnny?"

"Well, no, not exactly," he said, reaching for his glass. "He didn't *answer* to 'Arthur,' you see, so if Uncle Dick really wanted to speak with him, he had to use 'Er Thom.' I don't mind 'Johnny'— my mother called me 'Shannie' more often than not—and Anthora was *always* 'Annie.' To the best of my knowledge, Nova never did answer to 'Nora.'" He sipped. "I hope Val Con doesn't feel he owes balance for the king routine. I rather doubt it. Whatever his faults, Uncle Richard is a master storyteller. And Val Con's addicted to stories."

Priscilla frowned down at the table, then glanced up. "Captain? What is a debt-partner?"

He set his glass aside and picked up his tongs, readdressing dinner. Priscilla hesitated, then returned to her own plate, wondering if she had offended.

"A debt-partner," the captain said slowly, "is one with whom you are engaged in a balancing of accounts." He glanced at her quickly from beneath his lashes. "There are, as I mentioned before, many rules governing revenge—balance—and how it might be achieved. One of them is that balance is only owing *respected persons.*

Animals, for instance, may not claim debt-right." He paused, watching her face carefully.

"It," Priscilla whispered, her spoon forgotten halfway to her mouth. "He called us 'it,' Gordy and me."

"So he did," the captain agreed carefully. "One of the least attractive things about the High Tongue is that it's so easy to deny worth." He looked at her closely. *"I* didn't call you 'it,' Priscilla. Of all the people in the galaxy, I'd be among the last to do so. But Sav Rid believes that people who aren't Liaden aren't—people." He raised his glass and took a sip. "What he had done to you on Jankalim, he would never have ordered done to another Liaden. Even one he considered a fool of the first order, completely careless of his personal honor, the honor of his Line, and of his ship." He grinned. "He thought he'd gotten away clean, Priscilla. Imagine his depression when I not only turn up to bail you out, after he thought you safely disposed of, but uttering threats about earrings, guilty consciences—little enough. But he knows he's gotten away with nothing. He may still doubt my ability to do it, but he knows I'll attempt balance."

She laid her spoon down carefully. "But an—animal—has no recourse."

He sipped, eyes on her. "But you're not an animal, are you, Priscilla? Aren't you a person? Isn't respect due you? You can be an animal, if you choose to say you are. Or you can show him quite clearly that you are a resourceful, intelligent *person,* worthy of the dignity accorded all persons." He set the glass down, his big mouth tight.

"He has stolen from you—possessions, money, personhood. And you speak of taking on the role of an animal, sacrificing your life for mine. Priscilla, don't you see that you are owed? How *dare* he order violence against your person? How *dare* he steal the money you earned, the things you own, your reputation? And by what right did he place your personal honor in jeopardy in the first place, hiring you as master over a cargo of contraband?" He held out a hand. "Wouldn't you rather stay, Priscilla? We'll bring him payment together."

With no hesitation at all, she slid her hand into his.

"Yes," she said clearly. "We'll do that."

SHIPYEAR 65
TRIPDAY 143
FOURTH SHIFT
18.00 HOURS

Priscilla laid her hand against the door. It slid away to a soft "Enter" from within.

Smiling, Lina bounced up from her seat at the desk. "Priscilla! How are you, my friend?"

"Fine." Priscilla smiled back, sliding her hands into the small ones stretched out to her. "You're busy? I'm not on urgent business."

"No, come and talk with me! If I look at that terrible report another minute, I shall develop a *severe* headache." She laughed, tugging on Priscilla's hands. "Save me!"

They sat on the bed, Lina cross-legged in the center and Priscilla on the edge.

"So, now, what is this not-urgent business?"

"I'm afraid it isn't going to make any sense," Priscilla apologized, toying with the quilt. "At least, I can't think of a sensible way to ask it. Lina, isn't Shan yos'Galan the captain?"

The smaller woman blinked. "Of course he is. Are you having a joke, my friend?"

"I said it didn't make sense," Priscilla pointed out. "I just had dinner with the captain—" She stopped. Lina folded her hands together, waiting.

"I had dinner with the captain," Priscilla repeated slowly. "As I was leaving, I asked him about having returned my things. He said the ship bore the expense of buying them back, that I was to consider it my bonus for having been put in danger." She paused, frowning a little. "Then I asked about the earrings, because they *weren't* mine."

"And?" Lina prompted softly.

"He said the earrings were a gift from Shan yos'Galan, and the captain had nothing to do with it."

"He said so?" Lina moved her shoulders. "Then it is true."

Priscilla sighed. "Yes, I'm sure it is. But Lina, if Shan yos'Galan is the captain..."

"Surely you know that the captain speaks—acts—for the ship," her friend said carefully. "Yes? So, Shan speaks for himself. It is— I do not know the Terran word. Shan yos'Galan has many...roles! He is captain, Master Trader, pilot—three voices with which to speak on the *Passage*. On Liad he is also Lord yos'Galan. He only made certain that you understood which face he used—from which role he acted—when he gifted you."

Priscilla stared at her. "It makes a difference? But he's the same man, no matter what title he's using!"

"Of course he is. But the captain has specific duties, responsibilities, different duties than the Master Trader. A pilot has yet another set." Lina chewed her lip uncertainly. "It is only melant'i, Priscilla." She sighed at the blank look on her friend's face and tried once more. "It is true that Shan yos'Galan is the captain. But the captain is not Shan yos'Galan."

"I'll work on it," Priscilla said, smiling apologetically. "There might not be a Terran word, Lina." She tipped her head. "Is my Liaden accent horrible?"

"No. Who said it was? You are very careful and listen hard, but it is true you are just learning."

"The captain—at least I *think* it was the captain, but it might have been Shan yos'Galan—told me my accent was execrable and that he was going to introduce me to his aunt—his brother's aunt."

"To Lady Kareen? Illanga kilachi—no. Priscilla, did he *promise* that he would do so?"

"He said he would *engage* to," she said, somewhat amused. "How awful can she be?"

"You cannot imagine. She is very proper—ah, he is bad! We will practice, the two of us, very hard. And tomorrow I will choose enhancement tapes. You can sleep-learn? Good. Also protocol lessons." She looked up at her friend, hands fluttering. "What made him say such a thing? To Lady Kareen—"

"I told him he was high-handed," Priscilla confessed.

"So he now wishes to show you what that is." Lina grinned. "You are well served, then. However did you come to say something so rude?"

"It slipped out right after he told me I had a tendency toward melodrama."

Lina laughed. "It sounds as if you had a fine dinner! Compliments all around."

"Protocol lessons are a necessity," Priscilla agreed, smiling. She sobered. "Lina? Why is it wrong for me to tell the captain—the Master Trader—that I am all joy to see him?"

Lina looked at her in horror. "You said that? To Shan? In public?"

"And in the High Tongue," her friend admitted sheepishly. "Am I beyond redemption?"

"No wonder he gives you earrings!" Lina cried, taking her hand. "Priscilla, you must never do so again! It is a phrase reserved for...a brother, perhaps, or an individual one has grown up with...a lifemate."

"Really? I'm glad I said it, then. It was exactly right."

"Priscilla," Lina pleaded. "It is most improper! You must not do so again."

"All right," she agreed sunnily. "I don't think I'll ever need to again." She laughed then, very softly, and Lina held her breath. "Poor Sav Rid!"

Lina found Shan in the gym. Just inside, she stopped to watch him swing the paddle, strike the ball, spin, connect, dive, connect— faster and even faster, the ball a white blur trapped between wall and paddle, the man moving with lithe intensity, never missing, never pausing.

After a moment, she walked forward, angling toward the wall, then heard the ball strike just beyond her shoulder.

"Lina! Are you courting suicide? You could have been hit!"

"No," she told him calmly, changing her course. "You are far too quick for that, my friend."

"Accidents happen." Shan walked to meet her, paddle in one hand, ball in the other. His hair stuck in wet points to his forehead, lending him a slightly satanic air; he was breathing hard, and the wine-colored shirt showed darker patches. Lina set aside a spurt of fond sympathy; she stopped at precisely the proper distance and looked sternly up at him.

"You are meddling!" She spoke in the High Tongue, as senior to junior.

"I always meddle," he returned in mild Terran. "You know that."

"You will cease to do so in this instance. Immediately." Her words were still in the High Tongue, commanding, as was proper.

"Dear me," Shan murmured, looking down with a fine show of bewildered stupidity. "Do you mind if we sit down?"

She laughed and turned with him toward the side benches. "You are impossible!" she told him in Terran. "You deserve to be scolded!"

"Often," he agreed cordially, flipping paddle and ball into the wall slot and dropping into the first chair he came to. He thrust his long legs out before him. "Scold me."

She frowned. He was in a chancy mood. She began tentatively. "Shan, it is serious. Please. You could do harm." She extended a mental tendril.

She was met with opposition, the familiar Healer's barrier. He rarely took such complete refuge; never in all their years of friendship had he done so with her. Not at the time his mother had died so tragically, nor when Er Thom yos'Galan had turned his face from kin and from duty to follow her.

Lina withdrew the tendril and considered him quietly. "It is a bad thing," she offered, "for Healers to argue over a proper approach. Most especially when Healing has begun."

"I agree," Shan said.

"That is good. Now, I will tell you that I am puzzled. We spoke, did we not? And it was agreed that I should proceed, though Priscilla was drawn as much to you as to me. You insisted, old friend, saying you were captain, not Healer."

"True. I do not act as Healer in the matter."

Lina stifled a sigh. This was Shan at his least tractable, showing the streak of stubborn reticence that characterized Korval at the fore. In a way it was a blessing—if she could not read him through the protective barrier, neither could he read her. The Wall, like so much of healing, was reciprocal.

She considered that last thought. One did tend to become entangled with those one Healed. Priscilla...He may have feared reciprocity, having felt the strength of her—even half-crazed with pain. And if he had been drawn enough to fear the Healing process...

"What is it that you want, old friend?" she asked.

He stirred. "I want to be her friend."

So. "And her lover!" She put a lash to that. If he did not yet know...

"I am not," Shan said carefully, "made of stone. You will have noticed this."

"Better you should have taken her to Heal yourself, then! The bond was there, from the beginning! Healing across sex is more rapid—you know that! Why—"

"And have her think herself hired to be the captain's slut? Thank you, no." There was Korval ice in that.

Lina blinked and gave a flickering thought to her own protections. "Why should she have thought so, old friend?"

Shan sighed. "She came to me—as captain—for protection. One Liaden had already robbed her of status as a person. It would not have seemed at all wonderful to her if another continued—" He shifted irritably. "Priscilla's Terran, Lina. She wasn't raised to melant'i. I *am* the captain to Priscilla. She believes it. It would have been nothing short of rape, a violation of trust so basic..." He took a breath and ran his fingers through his hair, standing it up in sticky spikes. "I was in error, old friend. I act as Healer in the matter, in that I refused to act as one."

"I am Liaden," Lina said softly. "I am her superior."

"You are also friends. And I believe that the amount of influence a senior librarian exercises over a junior is somewhat less than what a captain may exercise over a crew member."

There was a silence that grew lengthy. Then Shan leaned forward abruptly and took her hands between his.

"I want her to be well. Joyful and complete. That most. I want her friendship, but I don't—won't—force it. A pair of earrings? Call it restitution for another wrong done her by Trader Olanek, if you like, Lina. If it will make all easier—"

"You have already said they are your gift to her," she reminded him. "But I do not think harm was done." She smiled warmly. "It is a good thing to have friends."

"I think so, too." He leaned back. "I leave the Healing in your hands. My word on it."

"So, then," she said, satisfied. She brought a finger to the side of her head. "I had almost forgotten the other. She did not mean it, Shan, when she welcomed you in esteem. I have explained, and it will not happen again. You must not be angry with her."

"Angry with her?" He laughed. "I'm delighted with her! She would have done no better if I'd coached her beforehand. What a devastating setdown for poor Sav Rid! The look on his face! I could have kissed her."

"You must not encourage her to behave improperly," she scolded him. "You talk of being her friend! It is important that she learn to behave with propriety. Especially if you will present her to Lady Kareen!"

"Yes, Lina," he said with wholly unconvincing meekness.

She shook her head. "No, *that* will not do. I know you. Priscilla and I will work on her accent, and she will use sleep tapes. Lady Kareen will find her above reproach."

"A matter of your own pride, in fact?"

She laughed and stood. "Completely impossible. Good night, old friend." She touched his cheek, very gently, noting that the Wall was yet in place. "Sleep well."

SHIPYEAR 65
TRIPDAY 144
FIRST SHIFT
1.30 HOURS

He did *not* sleep well. Nor did his interview with Gordy do anything to mend his badly frayed temper. He had begun by snarling at
the boy, and his mood was not improved by the realization that he
sounded rather like his father in that tone.

Irritably, he crossed to the bar and poured himself a glass of
morning wine. There were a few things to attend to here before
going worldside to begin a local week of trading. He dropped into
his chair and spun the screen around.

Buzzzz!

Shan looked up, not quite placing the sound.

Buzzzz!

Brutally, he rearranged the mob of documents on top of the
desk and eventually uncovered a shiny blue pad set with two unmarked keys. He depressed one at random. "Yes?"

Buzzzz!

Shan sighed and pushed the other key. "Yes?"

"Cap'n? Rusty here. Sorry to bother you."

"Rusty? Aren't you scheduled for world leave today? I thought
you'd be dancing in the streets with a lover on each arm."

"Well, I'd planned on it," Rusty said seriously. "But when we hit
port, there were two—oh, individuals—waiting for us. They say nobody from the *Passage* is allowed on-world and that they're coming
up." There was a tiny pause. "They say they've got a warrant, Cap'n."

"Do they? What are we to do with that very interesting piece
of information, I wonder? And what does it have to do with the
crew's leave? Do strive for clarity, Rusty—I'm afraid I'm a bit dense
this morning."

"Well, they say they want to see you. I guess they'll explain it
personally."

"Wonderful. What sort of...individuals, Rusty? Ambassadorial? Mere policepersons? Concerned citizens?"

"Ummm…" Rusty's voice drifted, then came back. "Didn't Cap'n Er Thom used to say that if your host wore a dagger, you should wear a dagger and a dirk?"

"It sounds very like him."

"By those rules, you ought to wear three daggers and a machete."

Shan grinned. "And these very formidable persons wish to call on me? How pleasant. Do me the favor, please, Rusty, of asking Seth to bring our visitors up as quickly as possible. Gordy will meet them and serve as escort. You needn't bear them company, if you'd rather not."

"Right you are. I'm not losing *my* breakfast. I'll catch a lift with Ken Rik, since they're evacuating him, too."

"Marvelous. Thank you for the call, Rusty. You always have such cheerful topics of discussion."

The other laughed and broke the connection.

Shan spun in his chair, hit the toggle that would summon Gordy, opened a drawer, and began to sweep papers into it.

The door opened to admit a subdued and rather pale cabin boy. "Yessir?"

Ruefully, Shan stretched out a hand. "Forgive me, acushla. My dreadful temper. I swear I didn't mean it to sound half as fierce as it did."

Gordy actually produced a grin, albeit a faint one. "That's okay. I should've been workin' at it all along. Guess I deserved to get my head bit off."

"That for me!" his cousin cried, snapping his fingers with a grin. Sobering, he shook his head. "An emergency, Gordy. Run to Selna and get a piece of the sample wood—so." He squared it off in the air with big, capable hands. "On your way back, stop and ask Calypso for the loan of his antique. Jet!"

Gordy was gone.

In an amazingly short time he was back, armed with the required items, which he placed on the pristine desk.

"Good," Shan said, surveying things. "Another task. Shortly there will be two individuals in the reception hall. Please bring them here."

"Yessir," the boy said, moving toward the door.

"Oh, Gordy!"

"Yes, Cap'n?"

Shan grinned. "Take your time."

The visitors were not pleased. They followed Gordy with rustling aloofness, their sulfur-colored robes brushing the sidewalls, and kept their hands on the hilts of their swords. They came finally to the red door—after having traversed the length of the ship twice, had they but known it—and Gordy activated the annunciator.

"Come!" Shan's clear voice was followed by a peculiar heavy *thump* just as the door slid open.

Gordy stepped into the room. Shan was lounging back in the chair behind the desk, which was clear except for a block of oak with a wooden-handled hatchet buried in it. He raised his glass and lifted his brows.

Mindful of the proprieties, Gordy bowed. "Cap'n yos'Galan, here are Budoc and Relgis come to speak with you."

"Good day; gentles. A pleasant one, isn't it? How might I serve you?"

Relgis, who was bald, stepped around Gordy and executed a grudging bow. "Good day, Captain," he replied in hoarse Terran. "We are officials of Arsdred Court. It is my duty to inform you that we carry papers denying your crew access to the planet surface for the amount of time required for the municipality of Arsdred to inspect and verify your cargo. Under this same order, you are banned from trade activities until such time as investigation retires charges brought against the *Dutiful Passage,* tradeship, and Shan yos'Galan, captain and Master Trader." He paused to glare sternly from beneath bushy eyebrows. Shan sipped wine.

"The charge," Relgis continued in a goaded voice, "is smuggling illicit pharmaceuticals and proscribed animals."

"The *Dutiful Passage* is accused of running contraband?" the captain inquired in the mildest possible tone. "May I know the name of the accuser?"

Relgis looked at him with suspicion, apparently formulating a reply. Into the silence stepped his partner, saying with ponderous affability that no such thing as *charges* had been leveled at ship or master.

"Relgis made a slip of the tongue, sir. The thing is, a complaint has been lodged with the court, citing *suspicion* of contraband. I'm sure you'll agree that this is a very serious thing."

"Oh, I do," Shan said, raising his glass, "Especially when suspicion names my ship."

Budoc had the grace to look discomfited. "Well, of course you're bound to feel that way," he allowed after exchanging a startled glance with his partner. "I'm sure it will be inconvenient for you to deny your crew leave and forfeit a few days' trading. But if you're innocent—as I'm certain you are—then there's no harm done, is there? You'll be allowed to go about your business, just as you normally would."

"The municipality," Relgis stated, revolted by this conciliating speech, "must be certain of either the truth or falsity of a suspicion of contraband. We cannot be too careful."

"I see. Any other suspicions, sir? Or is this the awful whole?"

Once again Relgis found that tone of vacuous amiability disconcerting. Budoc took over, clearing his throat noisily.

"We also bear a warrant for the detention of one Priscilla Delacroix y Mendoza, of the crew of the *Dutiful Passage*. She is to be questioned under deep probe and held, pending arrival of further information."

"On what charge?" Shan queried gently, leaning forward and setting the glass aside.

"Suspected thievery." Relgis was back in the game.

"Really?" Shan looked at him with interest. "Now *I* have found her to be scrupulously—no, make that excessively—honest. Who accuses her?"

"Trader Sav Rid Olanek brought the matter to the attention of the court, sir. When the balance of his information arrives, determination shall be made as to whether the matter would be most properly handled by local or galactic authorities."

"And if she's innocent?" Shan asked, resting his chin on his left hand. His right lay next to the wooden block.

"If she's innocent," Budoc said magnanimously, "she will be released."

"Which will," Shan said dulcetly, "do her a great deal of good if the *Passage* has moved on in the meantime." He ran an absent finger down the hatchet haft. "What is she suspected of stealing from Trader Olanek? The clothes on her back? She had nothing else when she came to me."

The two officials exchanged glances. "No doubt that will be included in—"

"Trader Olanek's further information," Shan concluded. "Of course. May I see the papers you carry, sirs? I must say that I think it extremely unlikely that Ms. Mendoza is a thief. As to allowing her to be removed from this vessel and placed in a detention block for—how long before this information comes forth? Stupid of me, but I don't seem to recall…"

"We didn't say," Relgis said quellingly. "No longer than ten days, local."

"Captain," Budoc added, with a warning glance at his partner.

Relgis glowered, produced the papers from the depths of his robe, and handed them over with scant grace.

"Thank you," Shan said, receiving them in the spirit in which they were offered. He glanced at the hovering cabin boy. "Gordon, fetch Ms. Mendoza, if you please."

"Oh, no you don't!" Relgis snapped, leaping between Gordy and the door in a swirl of fabric. He fingered his sword hilt menacingly. "A very sly idea, Captain, but it won't work! Send the boy for her! Warn her, more likely! Next we'll be hearing from him that she's escaped!"

"Escaped?" Shan blinked at him, striving for his best look of foolish interest. "Now, where would she escape to, I wonder? I do seem to recall rather clearly a statement to the effect that none of my crew would be allowed worldside." He picked up his glass and took a thoughtful sip. "Of course, the *Passage* is a large ship," he conceded. "But not that large, do you think? I'm sure you could run her to ground if she took a notion to hide from you."

Perceiving a sheen of dew on Relgis's bald pate, he relented somewhat. "Go for Ms. Mendoza," he instructed Gordy gently. "Say that I wish to see her immediately. Please do not mention the presence of these two persons."

Gordy goggled at him, then recovered enough to bow and mutter "Yessir" before turning toward the door.

Speared by a glance from his partner, Relgis let him go.

Shan had another sip of wine and began a leisurely perusal of the court's documents.

In just under five minutes, the door chime sounded.

"Come!" Shan called, eyes still on the documents he had already committed to memory.

The two officials turned, hands on swords, ready to confront the desperate criminal herself as she stepped unescorted into the room.

Relgis preserved his countenance. Budoc visibly gaped.

Priscilla gave each a friendly, though curious, smile and stepped around them. "You wanted to see me, Captain?"

He glanced up, sternly subduing the pang he felt upon seeing her ears yet unadorned. "Good morning, Ms. Mendoza. I'm sorry to have to call you to me so abruptly. These gentlemen, however—" He nodded at Budoc and Relgis and paused, frowning. "My terrible manners! Ms. Mendoza, these are Relgis and Budoc, officials of Arsdred Court. They have come to deliver this paper to you." He held it out.

She took it, directing a sharp glance at his face before beginning to read. Her cheeks flushed, then went white. Shan overrode the impulse to hold out his hand to her; instead, he picked up his glass and brought before his inner eye a Wall.

"Will he never stop?" Priscilla cried, slapping the paper onto his desk. "He hounds me, names me criminal, leaves me for dead—and now has me arrested! Questioned under deep probe! What good can he think it will do him? Trader on a ship crewed by lechers and motherless fools!" She spun, approaching the two officials with a tigerish tread. Relgis gave ground by a step. Budoc licked his lips.

"Whose palm was greased?" she demanded awfully. *"Suspicion* of theft? Information *forthcoming?* And I'm to be detained and questioned, treated like a thief on the strength of information that will never arrive, and so I swear!" She straightened haughtily. "I'm not going anywhere with you."

"Well," Budoc said carefully, "you've got no choice, miss. We've got the warrant, and you've got to come. It's the Law."

Priscilla sniffed. "This is a Liaden ship. You have no authority here."

"You're Terran," Budoc pointed out with a fair semblance of rationality.

"I should perhaps explain," Shan broke in apologetically, "that Ms. Mendoza serves on this ship because of a personal contract between her and the Heir Apparent of Clan Korval."

There was a moment's silence. Then, in accents between dread and wonder, Budoc asked if that wasn't the Tree and Dragon Family, trade representative for Trellen's World?

"Exactly the Tree and Dragon." Shan beamed at him. "Precisely Trellen's World. The contract between us extends back nearly two hundred Standards. How clever of you!"

That information might have impressed his partner, but to Relgis it conveyed nothing more than a blatant attempt to thwart the Law. He stiffened his resolve and advanced upon Priscilla's position by one step.

"Be that as it may," he said sternly, "the Law is still the Law. This woman's Terran, and she goes with us." He shifted his eyes to the man behind the desk and thrust out his chin. "She's not Liaden, even if this heir or whatever it is, is. We don't have a warrant for her contract—we've got a warrant for her!"

"Heir Apparent," Shan corrected gently. "Not, praise gods, the Heir. Ms. Mendoza is correct, you know. A personal contract of this kind assures her of the Heir Apparent's protection. Which amounts to the protection of Clan Korval. And Clan Korval is a legal Liaden entity." He finished his wine and set the glass aside. "An interesting point, isn't it? I'm sure the lawyers would be able to argue it for much more than ten local days, don't you?"

"Now, Captain," Budoc said nervously, "be reasonable. No one wants to get into that kind of protracted debate. Think of the expense! Better to just let her come along with us. Maybe the judge will allow her back right after the questioning—in light of her contract, you know!" He licked his lips again. "I'm sure we can work something out."

"Are you?" Shan asked. "Good. I think so, too." He picked up the disdained warrant and made a show of frowning perusal. "There doesn't seem to be anything here about bail," he murmured, feeling Priscilla's gaze bent on him in speculation. "An oversight on the part of the judge, no doubt. Who *was*—oh! Judge Zahre? What a delightful circumstance!" He smiled with exquisite stupidity at the two officials and avoided Priscilla's eye.

"We'll have everything settled soon!" he said gaily. "I'm acquainted with Judge Zahre. What a fortunate circumstance!" He flipped a toggle on the panel by his desk.

"Tower," a crisp voice informed him.

"Good shift, tower. Are you busy? Would it be possible for you to find Judge Abrahanthan Zahre of Port City, Arsdred, for me? I'd like to speak to him."

"Right away. Captain. Route the call to the office screen?"

"That will be perfect, tower, thank you. Do hurry. We have guests, and I seem to be wasting their time."

"Yes, sir." The connection was cut.

Shan nodded to himself and called the commlink from its slot, then turned to the infoscreen and tapped in a quick series. Out of the corner of his eye he saw Priscilla drift over and perch on the arm of the nearer chair, dividing her attention between the two officials and her captain.

Budoc and Relgis exchanged glances and remained uncomfortably silent. Relgis nurtured the hope that the judge would drop one of his thundering lectures on the heads of both captain and crew member.

The commlink buzzed gently.

Shan spun his chair, tapped the violet key set along the left margin of the screen, and inclined his head to the austere individual in ruby-colored robes. The other man also wore a ruby turban, held by a glittering nelaphan brooch. His eyes were dark and deep-set, and the authority of his nose exceeded that of Shan's own.

"I am Judge Zahre," he said emotionlessly.

"Yes, sir," Shan agreed easily. "W are acquainted, though I doubt you remember me. My father, Er Thom yos'Galan, and I guested you aboard *Dutiful Passage* several Standards ago, upon the occasion of your Honesty's succession to office."

The face in the screen thawed somewhat; the lips bent a trifle. "Indeed, I do remember you, sir, and most kindly. How does your father do? It would honor me if you and he would dine at my residence, if the length of your stay permits it."

Shan took a breath, hardly aware that it was deeper than the one before it. After so many repetitions, the phrase had become merely rote, and the inward voice that had keened "My father is dead!" was now but a wordless flicker of pain.

"I regret to be the first to inform you," he said evenly, pulling the words verbatim from the High Tongue, "that my father's heart ceased its labor nearly three Standards gone by."

The lines about the judge's mouth grew deeper as he bowed his head. "It grieves me to hear it. I am richer for having had his acquaintance, though it was for so brief a time."

"I will tell my family you said so, sir. Thank you."

The older man nodded. "Now, tell me what I may do for Er Thom yos'Galan's son."

Shan smiled. "A misunderstanding has occurred. At least, I think it must be a misunderstanding." He held the warrant up so that the other could read it. "This was delivered by two officials of Arsdred Court—Budoc and Relgis. It's a warrant for the detention and questioning of one of my crew members, Priscilla Delacroix y Mendoza. Apparently Trader Sav Rid Olanek accuses her of theft."

Judge Zaire nodded. "I remember him. I admit I did not like to let him swear out such a thing and then immediately depart the sector, but he pleaded urgent business and paid penalty and swear-charge. All was according to Law, as he promised further information by bouncecomm, within ten local days. I performed my office, as set out in the Book."

"I am certain you did," Shan said soothingly. "However, there are several points of which you could not have been aware. One is that Trader Olanek has taken Ms. Mendoza in severe dislike. I am not certain of the cause. It is a fact, however, that far from her stealing from him, he has stolen from her. A member of his command has within the last local day sold personal articles belonging to Ms. Mendoza at a shop in Parkton Way—Teela's Treasures. The proprietor is Frau Pometraf. She has a very good memory."

The judge inclined his head. "I am grateful. The information, of course, will be verified." He looked up, his deep eyes shrewd. "You have yet to say what I might do for you, Shan yos'Galan."

"A small thing, correction of an oversight." He rustled the paper. "There doesn't seem to be any mention of bail here, sir. Now, Ms. Mendoza is an important member of my crew. I can't spare her for ten days. Not for ten minutes! What shall I do?"

The older man's lips twitched, though he gravely agreed that it *did* seem to be an oversight. "You must understand that a warrant has been sworn to, sir. The Law must be served."

"Of course it must." Shan spun the infoscreen around. "I had nearly forgotten! This is Ms. Mendoza's record, sir. Now, I ask you: Is it likely that a person possessing such a record would sully her honor by stealing?"

After a longish pause, the judge said, "I believe bail of one cantra—cash, of course—is sufficient to this case. You will guarantee Ms. Mendoza's presence, should the matter in fact go to trial?"

"Korval guarantees," Shan said formally, and jerked his head at the gaped-mouth officials. "These two gentles may take the money with them? It will be secure?"

"Relgis and Budoc are completely trustworthy."

"I'm sure they are. No thought of their venality crossed my mind, sir. It's only—a cantra, you said? You're certain they won't want an armed guard to escort them?"

Relgis made an outraged noise; the man on the screen smiled.

"I believe that no guard will be necessary, sir. I appreciate your concern."

"One cannot be too careful," Shan said earnestly. "What with innocent persons being attacked by ruffians in the streets of the city." He sighed and spread his hands. "You've been very kind, sir. I find it necessary to impose upon you still further." He held the second document up.

The judge scanned it quickly and shook his head. "This matter is out of my jurisdiction. However, I am acquainted with Judge Bearmert, who is among those signed. Allow me to call him and ask if he will speak with you."

"You're very kind, sir," Shan said again. "Forgive me the trouble."

"There is no trouble. It is my duty to see that the Law is served, not that the innocent suffer." He bowed stiffly. "Be well, Shan yos'Galan. Will you come to dine tomorrow evening?"

"I would like nothing better, sir. But I believe that the ban on my crew visiting your pleasant world applies to me as well."

"Nonsense," the judge said crisply. "I will send my yacht for you, sir. You will be conveyed directly to my home. You will experience no difficulty."

Shan grinned. "In that case, of course. I'll be delighted."

"Good. Until then." The screen went dark.

Shan thumbed the yellow stud, and the screen slid back into the desk. Absently, he pulled open a small drawer on the right side and fished out a battered lacquer box.

"Cantra," he muttered, and dumped the box over.

Coins *tinged* and tumbled, rolled in tight circles, and sped away to catch against the block of wood supporting the hatchet: Terran bits of all denominations, Liaden coins, local money of half a dozen worlds, several rough-cut citrines, and a loop of pierced malachite.

"Cantra," Shan murmured again, conscious that Budoc was drawing closer. With clumsy care, he selected ten tenth-cantra from the jumble of money and beckoned the man still closer.

"One, two, three…" He counted all ten carefully into the sweaty palm and nodded. "Ten, are we agreed?"

"Yes, Captain," Budoc breathed.

"Good." He pointed at Relgis. "You, sir. A receipt, please."

Relgis glowered but did as he was bidden. Shan flipped a toggle by the desk. The door chimed instantly and slid away on his word to admit a grim-faced Gordy.

Shan smiled. "These gentles are leaving now, Gordon. Please conduct them to the reception hall and arrange for refreshment. Seth will conduct them worldside in good time." He turned his smile to the officials, striving for complete vacuity. "Thank you so much for your visit, sirs. I enjoyed it immensely. Good day."

"Good day, Captain," Budoc said, bowing low. Relgis sniffed and bowed, silently and slightly. Both turned and followed Gordy out.

The door closed, and Priscilla stood, holding out a hand. "May I refill your glass, Captain?"

He considered her warily. "Thank you, Priscilla. The red, please. And pour yourself something."

Priscilla stared a moment at the hatchet in the block of wood, then turned to busy herself at the bar.

"It's Pendragon," she announced suddenly.

Shan frowned at her beck. "Pendragon? Oh, the fellow with the table. One of Val Con's favorite stories, I recall. Named one of his infernal felines Merlin." His frown deepened. "It's only Uncle Richard's fancy, Priscilla. Coincidence. Dragon-analogs are fairly common around the galaxy, you know."

She nodded and handed him a glass before settling into the chair across.

"One hundred bits the night before last, a terrible scare yesterday, a cantra today. What am I going to cost you tomorrow?" Her tone was mild, but her eyes were very bright.

Shan considered the Wall; he left it in place and raised his glass. "I don't expect you'll cost me anything tomorrow, Priscilla. You didn't really cost me anything today. Sav Rid's thought was to cause me discomfort—so it seems I'm taken seriously! How gratifying." He sipped. "He has accused the *Passage* of running contraband. That's creative of him, isn't it? We're to be investigated—by officials of Arsdred Court."

"Unless the friend of your friend brings his authority to bear," she said dryly.

"Well, I don't think he will, do you? It's worth a try, of course. No sense rousing Mr. dea'Gauss until we need him. My sister the First Speaker prefers our man of business to stay close to hand. His tact and finesse are a good balance for her temper, you see. By the way, you were magnificent."

"I thought that was it." She considered him for a moment out of half-angry black eyes, then shook her head and smiled a little. *"Are* you Heir Apparent to Korval?"

"Of course I am. It's not the sort of thing one lies about, after all. You could find yourself in a great deal of trouble if you did. Besides that, if you want truth, I'd rather not be Heir Apparent. Especially with Val Con adventuring around the universe, busy being a scout and making no push at all to place an heir of his body between myself and destiny." He sighed. "I'm afraid I wouldn't be a very good Delm."

There was a pause while Priscilla tasted the wine, her eyes on the hatchet. Shifting her gaze to his face, she asked, carefully, he thought, "Will you do me a favor?"

"I'll certainly *try,* Priscilla," he said with matching caution. "What is it?"

"I wonder if you wouldn't make me a list of all the people you are, so I know who to ask for."

He grinned. "I'm afraid it might get a bit lengthy. And a few are so close that only a Liaden would make a distinction." He set the glass aside and began to count on his fingers. "Head of Line yos'Galan. Heir Apparent to Korval. Guardian to the Heir Lineal—that's a joke. Brother to Val Con, Nova, Anthora. Cousin to Val Con. Guardian to Anthora. Father to Padi. Master pilot…"

He sighed. "This is too tedious, Priscilla. You could call me Shan if you get confused, and I'll sort it out for you."

"Why don't I just call you Captain?"

"I *knew* you were going to say that," he complained.

Surprisingly, she grinned and pointed at the hatchet. "What's the idea?"

"My father used to say—so I was informed earlier—that if your host wears a dagger, you should wear a dagger and a dirk. I think he might have meant it in some other context, but Rusty did me the favor of calling it to mind this morning when he told me of the presence of our visitors." He wrenched the hatchet free, sending two sundered chunks of wood skittering across the polished desk top.

"My brother, now, says there's nothing will give one pause like the sight of a naked blade." He extended it, and Priscilla leaned back in her chair. "He's right, I see. That's comforting. I thought I would give our visitors a visible reminder of might." He grinned. "Liaden tricks, Priscilla. Forgive me."

She shrugged. "It worked, didn't it? And *they* were using tricks, too. Blustering and acting as if all justice were on their side."

"High-handed, in fact."

"I'll never live it down." She sighed. "Will it help if I say I'm sorry?"

"*Are* you sorry? You might ask me to forgive it, if you think I'm offended. But Liadens don't in general say that they're sorry. It's an admission of guilt, you see. Asking forgiveness acknowledges the other person's right to feel slighted, hurt, or offended without endangering your right to act as you find necessary."

She blinked at him. "Which is why Kayzin Ne'Zame was so infuriated with me when we met at the main computer! I kept saying I was *sorry...*" She sipped, working on the concept in silence.

Shan toyed with the weapon, turning it this way and that, taking note of its balance and the feel of it in his palm. Laying it aside, he took up his glass again and sipped, allowing himself the luxury of watching her face.

As if she felt his eyes on her, she glanced up, a slight smile on her lips. "Is there anything else, Captain? I'm supposed to be having a piloting lesson."

"Teaching me how to run my ship?" He waved his glass toward the door. "Go back to work, then. And thank you for your assistance."

"You're welcome, Captain," she said serenely. "It was no trouble at all."

ARSDRED PORT CITY
MIDDAY BAZAAR

Mr. dea'Gauss leaned back in the seat and allowed himself a moment of self-congratulation. Progress thus far was satisfactory. Not, he reminded himself, that he was in any way reconciled to being shipped harum-scarum off Liad and flung out into the galaxy with barely an hour's notice. If his heir had not just recently entered into a contract marriage that tied her to the planet, Korval would have found itself represented by the younger, less-tried dea'Gauss; and so the elder had informed Korval's First Speaker.

Lady Nova had acknowledged that statement with a slight tip of the head and continued outlining his task in her calm, clear voice. Mr. dea'Gauss experienced a reminiscent glow of warmth in the region of his mid-chest. She was a great deal like her father, and competent beyond her years.

She'll do, Mr. dea'Gauss thought with satisfaction. They would *all* do eventually. It was simply a sad pity that so powerful a Clan as Korval should have been left untimely in the hands of persons too young for the duty. Even the eldest, Shan, now Thodelm yos'Galan, had not attained his full majority. And young Val Con, the Delm-to-be, was barely more than a halfling, no matter how gifted a scout he might be.

The old gentleman laid his head against the cushion. It was his duty to insure that all continued as it should during this period of readjustment, just as Line dea'Gauss had kept Korval's business for generations—to mutual profit.

They were intelligent children, after all, he reminded himself with a shade of avuncular pride, and quick to learn. He and his would be unworthy indeed of the post they had held so long if Korval were to lose ground before Val Con placed the Clan Ring upon his finger.

The taxi glided to a stop. Mr. dea'Gauss opened his eyes and glanced out the window. Satisfied, he gathered up portfolio and travel desk, slipped the proper Terran coin into the meter's maw, and exited the cab as the door elevated. He blinked once at the din and the colors and the smells of the Offworld Bazaar, then turned his steps with calm dignity toward the shuttlecradles.

There was an armed guard before Cradle 712. Mr. dea'Gauss was untroubled; he had expected no less. What did puzzle him was the presence of two additional individuals engaged in vociferation with the guard.

"I don't care," the fat woman with the jeweled braids was saying loudly, "if you've got orders from the Four Thousand Heavenly Hosts! I am Ambassador Grittle of Skansion! You've seen my identification. You've verified my identification. I have urgent business onboard the *Dutiful Passage*—"

"Off limits," the guard interrupted laconically. "Judge Bearmert's orders."

The fat woman's face turned a curious purple color that contrasted not unpleasingly with the silver lines drawn around her eyes. The second individual addressed the guard.

"I am Chon Lyle, sector agent for Trellen's World. It is imperative that I be allowed onboard the *Dutiful Passage*. Clan Korval is the licensed representative of Trellen's World in matters of offworld trade. A charge of illicit dealing brought against its flagship must also be thought a charge brought against my world."

Mr. dea'Gauss's brow cleared. Unmistakable, here was the hand of Korval's First Speaker. He stepped forward, affording the guard a tip of the head, as was proper for a person of consequence addressing a mere hireling.

She surveyed him with boredom. "Don't tell me. You want to get up to the *Dutiful Passage*."

"Precisely," he said, undeceived by the apparent readiness of her understanding. He proffered a piece of orange parchment folded thrice. "I have here a manifest from Judge Bearmert allowing me that privilege, and also whomever I deem necessary to the commission of my duties." He moved a hand, encompassing ambassador and agent. "These persons are such. Pray verify the document. I am in haste."

The guard sighed, took the paper, and unfolded it with a flick of the wrist. Her eyes moved rapidly down the few lines, then returned to the top and moved downward more slowly. Eyes still on the page, she unhooked her belt-comm, thumbed it on, spoke into it briefly, then listened. She nodded.

"Okay, shorty," she said, handing the paper back to Mr. dea'Gauss, who folded it precisely and replaced it in his sleeve, "you're legit." She craned her head around the entranceway. "Hey, Seth! Customers!" Then she took up her official stance again, arms folded under her bosom, legs wide.

A tall, rat-faced Terran appeared at the edge of the ramp and glanced at the three before bowing to the elderly Liaden. "Yessir?"

He was awarded a slight smile and an actual, if shallow, bow. Korval employed persons of worth. It was as it should be.

"I am Mr. dea'Gauss, Korval's man of business. Lord yos'Galan expects me." He indicated his companions. "These are Ambassador Grittle of Skansion and Agent Chon Lyle of Trellen's World. His Lordship will be most gratified to receive them."

Seth nodded and stepped aside. "Welcome aboard, sirs, ma'am. We'll be lifting as soon as the tower clears us."

SHIPYEAR 65
TRIPDAY 147
THIRD SHIFT
15.00 HOURS

"That cargo is sealed!"

The taller of the two inspectors turned and sighed down at the cargo master before repeating for the ninth time that their duty was to inspect and—

"Verify the holds, goods, equipment, and general cargo of the *Dutiful Passage,* out of Solcintra, Liad, under the captaincy of Shan yos'Galan, Master Trader," Ken Rik singsonged, and threw up his hands in exasperation. "I *know.* I also know that this cargo is sealed. Do you understand what sealed means?

"Sealed means—one, that this cargo was delivered by the agency that leased the hold, made secure to their satisfaction and sealed with their lock.

"Two. It means that, having sealed the cargo at their end, the agency expects—has paid for the certainty—that the hold will still be sealed when the cargo reaches its destination.

"Three. It means that, if you two—people—unseal that hold, the *Dutiful Passage* will lose a shipping fee of approximately fifteen cantra—that's five hundred twenty-five thousand bits to you!—and very likely ten times that amount in commissions she will not receive for shipment of sealed cargoes in the future."

The taller inspector sighed. "I am aware of the exchange rate, sir. I am also aware of my duty. Surely you understand that in cases of contraband, to rely upon the ship's own records is sheer folly."

Ken Rik gasped. "How *dare*—" The Terran words were insufficient, he realized suddenly. Setting his jaw, he marched forward, placed himself before the hold in question, crossed his arms, and rooted his boot heels to the floor. "This hold is sealed," he said with a calmness his captain would have instantly recognized as highly dangerous. "And it will remain sealed."

"Quite proper," a dry voice said from the left. "Unless, of course, one of these individuals is a certified representative of the company whose seal is upon the cargo."

"Mr. dea'Gauss!"

Korval's man of business bowed. "Mr. yo'Lanna. I am pleased to see you well."

"And I'm pleased to see *you,* sir," Ken Rik said, throwing a grin of pure malice over his shoulder at the inspectors. "How may I serve you, Mr. dea'Gauss?"

The other man considered. "I will need a place to work. I apprehend these persons are inspectors from, ah, *Arsdred Court?*"

"Indeed, we are," the taller one asserted, coming forward with hand held out. "I am Jenner Halothi; my associate is Krys William. It is our duty to—" He cast a wary eye in the cargo master's direction. "—search this vessel for contraband and illegal goods."

"But not, I think," Mr. dea'Gauss said, ignoring the hand, "the holds sealed by companies independent of Korval or the *Dutiful Passage,* unless a representative of that company is present." He surveyed the inspectors with the air of one sizing up the opposition. "The purpose of this, of course, is twofold. The representative will be present to oversee the unsealing and search of the cargo and will be able to make testimony that it is, in truth, the proper cargo. Also, should the cargo prove to be—or to contain—illegal items, you, sirs, will have your culprit. Is there a representative of—" He glanced at the device on the hatch. "—Pinglit Manufacturing Company on board, Mr. yo'Lanna?"

"No, sir, there is not," the cargo master replied happily. "There is, however, Ambassador May of Winegeld, Pinglit's world of origin. Also Ambassadors Sharpe, Suganaki, and Gomez, from trade-linked planets."

"Excellent, excellent." The old gentleman's eyes were seen to glow with what Ken Rik knew to be the light of battle. "If these gentles will but follow—Mr. yo'Lanna, I regret. Is there a place I may work?"

"You may use my office, sir," Ken Rik offered with exquisite cordiality. "This way, please."

"With all due respect, Mr.—umm—dea'Gauss?—we have our duty."

"Of course you do," he agreed. "We each of us have our duties. At this present, however, yours must wait upon mine." He executed a stiff, barely civil bow. "Attend us, please, sirs."

Shan yos'Galan rounded the corner with lazy haste, a glass of wine in his right hand and a large green plant cradled in his left arm. Suddenly he stopped, plant fronds swaying over his head, and blinked with consummate stupidity.

"Have the inspectors gone, Ken Rik? Or is it time for your midshift tea? Please don't think I begrudge you anything, but—"

Ken Rik grinned at him. "Mr. dea'Gauss is here."

"Is he? How delightful for us. Has he been shown his room? Oh, are you going visiting? Silly of me—of course you are. Very proper, since the two of you are such fast friends. A game or two of counterchance, a few glasses of wine, a bit of gossip. But the *inspectors,* Ken Rik?"

"Mr. dea'Gauss is with the inspectors. He came directly to the holds, looking for your Lordship, and has taken matters into his hand. I am sent for a ship-to and a colorcomp, that he may do his work the better."

"You left the inspectors *alone* with Mr. dea'Gauss?" Shan grinned widely. "Poor inspectors. Should I succor them, do you think, Ken Rik? It wouldn't do if a charge of cruelty to those of limited understanding were lodged."

"Mr. dea'Gauss summoned four ambassadors pertinent to the present situation to my office, where he is instructing the inspectors. I think they'll be safe enough for this while." He sniffed. "Did you know that we've engaged the services of a local accounting firm to tally the losses to port and to ship while the *Passage* is off limits?"

Shan regarded him with awe. "Have we? That was clever of us, wasn't it? How did we do it?"

"We put an advertisement," the older man explained, a bit unsteadily, "in the port business publication."

Shan gave a shout of laughter, the plant shivering alarmingly in his arms. "Oh, dear. Oh, *no!* In the port business paper? Ken Rik, we have a blot upon our immortal souls: We've brought an expert to an amateur's game! Speaking of which, I believe I should be present, as referee. My Lordship wouldn't miss such a show for— never mind." He held the plant out. "Do me the favor of taking this along to Ambassador Kelmik's quarters. She tells me that she cannot feel comfortable without a bit of greenery about."

Ken Rik sighed. "How are matters in the pet library?"

"Lina and Priscilla seem to be holding their own. Really, we have a most remarkable crew. When I left, the inspectors were bloody, but game. Neither of the ladies had yet been touched."

"Nor will they be," the cargo master predicted with delight. "Please tell Mr. dea'Gauss that I have not forgotten him, and that he will have his equipment very soon."

"I will, indeed," Shan promised, moving off with his big, loose stride. Ken Rik grinned and proceeded toward the guesting hall, plant fronds bouncing over his head with each step.

"Also," Mr. dea'Gauss was telling an attentive audience when Shan entered the cargo master's sanctum, "it must be taken into account that persons employed by Clan Korval receive wages that are between ten and fifteen percent higher than wages received by persons employed in similar positions on other vessels. This, of course, means greater in-port spending on the part of Korval's crews. I expect to have the precise extrapolations in—your Lordship." He rose immediately and bowed low.

Shan stilled a sigh and inclined his head. "Mr. dea'Gauss. I am happy to see you. Forgive that I was not on hand to greet you personally when you came aboard."

"Your Lordship is gracious. It is understood that there are many demands upon your attention. Mr. yo'Lanna has seen to my needs. I believe it is not overoptimistic to state that matters progress well and an end to this misunderstanding will be speedily attained."

"I am sure we all hope for that," his Lordship responded gravely. "Please continue. It's always an inspiration to watch you at your work."

Mr. dea'Gauss acknowledged this with a tip of the head and reseated himself. Shan drifted to the left, exchanged polite smiles with the four ambassadors, and took up a position where he could watch the faces of the inspectors and Mr. dea'Gauss's workscreen.

"We should shortly," Korval's man of business resumed, "have a response from Pinglit Manufacturing Company. If they agree to the proposal offered—that is, your Lordship, to allow the presence of these four persons, Ambassadors May, Sharpe, Gomez and Suganaki, to equal the presence of one of their agents—then we will proceed with the unsealing and inspection of Hold Forty-three. In the meantime, sirs..." He turned to the befuddled inspectors. "I shall require from you a list of areas inspected and a certification for each."

"Certification, sir?" queried the shorter one—Inspector William, Shan recalled—with trepidation. "What sort of certification?"

Mr. dea'Gauss regarded him from under drawn brows. "Why, certification that you found nothing illegal within the stated area, of course. I do not ask if that was indeed the case. It could not have been otherwise."

Inspector William exchanged a glance with his partner.

"Was it otherwise?" Mr. dea'Gauss demanded.

The shorter inspector swallowed. "No, sir, of course—that is to say, we found no illegal substances in the holds thus far inspected. However, sir, it is our instruction to search the vessel entire and issue certification at the end."

"Insufficient," Mr. dea'Gauss judged, turning back to the screen. "Also, I find it incredible that two teams of inspectors are assigned to this task. A vessel the size of the *Dutiful Passage*—it is laughable. And while you pursue your efforts, Korval loses on the order of—" He touched a key with the reverence another man night reserve for stroking the cheek of his beloved. "Seven cantra per trade-night. Arsdred Port loses four point eight cantra per trade-night. This does not include the loss to those merchants who have offered guaranteed delivery for the goods we carry, based on our reliability. We must have at least two more teams of inspectors."

"I," Ambassador Suganaki said quietly, "would consider it an honor to be allowed to supervise one of those teams. It is absurd that the crew bear all the burden when there are so many of my colleagues here, pledged to aid. I am sure the crew has its scheduled round of duties, which must go on, regardless."

Shan bowed. "I thank you, ma'am. That's exactly the sort of assistance we do require. If I'd had any indication that the *Passage* was to have been boarded in this way, I would have signed on extra crew at the beginning of the trip."

"It is, of course, an unlooked for and unprecedented event, Captain," Suganaki agreed gravely, though there was a twinkle in her eye. "Perhaps an announcement at the reception this evening will alert my colleagues to the need." She turned to Korval's man of business. "It is possible, I think, sir, that even *four* more teams may not be excessive. The *Dutiful Passage* is a large ship."

"A worthy suggestion, Ambassador. My thanks to you. I shall inquire of Judge Bearmert how best to obtain additional inspectors.

Now—" The in-ship buzzed, and Mr. dea'Gauss tapped the speak key. "Yes?"

"Tower here, Mr. dea'Gauss," Rusty's voice said formally. "Pinglit Manufacturing Company agrees to your suggestion. Hardcopy verification arrives via courier ship soonest. If there is anything else they may do, they beg you not to hesitate."

"Excellent, tower. My thanks to you." He cut the connection and gazed around in satisfaction. "Let us repair to Hold Forty-three."

Much later, after the inspectors had departed for the night, Shan walked with Mr. dea'Gauss toward the guesting hall.

"I have a message from the First Speaker, your Lordship," the old gentleman murmured in the High Tongue. "She bade me inform you that the Clan bears all expense in this situation, since the blow seems aimed at Korval entire, not only at the *Passage*— or yourself."

Shan nodded absently. "The First Speaker, my sister, is generous."

His response was most proper. Mr. dea'Gauss cleared his throat as a prelude to speaking further. It was not often that one found his Lordship so biddable. He did not at the moment recall that every period of docility he had previously observed in Shan's career had been immediately followed by some mad start. "I have also a message from Lord yos'Phelium."

The big mouth curved in a smile. "Do you? And what has my brother to say?"

Korval's man of business paused. The message was an odd one—flippant to the point of outrage. However, it seemed certain that young Val Con had inherited his father's devious directness, and Mr. dea'Gauss believed the true message lay far within the one he was bidden to deliver. Carefully, striving for the original phrasing, he said, "He asked me to tell you that he believes a successful scout and a successful thief must share certain vital characteristics. He thanks you for the suggestion of an avocation and asks further what he may be honored to steal for you first."

Shan laughed. "Renegade. He should have been drowned at birth. How long does he stop at home?"

Mr. dea'Gauss allowed himself a sniff to indicate his disapproval of this manner of speaking of Korval's Heir and replied stiffly. "He had been on Liad a bare quarter relumma when he

was suddenly recalled to his duties as scout. He left the planet, I
believe, the very day I was called before the First Speaker. It was
only by chance that I was privileged to see him for a moment and
exchange greetings."

Shan considered him. "Suddenly recalled by the scouts, was he?"

"Yes, my lord, and a sad blow it was to Lady Nova. She had
invited Lady Imelda to guest. I believe she looked for a contract
marriage in that direction, so that his Lordship might fulfill his duty
to the Clan."

"Is she feeling better now?" Shan asked solicitously.

Mr. dea'Gauss blinked. "I beg pardon, your Lordship? Is
who feeling better?"

"My sister. Of all the ladies she might have tried to force down
Val Con's throat!"

"Lady Imelda," the old gentleman said severely, "is from a good
Clan. She is honorable and quite complaisant."

"*Quite* complaisant. And neither stupid enough nor brilliant
enough to pull it off. Val Con would have been at the screaming
point within a relumma." They paused by an indigo-colored door.
"I will give you any odds you name, sir, that that sudden recall by the
scouts came after a personal request to be recalled."

There were several answers to this, none of them proper. Mr.
dea'Gauss maintained an icy silence. His Lordship grinned and
bowed. "Your room, sir. I trust you will find everything exactly as
you wish it. The ambassadorial reception will be at Twenty Hours. I
hope to see you among the merrymakers."

There was nothing for Mr. dea'Gauss but to make his bow and
enter his room.

Shan moved toward his own quarters, his long stride eating
distance while he frowned in thought.

It was true that the lad must do his duty to the Clan. Everyone
must provide the Clan with his or her personal heir. Even Shan, the
reprobate, the cynic, had given Korval a daughter who would in
time take his place at the head of Line yos'Galan; at the head of the
Passage...Damn them both for being at such loggerheads! If only
Nova would try to enlist Val Con to the task of discovering some
suitable lady, all might yet come out right.

Shan sighed, stopped in the middle of his sleeping room, closed
his eyes, and breathed deeply and evenly, as he had been taught so

long ago by the Master Healers. Slowly, the worries—familial, professional, personal—stilled.

One thing at a time, he reminded himself with forceful calm.

An image of Priscilla as he had last seen her, the light of battle in her face as she confronted two harried inspectors, rose before his inner eye.

With a groan, he dropped onto the bed and closed his eyes.

You want too much, your Lordship, he told himself. Try to be worthy of her friendship. If you're very lucky, you'll manage it.

He rose from the bed and wandered toward the 'fresher, stripping off his clothes as he went. He stepped into the needle spray, resolutely turning his thoughts to the coming reception and what profit might be earned from it.

SHIPYEAR 65
TRIPDAY 148
FOURTH SHIFT
17.00 HOURS

"You must have a dress!"

"Lina—"

"No!" the small woman cried, taking her friend's hand. "You attend the reception properly attired. I will hear no more!"

Priscilla stood her ground and bit her lip. "Lina, I'm sorry— *truly* sorry. But I don't have any money, my dear. None. And I'm already into my wages for the cost of the clothes I'm wearing now. A—party—dress..."

"Bah!" Lina flung up a tiny hand, then swung close, pressing lightly against the taller woman's side. "I shall provide the dress, and you shall wear it to please me, eh?" She smiled. "All is arranged!"

Priscilla smiled and shook her head. "I can't ask you to do that, Lina. Why should you—"

"Why should I not?" Lina interrupted. "We are sisters—you said it yourself! Should I allow my sister to go improperly clad? And far from asking, you make it astonishingly difficult to gift you!" She laughed and pulled on Priscilla's hand, urging her to the entrance of the general stores. "Come, denubia. You must learn to accept a gift with grace."

The Terran woman chuckled. "Another protocol lesson? Next you'll be telling me to wear the earrings the captain gave me!"

"And why should you not?" Lina demanded. "The design is pleasing; I think they will look very well on you. Shan is honorable—he does not gift and then cry 'owed!'" She looked up into her friend's face. "The earrings are *yours,* Priscilla. A gift, freely given. No hurt can come from wearing them." She pulled her companion through the first storeroom, past the working clothes and everyday boots, past even the festive tunics and softshoes, into the room beyond, where dream fabrics drew the eye from all directions and the air smelled of Festival-time.

"I don't think..." Priscilla began, staring about her like a thing half-wild.

"Bah!" Lina said again, allowing no time for refusals. "Why should you not have a dress that becomes you?" She came close once more and extended both a hand and a mental touch of comfort to still the beginning panic. "Priscilla, you are lovely. It is added joy that you are so. Why not pleasure yourself—and those who see you—by wearing beautiful clothes? The occasion demands it!"

But Priscilla was no longer listening. She bent and stroked Lina's hair lightly, then slid a hand beneath the small chin and tipped her face so the light fell on it. Lina met the sparkling black gaze calmly, all Roads open and clear, the Wall at her back.

"You are of the Circle," Priscilla murmured, perhaps to herself. "I can feel the warmth coming out of you, like a hearth fire, my friend. And before—the pain—then the healing..." The hand withdrew; Lina kept her face tipped fully up, eyes steady.

"Are you Wife, Lina? Or Witch?"

"I have been a wife—twice by contract, as is proper. And I am mother of two sons: Bey Lor and Zac. By trade I am librarian; by training I am Healer. I do not know what a Witch is, my friend."

"Healer?" Priscilla frowned. "A Healer is—Soul-weaver, we say, on Sintia. When someone is sick in spirit..."

"When one does not accept joy," Lina agreed. "Shan says the proper Terran word is 'empath.'" She hesitated. "I am not sure. It seemed from my readings—for a Healer may not aid everyone. There are those I cannot feel at all. And there is training to be undergone, protections to be learned, techniques to be mastered."

"Yes, of course." Priscilla was still frowning. "But I—"

"You," Lina interrupted, "were fighting joy, denying both laughter and the possibility of kindness. It could not continue so! I had the means to aid you. Why should I not?" She swayed close, regardless of other persons in the room, all Roads open yet. "Priscilla? Sisters. You said it. I do not deny it."

There was a flare of pain like thrown acid, followed by a surge of joy nearly as searing. Lina put her arms around her friend's waist and hugged her tight, feeling Priscilla's arms pull her tighter.

"Sister and friend..." After a final, nearly bone-crushing squeeze, Lina felt herself released and realized that the Roads bore the other woman's clear, singing happiness; she retained enough wit to shut herself away from the intoxication.

"Come," she said, smiling and taking Priscilla's hand. "Let us choose you a *magnificent* dress!"

SHIPYEAR 65
TRIPDAY 148
FOURTH SHIFT
20.00 HOURS

Long after Lina left, Priscilla stood before the mirror, oscillating between terror and delight.

The dress *was* magnificent: black shimmersilk, shot with random silver bolts that glittered and danced as she moved. The fabric covered her from knee to neck, from shoulder to wrist, meticulously reproducing every line it adhered to. The slit on the right side made her accustomed stride possible while allowing a tantalizing glimpse of creamy thigh. Goddess knew how much it had cost. Lina had not answered when Priscilla had asked.

She frowned at her reflection. She wore her three remaining bracelets on her right wrist, and a blue enameled ring borrowed from Lina on her left hand. A silver ribbon wove like lightning through her storm-cloud curls. Yet there was something missing.

Slowly she went back to the wardrobe and rummaged within. The velvet of the box was warm in her hand. She worked the catch on her way back to the mirror, then carefully hung a hoop in each ear and stepped back to observe the effect.

In a moment she nodded, which set the hoops dancing; laying the box aside, she left the room.

Rusty frankly stared before coming forward and offering his arm. "'Cilla, you're gorgeous. How 'bout a cohab contract?"

She grinned. "You've been in the tower too long, friend."

"Well, that's true," he said morosely. "Between the cap'n and Mr. dea'Gauss, I thought I'd never get off that damn beam! We've got the fourteen prime points covered, I swear."

"Sounds rough," she sympathized. "Try coming to the pet library and defending Master Frodo's right to live."

Rusty snorted. "Busybodies. Why don't they find something real to do? As if we'd ship contraband! Must've lost all their aces to try and pin that on the *Passage.*"

Just then Lina approached, arm in arm with an elderly Liaden gentleman in formal dark tunic and strictly correct ash-colored trousers. "Priscilla, here is Mr. dea'Gauss, Clan Korval's man of business," she said with a stateliness made tolerable by her smile. Turning to the gentleman, she repeated the formula. "Mr. dea'Gauss, here is Priscilla Mendoza, my good friend."

Both pet librarian and man of business bowed.

Straightening, Mr. dea'Gauss was seen to smile. "Lady Mendoza, I am delighted to make your acquaintance. Lady Faaldom has spoken most warmly of you."

"I am happy to meet you, Mr. dea'Gauss," Priscilla said cordially; she added a diplomatic rider. "I am certain that Lina's friendship must be a bond between us."

"So I thought, as well," the old gentleman said, delighted to find her so well spoken. He inclined his head to her escort. "Mr. Morgenstern. How do you go on?"

"Pretty well, sir," Rusty returned as if he had not spent the greater part of his day executing the old man's instructions. "How are you?"

"I find myself in the best of good health, thank you, sir, in spite of the fact that I have recently been constrained to travel. Ah, there is Ambassador Kung." He executed a nicely gauged bow between Priscilla and Lina. "I beg to be excused. Duty must ever come before pleasure."

"Pity Ambassador Kung," Rusty muttered as Mr. dea'Gauss moved off after his quarry.

Lina laughed. "Ah, he is not so bad, the old gentleman. He sincerely tries to care for people. It is not his fault that he loves work more."

"If you say so," Rusty said doubtfully. "At least he's not as strung-up as Lady Whatsis—Kareen? You remember that run we had her and her son? I don't think Shan showed his nose in the halls the whole time she was here! Even Captain Er Thom looked nervous."

Lina smiled. "But it was only for a few weeks, after all. And the rest of the trip was very nice. Bah! Now *I* must ask to be excused! I did promise to speak with Mr. Lyle. And it is true that we should be pleasant, since we wish them to work for us." She executed the bow between equals and slanted a grin up at Priscilla. "Lady Mendoza. Mr. Morgenstern."

Rusty shook his head and sighed down at Priscilla. "Well, she's right. I'd better find that silly woman who was so excited about the pin-beam and show off my manners." He raised a hand, grinning ruefully. "See you later."

Priscilla looked about her. Mr. dea'Gauss was in earnest conversation with an emaciated and exceedingly tall Terran. Janice Weatherbee and Tonee had engaged the attention of three or four lesser officials; the conversation was liberally laced with laughter. Ken Rik listened politely to a fat woman with a painted face and a multitude of jewel-tipped braids, while Lina smiled winningly up at a clearly captivated gentleman who was, Priscilla supposed, Mr. Lyle. Rusty had disappeared into the crowded back of the room. And she did not see the other person she was looking for.

Irritably, she shrugged her shoulders and moved at random into the crowd. What difference did it make to her if Shan yos'Galan chose to absent himself from the reception?

"It would, of course, be unfortunate," Ambassador Gomez was saying confidentially to an elder in the robes of an Arsdredi, "should Clan Korval send word to its allies and trade-partners that it no longer stops here."

"Generations to recover," another person murmured as Priscilla eased by. "Economic tragedy…second-rate port…"

Was Clan Korval as powerful as that? she wondered, slipping by Janice and Tonee with a smile. Could they ruin a spaceport? Make thousands jobless? By refusing to stop? Merely by letting it be known that they would no longer stop there? It seemed incredible. And yet Shan yos'Galan had lost a middling fortune at the hands of Sav Rid Olanek and claimed the money as the least part.

He's a truthful person, Priscilla thought. He'd have told me if the coin-loss was desperate.

Spying a lone ambassador, important in beribboned tunic and sash-belt, she smiled and bowed. "Good evening. I am Priscilla Mendoza, of the crew of the *Dutiful Passage.*"

The ambassador, it turned out, had a thirst for knowledge. He wished to know everything concerning the *Passage,* her captain, Clan Korval, the pet library, and the crew. Priscilla obliged him, editing where it seemed appropriate, thankful for once that the possession of a comely face allowed her room to be just a trifle stupid. While she could not feel that her interpretation of the role was as inspired as Shan yos'Galan's, it was perfectly adequate for the audience.

The patterns of the party altered, partnering Priscilla's ambassador with one of his own. Liberated, she moved off. She saw Seth bent almost double, speaking into Tonee's ear; Rusty was near the bank of green plants with Kayzin Ne'Zame, his stance formal as he spoke to a half circle of listeners.

And leaning against the far wall, beneath the very wings of the dragon, closely attending a blond woman in ambassadorial dress, was Shan yos'Galan. He wore a blend of Liaden and Terran formality: ruffled white shirt, brocade jacket, dark, form-fitting trousers. The amethyst drop hung in his right ear. Priscilla was aware of a feeling of relief and took an unconscious step in his direction.

He glanced up, his big mouth curved in a smile. Priscilla froze, feeling her face flush.

"Ms. Mendoza?" The voice at her elbow was unpleasantly shrill.

She turned and smiled at the fat woman of the many braids. "Yes? How may I serve you, ma'am?"

The woman smiled, creasing the intricate pattern of her facial decoration, and made a jerky forward motion, which Priscilla interpreted as a bow. "I am Ambassador Dia Grittle of Skansion. Cargo Master yo'Lanna tells me you are a native of Sintia."

Her smile felt stiff on her face, and she was certain that she had lost color. Fortunately, Ambassador Grittle did not appear to notice.

Priscilla cleared her throat. "Indeed I am, ma'am..." She let the sentence trail to a tiny note of inquiry.

The ambassador nodded sharply. "Thought as much when I saw you walk in. Got the look of your mother."

Priscilla took a breath, forcing air down her constricted throat. Not here, Goddess, she prayed. Not *now.*

"Lady Mendoza. Ambassador Grittle. Forgive the interruption. I have here one who is anxious to meet you, lady." The speaker was Mr. dea'Gauss. Priscilla felt her knees sag in relief. Silently she thanked the Goddess.

The smile she gave Korval's man of business was genuine. "Of course, sir." Ambassador Grittle muttered something inarticulate but no doubt proper. Mr. dea'Gauss bowed, indicating the gentleman at his side.

"Priscilla, Lady Mendoza, may I make you known to Judge Abrahanthan Zahre."

The gentleman stepped forward, his ruby-red robes rustling, and held out a smooth, thin hand. "I am pleased to meet you, Lady Mendoza. Especially as it affords me the opportunity to make my apologies in person."

"Apologies, sir?" Priscilla's forehead puckered, then cleared. "The warrant!" she exclaimed, striving for a look of vacuous enlightenment. "I had forgotten, sir. Please do the same."

"You are kind." The judge bowed, smiling. "But I do wish you to know that it is not my practice to brand one a thief on such flimsy evidence as was presented to me by Trader Olanek. He was very persuasive, it is true. But I serve the Law, and I hold myself responsible. That warrant should never have been issued."

"Warrant!" Ambassador Grittle was staring at the judge in what seemed to be disbelief. "You issued a warrant! Did you take no time to *think,* sir? Did you take no time to consider with whom you dealt?" She took a deep breath, her voice rising ever more shrilly over the room at large. "To think that a *Mendoza of Sintia* might be a thief—it is an outrage, sir! We of Skansion are trade-partnered with Sintia. I am myself acquainted with the Mendoza family. It is an insult, sir! And one nearly past bearing! Of all—was there bail set?" she shot at the white-faced and rigid Priscilla.

"A cantra was set as bail," the judge murmured in a moment, "and has been paid by *Dutiful Passage.* Clan Korval guarantees Lady Mendoza's appearance, should the matter go to trial." He smiled faintly. "Which I am certain it will not."

"A Mendoza of Sintia needs no one to guarantee her word!" the ambassador snapped. She reached into the velvet pouch hung at her ample waist, produced a single dully shimmering coin, and slapped it in the judge's hand. "Skansion doubles the bond! Thus do we stand by our allies!"

Priscilla ran her tongue over dry lips, then opened her mouth to say—what?

Again Mr. dea'Gauss rescued her. He stepped forward and offered the ambassador his arm, smiling coolly. "Lady Mendoza is fortunate indeed that her home-world has so staunch a trade-partner. Allow me to procure a glass of wine for you, Ambassador."

Priscilla inclined her head to Judge Zahre, then raised her eyes to find him smiling in real amusement. Her own lips bent in response. "Now I must beg *your* pardon!"

His smile widened into a grin. "Without cause, Lady Mendoza. *You* were not rude." He glanced over her shoulder. "I see that refreshments have arrived. Allow me to escort you."

"You're kind," she said breathlessly, "but I—I must see someone just now. Perhaps we'll talk again later."

The judge's face turned quizzical. "Yes, perhaps we will." Bowing formally, he left her.

Moving with pilot swiftness, pilot grace, she slipped through the press of people and into the corridor. She strode clown the hall, turned a corner, and leaned against the wall, listening to the pounding of her heart.

That dreadful woman! Who had heard? The entire room, most likely. And she claimed acquaintance with Anmary Mendoza! Allmother, what shall I do?

"Good evening, Priscilla. Asleep? It's a terrible crush, isn't it? My Lordship isn't good for much of this kind of thing. I'm a sad trial to my sister—no manners, no address."

She opened her eyes, breath snagging. "Captain."

"Sometimes," he agreed, light eyes mocking. "Don't you like the party? Mr. dea'Gauss seems very impressed."

Her face relaxed a little, her mouth curving toward a smile. "I didn't have the nerve to tell him I'm not a lady," she confessed, striving for lightness. "I'm afraid it would embarrass him."

Shan laughed. "Mr. dea'Gauss never errs in these matters. I suggest you accommodate yourself to ladyhood." He tipped his head. "That won't be so hard, will it, Priscilla? After all, a Mendoza of Sintia—"

Her face went white, eyes widening, one hand moving up and out, warding him away. "No."

"Priscilla!" He snapped forward, hand outstretched. "Priscilla, it was a joke! I—I never wanted to distress you!" He took another step as he bit his lip. "I'm *sorry,* Priscilla."

Her hand wavered, fell, and closed about his. "It's all right," she said unevenly. Her hand trembled in his as she took a ragged breath. "Please, you mustn't ask…"

"I don't ask. I have no right to ask, Priscilla. It was only a joke. You looked as if you needed to laugh so badly." He smiled ruefully. "My wretched tongue!"

Her mouth wobbled on the edge of a smile. "Ambassador Grittle…"

"Makes you stop and wonder, doesn't it? How could she have become an ambassador? Do you think she might have assassinated someone?"

"There's a chance, if she did." The smile was there, finally; nor did she take her hand from his. "Maybe someone will assassinate *her.*"

Shan laughed. "We can hope." Then he sighed. "My Lordship is expected to return to the festivities. Will you come with me? Or are you retiring?"

She removed her hand, though the smile remained. "I'll stay here for a moment or two, I think. Then I'll go back."

"All right," he said, moving reluctantly away. At the corner he turned back. "Priscilla?"

"Yes, Captain?"

A shadow crossed his face but was gone before she could name it. He bowed slightly. "It was nothing. I'll see you later, Priscilla." She was alone.

Leaning against the wall, she closed her eyes and breathed in the way that was taught to every Initiate: breathe in serenity, breathe out confusion. Breathe in strength, breathe out weakness. Breath in hope, breathe out despair.

In a little while she opened her eyes, stood away from the wall, and went back to the reception.

SHIPYEAR 65
TRIPDAY 155
FIRST SHIFT
4.00 HOURS

Shan groaned and rolled over. One long arm swung out, smacking the alarmplate unerringly. Obedient to this prompt, the cabin lights came up and music began to play. Loudly.

"Give me a break," he muttered, sitting up and running his fingers through his hair. The music abated somewhat, a boon to his pounding head. "Damn that stuff! Floats you on a cloud, then hits you over the head with a rock. Why would *any*body want to smoke it?"

The room offered no answer.

Well, it had been a profitable week of trading, with the Arsdredi seemingly bent on recouping every cantra of "loss" the port business paper had kept such careful track of. It was merely a sad pity that profit had not yet been known to cure a headache.

Shan groaned again, and the pounding intensified as memory returned. Mr. dea'Gauss wished to speak with his Lordship this morning on business concerning Clan Korval. Wonderful.

He placed his feet carefully and stood, grimacing. Perhaps it's not too late to resign as a lordship? But there was no conviction in the thought. His brother and sisters needed him, so a lord Shan would be.

"A shower," he told himself firmly. "And breakfast. Coffee. Lovely, hot coffee."

Breakfast had been the right idea. Coffee had been inspired. Armed with a second steaming mugful, Shan moved back toward his office, nodding to and exchanging greetings with the crew members he encountered.

The good news, he reflected, laying his hand against the plate, was that his interview with Korval's man of business must of necessity be brief. The *Passage* had received permission to leave Arsdred orbit in one ship's hour.

The bad news was that Mr. dea'Gauss could pack more well-mannered moralizing into an hour than a Moreleki proselytizer. The phrase "business of Clan Korval" was especially ominous.

Unless he very much mistook the matter, Shan was in for a masterly rake-down.

It was odd, he thought, setting his cup on the desk and disposing himself comfortably in the captain's chair, how lordhood's vaunted powers and privileges did nothing at all to protect one from the righteous nagging of those who held one's best interests at heart.

The door chimed, and Shan sighed. He toyed briefly with the notion of remaining silent, then regretfully decided that it would not be seemly and picked up his mug. "Come."

Mr. dea'Gauss walked three steps into the room and bowed low, as agent to lord.

Shan inclined his head and took a sip of scalding coffee. "Mr. dea'Gauss. How delightful to see you looking so well! Adversity always did agree with you, sir. Please, sit down."

"Your Lordship will have his joke, I suppose," the older man said repressively. "The business I come on is quite serious, however. I am certain that your Lordship will give me the closest attention for the next several moments."

"Of course." Shan murmured politely.

Mr. dea'Gauss regarded Shan steadily, feet flat on the carpet, hands folded, spine stiff and inches from the back of the chair. "In the course of following the instructions laid upon me by Korval's First Speaker," he said crisply, "I found that which seems to indicate that you have undertaken debt-balance with Sav Rid Olanek of Clan Plemia. I ask if this is so."

Here it comes, Shan thought. He inclined his head slightly. "It is so."

Mr. dea'Gauss exhaled sharply. "It is perhaps unfortunate," he suggested, though Shan failed to observe any note of delicacy in his tone, "that your Lordship took it upon himself to enter into such an enterprise without first consulting those of us who are more knowledgeable in affairs of this nature. If I had been apprised of the situation at its first occurrence, balance might have been quickly and, I will say, cleanly achieved. As it stands—"

"As it stands," Shan interrupted, allowing an edge of irritation to be heard, "I am captain of this vessel. As captain, it is my duty to guard her honor, the honor of the crew, and my own honor *as* captain."

"Very true," Mr. dea'Gauss agreed. "However, the situation is not so clear. It is not your responsibility as captain to plunge ship and crew into debt-balance without making the First Speaker aware. It is the First Speaker's duty, after all, to protect the honor of the Clan. And I believe this to be a strike at Korval entire." He paused, rubbing his hands together dryly. "You are aware, I think, that Sav Rid Olanek had previously given your sister, the First Speaker, cause to feel that she was owed?"

Shan drank coffee and shrugged. "I think the case is that my sister, the First Speaker, gave Sav Rid Olanek cause to feel that *he* was owed. But, yes, I was aware. It did not appear to alter things significantly."

"Wherein," the old gentleman said with asperity, "lies the meat of my comments. I have grown old minding Korval's interests. It is vainglory for one as young and as inexperienced as yourself to think he might take up so weighty a matter, unaided by older, wiser counsel." He paused. It occurred to him that perhaps this was not the best tone to take with Shan, who was well known for his unpredictability.

"It is true," he continued in a more conciliating mode, "that your Lordship is yet young. Experience comes with age, with observing the actions of one's elders and studying their thoughts. It is my dearest wish to aid you, your Line, your Clan. I have done so my life long. If I speak too freely, it is from the knowledge that youth errs most greatly when it strives to do what is most proper."

There was a pause long enough to inspire Mr. dea'Gauss with the fear that he had indeed badly overstepped himself. It was within Shan's power—and certainly within the scope of his character—to refuse the aid offered and send his man of business straightaway back to Liad. In such a case, Mr. dea'Gauss's interview with the First Speaker could only be painful. Nova yos'Galan had a clear sense of her duty as First Speaker in Trust. She would not brook failure.

"So, then," Shan said conversationally. "What do you want from me, sir? Shall I give the captaincy of the *Passage* over to your capable self? Or call a halt to the balancing with what has already been done and hope that it suffices?"

Shan's unpredictability, Mr. dea'Gauss reminded himself carefully, could run both ways. "I hear from all only that you are a most excellent captain," he answered quietly. "A Trader of the first rank. For this present...If your Lordship would apprise me of what steps have been taken?"

"Pin-beams have been sent to four hundred twenty-eight worlds, issuing social and civil warning and citing *Daxflan's* unfortunate link with port violence. To date, three hundred have responded positively, via pin-beam and bouncecomm. The Trade Commission has likewise been notified and responds with thanks and a promise to investigate." He paused. "I trust you find these efforts not completely ineffective."

Mr. dea'Gauss drew a careful breath. "I will, of course, desire to study your Lordship's records, for my own edification." He considered a moment before venturing further. "Lady Mendoza is partnered in this enterprise?"

"Lady Mendoza," Shan said, his mouth suddenly tight and grim, "has had her person abused and her honor jeopardized—by order and by direct action of Sav Rid Olanek. You may find the details in her file." He leaned forward, tapped a one-fingered sequence into the keypad, and rose to his towering height. "If you will sit at the desk, sir, you will see what efforts have been made thus far. I hope you won't find them entirely without merit." He bowed slightly. "I'm sure you'll forgive me, sir. Duty calls me to the bridge. The *Passage* leaves orbit shortly."

"Certainly, your Lordship," Mr. dea'Gauss said, coming to his feet. He bowed as Shan swept out of the room and then moved behind the desk, pulling a notecorder from his sleeve.

SHIPYEAR 65
TRIPDAY 155
SECOND SHIFT
6.00 HOURS

"Leaving Arsdred orbit," Rusty said pensively. "'Bout time. I tell you, 'Cilla, I don't think I've ever been so sick of a port before. Lost money hand over fist—well, not the *ship*. Kayzin was saying at breakfast that the port-profit appeared to be adequate." He grinned. "That means 'the cap'n made a killing.'"

Priscilla gave one of her nearly noiseless laughs. "But that's good news, isn't it? Your share will be more at Solcintra. And you didn't lose money on the spec cargo, did you? I thought the wood was preordered."

"Yeah, that's all okay. Point is, we had to pay a stiff fine to— umm, convince the inspectors that Lina's damn perfume wasn't illegal in *some* places, even if it is on Arsdred, and that we never had any intention of trading it on Arsdred." He stopped, a riveted expression on his round face. "You know what, though? We'd been going to try and trade some here, except the cap'n nixed it. Whew! Close one! I tell you what, 'Cilla: Shan's damn good."

"Well," Priscilla said as the door to the bridge slid aside to admit them, "he *is* a Master Trader."

"Sure is. What're you doing after shift? Want to pick up Lina and have a picnic in the garden? My treat."

"That sounds good. But Lina might have other plans."

Rusty set his coffee cup on the comm island. "I'll check before we get started. See you later, Pilot."

"Carry on, Radio Tech." She continued across the bridge, past Navigation and around Meteorology to Piloting. Smiling, she slid into the chair and inclined her head to Third Mate Gil Don Balatrin. He returned an absent half bow.

"Early, aren't you, Mendoza?" Janice Weatherbee asked; she, too, was early. "Might as well start calculating." She leaned back in her chair and folded her arms over her chest elaborately, her eyes ostensibly on the blank screen over the co-pilot's board.

Priscilla nodded, slid her card into the slot, logged on, and began to run the figures, building an image on her screen. She checked it frowningly, made several adjustments, checked again, and nodded. A slim finger touched the send key and the image coalesced on the coscreen. Priscilla leaned back and deliberately closed her eyes.

"Looks okay to me, Mendoza. Feed it and lock it."

She nodded, stifling a sigh as her fingers flew across the board. "Looks okay to me" was an accolade when Janice said it. It's childish, Priscilla thought, but it would be nice to hear that I'd done this or that *well*.

A chime sounded, and the minor hum of voices faded, to be replaced by one voice, clear and soul-warming "Good morning, all. Station reports, please. I assume everyone's ready to leave?"

The screen was a uniform gray except for the red digits in the bottom right-hand corner, busy counting the "real time" they spent in hyperspace.

Priscilla shifted in the pilot's chair, conscious of a glow in the vicinity of her stomach. From orbit-break to Jump-entry, the piloting had been hers. Janice had sat, watchful, throughout the shift but had given neither instruction nor assistance.

Janice stood and stretched. "Okay, Mendoza. I'm gonna run down and snap a cup of coffee. Should be back before Jump-end. If not, you go ahead. This place is a real backwater. Nothing tough. You want anything?"

"No, thanks."

The second mate nodded. "Okay. Back in a couple minutes."

"Your Lordship? May I speak with you a moment?"

Shan sighed and stopped, waiting for Mr. dea'Gauss to come alongside. "Good afternoon, sir," he said politely. "How may I assist you?"

"A few words on the matter lying between Korval and Sav Rid Olanek, your Lordship. I have taken the liberty of ordering credit checks on *Daxflan* at all ports in this sector. This is in the nature of a supportive effort to your Lordship's own tactic."

Shan raised a hand. "Mr. dea'Gauss, I regret. We are due to break into normal space in less than five minutes. Duty calls me again to the bridge."

"Of course," the old gentleman murmured. "May I walk with your Lordship?"

There was no escape. Shan inclined his head. "Certainly, sir." He began to move, sternly suppressing a desire to continue at his usual long stride.

"I am certain," Mr. dea'Gauss said, "that your Lordship will inform Lady Mendoza of the action I have taken. Also, it is necessary to ascertain whether she has notified her House of the fact that it is partnered with Korval in a venture of honor. I retain the impression that upon Sintia, Mendoza is a House of power, enclosing a varied melant'i. It would be wise to establish amicable relations." He paused, and Shan nodded absently. Matching the old gentleman's pace had kept him from reaching the bridge before Jump; the Jump alert sounded peacefully.

They rounded a corner, entering the long hallway that led to the bridge. Mr. dea'Gauss cleared his throat as the tingle of pretransition raced though the ship.

"Your Lordship has done quite well in the initial moves. The warnings will cost Trader Olanek much in time, in flexibility, in money. Of course, in this, as in chess, which I believe your Lordship studies, it is important for us to cast our minds ahead, considering the possible countermove open to our opponent."

The Jump-quiver came. From nowhere, from everywhere— the shriek of a siren. Above Shan's head, a lightplate snapped from yellow to red—and Shan himself was suddenly gone, running flat out toward the bridge.

The digits in the corner of the screen told their final tally and faded as the break-Jump chime rang across the bridge. Priscilla extended a hand toward the board.

COLLISION COURSE the red letters screamed. Abruptly her hands were flashing over the keys, calling up defense screens, demanding data as her eyes scanned the instruments, assessing what it was, how big, how fast and—

HOSTILE ACTION

Second screens up, Jump alert, coords locked back in, coils— Hurry up, coils! She saw it now, the screen providing maximum amplification: a tiny ship, bristling guns, in position for a second run-by. Coils...coils—up!

Her hand was at the Jump control, eyes on the distance dial. There was enough room—just. Now...

"Well done, Priscilla." A big hand closed around her wrist, pulling her away from the switch even as he slammed into the copilot's chair and rammed his card into the slot. "Series A29, shunt 42—second screens up? Of course..."

Priscilla's fingers flew in obedience, assigning control to him; she heard him snap an order to Rusty for a visual and another to someone unknown, regarding Turret 7.

"Hurry up, please, Rusty."

"Got 'em, Cap'n—your screen."

The image filled both their screens: the bridge of the other vessel, smaller than the *Passage* by several magnitudes. A man was at the board. From off-screen, a woman's voice, initially inaudible, was becoming rapidly clear: "...tell Jury to start her run?"

"You will observe," the captain said from Priscilla's side, "the position of the gun turret on our off side."

The pilot of the other ship looked up in shock, made lightning adjustments to his unseen board, and swore. "Tell Jury to hang where she is!" he snapped over his shoulder.

"A wise choice," the captain said gently. "I hate to belabor the point, but I believe we now have five turrets trained on your vessel. Do correct me if I'm wrong."

The man took a deep breath. "You're right." He glanced behind him as another man came into the screen, a man older than the pilot, hard-faced and calm.

"What goes, Klaus?"

Wordlessly, the pilot pointed at something out of the range of the watchers on the *Passage*. The boss considered for a moment before turning back to the screen and inclining his head.

"Nothing personal, Captain. A contract."

"A contract," Shan repeated. "With whom?"

The boss grinned and shook his head "Confidential. But I'll tell you this: he wanted you out of the race real bad."

"Did he? I hope you got your money in cash and up front, sir. No?" He shook his head at the look of sudden dismay on the mercenary captain's face. "That was careless of you. I suppose you're sure that you have the right ship?"

"He gave me your break-in pattern, a time frame for arrival, approximate mass—real approximate."

"But he gave you no name? And you didn't ask—no, why should you? This is the *Dutiful Passage,* sir. Clan Korval. Tree and Dragon Family. Stop me when you hear something familiar."

'I Dare.' The voice of the unseen woman was breathless with awe.

"A student of heraldry? Exactly. 'I Dare.'"

The other captain seemed uncomfortable. His eyes strayed from the screen back to the pilot's unseen instruments, then came back to the screen again. "All right, Captain, what's the deal? You've got weaponry and the mass to back it. You gonna use it?"

"That depends on you, doesn't it? I suppose you wouldn't be betraying a confidence if I asked if the name of the man you dealt with was Olanek or the ship *Daxflan?* You needn't say yes, only no."

There was silence.

Shan shook his head. "I hope you got at least half of your money in advance, sir. No? Forty percent? Thirty? *Twenty-five?*" He laughed suddenly at the acute distress on the other man's face. "I'm ashamed of you sir! Didn't your mother tell you never to sign a Liaden's contract? Twenty-five percent down on a job that would mark you all for the rest of your lives? Ask your crew member there if she believes a family with 'I Dare' for a motto would let you rest if you'd completed your mission successfully."

The mercenary captain shrugged. "There wasn't a contract," he said sheepishly. "It was a gentleman's agreement. But I know where to find him."

"No doubt you do," Shan said cordially "I should perhaps mention that *Daxflan* is also capably armed. And the captain is counted a very fair shot."

The boss bowed his head. "What's the price?"

"Get out of here," the captain snapped, his voice suddenly hard-edged and cold. "We have your ships recorded and filed. The information is being pin-beamed this moment to the Federated Trade Commission. I advise you to take up a different line of work."

The boss glanced over his shoulder. "Tell Jury and Sal to scram. We'll do the same, if the captain'll deflect his guns."

The last ship reached its Jump point and blinked out of existence. Priscilla's instruments showed empty space around the *Dutiful Passage* for several light-minutes in all directions. In the chair beside her, Shan yos'Galan took a deep breath and spoke, voice glacial. "Second Mate."

There was a slight hesitation before Janice answered from directly behind them.

"Captain?"

"You will report to the captain's office immediately before prime. You will bring hard copy of your contract. Dismissed to quarters."

Priscilla caught her breath at the other woman's shock; she thought for a heartbeat that one of them would cry in protest.

The second mate cleared her throat. "Yes, Captain." And Priscilla heard her go.

Relief flooded through her, shocking in its intensity, mixed with outrage, pain, and near-manic glee. She gripped the arms of the chair, seeking serenity, buffeted by emotion. Adrenaline high, she told herself, keeping to the search for the path.

"Ms. Mendoza."

She took a breath and found her voice. "Yes, Captain?"

"On behalf of this ship and of Clan Korval, Ms. Mendoza, all thanks. I could have done no better in your place, given the resources at your command. I only hope I would have done as well." He pulled his card from the slot and tucked it absently into his belt. "There will be a meeting of the crew immediately after prime. I would like to see you in my office following it, please."

"Of course, Captain." The inner chaos was subsiding somewhat. Daring to turn her head, Priscilla met a pair of quizzical pale eyes even as the feeling hit her again—differently, though as intense— an overwhelming impulse to fling back her head and laugh, to embrace the man beside her...

Just as she knew she must be lost, she found the pathway. She flew down the inner way, found the door, and slammed it hard behind her.

Beside her, Shan sighed sharply and snapped to his feet, spinning to face the incoming relief pilots. "Your boards," he said curtly.

Vilobar bowed. "The shift changes, Pilots." Priscilla pushed herself out of the chair, still giddy from too much emotion experienced too quickly. But she found her path blocked by the captain, who was glaring·down at Mr. dea'Gauss.

"Well, sir?" Shan demanded.

The old gentleman inclined his head. "Shall I draft a message to the First Speaker, your Lordship?"

"I believe," Shan said icily, "that is the captain's duty. I thank you for your concern."

Mr. dea'Gauss bowed low. "Forgive my presumption, your Lordship. It is, of course, exactly as you say."

"I'm pleased to hear it," the captain snapped, and swept by, heading for Communications.

Priscilla watched him leave; realizing that she was watching, she moved her eyes, cheeks flaming, but found her instinctive step away hindered.

Mr. dea'Gauss bowed to her, not as deeply as for the captain but with a hand flourish indicating profound respect. Priscilla forced herself to be still, to form the proper Liaden phrase.

"Mr. dea'Gauss. How may I serve you?"

"It is I who wish to serve your Ladyship. Will you accept my aid in contacting your family? They should, perhaps, be apprised of what transpires." He looked at her closely. "I ask indulgence, my lady, if the offer offends."

Priscilla stared at him blankly, then recovered herself and inclined her head. "You are all kindness, sir. I thank you for thought and offer, but no. There is no need to trouble House Mendoza with my affairs."

Mr. dea'Gauss hesitated fractionally. Then, recent contact with Lord yos'Galan having rendered him wary, he bowed again with no less respect. "As you will, my lady," he murmured. He stepped aside to let her pass.

SHIPYEAR 65
TRIPDAY 155
THIRD SHIFT
12.00 HOURS

"No," Gordy answered Lina, "I don't." He took an appallingly large swallow of milk. "I guess I'm just dumb, or way too weak. No matter how hard I try, I just *can't* hold on. Every day I go to the exercise room, grab on to the bar, and Pallin tries to pry me loose." He sighed. "Does it every time. And he keeps saying I've got to think about my strength being a river, all running down my arm and pooling in the hand that's hanging on, but you know what? That don't—doesn't—make any sense at all! Rivers don't hang on."

"Indeed they do not," Lina agreed seriously. "But perhaps Pallin only wishes you to understand that strength is a fluid thing. A—a variable."

Gordy stared at her blankly. "That doesn't make sense either," he decided. "You're either strong or you're not. I'm pretty fast, but Pallin says I've got to learn to hold on before I learn how to hit back or run."

"Ah," Lina murmured, momentarily stumped. She picked up her teacup and glanced at the third member of the dinner party.

Priscilla sat with her hands curved around a cup of coffee, her eyes plumbing the dark depths. She had put her dinner aside untasted and had appeared lost in her own thoughts. But now she looked up, giving the boy frowning attention. "I know something that might help," she said softly. "It might sound silly to you, but it works."

"I'll try *any*thing," Gordy said, thumping his glass on the table for emphasis. "Nothing can be sillier than trying to think about a river making you strong."

Priscilla smiled faintly and sipped coffee. "To do this," she said slowly, "you should close your eyes and sit up straight, but not stiffly, and take two deep breaths."

He followed her instructions, shifting to set both feet on the floor and squaring his round shoulders.

Lina froze, regarding both with Healer's senses. Gordy radiated trust and boy-love, untainted by alarm. And Priscilla...

Gone were the grays and browns of unjoy, the coldness of unbelonging. Priscilla was a flame—a torch—of assurance, compassion. It was as if a door hidden within a dark and joyless cellar had been flung open to the full glory of a sun. Lina watched as Priscilla extended herself and surrounded the child's love and trust, saw her pluck one well-anchored thread of confidence from the glittering array of Gordy's emotions and expertly begin the weaving.

"Now," she said, and it seemed to Lina that her voice had also taken on depth; a vibrancy that had not been there a heartbeat before. "You're going to become a tree, Gordy. First think of a tree—a strong, vigorous tree at the height of its growth. A tree no wind will bend, no snow will break."

The boy's brows pulled together. "Like Korval's Tree."

"Yes," Priscilla agreed, still in that supremely assured voice, "exactly like Korval's Tree. Think of it alive, with its roots sunk deep into the soil, pulling strength from the ground, rain from the sky. Think hard upon this prince of trees. Walk close to it in your thoughts. Lay your hand upon its trunk. Smell the greenness, the strength of it." She paused, watching Gordy's face closely.

Lina carefully set her cup aside, watching the weaving with amazement. A Master of the Hall of Healers would do exactly what Priscilla was...

The boy's face went from concentration to pleasure. "It's my *friend.*"

"Your friend," Priscilla reiterated. "Your second self. Walk closer. Lean your back against the trunk. Feel how strong your friend is. Lean closer; let the Tree take you, make you one with it. Feel how strong you are—you and your friend. Your back like a trunk, the strength running in you drawn up from the deep—clean, green, absolutely certain strength. You're so strong..."

There was a small silence as Gordy sat, face joyful, wrapped in love, taking the image into himself. Lina heard the image strike home then, with a chime so pure that outer ears could not have heard it, and felt it click into place in the next instant. Priscilla withdrew slowly; Lina could see nothing in the fabric of the boy's pattern to indicate the new weaving.

Beside her, Priscilla extended a hand to sketch a sign in the air before the boy's face.

"It's time to say good-bye to your friend now, Gordy. Take another shared breath...take a step...another...you may come to visit as often as you like. Your friend will always welcome you."

She picked up her coffee cup and took a sip. "Don't you want dessert, Gordy?" she asked, and her voice was entirely normal.

The boy's lashes lifted. He grinned. "Pretty good," he said, still grinning. "Do it for me again tomorrow?"

She lifted her brows. "Me? I didn't do anything, Gordy. You did it. All you have to do is close your eyes and think about your Tree whenever you need to renew your strength." She smiled. "Try it on Pallin tomorrow."

"Crelm! Won't he be surprised when he *can't* yank me loose?" Gordy laughed, then glanced at the clock. "Guess I won't have dessert, though. Got to get to the meeting room and make sure everything's okay before the crew gets there. See you later, Lina! Thanks, Priscilla!" He was gone.

"Will it work?" Lina asked carefully.

Priscilla smiled. "It usually does. A small spell, but very useful. It's one of the first things an Initiate's taught when she's brought to the Circle for training."

"Spell?" She was unsure of the word. Inwardly, Priscilla had shielded the flame, not hidden it. Lina wondered if her friend yet understood.

"That's what it's called at—on Sintia," Priscilla was saying apologetically. "A spell. Other people would call it hypnotism, maybe, or voice tricks and psychology. Whatever the right name is, it *does* work. The image is so easy and so strong." She smiled again.

"Is it so important for an—Initiate?—to be strong?" Lina wondered, feeling her way, taking care to keep all incoming paths open in case the other should reach out, Healer to Healer.

Priscilla sipped coffee and nodded. "Learning to make decisions, learning to use your voice, the power symbols...and later, the larger magics that might require the woven concentration of ten or twelve of the Circle. It's very important to be strong."

Lina tipped her head, groping for the best phrasing. The chime announcing the end of the prime sliced across her thoughts.

Priscilla stood and held out a slim hand. "Come to the meeting with me, friend?"

Lina smiled and slid her hand into her friend's larger one. The inner roads were empty. Priscilla would not approach her that way. "Of course," she murmured, standing. "We should also save a seat for poor Rah Stee. He is always late."

SHIPYEAR 65
TRIPDAY 155
THIRD SHIFT
12.30 HOURS

Janice had been stoic.

Yes, she understood the reason for her dismissal. Negligence of duty was a serious matter. No, she did not think she would accept a position as shuttle pilot on one of Korval's lesser ships, though she appreciated the captain's offer. She had friends on Angelus, fourth planet in the system they had just entered; she thought she would pay them a visit before looking for another job. After a small silence, she offered the opinion that Mendoza was a damn good pilot—ripe for first class.

Shan nodded, counting out the coins that bought back her contract. Janice informed him that she was packed and could leave the *Passage* immediately. She had no good-byes to say.

Again Shan nodded as he flipped a toggle and spoke quietly to Seth in the shuttlebay. Janice's departure was scheduled for Fourteenth Hour. They would be within shuttle distance of Angelus then.

The door chimed, and he whirled about, snapping to his feet. "Come!"

Kayzin Ne'Zame entered the room, checked, and bowed profoundly. "Captain."

"If you've come to remind me that I'm to attend the crew meeting, Kayzin, you'd no need. My memory is quite sharp, though I daresay it will begin to deteriorate very soon."

Covering her shock, her face neutral, she bowed again.

Shan sighed sharply and strode past her to the bar. Glancing over his shoulder as he poured a cup of misravot, he strove for a happier tone. "Kayzin? Will you drink?"

"Thank you," she said formally, "but no." She waited until he turned his face to her fully before continuing. "If it does not offend, Captain, I ask to walk with you. There is a thing to be discussed. A matter of reassignment of duty, to accommodate the lack of a second mate."

"Very well." He moved to the door and bowed her through before him. That was highly improper; rank earned *him* that privilege. But what could she do when he waved at her so imperiously?

"The case is," Kayzin pursued through her prickling hurt, "that the third mate does not wish promotion to second. He feels he lacks the proper qualifications, that his reaction time is insufficient to demands such as those present upon the bridge this shift just passed." She paused. Shan said nothing.

"I agree with his assessment of his strengths—and his weaknesses. He is willing to extend his hand to those duties of administration for which the second mate is responsible." She looked up at him gravely. "It is the first mate's recommendation to the captain that this be done. For a short time. And conditionally."

"The captain hears," Shan said unencouragingly. "The conditions?"

Another nuance had developed in the symphony of emotion that was Kayzin. A chilly fogging…embarrassment, Shan identified, and was amazed.

"In view of the first mate's imminent retirement," she said levelly, "and the lack of a second mate, coupled with the third mate's inability to step into that position, it is in the best interest of the ship that another be trained in the line of command as soon as may be. I request that the captain assign Priscilla Mendoza to the first mate, that she may be strenuously schooled in the duties of the second."

"Reasoning, please."

"She has the ability. You yourself placed her in a training position. I admit that track is not as rigorous as this proposed will be. However, it has been my observation that Priscilla Mendoza possesses a strong character, quick understanding, and sure judgment. I believe she may do well for the ship, were she but offered the means. And if she does not," Kayzin shrugged, "the ship is no worse off than it is at this present."

"There is a phenomenon which Terrans call 'personality conflict.' The captain has seen indications of this phenomenon between the first mate and Priscilla Mendoza."

"The first mate has mastered herself."

Shan nodded. "Your recommendations have merit. They will be put into effect tomorrow First Hour, assuming Ms. Mendoza's acquiescence. The captain will require from the first mate a daily report of training and progress—or lack." He paused at the door of the meeting room and bowed. "Forgive my hapless tongue, old friend. I regret having caused you pain."

Her relief was like a puff of Arsdredi smoke. She smiled and returned his bow. "It is forgotten."

"By both," he answered properly, and preceded her into the room.

Shan leaned back in his chair and sipped. The room was full. Those of the crew whose duties prevented their physical presence watched by monitor from their stations. The general hubbub indicated good spirits and confidence.

He considered his inner Wall, then carefully allowed the merest slit to part its impenetrable fabric.

Hot, scintillating, brilliant iciness assaulted him. He took a breath, narrowed the slit, and began a Sort of the larger threads, flickering among webs of burning color, neither apart from nor completely of them.

Satisfied, he closed the slit, took some wine, and held it for a moment in a mouth dry with effort. The crew was outraged, of course, by the attack. But there was no trace of panic, of terror. They were certain of their ship—of their captain.

He wished he shared their certainty.

He moved a hand, and the room's lights dimmed as the central screen glowed to life. The crew's chatter died.

"You are all aware," Shan began conversationally, "of the day's *second* Jump alarm. I'd like you to watch a tape of what led up to the pilot's activation of the alarm." From the corner of his eye he saw Priscilla start. Lina reached out, and the taller woman settled back, her expression wary.

"We're at minus twenty seconds of the final transition from the scheduled Jump. Pilot Mendoza is at the board. Now—normal space."

COLLISION COURSE the screen shouted as Priscilla's hands flickered, hitting the screens up. "First defense barriers active." HOSTILE ACTION "Second screens up, coords fed, alarm on. We're waiting for the coils to come back up. Coils up and we're ready to go." On the screen his own hand stopped completion of the exercise. The action froze and faded as the room lights came on.

"Reaction time," Shan said for the benefit of the pilots watching. "From time of first warning to full defense: one and one-half seconds. From full defense to Jump-ready, two seconds. We were ready to depart twenty-four seconds after the initial alarm. Most of that time was spent waiting for the coils to renew themselves."

The silence in the meeting room was broken by the soft flutter of pilot hands over imaginary boards as pilot brains counted seconds.

Over to the right, Seth stood. Shan nodded to him.

"Yes?"

"I move that Priscilla Mendoza be given an up-share bonus. She got us out of a tough one. That bomb was right on the drive sections. Would've done real damage if it'd hit."

Rusty was on his feet before Seth was off his. "Second."

"Third," Ken Rik said. "And a call for ship-points, Captain. The debt lies there."

Gil Don Balatrin seconded that diffidently.

Shan nodded. "Any comments? Disapprovals? Discussions? No? Show of hands, in favor?

"First Mate?"

"Unanimous, Captain."

"So I counted, also. Thank you." He initialed a paper on his pad. "Recorded and done." He smiled slightly over the room. "Also recorded and done—two points hazard pay for all crew, payable at Solcintra. More business?"

There was none.

"Thank you. Dismissed."

SHIPYEAR 65
TRIPDAY 155
THIRD SHIFT
14.00 HOURS

There was tension in the air, prickling the short hairs on her arm. She focused her attention on the tapestry over the bar.

"Brandy, Priscilla?"

She started, then managed a smile. "Thank you."

"You're welcome." He handed her the glass and went by, heading for the desk.

She followed and settled into the right-hand chair, with the tension still singing around her.

The captain took a sip of his drink. "Gordy tells me you've taught him to be a tree," he commented. "I don't say it's a *bad* idea, Priscilla. I only wonder how his mother will react if I deliver him into her arms all green and leafy."

Laughter escaped her, softly. "No, an inner tree. Pallin keeps telling Gordy to think of his strength as a river. But Gordy believes that strong is strong, without variation."

"I see." The light eyes were speculative. He inclined his head. "It was kind of you, Priscilla. Thank you for your care of my kinsman."

She moved a hand in a gesture learned from the tapes Lina had provided. "It's not a *kindness*. I like him. He reminds me of Brand— my younger brother—the last time I saw him."

"My sympathy to you. But perhaps you'll find he's grown into a young gentleman when you go home next. I remember when that particular metamorphosis overtook Val Con." He laughed, and the tension shimmered. *"Truly* terrifying."

She laughed also, softly and unconvincingly. Sipping, she noticed an undercurrent of warm admiration such as she had not felt since her days as a Sister at Temple.

"The reason I asked you to come to me," the captain was saying, "is to discuss the new administrative structure of the ship."

She waited.

He sighed. "Janice Weatherbee has left us, leaving the post of second mate vacant. A problem, you will admit. The third mate has been approached and has graciously—one might say with comic haste—declined the promotion. The first mate has thus applied to the captain for another trainee." He leveled a blunt forefinger. "You."

"Me?" She stared at him. "I'm not qualified to be second mate."

"Did I say you were? I do beg your pardon, Priscilla. What I meant to say was that Kayzin had asked me to assign you to her so she could teach you to be second mate. What *is* the phrase? My dreadful, dreadful memory—aha!" He snapped his fingers. "On-the-job training."

To tension and admiration was added confusion. Priscilla drank. "I don't—why me?"

"Why not you? You were in the track already, after all. I do admit that the training Kayzin proposes will be more demanding, but it's the same training. Merely a difference in intensity." He stopped. "Kayzin is a very good teacher, Priscilla. She's been on the *Passage* for over fifty years, first mate for thirty. And she handled much of my own training, thankless task that it was."

Priscilla took a breath. "She dislikes me."

"No. She distrusted you, I believe. But I also believe that it's passed. Even if it hasn't, Kayzin is not one to let mere personal prejudice stand in the way of doing the best she can for the ship." He sipped, eyes quizzical. "Well, Priscilla? Do you want the job?"

Want the job? Like she wanted breath. Shocked, she looked within and found the same surety that had allowed Gordy to find the Tree. "Yes," she said.

"Good. Now, then, there are a few things to be explained." He paused, then nodded. "First, it is imperative that you acquire your first class license. You will come to the bridge every day immediately following your duty shift. I'll teach you. There's no reason why you shouldn't be a first class pilot by the time we reach Solcintra."

She considered it. "Shan?"

The tension altered in some indefinable way, though the warmth was constant. "Yes, Priscilla?"

"Won't it work out…" She sighed and began again. "The captain."

"What of the captain, my friend?"

"If I'm to report for piloting lessons on my first off-shift, won't the captain be pulling a triple shift?"

"Occasionally." He grinned. "The captain's made of stern stuff. When I was learning the ship, I often ran double shifts, between tutoring from Kayzin and tutoring from my father—and then stayed up half the sleep shift studying for the next day." He tipped his head. "Do you object to the captain's instruction, Priscilla?"

"No, of course not..." She felt an echo of tension and an echo of warmth. The echo would overwhelm her if she did not take care.

"Fine, then that's settled. Other points: Second mate signs a standard ship contract. That means you'll no longer be under my protection, but under the protection of the *Dutiful Passage...*"

Not under his protection? Panic added a sheen of ice to the echoes. No longer to be under Korval's wing, where there was comfort and friendship and aid? To be cast out? To be—

"Priscilla." His voice was a flame of common sense, licking at the ice. "The *Passage* is owned and operated by Clan Korval. A ship's contract guarantees you assistance that a personal contract with Shan yos'Galan cannot. You will, of course, read it before you sign it."

"Yes, of course..." Feeling foolish, she drank.

"You'll want to know the rate of pay." He tapped on the keypad as he turned the screen to face her. "Second mate draws three cantra flat for the short run, plus one-half ship-share. Bonuses and increments—not applicable at present. You will, of course, be starting at the low end. We've got four months to go, so that's prorated...plus the amount owed under previous contract...crew's hazard pay...ship's points, can't forget them...oh, and the up-share...subtract ship-debt. Well, some of this can't be finalized until we hit Liad, but I think that's everything, Priscilla: the minimum. Is the sum agreeable to you?"

It was staggering. The glowing amber letters named more money than she had ever seen at once. Enough to repurchase her bartered bracelets three times over. She could buy a hundred hours for Lina and herself, and still there would be money for clothing, for books, for tapes, for lodging, for food. It might be more money than she had made in her life...for one trip!

"That can't—*can't*—be right."

"Can't it?" Shan frowned and turned the screen around. "Well, then, let's do it again. Base pay for second, prorated..."

She felt wave after wave of emotion: admiration, nervousness, exhilaration, exhaustion. Priscilla felt herself expanding under the assault, taking it in, sending it out, over and over. The exhilaration built, as it had not built since she and Moonhawk...

Moonhawk was dead.

And the echoes came faster, where there should never have been sound. Where there could be no motion. Dear Goddess...she pictured the Tree. She took a breath, hearing Shan's voice as he muttered the figures over and leaned into the familiarity—the comfort—of it. The Tree had worked. The Gyre might work, as well.

She began the opening sequence and felt the image click into place and take on its own momentum. Thank you, Goddess. She would need to be in her quarters within the hour. Sleep was the room beyond Serenity: the end of the Gyre's dance.

"No, Priscilla, I'm afraid the figure is correct. You do have to realize that this is the short run, and that we're less than four months out of Solcintra. If you renew your contract at the end of the trip, you'll net more. Simple matter of mathematics. You'll be on from beginning to end, and the next trip's the long one. Takes a year to finish the circuit. Priscilla?"

She had passed through the First and Second Doors. The next was the Door to Serenity, where she would abide awhile before she came to Sleep.

"The sum is more than adequate, Captain," she murmured. "I was surprised because it seemed like such a lot of money."

"Oh, well, the *Passage* is the flagship of Korval's fleet, after all. You wouldn't want us to pay on the same scale as an ore shuttle, would you?"

"No, Captain." Serenity was in sight...then achieved. Priscilla took a relaxed breath and a drink.

Across from her, the captain stiffened: he shook his head sharply and stood. "I think those are the important points, Priscilla. You'll begin your training with Kayzin at First Hour. I will see you on the bridge for pilot training at Sixth. There will be a copy of the second mate's contract on your screen when you wake. Good night."

Such abruptness was hardly like him. But he must be tired, too, she thought, and offered him a smile as she bowed.

"Good night, Captain."

The door closed behind her, and Shan's knees gave way. He hit the chair with a gasp and hid his face in his hands.

He mastered himself with an effort, levered out of the chair, and turned toward the red-striped door to his personal quarters. Then he stopped.

Turning away, he crossed the room and went down the hall.

The crew hall was quiet and dimly lit: a blessing to his pounding head. He found the door by instinct and laid his hand against the plate.

For a moment he despaired. She was not there...The door slid aside. Honey-brown eyes blinked up at him. "Shan?" Then she slid her arm about his waist and drew him within. "My poor friend! What has happened? Ahh, denubia..."

Allowing himself to be seated on the bed, he pushed his face into the warm hollow between her shoulder and neck and he felt the Healing begin.

"She shut me out, Lina. Twice, she shut me *out.*"

SHIPYEAR 65
TRIPDAY 155
FOURTH SHIFT
20.00 HOURS

The contract was extremely clear; attached was an addendum providing the amount the second mate was due at Solcintra and the formula by which it had been figured. The addendum stated that the sum was not fixed and would be refigured upon final docking using the same formula and taking into account any additional bonuses, finder's fees, ship-points, or debts.

Priscilla placed her hand against the screen and felt the slight electric prickle against her palm as the machine recorded the print. *Beep!* Contract sealed.

Her hand curled into a loose fist as she took it away from the screen; she stared at it. Then, grinning, she turned to put on her shirt.

Lina's door was opening as Priscilla rounded the corner; she lengthened her stride.

"Good morning."

"Priscilla! Well met, my friend. I thought myself exiled to eating this meal alone, so slugabed have I been!"

It had done her good, Priscilla thought. Lina was glowing; eyes sparkling, mouth softly curving, she radiated satisfied pleasure. "You're beautiful," she said suddenly, reaching out to take a small golden hand.

Lina laughed. "As much as it naturally must grieve me to differ with a friend, I feel it necessary to inform you that among the Clans one is judged to be but moderately attractive."

"Blind people," Priscilla muttered, and Lina laughed again.

"But I have heard you are to begin as second mate in only an hour!" she said gaily. "Ge'shada, denubia. Kayzin is very careful, but she is not a warm person. It is her way. Do not regard it."

"No, I won't," Priscilla agreed, looking at her friend in awe.

"It is a shame that you will not have time to come regularly to the pet library now," Lina was rattling on. "You have done so much good there. I never thought to see the younger sylfok tamed at all. Others have remarked the difference there as well. Why, Shan said only this morning—"

Priscilla gasped against the flare of pain, and flung away from jealousy toward serenity—

To find her way barred and a small hand tight around her wrist as Lina cried out, "Do not!"

She froze, within and without. "All right."

"Good." Lina smiled. "Shan and I are old friends, Priscilla. Who else might he come to, when he was injured and in need? And you—denubia, you must not shield yourself so abruptly, without the courtesy of a warning! It *hurts*. Surely you know…surely your instructors never taught you to treat a fellow Healer so?"

"Fellow—" She struggled with it and surrendered to the first absurdity. "Do you mean you're open *all the time?*"

Lina blinked. "Should I huddle behind the Wall forever, afraid to use what is mine? Do you deliberately choose blindness, rather than use your eyes? I am a Healer! How else should I be but open?"

Priscilla was bombarded with puzzlement-affection-exasperation-lingering pleasure. She fought for footing against the onslaught and heard her friend sigh.

"There is no need to befuddle yourself. Can you close partially? It is not this moment necessary for you to scan every nuance."

She found the technique and fumbled it into place like a novice. The pounding broadcast faded into the background. She took a breath, her mind already busy with the second absurdity. "Shan is a…Healer? A *man?*"

Lina's mouth curved in a creampot smile. "It is very true that Shan is a man," she murmured, while Priscilla felt the green knife twist in her again. "It is also true that he is a trained and skilled Healer. Do I love you less, denubia, because I also love others?"

"No…" She took another breath, pursuing the absurdity. "It— on Sintia, men, even those initiated to the Circle, are not Soulweavers. It's taught that they don't have the ability."

"Perhaps on Sintia they do not," Lina commented dryly. "Shan is Liaden, after all, and Sintia's teaching has not yet reached us. Those of us who may bear it are taught to pay attention, to use the information provided by each of our senses. Shan is not one of those who may do nothing but learn to erect the Wall and keep their sanity by never looking beyond; nor am I. And it hurts, denubia, to be in rapport with someone, only to be—without cause and without warning—shut out. You must not do so again. An emergency is another matter: you act to save yourself. Should you find that you must shield yourself from another Healer, it is proper to say, 'Forgive me, I require privacy,' before going behind the Wall."

Priscilla hung her head. "I didn't mean to hurt him. I meant to *shield* him. I thought I was generating a—false echo, because I was tired."

Reassurance, warmth, and affection flowed in. Priscilla felt her chest muscles loosen and looked up to find Lina smiling.

"He knows that the hurt was not deliberate. The best balance is simply not to do it again." She held out a hand. "Come, we will have to gulp our food!"

TREALLA FANTROL, LIAD
YEAR NAMED TROLSH
THIRD RELUMMA
BANIM SECONDAY

Taam Olanek took another appreciative sip of excellent brandy. Nova yos'Galan had been called from the party some minutes ago. "Business," she had murmured to Eldema Glodae, with whom she had been speaking. Olanek allowed himself the indulgence of wondering what sort of business might keep the First Speaker of Liad's first Clan—why, after all, dress the thing up in party clothes?—so long from the entertainment of which she was host.

True, there was Lady Anthora, barely out of university and comporting herself with the ease of one ten years her senior. She was at present listening with pretty gravity to Lady yo'Hatha. He toyed with the idea of rescuing the child from the old woman's clutches, but even as he did, Anthora managed the thing with a grace that filled him with admiration. Not the beauty her sister was—too full of breast and hip for the general taste—but no lack of brains or flair.

No lack of that sort in any of them, Olanek admitted to himself. Even the gargoyle eldest had wit sharp enough to cut.

Their fault—collectively and individually—lay in their youth. Gods willing, they would outgrow, or outmaneuver, that particular failing without mishap, and Korval would continue bright and unwavering upon its pinnacle.

While Plemia continued its slow descent into oblivion.

Olanek sipped irritably. It seemed somehow unjust.

"Eldema Olanek?" a soft, seductive voice said at his elbow. He turned and made his bow, no deeper than was strictly necessary, but without resentment. That she should address him as First Speaker rather than Lord Olanek or Delm Plemia was worthy of note.

He smiled. "Eldema yos'Galan. How may I serve you?"

"By your patience, sir," Nova murmured, pale lips curving in what passed for her smile. "I deeply regret the need. Is it possible that you might allow a moment of business to intrude upon your pleasure?"

Odder and odder. He inclined his head. "I am entirely at your disposal." Clearly Nova wished to treat with him as a colleague. Now, why should Korval wish to discuss business with Plemia when they moved in such different spheres? And why at such a time, in the midst of this vast and enjoyable entertainment? Why not a call to his office tomorrow morning? Surely the matter was not so urgent as that?

Still, he walked with her from the room, declining to have his glass refreshed. They went side by side and silent down the wide hallway to another, where the woman turned right.

This portion of the house was older, Olanek saw. Its doors were of wood, with large, ornate knobs set into their centers. Nova yos'Galan stopped at the second, turned the knob, and stepped aside, bowing him in before her.

The gesture was graceful—one could not accuse Korval of flattery. What could they possibly gain? Olanek inclined his head and passed through.

He stopped just inside to consider the room. It was a study or office, warm with wood and patterned crimson carpeting. Korval's device, the venerable Tree and Dragon, hung above the flickering hearth. He took a step toward the fire, heard a rustle, and turned instead to face his host.

She gestured an apology—a flicker of slender hands—and moved to the desk. Olanek followed.

"If you would have the kindness to read this message. I should say that it has been pin-beamed and arrived only recently."

GREETING FROM CAPTAIN SHAN YOS'GALAN TO ELDEMA NOVA YOS'GALAN, the bright amber letters read. It was a formal beginning for a message from brother to sister, surely—but this was business. Olanek sipped his remaining brandy and read further.

Finished, he stood silently. When he did speak, it was in icy outrage and in the highest possible dialect. "Plemia is not diverted by the jest, Eldema. We demand—"

"No," she interrupted composedly, "you do not. It is conceivable that my brother could frame and execute such a jest. It is not conceivable that he would bring formal charge in this manner, as captain of the *Dutiful Passage,* begging guidance from his First Speaker." She drew breath, and the sapphire rope glittered about her throat. "My brother is not a fool, Eldema. He understands actions and the consequences of actions. As was shown, I think, when he was himself First Speaker.

"You should know that Mr. dea'Gauss was on the bridge of the *Passage* at the time of the attack. I leave it to you to judge whether he, at least, would be party to such a thing, were not every reported particular correct."

"I would speak with Mr. dea'Gauss."

"Of course," she replied calmly. "I have sent word, recalling him for that purpose."

"It might be wise for you to recall your brother's ship as well," he suggested ominously.

She raised her brows. "I see no cause. The route is nearly done. Captain yos'Galan has received the tuition of his First Speaker, as requested. For this present, of course." She looked at him out of meaningful violet eyes. "It does not need to be said that Plemia will act with honor and good judgment, listening with all ears, seeing with all eyes. Korval depends upon it."

To be thus schooled by a mere child, when he had been First Speaker—aye, and Delm!—longer than she had had breath! He gained control of himself, essayed a small sip of his dwindling refreshment, then inclined his head.

"Plemia wishes only to make judgment for itself, as is proper, before negotiating further with Korval." He paused. "I would ask, if Korval's First Speaker has not yet in her wisdom done this thing, that Captain yos'Galan be...entreated...to stay his hand until the precise circumstances have been made clear to all concerned."

Nova yos'Galan inclined her fair head. "Such was the essence of the First Speaker's instruction to Captain yos'Galan. I am certain that Plemia will instruct Captain yo'Vaade in like manner."

"Of course," he said through gritted teeth.

The woman bowed and smiled. "Business is then completed, Eldema. My thanks for the gift of your patience. Do enjoy the rest of the party."

Somehow, Olanek doubted he would.

SHIPYEAR 65
TRIPDAY 155
SECOND SHIFT
6.00 HOURS

Kayzin Ne'Zame was a thorough teacher—and a determined one. Priscilla's head felt crammed to the splitting point already. And there was so much more to learn!

She was in a hurry, lest she be late for her piloting lesson with the captain.

The captain! She dodged into the lift and punched the direction for the core and inner bridge. Rattled for the last six hours by a storm of information, she had nearly forgotten about the captain.

He was a Healer—a Soulweaver—though no man she had ever heard of was master of that skill. He was constantly open, always reading, aware...

Aware of her emotions. From the very beginning, he had scanned her and touched her feelings—and knew her as intimately as a...Sister-in-Power.

No! It was not done. It was improper, blasphemous! The power to read souls came from the Goddess, through Her chosen agents. Moonhawk, who was dead, had been such an agent, and Priscilla Mendoza her willing vessel. To use the power consciously, without divine direction...

The door slid open, and Priscilla escaped into the corridor; she dived into the first service hall she saw and froze, heart pounding.

Mother, help me, she cried silently. Help me...I'm lost...

The Tree, the Gyre, the Room Serenity, the Place of watching—each had she used within the past day. She, who was nothing and no one, save that once a saint had lived within her.

Heedless of time, she closed her eyes and quested in the Inner Places, where the Old One's soul had sung in time gone past.

Moonhawk?

Silence surrounded the echo of the thought. There was no one there but Priscilla.

Priscilla knew no magic.

Magic had worked. She held to that thought and opened her eyes. Three times—four!—magic had worked. And the promise she had given Lina had held no taint of unsurety. She would not close the captain out. She would hold the Hood ready to muffle any strong outburst and spare him as much pain as she could.

The hour bell sounded, and she gasped.

Tarlin Skepelter, on her way to Service Hall 28 to replace a faulty sensor, was treated to the interesting sight of the new second mate running at top speed away from her, toward the inner bridge.

"No! Completely useless!"

She knew it before he said so and barely caught the blaze of self-fury in time to muffle it. Beside her, the captain snapped forward and swept his big hand across the board. He was out of his chair in a blur and towering over her.

"Are you *angry*, Priscilla?"

She winced at the volume and kept a firm hold on the Hood. "Yes."

"Then be angry! You're a better pilot than that! *Gordy's* better than that! Of all the inexcusable, sloppy, *ground-grubber* piloting I have ever seen—"

"And I suppose you could do better—keeping the board in half your mind and watching for echoes, too!"

"Did I tell you to watch for echoes? I told you to mind that board, Pilot! If you can't keep your whole mind right there and nowhere else, we'll suspend all lessons, now! I'll not have this ship endangered because the pilot at the board was thinking about something besides the business at hand!" He was a glittering buzz of anger. Priscilla fielded it unconsciously, even as the hold on her own rage slipped.

"I didn't ask to be on the board with a full-open empath! What am I supposed to do? Forget about the spill? What about—"

"Yes! That's precisely what you're supposed to do! Damn it—" He slammed into the copilot's chair and flung his hands out. "Priscilla, am I made of glass? Will I break, do you think, at the touch of a little well-earned self-rage?"

She was silent, seething without attempting to contain it.

The captain sighed, his pattern now containing less anger than frustration overlaying interest-admiration-warmth-friendship. "I'm not wide open, Priscilla. I don't need to be. You're coming through quite clearly without it. Also, I am not a cretin. I can adjust the level of reception, if things are so intense I find my mind wandering. Further, I am a pilot! I've worked with *dozens* of people since I began training. One of the finest pilots I ever knew was terrified every moment of duty. Another I worked with fairly often was as nearly asleep as she could be, no matter what the emergency—and her reactions were perfect. Ask her why she had done a certain thing, though, and she'd panic..." He shifted, offering a smile. "I'm not fragile, friend. My word on it."

It was a temptation to extend herself, to grasp his warmth and cuddle it about her. She shook her head. "I—Lina said that—Healers are open, except for emergency. On—I was taught to remain closed unless Soul-weaving was required, and to return to Serenity once the duty was done."

His response was outraged puzzlement. "Then how do you make love?"

"It's not for that!"

The captain moved his shoulders. "Forgive me, Priscilla. It seems our training has been very different. For *this* training, however, please be assured that I can take care of myself—except against slamming doors! You are here for lessons in piloting. The next time we meet, I expect your mind to be only on piloting! If you choose to remain outside of Serenity, then don't try to damp every little twitch of irritation or jubilation. If you wish to be closed, then please make sure you are behind your Wall before you arrive."

He stood. "Today's lesson is done. I'll see you tomorrow, Priscilla."

TREALLA FANTROL, LIAD
YEAR NAMED TROLSH
THIRD RELUMMA
CHELETHA SIXTHDAY

Taam Olanek was finding the way to truth uneasy. Even the testimony of so irreproachable a witness as Mr. dea'Gauss was insufficient to rescue him from his quandary.

In charity, Nova sat silent, though they had covered the salient points again and again. She found patience for the task by recalling the countless times Shan had befuddled her. When the charm of these palled, she could begin to list the occasions on which he had sent their father into fury with his ways.

All the world knew of the unpredictability of Thodelm yos'Galan. Recrimination was useless, of course. To remind Shan of his position as Head of Line yos'Galan was to invite a blizzard of outrageous behavior, all calculated, one would swear, to bring her to the blush.

But it never had been said that Thodelm yos'Galan was less than honorable.

Still, she thought, how much easier, in Taam Olanek's place, might it be to suppose that Shan had crossed finally into dishonor than to believe that Plemia had fired upon Korval?

"This person Mendoza," Olanek said to Mr. dea'Gauss now. "I do not properly understand, I think. Who is she, sir? What is her claim in the matter?"

So, they were at last beyond Shan and into deeper questions. Matters were progressing, she assured herself. Well and good.

Mr. dea'Gauss cleared his throat. "Lady Mendoza is of a high House on the world of Sintia, in the Thardom Sector. Ship's records indicate that she has been offered reasoned harm by Clan Plemia, in the person of Sav Rid Olanek. Or by those to whom he stands as lord. Verification is being sought. I am certain, however, that we will find the records from the *Dutiful Passage* accurate." He paused.

Delm Plemia inclined his head with Nova's silent approval. A lesser person would have murmured "Of course" to Mr. dea'Gauss in such a face. Plemia merely awaited further explanation.

It came. "There appear to be considerations of melant'i involved. Lady Mendoza is of Terran extraction; thus, it may be some while before matters become sensible. Word has been sent to House Mendoza, informing them of the situation as it was before my return to Liad. A response has not yet reached me. In the interim, Lady Mendoza is content to walk Korval's path, so I speak for her, as well."

"Her position?" Olanek pursued. "Some melant'i must be obvious, sir. For an instance: here it is said that she serves under personal contract. Do I learn from this that Captain yos'Galan extends the protection of Korval entire to a pleasure-love?"

A reasonable question, Nova admitted, from one unfamiliar with Shan's habit of rescuing every lame puppy and kitten in the galaxy. Certainly nothing so untoward that Mr. dea'Gauss should stiffen and draw sharp breath.

"At the time of my departure," he informed Plemia in accents of ice, "Lady Mendoza served the *Dutiful Passage* in the capacities of apprenticed second mate and second class pilot. It was she who was the pilot of duty when the attack came against the *Passage*, and she who prevented damage and life-loss. That she honors Captain yos'Galan with her friendship is clear. Lady Faaldom enjoys like regard. The person we speak of could bestow no honorless esteem."

Great gods, what a paean! Nova very nearly stared at Korval's man of business.

Taam Olanek gestured peace, light sliding off the bright enamel work of his Clan ring. "I meant no disrespect to the lady or to the captain, sir. In the service of clarity, the question demanded asking. You yourself mentioned complications of melant'i."

Mr. dea'Gauss inclined his head. "Melant'i enters in another guise, sir. Information from House Mendoza will no doubt make matters mere obvious. Are there other questions that demand the asking? Is there a way in which I might serve you further?"

Olanek wiped his screen with a sharp wrist twist and sighed. "I believe the questions remaining are those best asked of my kin. Eldema, I will go to *Daxflan* and ascertain what has, and what has not, been done. I ask, in the interest of both Korval and Plemia, that Mr. dea'Gauss be allowed to accompany me."

"I am," the old gentleman murmured, as one giving just warning, "Korval's eyes and ears."

"For that reason do I crave your company, sir. You are known as a person of long sight and careful counsel. In such a tangle as this, it is wisdom to see that Plemia will require both."

"Korval," Nova said calmly, "has no objection."

Mr. dea'Gauss caught her eye for a brief moment; almost it seemed that he smiled. He inclined his head to Olanek, gesturing his willingness to serve. "I am ready to travel at Plemia's word."

SHIPYEAR 65
TRIPDAY 171
THIRD SHIFT
14.00 HOURS

Priscilla came to him with pilot grace, one slim hand extended, a smile of dawning delight upon her face. Scarcely breathing, he waited, dizzy and joy-filled. She had erected no Wall, shut no door—and this her choice, freely made! He turned his face into the caress, eyelashes kissing her palm even as he moved outside his own defenses.

There was an intake of breath, expelled on soft laughter. "Shan..." Her hand slid along the other cheek, cupping his face for enrapt inspection. The feeling sang between them, soaring unbearably. He felt his heart pounding and knew that hers kept pace.

She kissed him.

For a frenzied heartbeat he simply stood there, prisoned in re-flected rapture, then he felt her question and turned his mouth more sharply; he stroking her body closer to his as their shared songs twisted each about the other, creating one.

An alarm began to scream.

She started—and was gone, even as he tried to hold her. "Priscilla!"

His own cry woke him, though the alarm's din was louder. Snapping around in the tumbled bed, he slammed a violent palm against the shutoff and collapsed, eyes screwed tight against the ris-ing lights. "Damn, damn, damn, *damn!*"

The music came up: Artelma's "Festival Delights," rendered with passion on the omnichora, by his brother Val Con.

"Damn," Shan said once more, and headed for the 'fresher.

Some time later he passed through the dining hall on his way back from the cargo master's office. Ken Rik had been a bit less testy this morning. Perhaps he was getting over his pet at Mr. dea'Gauss's abrupt summons back to Liad.

Priscilla and Rusty were sitting with their heads together at a corner table. Belly tight with jealousy, he helped himself to a cup of coffee and a ripe strafle melon.

Healer! he jeered at himself. You can't even control your own emotions. And what does she project that you dare be jealous? Friendship? Those small bursts of appreciation, of comfort perceived, of desire…He drew a hard breath and bit into the fruit with a snap. Those are the sorts of things one might feel about anyone. Do strive for some conduct, Shan.

"How do, Cap'n!" BillyJo greeted him from the door of the galley. "You'll be havin' a real breakfast, won't you? Can't live 'til luncheon on an apple."

He grinned at her, talked a few moments about kitchen operations, accepted the sweet roll she pressed upon him, and refilled his cup. He left the dining hall by the side door, resolutely keeping his eyes away from the private corner.

The message-waiting light was blinking on the captain's screen. He put the sweet roll on the edge of the bar and hit GO as he slid into the chair

No more pin-beams from his sister, he noted. That was one fear laid to rest. He sipped coffee and scanned the directly. Nothing urgent. Well, tag the letter from Dortha Cayle. Maybe this time they had a deal. What was this?

A pin-beam from Sintia, directed to Mr. dea'Gauss?

He queried the item, frowning, found it was in reply to a message sent, and called it up, his memory stirring. Priscilla was from a powerful family, wasn't that it? Mr. dea'Gauss had wished to apprise them of circumstances.

TO DEA'GAUSS CARE OF TRADE VESSEL *DUTIFUL PASSAGE.* FROM HOUSE MENDOZA CIRCLE RIVER SINTIA. RE QUERY PRISCILLA DELACROIX Y MENDOZA. DAUGHTER OF HOUSE BEARING THAT NAME BORN (LOCAL) YEAR 986, COMMENDED TO GODDESS (LOCAL) YEAR 1002. MESSAGE ENDS.

He stared at the screen. "Commended to the Goddess"? *Dead?* His heart stuttered as he thought of Priscilla dead, then he shook his head sharply.

"Don't be stupid, Shan."

He cleared the screen and demanded Priscilla's filed identifications as well as those requested from Terran census as a matter of mindless form.

The figures appeared side by side on the screen: retinal pattern, fingerprints, blood type, gene map.

The woman who called herself Priscilla Delacroix y Mendoza *was* Priscilla Delacroix y Mendoza, to a factor of .999.

A Mendoza of Sintia... He remembered the clammy wave of desperation, Priscilla's colorless face, her hand, warding him away: "You mustn't ask..."

But Mr. dea'Gauss had asked, damn him, and the answer returned was worse than none at all.

He had an impulse to destroy the message. But he knew that was childish—and useless. If a reply did not arrive within a reasonable time, Mr. dea'Gauss would merely query again.

Well, she was rather active for a corpse. He sipped coffee, staring at nothing in particular. Save the captain. Save the ship...

"What in space can she have done?"

He sighed and finished his coffee.

The easiest—simplest—explanation was that she had run away. It was not hard to see how Priscilla might have become disillusioned in a rigid societal structure, with all power belonging to the priesthood.

So, then. The young Priscilla departs; her family declares her dead, for honor's sake. What choice, after all, would they have? The local records reflect the "fact."

But Terran census, above mere local politics, still carries one Priscilla Delacroix y Mendoza alive, alive-oh.

Simple. Comforting. Even logical. Except something was missing.

"She could be a criminal," he told the room loudly. "I don't believe it. Lina wouldn't believe it. Mr. dea'Gauss, with no hint of empathy about him, wouldn't believe it. Ah, *hell...*"

Local crimes were varied and interesting, as any space traveler could attest. A felony on one planet was conduct that on the next would not cause even the mildest of middle-class grandmothers to blanch.

Ostracism. A crime earning that punishment would have to be extreme.

From world to world there was some variation in the most heinous crimes. Not much.

Kin slaying. Rape. Child stealing. Murder. Mind tampering. Enslavement. Blasphemy.

Murder? She had certainly been ready to wreak mayhem upon Sav Rid Olanek. He retained a vivid memory of that initial interview, with its racket of fury, terror, and exhaustion. Murder was possible.

Kin slaying?

Child stealing?

Mind tampering? Enslavement? She was an empath—and a powerful one. Those crimes, too, were possible.

Blasphemy?

He sighed. Wonderful word, blasphemy. It might mean anything.

An exact definition of her crimes was required—for the ship, and for the Clan. Korval owed her much. It was vital that the person to whom the Clan was in debt be known—in fullness. Priscilla Mendoza had demonstrated aboard the *Dutiful Passage* a melant'i both graceful and strong. She had not, however, come into existence two months ago, much as he might wish it. The captain of the *Passage* could order the necessary actions, or Mr. dea'Gauss could order them, for the good of Korval. In either case, Shan yos'Galan's wishes and desires meant nothing. Necessity existed.

Hating necessity, he tapped in a new sequence and turned to issue instructions to the tower.

SHIPYEAR 65
TRIPDAY 171
FOURTH SHIFT
16.00 HOURS

"Priscilla?" Gordy interrupted apologetically. "Morning, Rusty. Priscilla, I was thinking. Could you teach me to be a dragon?"

Rusty glowered; she caught the flicker of his irritation and let it pass.

"Dragons are possible," she admitted, considering the radiance of the boy's anticipation, "but very difficult. Some people work for years and never achieve the Dragon. It requires study and discipline." And the soul of a saint? Lina had been at pains these last busy weeks to demonstrate how empaths conducted themselves in the wide universe. Melant'i figured prominently in these lessons. Souls did not.

At her elbow, Gordy sighed. "But *you* know how, don't you?"

Did she? The Dragon was a spell of the Inmost Circle—but Moonhawk's soul was an old one. She had known the way...

Before her mind's eye the pattern rolled forth; the Inner Ear caught the first rasp of leather wings against the air. She took a breath and reversed the pattern.

"Yes," she said, around her own wonder, "I know how. If you truly want to learn, I can begin to teach you. But there's a lot of study between the Tree and the Dragon, Gordy, and no guarantee that you'll be able to master it."

"Could Rusty be a dragon?" Gordy asked, trying perhaps to establish a range.

"I don't *want* to be a dragon," that person announced with spirit. "I like being a radio tech just fine. Don't you have someplace you need to be, kid?"

"Not right now. I've gotta help Ken Rik in twenty minutes. Priscilla, how come not everybody can learn this dragon thing? The Tree's easy."

"So it is." The Tree, the Room Serenity—anyone might learn these. The larger magics? Lina claimed no soul but her own. "The

Tree is a very simple spell, Gordy. Only a good thing. The Dragon is both—a weapon and a shield. It's not to be used lightly. You could live a whole life without knowing need great enough to call the Dragon."

He frowned. "You mean the dragon is a good thing *and* a bad thing? That's as goofy as Pallin's river."

"Paradox is powerful magic. The River of Strength is a basic paradox. The Dragon is immensely complex, Gordy. You must learn to balance the good against the evil, the strength that preserves against the fire that consumes. You must be careful that the fire does not consume your will, or sheer strength override your...heart. You must not—soar—too close to the sun."

Rusty's uneasiness pierced the wordnet. She pushed away from the table and smiled at them both. "Or be late for your piloting lesson with the captain. Talk with me more later, Gordy. If you're still interested. Rusty, thank you, my friend. I won't see you at prime, I'm afraid. My schedule's blocked out for the next two shifts."

He whistled. "That's some piloting lesson."

"No time with Kayzin Ne'Zame today." She grinned. "A vacation."

Rusty's laughter escorted her to the door.

She reached the shuttlebay before him. Just.

"Good morning, Priscilla! On time, as usual."

"Good morning, Captain."

He stopped in his tracks, swept a bow that the carryall slung over his shoulder should have made impossible. "Second Mate. Good things find you this day. I perceive that I am in disgrace."

"As if it would matter to you if you were!" she retorted, receiving the first rays of his pattern with something akin to thirst. Two weeks ago she would have wondered at such temerity. It was incredible how quickly she had come to depend on a sense that could not be hers.

"It would matter a great deal," he said, waving her into the bay before him. "Nice day for a shuttle trip, don't you think?"

It was at least reasonable. The *Passage* was currently in normal space, ponderously approaching Dayan in the Irrobi System.

"If, in the judgment of the master pilot, one requires more board-time in shuttle," she said.

"High in the boughs today, aren't you? Practice makes perfect, as Uncle Dick is wont to say. Roll in, Priscilla. Won't do to be late."

He dropped the carryall by the copilot's chair and slid in, his eyes on the board as he adjusted the webbing. Priscilla strapped herself into the pilot's seat, feeling his excitement as if it were her own: sheer schoolboy glee at finagling a day without tutors or overseers, the thrill of some further anticipation riding above his usual pervasive delight. And a glimmer of something else, which she had first taken for his well-leashed nervous energy but now perceived as an edge, almost like worry.

"Board to me, please," he murmured, hands busy over the keys.

Obedient, she shunted control of the ship to the copilot's board and leaned back, watching.

Lights glowed and darkened; chimes, beeps, and buzzes sounded as he ran the checks with a rapidity that would have dizzied any but another pilot. Air was evacuated from the bay; the hatch in the *Passage's* outer hull slid down, and they were tumbling away. Shan laughed softly, executed a swift series of maneuvers, cleared screens and instruments with the same flourish, and reassigned the board to her.

"Screen, please."

She provided it, wary now that it was too late.

The *Dutiful Passage* was ridiculously far away, big as a moon in the bottom left grid. Irrobi's four little worlds hung placidly beneath her.

Shan pointed at the second planet. "I want to be there, please. In—" He paused for a swift silver glance at the boardclock. "—eight hours, I wish to be docking at Swunaket Port. See to it." He spun the chair, snapped the webbing back, and reached for the carryall. At his touch it became a portable screen and desk. Radiating unconcern, he began to work.

Priscilla clamped her jaw on a caustic remark and began the dreary task of determining where exactly they were in relation to where the captain wished them to be.

DAYAN
FIRST SUNRISE

"Swunaket Port, Captain. The pilot regrets that we have landed five Standard Minutes beforetime."

He looked up, blinking absently. Since his pattern for the past two hours had been the steady buzz of concentration—as perhaps when one played chess—this ploy failed to deceive her.

"Still steamed, Priscilla?" The absent look faded into a grin.

She willed her lips into a straight line. "It was a *rotten* trick."

"I remember thinking so when my father pulled it on me," he said sympathetically. "Other things, too. Most of them sadly unfilial. You did quite well, by the way, especially when we hit that bit of turbulence—all the lovely hailstones! Really, the local weather has cooperated beautifully!"

The laughter caught her unaware, filling her belly and chest, heart and head, and, finally, the cabin. "You are a dreadful person!"

Shan sighed and began to reassemble the portable desk. "My brother's aunt, my eldest sister—now you. I bow to accumulated wisdom, Priscilla."

"I should think so!" The webbing snapped back into its roller as she stood. "The pilot awaits the captain's further orders."

He set the box aside and stood, stretching with evident enjoyment. "The captain does not require the pilot's services at present, thank you. He does, however, desire the second mate to accompany him to a certain place in the town where business is to be conducted."

She regarded him suspiciously. "What sort of business?"

"Come, come, Priscilla, I'm a Trader. I have to trade *some*time, don't I? To preserve the illusion, if nothing else."

He bowed slightly, ironically. "And I have need of your—countenance—here. I will be walking a proper distance behind you. The address we go to is in Tralutha Siamn. The name of the firm is Fasholt and Daughters." He waved a big hand, ring glinting. "Lead on!"

She stopped in the shadow of the gate, Shan close behind her, and stared into the street.

Bathed in the butter-yellow light of the smaller sun, women hurried or strolled, singly or in pairs. Behind each, at a respectful three-pace distance, came a man or boy, sometimes two. One elderly woman strolled by on the arm of a younger one, both expensively jeweled and dressed, followed by a train of six boys, each heartbreakingly lovely in sober tunic and slacks.

Priscilla frowned after them. The boys radiated a uniform contentment. Playthings, she thought. Well cared for—perhaps even beloved—pets.

"Well, Priscilla?" His voice was very quiet, with mischief and something more sober spilling from him.

She turned her head to glare. "Am I suppose to own you?"

He nodded. "But don't repine." He felt the fabric of his wide sleeve between two judgmental fingers, tapped the master's ring and the intricate silver belt buckle, and stroked light fingers down a soft-clad thigh. "You obviously pamper me."

She flushed. "I can't think why."

"Unkind, Priscilla. I'm counted not unskilled. Also, I'm a pilot, a mechanic, a good judge of wines, fabrics, spices—"

"And an incurable gabster!" she finished with half-amused vehemence. "If you were mine, I'd have you beaten!"

The slanted brows lifted. "Violence? You might damage the goods, exalted lady. Best to attempt to barter for one less noisy if this one's voice displeases you."

"Don't," she begged him, "tempt me." Back stiff, she turned and marched off.

Head down to hide his grin, Shan followed.

Lomar Fasholt was round-faced and rumpled; her tunic was a particularly pleasing shade of pink. She smiled widely and dismissed her daughter with a nod as Priscilla entered her office.

"A good day to you, Sister Mendoza," Lomar said heartily, coming around the gleaming thurlwood desk and extending a fragrant hand. Priscilla took it and grinned with relief.

"A good day to you, also, sister."

Lomar laughed gently, her eyes going over Priscilla's shoulder. "Shannie! What a sight for old eyes you are! Have you decided to marry me, after all? Your room stands ready."

He laughed and came forward to bow: the bow of honored

esteem, Priscilla saw. "It's good to see you, Lomar," he said gently. "How many husbands do you have now?"

"Eight—can you believe it? But it's no use, Shannie, I can't *not* make money! And the more I make, the more husbands they insist I take." She shook her head. "The newest is only a cub, the same age as my youngest daughter! What do they—" Her hands fluttered. "Oh, well, I've set him to be schooled, poor lamb. Though it's hard to find tutors who don't feel it below their dignity to teach a boy. But here I'm rambling on, and you both standing! Come, sit down."

"I don't think I'd do well, do you," Shan pursued, "as the ninth? There are certain freedoms I'm accustomed to." He grinned and slouched into a chair, legs thrust out before him. "Besides, I have a minor skill at making money, too. How many husbands can you support?"

"Oh, a few more, certainly. Though not as many as they'll insist upon. If I were twenty years younger, I'd leave this silly planet and set up somewhere else. I don't know why my daughters stay—true speech!" She sat, embracing them with her smile. "Well, I thought you'd say no, my dear, but one can hope. You'd certainly keep me laughing. Why are you here, Shannie?"

Priscilla caught the flicker of his puzzlement before he replied.

"I'm here because I have items to trade. Korval has traded with Fasholt these last two generations."

"And will do so no more. I'd hoped my message was clear." The round face turned sad. "It's true, isn't it, Shannie, that your family—your Clan—is headed by a man?"

He frowned and straightened a little in the chair. "Val Con is Heir Lineal, surely—Delm-to-be. But the yos'Pheliums aren't traders, Lamar; the yos'Galans are. Two different lines."

She considered that for a moment, then: "Who is the mother of your—Line—then, Shannie? No, that's wrong, isn't it? I don't know the right word."

"Thodelm," he supplied, his puzzlement increasing. "I am. Lamar, what is this? Have we slighted you in some way? Have you complaint of our policy, our price? Surely it can be mended. We've dealt together so long."

"Do you think I don't know it? Long, mutually profitable, and always such pleasant visits! Your father, always willing to sit, take a glass or two, and tell me about goings-on in the wide galaxy. You the same as he..." She smiled wistfully. "Things would have been better, Shannie, if you had been a girl."

Shan was sitting very tall, intent on the woman's face. "Lomar, I'm at a loss. I've been male all my life, and my father before me! The trade has always gone well."

"Didn't I say so?" She sighed, radiating grief and affection. "It's a new law, Shannie. From the temple. The thrice-blessed have instructed us to have no trade with any families but those who are properly headed by a female. To trade with no ship, except when captain and Trader are women." She fidgeted with an oddment of stone on her desk, then looked up sharply. "It's *Law*, Shannie."

"Lomar." Shan was speaking very carefully. "The contract between Clan Korval and the Fasholt family dates back to our grandmothers. It reads—if memory will serve me today—yes: 'Between Petrella yos'Galan, or assignees, and Tuleth Fasholt, or assignees.'" He moved his shoulders—not quite a shrug—and smiled. "Assignees, both."

"I know," she said, shaking her head. "It seems to hold some hope, doesn't it? I put the case forth, adding that it is the custom among outworlders to consider women and men equal." She grimaced. "The thrice-blessed were quite clear: trade is permitted only with those families or ships which are now headed by women. Because outworlders follow unnatural custom is no reason for us to do the same."

"After all," Shan said softly, "the Goddess made us all in Her image."

"Don't blaspheme, Shannie."

Priscilla stirred. "That is what we are taught—on Sintia."

The older woman smiled sadly. "This is not Sintia, sister. Here we follow the temple's instructions. Or find ourselves broken into bits and scattered, mother from daughter, and sister from sister, across the world."

Priscilla raised her hand and traced the Sign to Forefend in the air between them. Lomar nodded.

"So, I hope, as well. But it seems that my wishes are not to be fulfilled in this lifetime. Perhaps the next turn of the Wheel will find me in a happier time."

"So might it be," Priscilla murmured and Lomar bowed her head.

Shan cleared his throat. "Is it permitted by the—thrice-blessed?—that I speak to you of an item which belongs to a member of my crew? Lady Faaldom, who is Head of her Line—and female! Priscilla will attest my word. Or shall we go away?"

She considered him. "Is this item truly the possession of Lady Faaldom, Shannie? Why didn't she come to me herself?"

He looked, Priscilla thought, a little hurt. "Of course it's Lina's cargo. I said so, didn't I? As to why she didn't come herself, why should she? I'm Master Trader, she's librarian. It's reasonable that I speak for her in the matter."

Lomar shook her head. "If she's sworn to you, Head of her Family or not—I'm sorry, Shannie. The Law is the Law. I don't dare."

With a flash of vivid concern, Shan leaned forward abruptly, extending a hand across the desk. "Lomar, come away!"

She reached out and patted his hand. "There, now, dear...What a good boy you are, Shannie! But it will be all right."

"It will not be all right!" he snapped. "You know and I know that it will become less and less right. Cut off trade with half the galaxy? It's insanity—worse! Suicidal. You'll starve. If the luck rides your shoulder. If not—a society that enslaves half its population? Lomar, what happens when the slaves see the masters are weak?"

"Revolution," Priscilla said in a low voice, feeling prophecy stir within her. "War. Hatred. Death."

"I have read history, sister." Lomar sighed and stroked Shan's hand again. "Should I go without a bit to buy a guidebook, Shannie? My assets must be liquidated. That takes time, careful planning. And my daughters. It's not possible. Not now." She sat back. Priscilla thought she looked older all at once.

Shan sat poised, tension singing through him. Then he, too, sat back, sighing. "Of course. You'll do as you think wise. Do you have my pin-beam code, Lomar?"

She laughed a little. "Your personal code and the code for the *Dutiful Passage*. Why?"

"A favor, for the friendship we hold each other. When you're ready, call me. Transport will be provided. Also, I'll engage to be second partner in any business you care to establish."

She laughed. "Absurd creature! Why, again?"

Shan did not even smile. "Your credit is here. To set up else-where, you'll need local credit. With me as your second partner, there will be no problem." He did smile then, tiredly. "You do make money, Lomar. I know it. Why shouldn't I lend you aid in return for a profit I don't have to work for?"

She shook her head. "But you're local on Liad, Shannie. I don't—"

"Korval's credit," he interrupted gently, "is local everywhere. Except, perhaps, here."

There was a brief pause before she spread her hands. "A silent partner, then. For; say, five years? Ten, it had better be. Then I'll buy you out."

He nodded. "Easily arranged. But a mere business matter. The important thing is that you move you and yours as soon as may be—forgive my presumption, old friend. Line yos'Galan will be happy—joyful—to guest you for a time, so you may look about and make informed decisions."

"You're a good boy, Shannie," she said again. "I'll remember. Now, my dear, I'm afraid I'm going to have to bid you both good-bye."

"Have we endangered you, sister?" Priscilla asked as they moved toward the door.

Lomar smiled and patted her hand, too. "Bless you, child, things aren't that bad yet. But it's best not to push what Shannie calls 'the luck.' Walk in Her smile, now, both of you."

Priscilla set a rapid pace through the morning streets, with Shan's uneasiness feeding her own. She felt the chill of worry at her back, eclipsing his warmth.

Mother, grant us safety, she prayed.

The port gate loomed, and she increased her stride, breathing a sigh of relief as she crossed into the outworlder's preserve. At her back, Shan's worry diminished somewhat.

Thank you, Goddess, she breathed silently. Then she sensed startlement—and outrage like a zag of lightning.

She spun in time to see the white-robed woman shake Shan sharply.

"Creature! How dare you pass by without obeisance?" Her staff snapped toward his head, calculated to cow, not to strike.

Shan's fury flared, and the woman shook him again. "What are you called, soulless?"

"Frost, exalted lady." The quiet voice was in sharp contrast to the din of his rage.

"Frost, is it? Exalted lady, is it? Have you no manners, creature, or are you too stupid to know one of the temple when you see her?"

Priscilla felt a surge of bruising power. Aspect! She extended herself, deflected the other woman's intention, and felt her own expansion...

"Enough!" she snapped.

Both spun, staring.

"Frost," she snapped. "An apology to the thrice-blessed. And then behind me!"

For a heartbeat she thought he would not play along. Then, stiffly, he bent, forehead brushing knees.

"Forgive this one, thrice-blessed. No insult was intended your holy self."

It was scarcely the most abject of abasements, with the highborn fury crackling from him like electricity. Nor was the thrice-blessed appeased. Her staff whipped out, slashing the air between him and escape.

"Forgiven, indeed. After punishments, as it is written. A public scourging—"

"I had said enough!" Priscilla cried, projecting stern authority, soul-strength, and awe. "Would you mete violence to this person, with the Mother's own mark upon him?" She extended a hand and traced the sign, glowing, before Shan's face for the other to read.

"This man is more than you can know. He has power, as a temple-sister might have it! Depth of learning, skill of use—a mystery. And more!"

The priestess was fairly caught—the wordnet enveloped her, glittering. Priscilla pulled strongly on awe, mystery, belief, and began to weave—then became aware of something else: a single, sustained note, building passion and power, swelling, scintillating, magnificent— a lance of greatness overwhelming in its majesty.

It was Shan, projecting on all levels.

Within the wordnet, the thrice-blessed gasped; she raised a hand to shield her eyes from his radiance.

The note built further as Priscilla made adjustments. He must be caught, held in the echo of the thrice-born's trap...

The note paused, then glissaded, power fading with each downward thrum, until the last hung, vibrating rainbows...and was gone.

The thrice-blessed hung in her net of glamour, reverberating mystery. The man was merely a man, radiating nothing.

"So have you seen," Priscilla intoned, loosing the net carefully. "So have you heard. So shall it be. We live in blessed times, young sister, when mysteries and miracles abound. Look closely at all you see and trust that the Goddess holds each of us protected."

"Ollee," the priestess murmured. "I am blessed beyond counting, having beheld this wonder. Elder sister, I ask pardon. And your blessing."

Priscilla's hand rose and traced the proper signs at eyes, ears, and heart. "In Her name, forgiveness, as She forgives each of Her children. Walk in Her grace. Live well. Serve long."

The other effaced herself, and Priscilla turned, motioning to Shan. Unhurriedly, and without looking behind, they walked away.

Shan collapsed into the copilot's chair, his head thumping into the headrest. He opened one silver eye. "I would appreciate warning, please, Priscilla, the next time you feel the need of such support." His voice held a thread of amusement, another of exhaustion. His pattern...his pattern—was gone.

No! She sat, graceless, and reached along the inner ways, seeking his warmth as a blind person would seek the sun's touch upon her face. The questing encountered smoothness, cool and slippery, like a mirror, denying without repelling. And he must be beyond it...

"Priscilla?"

She brought her attention to the outer ways, striving for calm. "I didn't think to ask. I thought—I was afraid you'd been caught in the echo."

He snorted. "I haven't been caught in an echo since I was twelve years old, Priscilla. Give me credit for some ability."

"Yes, of course..." But this was a nightmare, with him before her and she unable to hear, unable to *know*..."Shan—"

He leaned forward and extended a hand, the master's ring flashing its facets. "I'm here, my friend."

There was concern in his voice and on his face, while within there was only the horrible, unyielding coolness. She gripped his fingers, feeling that warmth. It was not enough. "Shan..."

"I'm tired, Priscilla," he said gently. "It's been a long time since I've needed to travel outward along all roads. Grant me rest." He considered her face, squeezed her hand. "I'm in your debt again."

"Please," she began, and drew a breath. She found a phrase in High Liaden. "Pray do not regard it."

He sat back, his fingers slipping out of hers. "Kayzin is a thorough teacher, I see." A quick glance at the board took in the white proximity light. "The *Passage* is in orbit. Wonderful. Let's go home."

Home. Even with him locked behind his private mirror she felt a sense of relief, and heard the sound of need.

"Yes, Shan," she said, and then, in urgent correction, "Yes, Captain."

SHIPYEAR 65
TRIPDAY 177
SECOND SHIFT
9.00 HOURS

Ken Rik stared in disbelief. "Prepare Hold Thirty-two to receive cargo?" he asked finally.

Shan raised his eyebrows and looked down his nose for good measure. "You're up to the task, aren't you, Ken Rik? Or is Hold Thirty-two already full?"

"No, it's not full," the old man snapped. "As you well know. You're not taking on that—ah, damn this language!—that lanza pel'shek! *His* cargo!"

"I'm not? Well, I'm pleased to know that, Master Ken Rik, thank you. But, do you know, I had the impression that I *was* going to take it." He paused, then delivered the punch line gently. "I had the further impression that the cargo master takes orders from the captain."

Ken Rik had tears in his eyes. "Shan—he tried to kill the *Passage.*" He spoke in the High Tongue now: elder to youngling of a different Clan. "Now you take up his cargo, guarantee delivery! Your father—"

"Would have done exactly the same!" Shan finished in ice-coated Terran. "This is outside of balance. The goods are needed—required—on Theopholis. The port master appealed to us because of need. We guarantee delivery—because of need. We're going to Theopholis, aren't we, Ken Rik? Have some sense, for pity's sake! A pretty set of sharks we'd look when it came known that the *Passage* was petitioned at Raggtown and refused to take the load."

"Yes, of course." The words were nearly whispered, but they were in Terran. He bowed the bow of one instructed to instructor. "Forgive—"

"Oh, bother, you annoying old man! You've been ripping up at me for years! Don't, I beg you, begin to act properly now!"

Ken Rik laughed. "It would be something of a strain, I admit." He made a second bow, as subordinate to superior. "With the captain's permission, I will now go to prepare Hold Thirty-two for cargo."

"Thank you, Ken Rik," Shan said gently. "I'd appreciate it."

MASTER'S TOWER, THEOPHOLIS
HOUR OF KINGS

Port Master Rominkoff eyed the elderly gentlemen. That they stood there at all spoke of resourcefulness as well as resources. The amount of cumshaw required to pass two persons up the ladder of subordinates and into her presence was no doubt large. She made a mental note to find out the current rate. One liked to know the value of one's services.

The younger of her two visitors bowed, not deeply. "I," he said in careful Trade, "am Taam Olanek, Delm Plemia. My Clan possesses a tradeship, called *Daxflan,* which was to have been in port at this present. I find it has not arrived."

The port master sat up. Perhaps the old gentlemen had not paid so much, after all. "I am in agreement with you, sir," she said urbanely. "*Daxflan* has not arrived."

"I had hoped," Taam Olanek, Delm Plemia, pursued, "that you might teach me what you know of circumstances. I have learned from other persons here that berthing space was reserved—that it was not canceled. That there are goods awaiting?"

"And goods awaited," she finished, shedding a little of her urbanity. "Just so. You seem to know all I can teach you of the situation, sir. *Daxflan* is late by some four local days. Reassure yourselves that nothing ill has overcome it, however. I have had reports of her within the sector, doing business at certain—ahh, *free-duty* ports. It appears previous commitments have not been recalled." She steepled her fingers in front of her. "This is unfortunate. It is, of course, unfortunate for you, but it is even more so for Theopholis. Among the things *Daxflan* was to deliver are two shipments from Raggtown, consisting of medical supplies imperative to the conclusion of our vaccination program, and the jewelry the regent will wear at his coronation next week. Our last information from Raggtown is that those shipments are still in the warehouses, awaiting pickup."

There was a moment's silence, during which the port master wondered if her explanation had been too rapid for the old gentleman to follow.

He bowed. "The situation is very serious. Plemia has guaranteed delivery. There will be delivery. If you would allow me use of your facilities, I will make arrangements to employ a subcontractor for the delivery of the goods from Raggtown."

Well, now. *Here* was something. The port master inclined her head. "I will have you escorted to the beam room, sir. One moment." Her hand approached the keypad, but hesitated as the door to her right clicked open, admitting a breathless adjunct.

"Port Master," he began. The belated sight of the two gentlemen gave him abrupt pause.

Master Rominkoff raised her brows. "Continue."

"Yes, Port Master. We have had a pin-beam from the tradeship *Dutiful Passage*. It tells us they carry the shipments from Raggtown." The adjunct took a deep breath and finished his message. "Anticipated docking time is within the next local day."

"So, then." She smiled at her visitors. "It seems the problem is solved for us, sirs."

But Taam Olanek did not seem appreciative of his good fortune. He rounded on the adjunct, his face set in anger. "How does *Dutiful Passage* carry *Daxflan's* cargo?"

The boy blinked and looked for guidance. She nodded. "The port—the port at Raggtown, gentle," he stammered. *"Dutiful Passage* was asked to transmit the goods that were urgent, that were perishable. There was room, and the—the captain did the kindness…"

"Quite proper," the second gentleman murmured surprisingly, and the first spun to stare at him. "I suggest that we await the morrow. Captain yos'Galan will certainly be happy to lay every detail before you."

There was a moment of singing tension before the first gentleman bowed to due second. "Even so," he said softly. He turned back to the port master and bowed more deeply this time. "I thank you for your kindness and ask forgiveness on behalf of my Clan. Contracts must, of course, be honored. I pledge that they will be so, in the future."

The port master thought without sympathy of *Daxflan's* Trader. The wrath in the old gentleman's eyes was well earned.

"I am glad that the present crisis has been resolved in so timely a manner, of course. It will not be forgotten that your first thought was of that, sir, and of the solution." She stood and bowed to both. "It has been a pleasure speaking with you. May we meet again."

"May we meet again," the second gentleman echoed, performing his bow with precision. He offered an arm to his companion and guided him gently to the door.

The port master nodded at her adjunct. "Inform me when *Dutiful Passage* takes orbit. I think I should greet Captain yos'Galan—personally."

RAGGTOWN
LOCAL YEAR 537

The sum was enormous. Standing at the Trader's shoulder, Captain
yo'Vaade was hard put to maintain her countenance. The trade at
Drethilit had not earned them half so much, besides having gone to
the port master to pay for the unused berthing. And the goods were
gone as well, so there would be that loss, and another bill was awaiting them at Theopholis.

"What do you mean," Sav Rid demanded, his voice beginning
to rise in that way she dreaded, "that my cargo is not here? You give
me a spurious invoice and in the same breath say that the goods are
not in your warehouse? Where are they?"

The warehouseman shrugged his wide Terran shoulders. "You
didn't show, the client got worried, asked somebody else to take the
stuff along. Shipped out yesterday."

"By what right—*who?* What ship took my cargo? Because I
say it is nothing less than theft!"

Again the man shrugged. "That's between you and your client,
Mac. Tree and Dragon took the stuff. Now, about the—"

"Tree and Dragon," Sav Rid repeated blankly. Then he shouted,
the Trade words nearly unintelligible. "yos'Galan! Thieves, whores,
and idiots! My cargo! Mine! And you release it to yos'Galan?
Fool!" He shredded the bill, flung the pieces into the man's startled
face, and stormed away, looking neither to the right nor to the left.
Chelsa yo'Vaade hesitated, tempted—strongly tempted—to let him
go. Then she spun back to the warehouseman, tugging the nireline
ring from her finger and stripping the heavy chased bracelet from
her arm. "They are old," she said quickly, pressing them into his
hands. "It will be enough, if you sell to a collector of antiquities."
She left him then, running.

Sav Rid was striding across the shuttle field, Second Mate Collier
hulking at his shoulder. He had not been unguarded, then. Chelsa
was aware of a certain relief as she laid a hand on his sleeve. "Sav
Rid? Cousin, I beg you—let it go. It is—you have let it prey upon
your mind. End now. Cry balance."

"Balance?" He shook her off, lips tight, eyes glittering. *"Balance?* In favor of that frog-faced, half-Terran lackwit? yos'Galan is the reason we lose in every endeavor we undertake! yos'Galan steals our cargo, slurs our name, hounds us from port to port—there can be no balance!" He held out his hand, fingers clenched tight. "I will crush them—both of them! The idiot and his whore sister!" He paused. "And the Terran bitch who puts her cheek to his!"

Chelsa's stomach clenched with fear—of him? for him?—as she cupped his shaking fist in her hands. "Sav Rid, it is *Korval!* Let be. Let it all be," she pleaded suddenly, her eyes tear-filled. "Let us go home, cousin."

"Bah!" He jerked away, his rings tearing her palms. "Korval! A pack of half-grown brats, born to wealth and ease—no more! But you are like the rest—say *Korval,* and they tremble lest they offend." He spat into the dust and marched off, the second mate keeping pace. "Coward!"

The tears spilled over. She struggled for a moment, then achieved control and started slowly after him.

CROWN CITY, THEOPHOLIS
HOUR OF KNAVES

Dagmar fingered the knife and gave her quarry a little lead time—but not too much. She had almost lost them, right at the beginning, when she had still figured that there was some kind of sense to their explorations, before she had understood that they were simply following the boy's whim.

She eased out of the doorway and sauntered after them, picking up speed as they turned a corner. The boy was tugging on the woman's hand—they were heading toward the port. Slowly, doubling back on their own tracks now and then, they were completing a rough circle. Dagmar lengthened her stride.

Soon. Soon Prissy would pay for setting the white-haired half-breed on *Daxflan,* eating their profits—eating *Dagmar's* profit. Dagmar's share. Yes, her share. Without her, the Trader would not have thought of shipping the stuff. She had been the one who had showed him how profitable it would be for the ship, and for his precious Clan. She had been the one with the contacts at first, the one who had shown him how to play the game. So she got a piece of the action. A sweetheart bargain. What a Liaden would call balance.

They had stopped again. Dagmar slid into an alley mouth, then edged out to watch. Prissy was laughing and pointing to something in the window of a shop six doors distant. The boy had his nose pressed against the glass.

It would be the boy. She had decided that. Satisfying as it would be to hurt Prissy, to purple that white skin, to snap fragile bones...Dagmar wiped wet palms down the sides of her trousers, savoring the thrust of desire that the image imparted. Maybe...

No. She would take the boy. That would cause the deepest hurt—both to Prissy and to her half-breed lover.

They were moving again. Dagmar fingered the knife and let them get a little ahead.

DILLIBEE'S DIGITAL DELIGHTS, the sign read. Gordy checked and drifted closer to the glassed-in display, joy flowing out of him in a purr so

strong that it was a marvel the outer ears did not hear it as well. Priscilla smiled and rested her hands lightly on his shoulders. He wriggled comfortably, his attention on the gaudy goings-on beyond the glass.

Five minutes went by without a sign that his rapture would soon pass off. Priscilla squeezed his shoulders. "Let's go, Gordy."

"Um."

She laughed softly and ruffled his hair. "Um, yourself. The shuttle leaves in exactly one ship's hour. Your credit with the captain may be up to missing it, but mine isn't. Let's go."

"Okay," he said, still gazing at the display.

Priscilla sighed and walked away by a step or two. "Gordy?"

"Yeah, okay."

Shaking her head, she went farther down the block, adjusting her awareness so that the matrix of his emotions remained clear.

A bolt of terror impaled her as his voice wrenched her about. "Priscilla!"

Pilot-fast, she was moving back toward the woman and the struggling child. A scant two steps away, the woman twisted, her shoulder against a garland-pole, the boy held across her thigh with one hand as the other snaked to the front over his shoulder and held something that gleamed beneath the uptilted chin.

"Freeze, Prissy."

The gleam was a vibroknife, not yet live.

Priscilla froze.

"Good. That's real good, Prissy. You stay right there." Dagmar grinned. "Where's the white-haired boyfriend? Not gonna bail you out today?"

Fury and terror poured from Gordy. Priscilla shut him out. She opened a thin hallway: her heart to Dagmar's. Then she heard, tasted and saw kill-lust, fear, rage, and desire, a fragmented cacophony that held no pattern but shifted, froze, and broke apart again and again.

Dementia.

Gordy twitched in Dagmar's grip, then gasped as it tightened brutally.

"You be a good boy," she snarled, "and I'll let you live." She made a sound like a laugh. "Yeah, I'll let you live—a minute. Maybe two."

Seeking a tool, Priscilla groped within and found a rhythm; she picked it up even as she felt another stirring and saw a flicker of light and darkness, outlining the Dragon's broad head. The vast wings unfurled as she passed the spell-rhythm to her body; she swayed to the right, not quite a step.

"Stay there! You want this kid to have as many seconds as are coming to him, Prissy, you freeze and stay froze!" Dagmar grinned and moved the knife but did not thumb it on. "An' don't you look away, honey. I want you to tell the boyfriend exactly what it looked like."

"All right," Priscilla agreed, her voice pitched for magic, the words like strands of sticky silk. "I'll watch, Dagmar. Of course I will. But should I tell him everything? That might not be wise. If I tell everything, then they'll have you, Dagmar. They'll know who you are. They'll know where to find you." The faraway wings filled, then hesitated. She dared another half step, her eyes watching Dagmar's eyes as her heart watched Dagmar's heart.

"Best to let him go. Let him go, and they'll let you go. Let him go and be free. Let him go and rest. Rest and be peaceful. Free and at peace. Let him go. Walk away. No hunters. No hunted. Let him go…"

Dagmar's pattern was smoothing, coming together into something reminiscent of sanity. Far off, the Dragon hesitated, wings poised for flight.

A heavy-hauler slammed by in the street beyond, shattering the circle she had woven. The knife straightened in Dagmar's hand.

"Freeze!" she hissed.

Priscilla stood calm, her eyes on her enemy, not allowing her to look away. "Dagmar," she began again, taking up the thread of the weaving.

"Boyfriend buy your stuff back, Prissy?" Dagmar across her words. "He did, didn't he? Except not earrings. Not the earrings. Nobody'll see them again. Bugged, were they? Not now. Took a hammer, pounded 'em to dust. Spaced the dust." She gave a jagged bark of laughter. "Let him try and trace that! Tryin' to follow where we're goin'. Tryin' to catch us sellin' the stuff—but he didn't! Not so smart, after all, is he?"

"It was a trick," Priscilla murmured against the sudden whirlwind of a Dragon in flight. She was cold. She was hot. She resisted, trusting yet to the power of voice and words. "Only a trick, Dagmar. He wanted to scare you, that's all. Like you've scared me. I'll tell him how it was. I'll tell him you mean business. That you wanted balance. That you have balance. The score's settled now, Dagmar. You can let the boy go. Let him go, Dagmar. A little boy. Only a boy. He can't hurt you. Let him go and walk free."

Footsteps in the street beyond cut the fragile strand. Dagmar shifted her grip on her hostage. "Little public here. Move it, boy. Nice and slow. Prissy, you stay put 'til I tell you to move."

"No!" Gordy twisted, and one hand shot out to grip the garland-pole. In her mind's eye, Priscilla clearly saw a Tree, green and vital, roots sunk through paving stone, soil and magma, to the very soul of the world...

Dagmar swore and yanked at Gordy, her already mad pattern splintering into a thing hopeless of order. She yanked again, then gave it up—and thumbed the knife to life.

Priscilla heard it hum, low and evil.

And within, the sound of wings was like thunder as a hurtling body blocked out heart and sight and sense and soul, screaming like a lifetime's accumulated fury—Dragon's fire!

MASTER'S TOWER, THEOPHOLIS
VISCOUNT'S HOUR

It will be interesting to see how she contrives to send Mr. dea'Gauss away without me, Shan thought, sipping wine. The port master's desire washed him with warmth, and he curled into it shamelessly. Mutual pleasure was intended, neither hinged upon old friendship nor waiting on richer desires—the very thing he needed.

Healer, he instructed himself wryly, heal yourself.

The wine was excellent.

"Confess then, Captain," the port master drawled lazily. "You're intrigued by the proposition."

That was a masterly move. They had been discussing a possible investment of her own, the talk shared evenly between himself and Mr. dea'Gauss. Shan smiled, slanting his eyes toward her face in a sweep of black lashes.

"I am always intrigued," he answered audaciously, "by a lady's proposition."

She laughed, well pleased with him. "Perhaps you and I might meet to discuss the matter more fully." She inclined her head, including the old gentleman in her smile. "Mr. dea'Gauss must accompany you, of course. I'm sure we will both require his counsel."

He raised his glass. "The trading will keep me—tomorrow, the next day. You understand, ma'am, that there are persons I must see, in the normal course of business."

"Of course," she said appreciatively. "Perhaps I should stop by your booth in the Grand Square in a day or so. By then you may know your commitments more fully."

"Why, that would be lovely!" he exclaimed, smiling widely. "I'd be delighted to see you there, ma'am." And so he would, though he would be more delighted to see her this night—as she yet intended.

"Then naturally I will come." She began to add something more, then checked herself as the door to her right opened, no doubt admitting the third course.

But the individual who stepped into the room bore no tray, pushed no cart, and looked not a little worried.

The port master frowned. "Yes?"

"I beg your pardon, madam," her aide said formally. "Precinct Officer Velnik calls on your private line. He assures me the matter is one of urgency."

After a moment's frowning hesitation, a hand flick directed the aide toward the wallscreen. She turned back to the table. "Do excuse the interruption, sirs. This post has many privileges. Privacy is not one of them. It will be but a moment. Please do not regard it."

"That's quite all right," Shan assured her, smiling sympathetically. Mr. dea'Gauss inclined his head.

The precinct officer looked nervous. As well he might, Shan thought. The port master's displeasure was plain on her face.

"Well?"

The officer swallowed. "I'm sorry to disturb you, Thra Rominkoff," he said breathlessly. "It seems routine on the surface. But the boy insisted we call. Says he's the ward of a—Captain yos'Galan?"

Shan stiffened, all attention on the screen.

The port master nodded sharply. "He is here. Is the boy injured?"

Relief flooded Velnik's face. "No, Thra Rominkoff, he's just fine. But we've got a dead Terran female—"

No! And then he was expanding in all directions, an explosion of seek-strands, streaking past the port master's pattern, and Mr. dea'Gauss, and the liveried servant here, and those in the kitchen beyond, stretching, stretching as no Healer could, trying to read the city beyond the walls, searching for one signature, one life—*Priscilla!*

In his far-off body something snapped, followed by pain and more pain as the search slammed hard against its limits, rebounded...

He dropped the shattered stem next to the sharded crystal bowl in its puddle of bright wine and blood, and wrapped a napkin around his hand as the port master spun back to the screen, snapping her fingers.

"Quickly! Who has died?"

"Dagmar Collier, Port Master." The man was stumbling over his own words, his eyes flicking from Shan to the woman and back. "Native of Troit. Second Mate on *Daxflan,* out of Chonselta."

Which should not be here! Shan swallowed his curse and saw the thought reflected in the port master's face.

"Bring the boy here," she instructed the precinct officer.

He shook his head. "We have the woman who killed Collier, Thra Rominkoff. She confesses. But murder requires a formal trial, since rehabilitation is the fee—"

"No!" That was out before he could stop it.

The port master slanted a quick glance at Shan's face and returned her attention to the screen. "The woman who confesses is a friend of the boy's? He refuses to come away without her?"

"Yes, Thra Rominkoff."

"Port Master." Somehow he had control of his voice against the tearing pains in hand and head and the terror in his heart. "The person in question is a member of my crew. Am I not allowed to speak for her?" Rehabilitation. Gods, rehabilitation *here*. "It is possible that she does not understand. She is not native here. And perhaps not all of the—circumstances—have been made clear to the precinct officer."

She nodded. "It is, of course, your right to speak for your crew member, Captain." Her eyes were back on the officer. "We shall arrive within the hour. So inform the captain's ward. And arrange for the guard to pass us without delay."

"Port Master." He gave a formal salute, and the screen went dark. The port master rose.

"A medkit," she snapped at the frozen aide. The woman scurried off, returning in a bare moment. Mr. dea'Gauss took it from her and himself applied the lotion, sealed the sharp edge of the cut, and wrapped it in soft cloth, radiating concern.

The old gentleman's pattern set Shan's teeth on edge with anguish: the complex spill of rage, puzzlement, and—admiration?—from the port master nearly had him in tears. Painfully, he began the sequence to seal himself away, to leach the worst of the pain from the rebound shock so that he might unseal himself in an hour, perhaps even to some purpose.

"My car awaits, sirs," the port master said, concern her face.

"You are all kindness, ma'am." He managed the formula, stood, and made his bow.

"Nonsense!" she snapped. "It is my duty to monitor what goes on in this port, Captain. That includes seeing justice done." She indicated the patient aide. "Melecca will see you to the car. I will join you very shortly. There is an urgent matter I must attend to."

She was gone in a swirl of bright fabric.

"Daxflan's in port," Shan murmured to Mr. dea'Gauss as they followed Melecca to the car. "That's interesting, isn't it?"

"Very," the old gentleman agreed. He sighed.

PRECINCT HOUSE
CROWN CITY, THEOPHOLIS
HOUR OF DEMONS

There were far too many people in the room. Port Master Rominkoff paused to sort out the crowd. The young captain never broke his stride.

"Shan!"

The boy was smallish and pudgy, running pell-mell toward them. The young captain went down on one knee, caught the child as he skidded to a halt, and returned a hug just this side of savage.

"Gordy." He set the boy back, ran his hands rapidly over the plump frame, and touched a smooth cheek. "You're all right, acushla?"

"Crelm!" the boy snorted. *I'm* okay." The round face clouded. "Shan—they wouldn't listen! I told them—I did! They wouldn't fix her arm and—"

"Hush." He stroked the boy's cheek again, then laid a gentle finger over his lips. "Gordy. Just relax for a moment, okay?" The small body lost some of its tension, as if those words were all it took. "Good. Where's Priscilla now?"

Tears filled the brown eyes. "I tried to make them not—" He took a ragged breath. "They put her in a cage."

"Here now, young man!" the precinct officer said, approaching warily, his eyes flicking from the port master's face to the man and boy, then back to her face. "Not a *cage!* Just a holding cell, I promise!"

The captain rose smoothly and inclined his head. "A holding cell," he repeated softly. The precinct officer ran his tongue over his lips. The port master forbade herself the smile.

"I am captain of the *Dutiful Passage,*" Shan continued clearly. "Ms. Mendoza is a member of my crew. I am here to speak on her behalf, as set in the trade compacts. You will liberate her from the— holding cell—and guide her here so that all may be done...lawfully."

The port master denied the smile more sternly. Really, the young captain pleased her more and more.

The precinct officer was shaking his head. "I'm afraid I can't do that, Captain. She's a confessed murderer. We asked her twice, according to law. She understood the questions and answered them. Twice. She talked crazy about other stuff, but not about that. The law says in those circumstances, we hold the prisoner for a next-day trial. It's most likely the judge will rule rehabilitation in light of the confession, and lacking witnesses—"

"What do you mean, lacking witnesses?" the captain demanded. "The child says he told you what happened—and that you refused to listen!"

Officer Velnik held up a hand. "Not admissible, Captain. He's underage."

"On his home-world," came a dry voice from the port master's side, "Master Arbuthnot is of an age where his testimony is considered admissible."

"I'm sure it is, Mr.—ah?"

"dea'Gauss," the old man supplied, going forward. "I am the man of business for Clan Korval, of which Captain yos'Galan and, by wardship, Master Arbuthnot are members. Pray elucidate the reason for your refusal to admit testimony from a witness of sound mind and honorable character. You have yourself cast doubt by stating that Lady Mendoza spoke irrationally of subjects other than the specific mischance. It behooves you to place before a judge all interpretations of the event that are available. Justice could hardly be served in any other way."

"See here—"

It was time for the port master to take a hand. "Mr. dea'Gauss raises a valid point and asks a pertinent question," she drawled from the doorway. "Why is the boy forbidden to testify, Velnik? I have monitored trials where children much younger than he appears to be have spoken and been heard."

"Thra Rominkoff, it is law that all witnesses in cases of violent crime must testify under the same drug administered to the accused. Persons under majority—nineteen Standard Years—may not be compelled to submit to the drug."

"What drug?" the young captain asked very quietly.

"Pimmadrene," she replied. "It's been used for many years. The ego is temporarily dissolved, which nets quite truthful answers." She considered the precinct officer. "And yet it does still seem to me that I have seen very young children testify. The law speaks of 'impel.' What if free choice is offered?"

He moved his shoulders. "The parents gave permission for the drug in the cases you mention, Thra Rominkoff."

"Or guardian of record?"

He bowed.

"But it is dangerous?" the captain asked quietly.

"Dangerous? No. The doctor adjusts the dose to body weight and stays by to monitor. But it's unpleasant. Not the sort of thing to force on a person who can't—a child. The side effects are dizziness, stomach cramps, fever, disorientation. Some people go blind for a few days, but that's not common. Doc over there could tell you specifically."

"I'll do it," the boy said suddenly, and tugged on the captain's sleeve. "Shan? Tell them I'll do it. I'm your ward. Grandpa told me!"

"Acushla, think carefully. The side effects sound very bad. And the intended effect isn't good, either. I'll do what you tell me to do. It's your decision. But be sure, Gordy."

"Shan, it's *Priscilla.*" He grabbed on to a big hand, looking up worriedly. "They said—do you know what they're going to do to her, if the judge says she's got to be—to be rehabilitated?"

"I know, Gordy. Hush."

But Gordy would not be hushed. He hung on to the captain's hand and looked at Mr. dea'Gauss, making the explanation to him in a voice that washed against every wall in the room.

"They said—since she's a *murderer*—she'll go to the organ bank. They'll float her in a tank and feed her through tubes and stuff until somebody maybe needs an eye. Then they'll take one of Priscilla's eyes. And she'll float some more 'til somebody needs another eye, or a kidney, or a lung, or a leg, and they'll cut her up, piece by piece..."

"Gordy!" The captain was on his knees, pulling the boy tight against his shoulder and rubbing his face in the sandy hair. "Stop it, Gordy. Please."

There was silence.

The boy pulled back, lifted a tentative hand to the man's stark cheek, and snuffled. "Shan, you better tell them I'll be a witness. They can't—Priscilla's *good.*"

"Yes," the captain murmured, coming slowly to his feet. "I know that, too."

He bowed to the precinct officer very slightly. "It has been determined that my ward will testify at Ms. Mendoza's trial. Please tell us its time and location, as well as the proper manner in which to present ourselves."

"There is no reason," the port master cut in, "why the trial should not be held at once. I am empowered to act as judge in affairs of the port—as soon as my robes arrive and a room is made available." She glanced at the desk officer, who hurriedly placed a call.

The robes were heavy on her shoulders. Perhaps it was their unaccustomed weight: she rarely took part in such affairs, usually letting things run the legal course in their own time. Perhaps it was the boy's involvement, or the young captain's. They sat together by special permission, the giant, white-haired Liaden austere, and the boy with his empty, drug-toned eyes.

She sighed heavily, rang the bell to order, and read the preliminaries without expression. Having established the identities of those present, she glanced at the monitor; she nodded satisfaction and looked back at the boy. His face was slightly damp, eyes wide open, pupils dilated black with a thin ring of brown iris.

"What is your name, boy?"

"Gordy." His voice was blurry, like a sleep-talker's.

The port master consulted the card and frowned. She addressed the boy again. "All right, Gordy. What is your full, *legal* name?"

"Gordon Richard Arbuthnot."

She nodded. "What is your planet of origin?"

"New Dublin."

"In Standard Years, what is your age?"

"Eleven."

"What is your father's name?"

Silence.

She frowned. "Gordy, what is your father's name?"

"His father," Mr. dea'Gauss whispered in her ear, "is dead."

"I see." Damn this drug! It was clumsy—misleading. "Gordy, what *was* your father's name?"

"Finn Gordon Arbuthnot."

That was another match. "What is your mother's name?"

"Katy-Rose Davis."

And another. She turned her head. "Doctor, have we established that the drug is in force?"

"Yes, Thra Rominkoff."

"Excellent. We shall proceed with the testimony."

She paused to order her thoughts, mindful of the drug's limitation. "Gordy, when did you and Priscilla Mendoza arrive on-world?"

"First shuttle."

First shuttle? What sort of time was that? "Approximately Regent's Hour," the young captain said softly, and she nodded her thanks. "Why were you with Priscilla Mendoza, Gordy?"

"We were leave-partners."

"You were assigned to each other?"

"No."

She sighed. "How did you become leave-partners?"

"I asked Priscilla if she'd be partners, and she said okay."

"Who chose where you went in town?"

"I did."

"You chose to be in Nietzsche Street?"

"Yes."

"Why?"

"It looked interesting."

"Did Priscilla Mendoza ask you to go down Nietzsche Street?"

"No."

"Did Dagmar Collier ask you to go down Nietzsche Street?"

"No."

"Did Priscilla Mendoza kill Dagmar Collier, Gordy?"

"Yes."

She swallowed a curse at that simple damnation; she heard Velnik shift beside her, and saw the young captain's lips shape one word. She gave it voice.

"*Why* did Priscilla kill Dagmar, Gordy?"

"To save me."

On the other side, Mr. dea'Gauss leaned forward infinitesimally, his attention centered on the blurry young face.

"Were you in danger, Gordy?"

"Yes."

"How did you come to be in danger?"

"I didn't come when Priscilla said to."

The port master made a mental note to explore drugs other than Pimmadrene for use in interrogation.

"Gordy, I want you to tell me exactly what happened from the time you didn't go with Priscilla in Nietzsche Street to the time the arresting officer came."

"Priscilla said the shuttle was leaving in a ship's hour and if my credit with the captain was up to being late, hers wasn't and we had to leave. She went two steps away and said 'Gordy?' I said 'yeah,' and she went further away and I was getting ready to go with her when I got grabbed and it was Dagmar and she yanked and held on when I tried to run and held us against a pole and held me over her knee and Priscilla was running toward us and Dagmar had a knife and she said 'Freeze, Prissy.' And Priscilla stopped." There was a tiny pause as the boy licked his lips.

"Where did Dagmar hold the knife, Gordy?"

"Across my throat. Under my chin."

"All right, Gordy. Priscilla stopped. Then what?"

"Dagmar said Priscilla had to stay there. She asked where Shan was. I tried to get away again, and she—she hurt me. She said if I was good she'd let me live for a minute or two." There was another small pause. The port master snapped her fingers, never taking her eyes from that damp face.

"She said Priscilla had to watch. To tell Shan what it looked like." An aide arrived with a glass of water. The port master waved her to the boy.

"Rest a minute, Gordy, and drink."

He did, draining the glass thirstily.

"All right, Gordy. Dagmar said Priscilla had to watch, so she could tell Shan what it looked like. Then?"

"Priscilla started to talk. I don't remember what she said, but it made my head feel funny. She talked and walked forward a little bit and Dagmar's arm got loose and I thought about running away but then there was a noise in the next street and Dagmar's arm got tight again and she made Priscilla stop. Priscilla tried to talk some more, but Dagmar asked if Shan had bought Priscilla's things. She said she broke Priscilla's earrings into dust and then spaced the dust. She said Shan wasn't smart and that he wouldn't catch them selling the stuff.

"Priscilla started to talk again and my head felt funny again and then there were footsteps and Dagmar tried to make me go with her 'cause it was too public, she said. But I was scared and I didn't want to go with her and I grabbed on to the pole and held on and thought about the Tree like Priscilla'd taught me and Dagmar turned on the knife. I heard it hum and I was scared and I hung on and thought about the Tree and I heard a—roar. Like a big animal. And Priscilla was running fast—faster than Shan runs and Dagmar let me go and Priscilla—it was so *fast!* She grabbed Dagmar and twisted and did something with her hands. I heard a snap, like a stick breaking. Dagmar fell down. Priscilla stood for a minute and then she fell down, too." He swallowed.

"I went and kicked the knife away from Dagmar and then I tried to make Priscilla get up. It was hard and I thought she was— I thought she was dead. But she woke up and called me 'Brand' and her voice was all funny, like it hurt her to talk. Then she stood up and told me to go back to the *Passage*. I told her Shan wouldn't like it if I left her alone when she was in a scrape and she hugged me and threw a stone into the window of Marcel's Tailoring Emporium. Then she said she'd killed Dagmar and the cops would come in a minute and arrest her for murder. She told me to leave again, but I wouldn't. Then the cop came."

The port master leaned back in her chair and counted to twenty-five, eyes closed. She opened her eyes.

"Precinct Officer Velnik," she said very carefully. "I will now see the recording of Priscilla Mendoza's...confession."

The woman was slim, middling tall by Terran standards, doubly dwarfed by Velnik and the arresting officer. Her hair was short and black and curly, her face dirt-smeared; her eyes were enormous, ebon—and exhausted. "Priscilla Delacroix y Mendoza," she answered the precinct officer. Her voice was a ragged whisper.

"Planet of origin?"

"Sintia."

"Are you employed on a trading vessel?"

"Yes."

"State the name of the vessel, its home port, your rank."

"*Dutiful Passage.* Solcintra, Liad. Pilot, first class pending. Second mate."

"Did you kill the woman Dagmar Collier?"

"Yes."

"Did you deliberately murder the woman Dagmar Collier?"

"Yes."

"Where did you kill Dagmar Collier?"

"In front of Dillibee's Digital Delights in Nietzsche Street in Crown City on Theopholis."

"When did you kill Dagmar Collier?"

"One hour ago."

"Did you attempt escape after you killed Dagmar Collier?"

"No."

"Why?"

"There was no place to go."

From the young captain came a wordless protest. As if cued by that slight sound, Precinct Officer Velnik asked Priscilla Mendoza, "Why didn't you return to the *Dutiful Passage?*"

"No murderers are allowed on the *Passage.*" The captain drew a sharp breath. "Your name," the precinct officer pursued, "is Priscilla Delacroix y Mendoza?"

"Yes."

"Did you intentionally kill the woman Dagmar Collier?"

"Yes."

"Describe your actions that brought the death of Dagmar Collier."

"I called the Dragon. When it was with me, we roared and threw a fireball to distract Dagmar's attention from Gordy. Then I broke her neck."

There was a slight pause while precinct officer and cop exchanged glances.

"You, Priscilla Delacroix y Mendoza," the precinct officer said carefully, "broke the neck of Dagmar Collier, fully intending to bring about her death?"

"Yes."

"Are you a native of Troit?"

"No."

"What is your legal name?"

"Priscilla Delacroix y Mendoza."

"What is your planet of origin?"

"Sintia."

"Did you kill Dagmar Collier?"

"Yes."

There was a small pause. "Where is the Dragon now?"

"Above the Tree."

"How much is two plus two?"

"Four."

"Have you said any lies since you were brought here by the arresting officer?"

"No."

"Did the dragon kill Dagmar Collier?"

"No."

"Who killed Dagmar Collier?"

"I did."

"You see," Velnik said to the room in general as the lights came up. "Dragons, trees..."

"The Tree and Dragon," Mr. dea'Gauss cut him off, "is the shield of Clan Korval. It depicts a dragon, guarding a full-leafed tree. The motto is 'I Dare.' Lady Mendoza is quite familiar with the shield. It is displayed prominently on the *Dutiful Passage.*"

"So they had meaning for her; she was self-aware."

"Yes," the port master snapped, coming to her feet. Velnik retreated a step. "She knew what she was doing. The boy is alive. The person he names his potential assassin is dead. Priscilla Mendoza was not asked *why* she willfully and intentionally killed Dagmar Collier, Precinct Officer. Your interview was less than thorough."

Velnik licked his lips and came to rigid attention.

"Doctor, is the serum you gave Mendoza still in force?"

He shook his head. "It runs through the system pretty fast. She'll be on the downside by now." He glanced at the bench. "Can't give her another shot for two days. That's a medical fact. She mightn't recover."

She nodded. "It won't be required, thank you. My ruling in this case is that Priscilla Delacroix y Mendoza is found not guilty of murder. Defense of a child is not a crime here! Arresting Officer, bring Priscilla Mendoza here, so that she may be released into the care of her captain."

Mr. dea'Gauss caught the young captain's eye. *"Daxflan—"*

"My office is currently dealing with that difficulty, sirs," she said, turning back. "Granting even unheard of levels of inefficiency, it should at this moment be sealed in close orbit. And there, I think, we may all let it wait until the morrow."

The old gentleman bowed. "It is as you have said, madam. I should mention that the feud between Lady Mendoza and Dagmar Collier is one of long standing. Dagmar Collier threatened her ladyship and Master Arbuthnot with violence once before to my certain knowledge. On Arsdred."

"I would appreciate receiving the particulars of that event, sir. Also—Captain. I am deeply ashamed that my inefficiency has caused this circumstance. Dagmar Collier should never have been in this port. I am responsible, and I am grieved. Please consider me at your disposal in the resolution of the matter."

"You're very kind, ma'am," he replied, smiling wearily.

"Port Master," the arresting officer said, arriving alone and looking very nervous. "Port Master, she—won't move. I open the door and call, but she just sits, Port Master."

"I'll come." The young captain slid away from the boy, beckoning to the old gentleman. "By your kindness, sir."

"Certainly." Mr. dea'Gauss sat carefully and slid an unaccustomed arm about young shoulders, enduring the head resting upon his chest.

"Let's go," the captain snapped at the cop as he strode by. She had to run three steps to catch up.

PRECINCT HOUSE DETENTION HALL
CROWN CITY, THEOPHOLIS
HOUR OF FOOLS

The room was mercilessly bright—shadowless. In the center of the
cot huddled a ragamuffin creature, legs crossed, arms hugging her
waist, head leaning against left knee. She was trembling minutely
and constantly.

"Let's go, Mendoza!" the cop called briskly, unlocking the
cell port.

The bundle of misery did not stir.

The cop licked her lips and tried again. "Come on, Mendoza!
Your boss is here!"

Nothing.

Shan laid his hand on the cop's arm. "Leave us. I'll bring her."

She began to shake her head, lips parting to prate some senseless law.

"Go!" He augmented the command with a lash of fury. The
cop jumped—and fled.

The anger was blue-hot in him—Korval rage. With an effort
he contained it, banked it, and shut it away until it might be used.
Calmed, he went to the edge of the cot. "Priscilla."

She flinched, and he caught his breath; he calmed himself again
and hunkered down before her, his hands resting on the edge of the
mattress. "Priscilla, it's Shan."

"Shan." There was anguish like a knife in the ragged whisper.
"Shan, there wasn't enough time to be sure!"

Her agony caught him by the throat, even shielded as he was.
The next moment he had cast protection aside, spinning a line of
comfort, of love...

He was met by terror-desire-longing-grief-shame-love—a whip-
ping windstorm of emotion, punishing in its intensity. He gasped,
fingers clawing into the mattress as he scrambled for the line he had
spun for her—he gripped it, following it back into himself by painful jerks, and finally called up the Wall.

It slammed into place with a force that drew a soft moan from Priscilla, though she did not lift her head.

"My dear friend..." Slowly he unclenched his hands. "Priscilla, please look at me."

She was silent, motionless but for the constant shivering.

"Priscilla?"

"I'd rather—talk—to you. Please, Shan...They're going to—to kill me. I—can you stay with me? Please...Until they come..." She drew a shuddering breath. "You keep—going away..."

He forced his brain to work, to consider that last. "Have I been here before, Priscilla?"

"I think—yes. I was talking to you—trying to tell you...I tried to—to reach athetilu, but you were closed and I tried to—to hold you and you went away and I thought I'd made you angry..." She moved a fraction, tightening her arms about her waist. "Cama se mathra te ezo mi..."

Sintian. He was losing her, crippled as he was, not daring to step beyond the Wall. Shaking, he extended a hand and stroked the bedraggled curls.

"Priscilla, *please* look at me. I grant I'm hardly a feast for the eyes, but it would spare my feelings."

She gave no sign that she had heard him. Then, slowly, almost clumsily, she unbent and sat straight, her right arm cradled in her left, her eyes bottomless ebony pits in a filthy, exhausted face.

He smiled and dropped his hand from her hair to her knee. "Thank you. Now, since I seem prone to this fading in and out— your hand, please, Priscilla."

It took a moment for her to manage the movement, but she held a quavering left hand out to him.

"Good." He tugged the master's ring from his finger and slid it onto her thumb, where it perched precariously. "If you find I've gone away again, notice that you have my ring. I'll come back for that, at least, won't I?"

She considered it. "Yes."

He sighed, holding her hand lightly. "What a brute I am! It's a wonder I'm allowed your friendship at all, Priscilla; I marvel at you. What's wrong with your arm?"

"I burned it."

"Throwing fireballs?"

She jerked. His fingers tightened on hers, and she relaxed, licking her lips. "Yes. I'm not—accustomed—to throwing fireballs."

"I'd think not. Are you well enough to walk?"

"Yes."

"Good." He stood. "Let's go."

She stared up at him, her hand moving in his. "Go where?"

"To the *Passage*. You're hurt and sick and tired, and I'm tired and Mr. dea'Gauss is tired and even Gordy's tired." He grinned. "The port master's tired, too, but she doesn't come with us."

She tried to pull her hand away. He did not allow it.

"I can't."

He frowned. "Can't?"

"Shan…" Tears welled out of her eyes and spilled over, making streaks down her face. "Shan, I killed Dagmar."

"Yes, I know." Bending to take her other hand, he found her face close, so that he might lay his cheek against her— *Priscilla, I love you*…He fought the emotion and found the control to address her gently. "I'm *sorry*, Priscilla. It should never have come to that. You should never have had the need. Forgive me, I've taken poor care of you."

"You said—"

"I said 'no murderers,' may my tongue be damned! But self-defense isn't murder—nor is protecting the life of a friend." He took a breath, cooling the sharpest of the pain. "Please, Priscilla— for the friendship we have between us—allow me to take you to the *Passage*. You need care, healing—a sheltered place to sleep. When you are able, I will personally escort you anywhere you choose to go. Let me aid you."

There was confusion in her face and in her eyes. She was silent.

He raised a hand to touch the platinum hoop in her right ear and stroke the curls above it. "Please, Priscilla."

"The trial…"

"Has been performed. Gordy testified. The port master sat as judge. You are acquitted of murder. No one is going to come and take you away to die. Only Shan is come, to take you home."

"Home." Her hands clutched his, then relaxed. She looked into his face, her expression unreadable through the grime. "Please, Shan, take me home."

"Yes, Priscilla."

She staggered when she stood, clutching his arm for support. "Are you well enough to walk, my friend? Or shall I ask the port master to provide a chair?"

"No." She straightened, face set.

"Very well." He slid his arm around her waist, turning her toward the door. "Mr. dea'Gauss," he predicted with a merriness he did not feel, "will be appalled."

If Mr. dea'Gauss was appalled, he hid it well. The bow he performed was profound. "Lady Mendoza."

She inclined her head, which was all that dizziness and Shan's arm about her waist allowed. "Mr. dea'Gauss. I'm pleased to see you."

"You are kind." He glanced at Shan. "The physician has given Master Arbuthnot a drug he feels may counteract the worst of the side effects, or at very least allow him to sleep through them. He has also provided a printout of the structure of both drugs."

"Well enough," Shan said calmly, as if it were no surprise that Gordy should be lying so white and quiet upon the bench.

"I don't—" She shifted, half intending to go to the boy. The arm tightened about her fractionally, and she turned to look into silver eyes. "He was all right! They were going to send him to the *Passage.*"

"But he would not go without you," a new voice explained. "Afterward it became necessary that he be given the drug, that his testimony might be heard."

Priscilla blinked, clearing her vision. The tall, handsome woman in glittering evening dress smiled formally and bowed. "Ms.— Lady—Mendoza. I am Elyana Rominkoff, port master in the regent's service. Allow me to present my apologies: this should not have befallen you in the city under my care. When you are rested—at your convenience!—please contact me, that we may sit together and discuss fair recompense."

"Yes, of course," Priscilla mumbled, unable properly to attend to what the woman said to her. She was sinking into an indigo blur where the only realities were Shan's arm about her and the warm strength of his body steadying hers. Abruptly she pushed at the creeping indigo and reached out, tapping that near source of energy.

Strength flowed unstintingly from him to her, clear and bracing. She straightened as the room came back into focus and inclined her head to the woman before her. "Port Master, forgive me. I am—unwell—at the moment. I will call you, and we will talk."

"That is well, then." The woman shifted her gaze beyond Priscilla, smiling with warmth rather than mere formality. "Captain yos'Galan, remember what I have said. I am entirely at your disposal in this matter. My eyes and ears are yours to command at any hour." She bowed then and moved back, cutting off his reply with a wave of her hand. "At this hour, you have folk to care for. My car awaits you. If you allow, the precinct officer will carry the boy. Lady Mendoza, Mr. dea'Gauss holds your license and your papers."

"Thank you," Shan said gently. "You're all kindness, ma'am."

The walk to the car was blessedly short. Priscilla settled into the seat, Shan's arm still about her waist, his strength buoying her. She curled her fingers around her thumb, gripping his ring tightly. Then she reached within and turned off the tap.

The last thing she remembered was resting her head upon his shoulder.

SHIPYEAR 65
TRIPDAY 181
THIRD SHIFT
14.00 HOURS

He poured unsteadily, brandy splashing the bar top and, incidentally, the cup. Gritting his teeth, he managed to fill the thing halfway and set the decanter decently back into the rack.

Priscilla was in sick bay, under Lina's capable eye, and Gordy was there too. Both were asleep and abed—which was where he should be, working through the exercise that would grant his pounding head relief and rest. Brandy was not the best cure for an empath in his condition.

He sipped, frowning in momentary puzzlement at the stain on his cuff. Blood.

Yes, of course. Must remember to send the port master a set of crystal. Stupid Shan. Doesn't know his own strength.

Sav Rid Olanek. Gods, to have his hands about Sav Rid Olanek's slim throat...

And then? He jeered at himself, drinking again. The flaming ice of Korval rage stirred behind the barriers he had built about it. And then he would pay balance with his life! Shall he threaten lady, fosterson, ship?

Priscilla. That punishing outage of self-hate, terror, and confusion. A trace effect of the drug? Or something more permanent? Lina would know.

He stopped himself on the way to the comm. Lina would know, sooner or later. And when she knew, so would Shan yos'Galan. He would do nothing now but distract her from an essential task.

"Go to bed. Shan," he told himself.

But he tarried, sipping his drink, staring sightlessly at the tapestry above the bar.

When the annunciator chimed, he jumped.

"Come!" he called.

Mr. dea'Gauss entered, papers rustling in hand, face full of import. It was indicative of his weariness or the value of his news that he broke at once into speech, neglecting even his bow.

"Your Lordship, I have received the report of Ms. Veltrad, whom you sent to Sintia on the matter of Lady Mendoza. It is—"

"No!"

Mr. dea'Gauss blinked. "I beg your Lordship's pardon?"

"I said," Shan explained, voice thin with strain, "no. No, I do not wish to hear Ximena's report. No, I do not wish to hear the name of the crime Priscilla is supposed to have committed. No, I do not wish to find the report on my screen next on-shift. No, I do not want Ximena to call or visit so that she may tell me in her own voice what she has reported. No."

Mr. dea'Gauss took stock. Shan stood near the center of the room, holding a quarter-full glass in his bandaged hand, the blood-stained ruff falling gracefully about taut knuckles. The stark brown face might have been hewn from strellwood, and there was a slightly mad look around the silver eyes.

"The report from Sintia," he began again, "indicates that—"

"*No!*" Shan was across the room in a blur, was towering over Mr. dea'Gauss, his face set in cold fury, the syllables of the High Tongue crackling. "I do not hear you! Go."

Mr. dea'Gauss gave no ground. He had seen this before—from Er Thom yos'Galan. The proper answer had never included giving ground.

He drew himself up and took a firmer grip on his papers. "Will you hear it from me? Or from your First Speaker? It is a matter of ship's debt. The captain's attention is required."

For perhaps a heartbeat Shan was utterly still. He turned, went to his desk and sat, placing the glass precisely aside.

"yos'Galan hears," he said in the High Tongue, Thodelm to hireling.

Mr. dea'Gauss walked forward. He was not waved carelessly to a chair. Shan's face was expressionless, waiting. Mr. dea'Gauss bowed.

"Thodelm, it becomes my knowledge through the words of Ximena Veltrad, who was offered coin in return for verified truth, that Priscilla Delacroix y Mendoza was ostracized from her world for the crime called 'blasphemy' ten Standard Years gone by. The details of this crime are covered most fully by Ms. Veltrad's report. I wished only to assure you at this present that Sintia's melant'i suffers greatly by the reported incident. Lady Mendoza's actions were, as always, above reproach."

"And yet someone reproached her. Strongly." The High Tongue exuded no warmth. "You will explain this paradox."

"Yes, Thodelm. I am not conversant with the depth of the situation reported by Ms. Veltrad. My understanding is that Lady Mendoza, as an apprentice in Circle House—what is called there a 'Maiden' or novice priestess—called recriminations upon herself for an act of heroism. I confess that I do not understand why the saving of three lives should have caused these recriminations. Ms. Veltrad's report indicates doctrinal, rather than rational, causes. In any wise, Lady Mendoza was called before the masters of the craft and offered a chance to disown her act and be properly chastised. Lady Mendoza refused to recant. She was then stripped of her goods and her title, and banned from the craft. In order to keep face, her House cast her forth as well." Mr. dea'Gauss paused, considering the icy eyes. "Politics, Thodelm. Not balance."

"So." Shan drank the rest of the brandy slowly, then replaced the glass. "yos'Galan has heard. You will leave the report with me. Have you anything else that I must hear at this present?"

"No, Thodelm."

"Good. You are dismissed."

Korval's man of business bowed, then turned away.

"Mr. dea'Gauss."

He turned back. "Thodelm?"

Shan smiled wearily, his bandaged hand resting on Ximena's report. "Sleep well, sir. And thank you."

Mr. dea'Gauss felt absurd relief as his lips bent in reply. "Sleep well, your Lordship. You are quite welcome."

SHIPYEAR 65
TRIPDAY 181
THIRD SHIFT
16.00 HOURS

Shan lifted his head, groping after the sound. Surely...Ah. The door chime.

"Come."

The door parted, and she entered, slight and small, her face Liaden gold. "Old friend."

"Lina." Memory returned with a force that shuddered pain through his misused head, and he was half out of the chair. "Priscilla—"

"Resting. And well." Her small hands flickered, soothing. He sank back as she came around the desk. "More—she is herself. We spoke. She is rational; she knows what has transpired; she knows that necessity existed and that she acted as best she might." Lina sighed. "Much of the confusion you reported must be counted an effect of the drug—and of despair. Life has taught her to expect neither rescue from trouble nor surcease from pain. Healing had gone far, but that lesson is not easy to unlearn."

Shan had closed his eyes. Now he opened them, and Lina felt shock at the depth of weariness there. "She'll be all right," he murmured, his beautiful voice blurred and uneven. "Thank you, Lina, for coming to tell me. This is your rest shift, isn't it?"

"And yours, as well," she said briskly. "Priscilla sent me to make sure you slept. You were angry, she said, and hurt."

He rubbed his forehead absently. "Stupid. Trying to scan the whole planet..." He tapped a sheaf of papers. "Had to read Ximena's report. Mr. dea'Gauss...An act of heroism. She'll have to stop that, Lina. Get herself hurt. Saves three lives, using some sort of thing she wasn't taught yet. But she said the old soul—give 'em old souls, the Initiates, with the old names attached. Priscilla's soul was named Moonhawk. Very powerful lady. Much respected. Said the old soul had done it, for the glory of the Goddess and—and...who knows? Long and short, she gets thrown out. All very well and good to have a tame dramliza on your hands, but when she starts demanding her due, that's dangerous."

Lina frowned, noting the empty glass by his hand. "Is Priscilla a wizard, Shan?"

"Very good chance. Should see her—no, I hope you don't see her. Does things above and beyond us mere Healers. Got a definite flair..." He rubbed at his face again. "Gods, gods, she's *strong.*"

She leaned forward and stroked the warm, thick hair. "Shan. Come to bed."

He blinked at her. "Bed?"

"You are tired. You must rest, let yourself heal. How much brandy have you had?"

"Half a beakful," he muttered, and then grinned. "But it's quite a beak, eh?"

She laughed, between frustration and relief. "Come to bed, denubia." She grabbed the unbandaged hand and tugged. "Shan, have pity! I have promised my cha'leket to see you resting. Would you have me turn my face from her need?"

"Cha'leket?"

"Priscilla herself named me sister. I find my heart agrees. *Will* you come to bed?"

"Since you ask so nicely. Not likely to do you much good though, my precious." He wobbled to his feet but would not lean his weight upon her. Unsteadily, he laid his hand against the inner door.

She coaxed him to lie flat, unsealed the tight dress shirt, then sat stroking his hair and murmuring, weaving a net of warm comfort and loading it with the desire to sleep deeply and long.

After a time his eyes closed, his breathing lengthened.

Lina continued her weaving and stroking until she sensed that he had reached the first depths, where prime healing begins. She slid from the bed and spread the coverlet gently over him, dimmed the lights, and disarmed the alarm. Kayzin had agreed that the captain's rest should not be interrupted untimely.

Affairs ordered to her satisfaction, Lina bent and stroked his cheek. "Sleep well, old friend." And then she was gone.

CROWN CITY THEOPHOLIS
JUDGE'S HOUR

The cab pulled to the edge of the pedstrip and stopped. The driver looked over his shoulder and said something in a barbaric garble. Sav Rid stared at him coldly.

"The vehicle can go no farther," the driver announced in abrupt Trade. "Pedestrian traffic only inside the port. The fare's fivebit."

Sav Rid extended the proper coin silently and exited the cab. Behind him the driver spat between his teeth and muttered, "Louse!" But the action was beneath Sav Rid's notice, the single word in Terran.

He walked cautiously through the crowded port, intensely aware of his lack of guard. Dagmar Collier had not been at the rendezvous point this morning. He wondered what might have happened to the creature, then put the thought away with an impatient shrug. Who, after all, really cared? If Dagmar Collier chose to jump ship before the run was through, that was certainly its own affair. *Daxflan* would make good use of the unclaimed wages.

A man was coming purposefully toward him down the pedstrip: older with more gray than black in his thinning hair. Sav Rid froze.

His Delm continued briskly forward, then stopped at the proper distance and inclined his head. "Kinsman. I give you good day."

He managed a bow. "As I give you good day, kinsman and Delm. It surprises me to find you here, so far from home and House."

"No more," the elder said dryly, "than it surprises me to find you here, when the port master reports *Daxflan* absent."

"We hold orbit about the fourth planet out, my Delm. It has been found more—convenient—to use another vessel to bring goods from *Daxflan* to prime orbit."

"Indeed." Taam Olanek extended an arm, smiling coolly. "Walk with me, I beg you. I am curious about this so convenient method. Have you subcontracted your cargoes to others, Sav Rid?"

They walked a few paces in silence.

"It became necessary," Sav Rid murmured, "for *Daxflan* to purchase a subsidiary vessel to act as shuttle from *Daxflan* to berth. The method is quite simple, sir, and serves us well."

"Am I to understand," Plemia demanded, "that you have made *Daxflan,* in essence, a *warehouse?*"

"Exactly so," Sav Rid said, pleased.

His Delm drew breath. "I see. Forgive my question, kinsman, but such a purchase as a trading vessel...It seems that I surely would have noted the passage of a so large a voucher across my desk. Yet I recall nothing."

Sav Rid smiled, triumphantly oblivious to the worry in the other's face. "It was a small matter, sir; there was no need to resort to credit vouchers. We paid cash."

"Cash," Plemia repeated tonelessly. He was silent a moment or two as they walked. Then he straightened abruptly, renewing his grip on Sav Rid's arm. "It only now returns to me, kinsman—the matter of which I wished to speak. I have heard from the port master that a member of your crew—one Dagmar Collier—has been found dead in the city outside the port."

"So, that is what became of it," Sav Rid said calmly. "I had wondered. Well, it always had a quarrelsome nature."

"Had she?" Taam asked softly around the sudden ice in his throat. "And how long had Dagmar Collier served you, kinsman?"

Sav Rid moved his shoulders. "Two or three trips, I believe."

"Ah." Taam stopped, whirling on the other. "Sav Rid, a woman who has been in your service these four years has died! Do you not at least go to the precinct house and claim the body, that it might be sent properly to her kin?"

There was honest puzzlement in the young face. "No, why should I? I doubt it had kin. It was Terran, you see," he explained more fully in the face of his Delm's further silence.

"Terrans are not all kinless folk, Sav Rid," Taam murmured, his eyes filling as pity unexpectedly overtook dread. "They are people, even as we are." Still there was only puzzled confusion in the eyes watching his. He touched the smooth cheek gently. "And if they were not, my child, *we* are people. It is our burden and our pride to behave with honor, always."

"Yes, surely. But a Terran, sir..."

"Never mind, child. It will be attended to." He took Sav Rid's arm again and resumed the walk. "I hear from Korval that you and young Shan attempt to balance some puppy accounts. Are you not too old for such mischief, Sav Rid?"

The arm in his had stiffened, as had the young face. "It is not mischief, sir; it is earnest. I will have yos'Galan on its knees—hideous brother and first sister! Aye, and young Val Con, as well! How dare he treat a guest so? It was sheer insult, sir! They gave no consideration to that due one of Plemia! They will learn—and not soon forget! 'Korval,' Chelsa bleats, with fear in her face! A rabble of ill-raised brats! There is balance owing, sir, and it will be obtained. That I promise!"

"I see," Taam said again sadly. He took a breath. "Then you will not be adverse, I think, to this other news I bring. Korval demands a meeting, in sight of port master and witnesses, to establish balance and put paid to all accounts. The time is set for this local evening, if you find yourself able to attend."

"Korval demands a meeting!" Sav Rid laughed. "But they must, after all! How could they allow the idiot eldest to ruin himself?" He disengaged and bowed gravely. "I will accompany you with the greatest pleasure, sir."

SHIPYEAR 65
TRIPDAY 182
SECOND SHIFT
8.30 HOURS

Sleep receded, and she opened her eyes. The room had an uncertain familiarity—not her own quarters, nor yet the prison cell...*Sick bay,* memory provided. Lina had sent her into sleep, riding the wave of one resounding note, to wake when the healing reverberation was at last still.

How many hours? she wondered without urgency. She stretched, catlike, where she lay, noticing the cramp in her right hand, her thumb tucked tightly into her fingers.

Slowly, she eased the tension, the great amethyst of the master's ring sparkling in the room's dim light. Priscilla smiled. *Goddess bless you, my dear, for bringing me home.*

She stretched again, relishing the sensation, then sat up, pushing the thin cover away. Time to be about, whatever time it was. And she was *starving.*

The door to her left opened with a soft sigh. "Morning, gorgeous!"

She started, then grinned at the gangling medic. "Vilt. Do you always terrify your patients when they wake up?"

"Makes sense," he pointed out, taking her arm and beginning to unwrap the gauzy dressing. "If they're gonna have a heart attack, might as well have it here, where there's somebody to take care of 'em."

"Who?" she wondered, and he laughed, laying the dressing aside.

"Go ahead, do your worst. Just remember who runs the inoculation program around here. Arm looks great. Damnedest burn I've ever seen, though: inside, between wrist and elbow." He shook his head. "How'd you do it?"

She looked him in the eye. "Throwing a fireball."

"That a fact? Lucky you didn't lose some fingers. Better use a glove next time."

"Goddess willing, there won't be a next time."

"If you say so. How's the throat?"

"Okay."

Vilt shook his head in mock severity. "Think I'm taking your word for it? Open up, gorgeous—and don't even think about biting."

She submitted resentfully. Vilt made a thorough and, she suspected, leisurely exam, then grunted and stepped back.

"Looks good. Be careful of the voice for a couple days, just in case."

"Let the captain do the talking," she suggested.

He laughed again. "He will, anyway. I've known Shan since I was apprentice medic on this ship and he wasn't any older than Gordy. Been talking nonstop all that time. Likely born talking. His mother was a linguist, which probably accounts for it. Genes, you know," he explained sagely as Priscilla chuckled. He stepped back, abruptly sober. "All right, gorgeous, pay attention. Sometime between leave-time yesterday and arrival time, you lost one-tenth of your mass. The kitchen has been provided with special menus, just for you. You will eat everything on your tray until you've regained that weight. And just to keep you honest, you'll weigh in before you begin each duty-shift." He glanced at his watch. "A tasty, high-caloric breakfast will be here in three minutes. After you've eaten everything on the tray, you can use the 'fresher across the hall. Lina put fresh clothes in there for you. Any questions?"

"No."

"Great." He slapped her shoulder lightly and grinned. "See ya later."

"Vilt!"

"Yah?"

"Is Gordy okay?"

He snorted. "That kid? Been up for hours. Demanded to see you. Lina took him off to help in the pet library. Said you'd call him there when you woke up."

"I'll do that, then."

"You'll eat that breakfast before you do anything. Aha!" He stepped triumphantly to one side, allowing the orderly to push the meal cart up to the bed. "Enjoy!"

Priscilla stepped out of the dry cycle, running her fingers through unruly curls and frowning at her reflection. Her teachers had ever been anxious about her slenderness, saying that her body—

Moonhawk's vessel—was not robust enough to endure the working of larger magics.

True enough, by the mirror's testimony. Fourteen pounds lost meant countable ribs and jutting hipbones, the knobs at wrist and collar painfully apparent. She cupped a breast, sighing. She looked like a disaster victim. She turned sharply away to rummage in the closet.

The fresh clothes were unexpectedly fine. Priscilla wondered where Lina had gotten them, for they had the air of things handmade to personal specification rather than bought from general stores. Wonderingly, she unfolded the silky shirt, noting the flaring collar and the wide, pleated sleeves gathered tightly into ruffled cuffs. Its color was a pure and shimmering rose. The trousers were river-blue and soft. Velvet? she wondered, running light fingers down the nap. They belled slightly at the knee and fell precisely to the instep of the new black boots. She ran the tooled leather belt around her waist, fastened the rosy agate buckle, and turned again to her reflection.

"Thodelm," she breathed, touching the collar that framed her face and lent blush to her cheeks. Lina had provided clothing that the Head of a Liaden Line might wear when about the business of the Line.

Hesitantly she approached the mirror, and put out a finger to trace the features of her own face: the slender brows, the straight nose and startling cheekbones, the stubborn chin, the full mouth, and all around them the tumbling mass of midnight curls, relieved at each ear by the pure curve of a platinum hoop.

"Priscilla Mendoza," she said aloud.

On her hand the borrowed amethyst glittered—and that was wrong. She was not Master Trader.

Nor was she outcast.

She stared into the purple depths, considering that thought. "Moonhawk is returned to the Mother."

Truth.

And what did that truth mean, after ten years, a double-dozen worlds—a death? What did it mean here, in the place her heart called home, surrounded by friends, buoyed by a power she thought had fled?

Lady Mendoza, the old gentleman invariably addressed her with profound respect. Lina had not found it unusual that her friend possessed power, only that she had not been taught courtesy in its use. Shan...

But it was not possible to think clearly of Shan. Certainly he regarded her abilities, like his own, as natural and acceptable. "How do you make love?" she recalled him asking, and she put a hand to a cheek suddenly flaming. Don't do that, Priscilla...

Last night...How much had been drug-dream, how much true actions? He had come—she wore the proof on her hand even now! He had brought her home. What else besides these was fact?

Disturbed, she turned slowly and left the 'fresher.

In the hall she hesitated. It was time she reported for duty. Yet Vilt had not released her, and the finery she wore was not meant to withstand a second mate's rounds.

"Hello, Priscilla. Can you spare me a few moments?" Shan's voice interrupted her thoughts.

"All the moments you like," she told him gladly even as she groped for his pattern.

It was subdued, though she caught an indefinable jolt of something as he paused and looked at her closely.

"Are you well, Priscilla? Tell me the truth, please—no heroics."

"Well," she caught doubt and drifted an unconscious step forward, smiling reassuringly. "I lost some weight—strong magics have that effect. Vilt has me eating the most incredible amount of food! But I am well. In fact, I was getting ready to sign out of here and go back on duty."

"Duty? Priscilla..." He paused, glancing about. "Is that the room you were in? Do you mind if we speak there? I..."

Something was wrong. She expanded her scope, trying to read it from his pattern, but received only a discord of pain, bitterness, anger, despair—a medley so unlike Shan that she would hardly have known him had her outer eyes been closed.

"Of course."

He stood aside to let her enter first, then closed the door behind them and dropped into the single chair. Uncertainly, she sat on the bed.

The silence was uneasy; scanning was worse than useless. She pulled the Master Trader's ring from her thumb and held it out.

He stared, despair increasing: taking the ring, he sat holding it between thumb and forefinger, toying with the lights among its facets.

"Have you decided," he asked, looking at the ring, his voice husky, "where it is I shall take you?"

She stared at him, ice blossoming in chest and belly.

"Why," she managed, "should you take me anywhere?"

"I gave my word," he told the amethyst. "You only said you would stay until you were—*well*, Priscilla."

Through the isolated, tangled scenes of the night before, she recalled it and licked her lips. "You said you—had come to take me home."

"Did I?" Still he did not meet her eyes, but stared at the ring in his hand. "I will then, Priscilla. But you must tell me where that is. Home."

"Shan!" Anguish knifed through her; she made no attempt to damp it, and felt his answering surge of concern as he at last raised his face.

"You don't want me to go!" she cried, knowing it was truth. "Why—"

"It doesn't matter what I want, Priscilla! What matters is what you want! If there is a place that is home to you, where you know, if you are in need, that there is someone—anyone !—who will aid you, I'll take you there. See you safe—settled..." His voice cracked on the unaccustomed harshness. Instantly the black lashes flicked down, shielding him.

He took a breath, then another, his emotions an unreadable riot. "That a member of this ship's complement should feel there was no place to go when she was in direst need...I am ashamed, Priscilla. I've failed you as a captain...and as a friend."

"I want to stay." Her words came as barely a breath of sound. She gripped the mattress and tried again. "Captain, please. You never failed me. I failed, by not learning soon enough...by not understanding what it means to be a crew member." Tears ran her cheeks, unheeded. "Shan, by the Mother! The *Passage* is my home. Don't—don't make me leave!" She drew a shuddering breath and loosed the mattress to wipe her face with shaking fingertips.

"Really, Priscilla, you might tell me in advance if I'm expected to provide handkerchiefs for us both."

She gave a startled gasp, groping perhaps toward a laugh, and took the proffered cloth. "Thank you."

"Don't give it a thought. I have dozens. I just don't happen to have them all with me at the moment." He leaned back, his face less bleak, his pattern showing a glimmer of what might be hope.

"The ship would miss the services of the second mate," he said carefully. "The captain's information is that the second mate progresses excellently in her training, taking over more responsibilities each shift. The first mate is pleased. The captain is also pleased."

Melant'i. She drew a deliberately even breath, relaxing tight chest muscles as she recalled sleep-lessons and Lina's tutoring. "The second mate wishes with all her heart to continue serving the ship and the captain."

Relief like a draught of ice-cold water cascaded from him to her. "Good. You will take your duties up again in four shifts." He raised a hand to still her protest. "There is a meeting at local midnight in the port master's office, Priscilla. Since you are intimately involved, it's best that you be there. Also present will be Delm Plemia, Sav Rid Olanek, Port Master Rominkoff, Shan yos'Galan, Gordon Arbuthnot, Mr. dea'Gauss, and Lina Faaldom, as observer."

"Balance?"

"Balance, indeed. Which reminds me, Thodelm. Mr. dea'Gauss wishes to meet with you in a very few moments now to ascertain the extent of debt owed you by Plemia and Korval——"

"Korval owes me nothing!" she cried. "If anything, I owe Korval for giving me a job, for——"

"Priscilla, do be reasonable. If you hadn't been on this ship, there quite possibly wouldn't be a ship right now, whether or not there was a captain. Ship's debt exists. As well as a personal debt."

"No," she said stubbornly. "I won't take payment from you. There's no debt now, if there ever was one." She leaned forward, extending a tentative hand. "Shan? You gave me—a life. I gave you a life. Balance."

He hesitated, then put his hand into hers. "Balance, then, Priscilla." He smiled. "You drive a hard bargain. Mr. dea'Gauss awaits us. May I escort your Ladyship to the meeting?"

"No," she said, gripping his hand and drinking in his lightening pattern with giddy joy. "But you may escort your friend."

Shan grinned and stood. "Much better, I agree." He flourished the bow between equals. "After you, Priscilla."

MASTER'S TOWER, THEOPHOLIS
WITCH'S HOUR

Ten minutes before the hour.

Taam Olanek sternly forbade himself the luxury of fidgeting with the papers before him. It was not expected that a Delm betray uneasiness. At his right hand, Sav Rid sat silent. He still did not grasp it, Taam knew, pity warring with anger. He wondered briefly what had caused the younger man's madness, and set wonder aside. It hardly mattered.

Across the room, Mr. dea'Gauss was in quiet conversation with Port Master Rominkoff. The balance of the group had yet to arrive.

The door buzzed and was opened by the guard stationed there. Taam Olanek felt his breath snag.

A plain-faced Liaden woman in the costume of Thodelm entered, a tow-headed Terran child at her side. Taam Olanek's breathing eased. Of course Korval would arrive last. It was proper.

"I'm not sitting at the same table with him!"

The child had stopped, eyes fixed on— *Me?* Taam thought. No. On Sav Rid.

The woman had her hand on the boy's arm and was speaking in gentle Terran. "Gordon? We are here to settle past difference. You know this. To do so we must sit and speak together."

"I'm not," Gordon said through clenched teeth, "sitting at a table with him. He called me 'it,' and he said Priscilla was a thief."

With a feeling of infinite sadness, Taam Olanek rose and went across the room. A child, Sav Rid? he thought.

He and Mr. dea'Gauss reached the spot at the same moment. Asking permission with a flicker of fingers, Taam bowed to the child: elder to young person of rank. The boy eyed him narrowly but returned the bow properly, then straightened and stood waiting.

"I am," Taam said, speaking the unaccustomed tongue with great care, "Taam Olanek. The person you object to is one who will obey my word. Will it satisfy you, young sir, if I pledge that my kinsman Sav Rid will behave with fitting courtesy during the time we meet together?"

The brown eyes looked into his: a weighing glance. Taam returned it calmly. The boy looked to Mr. dea'Gauss.

"Is that true?" There was no insult in the tone; he was merely requesting information. Taam Olanek found himself amused.

Mr. dea'Gauss inclined his head. "The word of Delm Plemia is above reproach, Master Arbuthnot. What he has said will be."

"Okay." The boy inclined his head. "Thank you, Delm Plemia."

Taam bowed graciously. "Thank *you,* Master Arbuthnot."

Mr. dea'Gauss indicated the patient woman. "Plemia, here is Thodelm Faaldom, Clan Deshnol."

He inclined his head. "Thodelm, I am pleased to meet you."

She bowed, as Head of Line to Delm of another Clan. "I am pleased to meet you, Plemia." Neither voice nor face betrayed her thoughts. Her behavior was most proper.

As observer, Thodelm Faaldom sat at the bottom left of the table. The boy sat to her right, near Mr. dea'Gauss. Sav Rid eyed both coldly; he made neither overture nor introduction.

The hour struck on the clock above the door, nearly covering the sound of the door buzzer.

The woman was tall, though not much taller than Shan yos'Galan, who walked just behind her right shoulder, and black-haired and slender. But for its paleness, her face might have been Liaden. She wore calm authority like a silken cloak over the clothing of Thodelm.

Gliding, she crossed to the port master and bowed as between equals.

Pilot, Taam Olanek thought, seeing the woman's grace mirrored in her white-haired escort. He understood now Mr. dea'Gauss's moment of outrage. Pleasure-love she might be, but this regal lady was no one's plaything.

"Port Master," she was saying, her voice soft and deeper than one expected, "I'm happy to see you again. Please accept my gratitude now for your kindness to myself and my friend."

The port master smiled in momentary pleasure, then waved a dismissing hand. "You owe me no gratitude, Lady Mendoza. My duty was clear. I believe there are still amends to be made; we must meet again before you leave."

The black-haired woman murmured assent and stepped aside.

Shan yos'Galan made his bow to the port master. "I'm pleased to see you again, ma'am. Please accept my gratitude as well, to be flung aside with Lady Mendoza's."

She laughed. "A lesson in manners, Captain? Very well, I accept the gratitude of all—including the boy's, though he hasn't offered it. Perhaps he's a realist." She indicated the rest of the table. "We are all gathered now. Mr. dea'Gauss?"

Korval's man of business rose to his spare height and bowed profoundly to the two just arrived.

"Thodelm yos'Galan. Thodelm Mendoza. Here are Elyana Rominkoff, port master; Taam Olanek, Delm Plemia; Lina Faaldom, Thodelm and observer; Gordon Arbuthnot, fosterson and witness; Sav Rid Olanek, Trader."

Plemia inclined his head. Beside him, Sav Rid shifted and snapped, *"Lady* Mendoza!"

The woman's face remained coolly serene; she might not have heard. Certainly yos'Galan had heard; the light eyes glittered steel.

Plemia turned his face. Deliberately, using the Command mode of the High Tongue, he instructed for the ears of all, "You will exercise fitting courtesy here!"

Impossibly, Sav Rid looked hurt. "Certainly, sir."

Taam sighed to himself and saw a flicker of a reaction cross Lady Faaldom's face. At the top of the table, Lady Mendoza sat, Lord yos'Galan at her right. Plemia very nearly sighed aloud. Korval thus demonstrated its support of Thodelm Mendoza's demands and subordination of its claims to hers.

"It must be known," Mr. dea'Gauss announced, "that a pinbeam has been received from Eldema yos'Galan. It reads thus—" He plucked a sheet of hard copy from the pile before him. "'In the present affair between Plemia and Korval, it shall be that Thodelm yos'Galan speaks with the very voice of Korval. I, Nova yos'Galan, First Speaker in Trust, Clan Korval.'"

yos'Galan inclined his white head, his ugly face austere. "It shall be done as the First Speaker instructs."

Mr. dea'Gauss laid the sheet aside. "For the purpose of balance, it shall be considered that Priscilla Delacroix y Mendoza is indeed Thodelm. Since she has chosen to disassociate herself from House Mendoza, Sintia, she must also be considered Delm Mendoza Offworld—"

"Offworld?" Sav Rid cried, cutting the old gentleman off. "Outlaw, more like!"

"Sav Rid!" Plemia allowed irritation to be heard. "I remind you again that I will have courtesy from you, for every person here."

"What difference," the younger man demanded, eyes glittering fever-bright, "if the bitch chooses to style itself Thodelm? Our business is with Korval, which has the ill judgment to allow the fool to speak for it—"

"You are silent!"

A wave of heat washed past Taam's cheek, gone even as he understood the words to be in the High Tongue—ultimate authority to rankless person—and recognized the voice to belong to Thodelm Mendoza.

Beside him, Sav Rid opened his mouth, throat working. No sound emerged.

"Your Delm," the woman continued in faultless Liaden, "will speak for you. When your words are required, you will be permitted speech."

"Most proper," Mr. dea'Gauss murmured.

Taam looked quickly around the table. Shan yos'Galan was expressionless; the port master was puzzled but unshaken. Gordon Arbuthnot's brown eyes were stretched wide. Lady Faaldom was staring at the black-haired woman, awe and consternation in her face.

"Korval," Lord yos'Galan said in quiet Trade, "acknowledges a subordinate position in these negotiations. Debts owed Lady Mendoza are by far the greatest and must be met. We support her claims and are guided by her thoughts."

"Just so," Plemia inclined his head, carefully not thinking about the impossibility of what he had just witnessed. Beside him, Sav Rid sat mute and shivering.

"Thodelm Mendoza. I have seen information provided by Mr. dea'Gauss regarding your grievance against Plemia. Also, I have heard privately from my clansman that which convinces me of the justice of that grievance. Without doubt, Plemia owes. The amount must yet be ascertained. I am interested in hearing your thoughts on this."

The black eyes considered him calmly. "Sav Rid Olanek must be removed as Trader on *Daxflan* immediately."

He stiffened. "That is a Clan decision, Thodelm."

"Then it is a decision I require of the Clan," she returned serenely. "Sav Rid Olanek is unfit. If he were examined by the Trader's Guild tomorrow, sir, he would be found wanting and his license revoked. More." She lifted a hand, forestalling his protest. "I tell you now, sir, your kinsman gave scant attention to the honor of his crew—Liaden as little as Terran. His cargo included illegal pharmaceuticals: Bellaquesa, I will swear to; others I might guess. He is a danger to the honor of your Clan, the honor of your ship...and to himself." She glanced at the man on her right. "Is it permitted that I ask Lady Faaldom to speak—as a Healer?"

"If Plemia agrees."

Taam inclined his head. "Plemia agrees."

"Healer Faaldom."

"Lady Mendoza?"

"I feel that Sav Rid Olanek is not—rational. Are you able to form an opinion? Would you tell us what it is?"

The Healer gave the softest of sighs. "My opinion parallels your own. Sav Rid Olanek is deranged. The pattern is one I have only occasionally seen, most often in connection with ingestion of harmful drugs. Bellaquesa addiction, for instance, might cause such a pattern."

"Can he be Healed?" There was hope in the Terran woman's voice. Taam Olanek looked at her in wonder.

The Healer hesitated. "It is beyond my skill."

"Beyond everyone's skill, Lina?" She spoke insistently, and Olanek felt his wonder grow.

"On Liad, perhaps. The path would be a long one, I think, and tedious." She sighed once more. "If Plemia desires, I will provide names, an introduction."

"You are kind, Healer. My thanks to you."

"You will need that list, sir," Lady Mendoza informed him. "My second demand is that he be Healed."

"Thodelm," he said with dignity, "you do not need to demand it. The child shall have what he requires."

She bowed her head. "Forgive me, sir. I meant no offense."

"None was taken, Thodelm. May I know what items further go to balance Plemia's debt?"

"It must be recalled," yos'Galan said smoothly, before the lady could speak again, "that several attempts have been made on Lady

Mendoza's life—which is the life of her House, entire. The first attempt must be laid directly upon Sav Rid Olanek, who ordered Dagmar Collier to strike. The second and third incidents must also be laid upon Trader Olanek for his inability to control the actions of one sworn to his service."

"There are practicalities as well," Mr. dea'Gauss put in. "Unpaid wages, contract fee, clothing, hazard pay, recompense of personal indignities suffered while employed on *Daxflan*, family heirlooms lost—"

"Korval," yos'Galan broke in, "owes for the heirlooms, sir. Evidence indicates they were destroyed in retaliation for words spoken by Captain yos'Galan."

Mr. dea'Gauss made a notation. "So then. The sum owed, were there no further balance to be established: two cantra."

Plemia inclined his head. It surprised him that the woman should have drawn so low a wage, that she should have possessed so little. "Plemia agrees to a payment of two cantra in balance for these things."

"Lady Mendoza," yos'Galan said gently, "has declined her right to Trader Olanek's life as balance for his attempts on her own. The life-sum agreed upon by the Council of Clans for a first class pilot is three hundred cantra. It must be remembered that Lady Mendoza is currently the sum of her Line and Clan. It is to be assumed that one in her position would desire to establish a solid base for her House. Three children, I think, is not an unreasonable number. Nor is it unreasonable to suppose these offspring would inherit pilot reactions. Nine hundred cantra, then, for the children unborn."

Twelve hundred cantra.

"A just sum," Plemia murmured around the sinking feeling in his stomach. "Precise balance is intended. However, if Lady Mendoza permits, I would propose this alternate plan: Plemia pays a sum of fifteen hundred cantra, over four Standards, the money to derive from *Daxflan's* profits—"

"No!" she said sharply. "I want no money from *Daxflan*."

Wearily he raised his eyes to hers. "Lady, I assure you, not all of *Daxflan's* profits come illegally. A guaranteed payment of three hundred seventy-five cantra per Standard would be made, even should *Daxflan* fail to earn that sum. Is this plan acceptable?"

She looked at him for a long moment, then glanced beyond. "Mr. dea'Gauss."

"Thodelm?"

"If Clan Korval permits, sir, I would like you to take charge of these—details. The sum of twelve hundred cantra at once or fifteen hundred over several Standards is agreeable to me. Otherwise, it would be—comforting—to know that you act in my interest."

"Korval raises no objection," Lord yos'Galan put in, "if Mr. dea'Gauss feels he can undertake the task."

"I accept the commission, Thodelm Mendoza. I am honored to give service." He inclined his head. "Perhaps Delm Plemia and I might meet on the morrow and discuss the matter more fully."

"Certainly, sir. At your convenience."

"We come now," Mr. dea'Gauss said, "to that owed Korval. There is deliberate loss engineered by Sav Rid Olanek. There is the paid attack upon the *Dutiful Passage*—"

"Korval," yos'Galan broke in, "makes the following demands for balance: From Plemia, twenty cantra toward the loss on the mezzik-root purchase. Captain yos'Galan will likewise pay twenty cantra to the ship, to remind him to hear more fully. Also, Korval does likewise insist that Trader Olanek be removed from *Daxflan* immediately and sent home, that Healing may commence.

"Last, Captain yos'Galan would speak with Delm Plemia and Captain yo'Vaade regarding the management of tradeships and the planning of trade routes. Plemia may reap profit from the discussion."

Taam Olanek felt himself adrift. He managed to incline his head. "Plemia agrees to all terms of Korval's balance."

"So be it," Mr. dea'Gauss said formally, and made notation.

"I believe that Master Arbuthnot also holds a just claim," Taam ventured, still unsure of what had occurred.

"Me?" The boy looked up in surprise. "Shan? Does this—does Delm Plemia owe me something?"

"You were in quite a bit of danger through the Trader's mismanagement, you know, Gordy." From the mildness of the tone, yos'Galan might have been discussing a rather mediocre play.

The boy frowned and shook his head. "The only thing he owes me is an apology for calling me 'it.' But if he's going to see a Healer, I guess he'll learn better, so that's okay. Dagmar's the one put me in danger, and she paid as much as she can." Surprisingly, then, he inclined his head, speaking in tolerably accented High Tongue. "Thank you, sir, but I believe our accounts are in order."

Taam bowed his head. "Thank you, Master Arbuthnot. Should you have need, Plemia's name is for you to use."

"Thank you," Gordy said again in response to a glance from Lady Faaldom.

Plemia glanced at the port master. "Madam, I would ask assistance. *Daxflan* must be searched, and all illegal substances must be removed. Is it possible you could instruct me in the proper procedure?"

She nodded gravely. "Delm Plemia, I would be honored to assist you. Allow me to call on you tomorrow midday for the purpose."

"You are kind, madam. I thank you."

"I believe," Mr. dea'Gauss said dryly, "that the meeting may be adjourned." Seeing no dissent, he turned down his papers.

At the head of the table, both tall Thodelms stood, bowed, and glided toward the door. On the threshold the woman turned and raised a hand, tracing an invisible pattern in the air.

"Sav Rid Olanek," she announced in the High Tongue, "you may speak now."

Then they passed through the door and were gone.

Taam Olanek felt a sigh pass him, as if a bubble had given way. Beside him, Sav Rid burst into tears.

SHIPYEAR 65
TRIPDAY 287
THIRD SHIFT
16.00 HOURS

Acting First Mate Mendoza strode toward the captain's office. Hold 6, empty for the past two months, tantalized memory with the odors of leather, resin, spice. She took a deep breath, then sighed it out with a grin. It was hard to believe that they would establish orbit about Liad in five hours; hard to believe that so much had happened in five months. From pet librarian to acting first mate—she nearly laughed as she laid her hand against the captain's door.

He was frowning at the computer screen, his mental signature laced with irritation. At her entrance he looked up, irritation fading. "Hello, Priscilla."

She smiled, relaxing into the familiarity of his inner self. "You wanted to see me?"

He grinned. "Very good. When in doubt, hedge. The captain has several things to discuss with the first mate. Also the first mate was to have discovered what Lina Faaldom was going to do with that damn perfume of hers."

Priscilla laughed. "She's got a buyer in Chonselta City. They're going to package a distillate and sell it for a cantra the quarter ounce. The name is 'Festival Memories.'" She stopped because Shan was laughing.

"Oh, no! Shameless, shameless! She'd have done better to turn her hand to trading than librarying, Priscilla. 'Festival Memories,' in fact! The woman's dangerous." He leaned back, grinning hugely. "She's reserved a quantity for the crew, I hope?"

Priscilla nodded, lighthearted with his pleasure. "Anyone who wants part of their profit in perfume may take it that way, up to two bottles."

He chuckled. "Wonderful, wonderful. Pour yourself a drink, Priscilla, and come sit down."

She moved to the bar. "What are you drinking?"

"Nothing at the moment. But I would like a brandy, if you'd be so kind."

She poured them each a drink, brought him a glass, and settled into the right-hand chair.

Shan sipped, his light eyes on her. "Have you decided what you will do, Priscilla?"

"Do?"

He waved an apologetic hand. "Of course, it's true that you're rather well off now. You might choose to do nothing at all. But I'll tell you frankly, Priscilla, doing nothing is a very boring line of work." He sipped thoughtfully. "Not that there aren't a great many people who don't seem to find it arduous at all. My cousin Pat Rin, for an instance. The first jewels, the most fashionable companions...Why, if he didn't play the wheel with suspiciously consistent luck, he'd have no money at all to call his own, and live within his quarter-share he could not."

She smiled. "I don't think I'd do well as a gambler."

"Well, neither do I, frankly. But there are other things you might be about. Buy a house, a bit of land, start talking to people—lay the foundation for possible contracts and alliances."

"To set up my Clan," she surmised.

"Exactly to set up your Clan. Nothing wrong with that, is there?"

She sipped her drink, considering him. Emotive patterns told too little. He was not desperate, but there was a—tentativeness—mixed somehow with the desire she had found herself responding to more and more of late.

"I thought I'd invest my money," she said quietly. "Mr. dea'Gauss kindly offered his services."

Shan raised his glass. "I see that Korval will have to begin casting about for a new man of business. Mr. dea'Gauss is clearly smitten. I had hoped it would prove to be merely a case of calf-love, Priscilla, I confess."

She laughed. "More likely he thinks I'm too young to manage my own affairs! He helped me gain funds and status; how can he leave me alone to botch things now?"

"A fair summation of Mr. dea'Gauss's melant'i in the situation," Shan acknowledged. "But you still don't tell me what you'll be doing, Priscilla."

"Have you heard from Kayzin Ne'Zame?"

The slanted brows pulled together. "She brought *Daxflan* safely home and continues to work closely with Plemia to revise ship's procedures and work out a route that will not unduly tax available resources. I believe she had hopes of showing him the advantages of belonging to a cooperative, with which project I wish her luck. Plemia was rather resistant to the idea when I brought it up in our discussions."

"Does she think she'll be able to finish her work there in time for the *Passage's* next voyage?" More tentativeness. She knew it for her own.

Shan was surprised. "Kayzin warned me some time ago of her intention to retire at the end of this trip. Most properly, as Mr. dea'Gauss would no doubt agree. In a way, it was good that *Daxflan* and all its troubles came along. It gave her thoughts a new direction, away from—endings." He sipped. "Kayzin's captain was my father, Priscilla. They ran this ship together thirty years. It's not easy for her to see another in his place, even though she helped train me for just that purpose. She only stayed this long to be certain I was able. Her last duty to her captain."

"You'll be needing a first mate and a second?"

"Indeed I will. Which brings us back at last to my original inquiry, Priscilla. Have you thought of what you will do? Your contract runs out in—what? A day?"

"Fourteen hours," she replied, her mind racing. There was so much she did not know, so much training she would need; and there were people on the *Passage* who had been there all their lives, child and adult. Kayzin Ne'Zame, working on the ship for fifty years, at the captain's side for thirty of them, a captain she served even after his death...

Shan sipped brandy. She sensed tension in him, and restraint. The decision was hers. *Goddess, I'm a fool. How can it be easier to conceive of looking at his face, hearing his voice, sensing his moods for all of thirty years, than to consider myself without those things for even a week?*

She licked her lips. "If—I would prefer not to renew my contract as second—" she sensed shocked pain from him, quickly damped, as she hurtled on, "—and to sign a new one, as first mate!"

She was swept by singing triumph and a tangled knot of other feelings, from which she isolated lust, and relief, and joy, and something that seared so she could not find its name before the whole concert was controlled and shackled into the merest background hum.

"Thank you, Priscilla."

Her heart was pounding; she was gasping with the force of his emotions, her own powerfully evoked. Mother, the echo...she thought. But it was no echo.

"Priscilla?" He was before her, radiating concern. "Forgive me."

"No." She set the glass aside, hand questing. He took it in his. "Shan..."

"Yes, Priscilla?"

She translated it from the High Tongue, because protocol said it was done this way between Liadens, and it was imperative that he understand, that he not think her grasping or unaware of her place as someone all but Clanless. "Will you share pleasure with me, Shan?"

His fingers tightened as astonished joy flickered between them, weighted, though, with something else. Seeking, her inner eye perceived a wall, thick and impenetrable, with only a tiny slit in its smooth surface. As she watched, the slit enlarged, eating the wall until it was gone and there was only—Shan.

The impression was not just sound now, or pattern, or even an occasional whiff of elusive spice. It was all: a woven whole spread before the inner senses—Shan without defenses, open for her to know completely.

Priscilla cried out, jerking to her feet, gripping his shoulders. "No! Shan, you mustn't!"

Then there was sadness, though not despair, and the inner landscape faded, becoming again the barely breached Wall as she sagged against him, craving what she had just denied, and pushed her face against his shoulder.

"Priscilla, I ask your forgiveness yet again." His voice was very gentle in her ear. "I didn't want to distress you."

She drew a shaky breath and stood away. "I—" Words failed her. Goddess, she thought, twice a fool.

He sighed and guided her to the couch. Sitting beside her, he took her hand. "When I came to get you from the precinct house in Theopholis, Priscilla, you said something." She tensed. What *was* real from all she thought she remembered of that night?

"What you said," he pursued gently, "was, 'Shan, there wasn't enough time to be sure.'"

She relaxed. She did remember that. "True."

"It might still be true, Priscilla. There's no need for haste. And many reasons to be…sure."

She struggled with it, trying to balance the Liaden concept of pleasure-love with what she felt in him even now, with what she herself felt. "I asked…pleasure. And you want it!"

"Priscilla, my very dear." He raised her hand, lips brushing her palm, cheek stroking her fingertips. "Of course I want it. But not at the expense of your certainty. I'd be a poor friend if I made that trade." He sighed. "And I've already made you angry with me."

"Not angry," she protested, knowing he could read that lack in her. "It's—Shan, it's *wrong* to—to open up so far. To let someone see your—allness."

"Even when that someone is my dear friend? Even when I wish to give the gift?"

She opened her mouth, then closed it. "It is how I was taught," she told him humbly. "I never thought to question it." She had the name of the searingly bright emotion then, and felt tears forming. Too little time, indeed…

He sensed her understanding and nodded. "There are other reasons not to rush, as I said. Consider your new position, for one matter. Will you have people say that you are first mate because you and the captain are lovers?"

Her chin rose. "It's our business, not theirs!"

"Theirs," he corrected. "It's a matter of melant'i, and of ship's administration. The crew must know that the two people who run this ship are honorable, are trustworthy—are *capable*. That proved, you may take any lover—and as many!—as you wish. You do have an extensive amount of training to undergo, you know, before you'll be up to Kayzin's level."

Impossibly, she laughed. "As if I didn't know it!"

He grinned, relieved and admiring. "Will you be staying on Liad, Priscilla?"

She nodded. "I'm guesting with Lina until I find a house of my own."

"Good. Then you'll be able to get a firm grounding during the time we're docked. And the next run is the long one—one full Standard. Enough time, I'd think, for everyone to know what works and what doesn't." He squeezed her fingers. "We might not make a very good team in spite of it all, Priscilla. That happens sometimes."

"We're a good team," she said, startled to hear the Seer's lilt in her voice. "We'll be a better one. The best."

The silver eyes glinted mischief. "You sound sure of yourself, Thodelm. Would you care to place a small wager? Say, a cantra? Issue to be decided at Solcintra docking, next run-end."

"Done." She grinned, surprised at finding herself so easy, and read the same deep serenity in Shan. On some level, then, they understood each other. The pattern of the Goddess's dance would see to the rest. She gripped the big hand tightly, then let it go and stood. "Sleep well, my friend."

"Sleep well, Priscilla."

She moved to the door.

"Priscilla!"

"Yes?"

"May I call on you at Lina's, Priscilla? It might aid certainty."

She smiled, peace filling her utterly. "I'll be all joy to see you."

AGENT OF CHANGE

CHAPTER ONE
Standard Year 1392

The man who was not Terrence O'Grady had come quietly.

And that, Sam insisted, was clear proof. Terry had never done anything quietly in his life if there was a way to get a fight out of it.

Pete, walking at Sam's left behind the prisoner, wasn't so sure. To all appearances, the man they had taken *was* Terrence O'Grady. He had the curly, sandy hair, the pug nose, and the archaic black-framed glasses over pale blue eyes, and he walked with a limp of the left leg, which the dossier said was a souvenir of an accident way back when he'd been mining in the Belt of Terado.

They stopped at a door set deep into the brick wall of the alley. Up in front, Russ raised his fist and struck the heavy kreelwood twice.

They waited, listening to the noises of the night city beyond the alley. Then the door opened silently on well-oiled hinges, and they were staring down a long hallway.

As he stepped over the threshold, Pete gritted his teeth and concentrated on the back of the man before him. The man who was not Terrence O'Grady. Maybe.

It was in no way a remarkable back: slightly stoop-shouldered, not quite on a level with Pete's own. Terrence O'Grady, the dossier noted, was short and slender for a Terran, a good six inches below the average. This made him a valuable partner for bulky Sam, who handled the massive mining equipment effortlessly, but was not so well suited to exploring the small gaps, craters, and crevices where a rich vein might hide.

Sam and Terry made money in the Belt. Then Terry quit mining, bought himself some land with atmosphere over it, and settled into farming, child raising, and even politics.

Eight years later Sam got a bouncecomm from Terry's wife: Terrence O'Grady had disappeared.

Sam went to talk to wife and family, as an old friend should; he asked questions and nosed around. No corpse had been found, but Sam declared Terry dead. He'd been too stubborn a dreamer to run out on all of them at once. And, given Terry's luck, someone would have had to kill him to make him dead before old age.

Sam said Terry had been murdered three years ago.

But recently there had been rumors, and then this person here—wearing a dead man's face and calling himself by a dead man's name.

Pete shook himself as they rounded a sharp corner and barely avoided stepping on the prisoner.

"Look sharp!" Sam whispered harshly.

They turned another corner and came into a brightly lit, abandoned office.

The man who was not Terrence O'Grady nearly smiled.

From this point on, he knew the layout of each of the fourteen suites in this building, the voltage of the lighting fixtures, the position of doors and windows, the ambient temperature, and even the style and color of the carpets.

Within his mental Loop, he saw a number shift from .7 to .85. The second figure changed a moment later from .5 to .7. The first percentage indicated Chance of Mission Success; the second, Chance of Personal Survival. CMS recently had been running significantly above CPS.

His escort halted before a lift, and both numbers rose by a point. When the lift opened onto an office on the third floor, the Loop flickered and withdrew—the more imminent the action, the less precise the calculations.

The desk was beautiful, made of inlaid teak and redwood imported from Earth.

The man behind the desk was also imported from Earth and he was not beautiful. He had a paunch and an aggressive black beard. Soft hands laced together on the gleaming wood, he surveyed the group with casual interest.

"Thank you, gentlemen. You may stand away from the prisoner."

Russ and Skipper dropped back, leaving the man who was not O'Grady alone before Mr. Jaeger's desk.

"Mr. O'Grady, I believe?" Jaeger purred.

The little man bowed slightly and straightened, hands loose at his sides.

In the depths of his beard, Jaeger frowned. He tapped the desktop with one well-manicured finger.

"You're not Terrence O'Grady," he said flatly. "This readout says you're not even Terran." He was on his feet with a suddenness surprising in so soft an individual, hands slamming wood. "You're a damned geek spy, that's what you are, Mr.—O'Grady!" he roared.

Pete winced and Sam hunched his shoulders. Russ swallowed hard. The prisoner shrugged.

For a stunned minute, nobody moved. Then Jaeger straightened and strolled to the front of the desk. Leaning back, he hooked thumbs into belt loops and looked down at the prisoner.

"You know, Mr....O'Grady," he said conversationally. "There seems to be a conviction among you geeks—all geeks, not just humanoid ones—that we Terrans are pushovers. That the power of Earth and of true humans is some kind of joke." He shook his head.

"The Yxtrang make war on our worlds and pirate our ships; the Liadens control the trade economy; the turtles ignore us. We're required to pay exorbitant fees at the so-called *federated* ports. We're required to pay in cantra, rather than good Terran bits. Our laws are broken. Our people are ridiculed. Or impersonated. Or murdered. And we're tired of it, O'Grady. Real tired of it."

The little man stood quietly, relaxed and still, face showing bland attention.

Jaeger nodded. "It's time for you geeks to learn to take us Terrans seriously—maybe even treat us with a little respect. Respect is the first step toward justice and equality. And just to show you how much I believe in justice and equality, I'm going to do something for you, O'Grady." He leaned forward sharply, his beard a quarter-inch from the prisoner's smooth face. "I'm going to let you talk to me. Now. You're going to tell me everything, Mr. O'Grady: your name, your home planet, who sent you, how many women you've had, what you had for dinner, why you're here—everything." He straightened and went back around the desk. Folding his hands atop the polished wood, he smiled.

"Do all that, Mr. O'Grady, and I might let you live."

The little man laughed.

Jaeger snapped upright, hand slapping a hidden toggle.

Pete and Sam dove to the left, Russ and Skipper to the right. The prisoner hadn't moved at all when the blast of high-pressure water struck, hurling him backward over and over until he slammed against the far wall. Pinned by the torrent, he tried to claw his way to the window.

Jaeger cut the water cannon and the prisoner collapsed, chest pounding, twisted glasses two feet from his outflung hand.

Russ yanked him up by a limp arm; the man staggered and straightened, peering about.

"He wants his glasses," Pete said, bending over to retrieve the mangled antiques.

"He don't need no glasses," Russ protested, glaring down at the prisoner. The little man squinted up at him.

"Ah, what the hell—give 'em to him, then." Russ pushed the prisoner toward the desk as Pete approached.

"Mr. Jaeger?" he ventured, struck by an idea.

"Well?"

"If this ain't O'Grady, how come the water didn't loose the makeup or whatever?" To illustrate, Pete grabbed a handful of sandy curls and yanked. The little man winced.

"Surgery?" Jaeger said. "Implants? Injections and skintuning? It's not important. What's important—to him and to us—is that the readout says he's a geek. Terry O'Grady was no geek, that's for sure." He turned his attention to the prisoner, who was trying to dry his glasses with the tail of his saturated shirt.

"Well, Mr. O'Grady? What's it going to be? A quick talk or a slow death?"

There was a silence in which Pete tried to ignore the pounding of his heart. This was a part of the job that he didn't like at all.

The little man moved, diving sideways, twisting away from Russ and dodging Skipper and Sam. He hurled a chair into Pete's shins and flung himself back toward the desk. Sam got a hand on him and was suddenly airborne as the little man threw his ruined glasses at Jaeger and jumped for the window.

Jaeger caught the glasses absently, standing behind his desk and roaring. The former prisoner danced between Russ and Skipper, then jumped aside, causing them to career into each other. He was through the window before Pete caught the smell of acronite and spun toward the hallway.

The explosion killed Jaeger and flung Pete an extra dozen feet toward safety.

CHAPTER TWO

Dripping, he kept to back streets, passing silently through the deepest shadows. Sirens shrilled distantly in the west, but he had not seen a police car for several blocks.

He ghosted down a side street and vanished into a dark vestibule. Two minutes later he opened the door to his apartment.

The telltales had not been altered, and the little man relaxed minutely. The landlord had seen nothing odd in his story of needing a place for "an occasional night out, for when a man wants a little variety." He'd been more interested in the prospect of earning a few untaxed bits.

The lights came up as the man crossed into the bedroom. He pulled the shirt over his head, unlaced the belt from his waist, and headed for the bathroom.

He let the water run in the shower as he stripped off boots and trousers. Naked and shivering slightly, he opened the box by the sink and fished out three vials.

The Loop showed a gratifying .9 on the CPS now that the mission was a success. He sighed and upped the odds by opening the first vial.

He worked the smelly purple goo into his sandy curls, wincing when he pulled knots, nose wrinkled in protest. Carefully, he coated both eyebrows and resealed the tube with relief.

He looked at the second vial with loathing. Leaning toward the mirror, he stared into the wintery blue eyes beneath the purple eyebrows for a dozen heartbeats before taking up the dropper-topped bottle and reluctantly breaking the seal. He administered two quick drops to each eye, hand steady, breath hissing between his teeth.

Tears ran down his cheeks as he counted and blinked. After his vision cleared, he bent to the mirror again, reaching a probing finger into his mouth. From inside each cheek came a curve of flexible material; he worked the caps from his teeth and spat them out before beginning on the brace that had squared his chin. That out, he gingerly adjusted ears and nose, pleased to see the normal shapes reappear.

He carried the last vial into the shower with him. The contents of this were green and sticky and even more foul smelling than the other chemicals. He rubbed the goo over every bit of skin, trying not to breathe as he coated his face. On the count of five he stepped into the dash of steaming water, gasping at the ache in cheeks, chin, and nose.

Ten minutes later he was toweling himself dry: a slender young man with straight dark hair and green eyes set deep in a high-cheeked, golden face. He finger-combed his hair and went quickly into the bedroom, shoulders level, carriage smooth and easy.

He dressed in dark leather trousers and vest, cloth shirt, and high, soft boots; ran the wide belt around his waist and checked the holstered pellet gun. The most important blade he slid into his left sleeve; the throwing knife went into the sheath at the back of his neck. The belt pouch contained sufficient funds and convincing papers; he snapped it shut and looked around.

Terrence O'Grady's papers and the depleted chemicals were disposed of with a hand incinerator. He bundled up the used clothing, but a wary glance at the smoke detector convinced him to dispose of the clothing differently.

Another quick tour of the tiny apartment satisfied him that all was in order. It was time to move on, if he intended to catch the late shuttle to Prime Station.

He dropped tenbit on the counter for the landlord to find, gathered up his bundle of clothes, and turned out the lights.

Three blocks closer to the Port he stepped firmly through a pool of light, to all appearances a night-guard or a shuttle-ape on his way to work. The clothes had been scattered in three separate alleys, and he felt confident that, on such a world as Lufkit, they would not remain ownerless long.

The night was very quiet; the street he walked, empty. Abruptly, he chose a side street. His hunch had it that things were unnaturally quiet in the area. Noting that the vehicle parked at the far end of the street bore a strong resemblance to a police cruiser, he melted into the shadows and turned down the next alley, striking diagonally for the Port.

The way was twisty and unlit, the glow from the Port cut off by towering warehouses. Relying on his ears and an excellent sense of place, the little man proceeded soundlessly, if not quickly.

He froze at the first sound of pellet fire, sorting echoes and waiting for a repeat. It came. There was more than one shot: a fusillade, coupled with shouts. He drifted toward the ruckus, hand on gun.

The alley twisted once more and widened into bright spaciousness, showing him a loading dock and five well-armed persons protected behind shipping containers and handtrucks. Before the dock a red-haired woman held a gun to the throat of a Terran, using his body as a shield between herself and the five others.

"Please guys," the hostage yelled hoarsely. "I'll give you my share—I swear it! Just do like she—"

One of those behind the containers shifted; the hostage stiffened with a throttled gasp, and the woman dropped him, diving for the scant cover of a wooden crate. Pellets splintered it, and she rolled away, the fleeing hostage forgotten, as one of the five rose for a clear shot.

The little man's gun spat once, and the assassin slumped over his erstwhile concealment, weapon sliding from dead fingers.

"Over there!" one of the hidden men screamed. "There's someone—"

A pellet whined over the little man's shoulder and he jumped for cover, swearing alike at reactions and hunches. At the dock, the woman had come to her feet, accounting for another of her opponents with casual efficiency. The little man found himself the recipient of an assassin's sole attention and calmly put three holes through the container sheltering her. There was a scream—and then nothing.

Suddenly, the two remaining assassins were up, rushing the red-haired woman and firing wildly. She dodged behind a container and fired, but they came on, though a red stain had appeared on the lead man's sleeve.

The little man took careful aim. The leader dropped. Half a heartbeat later, the woman's shot accounted for the last of the five.

Warily, the man came out from his cover, beginning to salute the woman.

The blow that knocked him unconscious took him entirely by surprise.

One had gotten away, which was not good.

The red-haired woman came back down the alley and stooped to run probing fingers over the dark head and touch the pulse at the base of the slim throat. She froze, counting the rhythm for a full minute, then settled back on her heels, hands hanging loosely between her knees.

"Ahhh, damn."

She stared at the dark lump of the stranger, willing him to come to, pick up his gun, and go away.

No luck today, Robertson, she said to herself. Man saved your life. You gonna leave him here?

Cursing herself for a seven-times fool she scooped up the fallen weapon and stashed it in her belt. Then she bent to get a grip on the stranger and heaved.

Thank the gods for robot cabs, she thought sometime later, letting her burden slide to the shattered tile floor. Thanks be, too, for sheer, dumb luck—the street had been empty when the cab pulled up, and had remained empty while she maneuvered the man's body across the walk and into the building.

She sighed now, stretching back and shoulder muscles and acknowledging in advance the stiffness she'd feel tomorrow. She hadn't expected such a little guy to weigh so much, though at that he was bigger than she was. *Everybody* was bigger than she was.

Bending, she worked the catch on the man's pouch and pulled out a sheaf of papers. She whistled soundlessly at the verification of the obvious and refolded the sheaf, eyes on his unconscious face.

She saw high cheeks curving smoothly to a pointed chin, a generous mouth, straight brows above the shuttered eyes, thick, glossy hair tumbling across a smooth golden forehead—a boy's face, though the papers claimed thirty Standards for him. Liaden citizen. Damn, damn, damn.

She replaced the papers and snapped the pouch, then moved a safe distance away, folded her legs, and sat on the floor. Absently, she unpinned the braid wrapped around her head and began to unweave it, eyes sharp on the still figure of the man.

Very likely, he told himself, your skull is broken. More likely, his money was gone, as well as his gun and his knives—which was a damned nuisance. If his Middle River blade were lost, he'd have a hard tale to tell. Still, he thought, keeping his eyes closed, having a chance to wake up is more luck than a man with a broken skull and no brains at all should expect.

He opened his eyes.

"Hi there, thrill-seeker."

She was sitting cross-legged on the blasted tiles, weaving her copper-colored hair into one long braid. Her leathers were dark, like his own; her white shirt was loosely laced with silver cord. A black scarf was tied around one forearm, and the gun strapped to her thigh looked acceptably deadly.

She grinned. "How's the brain-box?"

"I'll live." He sat up slowly, noting with surprise that the knife was still in his sleeve.

"Interesting theory."

He regarded her blandly, noting the set of her shoulders and the deceptively gentle motion of her hands as she braided her hair, and recalling her efficiency during the fire-fight. The Loop indicated that he could take her—if he had to. But he'd have to kill her to be sure; she meant business, and no simple rush to disable would suffice.

He let the calculation fade, mildly astonished to find that he was disinclined to kill her.

Sighing aloud, he crossed his legs in deliberate reflection of her pose and rested his arms along his thighs.

She grinned again. "Tough guy." It seemed a term of admiration. She finished her braid, put a knot at the end, and flipped the length behind her shoulder, one slender hand coming to rest on her gun.

"So, tell me, tough guy, what's your name, what're you doing here, who do you work for?" She tipped her head, unsmiling. "Count of ten."

He shrugged. "My name is Connor Phillips, Cargo Master, formerly of free-trader *Salene*. Presently I am between berths."

She laughed, slid the gun free, and thumbed the safety.

"I got a weakness for a pretty face," she said gently, "so I'm gonna let you try it again. But this time you tell me the truth, tough guy, or I blow the face to the fourteen prime points and you along with it. Accazi?"

He nodded slowly, eyes on hers.

"Go."

"My name—" He stopped, wondering if the blow to the head had scrambled his brain. The hunch was so strong...

"My name is Val Con yos'Phelium. I am an agent for Liad. I am here because I have recently finished an assignment and was hurrying to catch the shuttle when I happened by a loading dock where there was a lone woman and some others having a disagreement." He lifted an eyebrow. "I assume the shuttle has lifted?"

"Quarter hour ago." She stared at him, gray eyes expressionless. "An agent for Liad?"

He sighed and tipped his hands out, palms up, in his own gesture. "I think you might call me a spy."

"Oh." She thumbed the safety, slid the gun back home, and nodded at him. "I like that one. I like it a lot." Yanking his weapon from her belt, she threw it to him, then jerked her head at the door. "Beat it."

His left hand flashed out, snagging the gun. As he slipped it into its holster, he shook his head.

"Not a return introduction? Who you are, what you do, for whom?" He smiled suddenly. "The headache I suffer for you…"

She pointed at the door. "Scram. Get out. Begone. Leave." The gun was back in her hand. "Last chance."

He bowed his head and came to his feet with swift fluidity—to find her standing, her gun steady on his gut.

A most business-like lady, indeed, he thought with a smile. "You wouldn't have a shuttle schedule, perhaps? My information seems out of date."

She frowned. "No. Just get moving, tough guy. Schedule's carried in every infobooth in this rathole." The gun moved infinitesimally toward the door. "I'm tired of your company, accazi?"

"I understand," he murmured. He bowed as between equals. Then he was through the door and out, seeking location, listening to the night.

In a moment he had his bearings; the heavy glow to the—east, it was—that was the shuttleport. It was rather farther away than it had been before he'd taken his impromptu nap; he thought he was close to the area where Terrence O'Grady had rented his second apartment.

The sounds from behind the door spoke of someone efficiently in motion. He recognized the movement pattern of a person with no time to waste, acting with rapid. purposeful calm, and his respect for the red-haired woman increased.

He turned his attention to the street. Halfway down the block two men stood beneath a street lamp, heads together. From the breezeway to his right came the sound of two unhurried sets of footsteps: friends strolling.

He left his shadowed wall and went down the street at a brisk walk, a man with a destination, but without urgency.

The men under the streetlight seemed to be discussing the betting on a sporting event, comparing official odds against their own notions. He passed with barely a glance, heading for the blue glow of an infobooth at the end of the block. Another pair of companions passed him, walking arm-in-arm toward the building he'd recently left.

He went on, and presently his ears told him that a set of quiet footsteps paced his own silent ones. The Loop flickered into being, diagramming the chances of an imminent attack—.98 surety. His outlook for survival over the next ten minutes was .91.

The infobooth loomed to his right, its blue dome light making garish ghosts in the evening mist. He turned firmly in that direction, quickening his pace. The escorting steps quickened, as well, attempting to overtake him.

He reached the door and fumbled with the catch. A hand fell on his shoulder and he allowed himself to be spun around. His hands moved with deadly precision.

The man dropped without a sound. Val Con went to one knee, made sure that the neck had broken, and was on his feet, running back the way he had come.

He streaked by the abandoned streetlight and dived for the deeper shadow the light created, smelling clean night air and a touch of heavy cologne.

They were grouped in a rough semicircle before the building, emulating the approach that had been so disastrous earlier. One pair was near the fence by the alley, while three more stood wide, farther from the light. The shifting shadow of the man who wore cheap cologne was at the door itself, in position to either slay her as she left, or surprise her if she ran.

Val Con did not think she would run.

He dropped to one knee, waiting for the watchers to take action, hoping that the woman had anticipated this much trouble and prepared another exit. Perhaps she was already in another safe place and would laugh if she knew he had returned.

Would she have sent him out to die—to be a diversion while she escaped? He wondered and then forgot, for the door opened and she stepped out.

He flashed to his feet, running soundlessly.

She closed the door and the assassin in the shadows moved. Something—a noise? a motion in the dim light? a thought?—betrayed him an instant too soon and she dove, hitting the ground on her shoulder and rolling. Her gun flashed up too late. The man was nearly on top of her—

He gasped, dropping his weapon and clutching at his throat with clawed hands as she continued her roll, gun coughing twice in quick succession, counting a pair of slow-moving men among the dead. Distantly, she heard three sharp cracks and knew without doubt that three more lay dead nearby.

To the right, two dead; to the left, three huddled lifelessly against a fence as a fourth stood upright, hands held out at waist level, palms toward her.

She stood warily in the shocking quiet and motioned him over with a wave of her gun.

"Hey, tough guy." Her voice was a raspy whisper.

He came, hands empty at his sides, and walked within grabbing distance. She stepped back, then laughed and took a half-step toward him.

"Thanks," she said, and her voice was stronger. She slid her gun away and nodded at the single assassin.

"What's with him? Thought for sure he had me. Then he just falls over!"

Val Con moved past her and knelt by the dead man, avoiding the pooling blood. She came and stood by his shoulder, bending forward with interest.

He turned the man over and pulled the hands from the sticky throat.

"Knife," he murmured, slipping it from its nesting place and wiping it clean on the dead man's shirt.

"Not even a laserblade," she said, wondering. "Unusual toy, ain't it?"

He shrugged and slid the blade into its neck sheath.

She wrinkled her nose at the dead man. "Messy." She felt him tense beside her and shot a glance at his face. "More company?"

"You seem to be a popular young lady." He offered her his arm. "I suggest you have dinner with me," he said, smiling. "We can lose them."

She sighed, ignoring his arm. "Right. Let's move."

A moment later the dead had the street to themselves.

CHAPTER THREE

The bargrill was near the shuttleport, a smoky, noisy place crowded with grease-apes, shuttle-toughs, fuelies, and any number of local street-livers. Two women played guitars, providing music of the driving, inane variety and eating and drinking their wages between sets.

The red-haired woman settled a little more comfortably against the wall, hands curved around a warmish mug of local coffeetoot, watching her companion watch the crowd. They had arrived here via the appropriation of three robot cabs, as well as several private cars. As self-appointed lookout, she was sure they'd lost their pursuers, but apparently the man beside her was taking no chances.

"Now," he murmured, eyes on the room, "you may begin by telling me your name, and continue down the list."

She was silent, drinking 'toot, and he turned to look at her, his face smooth, green eyes expressionless. She sighed and looked away.

Two fuelies were rolling dice at a corner table. She watched the throw absently, automatically counting the sides as they flashed.

"Robertson," she said in a cracking whisper. She cleared her throat. "Miri Robertson. Retired mercenary soldier; unemployed bodyguard." She flicked her eyes back to his face. "Sorry 'bout the bother." Then she paused and sighed again, because this was much harder to say—something she did not say often. "Thanks for the help. I needed it."

"So it seemed," he agreed in his accentless Terran. "Who wishes you dead?"

She waved a hand. "Lots of people, it seems."

The green eyes were back on hers. "No."

"No?"

A muscle twitched near the corner of his mouth. He stilled it and resumed his constant survey of the bar.

"No," he said softly. "You are not stupid. I am not stupid. Hence you must find another way to lie to me. Or," he added, as one being fair, "you might tell the truth."

"Now why would I do that?" she wondered and drank some more of the dreadful 'toot.

He sighed. "You owe me a debt, I think?"

"I knew you were gonna bring that up! You can forget that stuff right now, spacer. *You're* the Liaden in this skit. Terrans don't count coup."

She almost missed his start; she snapped her eyes to his face, only to find him expressionless, watching the patrons of the bar.

"What?" she demanded.

"It's nothing." He shifted his shoulders against the wall. "A better reason, then. Whoever wishes to kill you most likely has us linked by now, and so hunts us both. Is my new enemy one individual with the means to buy service? Or a group, most of whom we have dispatched already? Can I safely go off-planet, or will I find assassins around my Clan fire when I return home?" He paused. "Your danger is my danger. Your information may save my life. I wish to stay alive. It is dishonorable for a soldier not to know the enemy!" He turned his head to look at her, one eyebrow askance. "Is that reason sufficient?"

"Sufficient." She drank off the rest of the 'toot and set the mug on the table. Eyes on the cracked blue plastic, she resettled against the wall.

"Half a Standard ago I left the Merc," she began, voice perfectly even. "Felt like I wanted to settle down, I guess, learn about one world…relax…Got a job as a bodyguard on this place called Naome. Lot of rich paranoid types go there to retire. All of 'em got bodyguards. Status symbol.

"Anyhow, I was hired the third day on the Lists by a man who called himself Baldwin. Sire Baldwin. Paid me three months in advance. To demonstrate good faith." She shook her head.

"He needed help, okay. I worked for him five—six local months. Used to wonder once in awhile what he used to do that made him need so much protection now…"

She let her voice drift off as the waiter came and refilled the cups, hers with more 'toot, Val Con's with tea.

"And?" he prompted as soon as the waiter was away.

She shrugged. "Turned out Sire Baldwin had been somebody else before. Somebody who'd worked for the Juntavas. You savvy the Juntavas, tough guy?"

"Interplanetary crime net," he murmured, eyes on the room. "Drugs, gambling, prostitution, contraband." He flicked his eyes to her face. "Bad trouble."

"You're the one wanted to know."

"Yes. What happened next?"

"He got tired of the work, I guess. Resigned without paying his severance money. Took some cash and some confidential info— guess a man's gotta eat..."

"It was the people from his old unit I'd been protecting him from. They'd tracked him down and were asking for 'restitution.'" She took a swallow of 'toot that she didn't want, then shook her head.

"Baldwin told 'em to come ahead, that he was tired of hiding out and wanted to make everything square. He invited 'em to come to the house on Naome."

She paused, staring into the depths of the mug.

The pause lengthened. Stifling an impulse to touch her shoulder, Val Con tried a soft "And?" When a second "And?" brought no response, he snapped his voice like fingers in her face.

"Miri!"

She started and looked at him, face wry. "It was a doublecross. A bamboozle. Baldwin called the house staff together, from the cook to the upstairs maid. Told us we were being invaded. That we'd have to fight.

"The whole staff fought—and most of 'em had never carried a gun before! We refused Baldwin's buddies entrance, and when they insisted, we insisted right back. Bad, seeing untrained people fight that way...When it was sure we couldn't hold it, I went off loyally looking for my boss so I could perform my last duty—I *was* his bodyguard, wasn't I?" She shrugged and drank some 'toot.

Val Con looked at her.

"Don't you see? Gone. Bolted. Flew the coop. Left us to fight and die. I *think* five of us got away. Means fourteen didn't. Gardener didn't. Maids didn't. Cook—I don't know. He looked pretty bad, last time I saw him." She moved her shoulders again in a gesture that was not quite a shrug.

"Don't know who else they might've tracked down, but I was his bodyguard, all legal and certified and recorded. Took 'em about two hours to get on my trail."

She looked hard at nothing for a couple of minutes, then took another slug of her drink. "I came here 'cause there's a man who owes me money and a friend who's keeping some—things— for me. I better take everything. Not sure I'll get back in this Quarter again..."

The man beside her was quiet. She relaxed deliberately, her thoughts touching people she'd known as she sipped the 'toot for something to do and wondered where she might spend the night, now that she had one to spend.

The bench creaked, and she looked up into decisive green eyes.

"You come with me," he said in the tone of someone who has weighed odds and reached a decision.

"I do what?"

He was fishing in his pouch. "You come with me. You will need new papers, a new name, a new face. These will be provided." He raised a hand to cut off protest.

"Liadens count coup, remember? The debt runs in two directions."

He scattered a handful of Terran bits on the table to pay for the meal, then rose and moved off, not waiting to see if she followed.

After a moment, she did.

The cab deposited them before a modestly lit whitestone building in the affluent side of town. The door to the lobby swung open on silent hinges, and Val Con moved across a wilderness of Percanian carpet, his reflection keeping pace in the mirrored walls.

Miri paused just inside the door, mistrusting the light. Cursing herself for more of a fool, she set off across the carpet and arrived at her companion's shoulder as he removed his finger from the keyslot and said "Connor Phillips" into the receptionist's mike.

The desk hummed as a slot slid open and a large, ornate key emerged. Val Con crooked his left index finger in the loop and half-smiled at her.

"Two floors up," he murmured, moving toward the bank of sliding doors.

Miri trailed by half a pace, letting him summon the lift, enter it before her, and exit the same way when it stopped.

This hall was somewhat dimmer than the lobby and he paused, listening, she thought, before moving on. His head swung to the left and to the right, some of the tension leaving his shoulders as he used the ridiculous key on the second door on the left.

The door sighed open and lights came up in the room beyond as they stepped through. Miri stopped just over the threshold, hand dropping to her gun.

The door sighed shut behind her.

Halfway into the room, the man turned to look at her, one eyebrow raised, empty palms up. "I won't hurt you." He dropped his hands. "I'm too tired."

She stayed where she was, surveying the room.

Before her, a large double window showed the city night; a pillowed couch sat to one side, opposite two soft chairs and a table. To her right was an omnichora, its keyboard covered against dust. Beyond that, surrounding a closed door, were floor-to-ceiling shelves lined with tape boxes, and a comm unit—an oasis of practicality.

To her left were more shelves, filled with tape boxes interrupted here and there with figurines and bric-a-brac. Beyond the unit bar and its two upholstered stools was another closed door, and past that, through an elliptical archway, she caught the shine of kitchen tile.

"Pretty fancy for a cargo master."

He shrugged. "It was a profitable ship."

"Um." She gestured vaguely behind her. "That the only way out?"

He tipped his head at the windows, moved to the right, pulled open the door, and waved her inside.

A bedroom—with a sleeping platform adequate for the demands of a small orgy—connected to a bathroom that included wet and dry cleaning options and a valet for care of clothes. There were no windows.

She stepped out and the man guided her across the central room to the second door and a suite that was a mirror twin to the right-hand bedroom.

In the kitchen there was a small, high window, and another door.

"Beyond is a service corridor, which empties into another, which ends in a staircase, which—"

"Gets me to the cellar?" she guessed.

He smiled, moving back into the big room. "Would you like something to drink?"

"Would I. And then a shower. And then about twelve hours' sleep. Or maybe sleep and then shower—kynak," she said to his lifted brows, naming the mercenary soldier's drink.

He frowned at the display. "The bar appears to be understocked," he apologized. "I can offer Terran Scotch?"

"Scotch?" she repeated, voice keying upward.

He nodded, and she sat gently on one of the stools.

"Scotch'll be fine," she told him. "Don't put ice in it. A religious experience shouldn't be diluted."

He punched the button, then handed her a heavy glass half full of amber liquid.

Eyes closed, she sipped—and was utterly still before exhaling a sigh of soul-satisfaction.

Val Con grinned and punched in his own selection.

"What's that?" Her eyes were open again.

He swirled the pale blue liquid in the delicately-stemmed goblet. "Altanian wine—misravot."

"Limited selection on this model, ain't it?"

"It's not so bad, for a rental unit."

"Well," she conceded, playing it straight, "but when you go to buy, remember it's things like these cut-rate bars they try to stick you with every time. Put 'deluxe' on it in gold letters and stock it with grain alcohol."

"I will remember," he promised solemnly, moving around the bar and heading for the window. He stopped before he got there, settling instead into a corner of the couch and nearly sighing as the cushions molded themselves to his body. He sipped wine and *did* sigh. His head hurt abominably.

Miri moved behind him. He let his head fall back on the cushion. Glass in hand, she bypassed the couch at a cautious distance, circled the chairs, and approached the window from the side. Standing back, she looked out at the street, now and then tossing Scotch down her throat with well-practiced smoothness.

Tired, he thought suddenly. No way to know how long she's been running. And I'm too tired for any more questions. He half-closed his eyes. The effort of trusting another person was not best made in the teeth of headaches and exhaustion.

She turned from the window, surprise flickering over her face as she saw him lounging half-asleep on the cushions, long lashes shielding green eyes, throat exposed.

She sees me vulnerable, he thought, and the phrase struck something within his aching skull. He moved his head and opened his eyes.

"I'm beat," she said quietly. "Where's to sleep?"

He waved a hand. "Choose."

After a moment, she nodded and went off to the right. As she reached the bedroom door, she turned back to look at him.

"Good night." She was gone before he could reply.

He sighed as the door closed, and took a deeper sip of wine. He should go to sleep, as well.

Instead, he snapped to his feet and moved to the window as a free man would, gazing out as if he were safe and had no enemies to watch for.

The street was brightly lit and empty; a fledgling breeze tossed an occasional bit of plastic trash about.

It's good, he thought, that this place has not been found. I need a rest, need not to be O'Grady or Phillips or whoever. I need time to be—me.

He raised a hand to comb fingers through the lock that fell across his forehead, and in a moment of aching clarity recognized the gesture as one of his own. Unexpectedly, the Loop loomed in his vision, blocking out the street before him. CMS was .96. CPS flickered and danced, then flashed a solid .89 the instant before it faded away.

He swallowed wine and again stroked hair away from his eyes. Val Con yos'Phelium, Clan Korval; adopted of the Clan of Middle River...He thought every syllable of his Middle River name, as if it were a charm to hold thoughts at bay.

The face of Terrence O'Grady's wife intruded, sharpening and fading to the echo of the battering music from the bar he and Miri Robertson had been in.

He drank the rest of the wine in a snap that did it no justice. How many faces had he memorized, how many men had he been, in the last three Standards? How many gestures had he learned and then cast off, along with the names and faces of lovers, parents, children, and pets?

How many people had he killed?

He tuned sharply from the window, moving blindly across the room, seeking the omnichora.

The light on the keyboard came up as he touched the pressure plate. He found the echo of the bar music in his head, picked it up in his fingers, and threw it into the 'chora with a will, driving out the face of the woman who was not *his* wife and replacing it with the vision of the song.

His fingers fluttered up and down the scales an instant, then found the harsh beat again and filled the room with it, the sound echoing in his throbbing head. His hands fumbled, then recovered. He captured the rhythm with his right hand and began to weave melody around it with his left. He increased the tempo, found a suggestion of an older rhythm, moved into that *there*...

His right hand left the beat for a moment, switching stops and ranges, intensifying sound. The images drew back from him. The names of the dead he'd known and the faces of those who'd died nameless lay back down, battered into restless submission, into uneasy sleep, by the force of the music.

There came another recognition, almost lost in the music's swirl: *this* was a talent that belonged to Val Con yos'Phelium, learned and nurtured from joy, not from need.

The driving beats slowed into others; he played what his fingers found and realized that he was playing a lament from a planet he had visited in his early Scouting days. He added to it; he dropped it to its sparest bones, and slowed it even more. He reached an end of it and found that his hands had stopped.

The sound remained in the room for a few moments more as the 'chora slowly let the dirge go, then he dropped his head against the stopfascia, drained. Emotionless.

Bed, he thought with crystal clarity. Rest. Go now.

He stood and she was there, the stranger who had saved his life, standing at the open door to the bedroom, red hair loose, vest and gun gone, shirt unlaced. Her gray eyes regarded him straightly. He did not recognize the expression on her face.

She bowed slightly, hands together in the Terran mode.

"Thank you," she said, and bowed again, turning quickly to enter her room.

"You're welcome," he said, but the door was closed.

He walked carefully across the room to the second closed door. He did not remember passing through or lying down to sleep.

CHAPTER FOUR

Miri woke and stretched slowly, eyes focusing on the clock across the room. Ten hours and change had passed since she'd lain down to sleep. Not too bad. She rolled out and headed for the shower.

Half an hour later, sun-dried and refreshed, she pulled her gun from beneath the pillow, slipped it into the deep pocket of the coverall the valet had supplied, and went in search of protein, carbohydrates, and ideas.

What she found first in the kitchen was coffee! Brewed from real Terran bean, this beverage sat steaming at her right hand as she ordered food and then dialed up the mid-morning local news on the screen set into the table.

The lead story bored her. Something about an explosion at local Terran Party headquarters. One man killed, two injured, one Terrence O'Grady sought in the apparent bombing. An image of O'Grady appeared—it bored her, too, and she hit the REMOVE key in search of something useful.

Transport crash. No lives lost. Robotics Commission to convene today...REMOVE, she said to herself and punched the key.

She took a sip of coffee, savoring it as much as she had the previous night's liquor. Some people get the right jobs, she thought. Scotch and coffee...

She canceled three more articles in rapid succession, then paused to scan the brief story about six bodies found in an alley in the warehouse district. Juntavas work, police speculated.

A little farther on she stopped the text to read about a rash of vehicle thefts, including four robot cabs. All the cabs had been found in a lot at the spaceport, engines running, memories wiped. She smiled—he hadn't told her where he'd sent them—and hit REMOVE. The paper scrolled across the screen, through Obits and into Classified, as she continued with breakfast.

Juntavas work.

It was unfortunate that anyone had connected the incident to the Juntavas. If she'd been found dead by herself, it would just have been an unsolved murder. Something was going to have to be done about her not being found dead in the near future.

The tough guy seemed to think he had the pat answer for that. A quick and total overhaul, courtesy of Liad: new papers, new name, new face, new life. Good-bye Miri Robertson. Hello—well, did it matter?

Somehow, she admitted to herself, it does. She finished her coffee, leaned to place the cup on the table, and froze, eyes snagging on a familiar phrase.

Wanted: CARGO MASTER. Expd only, bckgrd with exotic handcrafts, perfumes, liqueurs, xenonarcotics. Apply Officer of the Day, Free Trader *Salene.* No xenophobes, no narcoholics, no politicians. Bring papers. All without papers stay home.

She was still staring at the screen when Val Con entered the kitchen a full two minutes later.

"Good morning," he told her, moving to the chef panel and making a selection.

Miri leaned back in the chair, eyes on the screen. "Hey, you. Tough Guy."

He came to her elbow. Without looking up, she waved her hand at the ad. Arm brushing hers, he bent forward to see, exhaling softly as he straightened, his breath shivering the gossamer hairs at her temple. He sat on the edge of the table and took a sip of milk, swinging one leg carelessly off the floor. She noted that the pockets of his coverall were flat. Gunless.

He raised an eyebrow.

She hit the table with her fist, clattering the empty coffee cup, and glared up at him.

"Who *are* you? The question was gritted out against clenched teeth. She felt her heart pounding and forced herself to relax back into the chair.

He drank some milk, his eyes steady on her face. "My name is Val Con yos'Phelium, Second Speaker for Clan Korval. I work as an agent of change. A spy."

She pointed at the screen. "And that?"

He shrugged "A tissue of lies tears much too easily. There must be meat and bone beneath." He paused to sip his milk. "I came to this world as Cargo Master on *Salene.* My papers said I was Connor Phillips, citizen of Kiang. When *Salene* took orbit, Connor Phillips had an argument with the Chief Petty Officer and as a result of this sudden feud tendered his resignation, effective off-loading of all local cargo. In the meantime, for the sake of ship's morale, he rented this place while he searched for a more convivial berth. And so we have this comfortable refuge in a time of stress." He offered her a smile. "Not too bad a sort, Master Phillips."

She closed her eyes. Every time you get the world by the tail, she thought, you gotta remember there's teeth on the other end.

"Where'd a spy learn to play the 'chora like that?"

His brows twitched together in surprise, and he answered carefully. "My kinswoman, Anne Davis, taught me. It gave her joy to see that I had the talent, when none of her own children did."

"Your *kinswoman.*" She wasn't sure she'd meant it as a question, but he answered it.

"Yes. My—is it aunt? The wife of my father's brother?"

"Aunt," she agreed, puzzled by this lapse in his smooth command of Terran.

"More," he said thoughtfully. "She was my—foster-mother. After my mother died I went into her home, was raised with her children."

"Is this any more—or less—real than Connor Phillips?" she demanded. "Do you really know who you are?"

He looked at her closely. "If you are asking if I'm insane, which of the answers I may give will comfort you more? I know who I am, and I have told you. Even when I am on assignment, I know who I really am."

"Do you? That's comforting." She said it without conviction, aware that she was tensing up again.

"Have you a problem, Miri Robertson?"

"Yeah. I do. The problem is that I don't know why you're helping me. Your logic don't hold up. If you *were* Connor Phillips, why can't you *be* him again, find a ship, and go away? You can get out of it! The Juntavas don't know who you are—what kind of description can they have? That you're short? Skinny? Dark?" She moved her shoulders to throw off some of the tension.

"The clincher is that you're with me. Without me they look—" She spread her arms. "—and they look away."

The equation had formed in his head, showing him how he might get away, her death balancing his escape. She knew much about him and could be a danger. In fact, he thought, if I—no! He forced the Loop back and down, refusing to know how useful she would be, dead.

Setting his empty glass aside, he began to read the breakfast selections.

She studied his profile, but saw nothing more than polite interest in the information imparted by the selection grid.

"Well?" she demanded.

He lifted a slender hand to select an egg dish, then glanced at her. "I think that last night's reasoning is sound. The Juntavas may have an imperfect description of me. Or they may have a photo image. I cannot afford to ignore that possibility."

Another equation showed itself, this one concerning not her death, but her betrayal. It noted that it was an approximation; the odds were good that her life would buy his own from the Juntavas.

The long lashes dropped over his eyes and he turned back to the panel, choosing hot bread and a fruit. Gathering the plates from the dispenser, he moved back to the table and took the seat across from Miri.

She got up silently, selected a slightly stronger brew of Terran coffee, and returned to her chair.

"So where does that leave me? Instead of wanted by the Juntavas, I'm a political prisoner of Liad, right?"

He shook his head, attention seemingly more than half occupied by slicing a ripe strafle into two equal portions. He offered her half. When she made no move to take it, he placed it on the table by her hands.

"Where does that leave things?" she insisted, an edge in her voice.

"I think," he replied, swallowing a mouthful of eggs, "that it leaves things where they were in the beginning. We are thrown together. We wish to live. Already each of us has brought something useful to the task of surviving. If we are fortunate, we shall live through the experience. In fact, we make our own fortune simply by doing what must be done, as it needs to be done."

He took a bite of bread, frowned as he reached for the glass that wasn't there, and combed a hand through his forelock, sighing.

"Mutual survival being the goal, I think you should tell me about these people—the man who owes you money and the friend who keeps your things—so that we may plan usefully."

He pushed back his chair and went to ask the chef for more milk.

Miri drank coffee, acutely aware of the weight of the gun in her pocket. She understood about mutual survival: it was why so many of the Gyrfalks had partners. Trust wasn't something that came easily to her; still it was obvious that her companion knew what he was doing in a tight spot.

"Okay," she said slowly. "The man who owes me money—that's Murph. Angus G. Murphy. The third. He was in my unit in the Merc. Decided he couldn't take all the killing." She smiled at the man across from her. "Thought there'd be lots of glory and romance. Anyhow, he wanted out, and it was safer to have him out, if he felt that way about it."

Val Con ate, watching her face as she spoke.

"So, I lent him most of his severance money," Miri continued, "with the understanding that he'd pay it back with interest in three Standards. Been damn near four."

She leaned farther back in the chair, leaving the untouched fruit between them like a challenge. He did not appear to see it.

"Murph is recalcitrant?"

"Absent," she corrected. "Address listed in the poploc. Nobody home." She shook her head. "I didn't have time to buttonhole all the neighbors. Somehow, from the way I remembered him, I figured he'd be home." She sipped her coffee.

"The friend who's keeping my things is Liz. Friend of my mother's, first. Lives closer to where we met than where we are now. Plan is to call her, make sure she's home and gonna stay there so I can drop by and pick up my box."

"And then pursue the search for the absent Murph?"

"Say!" she said, opening her eyes wide and smiling. "You've got almost as many smarts as a *real* person!"

To her surprise, he laughed—a sound oddly at variance with his tightly controlled face and unemphatic voice. There was *joy* in his laugh. Miri filed that information away with the echoes of the music he'd pulled from the 'chora.

"The best course," he said, "is for you to call your friend Liz and explain that you will need your things. Explain also that you will not be coming yourself but will be sending an associate—"

"Wrong."

He shook his head. "Consider it. The risk is less—they *may* know me; they *do* know you. And in the time it takes me to accomplish the errand you may be profitably employed in locating Murph." He waved his hand toward the common room.

"The comm is quite adequate. The planet is at your disposal."

She stared into the dregs of her coffee, considering it. Her own life was one thing, but to gamble Liz on the feeling that an undoubtedly deadly stranger meant her well? A Liaden stranger, just for fun. Liadens were known for playing deep: it seemed a source of racial pride. Miri closed her eyes.

Judgement call, Robertson, she said to herself. You trust him at your back or you don't.

She opened her eyes. "Liz hates Liadens."

The straight brows pulled together, his mouth nearly twisted, and he thumped the half-full glass on the table.

"It seems that all the galaxy hates Liadens," he said. He pushed his chair back to balance on two legs, taking a sharp bite out of his strafle.

Somehow, that decided it. Miri rose, deposited her cup in the clean-up slot and headed to the big room.

"I'll call her," she said over her shoulder.

Liz was at home. She was also unhappy to learn that Miri would be sending her "partner," rather than coming to collect the box herself.

"Since when have you had a partner, anyway?" she wanted to know, brown eyes shrewd. "You always played single's odds."

"Times change," Miri told her, trying to sound as if they had.

Liz snorted, eyes softening. "How much trouble you in?"

"More'n last week, less than next. You know how it goes."

Liz did know; she'd been a mercenary herself, after all.

"It can stay here, you know. Might slow you down if you need to get a move on."

"That's so," Miri said. "But I'm going on the Grand Tour. No telling—"

"When you'll be back," Liz finished for her. "Okay, send your partner around. Description? Or do I just hand it over to the first slob says they're here for Redhead's box?"

She grinned. "Short, I guess. Skinny, maybe. Brown hair—

needs to be cut. Green eyes. Male." She bit her lip and looked Liz full in the face. "Liaden."

But, to Miri's surprise, Liz only nodded. "I'll be watching for him. Take care of yourself, girl." Her image faded.

Miri turned away from the comm to see Val Con behind her, positioned so that he could see the screen, yet not be seen himself. He had exchanged his coverall for dark leathers and dark shirt. A worn belt was around his waist; equally well-used boots were on his feet.

He did not appear to be armed.

Miri opened her mouth, remembered the primitive little blade that had saved her life, and closed her mouth without comment.

"Your friend expects me."

"You heard it." She hesitated. "Make sure nobody follows you there, okay? Liz and my mother…" She moved her hands, shapelessly. "Liz is all the family I got."

His smile flickered into being. "I will be careful." He gestured, enclosing the apartment in a hand-sweep.

"This is a secure place. There is no need for you to leave. No need for you to let anyone in. I let myself out and let myself back in. You are free to search for Murph via the comm. It is scrambled and traceless."

She tipped her head to one side. "You're telling me I'm safe?"

He half-smiled, shoulders dipping in a gesture she was unsure of. "Forgive me," he murmured, "but, yes, I think so."

She grinned, shaking her head as she turned back to the comm.

"Just get me that box without getting killed, okay? I'll have Murph nailed by the time you get back."

"Okay."

She turned in time to see the door to the hallway closing behind him.

The call to the residence of Mr. Angus G. Murphy III was less than satisfying. Mr. Murphy's direct-comm had been temporarily disconnected, the visual told Miri, and messages might be left at another number. She dialed that number, found it to be an answering service, and broke the blank-screen connection instantly.

"Don't call me, I'll call you," she muttered, frowning. It would be best if he didn't know she was on-world.

Well, it would have to be the neighbors, then, though she disliked that tack. With her luck, the next-door neighbor would be a local Juntavas boss, with her picture on his desk. She could blank the screen, of course, but who would give info to a blank screen?

Blank screen was out, she decided. But her own face was also out.

She snapped forward in frowning study of the commboard. Fancy, she decided, after a few minutes. Sire Baldwin had had no better in his palatial home. Leaning back and letting her eyes rest on the understated luxury of the room around her, she was reminded that money and taste were very different matters. After all, look at the lovers Baldwin would bring home.

Suddenly grinning, she bounced to her feet and ran to her sleeping quarters.

Standing before the floor-to-ceiling mirror in the valet-room, she let down her hair and combed it straight. A few moments later the valet supplied a quantity of glittering jeweled pins and nets to confine the whirls, knots, and bunches the copper-colored mass had assumed. Likewise, she obtained cosmetics, gilded earbobs, rings of eight different sizes and metals, and a necklet of glazed silver flowers.

After some thought, she decided the coverall was just right for the occasion, but she unsealed the neck seam a little farther—and a little farther again, after consulting the mirror. She grinned at her reflection, paused to add just a dash more emphasis under each eye, and headed back to the comm.

She chose a firm with its single office in the most prestigious of high-rent facilities. Setting her face into what she hoped was simpering unease, she punched up the code.

"Mylander and Zanthal Collections," the receptionist told her.

Miri stretched her mouth in a closed-lip smile. "Good afternoon," she said in her best Yark accent. "I'd like to talk to somebody about—'bout this guy, see? He owes me a bundle an' won't pay."

The receptionist blinked, then recovered. "Why, surely. I'm certain that our Mr. Farant would be delighted—"

"Naw," Miri said. "Naw. Look, honey, this is—delicate, y'know? You got a woman up there can talk to me?" She stretched her mouth into the unsmiling rictus again. "Girl stuff, honey. *You* know."

The receptionist swallowed. "Well, there *is* Ms. Mylander."

"Aw, geez," Miri protested. "Not the boss herself?"

"Not exactly," the receptionist admitted, shakily. "Ms. Susan Mylander is Ms. Lavinia Mylander's granddaughter."

"Oh! Well, hey, that's great! I'd be real pleased to have a little girl-talk with Susan, honey. You just tell her Amabel Gleason's on the screen, okay?"

"Certainly, Ms. Gleason," the receptionist said, falling back on the comforts of training. "If you'll hold just one moment—" The screen offered an abstract in soft pastels to soothe Miri's eyes while she waited. She moved a hand, pushed two keys, and settled back into an attitude of watchful expectation.

The screen cleared after a time sufficient for the receptionist to have located Ms. Mylander and imparted all the details of her caller's manner, with embellishments. Miri performed her smile for the dark young woman in sober business attire.

"Ms. Gleason?" the young woman asked. Her accent was the cultivated drawl of the elite.

Miri ducked her head. "Ms. Mylander, it really is nice of you to talk to me and everything. I just didn't know where to turn, y'know, and when that pretty young lady who answers your phone said you were in—" She fluttered her jeweled hands, rings flashing. "Some things you just *gotta* talk to another woman about."

"Indeed," the other woman said. "And just what did you wish to speak with me about, Ms. Gleason?"

"Well, Ms. Mylander. I—could I call you Susan? I mean, you're so friendly and everything—" Miri leaned forward, jumpsuit gaping.

The woman in the screen took a deep breath. "If it makes you feel better, Ms. Gleason, by all means call me Susan."

"Thanks. So, Susan, there's this guy, y'know," Miri waved her hands again, rolling her eyes. "There's always a guy, ain't there? Anyway, we date for awhile and he likes me and I like him Okay—I mean, he's got some money, an' a steady job on the shuttle as a grease-ape. Don't mind buying a girl a few presents, taking her out to nice places…" Miri shrugged, taking her time about it. "Asks me to marry him— standard hetero contract; progeny clause says he'll take care of any kids we have while we're married, even if we don't re-up." She paused.

"I am familiar with the standard co-habitation/progeny contract, Ms. Gleason. Did you sign it?"

"Well, yeah, we did. I moved into his place. 'Bout three months later, shows I'm pregnant. I figure everything's okay, 'cause of the progeny clause—" She broke off, bowing her head sharply and raising a hand to wipe at her eyes. "Bastard walked out on me."

There was a short silence. Miri raised her head again, bravely displaying her smile.

"I don't quite understand, Ms. Gleason, what this has to do with Mylander and Zanthal," Susan Mylander said with professional puzzlement.

"I'm gettin' to that," Miri said, visibly getting a grip on herself. "It's that he left. Contract had three years to run. I have the baby and he says forget it, contract's no good, 'cause it ain't his kid!"

"Is it?" Ms. Mylander asked, staring in what seemed to be fascination.

Miri wriggled her shoulders. "I *think* so. 'Course, there's a problem with it being so close to the time we signed and all. I didn't know he was gonna propose contract and—well, I ain't *dead,* y'know, Susan. An' grease-apes work the shuttle two weeks on, two weeks off."

"I'm still not sure I understand why you need a collection agency, Ms. Gleason."

"He owes me *money,*" Miri cried, voice rising. He signed a contract said he'd pay for any of his brats I had while we were married. Could've been his as much as anybody else's. An' we were *married.*" She took a deep breath and let her voice even out a little. "He owes me a bundle of cash. An' he says he won't pay. That's why I need a collection agency, Ms. Mylander. To get my money for me."

"I—see." Ms. Mylander paused. "Ms. Gleason, I'm afraid that you do not need a collection agency at this point. What I advise you to do is engage legal counsel. If you speak to a lawyer, and he deems it proper for you to bring suit against your husband for breach of contract, wins the case for you and has your husband ordered to pay you a specified sum, and if your husband then refuses to pay that sum, Mylander and Zanthal will be happy to assist you." She steepled her fingers under her chin. "You must really engage counsel first, though, Ms. Gleason, and abide by the judgment of the courts as to whether your husband is responsible for your child or is liable for voiding the contract. We are not able to help you with those matters."

"Oh," Miri said, bright mouth turning down at the corners. She forced another horrible smile, though her face was beginning to ache. "Well, that's fine, then, Susan. I know a couple lawyers. Real go-getters." She bent to the screen once more and reached out as if to touch the other woman's hand.

Ms. Mylander was made of stern stuff. She did not flinch from the impossible caress, though her mouth tightened.

"Thanks an awful lot for your help, Susan," Miri cooed, and hit DISCONNECT.

She laughed for five minutes, leaning back in the embracing cushions and howling, tears running out the corners of her made-up eyes. When she was sure she could navigate, she went to the kitchen for a cup of coffee.

Resuming her seat in front of the comm, she began to edit her tape.

Liz answered the door herself and stood looking down at him.

Val Con made the bow of youth to age, straightening to find her still frowning at him from her height.

"I am here," he said softly, "for Miri's box."

Wordless, she pulled the door wider and let him in. After making sure the locks were engaged, she led him down a short, dark hallway to a bright living room. He stood in the entranceway as she moved to what seemed the only chair—indeed the only surface— not piled high with booktapes.

"Come here, Liaden." It was a command, delivered harshly.

He made his soundless way across the room and stopped before her, hands folded loosely.

She surveyed him silently and he returned the favor, noting the dark hair shot with gray, the lines about mouth and eyes, the eyes themselves, and the chin. This was, he saw, a person used to command, who knew command as responsibility.

"You're here for Miri's box."

"Yes, Eldema," he said gently, giving her the courtesy title of the First Speaker of a Clan.

She snorted. "Tell me Liaden: Why should I trust you?"

He raised his brows. "Miri—"

"Trusts you," she cut in, "because you're beautiful. It's a fault comes with growing up where nothing's beautiful and everything's dangerous—real different from sunny Liad."

He stood at rest, waiting.

Liz moved her head sharply. "So, you grow up on a world like Surebleak, manage, somehow, to get off, finally encounter beauty. And you want to give it every chance. You don't want to believe that a pretty rat's still a rat. That it'll bite you, just as sure." She clamped her mouth into a straight line.

Val Con waited.

"I don't care if you got three heads, each one uglier than the next," she snapped. "I want to know why *I* should trust you."

He sighed. "You should trust me because Miri sent me here. You must judge whether she would do so—besotted as she must be with my beauty—were I a danger to you."

She laughed. "A little temper, is it? You'll need it." She sobered abruptly. "What kind of trouble's she in, she needs to send you at all? Why not come herself?"

"It is not the kind of trouble it is safe to know by name," he said carefully. "It is only…trouble."

"Ah. So we all get in that kind of trouble once, now, don't we?" There was no particular emphasis; he thought she spoke to herself. Yet she continued to stare at him until Val Con wondered if he *were* growing another head.

"You're going with her when she leaves? Eh? To guard her back? She called you her partner."

"Eldema, when we go, we go together. I think it very likely that we will outrun the trouble. Lose it entirely." There was no flicker of the Loop, giving the lie to this piece of optimism, for which he was grateful.

She nodded suddenly, then reached to the overflowing table at her side and produced a black lacquer box from amidst a pile of tapes. It was a double hand's width of his small hands wide and twice that long—too odd-shaped to fit comfortably into pocket or pouch.

Liz frowned and fumbled further on the table, locating a less-than-new cloth bag with a drawstring top. She slid the box inside, drew the string tight, and handed him the sealed package.

He stepped forward so claim it, slipping the string over his shoulder.

"Thank you." He bowed thanks. When it became apparent that she had no more to say to him, he turned to go.

He was nearly to the hall when she spoke. "Liaden!"

He spun in his tracks, quick and smooth. "Eldema?"

"You take care of Miri, Liaden. None of your damn tricks. You just take the best care of Miri you can, as long as you can."

He bowed. "Eldema, it is my desire to do just that."

He turned on his heel and was gone.

Liz sighed. She had had nothing else to say, except—but the girl knew that. Didn't she?

She heard him work the lock; heard the door open and close, gently.

After a while, for old times' sake, she went to make sure he'd locked the door on his way out.

Mrs. Hansforth was excited. It had been years since she'd received a ship-to communication, but still the circuit was as she remembered it: a little scratchy, with occasional odd delays and the constant feeling that the mouth wasn't quite saying what it looked like it was saying.

Of course, it was disappointing that the beam wasn't meant for her, but disappointment was outweighed by the excitement of the event and the chance to gossip.

Yes, she told the dark-haired and serious young lady in the screen, she knew Angus quite well. A nice boy, not given to wild parties or exceptional hours. And his fiancée was a lovely girl. It was really a shame he wasn't in town to receive the message himself...

Where? Oh, with the students off at the University, he and his fiancée had taken several weeks to go to Econsey. They'd wanted some time alone and hadn't had the calls forwarded. Surely, they couldn't have been expecting...

Hadn't known she was going to be in-system? Oh, such a shame...But Mrs. Hansforth got no further; after all, this was ship-to, and such things were fabulously expensive. The serious young lady said something about some research Angus had done in his traveling days. Well!

Mrs. Hansforth asked the young lady to leave a message, and was so sorry to find that she'd only be on planet for a few hours. The chance of reaching Angus in that time did seem very small...

Perhaps on the return trip there would be time, Mrs. Hansforth heard. Or perhaps Ms. Mylander would be able to beam ahead next time. But research—you know how it *does* take one about...

Mrs. Hansforth agreed, though she'd never been off-planet, herself.

When the connection was cut, Mrs. Hansforth was sorry. But, still, a ship-to! Why, Angus must be more important in his field than she had realized. Imagine!

Miri leaned back in the chair, flipping switches and smiling slightly. Engineering the delay hadn't been hard at all—simply a matter of bouncing her signal off seven different satellites and across the single continental landline about three times. Her new partner had called the unit "adequate." She wondered if understatement was his usual style.

Now, sipping some exquisite coffee, she considered the information gathered. Not much, but maybe something. Flipping another series of toggles, she tapped "Econsey" into the query slot.

The door cycled at her back and she was up, spinning, hand on the gun in her pocket, as Val Con entered, a blue drawstring bag slung over one shoulder. He stopped just inside the room, both eyebrows up and a look of almost comic horror on his face.

She pouted and took her hand off the gun. "You don't like my makeup!"

"On the contrary," he murmured. "I am awestruck."

He slid the string off his shoulder and held the bag out. She nearly snatched it away from him, plopping crosslegged to the floor by the 'chora. The box was out in a flash, and she ran her pale fingers rapidly over the shiny black surface before cradling it in her lap and looking at him.

"How'd Liz do?"

"On the whole, I'd say she came off better than I did," he returned absently, staring at her as he drifted forward to sit on the 'chora's bench.

The hair. Was it really possible to twist, torture, and confine one head of hair into so many unappealing knobs and projections? But for the evidence before him, he would have doubted it. She'd also smeared some sort of makeup on her face, imperfectly concealing the freckles spanning her nose, and done something else to her eyes, making them seem larger than usual, but exquisitely lusterless. The color of her cheeks had been chosen with an unerring eye to clash with the color of her hair, and the blue on her lips was neon bright. Every piece of jewelry—and there was far too much of it—vied with the other for gaudery. He shook his head, lost in wonder.

She caught the headshake and smiled a ghastly smile that consisted only of bending her sealed lips and creasing her cheeks.

"You *do* think I look nice, doncha?"

He folded his arms on top of the 'chora and nestled his chin on a forearm. "I think," he said clearly, "that you look like a whore."

She laughed, clapping ring-laden hands together. "So did the woman at the collection firm!" She sobered abruptly, slanting lusterless eyes at him. "Your face was wonderful! I don't remember the last time I saw somebody look so surprised." She shook her head. "Don't they teach you anything in spy school?"

He grinned. "There are some things that even spy school cannot erase. I was raised to be genteel."

"Were you?" She regarded him in round-eyed admiration. "What happened?"

He ignored this bait, however, and nodded toward the comm. "Murph?"

She sighed. "On vacation with his fiancée in some place called Econsey—southern hemisphere. That's what I know. I was gonna see what else the comm knew when you came in and insulted my hairdo."

"Econsey is situated on the eastern shoreline of the southern hemisphere," he told her, singsonging slightly as he read the information that scrolled before his mind's eye. "It sits at the most eastern point of a peninsula and is surrounded on three sides by the Maranstadt Ocean. Year round population: 40,000. Transient population: 160,000, approximate. Principal industries: gambling, foodstuffs, liquors, hostelries, entertainment, exotic imports." He paused, checking back, then nodded. "Juntavas influenced, but not owned."

Miri stared at him; whatever expression may have been in eyes and face was shielded by the makeup.

"Mind like that and it's all going to waste."

Irritation spiked from nowhere and he frowned. *"Will* you go wash your face?"

She grinned. "Why? You think it needs it?" But she rolled to her feet, box in hand, and headed for her room. Behind her, Val Con flipped open the cover and touched the keyboard plate.

In the bathroom, Miri stripped the rings from her fingers and the bobs from her ears, jangling them along with the necklet and hair jewelry into the valet's return box. A glance at the readout showed that her leathers were at long last clean and the jumpsuit joined the gaudy jewelry. She closed the lid, hit the return key, and turned to the sink.

It took longer to scrape the gunk off her face than it had to put it on—the eyeshadow was especially tenacious—but a clean face was eventually achieved and, moments later, a braid was pinned in a neat crown around her head.

Her leathers slipped on smoothly, sheathing her in a supple second skin; she stamped into her boots, tied the knot in the arm-scarf, and carried the belt with its built-on pouch back to the sleeping room.

Sitting on the edge of the tumbled platform, she picked up the lacquer box and spun it in her hands like a juggler, hitting each of the seven pressure locks in unerring sequence. There was a *click,* loud over the soft drift of 'chora music from the other room. Miri set the box down and raised the lid.

Opening the belt-pouch, she pushed at the back bracing wall until she coaxed the false panel out, and laid it aside.

From the box she took a key of slightly phosphorescent blue metal, a thin sheaf of papers, a badly-cut ruby the size of a Terran quarter-bit, a loop of pierced malachite, and a gold ring much too big for her finger, set with a cloudy sapphire. She stowed each item in the secret space in the pouch. Then she removed the last object, frowned, and sat balancing it in her hand.

The room's directionless light picked out a slash of red, a line of gold, and a field of indigo blue. She flipped it to the obverse, and light skidded off the polished metal surface, snagging on the roughness of engraving. As she'd done a hundred times since she'd gotten the thing, she ran her finger over the engraving, trying to puzzle out the alien characters.

In the room outside her door, the comm unit buzzed once…twice.

Miri dumped the disk among her other treasures, sealed the hiding place, and was on her way to the door, threading the belt around her waist as she went.

Val Con was on his feet and moving as the comm buzzed a second time. He touched BLANK SCREEN and GO.

His eyebrows shot up as he saw one of his four captors of the night before standing in the lobby below, a squad of six ranged at his back, and he shook his head to banish the feeling of creeping déjà vu.

"Mr. Phillips?" demanded the man he recognized.

"Yes," Val Con said, taking the remote from its nesting place atop the comm.

"Mr. *Connor* Phillips," the leader insisted. "Former crew member on the *Salene?*"

Val Con strolled across the room to the bar. "It would be useless to deny it," he told the remote. "I was Cargo Master on *Salene.* To whom am I speaking? And why? I left instructions that I was not to be disturbed." He set the remote on the shiny bartop and activated the refreshment screen.

"My name is Peter Smith. I'm working with the police in the investigation of the explosion that took place at Terran Party Headquarters last night."

Val Con dialed a double brandy from the selection list "I am unenlightened, Mr. Smith. Unless I understand you to say that I am suspected of causing an explosion in—where was it? Terra Place?"

"Terran Party Headquarters." There was a real snarl in that correction, then a pause, as if for breath. "We're looking for a man named Terrence O'Grady, who caused the explosion and disappeared. We're asking everybody who's come on-world during the last fifteen days to answer a few questions about the—incident. Refusing to assist in a police investigation, Mr. Phillips," Pete said, with a very creditable amount of piety, "is a criminal offense."

Val Con dialed another brandy. "I am chastised."

Across the room, the door to Miri's bedroom opened and she came out, buckling her belt as she walked. She paused briefly in front of the comm screen before continuing on to the second bedroom.

"Mr. Smith," Val Con said, dialing yet another brandy. "It is really of no interest to me whether or not you catch this—individual—who blew up these headquarters. However, since you have already disturbed me, and since I have no wish to be treated as a criminal, you may as well ask your questions."

"That's fine," Pete said. "Now, if you'll tell the receptionist to let us up, we'll just take a few minutes of your time—"

"Mr. Smith, please. I said you may as well ask your questions. I did not say that I would welcome you into my home. The presence of a police representative would place me in a very awkward negotiating position at this moment."

Miri laid his gun silently on the bar and was gone, vanishing into the kitchen. Val Con dialed a brandy, clipped gun to belt, and waited.

After a pause, Pete's voice came again. "Okay, Mr. Phillips, if that's how you want it. Where were you last night between 10:45 p.m. and midnight?"

Miri reappeared, raised her brows at the row of brandy snifters on the bar, and passed silently on to survey the comm screen.

"Last night," Val Con said easily, "I was engaged with friends. There was a party, with fireworks and conversation." He dialed another brandy.

"I see. You can, of course, supply the name and address of your friends," Pete said. In the lobby, he jerked his head and two of his squad moved toward the elevators. Miri walked back to the bar.

"I can," Val Con was saying. "I won't. But I can."

"I see," Pete said again. "Mr. Phillips, do you know a man named Terrence O'Grady?"

"No." Val Con handed two brandies to Miri and waved toward her bedroom. She stood still, frowning; he reached into the depths of the bar, produced a flamestick, and tucked it in her belt. Enlightenment dawned with a grin of delight, and she departed on her mission.

"Mr. Phillips, I'm going to have to insist that I see you."

"Mr. Smith, I'm going to have to insist that you produce a legal document giving you the right." Miri was back for two more brandies, which she carried into the other bedroom. Smoke was beginning to waft from the doorway across the room.

"Have you any other questions?" he asked Pete.

"Why did you leave your post on the *Salene?*"

"It was not as profitable an association as I had hoped for, Mr. Smith. But I fail to see what that has to do with your problem. *Salene* did not ship explosives. I met no one there named O'Grady. I have met no one named O'Grady since I have been on Lufkit. I doubt if ever in my life I have met anyone named O'Grady, but I give you leave to explore the possibility." Smoke wisped sweetly from his former bedroom to billow with the smoke from Miri's.

He stopped dialing brandies and splashed the contents of one of the remaining snifters on the carpet around the bar. Miri appeared, picked up two more glasses, and carried them to the comm chair and the sofa, touching the flamestick to the cushions.

"Mr. Smith?" Val Con asked the remote.

Miri came back for the remaining snifters and began to splash the carpet.

"What?" Pete snapped.

"Have you other questions? I really must return to my own business." He held up a hand, stopping Miri from igniting the carpet.

"Any other—yeah, I do." Pete took an audible breath. "Are you a geek, Mr. Phillips?"

"Are you a horse's ass, Mr. Smith?" Val Con hit DISCONNECT. Miri touched the flamestick to the carpet.

Somewhere within the building, bells began to ring; a hiss of water striking flame came from Miri's bedroom as the sprinkler system activated itself. There were shouts from the hallway.

Miri and Val Con were already through the kitchen escape hatch. He slammed it to, twisted two knobs, and spun to find her shaking her head.

"Real genteel."

He grinned. "Thank you."

Then they were moving without haste down the small service corridor, toward the larger world beyond.

CHAPTER FIVE

He was male, though that rarely mattered to him. Indeed, he was hardly male at all, in the sense of lyr-cat, bearded Terran stud, or mouse. What mattered more to him was his name, which might take up to three hours of introduction when spoken to humans and, spoken fully, might consume nearly twelve hours. For purposes of the visas and other official papers that hasty humans required of one, there were several short forms of his name, which pleased him.

He was regal, as befitted a T'carais and a being more than nine hundred Standard Years old, though among his race he was known for his occasional hasty action. On visas he was thus: Twelfth Shell Fifth Hatched Knife Clan of Middle River's Spring Spawn of Farmer Greentrees of the Spear-makers Den, The Edger.

Some few of the Clans of Men—Terran and Liaden separately they named themselves—knew him reasonably well as Edger. He enjoyed this informality; it reminded him of those early days of learning his trade and life role.

With him now traveled other functionaries of his Clan: The Handler, The Selector, The Sheather, and, off-planet, The Watcher. Most of the Clan was home, growing knives in the cold, beautiful caverns of Middle River. His group of five had been sent by the Elders out into the wide universe to discover what knives were required. "Market research" his visa named this vast adventure, though Edger himself thought of it more fully as "Education." After all, one had to discover the uses and users of a knife before one could know what blade to grow, what edge to encourage, what handle to smooth, what sheath to mold. He never doubted that knives were needed, or that knives from the Knife Clan of Middle River were needed most of all.

So far, they'd been seven years on this hectic trip. Edger felt confident that another seven would yield all the information the Elders required.

Being relatively young, Edger did not regard himself as large; his twelfth shell had been still dangerously soft when they'd begun their journey, and even now was barely set. Yet people not of the Clutch regarded him with awe, for few of the working class traveled, and his four-hundred-pound bottle-green frame was fully one-third larger than the svelte and speedy persons the Ambassadorial Clans sent to human worlds.

Being young, Edger was fond of entertainment. In fact, it was for this purpose that he and his three companions were now moving with ponderous haste down the wide walkway of a neighborhood consisting of very tall, pastel-colored buildings. There was a piece of music to be performed in a building just a little farther down this street and then somewhat farther down the next. One could have argued that the briefness of the piece—barely longer than the speaking of Edger's full name in Terran—hardly justified walking such a distance at such a pace. But Edger's delight in music was well-known to his kin, and they were disposed to accompany him to this pleasure.

Thus they walked, taking care to keep to the strip of soft material Terrans lined their walkways with. And why not use stone, which endured at least a generation or two, demanded Selector, who had an acid tongue. Why use this—this *concrete,* which wore so quickly? Were the Clutch to use such material, nothing would be accomplished save the constant repaving of the roads.

Handler reminded Selector of the briefness of human lives. "Therefore, many of their own generations may walk upon this surface before it wears to nothing. And, in their hastiness, they may by then have decided upon the use of another material altogether so that it is not a waste for them, brother."

What reply Selector may have made to this gentle reproof was not to be known, for it was at that moment that the howl of a siren sounded behind them, echoed by another in front. Directly across the street from the group of Clutch members, a building chimed a shrill song to itself.

Edger stopped, enchanted.

The building continued its song while people gathered around it, each crying out in what could very possibly be some hasty new harmony. This was counterpointed by the screaming sirens atop the two bright red vehicles which had so recently arrived on the scene.

Edger left the walkway and moved across the crowded street toward the building that sang. His Clan members, seeing him in the throes of his passion, followed.

They moved through the crowd at the entrance very like a herd of elephants moving through grassland, and they did not stop at the policeman's order. Possibly, he had not been heard. Or his voice might merely have been approved for its place in the song, the words disregarded in the present of the experience.

Rapt, Edger came into the lobby, kin trailing after. Here, he noted, the sound of the sirens was not so shrill; the rich counter-harmony of the singers faded to a primal growl over which the solitary, single-noted song of the building soared triumphant, nearly incandescent.

And there were other textures herein encountered, doubtless meant as a frame to the piece: the softness of the carpeting beneath his feet; the clearness of the colors; the harshness of the light reflected from the framed glass surfaces. Edger stepped deeper into the experience, opening his comprehension to the wholeness of this piece of art.

Patiently, his Clan members waited.

Too damn easy, Miri thought with habitual distrust of easiness. The service corridor formed a small cul-de-sac off the first-floor hallway, and they had loitered there until the evacuation team arrived and began knocking on doors and hustling people to safety. Val Con had stepped quietly into the group of refugees, Miri at his shoulder, and so they had gotten rescued, too.

When the group hit the lobby, he as quietly dropped out, slipping ghostlike into the foliage of an artificial oasis. Intrigued by this return to complexity, Miri dropped out with him.

In the next few minutes, the situation in the lobby had grown noisier and more confused. Cops and firefighters were everywhere, yelling and pushing people around. Miri caught sight of two rescue workers shoving Peter Smith toward the door, and grinned.

"Tough Guy?"

"Hmm?" A gaggle of turtles had wandered into the lobby and he was staring at them, brows pulled together in a half-frown.

"*Do* you know Terrence O'Grady?"

The green eyes flicked to her face, his frown smoothing away to that look of bland politeness. Miri braced herself for a lie.

One of his eyebrows slid slightly askew and he took a deliberate breath, then released it.

"I don't *know* Terrence O'Grady," he said slowly. "But, for a few days, I *was* Terrence O'Grady."

The truth, after all. Miri blinked.

"I was afraid of that." She jerked her head toward the aliens in the lobby. "Friends of yours?"

He returned to his study. "It is difficult to be certain at this distance. They may actually be—kin."

She looked at him blankly and saw his face go from intent concentration to extreme pleasure as one of the Clutch began expounding incomprehensibly in its foghorn voice.

"That's Edger."

"It's *what?*" she demanded, dropping a wary hand to his arm.

"Edger," he repeated. "The big one in the middle is my brother Edger."

"Oh." She frowned at the group, and then at him. Maybe he's flipped, Robertson, she thought nervously. Don't look it, though.

The Clutch members were standing together, three of them waiting with visible patience, looking at nothing in particular, while the fourth—the loud one who stood a large head taller than his fellows—was in an attitude of animated attention. *Edger,* Miri reminded herself.

"Okay," she said, going with the gag for the moment. "What's he doing here?"

"I think…" He paused, eyes on the four aliens. "I think that he must be listening to the music."

Miri grabbed at the ragged edge of her patience. *"What* music?"

Her partner waved a slim hand, encompassing the pandemonium within and without. "Edger is a connoisseur of music. I met him when I was training as First-In Scout. I had a portable 'chora with me…" He shook his head, eyes still on the Clutch members, face relaxed, lips half-smiling.

"He enjoyed my playing. After I—got to know him, he offered me a place in his household, as Clan musician." The half-smile became a full smile briefly. "He also offered to import a lifemate for me, or a series of pleasure-loves, so I wouldn't sicken for my own kind."

Miri was staring at him. "First-In Scout?" she repeated, in whispering awe.

His face closed like a trap, skin pulling tight over his cheekbones and tiny muscles tensing around the eyes; the smile was gone as if it had never been.

Damn your tongue, Robertson! "What's next, boss?" she asked, fighting to keep her voice matter-of-fact.

He was already out of the tiny jungle. "Let us talk with Edger."

They moved quickly across the lobby, dodging firefighters and crowds of tenants being rescued. Val Con stopped before the largest of the Clutch people, Miri at his shoulder.

Slowly, hands hanging loose, he performed the bow of youth to age, as was proper when one who was yet shell-less would address the magnificence of one whose twelfth shell has set. He bent with the suppleness of a dancer until his forehead brushed his knee, then unbent as slowly and stood waiting to be acknowledged.

The measured pace of the bow, delivered with correct timing and in counterpoint to the frenziedness of the performance all about, drew Edger's eye. He studied the small figures before him: the brightly furred one standing in motionless respect, and the one who had performed the bow which had drawn the eye bearing a distinct resemblance to—

"By the first Egg of the first Clutch!" he boomed in joyful Trade. "It is my brother the musician! The dragonslayer! The stranger who teaches! Ahh, I had had suspicions, I will allow, but now they become certainties! Tell me, brother," he continued, lowering his voice to a mere bellow as he gestured about him with a three-fingered hand the size of a child's head. "This is yours, is it not?"

Val Con performed another slow bow, less profound than the first.

"I am honored that you recognize the workmanship," he murmured in soft Trade, "but I ask that you humor your soft brother. The work, which I had not known you might witness, is a specialty. It is to remain anonymous, known only to myself—and you, now, brother—and this lady, who assists me."

Edger sighed a tornado.

"What genius dwells within my brother! What nobility of purpose is his, who recognizes that art may be set free and allowed to pursue its own destiny and fulfillment!

"I am in your debt yet again, and I ask that you forgive my attention to the work which required you to bow such a bow. As your brother I ask that you not bow so to me again."

He paused to gaze at his brother the musician with wonder in his saucer-sized eyes.

"Frequently, I meditate upon that last work you played for the Clan, wherein you juxtaposed elements of the music of your people with the music of my own. That you could achieve such a thing without prior composition is a continuing astonishment to me. It is my opinion that most members of your race would rest, had they achieved such virtuosity upon an instrument. But you—I find you exploring other dimensions, tying the filaments of your work together with strands of discord and rhythm..." He let this drift away in order to sample again the music happening *now.*

"It is I who must bow to you!" he announced suddenly, nearly knocking over a passing firefighter as he attempted so do just that.

His brother waved his many-fingered hands, as if he would hold back the torrent of praise.

"It is too much—I thank you." The hands turned up to show the palms in his well-remembered gesture. "You permit?"

"Speak on. I permit all to such a brother, and such an artist."

"I would ask that you grant the boon of your company to myself and my companion for the space of a few days. It is that we must travel and there have been—hindrances. I feel we would be passed to our destination without molestation, if you grant us your cognizance." Val Con paused, head tipped slightly to one side.

"If you will," he continued slowly, "the art you see here is but part of a larger and more complex work we perform."

"It shall be done!" Edger declared, turning to his kin, who had been patiently standing by. "It shall be done!" he said in the highest of the Clutch dialects.

The others sketched quick bows, silently taking fresh note of Edger's lamentable haste. Still, a T'carais may have a brother, and who is to deny the brother of a T'carais when the request is reasonable?

"It is arranged," Edgar said in Trade. "A few days at the disposal of my brother. It is too little, yet it begins to repay the debt. I—"

"Will you damn turtles get the hell out of this hobby?" The policewoman who demanded it, stungun at the ready, was a towering, muscled brute, a scarred veteran of a multitude of riots and street fights. She loomed over Val Con like a mastiff over a lynx.

Edger looked down at her from his height, astounded by the temerity of such a small, soft person.

The small, soft person, blissfully unaware of her transgression, continued her tirade. "Don't you stupid reptiles know that this building's on fire, that there's a desperate criminal loose, that we're evacuating the tenants, and that *you* are obstructing *all* of it? You—" A jerk of the stungun at Val Con. "Who're you?"

"Linguistic Specialist Nor Ton yos'Quentl, of the—"

Miri closed her eyes briefly.

"You registered here?" the cop cut in.

"No, I'm with these—"

"Then, for the sake of Heyjus, get your butt *outta* here!" the cop yelled, tripping the safety on the stungun and waving it in emphasis. "And take this *zoo* with you; the building's being evacuated. If you wanna stand here and have the roof fall on you," she continued, as one suddenly struck by the brighter side of destiny, "I guess nobody'll be too upset over losin' a couple geeks and a herd of turtles."

She turned and strode away, slamming her gun into the holster as she went.

Val Con glanced up at Edger. "It is recommended that we make haste, my brother, before the roof falls on us with assistance from the local constables."

Edger sighed. "I had hoped to enjoy the last of your composition, but you are no doubt wise. It saddens me to find so many people unappreciative of art."

So saying, he turned in a wide circle—like a steamer making a mid-ocean change of course, Miri thought—and set off for the door, one of the waiting trio at his side. The other two remained where they were.

Val Con caught Miri by the arm and pulled her with him as the second pair of turtles fell in behind, acting as escorts.

"What's going on?" she hissed at him in Terran as they moved toward the door. "Who in hell is Norton Quentin? Why are we—"

"Nor Ton yos'Quentl," he corrected, "is a Linguistic Specialist at the local—"

She jabbed him in the side with an elbow. "Listen you—you *turtle-brother!* This is crazy, all of it! First, you get us out of the room and into the lobby and nobody knows who we are. *Then,* you gotta attract attention to us by being related to some weird Clutch standing in the lobby—and *then* you're somebody else again! Damn chameleon, that's what you are."

He grinned at her, enjoying the sensation of looking down on someone with all the tall company around. "I'm your partner, just as you told Liz. A rose by any other name…"

For the next few minutes, he found out what kind of a vocabulary life in the mercenaries can foster in a young girl.

Clutch people, Miri learned with surprise, were persons of consequence. Rooms for the two human members of Edger's party were bespoken and produced upon the instant at the hyatt where the marketing research team stopped. A private dining room was likewise provided, and, shortly, a meal of Clutch food and human food, with suitable beverages and utensils for each species. A concert-sized omnichora was shanghaied from some distant function room and placed also within the dining hall.

While they waited for the meal, and even before the beverages were poured out, Miri was formally introduced to Edger, Handler, Selector, and Sheather, each by his abbreviated, visa name.

"And your own?" Handler asked her.

Miri chewed her lip, working it out. "Miri Robertson Mercenary Soldier, Retired, Personal Bodyguard, Retired, Have Weapon Will Travel." She heard a small sound to her right, as if the other human member of the party had stifled a sneeze. Edger and Handler blinked solemnly.

"It is a well-enough name," the T'carais judged, "for one yet young."

Miri bowed in thanks, which pleased Edger, who thought her very pretty-behaved, and began to speak to her of music, asking, in his eventual way, if she played an instrument, as did his young brother.

She shook her head and confessed that, though she could pick out a tune, one-fingered and limp-timed, on a 'chora, it could not in justice be called playing. "I can sing some," she told Edger as they sat to dinner, "but Tough Guy says you're a connoisseur. My voice ain't anything special."

Edger paused, considering this message. Much of it was clear, but he was puzzled. "I believe I am unacquainted with this person who holds me in such esteem. My memory does not provide a face to match the name 'Tough Guy.' It is not often that I am so lax, and it troubles me."

"It is sometimes the custom among Terrans," Val Con explained, handing Miri a glass of wine and shaking his head at her, "to provide a person with what is known as a 'nickname.' This is most often suggested by a characteristic displayed by the person which seems very strong, yet is not touched upon by the person's official name." He paused and poured himself a glass of the canary before sliding into the seat between Edger and Miri. "For reasons best known to herself, Miri names me 'Tough Guy.'"

"I understand," Edger said, accepting in his turn a beaker of milky beverage from Sheather. "It pleases me that Terrans continue to adjust their names. It is not a tendency I have heretofore observed in them. But it is good to know of it." He quaffed his drink with apparent relish.

"I would be pleased," he continued, "if you and Miri would play and sing when the meal is done."

Val Con inclined his head and, after a slight hesitation, Miri copied the gesture.

The talk shifted to the mission of the four Clutch members. Miri let the conversation slide over and around her, not really listening to the words, but letting the slow voices, the grandiose phrasing and rolling periods, soothe her.

She broke a piece of bread from the loaf and buttered it leisurely. Edger's okay, she thought lazily. And Handler's sweet. And Selector— she grinned. As an ex-sergeant, she had a special feeling for Selector.

She became aware that shy, little—in a relative way, of course— Sheather was staring at her out of eyes the size of her salad plate, and smiled at him. He ducked his head and was suddenly very busy with his meal.

Miri ate her bread, luxuriating in the feeling of—safety? She sipped wine and decided that she liked the turtles.

"You will be pleased to know," Edger was booming to her partner, "that when you again come to us you will be able to eat of food and partake of drink designed for those of your kind. It was a source of shame to me that our Clan could provide you with naught but soups of which you must be unsure and which did not provide all the nutrients your body demands; and only water to drink, as our beer was too potent.

"To mitigate this shame, I have procured along our route foodstuffs prepared by your kind for your kind. And I am assured that these things are preserved for more than two hundreds of these standard years."

He paused, then, as delicately as the big voice could manage, asked, "Do you think you will return to us, as you promised, within two hundreds of years?"

Next to her, Val Con hesitated, and the glance Miri slanted at his face surprised an expression she recognized as sadness.

"Certainly before two hundred years," he said with strained lightness. "Liadens are not so long-lived as you." He lifted his glass and took a healthy swig of wine. "But how may I come to you at all, when you are adventuring around the galaxy?"

"Ah," Edger said, "but the expedition is nearly complete! We will be back in the caverns of Middle River in less than seven Standard Years."

Val Con laughed. "I had no idea you were so close to the end," he said, and the talk passed on to other things.

Presently, it was judged time for entertainment. Bowing to their hosts, Miri and Val Con moved to the 'chora. He ghosted his fingers down the keys, releasing a shower of sound, and glanced at her from under long lashes. "What song, oh, Traveler?"

She ignored that, frowning in concentration. "You know 'Jim Dooley Blues'?"

His brows twitched together. "I am not certain."

She came around his side and leaned over to pick out the schmaltzy melody line. He listened for a bar or two, then his right hand began to pick up the rhythm; his left hand shifted further down the keyboard, grabbed her lagging melody, shook it firmly, and set it upon its feet.

Miri straightened. "Show-off."

Grinning, he flipped stops, adjusted frequencies, and slowed the lines she had shown him until they were obviously an introduction.

Miri turned toward the audience and begun to sing.

She sang well, he conceded, adjusting the 'chora to fill the spaces her voice left within the song. She did not have remarkable range, it was true, but she knew the limits of her voice, and the song she had chosen, with its overstated lament of the problems encountered by Programmer Dooley, fit her abilities perfectly.

The song ended at an even dozen verses, which he also appreciated.

The Clutch members sat motionless at the oversized table; Edger's eyes were glowing.

Val Con adjusted the stops and began the introduction to that ever-popular ballad of the spaceways, "Ausman Overboard." Miri laughed and nearly missed her first line.

The party lasted until very early the next morning.

CHAPTER SIX

The staff of the hyatt in Econsey were even more impressed with the members of Edger's group than the staff at the City House, where they'd spent the previous night, had been. Of course, the Clutch had been staying at City House for several weeks—it was possible that the novelty had worn off.

A suite of rooms, arranged in a six-pointed star around a spacious common room, was provided. An omnichora, the stammering manager explained, was standard equipment in this apartment.

The suite was pronounced adequate, and the manager was requested to guide Handler and Sheather to the kitchens, where they could arrange the details of comestibles while Edger and Selector made a preliminary tour of Econsey's import shops.

Miri stared at Val Con and cleared her throat. "I'm gonna try the comm-net for Murph's registration," she said, jerking her head at the door to her bedroom.

He nodded wordlessly and drifted toward the 'chora.

Murph's name was readily regurgitated by the net; the comm connected her with his hyatt's front desk immediately.

"Mr. Murphy and his guest have rented one of our island hideaways for a few days," the smiling young man at the Archipelago told her. "They should be back on the mainland—let's see...Yes. Tomorrow afternoon. Would you like to leave a message for him?"

"No, thanks," Miri said through gritted teeth. "My plans ain't fixed yet. I'll give him a call back when I know what I'm gonna be doing. I just thought, if he was free tonight..." She let it trail off, and the young man dimmed his smile by a kilowatt or two in professional sympathy.

She thanked him and broke the connection, seething.

Spinning slowly on her heel, she surveyed the bedroom. It was not, she thought, as luxurious as the apartment rented by Connor Phillips in Mixla City, though the private comm built into the desk was a nice touch. And the bed was *enormous*.

The bathing room offered a choice of wet or dry clean, as well as a sunroom; the valet was in a room of its own, flanked by floor to ceiling mirrors. On whim, because any occupation was better than thinking up ways to ruin Murph's nature, she called for the valet's catalog.

A low whistle escaped between her teeth as the pictures began to form in the screen. Hot damn, but you're in the wrong business! she told herself. A person didn't get rich being a soldier—not unless she got real lucky. And personal bodyguards didn't get rich either, unless the boss died grateful—of natural causes. Miri puzzled briefly, trying to figure out what line of work one could get into and afford to dress in the clothes offered by the hyatt's valet.

Sighing, she hit CANCEL. There was one thing for sure—any gimmick that let a person dress like that was not a gimmick that a mercenary from a ghetto world was likely to fall into.

That thought touched another, and then her fingers were working the catch on her pouch, pulling at the false wall. The enamel work of the disk was nearly blinding in the spotlights of the valet chamber, but extra illumination did not make the marks more meaningful.

She stood for a long moment, frowning down at the thing. Then, with a sharp nod, she went in search of her partner.

The manager of the second shop was appreciative. She turned the one knife they carried with them for such purpose—their "sample" Edger called it—this way and that, letting the light illuminate and obscure the crystal blade in artistic series.

"It's beautiful," she breathed, laying it with gentle care on the velvet pad she used for showing off fine pieces of jewelry. "I'm quite sure I could sell a few hundred every year. Why don't we start with an immediate shipment of fifty? In six months I'll have a better idea of how they're moving and be able to reorder." She looked up at the larger of the two aliens, who seemed to be the boss of the venture. "Will fifty percent up front and fifty percent on delivery be satisfactory?"

"Quite satisfactory, " Edger replied politely. "But it appears that I have not made myself perfectly clear. I am mortified to display such a lack of proficiency in your language. The case is this: 'Immediately,' as I understand you to mean the word, is not possible. It takes a space of time to encourage knives to grow in the desired form for the proper edge to be induced, for handles and sheaths to be formed and grown..."

The manager frowned. "How long?"

Edger waved a hand. "For such a knife as that, do we notify those at home this day—twenty of these Standard Years."

"Twenty—" She swallowed and stared down at the lovely thing resting on the velvet. "What if you were to—ah, *encourage*—a smaller knife? Say one half as large as this? How long would that take?"

Edger considered. "Perhaps fifteen years. Some effort, you understand, cannot be hastened, though there is a saving in time due to the fact that the knife need not be encouraged to grow so large."

"There's nothing you can do to hurry the process a little? I mean—twenty Standards..." The bell rang in the front of the shop, announcing the arrival of another customer. *Two* customers, she saw around the curve of the silent turtle's shell, both well-dressed and cultured.

"Excuse me," she murmured to Edger and moved a bit down-counter. "Yes, sir? Is there something in particular you'd like to see?"

The older of the two smiled and flipped a hand. "Nothing particular. A birthday gift for my daughter. I'd like to look around, if you'd care to finish with those gentles."

She smiled and nodded. "Please take all the time you need. And if I can be of any assistance..." The phrase drifted off as she walked back to Edger and Selector.

"You must understand that it's not possible for a—a *human*—to wait twenty Standards for the filling of an order. Are you certain," she asked Edger very earnestly, "that there is nothing you can do to speed the process up?"

Edger moved his massive head from side-to-side in the gesture that he understood to mean negation. "I regret not. Were we to attempt such a thing—as has been done in the past, when knives were encouraged at a lightning pace—perhaps three Standards from thought to blade..." He sighed a huge sigh. "Such knives are flawed. They do not withstand the rigors we of Middle River Clan demand of our blades.

"That one before you—it will not shatter, no matter the provocation. Excluding, I should say, massive trauma, such as one would expect in the wreck of a land vehicle or collision of asteroid and starship. A flawed blade will shatter and be only dust upon the second strike against ordinary stone. We cannot, as craftpersons proud of our work, encourage a blade ahead of its time, knowing that it will perform as poorly as that."

He motioned, and Selector stepped forward to return the sample to its sheath of soft vegetable hide.

"Well," the manager said, putting her bravest face on it. "I'm sorry. I would've loved to have had some of your knives in the shop." She dredged up a smile. "Thank you for your time."

Edger inclined his head. "Our time has been well given. My thanks for the gift of your own." He and Selector turned—carefully, in this place crammed with fragile things—and started for the door.

"Your pardon, Gentles," the elder of the two well-dressed men said. Edger paused. Behind him, Selector paused also, there being no place to go with his brother blocking the aisle.

The man made a slight bow, as would a resident prince upon greeting another traveling through his country. "My name is Justin Hostro. I could not help overhearing your conversation just now. Much that you have said interests me, and I believe I see a way in which we both may prosper. I would be very happy, were you to have time to walk with me to my place of business, so that we may discuss the matter more fully."

Edger was pleased. Forsooth, a human of beautifully polished manner and splendid turn of phrase. Further, one who wished to learn more fully of the knives of Middle River. He inclined his head.

"My brother and I are happy to learn your name and would be pleased to discuss our craft with you. Let us, as you say, walk to your place of business and speak."

Justin Hostro bowed once more. "I am delighted by your willingness. If I might beg the favor of an instant, while I complete the purchase of a gift for my only daughter?"

"It is well," Edger replied. "My kinsman and I shall await you and yours without."

If their new acquaintance tarried longer than the requested instant, it was not by so significant a time that either Edger or Selector noted the delay. Justin Hostro and his companion rejoined them quickly, the companion bearing a large and ornately wrapped box.

"Ah!" Edger exclaimed. "What delicacy you show in your choice! What supremacy of color—the so-bold yellow, how subtly

Partners in Necessity

tamed by the soberness of the black ribands! It is my belief that your daughter will be well pleased with such a gift."

The man carrying the object of this acclaim stopped dead, blinking at his leader. But Justin Hostro merely laid his hand upon Edger's forearm and turned him gently down the street, murmuring, "Now, it does my heart good to hear you say so, for I see you have a discerning eye. I had had qualms, I will admit it. Perhaps the yellow was too bold? The black too severe? But that it draws such praise from you—I am content."

Shaking his head, Mr. Hostro's companion fell in with Selector, and thus they each followed their leader down the street.

CMS was at .90, CPS at .82. Val Con adjusted the stops on the 'chora as his fingers found an intriguing weave of sound, and the numbers in his head faded away.

Shrouded in the music, he did not hear the scant sound she made entering the room, nor did body-sense warn him of her nearness. The *thud* of disk to padded 'chora top was unexpectedly loud.

Trained reflexes stilled his startled reaction as his eyes snapped first to her face, then to the disk, and back to her face.

"Hello, Miri."

"What is it?" she demanded, voice harsh, finger pointing.

He dropped his eyes obediently and considered the bright design, hands folded in his lap as he sought the proper words, the correct inflection. It is heritage, he thought. It is home.

"It is a House Badge." He lifted his eyes again to hers, keeping his voice gentle and smooth. "The sign indicates Clan Erob, which is a House that chooses to seat itself elsewhere than upon Liad. They are respected Traders." He moved his shoulders. "It is what I know."

"There's writing on the back of it," Miri told him, her voice less harsh, but still carrying that edge he mistrusted.

He picked up the disk, flipped it in long fingers, and sighed.

"It is a genealogy. The last entry is incomplete. it reads: 'Miri Tiazan, born in the year named Amrasam.'" He let the badge fall gently back to the padding and looked up at her. "That would be approximately sixty-five Standards ago."

"Tayzin," she muttered, giving the name a Terran inflection. "Katalina Tayzin—my mother. Miri Tayzin—grandmother, I guess.

Mom might've named me for my grandmother—she never said. Just that her mother'd died in 1358, back during the Fevers, when the fatcats..." She let her voice drift off, shaking her head.

"Didn't tell me a lot of stuff, looks like. When I told her I'd joined up with Liz's Merc unit, she gave me that thing there. Told me it'd belonged to her mother, and she'd be happy knowin' it was off Surebleak—and me, too." Her eyes sharpened suddenly.

"You knew," she said, and it was surety, not accusation.

He nodded. "I knew as well as I could, for whatever difference it might make. I was surprised to find that you did not know, and that you thought yourself so Terran." He offered her a smile. "Look at you. Everyone knows Liadens are short, small compared with other humans; that the heartbeat is a fraction off, the blood count a trifle different..."

She shrugged, and the smile she returned him was real. "Mutated within acceptable limits. Says so in my papers."

"Exactly my point," he murmured. "Because it makes no real difference. No reasonable difference. I have it that we are all the same seed: Terran, Liaden, Yxtrang."

"Yxtrang, too?" She was onto the other point before he could nod. "You have that officially?"

He ran a finger over the smooth enamel work of Erob's badge. "My father did. He had access to the best of the genetics data, and to—other—information. In fact, he gave the information to the Terran Party."

"He *what?*" She was staring at him. "The Terran Party? What'd they do, laugh at him?"

He moved his shoulders against the sudden tension. "They tried to assassinate him."

Air hissed between her teeth, not quite a whistle. "They would, you know. Especially if they thought it was true. But you said— they tried."

He glanced down, took up the disk, and turned it over in his hands. "They tried...He was walking with my mother—his lifemate, you understand, not a contract-wife. She saw the man pull the gun— and she stepped in front, pushing my father aside." He turned the badge over and over in his hands, light running liquid over the many colors. "She was hit instead. They'd used a fragging pellet. She had no chance at all."

"So," she said after a long moment, "you do have a vendetta against Terrans."

His brows twitched together in a frown. "No, I don't." He flipped the badge lightly to the padding. "What good would a vendetta against Terrans do? Because one man with a gun did as he was ordered? Perhaps—probably—he thought he was protecting his family, his Clan, his planet, all of them, from some horrible destiny. I would think that the death of one man would be a cheap price to end such a threat, then and there."

He flexed his arms and leaned back. "A vendetta? Anne Davis, who took me as her own, raised me as her own—she was Terran, though my uncle, her lifemate, was Liaden." He glanced up, half-smiling. "You and I could be partners were you full Terran; there is nothing between our people that makes us natural enemies. No. No vendetta."

He picked up Erob's badge and offered it to her.

"I think," he said slowly as she took the disk from his hand, "that there is little purpose to thinking things like 'the Liadens,' 'the Clutch,' 'the humans,' or even 'the Yxtrang.' I think the best way to think—and talk—is in particulars: 'Val Con,' 'Miri,' 'Edger.' If you need to think bigger because some things take more people, it might be wise to think 'Erob,' 'Korval,' 'Middle River'—a group small enough that you can still name the individuals; a group small enough that you can, in time, know the individuals, the parts of the Clan. Where is the threat in 'Handler,' 'Edger,' 'Terrence'?"

She stood holding the Clan sign loosely, puzzlement shadowing her gray eyes.

"You didn't learn that in spy school," she told him flatly.

He looked down and began to stroke the keys of the 'chora.

"No," he said, very softly. "I don't think I did."

She clicked open her pouch and dropped the Erob-link within, her eyes on the top of his head as he sat bent over the keyboard once more.

"So how come you're a spy and not a Scout?"

The Loop flared and he was up, hands flat on the keyboard, primed to stop the deadly danger of her; he saw disbelief flash across her face even as her body dropped into a crouch, ready to take his attack, a trained opponent, growing deadlier by the instant—

"Miri." His voice cracked and he swallowed air; he raised a hand to push the hair from his forehead and exercised will to banish the Loop from consciousness..."Miri, please. I would—like—to tell you the truth. It is my *intention* to tell you the truth."

He saw her make the effort, saw the fighting tension drain out of shoulders and legs as she straightened and grinned shakily.

"But I shouldn't push my luck, right?"

"Something very like," he agreed, pushing the hair on his forehead up again. It fell back immediately.

"You really do need a haircut."

The adrenal rush had left him drained, a little shaky, but curiously at ease. He flashed a quick grin. "I find that suggestion hard to take seriously from someone whose own hair falls well below her waist."

"I like it long."

"And you a soldier!"

"Yeah, but, you see, my commander told me never to cut it. Just following orders!"

He laughed and found within himself an urge to talk, to explain—to justify.

"Orders can be difficult, can they not?" he said, sitting down again before the 'chora. "I came to this world because there was a man who was a great danger to many, many people of different sizes and shapes. A man who thought anyone whose heartbeat and blood failed to match his own was a geek—worthless—and who killed and tortured the hopeless.

"I was *ordered* here, but having seen the man act, I believe that *I* did what was proper. The reason I was ordered here, I think, is that a vendetta claim would have been sufficient to stop an investigation of my further motives, had something gone awry." He paused, then went on more slowly.

"After all, spy or Scout, I am a volunteer, am I not? I have already agreed to go first, to make the universe safe. A Scout or a spy—it is the same thing. I am an agent of change in either case. Expendable—too useful a tool not to use.

"Sometimes," he continued softly, "tools are programmed to protect themselves. This 'chora, for example, can be moved about within the hyatt with no difficulty. Yet, if we attempted to move it off the grounds, it would start howling, or perhaps it would simply not function all." He looked at her carefully. "The 'chora may not even know what it will do when the boundary is crossed—some circuits are beyond its access. Tools are like that, sometimes."

Miri nodded warily. "But *people*—" she began and chopped off her words as the door cycled to admit Handler and Sheather.

"It has been arranged," Handler told them, "that we shall all six dine in the so-called *Grotto* located belowstairs in this establishment. There is said to be music, which our elder brother will find pleasing, and there is also dancing, which we thought might be pleasing to our human friends. And," he said, voice dropping to what Miri thought must be intended as a whisper, "the form of the Grotto may be pleasing to all of us, since it is a likeness of a cavern system found elsewhere on this planet. We have bespoken the table for eight of the clock, and we hope that there will be sufficient time before the celebration for you to refresh yourselves, adorn yourselves, and be ready. We would not wish the event to begin with unseemly haste."

The humans exchanged a glance, and Val Con bowed.

"We thank you for your thoughtfulness. Six hours is more than adequate for our preparations. We shall be ready in the fullness of time."

"That is very well, then," Handler said. "If you will excuse us, we shall take our leave so that we may make analyses and also prepare for the evening. It does bode to be a time of some discussion."

The humans bowed their thanks and acknowledgements, Miri attempting to copy Val Con's fluid style and finding it much harder than it looked. The Clutch adjourned to their own quarters.

Miri sighed. "Well, I don't know how much adornment I'll be doing, though the refreshment part don't sound too bad. Maybe I can order a fancy new shirt out of the valet." She was talking to herself, not expecting an answer; Val Con's reply made her jump.

"You can't go like that, you know," he told her seriously. "Not into the most exclusive resort on the planet."

"Yeah, well, I can't go in any of the clothes the valet's peddling, either! Have you looked at the prices on those things? I could mount an invasion of Terra for the price of a pair of shoes. I'm here to pick up my money, remember? It's gotten so I gotta water my kynak so I can have a second drink. I sure can't go into debt to finance something I'll wear once in my life!"

Val Con tipped his head, brows bent together in puzzlement. "You would be very conspicuous in what you are wearing now," he said simply. "And Edger has said that the expense of the trip is his, since he counts a debt owed me, and because he had not thought to come to Econsey to research the local need for knives. Even if he wished not to extend his cognizance to you, I might pay—"

"No." She frowned stormily. "That ain't the way I do things. I can just stay in my room, beg off that it's a holy day or something."

"Now that would be an insult, after Handler went to the trouble and thought of arranging a place where we can all eat and enjoy." He paused, seemingly studying the air.

"It would be best not to wear a gun." As he spoke, he opened his pouch and brought out a slender polished stick, something like a Drumetian math-stick.

"Perhaps you could wear your hair to accommodate this." With a flick of the wrist, the stick separated, becoming the handle of a thin, deadly-looking blade, smoothly sharp along the curved edge, wickedly serrated along the other.

Another wrist-flick and the slender dirk was merely a polished stick: knife to ornament. He reversed it and held it out.

Miri hesitated. "I ain't a knife expert—just about know how to use a survival blade."

"If anyone gets close enough to grab you," he said, all reason, "pull it out, flip it open, stick it in, and run. It is not likely you will be pursued." He extended it further. "Simplicity itself, and a precaution only."

She looked from the knife to his face; when she finally accepted the thing, she took it gingerly, as if she much preferred not to.

"I," she announced, "am being bullied."

"Undoubtedly."

"Lazenia spandok," she said, rudely.

His eyebrows shot up. "You speak Liaden?"

"Well enough to swear and pidgin my way through a battle plan. And if ever anybody was a managing bastard, you are. In spades." She turned toward her room, experimentally flipping the hidden blade out and in.

Behind her, he murmured something in Liaden. She whirled, glad the blade was closed.

"That ain't funny, spacer!" The Trade words crackled with outrage. "I ain't a young lady and I don't need you to tell me to clean up my talk!"

"Forgive me." He bowed contrition and dared a question. "Where are you going?"

"To refresh and adorn myself. I've only got about five hours or so, after I decide what shoes to wear."

And she was gone, leaving him to wonder at the sudden bite of bereavement and at the impulse that had led him to address her in the intimate mode, reserved for kin. Or for lovers.

CHAPTER SEVEN

The door closed with a sigh that echoed her own, and she spun, flipping the stickknife onto the desk.

Nasty little toy, she thought, wrinkling her nose as her hand dropped to the grip of the gun on her leg. Just as deadly, surely, but somehow—cleaner? More straightforward? Less personal, maybe?

She shifted slightly, then caught sight of herself in the bed mirror and stuck her tongue out.

Miri Robertson, Girl Philosopher, she thought wryly.

Ilania frrogudon...The echo of Tough Guy's murmuring voice contradicted her and she froze, biting her lower lip.

Liaden was an old language, far, far older than the motley collection of dialects that passed for a Terran language, and divided into two forms: High and Low. High Liaden was used for dealing with most outsiders, such as coworkers, strangers, nodding acquaintances, and shopkeepers. Kin were addressed in Low Liaden— long-time friends, children...But *never* a person considered expendable.

Yet at least twice he'd begun the motions that would have killed her, automatically, efficiently. She might have brushed her death a dozen times with him already; it had taken her time to realize what the mask of inoffensive politeness he sometimes wore was meant to conceal.

His other face—the one with the quirking eyebrows and luminous grins—was the face of a man who loved to laugh and who called heart-music effortlessly from the complex keyboard of the 'chora. It was the face of a man who was good to know: a friend.

A partner.

She moved to the bed and lay back slowly, imposing relaxation on trained muscles.

"A Scout ain't a spy," she informed the ceiling solemnly. "And people ain't tools."

She closed her eyes. Scouts, she thought. Scouts are the nearest there is to heroes...And he'd said *First-in* Scout. The best of the best:

pilot, explorer, linguist, cultural analyst, xenologist—brilliant, adaptable, endlessly resourceful. The future of a world hung on his word alone: Would it be colonized? Opened to trade? Quarantined?

Miri opened her eyes. "Scouts are for holding things together," she clarified for the ceiling. "Spies are for taking things apart."

And that babble he'd given her about tools!

She rolled over, burying her head in the basket of her crossed arms, and relived the moments just passed, when she'd known he was coming across the 'chora at her.

Gods, he's fast! she marveled. Suzuki and Jase would give a year of battle bonuses to have that speed for the old unit, never minding the brain that directed it.

Never mind the brain, indeed. She wondered why he'd checked himself those times she'd seen her death in his eyes. She wondered why he'd trusted her with that deadly little blade, why he'd spoken to her...And she wondered, very briefly, if he truly were crazy.

It seemed likely.

The thing to do with crazy people is get lots of room between you and them, she said to herself.

She rolled to her knees in the center of the great bed, bracing her body for the leap to the floor. Time to flit, Robertson. You ain't smart enough to figure this one out.

"Leave!" she shouted a moment later, when she'd moved no further. Damn Murph and the money. Damn the Juntavas and their stupid vendetta. Damn especially a sentence spoken in a language that might have been her grandmother's but never had been hers.

Yes, and then? Damn the man who had twice—no, *four* times—saved her life?

You're a fool, Robertson, she told herself savagely. You're crazier than he is.

"Yeah, well, it's a job," she said aloud, shoulders sagging slightly. "Keeps me busy."

She kicked into a somersault, snapping straight to her feet as the roll flipped her over the edge of the bed. On her way to the bathroom, she paused at the desk and picked up the little wooden stick. So easy to hide...She thought of Surebleak and the one or a dozen times in her childhood when such an instrument would have been welcome protection. Memory flashed a face she hadn't seen in years and her hand twitched—the blade was out, silent and ready.

"Aah, what the hell," she muttered and closed the knife, carrying it with her into the bath.

Sometime later, bathed, robed, and damp-haired, she called up the valet's catalog again. She frowned at the first selection, trying to place what was different, and nearly laughed aloud in mingled outrage and amusement.

No price was displayed.

All right, she thought, beginning the scan. If that's how he wants it. I hope I bankrupt him.

It took her longer to realize that she was trying to figure out which clothes might please him, which clothes might make him receptive to an offer to share that immense bed with her this evening.

"Pretty, ain't he?" she asked her reflection sympathetically, then sighed. Pretty and dangerous and fast and smart and crazy as the six of diamonds. She cursed herself silently, wondering why she hadn't recognized the emotion before. Lust. Not just simple lust, of the passing-glance variety, but lust of the classic Lost Week on Moravia kind.

Looking around her—and back at the clothes in the valet's tank—she wondered if he might be interested in a Lost Week sometime. Then she cursed herself some more. Since when did she have a week to lose?

Connor Phillips's service record, reluctantly provided by *Salene,* included a holo, which was duly copied and sent around to cops, firefighters, and disaster crews present at the "fire" at the Mixla Arms.

Sergeant McCulloh stepped forward immediately. "Yeah," she told Pete, "I seen him. Redhead kid, him, an' four turtles all left together." She corrugated her forehead in an effort to aid memory. "Said his name was something-or-nother-yos-something. Geek name. Dunno hers. 'Nother geek. Talkin' Trade with the turtles—something about all traveling together for a couple days..." She shrugged broad shoulders. "I'm real sorry, Mr. Smith. Coulda kept the whole bunch right then, if I'd known."

"That's all right, Sergeant," the Chief of Police said, forestalling Pete's frustrated growl. "Now, did you overhear anything that might have indicated where they were going?"

The sergeant shook her massive head. "Nossir. Only that they should all go together."

"Well," the chief said, "that's quite a bit of help, actually. Four turtles and two humans traveling together? They'll be easy to spot." He smiled at his subordinate. "That will be all, Sergeant. Thank you for coming forward with that information. You've been very helpful."

"Yessir. Thank you, sir. Thank *you*, Mr. Smith." The sergeant whirled on her heel and marched out of the room, shutting the door crisply behind her.

"Great," Pete swore. "All we got to do, I guess, is put out an all-points on four turtles and two geeks and wait till we get a report."

"Actually," the chief said, leaning back in his chair, "that's close. We send out a picture and a note to report any combination of turtle and human. Instructions to observe and report to Mixla Headquarters. Under no circumstances are they to be taken."

"What!" Pete stopped in mid-pace, staring at the other man.

The chief shook his head. "Think about it. The boy's inventive—got himself a nice little diversion there: limited property damage, no risk to life—and if he's linked to the O'Grady incident, like you think, he's probably a tad dangerous." He propped his foot up on the desk top.

"Turtles occupy a very ticklish diplomatic niche. We can't afford to make them mad. And they will be mad, if they count the boy as a friend and some poor joke of a cop comes to arrest him." He shook his head. "The girl's an unknown, but it's a good idea to assume she's as dangerous as the boy—and the turtles are her friends, too."

Pete blinked thoughtfully. "So we wait till they're spotted and nailed, then hit 'em with everything we got so fast the turtles got no time to yell 'ho!' We can say 'sorry' later."

The chief nodded. "Exactly."

"Flawed blades." Edger was saying when Miri entered the room in the early evening. "And only flawed blades, my brothers! All that we have now—warehoused, do you recall, Sheather? Nearest the river?—and all that thrice-accursed cavern can spawn! Who could have imagined such a thing?"

"What use can any being have for flawed knives?" Handler asked, squinting his eyes in puzzlement.

"Ah, they are to be given to certain special individuals in the organization of this Justin Hostro. These individuals are entrusted with tasks having much to do with the honor and integrity of the organization. It is Justin Hostro's thought that a blade used for such a purpose need be used for that purpose alone and never for any other. More, it should be a weapon of impeccable crafting, that it not fail during the task itself.

"These knives fit the criteria Justin Hostro has set down most admirably, is it not so, brother?" This last was directed to Selector, who inclined his head.

"It is, indeed, as if the Cavern of Flawed Blades were created and discovered only for this bargain we have struck with Justin Hostro."

Val Con, perched on the arm of a chair set a little apart from the circle of Clutch members, grinned at the undercurrent of venom in that comment and glanced up as Miri's door sighed open.

She was dressed in a dark blue gown that sheathed her like a second skin in some places, and flowed loose and elegant, like a fall of midnight waters, in others. On the right side, her hair was arranged in a complex knot through which was thrust a slender, gleaming stick; the rest of the copper mass was allowed to fall free. Her throat was bare, as was one arm; her hands were innocent of rings.

He stood as she approached Edger, and faded back toward his own room as she made her bow.

"Yes, my youngest of sisters," the T'carais boomed, recognizing her immediately. "That color becomes you—it sets off the flame of your hair. A wise choice, indeed."

Miri bowed her thanks. "I wanted to thank you for the chance to have this dress. It's the prettiest thing I've ever worn."

"The artistry of you is thanks enough. You and my so-beautiful young brother—where has he gone?" The big head swiveled.

"Here." Val Con smiled, coming silently back into the room. "I had forgotten something."

He was beautiful, Miri saw. The dark leathers were gone, replaced by a wide-sleeved white shirt, banded tight at the wrists, lacy ruffles half-concealing slender hands. There was lace at his throat, and his trousers were dark burgundy, made of some soft material that cried out to be stroked. A green drop hung in his right ear, and a gold and green ring was on his left hand. The dark hair gleamed silken in the room's buttery light.

He bowed to her and offered the box he carried. "I am sorry to have offended you."

"It's okay." She took the box and cautiously lifted the lid.

Inside shone a necklace of silver net, holding a single stone of faceted blue, and a silver ring in the shape of an improbable serpent, clutching its jaws tight around a stone of matching blue.

She stood very, very still, then took a deep breath and forced herself to meet his eyes.

"Thank you. I—" She shook her head and tried again. *"Palesci modassa."* That was the formal phrase of thanksgiving.

Val Con smiled. "You're welcome," he replied, since it seemed safer to stay with Terran. He touched the necklace lightly with a forefinger. "Shall I?"

Her mouth quirked toward a grin. "Sure, why not?"

First she slid the ring onto her left hand, then raised both hands to hold her hair off her neck.

He slid the necklace around her throat with a skill that hinted at past experience, then gently took her hair from her hands, arranging its cascade down her back. Miri bit down on a sudden surge of excitement and managed to keep her face expressionless as he came to her side and bowed to Edger.

"I think that we are prepared to celebrate, elder brother," Val Con said. "Does it please you to walk with us?"

CHAPTER EIGHT

Charlie Naranshek slipped his service piece into the sleeve pocket of his dress tunic. He always carried it there, though his employers at the Grotto had supplied him with a large and very ornate weapon, with instructions to wear it prominently. It was a matter of feelings. Charlie felt better on his shift as bouncer when he knew that his daytime gun was at hand. He got the heebie-jeebies whenever he thought about having to draw and aim the pretty piece he wore on his belt.

Feelings, Charlie thought, slamming the locker door, were important. Clues to the inner man. It was smart to pay attention to one's feelings, to act with them.

He raised his hand as he passed the desk. "Night, Pat."

"Hey, Charlie?" She waved him over, spinning the screen on its lazy Susan so he could see the bright amber letters. "Take a look at this, willya? Something you might run into down on the second job."

He frowned at the letters: Be On The Lookout...

"Four turtles and two humans? Are they crazy?"

Pat shrugged. "Who knows? Don't you think the turtles would eat the Grotto up? That fancy no-grav dance floor?" She wiggled her shoulders in a uniformed parody of a dance that may have been in fashion on some steamy jungle world where spears and canoes were still considered pretty radical stuff.

Charlie grunted. "Sure. But it's not no-grav; it's *low*-grav." He shook his head at the screen. "'Observe, but do not contact. Report whereabouts to Headquarters, Mixla City...continue observation...Considered armed and dangerous'?"

He looked at Pat, who grimaced and touched her keypad. Physical descriptions of the two human members of the party scrolled into place.

"'Male, brown hair, green eyes, slender build, approximately five-five, age eighteen to twenty-five. Female, red hair, gray eyes, slender build, approximately five-two, age eighteen to twenty-five.'" He straightened, pushing the screen back where it belonged. "This is armed and dangerous? Ain't neither one of 'em big enough to pick up a gun, much less use it. The turtles now—one of them could hurt you, if he stepped on you."

Pat laughed and flipped her hand at him. "Get out of here, you damn moonlighter. I don't know what I expected from somebody who can't live on a cop's salary."

He grinned, moving toward the door. "See you later, Pat. Try not to let one of them kids take over the station while I'm gone, okay?"

"Yah—just don't go dancin' with no turtles, old man."

The door slid closed on her laughter and Charlie sprinted for the nearest taxi stand. He'd have to step on it now, or he'd be late.

Handler had outdone himself. Not only was the Clutch party seated within an exclusive alcove with excellent sight of the musicians and the famous dance floor, as well as two of the six bars, but he had further arranged—since the Clutch, after all, were visiting human space—that the four nonhumans should eat their meal using Terran utensils.

One by one Edger extracted his set from the sheathing napkin, turning each fork, knife, and spoon this way and that, subjecting it to saucer-eyed scrutiny.

"What think you, brothers?" he asked the table at large, extending a spoon. "Is this also a knife? It has an edge, of sorts..."

Handler pulled one of his spoons free and tried the balance in one large hand. "It is true that it *could* be a knife, elder brother, and it is not beyond our skill to encourage such a shape. But this other—" He proffered a dessert fork. "*Three* points? Six edges, I fear me."

"A trifle!" Edger asserted. "Think if we but bring the problem to—" Here sense was lost in a sonorous rumbling that Miri realized must be Clutch-talk.

She leaned to her partner. "Are they serious, or what?"

"Hm?" He started slightly and turned to her, his full sleeve brushing her bare arm. "Of course they're serious. Middle River Clan produces the finest knives in Edger's society. Which is the same as saying that they produce the finest knives anywhere yet discovered."

"What does that mean—the finest? Does it mean pretty or useful or indestructible?"

He grinned and refilled their glasses. "Yes. Middle River knives are crystal, delicately crafted, superbly handled, exquisitely sheathed—

things of beauty, without doubt. Also useful, since a knife is, after all, a tool. Edger and his Clan encourage as many blades as there are uses for blades, from screwdrivers to grace knives." He sipped wine. "Indestructible? Edger is very careful to say that a Middle River blade *will* shatter, under conditions that he likes to call 'traumatic.' These being the total destruction of the building or vehicle the knife resides within, while the knife is so resident…"

She laughed. "But *spoons?*"

He removed one of the many folded in his napkin. Flippling the lace away from his hand in absent-minded grace, he held the utensil out for her inspection and ran a finger around the edge. "There is symmetry, you see. And purpose. Utility. A certain pleasing quality, indeed, to the form." He shrugged and lay the spoon aside. "Who can tell? Perhaps soon—within, let us say, the late middle life of your grandchildren—Middle River spoons may be the very rage among the wealthy and influential."

"Indeed," Edger boomed, "such was my thought, young brother! If these be things that are used daily, why then should they be wrought of soft metal, that so quickly wears out? Why not, indeed, of crystal from our Clan's encouragement, so that they may be used for hundreds and hundreds of your Standard Years?"

Miri laughed again, raising her glass. "No reason at all! Humans are just shortsighted, I guess."

"We do not blame you for it," Handler said quickly, "for it is true that you cannot help the shortness of your lives. But it does seem wasteful and somewhat chauvinistic to condemn your works to obsolescence only because you, yourselves—" He floundered, the end of his sentence in sight and no graceful exit apparent, but Edger rescued him noisily.

"Not so, brother, for ephemera is an art form. Indeed, it may be art at its highest form—I have yet to conceive an opinion and have heard no others. Have we not all seen the works of this, our younger brother, employing the mediums of sound, of movement pattern, and reflected light? Done, gone, changing as it goes. Art, brothers. And who is to say that…" Perceiving that Edger was in the throes of his passion yet again, his Clan members composed themselves to listen.

The remaining two members of the party exchanged glances, grins, and a sip of wine.

Charlie came through the East door of the Grotto exactly on time and hardly out of breath, waving at his day-shift counterpart.

"Hey, George! What's the news, man? All quiet in underground Econsey?"

"Pretty quiet," allowed the other, a thin, dark man who'd been thrown off the force for hitting a kid and killing him. "There's a party over in the South quarter might bear some extra attention. Group of genuine Clutch-type turtles and a couple humans."

"Say what?" Charlie stared, then quickly forced himself to blink.

"Turtles," George repeated patiently. "Four of 'em. Two humans: male and female. Young. No problems—just a little noisy. But that's turtles for you—can't hold a conversation without cracking the walls next door. I just like to keep an eye on 'em. Not that we get that many 'phobes in here."

Charlie nodded. "Yeah, but you never know. I'll check in on 'em every so often. What about the kids?"

"Pretty couple. He's dark. She's a redhead. Not orange," he elaborated surprisingly. "Kind of a reddish brown."

"Auburn."

"Yeah, auburn. Little thing. Seem to be having a good time— all six of 'em. Million laughs." He shrugged and shuffled a step toward the bar.

"Well, good," Charlie said, taking his hint. "I hope they enjoy their stay in beautiful Econsey." He raised a hand. "See you 'round, buddy."

"Take it easy." George was already waving at Macy behind the bar to set up his first drink.

Charlie's beat was the East and South quarters, with one eye tipped to the low-grav dance floor at the center of things. Janees Dalton patrolled West and North, one of her eyes also on the floor, and two floaters circulated, their eyes on everything.

East was quiet. Charlie intercepted a bill dispute before it got noisy and passed it to the nearest floor manager; he escorted an early drunk to the nearest exit and put her in a cab; he nodded hello to a couple of regulars and moved across to South.

Good mob tonight, he thought, flicking a glance to the dance floor and another to twin bars marking the gateway from East to

South. He spotted one of the floaters, Mark Swenger, and waved him over.

"How's it goin'?"

"Not too bad." Mark grinned. A nice kid, he worked the Grotto nights and went to school days, aiming to be a lawyer. Charlie hoped that wouldn't happen—law was a bad way to lose a friend.

"What about the turtle party?" he asked. "Still running?"

"Oh, yeah. It looks like they'll be there for the next year." Mark shook his head. "Man, you would not believe the beer and wine that table's going through! They might *have* to stay a year."

Charlie tipped his head. "Disorderly?"

"Naw, just having a good time. A little loud, but I think turtles just *are,* since they're so big and everything. It's wild, though, to walk past and hear the big one booming out in Terran to the girl, and the next littlest one booming just a little less loud to the boy in Trade, and the other two going to town in something I don't think anybody can speak!" He laughed.

"Real cosmopolitan, huh?" Charlie was grinning, too.

"Real circus," Mark corrected. "But not obnoxious. Kind of heartwarming, actually. They don't seem to have a care to care about." He scanned the crowd and lifted a hand. "I'd better be drifting like the tides, man."

Charlie nodded, moving off in the other direction. "See you later, kid."

South was starting to fill up, though there weren't many people on the dance floor. Early yet for dancing, Charlie thought; the band was barely warm. He saw an opening in the mob around the hors d'oeuvre table and slipped through, working his way back to the far wall.

And there they were. Four turtles, looming and booming. Two humans: She, pale-skinned and tiny, the blue of her dress feeding the flame of her hair; he, dark and in no way large, casual in the fine white shirt, as if these were the clothes he always wore. Charlie saw him lean close to speak into her ear. She laughed and raised her glass to drink.

Armed and dangerous? Charlie thought. Fat chance. He flicked his glance to the floor, then checked out the bars, the snack table, and the main entrance to the Quarter as he drifted back to the wall. It struck him that the boy sat where he could take advantage of that same view and he wondered if it were by design. He snorted and shook his head. Old man, you been a cop too long.

An acquaintance hailed him from a center table and he stopped to chat a minute; he looked up in time to see the boy leaving the turtles' alcove. Charlie nodded to his friend, promised to call soon, and moved away, frowning at the redhaired girl, and at the empty chair beside her.

He did one more quick scan of the area—dance floor, bars, exit, hors d'oeuvre table—and nodded, satisfied. Then he headed for the turtles' alcove. It was time for his break.

Miri leaned back in her chair, occasionally sipping from the glass in her hand as she let the low, soothing rumble of the Clutch's native tongue roll over her. The evening had taken on a dreamlike quality which was not, she thought, entirely due to the wine.

There was no reason for it not to seem that way—all the well-known fairy-tale elements were there. Herself in a lovely dress, a necklace around her throat, and a ring upon her finger, each worth more than she could hope to earn in a year of superlative bonuses—gifts from a companion who was himself beautiful, charming, and entertaining.

And bats.

She banished the thought with a sip of wine and heard, beneath the thunder of the Clutch's conversation, the sound of approaching footsteps. Alarm jangled faintly—her partner walked without sound, and these steps did not belong to their waiter. She set the glass aside and turned.

A tall, wiry man, dark brown and cheerful, grinned and bowed, hand over heart. "My name's Charlie Naranshek," he said, straightening. "I saw you sitting here and I wondered if you'd like to dance?"

She eyed him, noting the ornate gun on the fancy belt, and the glint of silver thread in his dress tunic, then looked back at his face. He was still grinning, dark eyes sparkling. She grinned back.

"Sure," she said. "Why not?"

He helped her up and gave her his arm to the dance floor. "Be careful now," he cautioned. "This thing can be a little tricky till you get the hang of it—'bout six-tenths normal gravity."

She slanted her eyes at him, grinning. "I think I'll be okay."

Charlie hung onto her as they crossed fields, alert for any sign of unbalance—and made a derisive comment to himself when she made the adjustment to the reduced weight without the slightest falter.

"Been in space some?" he asked as they took over a few square inches and began to sway with the music.

She laughed, spinning. "Naw. Just on an awful lot of dance floors."

"Really?" he asked when they next came together. "But not on Lufkit. This here's the one, the only, the *exclusive* low-grav dance floor on the whole ball of mud."

She waved her hand at the table where the four turtles still boomed. "Crew like that, you figure we're gonna be doing some space."

Charlie grinned, refusing to be slapped down, and took her arm for the next move of the dance. "They could just be friends from out-of-town, couldn't they? And you and your—husband?— just showing them a good time?"

"Brother." She tipped her head. "Did you wait for him to leave?"

"Well, sure I did," he said. "Not that I don't think you're pretty enough to fight a duel over, understand—"

She laughed and spun away from him, obedient to the laws of the dance.

Val Con re-entered by the South door and passed the two bars and the hors d'oeuvre table, not hurrying, but not dallying. The alcove was hidden by an eddy of people. As he broke through the crowd he heard the notes of Edger's voice, and then the table was suddenly in sight.

He froze, stomach clenching, then took an automatic breath and surveyed the room calmly, ice-cold sober. He caught a glimmer of blue in the pattern of the dance, saw a small pale hand join with a larger brown one, and moved deliberately over to the edge of the floor to wait.

The dance brought them together again.

"You never did tell me your name," Charlie said.

"Roberta." She accepted his hand for a full spin and bowed as she returned. "My brother's Danny. If you want the names of the rest of the bunch, we'd better go someplace where we can sit down, 'cause it'll take awhile."

"That's okay." He frowned, noticing her start. "What's wrong?"

"Nothing." She threw a grin at him. "Nearly lost my footing."

"What! And you an old spacehand!"

She grinned again and whirled away for the last figure, again catching sight of her partner where he stood at the edge of the floor, watching the dance with a sort of detached, polite interest.

She completed her swing, dipped, and came up, swearing at herself for having yielded to the wine and the music and the dreaming. Her hand met Charlie's for the final time and the music stopped.

She smiled and began to move off the floor. "Thanks. It was fun."

"Hey! What about another one?" He was at her shoulder, reaching for her arm.

She eluded the touch without seeming to do it consciously, and set her steps straight for the still figure at the edge of the dance floor. "Sorry, Charlie, but my brother's waiting for me." She flung him another grin, hoping he would miss the tightness underneath it—hoping he would go away.

He stayed at her shoulder. "Well, there's no reason for your brother to want your head, is there? Besides, I think I owe him an apology for stealing his sister when he wasn't looking."

Hell, Miri thought. And there was the end of the dance floor and the man with the cold, closed face—

Teeth gritted, she faked a stumble, locking her hands around his wrists. He did not sway when her weight pushed into him; she held tighter, creasing the fine lace cuffs, and forced a breathless little laugh.

"Here's my brother now, so we can both apologize," she said to Charlie, giving the wrists she gripped a small shake before releasing them.

"Danny, this is Charlie Naranshek," she said, squeezing brightness into her voice around the lump of dread in her throat. "He asked me to dance while you were gone and I said yes. I'm sorry. I should've known you'd worry." She tipped her head, slanting gray eyes at his cold green ones.

Charlie added his voice to this, frowning slightly at the boy before him. Pretty, and that was a fact. But there was more warmth to be had from the eardrop or the faceted ring-jewel than from the eyes that rested on his. He moved his shoulders, grinning.

"I'm really sorry, Mr.—? But I saw your sister sitting there looking so pretty and so lonesome and all. I thought we could maybe have some fun. Do a little dancing. Talk. You know." He smiled again. "I understand how you could he a little upset. Man can't be too careful of his sister these days, and I know that to be a fact. But there really isn't any harm in me and I never meant to get her in trouble with you."

One eyebrow had slipped slightly out of alignment and the eyes themselves seemed somewhat thawed. "My sister is certainly capable of taking care of herself, sir, and I very much doubt that she is afraid of my displeasure." He offered a smile that went a lot farther toward melting his expression.

"If she's been feeding you stories of my temper, I'm afraid I will have to assure you that my bark is considerably worse than my bite."

This was much better, Charlie thought. "Well, that's fine. I'd have been real sorry to make trouble between a brother and sister." He turned to the girl. "So what's say we give it another round?"

She laughed and shook her head. "Sorry, Charlie. I think we've left our friends alone long enough. Be a shame to offend them."

Charlie's eyes flicked to the table where the four turtles sat, silent now, saucer eyes turned toward—the dance floor? Or the three of them? Charlie didn't know, though his stomach seemed to think it did.

Carefully, he made his bows—a low one to her, hand over heart, a slighter one to him, hands folded at belt level—and received theirs in return. He watched until they were back at their table before turning again to his duties as bouncer and peacemaker, his feelings in disarray.

Val Con waited until they were both seated and the talk of Clutch began its sonorous weaving around them once more. He poured wine for the two of them and tasted his, playing for more time as he struggled to smooth out the unaccustomed emotion—anger, he told himself in vague consternation. He caught a glimmer of the Loop. CPS was at .79.

Taking up her own glass, Miri watched the side of his face. It was no longer the face she associated with lies and death, but neither was it the face of her charming companion of the early evening. Calling herself a fool did not improve matters, so she leaned back in her chair, sipped wine and waited for the storm to break.

Finally, he took a deep breath. "Miri."

"Yo."

"You must understand," he said slowly, watching the eddy and flow of people in the South quarter, rather than her face, "that I am a highly trained individual. This means that I react quickly to situations I perceive as dangerous. Given your present circumstance, to go while I am not in the room and dance with a man who carries two guns is—"

"*One* gun," she corrected. "You're seeing double."

"*Two* guns." There was very nearly a snap in the usually even voice. "Do not blame me because you are blind."

She sucked air in through her teeth, searched out and found Charlie in the crowd by the near bar, talking to a fat woman, and stared at him, considering.

"One gun," she repeated. "In the belt."

"Second gun," he instructed, still snapping. "Sleeve pocket, right-hand side. Also the belt itself is a weapon, in that it contains a device by which he may call for aid."

It was there—now she could see the flat outline of a pellet gun in the pocket of his right sleeve. It would be a more serviceable weapon, she thought absently, than the pretty toy in his belt. She picked up her glass and tossed back the rest of her wine, heaving a huge sigh.

"I apologize," she said as he refilled her glass. "And I'll arrange to get my eyes checked in the morning."

There were to be fireworks over the ocean at midnight.

When the meaning of this announcement had been made clear to him by his youngest brother, the musician, there was nothing for it but that Edger must attend. Here was yet another manifestation of what he was pleased to name the Art Ephemeral: Only think of something made but that it may unmake!

Selector and Sheather had no interest in this display of art and made known their joint desire to walk about the city and see what wonders unfolded. This decided, they took their leave of the rest of the party, who each had another glass of whatever it was they were drinking, to pass the time until midnight.

"Would you bear me company tomorrow morning, brother?" Val Con asked Handler. "I've an errand to run, and your assistance would be valuable to me."

Handler inclined his head. "I am at the service of my brother's brother."

"An errand, young brother?" Edger asked. "Of an artistic nature, perhaps?"

Val Con laughed. "Hardly. It only seems to me that Miri and I will soon require transportation and I wish to arrange for it before the moment is upon us."

"My brother is wise. But know that our ship, which is at dock at the so-named Station Prime in orbit about this planet, is at your command, should you have need." He paused, his large, luminous eyes on the small form of his brother. "You are an honored member of the Clan, Val Con yos'Phelium Scout. Do not forget."

Val Con froze in the act of placing his glass on the table, then completed the action slowly. "You are too generous. I am made glad by your goodness and thank you. But I do not think we will need to commandeer your ship, Edger."

"Nonetheless," the T'carais said, quaffing beer, "remember that it is yours at the speaking of a word, should the need arise."

"I will remember," his brother promised softly.

"It is sufficient," Edger announced. "Now then, who accompanies me to this fireworks display?"

"I shall, elder brother," Handler offered, finishing off his beer in a swallow.

Miri smothered a yawn. "I'm sorry, Edger, but I'm so tired I'm afraid I'd go to sleep in the middle and fall into the ocean."

"Ah. But that would not happen," Edger told her, "for your brothers would surround and protect you. If you are very tired, however, it would be wisdom to return to your room and sleep. That is, unless you long to see this wonder?"

"Fireworks? I seen fireworks before. Guess I can miss this batch."

"Have you so, indeed? We will have to compare observations upon the morrow, if you would honor me?" He heaved his bulk to a standing position, extending an arm to steady Handler, who appeared to have drunk one beer too many.

Miri stifled another yawn and grinned up at the hugeness of him. "Sure, we'll talk fireworks tomorrow. Why not?"

"It is well. Young brother, what will you?"

Val Con stood to help Miri ease back her chair and winced imperceptibly when she ignored the arm he offered. "I will go with Miri back to the rooms, I think," he told Edger. "I am tired, also."

"We will look forward to seeing you upon the morrow, then. Sleep deeply. Dream well."

Miri watched as Edger and Handler wove their majestic way across the crowded floor. That they did not bump into and seriously maim some innocent merrymaker, she noted, was not so much due to the elegance of their progress as it was to the vigilance of those same merrymakers. She grinned at her companion.

"Drunk as judges, as they say in my hometown."

"Why judges?" he wondered, allowing her to precede him around the table.

"Where I come from, Tough Guy, the only people dumb enough to be judges are drunks."

They threaded a less spectacular route through the bright swirls of people, arriving at the South door at the same time Charlie Naranshek came through the gateway of the two bars, on the second leg of his round.

"Aw, now, Roberta, you're not going to leave without one more dance, are you?"

Her brother, walking at her shoulder, spun quickly and neatly, his eyes locking with Charlie's. She turned more slowly, grinned, and shook her head.

"Charlie, I'm beat! Exhausted. Done in." She waved a tiny hand at the noisy crowd. "Whyn't you go find yourself a live one?"

"Am I gonna see you again?" he asked, putting as much schmaltz as he could manage into the question.

She laughed and took her brother's arm, turning him with her toward the door. "If you look hard. Take care of yourself, Charlie."

"You do the same, Roberta," he told the empty doorway, and turned back to finish his beat.

CHAPTER NINE

A coffee pot and a tea pot, with attendant pitchers, bowls, spoons, and cups, had been set out with a plate of biscuits on the table by the two softest chairs in the common room. Miri laughed when she saw them and moved in that direction.

"Whoever said there ain't guardian angels is a filthy liar," she said, pouring herself a cup of coffee. "Want some?"

He nodded. "Tea, please, though."

"Coffee ain't good enough for you?" she demanded, switching pots and juggling cups.

"I don't really like coffee," he said, taking the chair with the best view of the door. He accepted his cup with a smile.

"You, my man, are a maniac." She sank into the chair opposite, sighing deeply. "How much did we *drink?*"

He regarded his tea doubtfully, judged it too hot to drink, and set the cup on the table. "Three bottles between us."

"Three! No wonder I'm acting like a lackwit know-nothing. Oh, my aching head tomorrow—or is it tomorrow, now?"

"In a few minutes." He sharpened his gaze upon her face, picking out the tight muscles around her eyes, the smile held in place by will, not pleasure...

As if she felt the intensity of his study, she moved her head sharply, tossing her hair behind a bare shoulder. "You and me gotta talk."

"All right," he said amiably. "You start."

The full mouth flickered into a grin, then straightened. "I ain't going to Liad, Tough Guy. Straight dope. No lies. I like who I am. I like how I look. I don't *want* to be somebody else." She took a sip of coffee, made a face as she burned her tongue, and set the cup on the table.

"I know that probably sounds crazy to somebody's got three or four identities going at once—but, hell, I'm just a dumb hired gun. And that's what I want to stay. So thanks, but no thanks, for the generous offer. I appreciate it, but I can't approve it."

He sat at ease, eyes on her face, hands loosely draped over the arms of the chair, ankles crossed before him.

After a time, she leaned forward. "Ain't you gonna take your turn?" she asked softly.

He lifted a brow. "I was waiting for the rest of it."

"You were," she said, without any particular inflection. She sighed. "Okay, then, the rest of it is this: I'm grateful for your help—which has been substantial and timely. I know I would've been a deader if you hadn't come along. I owe you a life, and I can't pay except to give you yours by splitting. Now.

"So, tomorrow I'll get my cash from Murph and then I'll walk out, easy and slow, with nobody the wiser. I don't need a car, so you can let poor Handler off the hook. And I *sure* don't need a space-ship, so Edger can relax." She picked up her cup, took a less scalding swallow, and continued.

"I think that—with your help—the Juntavas is off the trail for the time being. I should be able to get off-world before they know I'm missing. I can handle it from here, okay? I've played singles odds my whole life long and I've managed to make it this far..."

In the chair across from her, he had closed his eyes. As she let her voice drift to silence his lashes flicked up and he sighed.

"Miri, if you follow your plan as outlined, your chance of getting off-world is less than two percent. One chance in fifty. Your chance of being alive this time tomorrow is perhaps point three: thirty percent—three chances in ten. Your chance of being alive the day after falls by a factor of ten."

"So you say!" she started, anger rising.

"So *I* say!" he overrode with a snap. "And *I* say because *I* know! Did I tell you I was highly trained? Specially trained? One of the benefits is the ability to calculate—to render odds, if you will—based on known factors and subconsciously and unconsciously noted details, extrapolating on an immense amount of data I have noted. If I say you will likely be dead tomorrow evening if you leave without my aid, believe it, for it is *so.*"

"Why the *hell* should I?"

He closed his eyes aid took a very deep breath. "You should believe it," he said, and each word was distinct, as if he were following a ritual, "because I have said it and it is true. Since you seem to demand it, I will swear it." His eyes snapped open, captured and held hers. *"On the Honor of Clan Korval, I, Second Speaker, Attest This Truth."*

That was a stopper. Liadens rarely mentioned the honor of their Clan: it was a sacred thing. To swear on the honor of the Clan said they meant business, down-and-dirty, one-hundred-percent-business, no matter what.

And the eyes that held hers—they were angry, even bitter; they were bright with frustration, but they told no lie. She flinched, the weight of his meaning falling onto her all at once. He *truly believes* you're gonna be dead tomorrow if you leave this menagerie, Robertson.

"Okay, you said it, and you believe it," she said, making a bid for some thinking time. "You'll understand if I find it a little hard to believe. I never met anyone who could foresee the future." It was scarcely an apology, nor did it appease him.

"I do not foresee the future. I merely take available data and calculate percentages." His voice was steel-edged and cold. "You are not a 'dumb hired gun,' I think, and I am puzzled by your insistence on behaving like one."

The crack of laughter escaped before she could stop it.

"Count score for Tough Guy," she directed some invisible umpire, then grew serious again. "You mind if I play with your odds-maker for a couple minutes? Just to satisfy myself? I might not be dumb, but I sure am stubborn."

He picked up his cap and settled back in the chair. "Very well. You may."

"What are the chances of Edger turning us in?"

"None whatsoever," he said immediately. "To be as exact as the calculations go, it is more likely that *I* would turn us in than Edger would—the answer closely approximates zero."

"Yeah?" she said, brows rising. "That's good to know. Edger's easy to be fond of, the big ox." After a short pause, she asked, "What were the chances I could've killed you, the first time we were together?"

He sipped tea, watching the numbers appear on the scoreboard behind his eyes, then tried to relay the data dispassionately.

"If you had tried while I was unconscious, on the order of point ninety-nine: approaching surety. After I regained consciousness, before you returned my gun, and assuming that your own survival was a goal: perhaps point one five—fifteen chances in one hundred. Assuming your own survival was *not* a prime consideration, the odds would have approached point three—nearly one third chance of success."

He paused, sipped more tea, looked at the figures his head developed for him, and continued the analysis.

"Once you returned my weapon to me, your chance of success dropped to something close to point zero three, if you wished me dead, no matter what. Three percent, by the way, is a significantly higher chance than most soldiers would have against me, but you have speed, as well as excellent sense of location and hearing. Also, I do not believe that you would underestimate me because of my size, as other opponents have done."

He might have gone on—the figures *did* interest him. He found that her chance of surviving the first Juntavas attack had been as high as twenty percent, had he not shown up. The chance of her living through the second wave was much lower.

"Wait," she said, interrupting these discoveries. "That means you *let* me hold you. Why?"

"I did not wish to kill you. You were not a threat to my mission, nor to myself, nor to any of the projects I have been trained—"

"I'm obliged," she said, cutting him off. She poured coffee and settled back carefully, cup cradled in her fingers, her gray eyes on his face. "What odds that Charlie guy could have killed me down on the dance floor?"

He sighed, closed his eyes, and added several conscious variables to the equations.

"Discounting Edger and his kin, who are more aware than many people credit, and recalling that the weapon is new to you, but that you are a skilled soldier and he a mere policeman or security guard...During the time I was not in the room there was a point four chance of him wounding you, a point three chance of your being severely wounded or incapacitated, and a point two—or twenty percent—chance that an attack would have succeeded. All of these are first attacks with a handgun. With the Clutch present, he would have had no opportunity to follow up."

He opened his eyes, drank tea, and closed his eyes again, concentrating. It had been a long time since he'd done full odds this way.

"Once I re-entered the room his chance of wounding you dropped to about one chance in twenty—perhaps four point nine percent."

"Think a lot of yourself, doncha?" She frowned and leaned forward a bit in the chair. "But, Tough Guy, what're the odds he *would* have?"

He moved his shoulders, unaccountably irritated. "Insufficient data. I don't know who he is or why he asked you to dance. He was armed with a hidden weapon, and although he is not a young man he is in good shape, has quick reflexes, and excellent eye use: a trained guard of *some* kind. That does not make him a murderer, it is true. But, in your precarious position, adding anything to the odds for the other side is very foolish."

"But," she insisted, "he *could* have asked me to dance because he thought I was cute and he wanted to dance."

Val Con nodded and poured himself some tea.

"You don't think so," she said. "Why not?"

"Something…a hunch, you'd call it."

"I see. And a hunch is different than that damn in-skull computer?"

He nodded again, pushing at his hair. "Hunches saved me a lot of times—perhaps my life—when I was a Scout: guesses, made with minimal information, or just feelings. The Loop is different—it takes a definite course of action or concern to trigger it. A hunch might simply make me uneasy of a certain cave, or wary of thin ice…It's not something I can see behind my eyes, plain and certain."

"Sure," she murmured. "It's obvious." She threw back the rest of her coffee as if it were kynak and sat the cup down on the table with a tiny *click*.

"Well, then," she began again. "Do you remember when we started our souls on the way to damnation by burning up that imported brandy?"

He nodded, smiling.

"How safe were we? The TP was all around, waiting for you…" She was watching him very closely, Val Con saw; he was puzzled.

"Once we reached the lobby, there was virtually no chance that we would be recognized. Pete didn't know who he was looking for—a faceless voice on the comm? The last time we'd met in person I'd had a blond head, blue eyes, and glasses on my face. You and I could have walked across the lobby without danger, I believe. No one would have stopped us. In fact, they would have been happy to have us out so quickly."

"But you knew Edger and his gang were going to be there."

He laughed. "I had no idea that Edger was within light-years! That was coincidence, neither deduced nor felt. It is also why the Loop is not one-hundred-percent accurate: I could trip on a piece of plastic trash and break my neck."

"Well, that's a relief," she said, and he could see her relax. "I was starting to think you were superhuman, instead of just souped-up." Her mouth twisted. "Tough Guy?"

And what was *this,* he wondered, when things had been easing between them? "Yes."

"What are my chances—now—of killing, maiming, or just plain putting you out of commission on any average day? Do you have enough information to run that one?"

He did, of course: The equation hung, shining, behind his eyes. He willed it away.

"You have no reason to do any of those things. I have helped you and desire to continue helping you."

"I'm curious. If I had to," she persisted, eyes on his face. "Indulge me."

The equation would not be banished. It hung, glowing with a life of its own, in his inner eye. He combed the hair back from his face. "I do not *wish* to kill you, Miri."

"I appreciate the sentiment, but that ain't an answer."

He said nothing, but leaned over to place his cup gently upon the table, keeping his eyes away from hers.

"I want those numbers, spacer!" Her voice crackled with command.

He lifted an eyebrow, eyes flicking to her face, and began to tell her the facts that she needed to know before the figures were named, or acted upon.

"The data is very complex. You have much less chance now than before, I believe: I am too familiar with your balance, your walk, your eye movement, your inflections, and your strength for you to surprise me by very much. The fact that you have asked this question reduces your chances significantly. That you have seen me in action, know of the Loop, and are esteemed by me increases your chances—but not, I think, as much as they have been reduced." He drew a deep breath, let it out slowly, and continued, keeping his voice emotionless.

"So, the answer is that you would have, in a confrontational situation, approximately two chances in one hundred of killing me; three chances in one hundred of injuring me seriously. In a nonconfrontational situation your chances are much higher than before: I trust you and might err.

"On the other hand, your chance of *surviving* an attack on me by more than five minutes is significantly lower now than before— it would be a somewhat emotional event for both of us—and if it occurred anywhere within the ken of the Clutch it is likely that you would die over a period of days, were you to survive the immediate assault."

She sat very still, hunched forward in the chair. Her eyes dropped away from his to study the pattern of the carpet, and she took a deep, deep breath.

He sat frozen, also, until he was certain of the emotion he had seen in her eyes. It was not something he had seen in her before, and that it should be there now sent a cold thrust of something unnamable through his chest and belly.

Moving with quick silence he came out of the chair and went to one knee before her, slanting his eyes upward to her face, extending a hand, yet not touching her.

"And now, you are afraid."

She winced at the remorse in his voice, shook her head, and sat up straighter.

"I asked for it, didn't I?" She looked at him for a long moment, noting the wrinkle of concern around his eyes and the grim line of his mouth.

He doesn't *know*, she thought suddenly. He doesn't understand what he's been saying...

On impulse, she reached out and brushed the errant lock of hair from his eyes. "But," she said carefully, "I ain't afraid of *you.*"

She stood, then, suddenly aware of her finery, the ring on her hand, the gifts, the confusion, and her early-evening plan of waking with him in the morning.

She rounded the chair, heading for her room.

Val Con rose to his feet, watching her go.

At the door, she turned, then paused as she saw the expression on his face. She waited an extra heartbeat as she thought she perceived the veriest start of a move in her direction, a flicker of—but that quickly it was gone. His eyes were green and formal.

"Good-night, Val Con."

He bowed the bow between equals. "Good-night, Miri."

The door sighed shut behind her. A moment later, he heard the lock hum to life.

CHAPTER TEN

It was cold and she shivered in the depths of the old wool shirt. It was a good shirt, with hardly any holes in it, a gift from her father in a rare moment of concern for his only child—brought on, indeed, by an even rarer moment of actually noticing her. She was so little, so frail-looking. Hence the shirt, which she wore constantly, inside and out, over her other clothes, sleeves rolled up to her wrists, untucked tail flapping around her knees.

It was damp, too, along with the cold—typical for Surebleak's winter. It was, in fact, rather too cold for a twelve-year-old girl to be out and walking, no matter how fine a shirt she possessed.

The wind yanked her hair and she pulled the shirt's collar up, tucking her pigtails inside. She unrolled the sleeves a little bit and pulled her hands inside. The wind blew some more and she laughed, pretending to be warm.

It was a good day, she thought, turning down Tyson Alley. She'd spent it running errands for Old Man Wilkins and had an entire quarter-bit in her pocket for wages. Her mother had the cough again, and the money would buy tea to soothe her throat.

The hand fell onto her shoulder out of nowhere, spinning her to the right. The blow to the side of her face sent her reeling into a splintering wall, dazed.

"Well, now, here's a nice tidbit, Daphne, ain't it? The buyers'll give us a sum for this one, won't they?" It was a man's voice, thick with dreamsmoke.

Miri shook her head, trying to clear it. Two figures wove before her sight—the man towering over her, his hand completely encircling the arm he held her by. His beard had once been yellow, but long neglect and an addiction to the 'smoke had turned it blackish and matted. He was grinning emptily. A gun hung on the right side of his worn belt.

"Scrawny as it is?" The woman stepped beside her mate, dressed like him in greasy leathers, but with a ragged blanket around her shoulders, serving as a cloak. "Besides, the buyers want 'em ready to use now, not in five Standards." She turned away. "Give it a couple slaps to scramble its memory and let's get out of this damn wind."

"Want to use 'em now? We can use this one now, Daphne. Yes, yes, we can—Look!"

He moved his other hand to pull at her fine shirt, tearing buttons and cloth. He yanked it down over her arms and flung it into the frozen mud against the wall. "Look, Daphne," he repeated, reaching out to tear at her second shirt.

Miri dove, grabbing for the gun in the shabby holster. His hand swooped for her neck, but missed, grabbing a pigtail instead. She screamed, twisting around like a snake, burying her teeth in the filthy leather behind his knee.

He yelled in shock and loosed his grip on her hair. She dove for the gun again, pulling it free with one hand as he swung in a swipe that bowled her sideways, bruising her ribs against the wall. He roared, and she saw the foot coming toward her; she swung with the butt of the gun and rolled, fumbling with the safety.

She heard another roar somewhere above her as she came to her knees and raised the gun, both hands locked around the grip.

"You goddamn brat! I'll brain—"

Miri pulled the trigger.

He staggered, eyes widening. She fired again, and the left side of his face was mush. He began to topple, and she scrambled out of the way, coming to her feet to spin, bringing the gun up and pointing it at Daphne, who was standing at the far wall, gaping, hands spread before her.

"Take it easy, kid," the woman started. Her voice was not steady.

Miri pulled the trigger. Again. And again.

The woman jerked with the first shot. The second slammed her against the wall. She was already sliding down with the third, and Miri thought she might have missed her mark.

Slowly, she let the gun fall to the mud. Gritting her teeth, she knelt at the man's side, avoiding as of the blood as she could, and opened his pouch, snatching at the few plastic coins loose in the bottom.

The woman's pouch had more money in it. Miri took it all, cramming it into the pocket of her trousers with the quarter-bit she'd earned that day.

She went back for the shirt, but when she bent to retrieve it, she began to shake. She started up, staring at the two corpses, her stomach churning. Gagging, she leaned over and threw up, then braced herself against the wall and shook some more.

Suddenly she heard excited voices, no doubt drawn by the gunfire, though in this part of town it was hardly a sound to wonder at.

Pushing away from the wall, Miri ran.

She woke, sweat-drenched and shaking.

Gods, but it had been a long time since that particular bogeyman had come back to haunt her. She forced herself to lie still in the wide, soft bed and breathe deeply until the shaking stopped. Then she rolled gently to the floor and padded across to the walldesk.

The clock told her it was morning. Latish morning. Arms crossed tightly over slight breasts, Miri went into the bathroom and turned on the cold water in the shower.

A voice cried out and woke him. He lay still, listening to the echo of the sound.

It had been his voice. The word: "Daria!"

Daria? A name, certainly. He lay quietly in the vast softness of the bed, eyes closed, waiting for his memory to provide the rest of it.

It was a time in coming. He dreamed so seldom, and he'd had to learn so *many* names...

Daria dea'Luziam.

He weighed it in his mind, brows drawn together over closed eyes. But nothing else surfaced.

Irritated, he rolled sideways, snapping to his feet the instant he opened his eyes, and strode to the bathing area to splash cold water on his face.

Too much wine and too little sleep, he thought, rubbing dry with a towel. Much too little sleep. He caught sight of his reflection in the mirror above the sink and frowned into the face frowning there.

Daria?

Her image arose, finally, before his mind's eye: A slender woman his own height, dusky hair short and curling, eyes a vivid sapphire, laughing. Older than he, though not by so much.

The face in the mirror tightened and the frowning eyes widened slightly.

One year older, to the very day—she'd been eighteen to his seventeen. It was forbidden that those of the graduating class take lovers from the junior classes, but there had been ways, and they had found them. They had made plans. She would pass her Solo—the final testing—and spend the year before he passed his gaining Single Scout experience. Upon his graduation they would become a team. Such things were not unknown. And who better? She was at the head of her class, as he was at the head of his.

On the day she had departed for the Solo, she had kissed him, laughing, promising a triumphant return on their birthday, half-a-year distant.

But she had not returned on their birthday, and a search of the sector to which she had been sent eventually yielded a few random shards of metal and plastics which were thought to once have been components of a Scout ship.

Val Con shook his head sharply; he leaned close to the glass and looked into the depths of his own eyes.

You loved her! he accused himself. And you scarcely recall her name?

The eyes in the mirror returned his gaze, lucent and green.

After a time, he turned away and went to ask the valet for his clothes.

CHAPTER ELEVEN

It felt good to be back in leathers, Miri reflected, yanking the scarf tight around her arm. She stood for a long moment, looking at the jumble of items on the counter before her: a polished stick, a blue and silver necklace, and a ring in the shape of a snake.

Hesitantly, she plucked up the necklace, folded it, and put it with the other treasures hidden in her pouch. The ring she slid back onto her left hand, smiling slightly, then she carried the stick with her into the bedroom.

She was nearly to the door when she caught sight of the wrongness and spun, knife flicking open, body ready to fight. When she saw that it was only a tray, holding a coffee pot, a cup, and a covered plate, reposing peacefully on the desk, she relaxed somewhat.

She frowned at herself, shaking her head, eyes moving from breakfast tray to door.

Locked. She had locked the door last might, and the telltale on the jamb informed her that it was locked right now.

Room service does not come into locked rooms.

Knife held ready, she approached the tray and looked cautiously down at its contents.

A curl of coffee-scented steam rose from the spout of the pot, and a breakfast of egg, roll, and broiled meat lay beneath the cover.

The note had been wedged between pot and cup.

She picked it up between thumb and forefinger—a single sheet of pearly hotel paper, folded in half, with her name written across it in a bold black backslant.

Frowning, she unfolded it, flipping the knife closed absently and thrusting it through her belt.

"Miri," the strong black characters read. "I have gone with Handler to procure a car and anticipate returning during the midafternoon. I will then accompany you on your visit to Murph and we will be on our way this evening. Enjoy your breakfast." At the bottom of the page marched several angular letters from another alphabet, spelling out what might have been his name.

Miri began to swear. She started in Liaden, which seemed appropriate to the occasion, switched to Terran, Aus-dialect, and moved methodically through Yarkish, Russ, Chinest, and Spanol. She flung the crumpled note to the tray, then shook her head and splashed coffee into the cup.

She drank while she paced, fuming; when she finished the cup, she clattered it back into its saucer. "Damn him to hell," she muttered, which left something to be desired as the climax to what had gone before. Turning her back on the cooling breakfast, she stamped to the door.

Edger and Sheather were standing near the 'chora, chatting loudly in their own tongue. Upon seeing her, Edger cut off his comment and raised a hand.

"My youngest of sisters! Good morning to you. I trust you slept well and profitably?"

"Well," she told him, smiling, "I slept. And you?"

"It is not yet time for us to sleep," Edger said. "Though it must be near, for I grow a bit yawnsome. Perhaps next month we will sleep for a space."

Miri blinked. "Oh." There was a movement to her right, and she turned to see Sheather shuffling forward, head bent at an uncomfortable-looking slant. He offered her something with his left hand.

She took it, wondering. It seemed to be a leather envelope of some kind, long and very thin, black like her leathers, but of a wonderful softness.

"For the blade you wore last evening," Sheather mumbled in his shy way. "It is my understanding that blades of that manufacture are metal, which is a substance much prone to rusting and edge-damage. It is important to protect it from such trauma. I regret that I was unable to offer you this last evening, but the youngest of my brother's brothers did not admit us to his thoughts.

"Please do not think us lacking in courtesy," he continued, "or suppose that we lament our brother's choice. It only sometimes comes about that the hastiness of human action leave us at a loss." He bowed his head even lower, in what Miri suddenly understood as an effort to make himself shorter than she. "We wish you great joy and long, warm days."

She felt a sting in her eyes, touched, though parts of this speech were somewhat confusing. "Thank you, Sheather. I'm—grateful.

You and your brothers are very kind and I can't imagine you lacking in courtesy."

"Thank *you,*" Sheather replied, "and know that we look upon the flame of your being with awe and much affection." He straightened finally and backed away, nearly knocking over the omnichora.

Miri pulled the stick-knife from her belt. It slid easily into the soft sheath, which she hung on her left side, wondering as she did so if it was proper to cross-draw a knife.

"My sister?" Edger said. She turned to him with a smile. "My brother?"

He inclined his head. "It would honor me, were you to bear me company to the place of Justin Hostro's business. We are to collect our portion in advance this day, which is why I go hence. I would have you accompany me because it is clear that you are an accurate judge of humans, where it is very possible that I may not be.

"My brother, whom you call Handler, has raised the question of purpose for these flawed knives Justin Hostro would purchase. He quite properly asks what being deliberately orders flawed tools, stating that he will have none but? My brother is concerned by this behavior and feels that perhaps Justin Hostro is a thief, who will seek to cheat us of our purchase price."

Miri eyed him. "You want *me* to tell *you* whether this guy's a crook?"

"That," Edger replied, "is the essence."

She shrugged. "Do my best."

"It is sufficient. Let us go."

Charlie Naranshek was not happy. He had expended a quantity of energy and lost quite a bit of sleep convincing himself that he did not have to report sighting the Kid and Turtle Gang by reason of the fact that be had not been on duty when the sighting occurred.

It was, after all, one of the silliest things he'd ever heard of. Turtles weren't desperate characters, just slow and funny. And the kids were just that—kids. A little bill-and-coo for brother and sister, maybe, but that wasn't the kind of thing the local force covered. Especially with a couple like this, who were from off-world.

Armed and dangerous. Sure. Somebody at Mixla 'quarters was having their little joke.

Having thus battered his conscience into submission, Charlie fell asleep, to be awakened moments later by his alarm. He stumbled through the morning routine, got to the station in time to pick up his partner and their cruiser and eased on down to the merchant's quarter to start the daily round.

As they turned the corner from Econsey into Surf, passing a snack bar and an amusement center, his partner suddenly sat up. "Hey, look at that!" he cried, pointing.

Charlie looked—and swore.

For there was a turtle coming out of the office of Honest Al's Rental Cars, with Al himself at his side. And trailing a few steps behind, in dark leathers and shirt, gun holstered efficiently on the right side of the belt, was brother Danny.

Still swearing, Charlie punched up the comm and called in the report.

Miri took a deep breath of salty air and grinned up at Edger. "Nice day."

The T'carais paused to cast an eye skyward and test the air in a mighty inhalation. "I believe you may be right," he conceded. "The sky is bright and the air is fine, though not so fine as the air at home. But that is expected, and one would be churlish to deny other planets their days of prettiness, simply because they are not home."

She laughed and stretched her legs to more or less match his stride. "It might be a good idea," she commented, "to tell Mr. Hostro I'm your aide. If he's a fatcat, he'll figure that to mean 'bodyguard' and you'll gain some points."

"A good plan," Edger decided. "For it has come to my attention that it is profitable to proclaim one's consequence loudly when there is money involved."

Miri grinned and then wrinkled her nose as her elbow bumped the unaccustomed protuberance on her belt. "Edger?'

"Yes, my sister?"

"Edger, I ain't trying to be rude, but I think I better ask, 'cause I'm confused. Maybe I should've asked Sheather, but he's so shy…"

"It is true," Edger said, "that my brother Sheather does not put himself forward as much as is perhaps desirable as one who would stride galaxies, but he is a thoughtful and meticulous individual, who seeks always to do what is proper." He looked down at her with luminous eyes. "Does our gift not please you?"

"Oh, no, it pleases me very much! But see—I don't know why I'm getting a gift at all and I'd hate for there to be a misunderstanding between us. 'Specially when it's so easy to open my big mouth and ask a question and hear what you got to say."

"My sister is wise," Edger announced as they rounded a corner and nearly bowled over two bejeweled ladies walking hand-in-hand in the opposite direction.

"Know then," he continued, not at all discomfited by the ensuing scramble, "that we have made you a gift to demonstrate our joy for and concurrence with our brother's choice of lifemate."

Miri blinked. "Which brother is that?"

"The youngest of my many, he whom you call Tough Guy."

"Right." She considered it. "Edger, did Tough Guy tell you he was going to—ah—marry me?"

"Alas, he did not, which I do not feel is like him. But I am persuaded that the matter slipped his mind, for he has no doubt been preoccupied with his art, planning, perhaps, his next composition." They rounded another corner, this time without incident.

"We were only made aware last evening, when it was seen he had given you the knife-within-a-stick, which he carried when first he came to us," he continued. "And then also was I assured that he had meant no insult by failing to speak, since he had chosen first to wed in our manner, with the gift of a blade. His own people, I believe, exchange gemstones or jewelry, which he gave later, in our presence."

"Hmmm. Is it okay for a person to take a lifemate without telling *anybody* they were going to? Even the person they were going to marry?"

Edger considered it. "I have heard of such things among humans," he said after a time. "But I am certain that my brother would not behave in such a manner, for he is kind and would wish to make certain his attention was not repugnant."

She stopped, staring up at the bulk of him. Edger stopped as well, creating an effective block to traffic. People detoured around them.

"He's *what?*" She heard her voice crack and swallowed.

"My brother's heart is gentle," Edger said, his big voice surprisingly quiet. "He would hurt no being, nor thing, that was not his sworn enemy. Nor would he willingly cause distress. I have seen him to weep with one whose mate lay slain and comfort in his arms a babe nearly larger than himself. It is not possible that he would wed you without your knowledge and goodwill."

There was a long silence during which Miri kept her eyes closed and concentrated on breathing. Crazy, crazy, a voice in her head repeated. Crazy as the six of diamonds.

Edger's voice rumbled over her head and she opened her eyes to look up at him.

"And have you not found him so?"

She extended a hand and captured two of his three fingers. "I guess I don't know him that good," she said seriously and shook her head slightly, as if to clear it. "Thanks, Edger. I'm glad we could talk."

He inclined his massive head, allowing his fingers to remain within her grasp. "I, also," he said.

"That's our boy!" Pete yelled, slapping the chief's shoulder.

The other man nodded and cut back into the net. "That appears to be him, Officer. Do not, repeat, *do not* approach the suspect. He is highly dangerous. We will be sending specialists from Headquarters. I want you to keep track of him, if it's possible without showing or risking yourselves. And find out where that turtle's staying. It's possible the girl's waiting there."

"Yes, sir," Charlie said, struggling manfully to keep his fume under wraps. "When do you think your specialists will be here, sir?"

"Three hours, at the outside," the chief said. "I'd get on the net to your Station commander and set up the timetable. You keep track of that boy. What'd you say they were doing?"

"They appear to be renting a car, sir. It might take 'em awhile, though, if they're looking for something the turtle can fit in, too."

"Right. Over—ah, Officer?"

"Sir?"

The chief considered Charlie's face rather more carefully than Charlie wished he would. "Just don't let them get in the car and drive away, Officer, okay? We want to clean this up fast, before the boy hurts somebody else." The chief leaned closer to the screen. "Just so you know—Charlie, isn't it?"

"Yes, sir." Charlie restrained himself from hitting the cutoff toggle and gave the chief his best wide-eyed wonder look.

"Well, Charlie, I know you're thinking that this boy doesn't look like much. Shows how deceptive looks can be. He's responsible for the deaths of five people in a robbery in Mixla City. Lined 'em up and shot 'em—just like that." He snapped his fingers. "One of 'em was a little girl—eight years old, Charlie."

Charlie made appropriate noises, which wasn't really necessary, since his partner was making enough for both of them.

"So be careful, but keep a line on him. Remember that he's a Liaden—don't have to tell you how slippery *that* bunch is, do I?" The chief nodded at the screen. "Carry on, officers." He touched the disconnect.

Pete whistled in admiration. "Wish I'd thought of that."

The chief grinned, leaned forward, and punched the line for Econsey 'quarters. "Pretty good, wasn't it? A little atrocity goes a long way, Peter." He frowned at the busy signal from the board, cleared the number, and tried again.

"Better get your guys ready. Fifteen of the best ought to do it. I'll add twenty Mixla cops and twenty from Econsey." The line was still busy and he punched the disconnect. "Have 'em here in an hour. Can do?"

"Can do."

The third car had possibilities. The little guy was leaning over the engine; the slender hand hooked around the edge of the fender was all that kept him from tumbling headfirst into the workings. With the other hand he tested connections, checked fluid levels, and poked at the various brain-boxes. This went on for some time, while Honest Al and Handler waited, Al trying not to wring his hands.

Finally he was through, having ascertained whatever it was he had been trying to ascertain. He slid off the fender and rubbed the palms of both hands down leathered thighs.

"The engine is sound," he said, speaking over Al's head to the turtle, "and of a strength sufficient to our purpose."

"Oh, yes," Honest Al broke in eagerly. "It's one of the earlier models, when there was a demand for speed *and* size. It's not as new as the other two vehicles we discussed, but certainly a very fine piece of equipment."

The little man smiled at him. "Age does not matter in this case. Utility does. You see the size of the T'caraisiana'ab. The others of the Mission are built on comparable proportions." He nodded at the car. "I think that this vehicle might serve the Mission well. However, there are one or two other requirements."

"Certainly, certainly," Honest Al said, beaming. "This car was at the top of its line. Royalty, she was."

The little man smiled again and waved a hand, indicating the interior. "One concern—I believe the seats are adjustable?"

"Why, of course."

"Of course," the customer echoed. "But are they individually adjustable, I wonder?" He pulled open a door.

"The case is this," he murmured. "While most of the Mission are rather—large and will require sufficient space in which to ride, there are others of the Interface Team who are somewhat smaller. One such as myself, for instance," he said, smiling at Al, "would be hard put to drive this vehicle, were all the seats adjusted to accommodate the prime members of the Mission."

"There is this control here." Al demonstrated, varying the heights of each of the six individual seats, as well as moving them back and forth.

"Ah," the little man said in admiring accents. "That is excellent."

"And, of course, there is a private comm, plus an auxiliary band, whereby you may monitor weather reports, stock market closings…" He twisted the dial as he spoke, demonstrating, while his customer murmured appreciatively.

"There is also, in this model, an environmental control—here— if their excellencies prefer, perhaps, a richer oxygen mix? More humidity? And this control polarizes the windows, if they find our light uncomfortable."

"Royalty, indeed," the little man said.

"And here," Al said, tapping a small dial set by itself in the far corner of the board, "is the emitter, which we will set to emit the proper code for the status of your Mission. In this way the police need only direct a reading beam at your vehicle to discover that you are persons of importance and should not be impeded."

"Wonderful," the other said, smiling. "I am certain that this vehicle precisely suits our need." He stepped back, frowned suddenly, and stood gazing at the mint-green exterior while Al's stomach sought refuge in his shoes.

"I am not sure that this color is as pleasing as it might be."

Honest Al's stomach returned to its original location. "How foolish of me!" He motioned to the little man, who attended him once again at the control board. "This device here—we manipulate it so. Now look."

The customer did as he was bid and, upon discovering that the exterior was now a brilliant yellow, grinned like a boy.

"Do you find that color pleasing?" Al asked hopefully.

"Let me speak with the T'caraisiana'ab." He moved away to where that person still stood gazing absently at the vehicle under discussion.

"We are almost decided, brother," Val Con said, switching to a liquid mix of Clutch and Liaden, "and I thank you for your kindness in accompanying me. Would you now care to watch the exterior of the vehicle and tell me when it has achieved a color that gives you pleasure?"

Handler rested his large eyes on the small form of his now-youngest brother. "I to choose the color?" he cried, gladdened. "It is you who are kind, brother, and I who am honored. I shall, indeed, watch and call out to you when the shade pleases me."

The little man came back to the car, throwing a smile to Al as he passed, and sat in the driver's chair. He manipulated the proper device.

The exterior of the car faded from bright yellow to gold to amber to bronze to tan to brown to sienna to—

A big voice boomed in a tongue Al did not understand, startling him out of his stupor. The vehicle before him was of a hue known to antiquarians as "fire-engine red."

The little man climbed out of the driver's chair and beheld what he had wrought, eyes narrowed slightly, as if he were staring into too bright a light. His gaze caught Al's and he shrugged.

"Ah, well. We will rent this car," he said, coming to Al's side and taking his arm. "The Mission is to be on-world for one local year. Let us pay you now for two years' rent, so that you have security on your investment. Is that satisfactory?"

Honest Al blinked, letting himself be gently guided back to his office. "Oh, yes," he managed. "Very satisfactory."

"Good. I am right in assuming that you will be able to adjust the emitting device now, so that we may drive the vehicle away?"

Al nodded, bereft of words.

"Excellent," the little man said amiably. "Now, about your fee. Would you prefer Terran bits or Liaden cantra?"

Justin Hostro had a nice operation, Miri thought. His office was nearly as classy as Sire Baldwin's, though the taste in wall art and knickknacks was different. More cosmopolitan, she thought. Baldwin had been a devotee of the Art Terran, primarily, though an original Belansium had hung in his library.

There were *two* Belansiums in Justin Hostro's inner office, each depicting a planet seen from space. The quality that made each a treasure was the evocation of the feeling of actually being in space, with this world hanging before you, filling the big window on the obdeck.

Miri moved her attention from the paintings to Justin Hostro, seated comfortably behind his rubbed steel desk.

"This is the sum we have agreed upon. Please count it and be certain that we have not misunderstood each other," he was saying.

Edger complied with this request, opening the pouch he was offered and removing the clear plastic rolls of coins. Liaden money, Miri saw, keeping control of her face. A bloody *fortune* in Liaden money. And this was just the fifty percent up front. For knives guaranteed to break.

Edger split the rolls into piles of seven each and brushed each pile back into the carrying pouch. He inclined his head. "The sum is correct in that it is the first half of the total agreed upon."

"Good." Mr. Hostro smiled and slid a sheet of printout from the folder before him. "This is the list of locations for the first shipments. I desire that three hundred go to each site, for a total first shipment of 3,000 blades. To aid you, the document lists each location by its Trade designation and by the local name." He passed the sheet to Edger, who took it carefully and scanned it.

"This shall be done," he said, folding the sheet and placing it in the pouch with the money, "within the next year Standard, as we discussed. The first shipment is required at the first location within three months Standard, is that correct?"

"That is correct," said the man behind the desk.

"Then," Edger said, rising and inclining his head, "we understand each other very well."

Mr. Hostro stood also, bowing his royalty-to-royalty bow. "I am pleased that it is so. It is rare to find camaraderie in business dealings. May we deal long and profitably together."

"May we so indeed," Edger replied. "It is very pleasurable, doing business with you. I hope in the future we shall deal as well." He began his turn and Miri, in her role as aide, moved to the door, going through first to check the hallway. Edger came after, and the door closed behind them.

Justin Hostro sat down behind his desk, the tiniest of lines between his fine brows. "Matthew."

His aide approached the desk. "Yes, Mr. Hostro?"

"That woman, Matthew. I feel that I have seen her face before. Perhaps in our files?" He made a steeple of his impeccable fingers. "Yes. In our files. Recently. Find out who she is, please."

"At once, Mr. Hostro." The aide removed himself to the file station in the corner of the room and began the search.

The manual was old and hard to read. Al squinted at the screen, trying to make out the index. White letters wavered on a flickering gray background, defeating his eyes. He sighed and looked apologetically at the little man, glad that the turtle had remained outside.

"Perhaps I'd better call the Registration Office. My eyes aren't as young as they used to be."

The little man was all concern. "Trouble, sir? Here, let me see if I can make it out. Of course: 'Diplomatic Uses, Y-1.'" He manipulated the advance. "I'll have it in just a moment, if you would care to write it down."

Honest Al scrabbled under the counter and came up with a piece of torn pink cardboard and an age-old stylus.

"Here it is," his customer said. "Much easier than bothering the Registration Office, don't you think? The code we need is: DY3-9736-X-7558-T."

"DY3," Al read back, "9736-X-7558-T."

"Correct."

"Well, that's fine. I'll just go out and program the emitter and you're on your way. Another five minutes, sir." He paused and made as much of a bow as his paunch would allow. "Thank you, sir, for your help."

The little man smiled. "It was no trouble," he murmured, turning off the manual. He waited until Al was safely outside before he spun the wheel back.

"Edger, I'm gonna leave you here, if that's okay. Got some business to take care of."

"It is permitted," Edger replied. "When will you return to us?"

Miri shrugged. "In a little while, I think. Nothing complicated, but it's gotta be taken care of."

"I understand. Go and resolve your business, young sister. I look forward to the time when we shall see each other again."

She grinned, shaking her head, and moved off across the street. She turned around once to wave, but Edger wasn't looking.

The bright red car pulled against the curb half a block ahead and discharged its passenger.

Charlie pulled off to the side and likewise discharged his partner, reminding him that his only job was to keep the turtle in sight and stay out of sight himself. Then it was time for Charlie to be after the red car again.

The driver of the car did not seem to be aware that he was being followed. He drove safely and within the speed limit to a self-service lot in the seedy edge of town backing onto the hyatts. He chose a parking space facing the exit and got out to deposit the proper number of bits in the box.

Charlie pulled the cruiser across the nose of the red car and popped out. By the time he got around to the front, the driver of the other car was leaning against the door, arms crossed over his chest, waiting.

Charlie approached unhurriedly, nodding. "Danny."

"Officer Naranshek," the boy returned with distant politeness. Charlie shook his head and sighed.

"Thought it might interest you to know," he said, "that the cops have an All-Point out on you and your sister. Calling you armed and dangerous." He glanced at his wrist. "In about two hours the big boys from Mixla 'quarters'll be here to round the two of you up."

Danny nodded. "Thank you. I appreciate your concern."

"Yeah, well, you can stop appreciating it," Charlie growled, "cause it ain't for you, it's for your sister,"

"I know," came the even reply. "But I am grateful, nonetheless."

"Are you?" He took a breath. Ah, what the hell. "Mixla Chief says you shot five people there, one of 'em a baby girl."

Both eyebrows rose. "Lies. But I thank you for that information, as well."

"I *know* he's lying," Charlie said irritably. "But the point is, nobody else will. Human nature just naturally wants to expect the worst. More fun hunting lions than it is pussycats."

The boy smiled faintly, unfolded his arms, and moved away from the car. "You'd best leave. It would be very dangerous, I think, if you were seen talking to me. Thank you again." He walked around the back of the car, heading across the lot toward the hyatts.

Charlie got in his car and backed it around. As he pulled out of the lot he looked in the mirror and was in time to see the boy vault to the top of the fence and drop to the walk on the other side, sure as a cat.

"Mr. Hostro?"

"Yes, Matthew?"

"If you would step over here a moment, sir, I believe I have the woman's file."

Justin Hostro slid back from his desk and walked leisurely to the file station to lean over his aide's shoulder.

"Yes, I believe so. Excellent likeness, don't you think, Matthew? Miri Robertson." He laid his hand lightly on the other man's shoulder. "Fax me a copy of the file, please. I feel I should review the case before deciding upon our course of action."

CHAPTER TWELVE

The young man in the alcove had never been happier in his life. Being endowed with a poetic cast of mind, he found that the conceit pleased him and set out to expand upon it as he sat next to the potted melekki tree, waiting for his beloved to appear.

Yes, life was a fine thing: pleasant slow days easing one by one into passionate nights filled with lovemaking, wine, and talk. Sylvia was a beautiful woman, loving, gentle, and giving. She was also quite wealthy—but that was hardly to be thought of. His feelings were such that they transcended mere finance.

There was a rustle from the back entrance to the alcove, and the young man smiled. The delightful creature was trying to sneak up on him! He eased out of his chair and turned to meet her.

The leaves shielding the back entrance parted and she stepped quietly through, right hand near her gun. "Hey, Murph. What's new?"

The smile fled, and his eyes made a fair attempt to leave their sockets. *"Sarge?"*

Both brows rose and were hidden by her bangs. "You weren't expecting me? I'm sure I wrote." She tipped her head, gray eyes thoughtful. "You look good," she said cordially. "Prosperous. No worries, either, huh? Sitting with your back to the door."

"There's more than one door," he told her, trying to ignore the sick feeling in his stomach. "Besides, I heard you coming."

She came another couple of paces into the alcove, and the look on her face was one he knew of old. He tightened his gut, determined to take his chewing-out like a trooper.

"You heard me coming, you stupid groundhog," she said, dividing her attention between his face and the portion of the lobby she could see over his shoulder, "because I let you hear me coming! And if I wasn't feeling softhearted today, you wouldn't be around to jaw off any of your damn guff right now." She pointed to the chair he had so lately quit. "Sit."

He sat.

She hauled another chair around to where she could keep tabs on the lobby, Murph, and the back entrance, then eased down and laid her hand alongside the gun. Leaning back, she considered him silently until he began to sweat.

"Look, Sarge," he began, thankful that his voice did not crack. "I've been meaning to make that bank transfer…"

"Yeah?" she said interestedly. "Well, I'm glad to know you had such good intentions. Shows you had upbringing." She absentmindedly caressed the butt of her gun with one finger. "Also shows you're a thief, my man, 'cause I still ain't got my money."

"I can explain—"

She held up a hand. "Is it *very* rude to point out that explanations buy no kynak?"

He licked his lips. "I'll make the transfer."

"Hey, you don't have to do that," she said reasonably. "Now I'm here, you can just give it to me in cash."

"Cash?" This time his voice did crack.

"Cash."

"Sarge, I don't have that much cash on me." He was beginning to feel desperate, as well as trapped.

"No? Too bad. How much *do* you have on you?"

"About four hundred fifty bits." It was useless to lie to her; he had learned that lesson well. "Most of it's in the room."

There was a short silence. "Okay," she said. "I'll take the four-fifty in cash and the rest in trade." She held out a tiny hand, palm up. "Earrings."

"What? Sarge, look, come with me to the room, I'll give you the cash I've got and call in the transfer for the balance, okay?"

She sighed deeply, regretfully. He swallowed hard.

"Angus," she said earnestly, "don't push your luck." She motioned with the outstretched hand. "Earrings. Now."

He slowly slid the hoops out of his ears and laid them gently in her palm. She closed her fingers around them, her gray eyes moving down his person. Murph made a convulsive movement with his hand, trying to hide the ring in the clench of his fist.

Her eyes caught on the movement; she nodded and extended her hand. "Ring."

"Dammit, Sarge—" he started.

She raised her eyes to his.

He gulped and began again, more quietly. "Look, not the ring, okay? It was a gift from my—from Sylvia." She did not look impressed. "Look, it's my troth ring—more sentimental value than pawn value."

The outheld hand did not waver. "Here's the deal, Angus: I get the ring; you get to live long enough to enjoy the girl. Give."

Tears standing in his eyes, he pulled it from his finger and laid it in her palm.

Her brows rose at the weight of it. "Platinum set with ponget and sapphire? Some sentiment." The ring vanished the way of the ear hoops as she continued her inventory of his person.

"Let's see…"

The clock in the lobby indicated that it was somewhat later than mid-afternoon. Val Con summoned a lift, rode to the third floor, and entered the common room by the hall door, braced for a blast of bad temper.

His brothers were seated in a loose ring in the center of the room, the sonorous phrases of their native tongue striking him with the force of thunder overhead as he closed the door.

Edger raised a hand to acknowledge his presence, but did not otherwise interrupt the flow of his speech. The low table to one side of the group supported heroic amounts of fruit and beer, as well as a new wheel of cheese and an unopened bottle of wine.

Miri was not in the common area. The door to her bedroom was closed.

He felt a slight prickle at the back of his scalp and wandered over to the door. Unlocked. He crossed the threshold cautiously.

The bed had been made and the room was professionally tidy, devoid of Miri. Likewise the bathroom. He left the room rapidly and made a whirlwind search of the rest of the suite, though he was already certain she was not within. The prickle at the back of his head had become full alarm.

Back in the common room, he approached the grouped Clutch and stood before Edger to make the obeisance that indicated he had urgent need to speak.

Edger responded with a flutter of the hand that told his brother that he would be heard next. There was nothing for it but to bow thanks and move away.

Choosing a piece of fruit and a chunk of crumbly golden cheese, Val Con hoisted himself to the edge of a higher table on the outskirts of the group and settled to wait his turn with what patience he could recruit, feet swinging above the floor.

Sylvia smiled at the young man and inclined her head as she passed by. She knew she was in her best looks, and knew that the costume she wore enhanced those looks. No assembly-line dresses out of the valet for her! This dress had been custom-made by an artist, and every line proclaimed it.

She paused to scan the lobby for the tall, athletic form of her betrothed, very nearly missing him in the alcove of greenery in which he sat. Smiling, she started across to him, then, seeing that he was not alone, she paused in the shelter of a pillar to study the situation.

His companion was a tiny woman, dressed in what seemed to be well-used leather clothing of the sort worn by laborers on space vessels or mercenary soldiers. Her hair was red, braided and wrapped around her head like a gaudy copper crown.

Angus had been a mercenary, Sylvia remembered; it had been a brief episode during his late adolescence. He had mentioned no friends from that period of his life, but perhaps this small person was such a one? Sylvia made as if to continue on her way, determined to be gracious to her fiancé's uncouth acquaintance.

Angus pulled the chain from around his neck and handed it to the small woman, who dropped it into her pouch.

Sylvia froze.

Angus was being *robbed!*

Outrage rose in Sylvia's breast. *No one* robbed her or hers. It was not done. Obviously, this small person badly desired a lesson in etiquette.

She stayed a moment longer, committing every detail of the woman's attire and person to memory, then turned on her heel and marched to the bank of public comms on the far side of the lobby.

She reversed the charges, since she never carried change, and punched in the code for her father's private office line.

His aide answered the summons immediately, inclining his head slightly as he recognized her.

"Hello, Matthew," she said, always gracious. "Please let me speak to my father instantly. It is quite important."

"Of course, Ms. Hostro."

"OK, Intaglia, take your group down to the entertainment level—I want the exits and the lift bank watched.

"Kornblatt, get this lobby cordoned off—I want somebody on the central comm station and somebody else on central power.

"Smith, you and me and this bunch here are gonna watch the lobby lift bank. Remember, now, all of you! These are highly dangerous individuals. We would prefer to have them alive, but shoot to kill if you have to. Stations!"

"Well, younger brother, I am pleased you have returned. This my brother has been describing your artistry in obtaining a vehicle, making it yet seem that you had not obtained it. Genius. You are an artist such as the worlds have not before known."

"You are very kind," the object of this praise murmured, brushing cheese crumbs from his fingers. He leaned forward. "Edger. Where is Miri?"

The T'carais took a moment to consider it. "I do not know, brother. She spoke of business to be resolved. Other than this…" He moved his massive head from side to side.

"We walked together earlier in the day," he said, "and spoke of things of importance to us. She was very surprised to find that she had been wedded to you, my brother."

Val Con froze, and the look of naked shock on his face would have surely earned a crow of laughter from Miri, had she been present. He took a deep breath. "So she might be," he agreed, though his voice was not perfectly even.

Sheather glanced up from his contemplation of the carpet on which he sat. "We wished only to increase joy when it seemed, last night, that you had knife-wed our sister. True, you had not said to us that you would do this thing, but we know humans to be hasty, and our eldest brother would have it that you could very well be so absentminded as to not inform your brothers, were you planning another of your compositions. Did we do ill, brother?"

He wet his lips, odds running in his head. "Yes," he said, "I am afraid that you have done ill."

"It sorrows me," Sheather said. "May we inquire how we have done so?"

There was a longish pause, during which Val Con banished the tickertape of calculations running before his inner eye. He sighed.

"It is very complicated, brother. Most of the ill would have been done when you hailed her as my mate. She fears me and this will have made her more afraid. It may, however, be mended."

"She *fears* you, brother?" This was Handler, but Val Con had turned back to the eldest of them all.

"Edger, please tell me when Miri left you and exactly what she said."

Edger blinked his huge eyes. "It was three of the clock when I entered the lobby of this hyatt, the youngest of my sisters having left me at the door but a breath earlier. Her words are in answer to my query of when she might return to us. She said: 'In a little while, I think. Nothing complicated, but it's gotta be taken care of.' Thus did we part company."

He let the breath he had been holding go: The odds were slim that she would lie to Edger. He closed his eyes and rubbed his forehead. "All right. But it is now five of the clock and she is not returned."

"It means only that her business has taken longer than she had anticipated," Edger rumbled.

Val Con opened his eyes. "So I hope, as well." He slid from the table and bowed deeply.

"Speak," Edger commanded.

"I would that you forgive my hastiness, brother. It is not thus that I would behave." He held his hands out, palms up. "Events unforeseen have entered the situation and it may mean that your ship, indeed, will be required to serve us. Is all in readiness? If the need is upon us, could we embark and depart this very night?"

"He Who Watches has been told to expect you, alone; with the youngest of my sisters; or my sister, alone. All is in readiness for you. There is food in plenty and of a kind nourishing to humans. There are books in many languages, as well as several kinds of musical instruments."

"You are kind. It saddens me that I must ask further."

"Speak," Edger commanded once more, large eyes glowing on his young brother's face.

"I go now to seek out the youngest of your sisters. Should it befall that she returns here while I am gone, pray tell her all that has transpired between us at this meeting and ask that she bide until six of the clock. Have I not returned by this time, she must go to the parking lot at Pence Street and Celeste and look for the red car. This vehicle she may enter by encoding '615' in the lock. She must change the color from red immediately and go to the nearest shuttle port. She must stop for nothing. Once on station, she must seek out your ship and depart." He bit his lip and closed his inner eye on the equation that denied it. "Say that I have computed the odds and that they are not good. But say also that she is a person with luck and, if she is wily and careful, all will be well."

"I will say these things to my sister," Edger promised. "Shall I say also that this last you do not believe?"

Val Con drew a breath. "Brother, I pray you will not. It is a matter of human definition—truth of another order."

"I understand, and all will be done as you have instructed. The name of our ship is—but you are in haste. Remember only that it is at Dock 327, Level F."

"Brother, I cannot say how the greatness of your heart makes glad my own." He bowed to Edger, then to the rest of the silent Clutch. "Gather much wisdom, oh, my brothers, and use what you have gathered well."

"A long life to you, young brother, and much joy in it," Edger replied, releasing him.

Val Con moved, not running, but quickly, the door opening and shutting like a conjuring trick—then he was gone.

Edger turned beck to his kin, motioning that Selector should pour him a beaker of beer. "Our brother," he said, taking a draft, "is a very great artist."

Justin Hostro nodded. "Yes, I see. A happy circumstance, Sylvia, though I am sure it is very sad that she has chosen to rob your friend…" He let his voice fade out as he glanced down at his desk and shifted papers. His daughter, used to his ways, held her tongue and waited with what grace she could muster.

He looked up again, smiling faintly. "Sylvia, my dear, I shall be sending a group of my associates to your hyatt to escort this lady to my office. In the meantime, please do me the favor of keeping her—available."

Her perfect brows twitched together. "Available, Daddy?"

He moved a hand, banishing details. "Available. Buy her a drink, invite her to your room, seduce her—but keep her in that hyatt for twenty minutes more. Then you may let her go. Understand?"

"Yes, Daddy."

He smiled. "Good. You and your friend are still planning to dine with me this evening, are you not?"

"Of course," she said, surprised.

He nodded. "Till then, my dear...Oh, and Sylvia—"

She paused with her hand on the disconnect. "Yes, Daddy?"

"Do be careful, dear. The lady in question has rather an—uncertain—temper, I fear. You don't want to make her angry with you." He smiled again and cut the connection.

Sighing, Sylvia left the booth and started back across the lobby.

Val Con summoned a lift, thinking hard. She would have gone across the street to Murph's hyatt, of course. To wait? Or had she arranged to meet him? The lift's door *swished* open and he entered, directing it to the lobby.

When the lift stopped, bell *dinging,* the door slid away and he took two steps out.

"There he is!" yelled a voice that had become all too familiar.

Val Con froze, his gaze flicking over the crowd of carefully placed individuals. Too many had guns. Far too many were pointing them at him. Directly before him stood Peter Smith.

In the charged silence, he heard the safety click off on Pete's gun.

He kicked, spinning as his foot connected with Pete's hand, diving back toward the open lift. A pellet whined past his shoulder as he hit the floor and rolled the rest of the distance. Another got through the doors before he had ordered them closed and slapped the 'rise' button.

At the fifteenth floor, he stopped, wedged the door open with a Terran half-bit, ran to the summons box, and demanded more lifts.

Three came immediately—one discharging a middle-aged couple who walked hand-in-hand down the hall, never seeing the slight young man who slid behind them and wedged open the lift's door.

Four out of seven lifts accounted for and the odds were nigh on to perfect that the three remaining were going to be bringing him lots of company in just a little while.

Well, then, what next? Into a room and out the window? He grimaced. From the fifteenth floor, with people no doubt shooting from below? No need to calculate that one.

Down the service ramp? If there was one. He had not committed every detail of this building to memory, more the fool he. He'd allowed himself to believe that he was secure, protected from harm by Edger's reassuring bulk.

He shook his head. It would have to be back the way he'd come then, striking for the Grotto and its dozen or so exits.

He spun slowly on his heel, surveying the empty hallway. Surely there must be something to aid him? Memory stirred after a moment and he moved off to the right, down a short dead-end hallway.

The cleaning station was locked, but that was easily remedied; he made his choices quickly, ears cocked for the sound of an elevator arriving on the floor, wishing he had a partner with eyes on that lift bank.

Gathering up his collection of bottles and paper, he went back to the lifts, leaving the door to the station unlocked and swinging gently to and fro.

They were leaving the alcove as she came near, and she could see Angus's shoulders drooping in depression. The little woman kept up with his pace easily, silent in her leather boots.

Hidden by an ivy-covered pillar, Sylvia watched them cross the lobby to the lift bank. When they claimed their car she followed and stood watching the floor indicator. Fourth floor—back to their rooms! The little bitch wasn't satisfied with taking what he had on him; she wanted more.

Shaking with rage, Sylvia summoned a lift.

Val Con frowned at the telltale. For reasons best known to the police, the three elevators not currently with him were grounded— two at lobby level and one at the Grotto. He had a theory regarding this maneuver, but it bore checking out.

Wadding paper into a tight roll, he soaked it with alcohol and touched it with flame. It flickered and caught, smoking nicely.

Gingerly, he tossed it into the first of four elevators and unwedged the door.

Murph sighed as the door to his room slid back. He sighed again, more deeply, as he went to the desk and inserted his finger in the lock. A drawer made a sudden dimple in the smooth plastic side, and Murph removed from it a money pouch, which he offered to the woman at his side.

She nodded at the desk. "Count it. I know you got the best intentions going, but your memory's rotten, my man."

He did as he was told, unsealing the pouch with a jerk and upending it over the desk. Bits rolled and clicked; one escaped to the floor.

Irritably, he bent and captured it, adding it to the first stack of ten.

There was a sound at the door.

Murph looked up as the panel slid back and his fiancée entered, lithe and elegant and high-colored in an evening dress picked out with gemstones. He was on his way to embrace her when he heard the unmistakable sound of a safety being thumbed off.

Sylvia froze, eyes wide, nostrils slightly distended.

Murph spun. "C'mon, Sarge, what d'ya think, she's got a bomb in her pocket?"

Eyes on the woman at the door, Miri shook her head. "Finish counting, Angus." She motioned slightly with the gun, indicating that Sylvia should close the door.

"Nice dress," she said, when this was done. "Me and Murph're just finishing up some business. Shouldn't be more'n a few minutes, now, and then I'll be gone and you two can comfort each other."

Sylvia swallowed, decided to ignore the gun, and turned her attention to her beloved, who was completing the last stack of coins.

"Four fifty-seven fifty," he said, straightening.

The woman with the gun spared a brief glance at the piled cash and nodded, eyes back on Sylvia. "Fine. Back in the pouch."

"Angus," Sylvia demanded in throbbing accents, "is this woman robbing you?"

"Robbing?" the woman in question repeated. "Not at all. Murph owes me money—his severance from the Mercs, plus interest, like we agreed when I made him the loan. He's been a little backward about paying, but I think we're all right and tight now, don't you, Murph?"

Angus held the refilled pouch out to her. "I still think it'd be better if you let me call in the transfer, Sarge, rather than taking all that jewelry. You're not going to get half what it's worth—"

"But I'll get it *now,*" she cut him off, sliding the moneybag into her pouch. "And I need it now! Hard cash—not a bank note I might not be able to collect on for awhile." She spared him a withering gray glance.

"I had money for you when you needed it, you miserable cashsutas! I don't wanna hear any bellyaching about paying me what's owed when I need it." She moved her gun, infinitesimally. "Out of the way, honey."

Sylvia licked her lips and stayed put. "But, Sergeant—it *is* Sergeant, isn't it?—if it's cash you want, I have some with me, as well." She smiled her most winning smile.

"At least let me buy Angus's ring back."

CHAPTER THIRTEEN

A lift sent upward should rise, not sink. Thus, the theory was confirmed.

Sighing gently, he entered the middle elevator, slid the knife from the neck sheath and began to work on the destination plate. It was a sinful use of the blade, but there was no help for it, and he worked with careful rapidity until he had loosened a corner of the metal plate. Sliding the knife away, he pulled a length of wire from within his vest and twisted one end into a hook.

Moments were squandered while the hook was caught and released by the workings behind the plate. Finally, the button that concerned him most drifted inward, obeying pressure from the wire in his hand. He nodded and carefully let the wire down to hang precariously in position.

Then, he went to prepare the remaining lifts.

Ring, stylus, and pin were bought back for a total of eight hundred bits, bringing the cash received to the sum originally borrowed, give or take a hundred. Miri kept the necklace and the earhoops for the unpaid interest.

"See you 'round, Murph," she said, sealing her pouch and turning to go. She frowned at the woman before the door and motioned with the gun.

"OK. honey, business complete. Outta the way."

Sylvia wet her lips. "You know, Sergeant? I think I could probably borrow another two hundred—if you wanted your interest in cash, too? It would take just another couple minutes. I'd need to make a call to my—"

"Angus, your fiancée talks too much. I'm done and I'm leaving. She's in my way. You can move her or I can move her. Choose."

Murph started, then moved a step toward Sylvia. "Let the sergeant go now, love. She's finished here."

"But Angus. it would be no trouble. If she'll just wait here while I call Daddy for the loan—"

"No!" the little woman snapped. "I been here long enough, honey. Move, or I shoot you. You won't," she confided, "like that."

Murph had heard this threat before and knew it to be in earnest. Putting chivalry aside, he pushed forward, wrapped his arms about his beloved and lifted her out of the way. She pounded on his shoulder with ineffectual fists as the woman in leather dove past, slapping the door open.

All was in readiness. He unwedged the doors in rapid succession and took careful grip on the wire sticking out of the control panel.

All right, Commander, he told himself, here's the plan: Bypass the lobby via homemade juryrig in hand. Exit on the Grotto level and get over to Murph's hyatt, fast. Do not speak to strangers, especially policemen. Simplicity itself.

He shook his head as the bell *dinged* outside his lift.

Commander, old son, you're an optimist. He smiled wryly.

They just missed nailing her in the room. As it was, one saw her as she slid around the corner toward the service lift and set up a yell.

Miri ran. The luck was in: a cleanbot hauling a load of supplies and paper goods was just leaving the lift. She grabbed its head and threw her weight into a spin that sent it bumbling out of control and into the shins of the man in the lead; then she dove into the lift, slapped *down,* and leaned on it.

Down it went, obedient to unceasing imperative, and stopped with a bump that would have made her nervous, if she'd had time for luxuries.

She was out before she'd gauged her surroundings, and the lift was closed and rising before she thought to wedge the door.

Well, can't help that, she thought. Look for the other way out before the cheering section gets here.

The light was dim, but that was to be expected in a sub-basement stacked with boxes of cleaning supplies and gods-knew-what else. She was in the guts of the hyatt, the tenement within the palace. Miri took a deep breath of dank air. Almost made a body feel at home. Now, which way was out?

Charlie Naranshek spun on his heel at the watchpost, almost dislodging his partner of the evening, one of Mixla City's specialists.

"What the *hell?*"

The specialist glanced incuriously at the group of men entering the hyatt opposite. "Some more of our guys, maybe, making sure he don't break for across the street."

But Charlie had seen a face. "Wrongo, chum. Them's Juntavas."

"Yeah?" the specialist said, returning to his bored surveillance of the street. "Busy night."

The door was locked, a circumstance that reminded her of the punch line to a very dirty joke. Across the basement, she heard the whine of the lift, coming back down.

She considered the lock: a shaft of metal extruded from the door, sunk deep into the jamb. No fancy computer lock had been used to protect the paper goods. But it was effective, real effective.

The lift-whine was louder. Miri shifted her shoulders, elbow bumping on the obstruction of sheath and blade—

The knife was in her hand before she had fully formed the thought. Carefully, she wedged the tip where bar entered the wooden jamb, probing.

Across the cellar, the lift door opened.

The lobby was filled with smoke; alarms began to scream and sprinklers to sprinkle. The racket reached the sharp ears of the Clutch, three floors up, and Edger so far forgot protocol as to cut short a question being posed by his brother Selector to rise and move, with haste, to the door.

"Come, my brothers! Did I not say he is great? Let us see what he has wrought in this present." So saying, he was gone, vanished into the hall.

Handler, Selector, and Sheather followed, though Selector did tarry a moment to wonder, for Sheather's benefit, at the excitability of their kinsman.

"For you would suppose," he said, "that by the time one has his twelfth shell—and is, besides, the T'carais of so mighty a Clan as our own—one would have put aside such childish hastiness and behave as an adult."

They were in the hallway proper before Sheather had framed his reply.

"Perhaps," he offered diffidently, for he was very conscious of his status as a lowly Seventh Shell, "it is that our brother, himself, is an artist."

They had split into groups and were prowling the rows of stacked goods one by one. Miri bit her lip and continued working the blade. She almost had it...

With a *click* too loud for oversensitive ears, the bar retracted into the door. Miri was through in the next instant and turning the key on the other side, firmly engaging the lock once more.

She took a deep breath and wrinkled her nose. The ramp she stood on smelled bad, though the 'bots probably didn't mind. And by rights, she shouldn't either, because the ramp led up and that was just what the doctor ordered.

So she'd head up, preferably to the Grotto level, where there was lots of access to outside. Once out, she'd find a comm and buzz Edger, who would no doubt tell her what Tough Guy had decided she should do next.

Which did raise an interesting point: What *was* she going to do next?

One thing at a time, Robertson. Don't get ahead of yourself.

The smell was getting less bad—or her nose had made an adjustment of heroic proportions—and she was hearing noises from above. Lots of noises. Well, maybe somebody was having a party. The more the merrier—and the easier for her to slip through and out, unnoticed.

The ramp curved and abruptly ended at a door. She worked the lock as quietly as possible and opened it a crack, peering through. The kitchen beyond was pristine, huge and empty; she slid through and eased the door shut.

The party in the next room was a doozy—both louder and not as loud as it had been from the ramp. She'd lost the vibration of feet on floor that she'd had from underneath, but there was something—

She froze and the sound came again. Party, indeed. *That* had been pellet whine, or her great-aunt Agnes had been hatched from an egg.

She made her way cautiously across the impeccable expanse of floor to the double chrome doors, eased one barely open, and peered out.

Men and women with guns—about thirty of them—deployed with more caution than tactics around the empty echo of the Grotto. Whatever it was they were after was holed up behind the eastern-most bar. And whatever—or whoever—it was could definitely shoot. Whenever one of the armed horde showed the slightest portion of body, that portion suddenly acquired a pellet-hole. Methodical. Which could only mean that the prize in this tiger hunt was her partner.

Miri frowned, then grinned as another of the enemy was punctured—hole in the shooting arm, very pretty.

Odds look about even, she noted. Wouldn't lay a busted bit on either side...

Her grin suddenly widened and she ducked back into the kitchen.

Policemen, Val Con thought, squeezing off another shot, had no sense of humor.

Or sense of futility, for that matter. Why in the name of all they might hold holy would they just sit out there, shooting and being shot at, taking loss after loss and inflicting no damage? Why didn't they just pack up and go home, call it a day, admit they'd been bested—any or all of the above? And soon. He was running out of pellets.

Miri propped the door at the top of the ramp securely open and a little time later did the same for the door into the cellar.

By the sounds, her pursuers were still beating the rows for her. She grinned and moved toward the nearest sound.

The man was peering into a carton that might have concealed her had it not been full of bottles of cleaner. Miri extended a hand and toppled a near bundle of brooms.

He whipped around, pulling his gun, and she was off, making a lot of noise as she ran.

The racket roused his buddies, who came racing to his aid. Miri rounded the corner farthest from the ramp door on one wheel, skidded to a stop in the face of five of them, then whirled and was going back the way she'd come before they had time to understand that she'd been there.

For good measure, she fired a shot over her shoulder, parting the hair of the man in the lead, then she was moving flat out, streaking past another bunch of them, knocking one into three others like tenpins and twisting around the corner to the ramp door.

Roaring, they came after. She checked for a moment, glancing back to make sure that somebody twigged to the vanishing act.

A lean man with no hair whatsoever rounded the corner, gun leveled. Miri dove through the door.

It was not possible that he could win. He supposed he would take a formidable honor guard with him, but the thought brought no comfort. Nor did the equation that hung before his mind's eye. He gritted his teeth in a final effort to banish it: Suicide is an unacceptable solution.

The equation faded, to be replaced by another bearing a strong resemblance to the one he had denied in Edger's presence. Very soon now he would be dead. Miri might yet be alive, but the end for her was also quite near.

He leaned out from his cover and fired, striking his man cleanly in the eye. A pellet screamed by, chipping the plastic by his head as he huddled back into protection. Cracking his gun, he loaded the last of his ammunition and eased his position a little, glancing around the corner of the bar to gauge the next shot.

There was a banshee howl that raised the hairs on the back of his neck, and out of the kitchen burst an apparition in dark leathers and white shirt, brandishing a gun, a squad of armed men at her back.

"We're coming, Tough Guy!" the figure in the lead screamed, firing into the group at siege.

Confused, they returned fire as the rushing squad broke up and made for cover, returning fire on their own while their erstwhile leader dove sideways, rolling, taking advantage of the shelter offered by tables, chairs, and bar to work her way toward his position.

Val Con grinned and waited, occasionally adding shots of his own to the melee to distract his attackers from her movement.

She was at his side in a ridiculously short time. Sighing, she slumped against the inside wall of the bar, peering out at the fight through a filigreed screen.

"Hello, Miri."

She shook her head at him. "I don't know how you get into these fixes. Leave you alone for five minutes—"

"*I* get into fixes?" He waved at the floor. "What do you call *that?*"

She opened her eyes wide. "Hey, I'm your rescue, spacer. And I want you to know I wouldn't do this for just anybody."

He laughed and snapped off a shot at a woman crawling toward their hiding place. She collapsed and lay still.

Miri peered out from her end, added a few pellets to the general merrymaking, and ducked back. "Nice party."

"You might think so," he told her, "but I've been here for some time and it's getting a bit rough for my taste."

"Yeah?" She jerked her head toward the most accessible exit, half a block down the room. "Wanna leave?"

"If you don't mind." He cracked his gun, showing her the empty chamber. "Give me some pellets and I'll cover you."

The call came over the emergency channel: All available units to the Grotto, immediately. The description, though terse, sounded more like pitched battle than the arrest of two half-sized bank robbers.

His partner was off at once, sliding his sidearm out as he ran. Charlie took two steps in that direction and stopped, near blinded by a flash of brilliance.

Spinning on his heel, he headed for the lot at Ponce and Celeste, moving at a dead run.

Miri went over the fence while Val Con circled around to the front of the lot, checking the street.

She dropped silently from the top and moved quickly in the deepening dusk, using the few vehicles there were for cover, striking out in a diagonal and wondering what she would do if there were *two* red cars parked in the front row, facing out.

She left the shadow of the last car enroute and stepped out into the open.

There was only one car in the first row. Between her and it loomed a figure, too tall and much too blocky.

She froze, hand twitching toward her gun in reaction before she stilled it.

"Hi, Charlie."

"Hello, Roberta." His own gun was out, steady on her gut. "Where's your brother?"

"Bound to be around somewhere," she said lightly, keeping her eyes on his face, not on the gun. "He usually is."

"He wouldn't be down the Grotto, would he? Shooting cops with the rest of the Juntavas?" He was coldly sure of it, and the certainty kept his gun hand from shaking.

Can you shoot her—kill her—if you have to? he asked himself. He didn't know.

She was shaking her head. "We ain't Juntavas, Charlie."

"No? The cops go in to get you, the Juntavas goes in across the street and—boom! A war. Juntavas protects its own, but it ain't much on helping out strangers."

"It was an accident. And the explanation's complicated." She decided to push it. "Charlie, look, I'm in a hurry, okay? How 'bout I give you a call next time I'm in town, we have a drink and tell you all about it?"

No reaction. She hadn't really expected one, not with him in uniform and all, but it had seemed worth the try. Where the hell was Tough Guy?

"The story out of Mixla 'quarters," Charlie was saying, "is your brother's wanted for killing five people—eight-year-old kid was one of 'em." He watched her face closely, trying to gauge her acting ability.

She frowned and shook her head. "Not since I've known him. Not a baby." She took a breath. "Not to say he wouldn't. Just that he hasn't. I think."

Her gaze sharpened, locking on a movement in the dusk beyond his shoulder. Almost, she sighed.

"Charlie," she said, very quietly. "I like you, which is why I didn't draw on you and why I'm telling you this: There's a man behind you with a gun. He'll kill you, without an instant's hesitation or a moment's remorse, unless you drop that piece now."

He hesitated, weighing the chance of it being a lie, keeping the gun where it was.

She flung out both hands, her face revealing something that looked like fear in the uncertain light.

"C'mon, Charlie!"

He dropped the gun and kicked it to one side.

"That's fine," she said gently. "I'm real sorry, but you're gonna have a headache when you wake up."

The blow clipped him just above the left ear, hard enough to do the job. He carried her face with him into unconsciousness.

The sleek brown car moved with sedate purpose through the streets of Econsey, toward the mainland and the shuttleport. The windows were opaqued so that the vulgar were denied a view of the vehicle's occupants. The emitter broadcast its message to all with the means to read it.

"Wasn't that just a bit harsh?" inquired the man in the seat next to the driver.

"Wasn't which?" she asked, slowing to a stop in obedience to a flashing signal.

"He will kill you, without an instant's hesitation or a moment's remorse…" he quoted flatly.

She glanced at him. He was sitting straight in the comfortable seat, staring out the window. The tension in him puzzled her. She eased the car through the intersection as the light steadied and shrugged her shoulders.

"You have shown that tendency in the past," she said as mildly as possible.

Perhaps he snorted. Or perhaps he only let loose a breath that had been too long held, all at once, and with a vengeance.

"I'll try to rehabilitate myself," he said, and there was no inflection at all in his voice. After a moment, he slid down in the seat, moving his shoulders until he found comfort within the cushions, and closed his eyes. "Don't stop for anything," he told her. "And wake me when we get to the port."

It was her turn to snort, but he did not appear to hear; the rhythm of his breathing told her that he was asleep.

Irritably, she yanked on the wheel, snapping the car from left to right. He rolled bonelessly with the jerk, his breathing unaltered.

"I guess you'll want tea and crumpets when we get there," she muttered. She smoothed the car through another curve and onto the main highway.

The best place for a roadblock was on the Econsey side of the last bridge to the mainland, and that was exactly where they'd set it up. Miri sighed and let the car slow fractionally.

"Hey, sleeping beauty."

He eased to a sitting position, in no hurry about it.

"Roadblock," she told him, stating the obvious.

"Maintain your speed."

She slanted a glance at his face. He didn't *look* crazy. But, then, he never did. Well, what the hell. She kept the car on course and steady.

The roadblock loomed closer, lights flashing, and she could make out the expressions on the faces of the people lining the roadway before them.

Then something very strange happened. The 'block began to move clear of the road and the guard fell back, holstering their pieces or bringing them to rest.

Miri took a deep breath, meticulously keeping the pace.

The roadblock lumbered clear a bare moment before impact. Miri let her breath out in rationed units as the brown car continued its stately progress across the bridge and onto the mainland.

"Tough Guy?"

"Yes?" He was settling back into the seat, no doubt arranging himself for another nap.

"Why'd they do that?"

"Possibly they judged an interplanetary incident too high a price to pay for stopping and searching the Yxtrang ambassador's private vehicle." He yawned.

"Oh." She was silent for a short time, digesting his words. "I don't want to pry into your private life or anything, but you didn't by any chance *steal* this car from the Yxtrang, did you?"

"To the best of my knowledge, the Yxtrang delegation for this sector is presently on Omenski."

"Good place for them," she agreed. "Hope they fall in love with the place and never leave." She made a left-hand turn into a wide thoroughfare and then the tower light from the shuttleport was directly before them.

"Sorry I'm so dense," she said, "but I didn't have a nap. What made the cops think we were the Yxtrang ambassador?"

"The emitter says we are." He shook his head and sat up straighter in his seat. "I'm afraid I must have read the wrong code out of the manual at the rental office. It was really very hard to read—grainy and flickering. One of the connectors loose, I should think."

She looked at him. "You wouldn't have had anything to do with that, I guess."

He turned to face her, eyes wide. "How could I have?"

"Never mind, I don't think I really want to know."

The port was less than a half-block distant now and she was beginning to feel loose for the first time since she and Murph had started their negotiations.

We just might pull it—

"Oh, *damn.*" She swung the car—easily, easily—into a side street, moved to the end, and turned into a wider avenue, heading away from the tower light.

"Did you see what I thought I saw?"

He nodded. "Yes. Checking people as they go in. I'm afraid neither of us can pass for Yxtrang at any distance."

"Funny, the things you live to regret." She took a breath. "Now what?"

There was a pause, which she was inclined to think was bad news.

"Let's get a bit closer to the port and leave the car. If we can mix with a group going through, we might have a chance to confuse things and get by."

She laughed and made a left; shortly thereafter a right turn headed them back to the port.

"No plan, but, sister, do we got guts!" She pulled to the curb and killed the power, grinning. "Okay, let's go crash the gate."

CHAPTER FOURTEEN

The situation looked even worse from the street than it had from the car. Even granting the two of them awesome powers of mayhem and confusion, Miri was ninety-five percent certain that they wouldn't be able to fade through the checkpoint. She didn't bother to ask her companion for the official figures.

Nor did he offer them, just stood at her shoulder in the pool of shadow they'd chosen as their observation point and silently watched the procedure.

After a time, she felt him shift next to her. "Let us get a drink."

She turned her head, but it was impossible to see his face in the inkblot they occupied. "Sounds like the most useful thing we can do," she agreed. "Maybe two or three. Then we can come back and try to bull on through. Won't hurt so much when we get perforated."

She heard the shadow of his laugh as he moved out onto the sidewalk. "No faith, Miri."

"None," she said, catching up. "My folks weren't real religious, either. Are we really gonna take a kynak break with the cops *and* the Juntavas within eight seconds in every direction?"

He turned down a slender alleyway at the far end of which multicolored neons promised cheap warmth and noise.

"Why not?" he asked.

Or, she translated, do you have a better idea?

She didn't, so she followed.

The third bar was noisiest, full nearly to overflowing with men and women in leathers and other work clothes. It was the perfect place for them to hide, though there seemed barely enough room to accommodate two more bodies, no matter how small.

Val Con hesitated at the door, weighing the scene, while Miri stood at his shoulder, watching the crowd absently. She stiffened suddenly and he snapped his eyes to her face, looking for a clue to the trouble.

She was grinning and leaning a bit forward, eyes squinted against the smoke. In a moment, she turned to him, grin undiminished.

"Tough Guy, you're a genius. Let's go." She started forward.

He dropped his hand, gently encircling her wrist. "Tell me."

"Part of that mob in there's the Gyrfalks—my old unit." There was no missing the excitement in her voice. She jerked her wrist and he let it go. *"C'mon,* Tough Guy."

He followed, afraid of losing her in the press of bodies and the eddying smoke as she pushed and wove her way through, moving with the stride of a person with a goal in sight.

What the goal was, Val Con couldn't tell. He was satisfied to keep her in sight, and re-established himself at her left shoulder when she caught up against a temporary body-jam.

The jam sorted itself out and she moved on, he maintaining his position as they broke out into the center of the room.

There it was less crowded, though a goodly portion of available floor space was taken up by the biggest Terran that Val Con had ever seen: Eight feet tall if he was an inch, shoulders wider than Edger's shell, chest and ribcage said his planet of origin had been just a tad light on oxygen, and there was not an ounce of fat on him. His shoulder-length blond hair was tied back with a black cord. His full beard was curled and very likely perfumed. He was drinking something brownish from a liter pitcher, an arm draped possessively across the shoulders of a slender dark woman who would have dwarfed any man but this one.

Miri strode straight up to the blonde godling, Val Con just behind her; she stopped with legs braced and hands on hips, head craned upward.

The godling finished the contents of the pitcher and extended a long arm to deposit it on the bar. His lapis gaze fell upon the face of the woman before him.

"Redhead! By the highest, iciest, most diamond of the Magnetas! By the deepest hellhole of Stimata Five! By—"

Words failed him and he reached down, encircled Miri's waist with his huge hands, and threw her upward as if she were a doll; he caught her and gave her a kiss that might have drowned someone less alert.

She captured his ponytail, yanking on it and smacking the side of his head with the flat of her hand.

"Jason! Put me *down,* you overgrown bumblebear!" She swatted him again and Val Con winced with the force of the blow. *"Put me—"*

"Down," Jason finished, placing her with the utmost gentleness atop the bar. "Of course, my darlin'. Down it is, and nicely, too. Ah, it's a sight for a man's heart to see you, my small—but there's something amiss! *Barkeep!* A kynak for the Sergeant, on the double! Or will you have a triple, my love?"

"A single," Miri said, collapsing crosslegged to the bar and waving a hand at Val Con. "And one for my partner, too."

Jason's eyes lit on the little man in dark leathers, noting the gun belted for a crossdraw from the right, but seeing no other hardware. The stranger was slender, though with a certain whippiness about him that said he'd do well for himself, hand-to-hand. A fighter, and no nonsense. The sort of person one would want at Redhead's back.

He shifted his attention to the beardless golden face, encountering eyes as warm and cuddlesome as shards of green glass: Jealous, then. Not the best trait possible, since partners were not always lovers, but who cared, if it kept him sharp?

"Partner, is it?" he drawled, turning back to Redhead. "Bit exotic for your taste, I'd have thought..." No reason not to hone the little man a shade finer. He looked around. *"Barkeeper!* Ah, here we are, my love..."

The barman shoved a glass into Miri's hand and held the other out to Val Con, who looked into the dark depths and dared a sip. He was not quite able to control the shudder that ran through him.

Miri laughed. "Like this—" she told him, knocking back a quarter of hers. "Don't *taste* it, for pellet's sake! It'll kill you."

"It may, in any case." He tipped a brow, half-smiling. "How well does it burn?"

She laughed again, then turned where she sat, holding both hands out to the woman who approached.

Small by Terran standards and built along the lines of a bulldog, her very short hair a glossy, unrelieved black, her blue eyes set at a slant in a rosy-cheeked, plain face, she looked efficient and practical. She took Miri's hands, leaned forward, and kissed her gently on the mouth.

Miri returned the kiss with evident pleasure and kept one of woman's hands captive as she turned back. "Tough Guy, this is Suzuki. She's my friend and Senior Commander of the Gyrfalks." She waved a casual hand at the blond godling. "That's Jase."

"Oh, cruel, my small," the godling cried. "Heartless, heartless. When I think of the nights I spent sleepless without you—"

"Without me *what,* you noshconner—on guard?" She turned back to the woman. "Why do you put up with him?"

Suzuki appeared to give it some thought. "I believe," she said finally, in a voice that should have been too soft to carry through the surrounding din, "that it is because of the beard. The care he takes of it! The hours spent grooming and perfuming it! Even in the heat of battle have I seen him fondle it. Yes." She nodded. "I do think it's the beard. Though, of course," she added, as one being completely impartial, "the snoring is nice, too. Do you remember, Redhead, when we were on that frontier—Sintathic?—and we needed to set no guards at night, because the animals were so frightened of Jason's snores?"

There was laughter from the group that had gathered around them and Jason dropped his massive head into his hands and moaned in mock agony.

More laughter from those around and Val Con allowed himself to relax infinitesimally, putting aside also the desire to set a knife into the godling, for the principle of the thing. He acknowledged a liking for Suzuki: It would be an honor, indeed, to serve in a troop of her command.

He shifted position to the left of the bar, put down the glassful of horrible stuff—and became aware of someone standing much too close, trapping him next to the counter. He turned the slight amount he was allowed and frowned at her.

She grinned: a mid-sized Terran; large, the way a lifter of weights is large; a gun on each hip and the hilt of a survival blade showing at the top of the right boot; breasts straining taut the cord that laced her shirt. Her grin broadened and she extended a blunt hand to stroke his arm from shoulder to shoulder.

"A pretty toy, Sergeant," she said over his head. "We fight for him, yes?"

Miri laughed, snapping off another quarter of her drink. "We fight for him, no. Go away, Polesta."

"Come, Sergeant, you know me. It will be fair, this fight—a thing for the songs, eh, no matter which may take the prize. Would you pass the chance of a meeting between two such as we?"

"With pleasure. Where's your partner? You're drunk."

Sensing an opening, Val Con shifted balance cautiously, but, drunk or not, Polesta was alert and blocked the escape route with a casual hip.

"The Sergeant will not fight me?" she demanded. There was a strong feel of ritual about the question. Val Con tensed, anticipating Miri's answer.

"Now you've got it!" she said admiringly. Then, dropping her voice and putting a snarl in it, she said, "Get out of here, Polesta. I don't fight drunks and I don't fight crazies, so you're safe on two counts."

"The famous Sergeant will not fight," Polesta announced to the room, which had grown much too quiet. "So, I take my prize by forfeit."

He dove, trying to get around to the right of her, lower than her normal reach—and was blocked for an instant by a pair of leathered legs. He felt her fingers knot in the hair at the nape of his neck to jerk him back, throat exposed.

Unbalanced, he didn't struggle; he got one leg where it belonged and braced himself for the twist—

She brought her mouth to his and kissed him—harshly, thoroughly, with lots of tongue and amid roars of laughter from the gathered onlookers.

He kicked and twisted, not giving a blazing blue damn if it broke his neck, but the move for some reason surprised her and she lost her grip.

He landed on his feet next to the bar, back stiff, eyes glacial. His face had lost color, Miri noted, and every line of him expressed outrage. Not the polite killer here, but a man in a towering fury. She rolled to her feet silently on the bar, ready to back his play.

Deliberately, he turned his back on Polesta and took up his glass from the bar. He turned back and took a swig of kynak. He rinsed his mouth.

Then he spat.

Turning away again, he gently replaced the glass on the bar.

Huge laughter burst from the crowd as Polesta's face went red as a Teledyne sunset. "No one insults me so!" she cried, and swung.

He dodged, making use of the space that had suddenly opened around them to get far enough away from her to have room to move.

She swung again, and he grabbed her arm as it rocketed past, twisting his body *so,* inspiring Polesta to the heights. At the last moment he clenched himself to take the sting out of the maneuver, and let her go.

She hit the floor six feet away with a sound like an infant earthquake. Val Con took a deep breath as a man separated himself from the now-silent crowd and went to the inert warrior. After some cajoling, including a few brisk slaps to the face, Polesta was gotten to a sitting position, though she still seemed rather groggy.

Val Con drifted back to the bar, people slipping out of his way, and settled his back against the solid plastic at Miri's right hand, ignoring Jason's gape. He felt drained—almost exhausted—and wondered briefly why this should be so. The throw had used very little of his own strength, trading as it did on his opponent's momentum.

Miri shifted at his side, and he looked up at her face.

"Pulled your punch." It was a statement, not a question.

"You wanted me to rehabilitate myself," he reminded her, hearing the snap in his voice. He held out a hand. "Give me some of that stuff."

She gave him her glass, and he drank what was left, properly. He drew a hard breath and let it explode out of him.

"Awful, ain't it?" she said, taking back the empty and handing it to Jase, who raised his eyebrows. She jerked her head slightly; he assumed a martyred look and went in search the bartender.

The crowd had split into other patterns now. Across the room, Polesta's partner had managed to get her to her feet. Suddenly, she pushed away from him and started purposefully, if unsteadily, toward the bar.

"Where is he? Run away, eh? Thinks it's done, does he? I'll—"

Her partner jumped in front of her, hands on her shoulders, heels braced. She shook like a mastiff and he held on; he continued to hold on even when she raised her fist—and lowered it.

"Well?" she yelled at him. "I'm insulted. And I should take it, eh? Be meek. Be mild."

The man shook her, though she did not appear to feel it. "Polesta, the Sergeant was right. You're drunk. You made a mistake. He showed you it was a mistake. It's all over, okay? No harm done." He glanced over his shoulder, catching the green gaze of the man at Redhead's right.

"A mistake," he repeated, urgently.

"A mistake," Val Con agreed gently. "No harm done."

Some of the dreadful tension left the man; he returned his attention to Polesta, pushing at her shoulders. "Come on. Let's get some coffee and something to eat. We're due to move in another hour. You'll lose your kit again if you don't sober up some before then..." Talking so, he led her away to claim a table near the back of the room.

Val Con took the glass Miri put in his hand and finished off half in a swallow.

"I think you're right," he said.

"About which?" she asked, noting with approval that his face once more had the proper depth of color and that his shoulders had loosened up a little.

He put the half-empty glass on the bar and twisted his head to grin up at her. "I need a haircut."

She grinned back. "Maybe. Might grow it a little longer, instead, and tie it up with a ribbon, like Jase."

"No, thank you," he began, but then the subject of this conversation was with them and he cut off what he'd been about to say.

"What say we all grub together," Jason boomed "We got a little over an hour before we shuttle out—"

Miri reached up and captured an ear. "Before you what?"

"Shuttle out. Did you think we were going to stay on Lufkit, my small? No wars here—Now, darlin', don't twist it off, I'm attached to it. Part of a matched set, as they say."

She released him and slid to the floor. "Where's Suzuki?"

"It's what I've been telling you, love. You and your partner have been invited by Senior Commander Rialto and Junior Commander Carmody to dine with them in the admittedly limited elegance of the back dining room of this establishment, there to talk over old times and weep into our kynak."

"Tough Guy—"

He was at her shoulder. "Let us, by all means," he murmured, "dine with Suzuki and Jason."

It's possible, Val Con thought, leaning back in an unsteady plastic chair and sipping carefully from a steaming mug, that the only reason people drink kynak is because even coffee tastes good afterward.

He set the mug back on the table and sighed very gently. Across from him, Suzuki smiled.

"I have not yet thanked you for saving Polesta's life," she said in her soft voice.

His brows twitched together. "Saving her life?"

"That kill has four moves, does it not?" She didn't wait for his nod. "All who watched saw that you executed but three—and so Polesta lives. I am thankful for that because she is one of the unit's strongest fighters—a berserker. It is unfortunate that the traits that make her so valuable in action cause her to be such a trial when we have been inactive." She paused to drink coffee.

"I admire the skill with which you were able to subdue her," she continued. "I would not have thought it possible, short of killing, which is why I believe Redhead would not fight."

Miri snorted. "That waste of time? Best thing anybody could do would be put her away. She's bats, Suzuki."

"Valuable, nonetheless. As you well know. I did not say you would come out the loser in such an encounter, my friend, but that you would not take from me what you know I consider essential to the unit." She laid a hand on Miri's arm. "You chose your partner wisely."

Miri laughed and picked up her mug, forestalling the need for an answer.

"Besides," Jason commented, "Polesta's probably so mad now she'll take on the other side all by herself when we hit Lytaxin. Give the rest of us a paid vacation." He shook his head at the little man, both admiring and envious. "My lad, you are *fast.*"

"Best remember it," Val Con returned, retrieving his mug and finishing off the contents.

Jason laughed and turned away. "So, then, Redhead, what about signing back on, taking that promotion we offered you? Lytaxin'll be a job o'work—I won't lie to you, my small—and we'll be in sore need of you. I don't doubt you've found civilian life a trial—and travel's expensive when the client's not paying." He held out a large hand. "What about it, Redhead? A lieutenant's badge and the chance to get shot at first? You'll not turn it down?"

Miri looked at Suzuki, who nodded. "We would welcome you back. You know that. We cannot offer your partner what he has not earned, but he is a skilled fighter and we would be happy to add him to the roster. There is no reason why he should not be at your shoulder."

No, Val Con thought, the equation flaring like iced lightning. No, it's a bad solution, Miri!

She touched Jason's and Suzuki's fingers lightly. "Ask me later," she told them. "I'm glad you want me back." She tipped her head. "Favor?"

Suzuki nodded. "If it is within our power."

Miri glanced at her partner; he was wearing his no-expression expression, and her stomach tightened a little as she turned back to Suzuki.

"We need to get to Prime without publicizing it," she said. "Port's got some kind of damn check going. We can't pass it—you can ask why, but it's a long story." She paused, waiting for the question.

Suzuki drank coffee. "You want us to sneak you through the checkpoint and onto Prime?"

"Yeah."

The Senior Commander of the Gyrfalks shrugged. "I see no reason why it cannot be done," she said, looking at her Junior.

Jason grinned hugely and leaned precariously back in his chair to stretch. "Piece o'cake."

"See to it, then." She glanced back at her friend. "Other favors?"

"No—yeah. Can the Treasury afford to buy some jewelry? I need cash, not geegaws."

Suzuki's eyes dropped to touch the snake-shaped ring and rose again, quizzically. Miri laughed.

"Other jewelry. Everybody's entitled to *one* geegaw."

"Well, let's go find Ghost and see what she says." Suzuki pushed away from the table and laid her hand on Jason's shoulder in passing. "Want to start getting everyone together? It's time."

"Nag, nag," he muttered, coming to his feet. "I'll just take Tough Guy with me, shall I? Have him ride up with Yancey's bunch."

Val Con rose slowly. "Miri."

He hesitated, then shrugged irritably. "Dock 327," he told her. "Level F. Meet me there, fifteen minutes after we hit."

She turned away, taking Suzuki's arm. "Sure," she said.

"How long," Daugherty demanded, "is this going to go on?"

"Until they tell us to stop?" Carlack hazarded.

"Which could be in the next twenty years. Or maybe not."

Daugherty had been on duty since early morning, just ten minutes short of finishing her shift when the order had come through: All Personnel to Man Port Access Yards Until the Present Emergency Has Been Resolved. She had cause to be bitter, Carlack thought, but none at all to be dramatic.

"The Chief of Police thinks they'll have 'em before the night's out. They're desperate criminals, I heard on the band. Every cop on-world's looking for 'em, so they've gotta try and get off. The Chief was real sure they'd try it as soon as they could."

Daugherty said something uncomplimentary regarding the Chief of Police's personal habits. She added, after a moment's further consideration, a rider that hinted at a far more accurate knowledge of anatomy than of practical genetics.

Carlack sighed and considered sending down for more coffee and some sweet rolls.

"Oh, blessed Balthazer," Daugherty whispered, but it didn't sound like a prayer.

Carlack looked up. "What?"

"Mercenaries," she snapped, on her way to the door. "Hundreds and hundreds of mercenaries, coming in the wrong damn gate!"

Senior Commander Higdon was in a foul mood. This was not necessarily a bad thing; certainly, it was not unusual. A methodical man and a high stickler, he did not relish being delayed, nor did he allow the considerations of mere civilians to outweigh the obligations of the lowest soldier in his troop. He so informed the two models of civilianhood who had dared stop him as he entered the port gate at the head of his unit, demanding that all wait, line up, and show papers.

Commander Higdon did not approve of papers.

Daugherty gritted her teeth. "Police orders, Commander. No one to shuttle out without showing papers and being cleared. There are desperate criminals on the loose and the police think they'll try for the shuttle. Chances of catching them once they're on Prime go way down. If they manage to get on a spacer, they'll never be brought to justice."

"And a good thing that would be, too!" the Commander said with obvious relish. "Society is killing off all its good stock—its 'criminals'! Hunting them down and killing them off. We'll be a society of cows, if the police and the lawmakers have their way. Ought to hunt *them* down and nail their hides to the shed! To hell with all of 'em." That settled to his satisfaction, he turned to his Junior to relay the march order.

"Be that as it may," Daugherty pursued, "we've got our orders and we're going to do our job. How do we know you haven't got those crooks mixed in with your outfit, there?"

"I wish I might!" Higdon returned. "Can always use a good fighter. As for your orders—to hell with them, too. I've orders of my own, and a deadline to meet, and I'm afraid I have the means to convince you that my necessities are the more pressing." He raised his hand.

There was a large sound in the night—the sound, Daugherty realized suddenly, of many, many pellet guns being brought to ready.

She opened her mouth, not at all sure of what she was going to say—and was saved by the appearance of a smallish round-faced woman in standard leathers who marched up to the maniac at the head of the line.

"What in the name of all that's damned is the hold-up?" she demanded. "We've got a schedule to keep, Higdon."

"This civilian and I were just discussing that, Suzuki," he said. "She seems to think we're required—that each and every one of us is required—to show papers before boarding shuttle for Prime."

"What?" The woman turned to Daugherty, who wished briefly that she'd never been born. "We are expected. We have a private shuttle. We are short on time. We take our own chances. No more delays." She walked away.

Higdon raised his eyebrows at the two before him. The man, he saw, was decidedly pale. The woman was made of sterner stuff, but she was obviously well aware of her personal inadequacy in the face of an armed and at-ready unit of seasoned mercs.

She stepped aside, dragging the man with her. "Okay, Commander. But I'm required to inform you that we will report your infringement to the Chief of Police."

Higdon laughed and brought his hand down. Safeties were snapped on and firearms returned to holsters. In good time, the Junior gave the order to march.

Line upon line of them marched across the field to the private shuttle, entering the hatch in good formation. In a much shorter time than one might imagine, the last of the mercs had entered the hatch; the door was sealed and the shuttle lifted.

Daugherty, who had been on the line with the nearest police unit, reported this fact. The cop on the other end looked bored.

"It's not real likely the mercs are hiding 'em," she told Daugherty. "The Chief's got 'em figured as loners. I'll let him know they wouldn't stop for the check, but it probably ain't worth a fuss. They've had this lift scheduled for the last ten days. No surprises."

Yancey, it turned out, was the slender brunette Jason had been with earlier in the evening. She grinned at Val Con, spoke a word of admiration for his skill, and handed him over to a man with bluish-black skin and a shock of bright orange hair.

"Tough Guy's your partner 'til we hit Prime, Winston. Don't let anybody break him."

He jerked a thumb at his charge. "Him? Better he makes sure nobody breaks me!"

Yancey laughed and went away, and Winston tapped Val Con on the arm. "C'mon, youngster. Gotta pick up my kit and get in line."

They did so, waiting in line rather longer than Val Con liked, though he spent a good deal of time craning his neck around tall Terrans, looking for a short, slender figure.

"Sonny," Winston told him finally, "you can leave off worryin' about Sergeant Redhead. First of all, she's the toughest somebody in this whole damn unit—that's counting Polesta. Second of all, Suzuki'd skin alive whoever let somethin' fatal happen to her; and then Jase'd stomp'em to a grease spot."

Val Con grinned. "I guess I'm wasting my time."

"Yours to waste, boy. It just does seem—uhp! Here we go."

They moved down the slender alley, out into the main thoroughfare, and down to the port—not so much marching as walking in rhythm, as a unit.

Short of the port gate, they stopped, and the sounds of an altercation came to them faintly. The sounds of weapons being armed was rather louder and Val Con felt himself draw taut. Where was Miri?

Winston dropped a light hand to his arm. "Just relax. It's only Higdon throwin' one of his tantrums. Man's got the rottenest temper this side of Yxtrang. Just ain't happy 'less he's feelin' mean. I don't know how he keeps his unit, and that's a fact—you gotta think about more'n bonuses and pillage-right when you sign on, *I* think. 'Course, there're lots of people around, an' every one of 'em's got their own idea 'bout what's right—" He paused, and the sound of safety catches being clicked back into place reached their ears.

"Now we'll get on."

They made their way through the gate, across the field, up the ramp, into the shuttle, and down a hall, where they had to find something to grab onto—standing room only.

Val Con stopped by a strap set too high in the wall and braced his legs. Shortly, the ship clanged as the hatch closed, the lights dimmed, and he heard the subsonic whine as the engine gyroscoped into full power

"You okay, boy?" Winston asked.

"I'm fine."

The shuttle lifted.

CHAPTER FIFTEEN

Prime Station.

Val Con moved with the rest of the troop through Docking Tunnel 6, Level E, and into the main corridor. He touched his companion's arm.

"I leave you here," he said. "Thank you for your care."

Winston grinned. "Son, I don't want Sergeant Redhead wastin' *me.*" He slapped the Liaden gently on the shoulder. "Be good now." He went on with the rest as Val Con dropped out of line and slid into DownTunnel Sirius, which accessed Levels F through L.

The DownTunnel was a slow, easy float, designed for tourists, not spacers. He drifted to F Level, snagged a loop, and rolled lazily into the corridor beyond. Docking Bay 327 was to the left and around the curve of the Station's wall; he set off at a light bound, savoring the slight reduction in gravity.

She was not at the entrance to the dock. He frowned, checking his inner clock. Seven minutes had passed since they'd hit.

Fair enough—he had told her fifteen.

Back against the corridor's inner wall, positioned so that he could watch the hall in both directions, as well as the entrance to Number 327, he settled in to wait.

According to Winston, the mercenaries were to rendezvous at Dock 698, halfway around the station on Level E. From there, they would board private transport and be en route to Lytaxin within twenty minutes of hitting Prime Station.

He frowned again, groping after some faint sense of importance attached to the planet's name. Lytaxin?

Footsteps sounded beyond the curve of the wall and he stiffened, hand flicking to gun. With a grating effort of will, he relaxed back against the wall and a moment later exchanged a casual nod with a woman in the uniform and utility belt of an electrician. The sound of her steps faded to nothing in the other direction, and he strained his ears to catch the slight clues of Miri's approach.

She wasn't coming. He was certain of it, though no numbers appeared to support the certainty. She'd thrown back in with Suzuki and the Gyrfalks: The mercs were her safety; she wouldn't believe the Juntavas would hunt her there.

Then he was running, streaking down the corridor, looking for an UpTunnel to Level E—and finally the numbers began, flickering and flashing like lightning before his mind's eye.

A mistake, Miri! he cried soundlessly. And the harm done only too clear.

He sighted an UpTunnel, grabbed the loop, and rolled inside, giving an extra kick to send himself rising faster; he ignored the loop at E level, tucking and rolling, spacer-style, and running on the bounce.

Val Con ran, dock numbers flashing by and the equations flickering, flickering. At Dock 583 a load 'bot was jammed cross-corridor, while three humans yelled instructions at each other. He pulled more speed from somewhere, kicked, rose, slapped the top of the 'bot with both hands, flipped, and hit the corridor beyond, running. The shouts were meaningless sounds, far behind.

Sixteen minutes.

Access Tunnel 698 was empty, though he heard voices ahead. The mercs were still in the holding room, then.

He was three feet into the room before a cry went up; and two more before the first of them moved to block him. He sidestepped, twisting, then parried an arm that came from nowhere, slapped aside a knife—

Seventeen minutes and the numbers within danced maniacally before his mind's tired eye.

A gun appeared in a hand before him; he scooped it away, spinning, into the crowd of bodies. There were fewer bodies now— he could see his goal and forced himself to slow the pace at which he moved toward her.

A large obstacle dropped into his path; he dodged, only then recognizing the blockage as something called "Jason." His goal was half a yard ahead, watching him inscrutably. He called her name as heavy hands fell on him and his arms were twisted behind his back.

"Suzuki!" Eighteen minutes.

"I hear," she said in her soft voice. "What do you want?"

"I must speak to Miri. She is in great danger if she stays with the unit."

He was breathing deeply, Suzuki saw, but not painfully, as might a man who had been moving so quickly and doing so much. He stood within Jason's grip as if it were too small a thing to regard, as if he barely knew he was restrained. His eyes were a bright and lucid green.

She shrugged. "We are all of us here in great danger. It is the nature of our business."

"A different danger. A danger that threatens the entire troop. The Juntavas would make little, do you think, of killing several others with the person they wished to destroy? And even if they proved squeamish, how could you be sure that the next soldier you hire is not an assassin hired to kill Miri?" He leaned forward infinitesimally in Jase's hold. "You cannot protect her against the Juntavas, Suzuki. Not if you must ever sign on another soldier or share quarters with another unit."

"And *you* can protect her?"

"Perhaps."

An aide appeared at Suzuki's shoulder.

"Commander? I—there's been a delay. We leave within the hour, not immediately, as planned."

Suzuki nodded absently, eyes still on the man whom Jase held captive. Or did he? Was it not rather, she wondered, that he suffered Jason to hold him, that she might feel secure and so hear him speak?

"If she chooses not to hear you?" she asked him. "If she comes with the unit, which is her right and her privilege?"

"She dies within the Standard, even if she never sees action. I swear to you that it is true."

There was a long silence, during which blue eyes measured green. He was insane, Redhead had said. Certainly he was to be feared...

"Allow me to speak to Miri," he said, and the measured voice sounded only sane. "I beg you, Suzuki."

And he was not a man who begged, whatever else he was.

Suzuki drew a breath. "Let him go, Jason."

There was a fractional pause before she was obeyed. The little man took as much notice of his freedom as he had of his captivity.

Suzuki raised her voice. "Redhead!"

"Here." And she was at her commander's shoulder, gray eyes blazing on his face.

"Can't you tell when you've been ditched, you scruffy midget? I gotta spell it out for—"

"Redhead."

Miri chopped off in mid-curse, eyes snapping to Suzuki's face. "What?"

"Hear him. It may be that he is truly insane, as you have said. This does not mean that he lacks information or that he holds less than your best interest next to his heart."

"Providing he has one." Her eyes were back on his. "Talk."

"Stay with the Gyrfalks and die within the Standard. True and certain. On my Clan."

Her brows rose, but she said nothing.

He flung his hands out, palms upward. "Miri, please. Take the ship—alone, if you fear me. But you cannot stay with the Gyrfalks and live."

"Odds?"

"None," he told her, flatly. "Point nine-nine-nine guarantee that you will be dead within the Standard. The Juntavas has this reputation." He drew a deep breath. "Take the ship, Miri."

"Odds if I do. Alone." Her eyes were hard on his.

"Point six against five Standards' survival."

"If we take the ship together?"

"Even odds over five Standards."

A brief silence. *"Your* chance of survival, if I take the ship alone. Figure it for five, if you gotta."

He opened his mouth—then closed it, brows pulling tightly together.

"There are no odds over five Standards. Point eight against my surviving nine months."

Her eyes widened slightly. "And if you go with me?"

"Over five Standards, sixty per cent against survival." He shook his head. "Miri, take the ship."

"If I leave you, you'll die!" she yelled. "Didn't you *hear* yourself?"

"I heard."

"Then *why?*"

He moved his shoulders. "When a man is insane, does he require another reason?"

She sucked in a deep breath and released it, then stepped to Suzuki and hugged her, catching the kiss on her lips. As she strode past the tall man and the small one, her fist flashed out to strike the larger in his treelike arm.

"Take it easy, Jase."

Val Con stood, watching her go. At the door she turned around. "Let's move it, Tough Guy. I ain't got all day!"

He followed her then, weaving his way through the silent mercs. At the door, he, too, turned.

"Jason!" His left hand flashed, throwing underhand.

Reflex extended Jase's arm; he snagged the spinning thing and swore.

"What is it?" Suzuki demanded, coming close.

He held it out. "My survival blade. Damn little sneak had it out o' my belt."

Suzuki lifted a shoulder. "Well, then, maybe she *does* have a chance."

"But she said he's crazy!"

"Isn't everyone?"

It had proved impossible to check out the mercenaries. First of all, there were just too damn many of them. Second of all, none answered questions, no matter how delicately put, except maybe to snarl an obscenity or show a sudden gun or laserknife in a hand trained to use it.

The other avenues of questioning normally open to him were closed in this instance: Mercenaries took unkindly to the murder of any of their number, and it was hardly in Costello's best interest to allow a soldier he had questioned under "persuasion" to stay alive.

So, though he disliked it, he sent a terse report of his failure on an extremely tight beam to the surface of Lufkit. He added that Lytaxin was the destination of the troops, more to show that he had the best interests of the organization at heart than because he believed it possible that the boss did not already possess the information. Odds were fairly certain that he had already alerted his contacts in Lytaxin's sector. It was just that he had had his heart set on stopping them before they'd gotten out of Lufkit's jurisdiction. A matter of pride. Bosses had a lot of pride.

Ah, well, Costello thought, there's just so much one man can do.

His board chattered to itself for the space of time it took the message to reach its counterpart on-world, and Costello extended a pudgy hand to cut the power. He stopped short, eyes disbelieving on the bright purple knob that had just lit: Stand By For Instructions Incoming. What the *hell?*

He Who Watches was in a dilemma. He had obeyed the commands of his T'carais and made ready the vessel for occupancy by humans, even to removing a container of beverage and another of food-stuffs from the nether hold and placing them where they could be easily seen, by the map table in the control room.

Certain things had been taken from their places and put into containers which were then moved to the storage facility attached to the docking area. The temperature of the water that flowed in the pools had been lowered to the normal blood temperature of humans, and the lighting had been adjusted so that their eyes might not take harm from journeying too long in dimness.

The temperature of the atmosphere within the vessel had been lowered—except, of course, in the Room of Growing Things—and the oxygen-nitrogen mix adjusted. All this had Watcher done, correctly and in great haste, as commanded by the T'carais, and now all was in readiness, waiting upon the arrival of the humans.

Wherein lay Watcher's dilemma.

Watcher loathed humans. They were soft. They were little. Their high voices squeaked across the ears like nails across a slateboard. They were forever rushing hither and yon, stopping neither for pleasantries nor protocol. It was no wonder, Watcher thought, that they died so soon after they were born. They were without cause or benefit to the universe, and Watcher regarded them—individually and as a species—with the fascinated horror of a man phobically afraid of spiders.

The T'carais had left further instructions, which Watcher was unable to fulfill until the advent of these humans. The instructions included demonstrating the drive and the ship's controls, as well as aiding in the setting of whatever course the humans deemed appro-priate. He was also to instruct them in the proper way to activate the autopilot so that the ship would return in its time to Lufkit Prime Station and He Who Watches.

Well and good. It would not be easy to be in the close proxim-ity to humans necessitated by the teaching of the controls, but he was confident that he could do it. Edger had further instructed—

and there lay the horror at the core of the dilemma—that, should it be requested by these humans, He Who Watches was to accompany them wherever they wished to go and to serve them as he was sworn to serve the brother of his mother's sister, the T'carais.

The thought of a time to perhaps be computed in months in the company of humans—even one human—caused Watcher to experience distinct feelings of illness, to the extent that he actually considered not opening the hatch when the summons let him know that they had, indeed, come. But steadying him was the thought of the punishment that would be his when it became known that he had refused the order of the T'carais.

Clenching his loathing to himself, Watcher went to open the door.

Shoulder to shoulder and silent, they walked Level E's long hallway.

At the DownTunnel, Miri stepped in first, floated down, and rolled out. Half a second later, Val Con also rolled into the corridor, using the loop and not hurrying. He landed on the bounce and tottered, catching himself not quite instantly.

She frowned, slanting a look at his face as they went on.

He looked bad, she decided. The skin was stretched tightly over his cheekbones, and his eyes looked as if they were too far back in his head; there were lines engraved around the generous mouth, and his shoulders slumped slightly.

"You okay?" It was the first either had spoken since leaving the mercs.

He spared her a sharp green glance. "I'm tired."

Very tired, he thought, forcing himself to keep her pace. Well, there was only a little farther to walk and a few moment's talk with Edger's watcher before he could rest—would rest. It was imperative that he rest...Shutting that thought away before the rhythm sapped the strength he had left, he lifted a hand to point.

"There."

"Let's go." She turned with him into the entrance tunnel. "What's this one's name?"

"He Who Watches, Edger called him."

"Watcher?" she wondered, brows knit.

Val Con shrugged. "It should do," he said. "I've never met him."

"Oh."

The hatch was before them, the summoner set dead center. Val Con reached up and pressed it, fighting the desire to lean forward and let the opaque crystal of the hatch hold him up.

Time passed. Miri reached past his shoulder and hit the summoner again. "What if he's asleep?" she muttered.

There seemed to be no reason to answer, for which he was grateful. Words were blurring in and out of focus, as if his mind were unable to deal with the process of converting sound to meaning.

The hatch began silently to rise.

When the opening was wide enough to accommodate them, they stepped through into the room beyond, where a Clutch person somewhat smaller than the smallest of Edger's entourage awaited them. He moved his hand on a control board set in the solid rock wall and the hatch slid down and sealed.

The Clutch person bowed—and Miri clamped her jaw on a gasp. No shell! she thought and then saw that she was wrong: a very small shell sat high like a knapsack between his shoulders. Maybe he was a kid.

Completing his bow, their host began to speak sonorously in what she recognized as Clutch speech. He had barely gotten into the first syllables of what could have been a first word when Val Con moved.

He bowed—not as deeply as he bowed to Edger, or even to Sheather, barely a heavy nod of head and shoulders—and cut across the other's speech.

"No doubt," he said in Trade, "the T'carais has informed you that we are in great haste. There is no time for the exchanging of names or other formalities. Please take us to the control room and show us what we must know."

Watcher froze, outrage warring with loathing in his soul. Regretfully, he put both aside. His T'carais, as the soft creature before him said, commanded. His was to endure and obey.

"As you will," he returned, dropping the jagged shards of the language called Trade from his tongue with what he hoped was seemly haste. "The control compartment is in this direction." He turned to lead the way, not looking back to see if they followed.

The control room was about the size of the Grotto, Miri thought, or maybe even bigger. It was hard to be certain because of the way the controls faced the large crystal suspended on the far wall. Star patterns were depicted within the crystal and Miri looked at it harder, giving herself a sharp mental shake.

Navigation tank, dummy, she told herself. Pay attention.

She pivoted slowly, taking in the rest of the area. A large table sat near the wall opposite the navigation tank, flanked with upholstered benches. Cubbyholes were cut into the wall to one side and in back—most were sealed, but a couple were open and empty—and two large cartons were pushed into the corner. Stenciled on the side of one was FRAGILE and on the other, THIS END UP.

The wall to her left was blank, though she thought a closer inspection would reveal more storage bins, and a wide shelf was built out from it at what might have been convenient sitting-height for Edger.

She frowned and continued her pivot. The room wasn't completely symmetrical; her mind kept trying to insist on the proportions she was most comfortable with, and the effort to really look at what she was seeing made her a little queasy. She tried to concentrate on the walls themselves, noting that they seemed to be made of seamless rock, rather than matched plate steel, and frowned harder.

From behind her she heard the rumble of Watcher's voice and the broken-edged sound that was Val Con's reply. She went quietly to the control board and leaned over her partner's shoulder.

"This is the recalibration device. When the ship is at rest you will remeasure and realign. Comfort requires it. If *this* has occurred, you must also recalibrate, utilizing this device—so."

Val Con nodded. "How often does the ship rest?"

"The ship rests four hours for every eight that it labors."

The man took a deep breath, forcing the air far down into his lungs and closing his eyes to better see the mental picture. The initial procedure was *thus*. To recheck, measure and align, one waited until the ship was at rest and made required adjustments *so*. The ship returned to labor when its rest was done, with adjustments or without them. He nodded and opened his eyes.

"Very good," he said, pushing aside that part of him that wondered what the sounds meant. "We must now set our course."

"Where is it that you wish to go?" Watcher inquired around the terror he felt. Only let it not be years!

"Volmer. Planet Designation V—8735—927—3..."

Behind him, Miri shifted. "That's a Liaden planet! I told you, Tough Guy, I ain't going to *Liad* and I ain't going to any world *controlled* by Liad!"

From somewhere he brought forth a last shard of patience and lucidity and made it her gift. "It is a planet of the federated interests of Liad, Terra, and Clutch." His voice was nearly even. "From it we can depart to any of the fourteen prime points. I know that you will not go to Liad."

She wasn't convinced. "I don't like it, and I ain't—"

But his patience was gone and time was running out. "Be silent!"

She blinked—and shut up.

Watcher was pushing at the pastel crystal buttons, lighting and extinguishing them in a pattern that looked random to her nonpilot eyes. After a time, he stood away from the board.

"Your destination has been set," he said. "You will arrive in approximately three weeks, ship time. Of course, you will have to recalibrate your chronometers at journey's end. When you disembark, assuming you have no further need for this vessel, you will press this." He pointed to a large red disk set by itself on the right side of the board.

"You will have sufficient time after you have depressed the disk to exit the ship before the return journey begins." Was it possible that they would not ask, he wondered, hope beginning to stir.

Three weeks? Miri frowned, laboriously working out the sector designation in her head. No. He was translating the time units wrong somewhere. The trip shouldn't take more than two days. Oh, well, he was just a kid. As long as he had the destination coded right, they would be okay.

Val Con pushed himself away from the board and made the slight bow once again. "I thank you for your assistance. I—" He paused, his intention clear and glowing within his mind.

"I would that you say to my brother Edger," he began, forming each word in his head before speaking it, "that, should it come to his attention that I have lived—less long—than others of my kind, it would—please—me that he extend to this, his sister Miri, all honor and—and aid—that he would have made mine, had I— lived—to return to him, as I had promised." He paused to review this. It seemed to contain the germ of his desire.

"Say also to my brother," he continued, the words coming more and more slowly, "that I have been honored and enriched by his acquaintance and that my—love—goes with him in his endeavors." It was insufficient, he knew, but he could go no further. Edger would understand.

Watcher stared at the small, soft, swaying thing before him. He almost understood why his T'carais so honored the creature. Then the red-furred one reached out its many-fingered hand to the one that had spoken; Watcher's stomach turned and the moment was gone.

"These things shall be said to my kinsman, the T'carais." He bowed. "I will signal you when I have reached the end of the tunnel. You will then press the disk that is blue, as you have been shown, and your journey will begin."

Val Con nodded, ignoring Miri's outstretched hand and forcing himself to stand unaided. "I must ask that you make considerable haste in gaining the end of the tunnel. We must be off within five Standard minutes."

Outrage again flared in Watcher, not quite overcoming relief. He would not have to serve these monsters, after all! He would only have to wait in the dim quiet of the corridor, with occasional forays out for food, until the ship returned to him. In the face of this reprieve, rudeness could be suffered.

"It shall be as you have said." He turned without further formality and left the control room.

A minute later, Miri heard the hatch slide up, then down. She looked at Val Con, who was swaying where he stood, his eyes on the blue disk.

"Boss, are you nuts? I don't need Edger's protection. You gave us even odds, remember?"

"Miri…" His voice faded off; he did not look at her.

She went to the nearest bench and sat. "Shut up," she finished for him. "Yes, sir."

A portion of the board lit and Val Con raised his hand, laid it over the blue disk, and pushed.

In the navigation tank, the stars went away.

"Already?" Miri demanded incredulously. "Maybe he meant three *hours.*"

Costello rolled out of the DownTunnel and moved along F Level, not running, but pushing the walk.

Turtles, for Panth's sake! As if he hadn't had enough trouble trying to talk to mercenaries, now he had to go and try to talk to turtles. Ah, well, he got paid by the hour and it was overtime tonight, for sure. Maybe even hazardous duty pay.

A largish green person was exiting the tunnel to Number 327. Costello quickened his pace. The green person did things to the door controls and pressed the summons stud. Costello started to run.

"Hey, you!"

The turtle did not turn around. Rather, it laid its head against the tunnel door and stood very, very still, as might someone who breathes free air again after a time in captivity.

Costello arrived panting, and laid his hand on Watcher's arm. "Hey."

Watcher opened his eyes. When he saw the horrid, misshapen hand resting upon his arm, he jerked back and whirled to face the perpetrator of that outrage.

Costello held his hands out, fingers spread placatingly. "Hey, I'm sorry. No harm meant. It's just that I'm looking for some friends of mine. Thought you might have seen them." He paused, but the turtle only stared at his hands.

"Two kids," Costello said, picking up the thread of his story. "Boy about—oh, twenty, twenty-five; dark brown hair, green eyes, thin. Girl—pretty little girl—eighteen, or maybe twenty; red hair, gray eyes. Thought you might've seen them," he repeated.

Watcher made no reply.

Costello decided to play it tough. "Look, you," he snarled, moving closer and jabbing with his finger. "I know you're hiding something. It ain't gonna do you no good to play dumb, see? 'Cause there's ways of making guys like you talk. So you just tell me where them kids—"

Enough! Enough of outrage and sickness and terror and too many fingers on hands too small! Enough and too much!

Watcher struck.

And Costello screamed, pulling back a hand from which two fingers had been cleanly bitten away.

CHAPTER SIXTEEN

Walls, Miri thought, should be stable things. They should not, for instance, be fuzzy one minute and translucent the next. Nor should they be shot, from time to random time, with sudden neon-bright color.

Her hands shouldn't seem to go into the wall when she touched it, and her feet shouldn't look foggy. In fact, things in general shouldn't be that—indefinite. And why did she feel so good? She wasn't drunk!

Miri sighed, which felt very good.

The good news, as far as she could tell, was that they wouldn't be on the ship very long—not the way they'd been able to slip away from Prime without a head start, clearing Jump or anything.

Yeah, that was pretty good, just sliding—

She couldn't concentrate on the thought. The wall she'd been staring at ghosted momentarily, becoming largely green fog, and she thought she saw a diamond the size of a dozen landcars on the other side.

Absently, she ran a hand down her arm. She did it again. How soft her shirt was! She stroked her arm a third time, eyes slitted in pleasure.

Putting her hands on her thighs, she immediately discovered the tactile delight of supple old leather, well-kept and clean—and snapped to her feet, holding her hands away from her body. There was a pattern in the floor she hadn't noticed before: layers and layers of large prints—the prints of Clutch feet—one on top another, pressed into the hard rock floor.

She half-laughed, then frowned as the idea struck her. She was assuming the semipsychedelics were drive-effects. What if instead there was something wrong with—her? What if she was sick? Or crazy?

Well, crazy'll be company for Tough Guy, she thought philosophically. Worse fates could befall.

Still, her fear needed to be checked out. On impulse, she unwound her braid and pulled the length of hair over her shoulder where she could see it.

It was as she had feared. Her hair was foggy, each strand a little brighter and a little less definite than normal.

Flipping the braid behind her shoulder, she turned and strode out of the bookroom, heading for the control area and her partner. When an entire wall went bright gold as she passed by, she stuck her tongue out at it.

Val Con got up when the control board began to shift.

Well, not *shift* so much as—fade? There was a rainbow iridescence at the edge of things that made him acutely uncomfortable; he tried hard to determine where one of his fingernails actually ended.

That experiment was interesting. He could touch edge of thumbnail to edge of thumbnail and *feel* it, except he'd swear he could feel it before they touched and after they were parted. Even more unsettling was that his thumbs and the fine hair that grew on the backs of his hands appeared to have a certain lack of substance.

Tired. He was very, very tired. He needed to rest.

But he hadn't been able to rest—and the so-called Survival Loop kept popping up, over and over, unbidden, each time giving him figures which seemed not to concern him, but still initiating bursts of energy as it insisted to that *this time* he might not get home.

Home? He closed his eyes, trying to picture the place, but the weird effects disrupted the efficiency of his memory's eye.

Shan? he thought, in something like desperation. Nova?

But the faces of his kin did not arise.

Edger? There was no difficulty recalling *that* person, down to the bone-rattling boom of his voice; and with it this memory brought attendant memories, of life with the Middle River Clan...

Go home, he thought. Rest. Go home and be musician for the Clan...

But there had been those equations when he'd played the 'chora— the Loop, showing him that the longer he played, the less chance he had of ultimate survival. And now these fadings and flashings, when things had been feeling so—unreal—in general...

Seated at the map table, he took quick inventory. The effects observed were not akin to any poison he had been trained to recognize: they seemed to be nearly psychedelic, yet *actual*—which argued against an airborne spore or something of that nature.

It had to be an artifact of the drive—he hoped.

He massaged his wrist gently, astonished at the intense pleasure the action gave him, and closed his eyes.

CMS: .2.

Not so unusual. Except that he hadn't given the Loop a mission to calculate.

Music. Edger had said there were instruments on board. Gods, I could use a 'chora now! he thought.

The display in his head dropped the CMS to .1 instantly.

There was no sense to that, was there?

Was there?

Why should music endanger him? He needed to relax; he needed sleep, rest, a chance to let stretched reflexes loosen. He'd used the 'chora for that quite successfully in the past.

If there was space—and there had to be space on a ship this size—he might begin a session of *L'apeleka.*

He shook his head. Composure was needed to practice that Clutch discipline. He had taken time, between missions, to enter as far as the Fifth Door without a partner, and had never failed to feel more—alive.

I have to go home, he thought.

But no, that wasn't getting him anywhere. The flashes behind his eyes showed a new reading on the CPS, a figure he didn't want to admit to consciousness.

His thirty-day chance of personal survival was down to .09.

"The mind must be composed for proper utilization of the Survival Loops," he recalled.

If only he could relax! He was certain the figures would be higher.

One wall flashed brilliant gold, went to streaked yellow with orange specks, then turned red as the floor flowed green; and his hand looked even *less* distinct.

It was good that Miri was not there, he reflected.

He would find it impossible to deal patiently with her questions, her demands for attention—yet he was glad that had gotten her out of Juntavas territory, that she'd have a chance to get on with her life when they raised Volmer. Glad that he'd gone back for her.

And why had he? What was she but a deadly danger, growing more deadly all the time? The things she knew—the things that he, himself, had told her! The things she had seen—and she saw much, he was sure. She was a threat and a danger, to himself and to his mission—

"What mission, dammit!"

He was on his feet, glaring around at the chaotic walls. Deliberately, he took a breath and combed his fingers through his hair.

Relax, he told himself gently. Stop thinking so hard. This was Edger's ship; likely it would take a Battlewagon a week to break in, if there were trouble. He had security, safety—for the moment. For the next week or two. He was secure. He could relax.

Carefully, refusing to look at the flowing floor, he crossed to the opposite wall and sat on the wide upholstered shelf. He lay down after a moment and began to review the plans he'd had for helping Miri, wondering if that were the mission the Loop was figuring.

No, he reminded himself, you're at low energy. Training tells you to be at your best before attempting long-range planning. Relax.

Closing his eyes, he reached for the simple relaxation drill he'd learned as a Scout cadet, so long ago: Recall the colors of the rainbow, one-by-one, and assign each a special property. Relax the body somewhat, then the mind; relax the body more and the relaxed mind would relax still further. Using that as a beginning, one could go to sleep, set goals, or enter special states for study, review, or reflex-reaction control.

Relax. He began the ritual, lying quietly, hands loose at his sides. Visualize the color red. Red is the color of physical relaxation...

It took concentration, with the other colors flashing in his head. Red. He held it before his mind's eye, using it to relax tight chest muscles; he felt the warmth of his blood, flowing; he eased tense neck muscles, then leg muscles—and moved on with the technique. He saw *through* the colors flickering behind his eyes, seeing only the color he desired as he went through the layers, relaxing physically, mentally, physically, mentally.

He felt as if he were floating, barely conscious of the comforting pressure of cloth and leather against his skin. Mentally, he approached the switch level, the depth of mind where he might assign his concentration to a project or merely go to sleep, if he chose that path.

His thought was focused on the color violet—the end of the rainbow. Behind the color another image began to form unbidden, undesired. He tried to suppress it, but it grew more vivid. He recognized the sequence; one of the training-review programs from The Lectures, the series of tortures and teachings that had graduated him from Scout to spy. Too late, he thought to break the rainbow's spell; found himself locked in, forced to watch: *There.* Before him: People dying. His targets. His *victims.*

That program rated the efficiency of kills; it was not supposed to impose itself after training.

But it was rating his last fight.

The man shot in the eye: That was rated highly efficient; the shoulders of a crawling man protect the heart and lungs, and a spine shot is unlikely.

The woman who had half-crouched: That was efficient, slightly off-center to the left in the chest. Even if not a death-shot, she would be out of action for the duration of the incident.

Now he was swept fully into the review: five, six, seven, ten, twelve—every shot he'd taken to save Miri, to save himself, all those people, dead yet recalled so vividly. Not many poor-risk shots, not many misses. Dead people. Blood on the floor, on the wall. The knife throw at the hidden assassin was rated circumstantially excellent: that man *and* the woman should have been shot.

No! That was Miri!

Relentlessly, the training-review went on, driving Val Con further and further into the dead past.

The walk to the control room convinced Miri of several things. One was that her shirt felt indecently delicious against her: soft and comfortable and erotic all at once.

Another was that the sheer size of Edger's ship hadn't really hit her before. So far she'd passed a room that was half swimming pool and half lawn, and another room that was a gigantic sleeping compartment.

The third thing she'd become convinced of was that the strange effects—the colors and the shifting fuzziness of things—were *real.* They were nothing like the hallucinogens she'd taken years ago, nor did they bear any resemblance to the truly weird stuff that had happened in her head that time she'd been poison-speared in the leg.

Comfortable in her certainty, she stepped into the control room—and stopped.

Val Con was not at the board.

She tried to ignore the strange colors of the floors and walls, the odd rainbows snowing out of the crystal in the center of the...it was hard to define things with all this *change* going on. She scanned the room again.

There! He was lying on one of the long slab seats, but he hardly looked restful. In fact, he looked poisoned, somehow, transfixed—muscles all in stark relief, mouth grimacing, eyes screwed shut.

Miri approached slowly and stood frowning over him. His fists were clenched, she noted. He was breathing.

"Hey, Tough Guy!"

There was no response.

"Pay attention to me!" she tried, raising her voice.

Nothing.

She put her hand on his shoulder. "C'mon, Tough Guy, this is important!" She shook the shoulder, lightly at first, then hard.

"Tough Guy! Let's *go!*" The command voice didn't work—and that was bad.

He was sweating, the renegade lock of hair plastered tight across his forehead, his face a muddy beige color.

Miri bit her lip and felt for the pulse in his wrist. It was strong and steady, but fast. That was all right for now, but it wouldn't stay that way if he didn't come out of it soon.

She yanked on his arm, pulling him into a sitting position, hoping to see a reaction. Any reaction.

Nothing.

"Val Con!" she cried, using her voice as a whip, making his name a command to return. "Val Con!"

He did not respond.

She swore, softly and with feeling, recognizing battle shock, otherwise known as hysterical paralysis. She'd seen enough of it to know the symptoms—and the cure.

Some people could be pulled out easily, by a familiar voice calling their name. Other people required more drastic measures. Pain, physical and immediate, worked best.

She hurled herself forward, shouting in his face. *"Val Con!"*

Nothing. Not so much as a stutter in the rapid rhythm of his breathing.

She stepped back, surveying the logistical problems. Several approaches seemed to guarantee certain death, assuming that this patient recovered with the quick completeness of the patients she'd treated in the past.

Probably he'd recover much, much faster.

In the end she decided for a kick to the shoulder, hoping the spin would have her out of range before he snapped out of it.

She tried calling his name and shaking him again, just in case the gods had had a change of heart, then took a deep breath and kicked out, spinning as she connected, moving to the left—

The impact hit her with the force of an enhanced bullwhip, smacking her and rocking her; her left arm was a dead thing, hanging useless in the socket. He was coming and she dodged; she knew he would grab her and as he threw her she began to roll, going with it, eating momentum with each revolution, trying to stay tucked with the arm that was dead—and slammed against the far wall, breath exploding out of her in a cry.

Far away, she heard a sound that might have been her name.

Tired, she thought carefully. He was tired. That was why she was still alive.

"Miri!"

She pried her eyes open and rolled awkwardly to sit against the wall, arm still numb. He was kneeling at her side, close enough to touch, and the muddy agony was gone from his face.

"I'm okay," she said, willing it to be so.

The horror eased from his face, but a tightness around the eyes remained. "Forgive me..." He let his voice fade away, shaking his head.

She tried a grin, to which he responded not at all.

"Hey, everybody makes mistakes," she said. She eased herself against the wall, gritting her teeth as sensation began to return to her arm, and laid her good hand on his sleeve. "How 'bout getting me a drink of water, friend?"

He rose and moved away. She leaned back and closed her eyes, trying to gauge from the quality of the pain whether or not her arm was broken.

Some obscure sense nudged her and she opened her eyes to find him kneeling beside her again, wordlessly offering a mug.

The water was cold, which felt luxuriously good on a raw throat. She set the empty mug on the floor at her side, and the grin she offered him this time was nearly real. "Thanks."

He did not reply; the horror was a shadow lurking far back in his eyes. "Miri, how can you be my friend?"

"Well," she allowed, shifting her shoulders, "it *is* more of a challenge some days than others."

But he was having no part of humor. She sighed and moved her arm, flexing the fingers. Not broken, then.

"You should have taken the ship without me," he told her.

"I don't waste my friends," she snapped. "And you were standing there, risking bloody mayhem because you figured me at less than a Standard and you had less—and didn't care!" She shook her head. "Tell me why you did that—why you saved my life this past three or thirteen times. No reason for *you* to be *my* friend!"

"And I lied to you," she added, after a moment. "Tried to run out and leave you to die."

"You did not know. And it is reasonable that my life expectancy be shorter than yours. You go into battle, fight an enemy pointed at you as you are pointed at him, collect your fee, and move on. Should you meet an old adversary in a bar a Standard or ten or twenty hence, what would ensue?"

"Huh? I'd probably buy him a drink, and then he'd buy me one, and we'd be cryin' into our third about the good old days."

"Exactly. Were I in the same position, however, my old acquaintance would immediately renew hostilities. With every assignment, I add one or two such enemies. Sooner or later, my luck will be down, while the luck of a person I wronged in the past will be up, and I will die. As such things go, I am on the wrong side of the wager—three years is a long time for a spy to live."

"You're telling me you're waiting to be gunned down?" She eyed him in disbelief.

He shook his head. "No. I was chosen to be who—what I am now because I am a survivor. I fight when there are no odds at all in my favor. I manage to stay alive, somehow, some way. It's a good trait in a Scout. Apparently it is essential in a spy." He tipped his head. "You still have not told me why you brought me with you, when you fear me, when you could have come alone."

"I told you: I don't waste my friends. Even a friend who's crazy, or who could kill me."

"No!" His reply was too sharp, too quick.

Miri raised her eyebrows. "No? Well, you're the oddsman."

She laid her fingers lightly on his forehead. He flinched away and she shook her head. "I don't think they did you any favor, putting that thing in your head. No wonder you're crazy."

She shifted again, raising her arm above her head. She felt as good as new, except for an ache high in the shoulder and another that spoke of bruised ribs when she breathed deeply. "Help an old lady get up?"

He stood and bent, settled his hands about her waist, and lifted her easily to her feet.

Fighting dizzy nausea, she made a grab for his arms and dropped her head forward against his shoulder. He held her patiently, and she suddenly noted how good his hands felt on her, how soft his shirt was and how warm, with the warmth of the skin beneath.

She pushed away and he let her go, though he stayed at her side as she walked across the room to the table, which was getting bigger and smaller in a rhythm she could almost hear.

"I think we both better get some solid, old-fashioned sleep," she told him. "Sleeping rooms down that hall. I'll show you."

She turned, staggered, and would perhaps have fallen, except he was there, hand on her elbow. The instant she was steady he withdrew his support and she turned to look at him fully.

Horror still lurked in his eyes. She was suddenly struck with a fear that it would never leave them.

Reaching out, she tucked her arm through his, pretending not to feel the slight withdrawal. "Maybe we'll do better if we lean on each other, huh?"

He did not answer, though he let her hold onto him and thus force him along the hallway.

She glanced at his face. "Val Con yos'Phelium, Second Speaker for Clan Korval."

"Yes."

"Who's First Speaker?" she asked, firmly ignoring the kaleidoscopic hijinks the walls and floor were indulging in.

"My sister Nova."

"Yeah? What's Second Speaker do?"

He almost smiled. "What the First Speaker commands." There was a slight pause before he elaborated. "Second Speaker has no power, except if the First Speaker is unable to perform her duties. In that situation, the Second Speaker takes these upon himself until the First Speaker is again able or until another has been chosen."

"How do you choose a First Speaker?" Miri persisted. "By age? Nova's older than you?"

"Nova is younger, a bit. Shan is eldest. He had been First Speaker after—after Uncle Er Thom died. But he is a Trader, you see, so he trained Nova for the task and then refused Second, saying he would be off-world too often." His voice was almost back to normal. "Nova is best choice for First: she is on Liad most of the time and is a Rememberer, which is an aid when speaking for the Clan before the Clans."

"You ain't on Liad much, are you? How come you drew second slot?"

He actually smiled. "It gives Nova just cause to complain that I am so seldom at home."

She laughed and nodded at a shimmering doorway. "Here we go."

They entered and he allowed her to lead him to the bed, finally retrieving his arm as she sat, feet swinging high off the floor. He turned to go.

"Val Con."

One eyebrow tilted as he looked back; the horror was still there.

She waved at the bed. "You're beat too, remember? That's what started this whole thing. And this bed's big enough for all the Gyrfalks to sleep on and not be crowded." She grinned. "Your honor's safe with me."

He shadow-smiled, sighed, and came back. "All right."

Sitting on the edge of the bed, he stroked the coverlet and glanced at the woman who already lay curled, eyes closed.

"Miri?"

Her eyes flicked open. "Yeah?"

"Thank you for your care. I was—trapped—in my thoughts…"

"No problem. Used to have to do it three-four times a year. Part of the joys of being a sergeant. Now go to sleep, okay? And turn off the light, if you can figure out how it works."

He laughed softly. "Yes, Sergeant," he murmured. He waved a slim hand over the flat plate set high in the wall above the bed. The light dimmed to two glowing bulbs, one red and one blue, miming alien moons.

He lay atop the coverlet, staring at them, afraid to close his eyes…

"Go to sleep, kid," Miri grumped at him.

Obediently, Val Con closed his eyes.

And slept.

He woke, unsure of what had called him back, and lay listening, eyes closed. Silence—no. The sound of someone breathing in sleep, nearby. His right arm was numb and appeared to be pinned.

He opened his eyes.

There was Miri, face drowned in sleep, head resting on his right arm, one hand beside her cheek, fingers clutching his sleeve.

He felt a surprising twist of something sharp in the center of his chest—painful, yet not painful. He clamped his teeth to contain the gasp and took several deep, slow breaths. The sensation became less sharp, though it remained, warm and cold together.

He had never seen her face at rest before; he noted the slim brows that curved above the lightly lashed eyes, and the spangle of freckles across her nose, spilling here and there onto her cheeks. Her full mouth was smiling faintly, as if what she dreamed pleased her.

Beautiful Miri, he thought and was surprised at the thought, even as he extended a hand to stroke her cheek.

Six hours before, he had tried to kill her.

He snatched his hand back, fist clenched, and flung his mind away, seeking that which had awakened him.

The ship has ceased its labor.

He shifted slightly. "Miri."

She stirred, lashes flickering, and tried to settle her head more firmly on his arm.

"Miri," he repeated. "Wake up."

The gray eyes flicked open, regarding him softly for the space of a heartbeat before they sharpened. "Why?"

"The ship has stopped, and I require the use of my arm."

She frowned, released his shirt, and twisted to a sitting position with a cat's awkward grace. "Stopped? Are we there?"

"No," he said, trying to rub feeling back into his numb arm. "The ship rests after eight hours in drive, Watcher said. It is out of drive now, which means we have four hours in normal space to recalibrate and measure and make necessary adjustments." A needling sensation signaled the return of utility to his arm; he swung his feet over the edge of the bed and dropped lightly to the floor.

Miri surveyed the room. The psychedelic effects seemed to have stopped while they slept, and she thanked the gods for their favor. She slid across the bed and jumped down

"Well, what're we waiting for? Are we going to the control room or ain't we?"

She stared at the navigation tank for several minutes before she walked over to the board and sat astride one of the benches, facing her partner.

"Val Con?"

He flicked a glance at her, then returned to the board. "Yes."

"Umm—I ain't a pilot or a navigator, so maybe I'm missing something, but—ain't that the same star pattern we were in when this tub went into drive?"

He sighed and straightened a little on the bench to ease his back. "No, not exactly. We are actually four light-years from Prime." He bent forward to check a dial and moved his eyes to her face again, half-smiling. "Or, put another way: We've just reached Terran short-Jump."

"What!" She stared at him, suddenly suspicious. "You're laughing at me."

He held up his hands. "No—or at *us*. Clutch ships are slow—rather like Clutch people. I don't remember how it is exactly that their drive works—one of those things people make you study but there isn't any real use for it..." He pushed three knobs in sequence, glancing up at the tank. "But it does work on an entirely different principle than Terran or Liaden ships—Electron Substitution Drive. For whatever good a name may do."

"Like saying you understand how a Terran ship works because of the Congruency Flaw," she agreed, frowning absently at the tank. "Boss, it's gonna take us a hundred years to get out of the sector."

"Not quite. Three or three-and-a-half weeks to Volmer, assuming Watcher has coded the destination properly."

"What I said." She tipped her head. "You don't remember anything about how this drive works—just that it's different?"

"I do sometimes forget things," he murmured.

"Just don't seem like you, somehow." She stood. "I'm going to the bookroom. Unless there's something useful I can do here?"

His attention on the board, he shook his head. She left, shrugging and trying to ignore the flare of irritation she felt.

CHAPTER SEVENTEEN

It had taken some time to get things sorted out. Happily, the victim's fingers had been retrieved intact and there was an excellent chance that they would be successfully replaced. The incisions, the doctor told Mr. Ing over the comm, had been almost surgically precise.

That out of the way, it had taken rather longer than Ing had hoped, though no longer than he had expected, to coax information from the young Clutch person seated on the other side of his desk, seriously taxing the structural integrity of the sturdiest chair available on the Station. Finally, however, Ing had the short-form name of a kinsman.

The blur on his screen became the head and shoulders of another Clutch person. "Yes?" it inquired.

Ing inclined his head. "May I have the honor," he began in Trade, "to speak with he who is named in the short form Twelfth Shell Fifth Hatched Knife Clan of Middle River's Spring Spawn of Farmer Greentrees of The Spearmaker's Den, The Edger?"

The big eyes blinked. "You are, please?"

Extremely brief, for Clutch. Ing began to entertain hopes of putting it all neatly to bed in another three or four hours. "This person is called Xavier Ponstella Ing, Dayside Supervisor Prime Station Municipality of Lufkit."

The person on the screen inclined its head. "I shall inform the T'carais. Please do not sever the connection." The screen was abruptly empty of Clutch persons, displaying instead an abstract design in blue, green, and orange.

Ing glanced over the comm at his prisoner. "Perhaps," he tried, "it would be well for you to come here, where your kinsman will be able to see you and where you will be able to speak with each other more easily."

There was a pause long enough to let Ing wonder if his words had been understood. Then the youngling levered himself out of the chair and came around the table, shuffling, to stand behind Ing's shoulder.

On the screen the abstract was replaced with the countenance of yet another Clutch person. This one was old, Ing saw: his shell nearly covered his shoulders.

"I am he with whom you requested speech, Xavier Ponstella Ing. To save your time, it should be said immediately that, among humans, I have no objection to the name Edger," the big voice rumbled through the speakers, picking up some static. Ing adjusted the gain and bowed his head profoundly.

"This person is most often addressed as Ing," he said. "I'm afraid there has been an altercation on Prime between your kinsman, whom you left to watch your vessel, and a human." He paused, but Edger seemed willing to hear him out completely.

"I am not sure how it came about," he continued, "for the human was in shock from his injuries when aid arrived, and your kinsman appears to have less than a good command of the trading tongue. The short of it is that your kinsman seems to have bitten two fingers from the hand of a human person on this station. This is a criminal offense—it is called Assault and Battery—for which we have punishments. Since this incident involves your kinsman, however, I would not presume to punish him without your knowledge and consent." Ing hoped the old boy was a reasonable sort.

"This human person," Edger said. "What was the name?"

"Herbert Alan Costello," Ing said, wondering.

"Ah. And the condition of Herbert Alan Costello? It seems that I have heard it dangerous for humans to experience the state called 'shock.'"

The old gentleman was really concerned, Ing thought. He hadn't expected that, considering the kid's attitude.

"I have recently spoken with the doctor, who assures me that the fingers will be able to be replaced and that function should return, perhaps wholly, but certainly to the ninetieth percentage. It was most fortunate that we were able to recover the fingers in such excellent condition."

"Most fortunate, indeed," Edger agreed. "You spoke of punishment. It is the custom of our Clan to mete punishment to members of the Clan. It would shame me to have it said that I am so lacking in propriety that I allowed a kinsman of mine to be corrected by one of another Clan, no matter how shamefully he had behaved. It would mean much to me, were you to honor this custom. I assure you that this person will be punished in full measure for his crime."

"It would also mean much to me," he went on, "if you would ascertain the sum of Herbert Alan Costello's medical expenses, as well as the cost of maintaining his household while he is unable to pursue his rightful occupation. I will pay this sum to Herbert Alan Costello, and also whatever blood-price is appropriate. I depend upon your advice in the matter, since I cannot presume to place a price on such damage to a human, who may not regenerate what he has lost. I would do everything that is proper, so that this disgrace does not mar the goodwill that exists between the Clutch and the Clans of Men."

Ing blinked. "You are very generous," he began.

Edger waved a large hand. "I am mortified that one of my Clan should have acted in such a manner. I repeat that he will not go unpunished. He is young and without experience, it is true, but there is no excuse for the lack of courtesy that you have brought to my attention. It is mine to rectify, and to hope that Herbert Alan Costello regains the full use of his hand."

Edger shifted his gaze upward and back, his large eyes hardening. Ing felt a moment's sympathy for the kid behind him.

"I am also ashamed," Edger said, speaking to Ing, though his eyes were on Watcher, "that you have somehow been led to believe that my kinsman does not speak Trade. His knowledge of that language is adequate. It is beyond my comprehension that he would not have spoken when addressed in that tongue and thereby made an accounting of himself to an Elder-in-Charge."

Ing would have sworn that Watcher cringed.

"Maybe," he offered, "your kinsman was also in shock of some kind. The condition does sometimes rob persons of language for a time, even the tongue they have spoken since birth." Hell, it was only a kid.

"You are kind," Edger said with awesome dignity. "I take note of your effort to soften the blow to our honor, but I am not persuaded that this was the case.

"Watcher!" he snapped, still in Trade. "You will come to me. You will come with whatever person or persons Xavier Ponstella Ing deems proper to send with you, so he might be assured that you will damage no other beings before you are under my eyes.

You will come in whatever haste or deliberateness Elder Ing adjudges proper. Above all, you will speak when spoken to, and answer all questions honorably and in the best fullness that time allows. You will think upon the uses of courtesy among and between all peoples, and you will have an accounting of yourself and your actions to lay before me when you arrive. Have you understood all that I have said to you?"

"Yes, T'carais." Watcher's voice was barely audible.

"And will you obey?"

"Yes, T'carais," Watcher replied even more softly.

"I leave you then to the care of Elder Xavier Ponstella Ing, to remove you to me within his own customs and traditions. Goodbye." This last had apparently been meant for both. The screen went suddenly dark.

The kid looked decidedly shaken, Ing thought. "Okay, Watcher, why don't you have a seat while I arrange transportation? We'll have you on-world within the next day."

No matter what other punishment awaited him should he show further lack of courtesy, Watcher could not bring himself to thank Elder Ing for this consideration of him.

Edger certainly had an amazing number of books, even granting that fewer than a third were written in a language that Miri could read. A brief search among those produced *The Young Person's Book of Space Drives,* by Professor Thos. Swift, and *A Beginner's Course in High Liaden,* by Anne Davis.

Anne Davis? The name was vaguely familiar. Miri scouted up a reader, curled up comfortably on the upholstered ledge that seemed to be the Clutch's answer to overstuffed chairs, and fed that tape in first.

"Anne Davis," the bio at the beginning told her, "was a Heidelberg Fellow and respected comparative linguist. Her work included compilations and cross-checks of the major Terran dialects, and is considered a touchstone of contemporary linguistic research. However, she is best known for her in-depth study of High Liaden, as well as the several grammars and self-paced study texts of this complex and beautiful language. A manuscript outlining the grammar and following the structural shifts of Low Liaden was left uncompleted at the time of her death. She is survived by three natural children: Shan, Nova, and Anthora yos'Galan; and a fosterchild: Val Con yos'Phelium."

Miri blinked, remembering his story of the aunt who had taught him to play the 'chora. Just your luck, Robertson, she thought. Leave off wondering who he really is and up pops verification.

She rewound the book and set it aside for later study, then fed the other into the reader, arranging herself more comfortably against the ledge and manipulating the forward control.

"There are four kinds of space drives in use in the known Galaxy at the present time," Chapter One informed her cheerily. "The three best known are the Terran, or Congruency Flaw Drive; the Liaden, or Quark Retraction Drive; and the Clutch, or Electron Substitution Drive. The fourth kind of drive is that used by the Yxtrang, but no one has yet been able to discover exactly what kind of drive it is."

"Bloody guess not," she commented. Yxtrang never let a ship fall to capture, instead destroying full battle crews if necessary. A few ships had, nonetheless, been taken—mostly by the sneaky Liadens who, to be fair, had been trying longer. Those captured ships had destroyed themselves when entry was forced, taking the boarding parties with them. The best thing about Yxtrang ships was that there weren't many of them. The worst thing was that there were any at all.

"Terran and Liaden ships," the text continued, "make use of a mathematical probability called the Similarity Constant, which allows ships to cover great distances very quickly. Since Terran and Liaden mathematicians envision this concept in slightly different ways, the Congruency Flow and the Quark Retraction Drives are not exactly equal in terms of the time it takes vessels to cover a given distance.

"For instance, a Terran cargo ship might traverse 50 light-years within 50 seconds. The same journey might take a Liaden freighter 50 hours. This comparison, of course, is for ordinary purposes of calculation.

"It has been reported that Liadens possess some vessels at the one- and two-man size which, though not necessarily faster than Terran ships, are able to perform close-in maneuvers that allow them a head start on a vessel that must put several light-hours between itself and the nearest planetary body before commencing the Congruency maneuver."

Yeah, so Liaden Scout ships are fast and do tricks and you're jealous, Miri thought. What about Clutch ships?

"The Electron Substitution Drive utilized by the members of the Clutch takes advantage of the ability of an electron to appear in a new orbit before leaving its original orbit." Huh? "This means that Clutch ships move along in a series of physical 'burps' of about one light-day, always making sure that there is room for it where it is going before it leaves where it is."

Miri closed her eyes and scrubbed her hands vigorously over her face before reading that last bit one more time.

"This method of travel," the book continued, "is extremely efficient of energy as it utilizes the mass available around the ship to aid propulsion. It is this aspect of the drive that accounts for the Clutch's navigation through densely populated starfields, rather than attempting to avoid these, as do Terran and Liaden vessels. The Electron Substitution Drive is also much, much slower than the other two drives we've discussed, but time is rarely of the essence to Clutch people…"

Working with the forward, she scanned the rest of the book quickly, looking for reports of side-effects of the Clutch's goofy drive. She found nothing. Apparently humans didn't ride in Clutch ships. Which made sense, in a way: Why take three weeks when another ship can make the trip in two days?

She shook her head and leaned back. That was another problem with being so short-lived, she guessed. One had to risk one's life for a chance to live more. She wondered what the psychedelics were like for Edger.

Pushing the reader to one side, she stretched and fished in her pouch for a ration stick, then stopped with her fingers on the seal-rip. There's supposed to be real food somewhere on this tub, she thought. Tough Guy—Val Con—probably he knows where.

She rolled to her feet and headed leisurely for the control room.

It took a little over half an hour to line up a special shuttle and guard. Watcher would be escorted on the shuttle from Prime to Econsey Port, and in the truck that would bear him from there to the hyatt where his kin awaited him. He should, Ing told Watcher, be with Edger within the next planet day.

Watcher bowed his head, as was proper when addressing an Elder-in-Charge, and spoke as politely as he was able, though the tongue called Trade barely lent itself to courtesy. "Thank you for your care of me. I regret the inconvenience."

"Well, I regret it, too," Ing said frankly. "But it's done now, and you'll have to take your punishment. Just take what's coming to you and then shape up, okay? Nothing like this needs to ever happen again."

Watcher murmured that there was no doubt much in what Elder Ing said. Watcher would devote thought to his words.

Ing left it at that and showed the kid to a holding area where he would be guarded by a nervous security woman until the transport personnel showed up to claim him.

Taking the left hand hallway from the library, rather than the right, Miri bypassed the swimming pool and came instead to a garden. Plants hung in pots, climbed trellises, and crept along the ground, surrounding artistic little clearings and comfortably shaped benchstones. It was a pleasant place, except that the light was a little dull and the temperature rather more sultry than Miri, bred on cold Surebleak, could like. Still, she lingered for a time, inspecting some purple and yellow flowers creeping along the floor, and studying a cheery red cluster of fruit on a trellis-climbing vine. She wondered idly if these were grapes and what sort of wine they'd make.

Eventually she moved out of the garden, going down a short corridor that intersected the hallway of the sleeping rooms, which in turn led very quickly to the control room.

Val Con was not in the control room. No reason why he should be, she allowed, with the facilities of a ship this size at his command. Still, she was irked and, spying the pile of—things—on the table, worried.

She approached the table cautiously and stood with her hands behind her back, frowning as she sorted the items by eye.

Well, there was his gun. And that was surely the throwing blade he'd shown her in the alley outside her hideout—how long ago? But *that* was only the cord from his shirt, and the flat metal rectangle looked for all the worlds like a creditcard, and *those* were his boots...

He entered the room silently at her back and she turned on the instant, eyebrows up.

"What've you been doing to your face?" she asked. "It's all red."

He smiled and came over to the table. "Edger's soap is *sand*. I'm pleased to have skin left of any color."

She surveyed him without comment: hair damp, face slightly abraded, shirt unlaced, sleeves rolled up revealing more abrasion on his arms, and she wondered about the force he'd used with the soapsand. He was beltless and barefoot. She flicked her eyes to his face and discovered no trace of last night's horror. He returned her gaze calmly, his eyes a clear and bottomless green.

Breaking that gaze, she waved her hand at the pile on the table. "Cleaning house?"

"These are weapons, Miri. I want you to hide them, please."

"How come I get all the fun jobs? And why? And even if I do, boots ain't weapons, friend. Neither is a belt, except under certain exceptional conditions I'm willing to risk. Man shouldn't walk around with his shirt unlaced—ain't genteel. *And* you oughta keep the creditcard—never know when you're gonna need cash."

He picked up the black cord that had laced his shirt, slid it through his fingers, and allowed his hands to go through the proper motions.

"Garrote."

The creditcard he used to shave a curl of rock from the wall behind him. He offered her the shaving.

"Guillotine."

He flipped the belt to reveal the inside surface and its three distinct layers.

"Explosives, electronic picklock, sawblade."

He laid the belt down and pointed.

"The right boot has an explosive charge built into the heel, as well as a climbing spike that extrudes from the toe. The left has the climbing spike and a manual picklock in the heel."

He sat, abruptly drained, and waved a hand to include the jumble of wires, pins, and metal doodads.

"Whatever the moment demands. Push a pin behind an ear; drive a piece of wire into an eye—death. Or—"

"I get the picture," she interrupted and then stood for a long, silent time, surveying the pile. Something caught her eye and she pulled it to her.

A black sheath of the finest suede, enclosing and caressing the blade within. The handle was made of something that gleamed like polished obsidian, yet was warm to her touch.

Gently, she curled her hand around it and pulled the blade free.

It glittered in the light, catching and dispersing rays—a live thing, she would swear it, made all of green crystal and black.

With reverence she slid the blade back into its nest—the fit was not proper for her hand, and she knew that the knife had been made for one grip alone. Silently, she held it out to him.

His hand jumped forward, clenched, then dropped.

"Edger gave you this." It was not a question. "Let's keep it simple, kid: You kill me with the knife Edger gave you, and I won't argue that I didn't need killing." She pushed it at him. *"Take* it!"

Hesitantly, he obeyed, running his fingers over the handle in a caress.

Miri turned sharply, flinging her hands out. "And all the rest of it, too! Put it on, put it back, throw it out—*I don't care!* It don't make sense to hide 'em, so I won't." And she suddenly sat, breathing a bit too hard and hanging on tight to her temper.

"Miri, listen to me. I can kill you—"

She snorted. "Old news, spacer."

He shook his head. "I-can-kill-*you*. At any time. I—believe you may be right and that I am—walking on the knife's edge." He paused to even his breathing. He had to make her understand! "You might take your gun out to clean it, and I would react only to the gun—not the cleaning—and you would die. Last night, I very nearly did kill you—"

Her fist hit the table as she snapped to her feet "With your *hands,* you cashutas! You never went for *one* of those damn things, and it's my belief you won't!"

She sat as suddenly as she had stood, swallowing hard in a throat gone dry, eyes fixed on the shine and glitter that was a silver snake holding a blue gem fast in its jaws. "I don't believe you'll kill me," she said. "I won't believe it."

He waited for her to look up, then spoke with utmost gentleness. "Miri, how many people have I killed since first we came together?"

She rounded her eyes. "Weren't *you* counting?" A sharp shake of the head followed. "Those were strangers. In self-defense. War conditions. And last night was a special case. You were out of your head—battle shock. I've seen it before. Knew you'd come out of it like a tiger fightin' a cyclone. My mistake was thinking I could get out of range in time. So we screwed up and we're alive to argue about it. Some people have all the luck."

"Miri—"

"No!" she yelled. Then she continued more calmly. "No. I don't wanna hear any more about it. The only way to convince me you'll kill me is to do it, accazi? I think you're the craziest person I ever met—and that's a compliment considering what you've managed to get done while quietly going bats. And I think the thing responsible, the thing that's making you so bats, is that damn—*estimator*—sitting in your head talking to itself.

"People ain't ciphers, and situations with people in 'em are by definition random, subject to chance, mischance, and happy circumstance. You can't calculate it." She rubbed her hands over her face and took a deep breath. "You derail that thing and you'll be sane as a stone; chuck this damn job and get one playin' the chora somewhere ritzy…" She let her words trail off and rubbed at her face again.

He waited, watching her.

"Aah, I talk too much." She pushed to her feet, waving a hand at the pile between them. "Here's the deal: You point me in the direction of food and I'll make us something to eat, okay? And while I'm doing that, will you for Great Panth's sake get *rid* of this stuff?"

CHAPTER EIGHTEEN

Volmer.

The price of obtaining that single word had been high, but orders had been to spare no expense. Upon being told what his money had bought, Justin Hostro nodded and issued more expensive orders yet.

A ship. Two dozen men of the first rank. Weapons. All to be assembled immediately and sent forthwith to Volmer.

Matthew bowed and saw that all was done as ordered.

In the end, he relaced his shirt, pulled on his boots and stood to wrap his belt around his waist. From the weapons pile he pulled back Clan knife, throwing knife, gun. Rediscovering in himself the strong distaste that he'd felt as an agent-in-training for the pins, doodads, and acid, he pushed those aside; he hesitated briefly before reclaiming the creditcard and wire.

Taking the pile of discarded junk to the far side of the room, he opened a compartment in the seemingly blank wall, piled everything inside, and shut the door. At the control board, he touched two knobs in sequence, nodding in satisfaction at the slight vibration that followed.

Miri glanced up from her labors with dinner as he returned to the table. "What'd you do?"

"Spaced it. I never liked them." He shrugged. "The first time I saw that little pillow filled with acid I nearly lost my last meal." He perched on the edge of the table, watching her.

She put the cover over the bowl that would eventually contain a mushroom soufflé, picked up two nearby mugs, and handed him one, waving at the bowl.

"Dinner takes about forty-five minutes to reconstitute. I hope you like mushroom soufflé a lot, 'cause that's all that's in that box. An' I hope the wine's okay, 'cause the other case is full of nothing but." She grinned. "Sorry 'bout the stemware—came with the kitchen."

"It looks fine to me." He sipped, one eyebrow lifting in appreciation.

"I was afraid it was gonna be real good," Miri said wistfully.

"It is good," he said, puzzled. "Taste it."

She sipped gingerly, then sighed. "Yeah. Trouble is, stuff like this tastes so fine you want to keep drinking it. Kind of ruins your mouth for kynak."

"Liz said you like fine things," he murmured.

"Liz *said,*" Miri corrected sharply, "that I got no sense about beautiful things. That I think pretty can't hurt as bad as ugly. It's an old line." She glared at him.

He endured it, sipping.

After a moment, she shrugged. "Edger says *you're* gentle and good. So what?"

His face tightened with the unexpected bolt of pain. "Certain people have thought so…"

"Yah." Her tone was disbelieving.

She did have some reason to doubt that, he thought. Who, indeed, might have thought such a thing?

"Edger," he began, suddenly needing to hear the names of those who loved him. "Shan, Nova, Anthora—"

"Relatives," she jibed.

"Daria—" Too late, he clamped his mouth on that name.

Miri raised her brows. "Daria? Who's that? Your first grade teacher?"

"We were lovers."

"And then she discovered your true nature."

He took a large swallow of wine and looked into the depths of the mug. "She died," he said clearly.

"Yeah? You kill her?"

He gasped, head snapping up, eyes sharp with outrage. His mouth twisted and he forced himself to take slow, deep breaths. "No," he told her. "I had not yet reached the place where I might slay what I love."

Slapping the mug to the table, he slid to his feet and walked out.

Miri stood for a long time, breathing—only breathing. When she was sure of herself again, she picked up the mug and went to find him.

He Who Watches was ushered into the presence of his T'carais by four human guards and roundly ignored while that exalted person offered them food and drink. They refused, politely enough, if briefly, saying that duty required them to return to port immediately they had relinquished Watcher to his kinsman's custody.

Thus they took their leave, and Edger at last turned his attention to the son of his sister's sister.

"Have you an accounting of your actions to lay before me?" he inquired in Trade.

"Kinsman," Watcher began in their own language.

"No." Edger waved a hand. "We shall speak in the tongue known as Trade, since you require practice in its use." He motioned permission to speak. "You may proceed with your accounting."

"Kinsman," repeated Watcher in the barbarous shortness of the language called Trade. "I am ashamed that I allowed myself to become so unnerved by the behavior of the persons to whom you found yourself indebted to the extent that they might claim the use of—of our ship—that I offered violence to a creature—a being— so much weaker than myself—"

"Cease."

Watcher obeyed and stood silent, striving to maintain personal dignity while the T'carais stared at him.

In the fullness of time, Edger spoke again. "It would perhaps be instructive for you to tell me further of the persons who came and claimed our vessel for their use. Do so."

"They came together, T'carais: one dark-furred, the other bright; both very small. The dark one interrupted me as I began to introduce myself, saying it was in too much haste for the exchange of names and that I must instruct it—"

"The proper syllable is 'he' in this instance, as the person you speak of is a male of the human species. The brightly-furred companion is a female of the same species and shall be referred to as 'she' or 'her' in accordance with rules of grammar applied to this tongue. Continue."

Watcher clenched himself in mortification—to be instructed so, as if he were an eggling!—and took up the thread of his tale.

"...that I must instruct him, T'carais, in the piloting skills necessary to take the vessel where he desired. This I did and set in coordinates for the planet named Volmer or V–8735–027–3, as he instructed. Then did he bid me to say to you this…" He paused, awaiting permission.

It came: a flick of the hand.

Scrupulously adhering to the original phrasing and inflection, Watcher repeated: "I would that you say to my brother Edger…" He paused once more when he reached the end of it. The T'carais waved at him to continue.

"Then he bade me go, saying that I must do so in the greatest of haste, as he would cause the ship to enter into labor within five of Standard minutes. At no time, kinsman," Watcher cried, unable to contain himself longer, "was I treated with courtesy or consideration by this person, who offered neither his name nor that of his companion nor asked after mine. Nor did he—"

"You will be silent," Edger commanded. He closed his eyes and, after a time, re-opened them.

"You are young," he said, "and it is perhaps possible that you have no knowledge of the person of whom you speak. This might account for something of your discontent with his behavior, though I feel that the fact that he is my brother should have borne more heavily with you.

"Know then, Uninformed One, that this person is named, in present fullness: Val Con yos'Phelium Scout, Artist of the Ephemeral, Slayer of the Eldest Dragon, Knife Clan of Middle River's Spring Spawn of Farmer Greentrees of the Spearmaker's Den, Tough Guy. Know also that I make no being my brother who is not worthy. And know at last that the person who tends this name is yet—*even yet*—of an age where he would not have attained the first of his shells, were he of our race." He paused, allowing Watcher time to think on what he had heard.

"Further reflect," he continued, "that the tenor of his message indicates that my brother was in danger of his life. Appreciate now that he paused in doing that which was necessary to preserve himself and his companion to make known to me his death desire, as is fitting between brothers, and to assure me of his honor and affection. I fail to find in this action discourtesy or aught less than what might be expected of an honorable and great-hearted person of any race. I am ashamed that one of my Clan should be so far lost to propriety that he could fail to see and understand this."

Watcher bowed his head. "I will think much on what you have said, T'carais."

"Do so. For the moment, however, continue with your accounting. How came it to pass that Herbert Alan Costello has been maimed by a member of my Clan?"

"After your brother dismissed me, T'carais, I passed down the tunnel at a rapid rate, sealed the inner door, and signaled that I was without. I felt the vibration of the vessel entering drive and at the same moment heard a person shouting in Trade. The words were 'Hey, you!' I did not understand that they were addressed to me until this person who is Herbert Alan Costello laid his hand upon my arm." Watcher could not quite control his blink of revulsion at the memory. Edger motioned for him to continue.

"He asked where your brother and his companion had gone and, when I did not answer, he spoke words which I feel were threatening, stating that, should I not say where these two had gone, that there were ways to make me do so. I was at that present upset by my inability to appreciate your exalted brother and when Herbert Alan Costello said these words and pushed his fingers at my face, I bit him." Watcher bowed his head. "That is what transpired, T'carais. I am ashamed."

"As is proper. You will now present yourself to your kinsman Selector and make known to him my desire that you serve him as he requires. Also, think on what I have said to you, as I will think upon what you have said to me. We will speak of your punishment at another time."

"Yes, T'carais."

He was in the atrium, lying on his stomach on a patch of springy blue grass, chin resting on his folded arms. If he heard her approach, he gave no sign.

Looking down at him, she considered slitting her own throat, but rejected that as a coward's answer and sat cross-legged at his side, where he might see her if he chose to turn his head.

He did not so choose.

Miri pinched herself to make sure she was really there, and wet her lips. "It is my sorrow to have caused you sorrow," she began in stumbling High Liaden, "and my pain to have incurred your displeasure. In my need to say that which I felt to be of importance, I wounded you. That my motives were of the highest does not excuse me." She took a deep breath and concluded in rapid Terran, "I'm a rude bitch."

His shoulders jerked and he turned his head to look at her. "Miri..."

"Hey, I'm sorry! But you could cut me some slack, y'know? I didn't expect you to fall for it! Could've knocked me over with a snowflake—"

He was laughing. "Miri, how can you be so absurd?"

"I practice," she told him earnestly. "Every day. Even when I don't feel good." She held out the mug. "Here's your wine."

He made no move to take it, though he rolled into a cross-legged seat facing her, arms resting on his thighs. "Liz *did* say that you were less than wary of beauty."

"Yeah, well, at least she didn't tell you I was good," she said, frowning down at the mug.

"Most likely she felt I would see that for myself."

She snapped her eyes to his face, unsure of the expression there. "Now you *are* laughing at me."

"Am I? Terran is a hard language in which to make a compliment."

"Not like Liaden," she agreed, "which it's impossible to make sentences in."

"The High Tongue can be inflexible," he conceded thoughtfully. "But that is because it's very like Terran in its purposes: imparting information, dealing with technical and trade concerns, keeping people at a polite arm's length. The Low Tongue is for expressing feelings, relationships—human things. Much of the meaning is in the inflection—something like working the sound stops on a 'chora, to get more mileage out of the words."

"Sounds hard to learn."

"Easier to learn than to explain, I think. Anne found that. I believe that is the reason she never finished her second grammar."

Miri shifted, irritably conscious of the mug she held. "Edger has her book on High Liaden in his collection. Thought I'd learn the language right, since I got almost three weeks to kill."

He looked at her closely. "Will you go to your family, then?"

"I ain't got—Oh. You mean Clan Whoever-they-are." She shook her head. "They ain't family."

"Erob is your Clan, Miri. I am certain they'd be honored to learn of a child such as you."

"Well, I don't know why they should be," she said, puzzled. "They don't know me from Old Dan Tucker."

He lifted a brow. "From who?"

"See? And we were even introduced."

He shook his head, frowning. "You are a daughter of the Clan, one who is courageous and strong, quick in perception and thought. I know of no House so wealthy in its members that it would shun you. You would be an asset to Erob. They would welcome you and provide you your birthright."

"It don't figure," she told him. "I don't know them and they don't know me. I sure wouldn't go to them if I was in trouble. I'd go to Edger before them."

There was a small silence. "Perhaps it would be best," he said softly, "to go to Edger, were you in trouble."

Miri set the mug carefully on the grass between them. He did not appear to see.

"How'd you get to be Edger's brother?" she asked, more because she was uncomfortable with the lengthening silence than because she had planned to ask the question.

He lifted a brow. "By right of the dragon we slew between us."

"Dragon?"

"Grant me some knowledge of the species; a dragon figures prominently in Korval's shield."

"And it breathed fire and everything?"

"It is possible," he admitted, "that we struck it down before it had completed its graduate work. Indisputably, however, a dragon. I believe it compensated for any handicap attendant to an inability to breathe flame by growing at least three times more teeth than were necessary, and growing them three times longer than I feel was strictly required. Quite terrifying."

She studied his face, sensing a joke of some kind; she caught the barest gleam of what might have been—mischief? "So you and Edger killed it between you," she guessed, "with just a crystal knife and a handful of pebbles."

"No, Edger had a lance. I had a pellet gun, of course, but the thing was so large that it was simply a waste of time to shoot it." He shook his head. "I was stupid with fear and reached for my belt, feeling for a bigger gun. The best thing I had was a flare gun, so I fired at its face. That distracted it long enough for Edger to make the kill. Luck."

"Some people got it all," she agreed, unconvinced. "You sure you're not leaving something out? Or making something up?"

"It happened exactly that way," he said, eyes wide. "Why should I invent it? Edger will tell you the same tale."

"Why do I doubt that?" she wondered and held up a hand. "Never mind. I'd hate for you to perjure yourself." She pointed. "You want that wine or don't you?"

"I would very much like to have the wine," he said, making no move to take it or, indeed, even looking at it. His face was completely sober now, and he kept his eyes on hers. "Miri. Why?"

Ah, hell, she thought. "Why which?"

Val Con pushed the hair off his forehead, brows up. "Shall I determine the order of the explanation, then?" He waited, but she waited longer, and his mouth twitched slightly.

"Very well. Why did you push, not to say entrap me?"

She hesitated, hearing his voice in memory: "It is my intention to tell you the truth..." So many debts, she thought suddenly, all to be paid in kind.

She licked her lips, and tried to explain.

"I wanted to make the point—to make sure you understood—that it might be true that you ain't the person you used to be. But I don't think you're the person you *think* you are, either." She paused, fighting for clarity. "Everybody who *does* things, sometimes does things they ain't proud of. It's just that you gotta—gotta learn from it and get on with things and try not to make that mistake again." She took a breath and resisted the temptation to close her eyes.

"And it ain't—*right*—for you to take the whole blame for the things you did 'cause somebody else forced you. 'Specially not," she concluded in a rush, "when it's clear they've been walking inside your head with combat boots on and screwing around mightily with the wiring!"

His smile flickered. "Why take the burden of proving this point upon yourself? When, whether you choose to believe it or not, I am dangerous and unpredictable?"

"I don't—I don't want you to die...Being made over to somebody else's specs—that's dying, ain't it?"

There was a small pause. "Perhaps. But why do you care?"

She moved her head, not quite a shake, not quite breaking eye contact. "You said you'd been a Scout—*First-In* Scout..."

"Yes."

She felt herself tensing and tried to ignore it. "You remember what it was like—being a Scout?"

His brows pulled sharply together. "How could I not?"

"Just checkin'." She kept her voice matter-of-fact. "Scouts ain't the same as spies."

"True," he said calmly. "A Scout must complete quite a bit of training in order to become a spy." He paused, then continued gently, "I have completed *all* of that training. Miri."

"So you said. But you remember what it was like when you were a Scout and that's more'n I expected—" She cut herself off and began again, on what seemed a tangent.

"You know about friends—there's Edger—and about partners...okay," she said, apparently now having it sorted to her satisfaction. "I care because you're trying to be my friend. Maybe you don't even know why—that's okay, 'cause I'm your friend and I'm damned if I know why I should be. And we're partners—though it don't look like either one of us is very good at it.

"People," she continued, as one spelling out basic truths, "help their friends. That's what holds it all together. If people didn't help their friends, then everything would fall apart. I'm in favor of holding things together, so I help my friends." She looked at him closely, wondering at the unease she saw in his face. "You understand all that, Tough Guy?"

He closed his eyes and bowed his head.

"Do I lose?" she asked after what her stretched nerves insisted was a very long time.

His shoulders jerked and he looked up. "I hope not," he murmured. He straightened abruptly, smiling into her eyes.

"It is good to have a friend." Picking up the mug, he drank deeply and offered it to her.

She paused with her hand half-extended to take it, searching his face. His smile deepened, lighting the depths of his eyes, and he nodded slightly.

Stomach fluttering, she took the mug and drank what was left, returning his smile.

He grinned and snapped to his feet, bending to offer her his hand. She slid her hand into his.

"Do you think dinner is ready by now?" he asked as they went down the garden pathway toward the flower-shrouded doorway.

"I think dinner's ruined by now," she said. "I never was a very good cook."

The drive had kicked in half an hour before. Val Con paused as he reached for his mug, his attention captured by a movement behind Miri's shoulder.

The floor was beginning to ripple, shading from brown toward purple. Sighing, he closed his eyes.

"Starting up already? Didn't it take closer to an hour last time?"

His eyes flicked open. "You, too?"

"Think you're special? Though I'm not getting any—oh-oh, here we go." The wall directly behind his head flared orange. "Ugly. Orange never was one of my favorite colors." She sighed. "Damned silly way to make a space drive, anyway."

Val Con sipped wine. "It seems I should have paid more attention in school." He gestured with the mug, encompassing the room at her back. "This is an effect of the drive, you think?"

"Have it on the best authority," she assured him. *"Space Drives for Dummies* says that the Electron Substitution Drive works on a principle that involves the ability of an electron to arrive in a new orbit before it leaves the old one. So the ship and everything in it— that includes us—must be in two places at once all during the time we're in drive." She took a drink and ignored the fact that the table was beginning to pulse and shimmer.

Val Con was staring, a look of stark disbelief on his face. "Correct me if I'm in error. That means that every electron in the ship and everything in it—including, as I am reminded, us—is firing *twice* for each individual firing in normal space?"

"Sounds right to me, but I'm a soldier, not a physicist."

He looked over her shoulder at the control room. The floor was flashing wildly now, torn by dark lightnings, while the board oozed violet and magenta vapors, and the pilot's bench glowed blue with serpentine streaks.

Taking a deep breath, he expelled it and said something softly in a language that sounded like glass breaking around a steel maul.

"Come again?" Miri asked, interested.

"Never mind. It is not fitting that the youngest of Edger's siblings hear his brother speak of him so."

"I was thinking about that," she said, finishing off her wine setting the mug on the shimmering table with care. "How different is Edger from us in how he—thinks about—things? Maybe all this stuff happens too fast for him to notice. Or maybe he can't see it at all." She frowned slightly. "Do *we* see it?"

He moved his shoulders. "If the mind processes something as experience, then it is experience. Reality is perhaps more difficult to define than truth…"

"The visuals ain't so tough," Miri offered after a minute. "Best thing seems to be to concentrate on something else and let 'em fade into the background. Or we could sleep for the next three weeks—maybe not. Had some real weird dreams last sleep. How 'bout you?"

He was contemplating the navigation tank, which seemed at this moment to be filled with busy multicolored fish of varied sizes. "I don't dream," he murmured absently, then shook his head slightly and returned his gaze to her face. "It is my feeling that—delicious though it is—mushroom soufflé will become just a bit boring in three weeks. Would you care to help me concentrate on a tour of the ship? Perhaps we can find a storeroom containing different kinds of human food."

Her eyes lit. "Coffee!"

He grinned and stood, stretching. "Stranger things have happened."

Yxtrang Commander Khaliiz considered the scan-tech's data: A single ship, poorly shielded, with three life-forms showing. No doubt Terran, and normally not worthy of the hunt, but booty had been scarce thus far, and the crew was hungry.

"Enter normal space."

The quarry was abruptly before them: a private yacht, with speed alone to its credit. The Commander had seen two of these in the past; both had been personal spacecraft, owned by individuals rather than a Troop. They'd had no weapons and only pitiful shields.

"Scan contact," the Adjutant announced as the low gong sounded. A moment later, he added, "Intruder scan. We are seen."

In the screen the vessel was turning and beginning to accelerate.

"Local radio," the Adjutant reported. "It seems they are calling for aid!"

"Signals responding?" Khaliiz asked.

"None." The Adjutant's voice was filled with the joyful anticipation of battle.

Khaliiz found an answering joy within himself. "Pursue."

Edger himself answered the comm and inclined his head in recognition of the caller. "Xavier Ponstella Ing. A pleasant day to you."

"And to you, sir," Ing replied, bowing his head deeply. "I have the information you requested concerning Herbert Alan Costello."

"You are kind. Is there further news, also, of this person's physical state?"

"The fingers have been replaced and the nerves are disposed to grow and the bones to knit. Another few days will tell the whole tale, of course, but the physician is most optimistic."

"This is welcome information. I shall inform my kinsman, who will rejoice."

Ing doubted it, but neglected to say so; it wouldn't do to offend the old gentleman. "In terms of the other things you wished to know: Herbert Alan Costello is employed by a man named Justin Hostro, who is a private businessperson in Econsey. I am sorry that I have been unable to ascertain from Mr. Hostro's assistant the precise amount of Herbert Alan Costello's wages—"

"This person Hostro is known to me," Edger said, cutting him off in a most un-Clutchlike manner. "We have done business together. I shall myself treat with him on this matter. Yes, I believe that will be best." He inclined his head once more to the man in the screen. "Xavier Ponstella Ing, you have been most helpful and courteous. I thank you for your care of my kinsman and for your willingness to allow us our customs. My Clan will not forget."

"It is mine to serve," Ing assured him, "and I rejoice to have served well."

"Joy to you, then, Xavier Ponstella Ing, and a good, long life."

CHAPTER NINETEEN

This, Val Con told himself sternly, must stop. There was no indication, however, that it would do so in the near future.

The visuals, as Miri had said, were easily ignored. One simply concentrated on the next order of business and refused to be turned from one's chosen course by fuzzy doors, edges, or ceilings, or by flaring colors. Such things could not be happening. Thus, one walked through them.

The physical effects were more difficult.

His shirt caressed chest and arms with every move as he delightedly slid his palms down leathered thighs. When he put up an exasperated hand to push the hair away from his eyes, the feel of the thick, silky stuff slipping through his fingers nearly had him weeping in pleasure. Irritably, he put his hand to the flickering wall and dragged it along for several paces before admitting defeat there, as well.

Everything felt so nice!

There was worse. At the moment, Miri was waking ahead, allowing him a fine view of her strong, slender shape and the tantalizing hint of sway to her hips. It was a sight that gave him delight, which was not of itself surprising. He had been aware for some time of taking a certain satisfaction in contemplating Miri's physical self; he had, indeed, noted a tendency to allow his eyes to rest upon her more and more frequently. It had not seemed particularly worrisome.

Now, with the beat of the drive calling forth multiple songs of sensuality from body and mind, it was very worrisome, indeed.

There was an inward flicker, and hanging before his mind's eye was the equation showing him how he might take her to his own—though not their mutual—pleasure. CMS wavered between .985 and .993.

Go away! he snarled silently, and it faded, leaving a taste of metal in his mouth.

A position of less jeopardy was required. Stretching his legs, he came alongside her, which put them both in greater safety—he hoped. She looked up at him, grinning, allowing a glance of the sweet curve of her throat down to what lay hidden by the lacing of the snowy shirt.

He slammed to a halt, eyes closed and teeth gritting. Wrong again, he thought. This is getting to be a habit.

Her hand was warm on his arm, and he snapped his eyes open to find her standing closer than he liked, yet not close enough, looking up at him. Sympathy seemed at war with laughter in her face.

"Little bit of lust never hurt anybody."

He shook his head, as if the motion would clear his brain. "It's been a long time."

"With a face like that? Don't lie to your grandmother." Laughter triumphed over sympathy. "Bet the galaxy's full of green-eyed kids."

"Countless numbers," he agreed. "None of them mine."

"Real waste," she murmured, slipping closer until her hip touched his. Slowly, seeming to take as much pleasure in the sensation as he did, she slid her hands up his arms to his shoulders. "It'll give us something to concentrate on."

His hands of themselves had settled around her waist, holding lightly; he noted that he was trembling. Yes, he thought suddenly, with the surety of a well-played hunch, with no taint of drive-effect attached. Yes and yes and—

No.

Easing back a fraction, be searched her face and found what he sought in the soft curve of her mouth and deep in her eyes. It had been there for a while, he realized with startling clarity, yet she had no notion. For all her life, Miri had played single's odds, and if she could deny what she was feeling before it was conscious, dismiss it as drive-induced pleasure...

He pulled back another inch. "Wait."

She stiffened, mouth tightening. "Guess I'm as bad as Polesta, huh?" Hurt showed on her face—but also relief.

"Oh, Miri..." He dropped his face to her warm, bright hair, rubbing cheek and forehead in its wonderful softness, rumpling her bangs and half unmooring her braid. His retreat was timed to a millisecond; and taking his hands from around her waist required more disciplined timing than the throw that had not broken Polesta's back.

"Well—" Her mouth twisted, and she half-turned away.

He caught one small hand and waited until she turned again to look at him. "When the drive goes off," he said.

She frowned. "What?"

"When we are again in normal space, let us speak of this." He tipped his head, half-smiling. "Don't be angry with me, Miri."

The ghost of a laugh eased the tightness of her face as she pulled her hand away and moved on. "You're a mental case, my friend."

"Watcher."

"Yes, T'carais?"

"Extend to our kinsman Selector my regret for any inconvenience I may cause him by requiring you to accompany me to the place where Justin Hostro conducts business."

"Yes, T'carais."

"Say also to our kinsman that, should he have heard nothing from us—either by comm or by our return to this place—within three Standard hours, he must inform my brother the T'caraisiana'ab of this event, instructing him in my voice that he is to act as he knows is proper in the case, always keeping in his thoughts that Justin Hostro has been adjudged by our failure to return guilty of capturing the knives of four of our Clan."

"Kinsman?"

"Such may overstate the case," Edger said more gently. "But when one deals with the Clans of Men it is well to be prepared for ill-thought action. Do as I have asked. We depart in fifteen of these things named minutes."

The meat had been easy, the pillage of no great worth. But the kill had put fresh heart into the crew, and Commander Khaliiz, satisfied that the luck of the hunt had changed, gave the order to take the ship into the underside of space.

"Which way now?" Miri asked at the branching of the corridors.

Val Con considered it with his new sense of clarity and gestured to the right. "There."

"You're the boss." She followed him down the indicated hall, grimly looking at the tricksy walls, which was not a good idea. Her eyes slid to Val Con, ahead of her. In some ways, that was not much better an idea, though it offered a more pleasing aspect than the walls. Vividly, she recalled the warmth and the slim strength of him and his hands curved with promise around her waist—and bit her lip hard enough to draw blood as she strove to keep her walk even, though she was shaking with desire.

He'd stopped and was bent close to the wall, seeming to study something. Though how anybody could study *anything* in the present sense-storm was more than Miri could fathom. She leaned against the opposite wall and waited.

Val Con had put his hands against the wall and seemed to be trying to square something off. After a few minutes of effort, he shook his head and straightened.

"What's up?" she asked.

"This is the storeroom we want," he said, not turning to look at her. "But it's locked, and I can't see the keyplate properly—it keeps running and shifting."

This was absurd! There was food and drink and music on the other side of the door—he knew it! To be thwarted now by something so minor as an inability of physical eyes to perceive—

The answer formed just behind his eyes, in the space reserved for Loop phenomena, and hung there, glowing, its aura strongly reminiscent of hunch. The keyplate configuration was clear. He thought of the pattern he saw, and the door slid open, untouched.

He stood staring.

"I didn't know you could do that," Miri commented from across the hall.

"I can't," he said and stepped forward. The open door to the storeroom was not an illusion. He walked through.

A moment later, Miri pushed away from the support of the wall and went after him.

That proved to be a mistake. The moment she crossed the threshold, odors of every kind assailed her: spices, wood-shavings, wool, mint, musk. Added to the visuals and the textual and the need, it was too much. Much too much.

She sat down hard on the first thing that looked like it might be real. Arms wrapped in a tight hug around her own chest, she hunched over, eyes closed, shaking like a kid in a fever.

She would never make it. Eight hours? Impossible!

"Miri. Miri!"

"What?" The word was a hoarse gasp.

"Put out a hand and take this. *Miri.* Put out a hand and take this. Do it now."

Obviously, she was not going to have any peace until she did what he said. She managed to get one arm unwrapped and, after a hard struggle, opened her eyes.

Val Con sat on the shifting floor at her feet, holding out an open bottle of wine. She took it from him, blinking.

"Now what?"

"Drink."

"Drink? Out of the *bottle?*" Her laughter sounded shrill in her own ears, but any joke was better than none.

"It was difficult enough finding wine without wasting time looking for glasses," he said repressively. "Drink."

She shook her head. "Always telling me what to do. No *reasons,* just—"

"Alcohol depresses the senses," he said. "Drink your wine."

"You go to hell!"

He drank. "I suppose," he murmured pensively, "I could pour it down your throat."

"Bully." But she took a pull, drinking it like kynak, not for taste, but to get drunk.

After a time she passed for breath, grinning and shaking her head. "And I had you figured for a kid from the right side of town."

He lifted a brow. "As distinct from the left side of town?"

"As distinct from the wrong side of town." She paused to gulp more wine. "*I'm* from the wrong side of town—no money, no prospects, no education, no brains."

"Ah. Then you figured correctly. Clan Korval is very old; we've had a great deal of time to amass wealth. Quite likely money accounted for the excellence of my education, which made it easier to qualify for Scout training." He took a long drink. "I don't think brains are the sole property of people from the—right side of town, however."

"Yeah?" She leaned forward, which was taking a risk, even though the shakes had largely departed. "Why'd you say no, back there?"

Both brows raised. "Enlightened self-interest. The drive is still engaged."

"Could've fooled me." She sat back and drank deeply. "How'd you pull that gimmick with the door?"

He took a slow swallow and set the bottle on the bucking floor at his side. "When I became halfling it was seen that I had an ability to—pick up objects—without physically touching them. Within my Clan, such abilities are not unknown. However, testing found my talent too insignificant to train, though I was given instruction in its control, so it would not affect my normal activities.

"The talent neither grew nor disappeared, merely remaining at the same level into my adulthood. I played with it occasionally, but it was too much of an effort to use seriously. By the time I had reached forth with my mind and brought a cup to myself from across the room, I could have walked the distance, picked the cup up in my hands, sampled the contents, *and* been much less tired." He paused to retrieve his bottle and drink.

"Then it vanished. I—" He took a breath, reviewing sequences in his mind. Yes, the timing was correct. There was much there that required Balance..."I believe that the—energy—generated by certain nonsurvival functions is what fuels the Loop."

Miri was not shaking anymore, though she was exceedingly cold. "Nonsurvival functions? Like, maybe, dreaming? Or sex-drive?"

He closed his eyes, nodding. "Or music. Or the very faintest of—paranormal talent." He opened his eyes. "The night we met was the first time I had made music in nearly four years."

She tipped her head. "If you didn't have it and now you do—does that mean the Loop's bust? Or—is it a machine or something in your head? What'd they do?"

"What they did—" he shrugged. "I am fairly certain it is not a physical artifact implanted in my brain—that would be inefficient, since the tissue tends to reject an implanted machine eventually." He drank, considering the problem.

"I believe that it must be more like a—master program, superimposed—" He stopped, aware of something akin to anger building in him, except that it was a thing of surpassing coldness, rather than flame.

"Superimposed and overriding," Miri continued, eyes focused tightly on his face, "that set of programs named Val Con yos'Phelium."

He did not reply. They had both found the correct conclusion.

"Val Con?"

"Yes."

"I don't much like your bosses."

His smile flickered briefly. "Nor I."

"But it's bust now, right?" she insisted again.

Was it? he asked himself. He was immediately answered by the flare of an equation, elucidating the latest figures for his survival. Thirty-day CPS was at .06 now.

"No."

"What then? Something's got to be causing—oh." She closed her eyes and reopened them immediately. "The drive."

He drank the last of his wine and stared at the writhing bottle for a moment before setting it aside. "It seems likely. Apparently I've enough ability to balance everything—that which was originally mine and that which has been forced on me—when the ship is in drive and every electron in my head is firing twice.

"Even more. I was never able to see with wizard's eyes so well that I could have picked up the image of the keypad and the pattern of the lock."

She finished her own bottle and put it down. "What's going to happen?"

"The ship will continue to labor yet awhile and then it will rest." He looked up at her, smiling slightly. "Do you feel better?"

"Better. Beat up. Knocked down. Stomped on. And rode over. But definitely better. What now?"

He rolled to his feet, remembering at the last instant not to offer her his hand. "I suggest we gather food and whatever else we can use from what is stored, while I have extra eyes to see with."

The Juntavas hit planet brief hours after Port clearance, despite the high rates of cumshaw required for such speed. Once on-world, money was spent with astonishing open-handedness for the purchase of clearance lists, ships parked, new arrivals, visas issued, and papers filed.

"They ain't here," Jefferson said some hours later, throwing the last fan of printout from him in disgust.

"Whaddya mean, they ain't here? Where else would they be? Maybe they hit and Jumped out again—you check that?"

Borg Tanser, second-in-command of the project, was a tight, smallish man, given to nagging; he was a good gunman and a quick thinker in a jam, and Jefferson was fortunate to have him along. He reminded himself of that now.

"We checked. No Clutch ships in or out of system for nearly six months. They ain't here. And they haven't been here." He shook his head. "Beats hell out of me."

"Yeah? Well, how's this, then? Let's split the team. Half checks the planet inside-out. Other half takes the ship and backtracks. Could be they're hanging a Jump or two back, waiting for the heat to cool."

Jefferson thought about it, reaching for the printouts and stacking them neatly together. "Yeah—we'll run it that way. The boss was real anxious to have both of 'em. Impolite, they were."

But Tanser was not a man known for his sense of humor. He snapped to his feet, nodding sharply. "Okay, then, I'll take the crew and get out of here. See ya." He was gone.

"See ya," Jefferson said absently. He sat for a moment, staring sightlessly at the stacked sheets, then pushed away from the table and went over to the bouncecomm to make his preliminary report to the boss.

Matthew looked up from his study of the latest data and regarded the two Clutch members expressionlessly.

"I am very sorry, sirs, but Mr. Hostro has given orders that he is not to be disturbed for any cause. I will be happy to give him a message—"

"I have no message to leave," Edger interrupted. "My business with Justin Hostro is of an urgent nature and will brook no further delay. Please allow him to know that I am here and must have speech with him now."

"I am very sorry, sir," Matthew repeated, "but I am not allowed to disturb Mr. Hostro for any cause."

"I understand," Edger said. "Therefore shall I interrupt him." He turned, moving around the comm station with a speed astonishing in someone so large, paused at the locked door long enough to extend a hand and push the panel—which screamed in protest—along its groove and into the wall, then stepped royally across the threshold into Hostro's office, Watcher at his back.

Justin Hostro was behind his rubbed steel desk, absorbed in a sheaf of papers. At the scream of the forced door, he looked up. At the advent of Edger, he stood.

"What is the meaning of this intrusion?" he demanded. "I left strict orders not to be disturbed. You will forgive me, I know, when I say that I have urgent business—"

"I, also, have urgent business," Edger said. "And it must be settled with you in this time and place." He moved over to the only Clutch-sized piece of furniture in the room, signing to Watcher with a flick of the hand to stay by the door.

Justin Hostro hesitated a heartbeat before sitting down also and folding his hands atop the desk with a creditable semblance of calm. "Very well, sir, since you are here and have disturbed me, let us settle your urgent business."

"I have come to speak with you," Edger announced, "concerning the proper bloodprice owed by our Clan for the damage we have done to Herbert Alan Costello."

"Costello?" Hostro frowned. "It is of no matter, sir; we shall take care of his expenses. I am sorry, however, if he has offended you."

"Ours was the error," Edger said, "and ours the payment. Our Clan is honorable. We pay what is owed."

"My clan is also honorable," Hostro snapped, striving to keep hold of his fraying temper, "and we take care of our own. Pray think no more of the matter, sir. The Juntavas shall care for Herbert Alan Costello."

"The Juntavas? This is the name of your Clan, Justin Hostro?"

"It is. A very powerful clan—one that spans planets and star systems. We count our members in the hundreds of thousands and we care for each of them, from the lowliest to the most high."

"Ah," Edger said. He inclined his head. "This gladdens me, Justin Hostro. It is true that I have not previously heard of your vast Clan—and I beg pardon for my ignorance. Happily, you have enlightened me and we may now deal together properly. Do you not feel that this is correct?"

"Of a certainty," Hostro agreed, forcing his hands to relax from the clench he had abruptly found them in.

"Know then, as an Elder of your Clan, that it has come to my attention that your kinsman, Herbert Alan Costello, has offered threats of physical harm—and perhaps termination—to three of my own kin." He waved a huge hand, indicating Watcher.

"That this my kinsman did grave harm to Herbert Alan Costello is not forgiven, and shall in the fullness of time be punished. However, the threat of danger was offered before he struck, which circumstance alters the punishment that must be meted. I ask," he concluded, "if you have knowledge of the nature of the disagreement existing between your kinsman and the two of my Clan who are not present."

Hostro took a deep breath and let the rein on his temper out just a bit. "If one of those with whom you claim kinship is the woman known as Miri Robertson, then I must tell you that Costello was acting in accordance with my instructions to him that she be detained, and also her companion, if he still traveled with her."

"Ah. And, if one Elder may ask it of another, in the interest of an equitable solution after fair judging: Why did you so instruct your kinsman?"

"The woman is declared outlaw by my Clan and has recently, along with her companion, been responsible for the deaths of some of my kinsmen—as well as causing discontent between my clan and the—Clan of policemen." Briefly, he considered the pellet gun in the top drawer of his desk; recalled the ruined door and sat still.

Edger was puzzled. "Was Miri Robertson then a member of your Clan? I would know the laws she has broken, that she adds 'outlaw' to her name while her life is made forfeit. Surely one or the other were sufficient punishment?"

"She hired herself as bodyguard to one who was himself outlawed, slaying in this capacity many of my kin. Her life is ours to take, though she was never a member of the Juntavas."

"She is not your kin, Justin Hostro, yet you pass judgment and seek to mete punishment?" Watcher looked at the T'carais worriedly: he did not like *that* note in the old one's voice.

"That is true," Hostro said.

Edger moved his massive head back and forth. "You baffle me, Justin Hostro. It is not so that we deal among Clans. Let me be plain, that there be no tragic misunderstanding between is: The woman Miri Robertson and the man Val Con yos'Phelium are adopted of the Clan of Middle River's Spring Spawn of Farmer Greentrees of the Spearmaker's Den. It is true that they are young and sometimes overhasty in their actions. Possibly, they have wronged you in some manner. As Elders of our Clans it is our purpose to determine what harm has transpired and what balance may be made. My Clan is an honorable Clan; we pay what is owed. We are a well-traveled Clan and as such have found it good to allow other peoples their customs.

"But know, Justin Hostro, that whatever wrong they may have done you, the knives of these two are not yours to take. If they are judged after deliberation to deserve death, their own kin shall deliver that punishment, not the Clan of the Juntavas. Is this thing clear to you?"

"The Juntavas," Hostro snapped, "is a mighty Clan. We take what we will, as we see fit. Including the knives of the kin of the Spearmaker's Den."

Majestically, Edger rose from the chair. Watcher dropped his hand to his blade.

But the T'carais inexplicably stayed his hand. "You are of the Clans of Men," he boomed, "and thus hasty. Hear me further: In our history was there a Clan that meted judgment to a member of the Spearmaker's Den, against all tradition and without justice. Two persons from our Clan were thus dispatched to construct balance with this renegade family." He paused, taking the half-step that put him at the edge of Hostro's desk.

"The name of that Clan is not now written in the Book of Clans," he said slowly. "Nor is that combination of traits any longer available to the gene pool. Think, Justin Hostro, before you take the knives of any of the Spearmaker's Den."

Hostro did not speak. Wipe out an entire family? And he had claimed the Juntavas as family—countless thousands, yes. But those of the Clutch lived two thousand years and more...

"Have you heard me, Justin Hostro?" Edger asked.

"I have heard you."

"It is good. However, it has come to my notice that those of the Clans of Men have memories shorter even than the span of their years. Allow me to leave you a reminder of our talk." The Clanblade was then in the hand of the T'carais, flashing down—to slice clean into the steel of Hostro's desk and stand there, quivering.

Justin Hostro managed to stare calmly at this for a moment before raising his eyes to Edger's.

"As Edger for my Clan, Justin Hostro, I know that our blades are worthy—the youngest no less than the eldest." He reached forth a hand, plucked the knife from its nesting place, and returned it to its sheath.

"Think on what we have spoken of, Justin Hostro. I shall return to you in one Standard hour and you may tell me what you have decided, so that we may talk further. Or begin to feud." He turned toward the door. "Come, Watcher."

Abruptly, they were gone, leaving Mr. Hostro to gingerly finger the razor-edged gash in his desk.

One Jump back from Volmer, a dead ball of dust circled a cold sun, bands of rubble marking the orbits of what had been three—or even four—additional worlds. The sensors reported nothing else.

Borg Tanser gave the order to initiate second Jump.

CHAPTER TWENTY

They emptied a box containing dehydrated escargot and filled it with dried eggs, vegetables, a quarter-wheel of cheese, dried fruits, and tea. There was, to Miri's vast disappointment, no coffee.

"What's wrong with Edger, anyhow?"

Val Con grinned. "Possibly he did not expect you—and I don't like coffee."

"Don't know why you didn't take him up on that offer and stay," she said, shaking her head. "I'd sure hang onto anybody took that much care of *me.*"

He bent to add a package of cocoa and another of dry milk to their supplies. "I didn't become a Scout in order to stay in one place all my life."

Miri shut up. She knew she was on dangerous ground and she wasn't feeling up to any danger just then. "See any bread?" she asked.

He straightened, frowning at the boxes piled high on all sides. "I don't think—" The frown lightened, and he pointed at a carton by her right hand. "Will crackers do?"

"Suits." She pried open the top, hauled out a metal tin, and handed it to him, trying to not see that yellow and turquoise sparks were raining over her hand. "That okay for awhile?"

"It seems to be enough food for a day or two," he said dryly. "Do you mind waiting here a moment? There is something else…"

"No problem." She waved him off, retrieving the bottle they had been sharing from beside a case of sardines. "But if I'm drunk when you get back, you gotta carry me home."

He grinned. "A fair bargain," he said, and then the towering boxes swallowed him.

Miri settled on the floor next to their supply box and closed her eyes, wine bottle forgotten in her hand. The ship had been in drive for—what? Four hours? There were only another four to live through. You're that tough, ain't you? she said to herself.

Her thoughts settled on Val Con, where they tumbled like the colors in floor and walls. Talk to me when the drive goes off, huh?

she thought. What the hell does that mean? Damn Liadens. Never straight with anybody...She shifted sharply, setting the bottle aside without opening her eyes, and revising her opinion of whether she could sleep for three weeks.

She might even have drifted off, for she was not aware of his return, nor of the hand that hovered for an instant over her bright head before he took it away and sank to his knees before her.

"Miri?" He spoke softly, reluctant to disturb her, but she started violently, eyes snapping open, shoulders tightening—and relaxing instantly.

Silently, he offered three things for her inspection.

The first was recognizable through its flowing iridescence as a portable 'chora. The colors of the second thing writhed and shimmered too much for her to wrest sense from them. And the third—

She took it from him, shaping her hands around it to be sure, then brought it to her mouth, blew a ripple of notes, and sawed them back and forth. She looked up to find him grinning, and she grinned back.

"I ain't asking, notice, how you knew I play harmonica."

"Is that its name? I had never seen one before. I thought perhaps you might know..." He was still smiling, delight showing in his bright green eyes.

"Harmonica," she affirmed, rubbing her fingers over the smooth metal sides. "Also, mouth organ." She squinted at the unidentifiable something. "What's that?"

He turned it over in his hands. "A guitar. I think. Something with strings and a soundboard, at least." He came smoothly to his feet and slid the two instruments into the food box. "Would you like to put the harmonica in here as well?"

"Do—" She frowned at him, loath to give the mouth organ up. "It's Edger's, ain't it? I better put it back."

Jerkily, she came to her knees, then stopped, because he was in front of her, hands out, inches from disaster.

"Miri, if it gives you pleasure, keep it. Edger named you kin, and this ship is Clan property, belonging to all equally. If you would repay Edger for the gift, play for him when next you meet."

"I don't steal from my friends," she insisted. "And Edger only said I was his sister because of—" She caught herself, dropping her head into her hands. "If this ain't the *stupidest* damn way to make a space drive!"

"Because of?" he asked, though he knew what the answer would be.

"Because of you," she said, and he longed to touch her, so worn did she sound. "He made a mistake. Said the knife you gave me—back in Econsey…" She couldn't finish it.

Val Con took a breath and let it out, very gently. "Edger thought I had knife-wed you," he said, keeping his voice even. "A reasonable assumption, from his standpoint, though I had not spoken to him, as would have been proper in a young brother. The fault is mine. I did not think. And I am sorry to have caused you pain."

He balled his left hand into a fist to keep from touching her and continued. "Of this other thing: Edger would not have named you sister only to rescind the honor. He has accepted you into his Clan. Whether we are wed or no, you carry a blade given you by one of his kin and he considers you worthy of it." He sighed when she still did not uncover her face, and tried once more.

"I can attempt to explain all I know of the tradition and customs of the Clutch and of Edger's Clan, though it will take a bit longer than either of us might find comfortable sitting on the floor here. Will it suffice you at this moment to know that Edger does not allow unworthy persons into his family; and that being named kin is a great burden and a great joy?" He bit his lip and leaned back, wondering if she had heard him at all.

"What this means in practical terms, right now, is: Does the harmonica please you? If so, you must take it and strive to master it, to the betterment of the Clan. It is no less than your duty."

"Yaaah!" Her whisper carried the inflection of a scream. She looked up suddenly and shook her head. "Well, it just goes to show you that things're never as bad as they look. When I started this run, I didn't have anything—no unit, no money, no place to go. Now, when I think I got even less, it turns out that somewhere along the line I picked up a husband, a family and a—what? hundredth share?— in a space rock powered by the looniest drive going. *Two* families," she amended and snapped to her feet, harmonica gripped tightly in her hand.

"Maybe they oughta lock *me* up, 'cause I sure don't know what I'm doing." She looked down at him for a moment, then waved her hands helplessly and spun away, marching unsteadily out of the storeroom.

Val Con came to his feet slowly and bent to retrieve the box. "*Three* families," he murmured.

The bouncecomm began to chatter, bringing Jefferson, cursing and on the run.

He scanned Hostro's incoming instructions and jabbed the button for a hardcopy. Cursing ever more fluently, he cleared the board and warped a message to Tanser. The machine chattered, went silent, and chattered again before spitting back the message he wanted to send. The ship was in drive.

Curses exhausted, he set the comm to resend the message every ten minutes until received by Tanser's ship, and then sat staring at the screen, stomach tight.

Abruptly, he thought of his son; and, shaking his head, he tried to assure himself that the message would reach Tanser before Tanser reached the prey.

The stuff Edger used for soap *was* sand. Miri used it liberally, relishing the minor pain, then unbraided her hair and washed that, too.

Music filled the poolroom, though she hadn't thought a portable 'chora had that kind of range on it. There was, as far as she could tell, no order to the play list. Terran ballads mixed with Liaden chorales mixed with bawdy spacing songs mixed with other things the like of which she'd never heard mixed with scraps of see-sawing notes that sounded like the melodies of children's rhyming games.

On and on and on and on it went: Val Con playing every shard of music he'd ever heard. In some ways, it was worse than the drive effects.

The music broke and came back together, jagged-toothed and snarling, reminding her of the language he'd cursed in. She struck out for the edge of the pool as he added a new element to the sounds he was making—a high-pitched, whispery keening, twisting and twining through the hateful main line, sometimes louder, sometimes not, resembling, it seemed to her as she levered herself onto the lawn, one of the Liaden songs he'd played earlier.

And then it changed, shifting louder, intensifying until the breath caught in her throat: a wail that rattled the heart in her chest and the thoughts in her head.

She reached her piled belongings and crumpled them to her chest. Slowly, bent as if against the stormwinds of Surebleak's winter, Miri sought refuge in the bookroom.

The ship had been at rest for perhaps fifteen minutes when she entered the control room, her hair still loose and damp from her bath.

"I give you good greeting, Star Captain," she told Val Con's back in what she hoped was much improved High Liaden.

"*Entranzia volecta, cha'trez,*" he murmured absently, his attention divided between board and tank.

Miri wandered over to the map table. Avoiding the silent 'chora and the guitar, she set down the cheese.

"How," she wondered, pulling out her knife, "am I gonna learn High Liaden if you keep answering in Low?"

"Do I? I must be having trouble with the accent."

Her brows rose. "You got the makings of a nasty temper there, friend."

He leaned back, hands busy on the board and eyes on the tank. "I am usually considered patient," he said softly. "Of course, I've never been tested under such severe conditions before."

She laughed and sliced herself a sliver of cheese. "Very nasty temper. Sarcastic, too. It ain't my fault you don't remember your milk tongue."

He made two more adjustments to the board and stood, then came over to the table. She whacked off a slab of cheese and offered it to him on knife point. He took it and sat down on the bench near the 'chora, one foot braced on the seat.

"Thank you."

"No problem." She sliced a piece for herself and sat astride the second bench. "What did you say, just then?"

One eyebrow lifted. "Are the roots so different?"

"Oh, I got 'good greetings' okay, but there was another word— sha..."

"*Cha'trez,*" he murmured, nibbling cheese.

"Right. What's that?"

He closed his eyes, frowning slightly. When he finally opened his eyes, he sighed a little. "Heartsong?" He shook his head briefly. "Not quite, though it has the right flavor."

She blinked and changed the subject. "How many languages you speak?"

He finished his cheese and dusted off his hands. "At the level at which I speak Terran—five. I know enough of nine more to ask for meat and bed. And Liaden. And Trade."

"All that?" She shook her head. "And you speak Terran better'n most born to it. Little weird, though, you not having an accent."

He shifted, reaching to take up the guitar and fidgeting with the knobs projecting from the top. "I had one once," he murmured, turning a knob and plucking a string, "but when I was put on— detached duty—it was not considered politic for me to speak Terran with a Liaden accent."

"Oh." She took a breath. "My friend, you ought to chuck that job."

"I am considering it."

"What's to consider?"

"How it might be done." He plucked another string. *Twong!*

She stared at him. 'Tell 'em you're all done now, detached duty is over and you'd like to go back and be a Scout, please."

Plonk! He shook his head, listening to the vibration of the string.

"It is not possible they would agree to that. I've lived too long, learned too much, guessed a great deal…" *Bong.*

"They'll kill you?" Plainly, she did not believe it, and he cherished the effort she made to keep her voice matter-of-fact.

He ran his fingers in a sweep across the strings near the bridge and winced at the ensuing discord. Numbers were running behind his eyes: He should not be having this conversation; he should not have helped Miri in the first place; he should not have gone back for her—that was what the numbers seemed determined to say. And now his life was forfeit. He tried to ignore the numbers. CMS was at .08.

"Val Con."

He looked up, holding the guitar across his lap by its fragile neck. The numbers were running faster, switching from one Loop to the other, almost too rapidly for him to scan.

Death and danger. Disgrace and death. Dishonor and destruction…

His muscles were tightening, his breathing quickened—and still the numbers raced.

"Val Con." Rising concern was evident in her voice.

He shook his head, struggling for words. "It is most likely that they will kill me," he managed, fascinated, watching the numbers flash, reverse themselves, and flash again as they counted the reduced chances of his living out the month, the week…"Though it is true that my Clan is a powerful one, which reduces somewhat—" It was hard to breathe; he seemed to hear himself *out there* somewhere, while back here, where the truth was, where *he* was, he felt heat and a need to hide. "—the chance that they would kill me outright." His mouth was too dry; the rushing in his ears amplified the sound of his heart pounding against nearly empty lungs.

He tightened his grip on the guitar and sought out Miri's eyes.

"They would not want trouble…trouble with Korval. So it is—possible—that they would only…" He was sweating, but his hands were cold.

"Only?" Her question was barely a whisper.

"Only wipe me…and let my body go home."

The air was too hot and too thin, but it wasn't happening to Miri; he needed to run from her to get out *get out—look at the numbers!*

CRR-RACK! The guitar's neck snapped in his grip and he jumped back, dropping it and gasping, looking for a way out. His shirt was choking him and the numbers were glaring behind his eyes: dead, dead, zero percent chance of survival. He grabbed a wall and held fast.

"No! No! Not here! Dammit, not here!" I won't die here! I'll get out…

"Val Con!"

The scream penetrated his panic, piercing the terror for an instant. It seemed so sure a name—Val Con. In fact: Val Con yos'Phelium Scout, Artist of the Ephemeral, Slayer of the Eldest Dragon, Knife Clan of Middle River's Spring Spawn of Farmer Greentrees of the Spearmaker's Den—and from somewhere her voice added, "Tough Guy!"

He sobbed and held on, then found himself gasping against the strong stone wall. Several feet away, hand outstretched and terror in her eyes, was Miri. He brought his breathing down slowly and calmed himself, feeling the air cool him as his hands began to warm.

The numbers were clear: zero and zero. No chance of surviving the mission. The mission itself a failure. Accordingly, he was dead.

He took another breath, leaned back against the wall, and accepted the slow slide to the floor as natural, even comforting; the sound he made verged on laughter.

"Val Con? You there?"

He nodded. "Here," he said raggedly.

She approached cautiously and knelt by his side, gray eyes intent on his face.

"Miri?"

"Yo."

His breath was still slowing; his lungs ached from the hyperbreathing he'd done, but he was calm. He knew his name and with that he knew he was safe. "Miri, I think I died just then."

Her brows twitched upward and she reached out to lay cool fingers on the pulse at the base of his throat. Shaking her head, she removed them.

"Sergeant Robertson regrets to report a glitch in the system, sir."

He laughed, a jagged stone of sound, then lifted both hands and ran them through sweat-soaked hair.

"Dead," he said. "The Loop showed me dead at the moment I told you I would be wiped." His breath was nearly back, and he felt at ease, though drained in a way he'd never been drained before. "I think I believed it—panicked or—something. I *believed* them…"

"The Loop," Miri asked, hoping. "It's gone? Or busted?"

"No…Still there. Not, I think, broken. But it may have been programmed to lie to me—do *you* understand?" he asked her suddenly. "They took so much—so I would survive, they said. Surely it's important to survive? My music, my dreams—so *much*—and all to give life to a thing that lies…" He rubbed his hands over his face. "I don't understand…"

Miri laid a wary hand on his arm; his eyes were on her face instantly, noting uncertainty and strain.

"Yes."

She bit her lip. "What's—wiped—please?" Her voice was small and tentative, most un-Mirilike.

He shifted slightly, bumping a leg against the fallen guitar. Awkwardly, he retrieved it and cradled the splintered neck. "Ah, poor thing…"

Looking up, he half-smiled. "Wiped is…" He shook his head, keeping a wary eye out for phantom equations. "A machine was made in answer to the thought that it would be—convenient—if, instead of impersonating someone, an agent could *become* that person. It was thought that this could be accomplished by—smoothing out the agent's own personality and overlaying a second." He saw nothing. The screen behind his eyes was blank. "When the mission was done, the second personality would be removed and the agent allowed to reemerge."

He paused for breath. Miri was watching his eyes closely, the line of a frown showing between her brows.

"It didn't work out very well. The only thing the machine did was eradicate, totally, the prime personality. No other personality could be grafted on to what remained. Nor could more conventional learning take place. The person was gone, irretrievably, though the body might live on to a very respectable old age."

A shudder shook her violently and she bent her head, swallowing hard and screwing her eyes shut against the sudden tide of sickness.

"Miri." Warm fingers brushed down her cheek, then slid under her chin, gently insisting that she raise her face. She gave in, eyes still shut, and after a moment felt him brushing away the tears.

"Miri, please look at me."

In a moment she opened her eyes, though she couldn't manage a smile.

His own smile was a better effort than the last; he shook his head. "It would be wisest not to mourn me until they bring the body before you."

"They bring me a zombie, I'll shoot it dead!"

"I would appreciate it," he told her gravely.

She dredged up a lopsided grin, looking closely into his tired eyes and grim face and hoping that this last little scene was the final drama his unnamed bosses had engineered. It had been ugly enough— and, potentially, deadly enough. What if he'd been in a shoot-out or one of the other tight spots he seemed prone to when that damned— panic—had hit?

Murder by extrapolation? She shook the thought away. "How are you now?" she ventured, aware that he had dropped his hand and twined his fingers lightly around hers.

He smiled. "Tired. It is not every day that one dies and lives to tell the tale."

She grinned and squeezed his hand. "Wanna get up? Or should I get you a blanket?"

"Up, I think." But that was easier said than done. Somehow, they both managed to rise; they stood close, leaning against each other.

Val Con moved, surprising them both as he hugged Miri to him and dropped his face to her hair, murmuring something that did not sound like Terran or Trade. Holding her away, he looked seriously into her cautious face.

"There are many things for us to talk about—but there are many things I must first say to myself, to hear what the answers may now be. I require time—perhaps a day, perhaps two—by myself. I will take food, find another room to be in..."

She stiffened. "Ain't no reason to run away from me—"

He laid light fingers over her lips, cutting her off. "Not *away* from you. But think: Twice in two days I have frightened us both—badly. I must take time—while there is so much time—to find the man I am, now that there are two I am not." He unsealed her lips and touched her cheek. "It is something we both should know, I think."

Not trusting her voice, she nodded.

"Miri Robertson." There was a glimmer of ritual in his voice. "Consider please if you wish to become my partner—to remain my partner. We will speak in a few days."

Quickly, he bent and kissed her forehead, then released her and turned to gather food for his time away. The broken guitar he left on the map table. One day, he vowed, he would repair it.

CHAPTER TWENTY-ONE

For the fourth time Miri sneaked back to the bookroom after having peeked in at her partner. She felt like a spy herself after having agreed that he should have his time to himself. But, despite her great joy at having all the marvels of Edger's library at her command, she discovered in herself a need to be sure that Val Con was all right.

For the second time, she was confused by what she'd seen: Val Con standing in the center of the large room, moving slowly, eyes closed. He would stop for a minute, two minutes, three—and then she'd realize that he'd done a half-turn in that time. His movements had been sinuous and twisting, like a dance, but so *slow,* as if he were Edger imitating a flower growing.

In the midst of this, he would suddenly run or jump or sit to relax or concentrate, and then get up and try the same thing again. Or maybe not *quite* the same thing.

That there was method here, she was certain. She refused to think that it could be madness, as well.

To pass the time, she did more ordinary calisthenics, making sure her body was in shape to fight, to act, when this time of fairy-tale safety was over.

And the books! She worked her way through the High Liaden grammar, then devoured, in rapid succession, a small book of poems by someone named Joanna Wilcheket, a rather longer volume illuminating the intricacies of a team game called bokdingle—which she thought sounded more like pitched battle than a game—then learned the proper way to veri-date Qontikwian tree carvings. She finished up with a history of some place called Truanna, which had self-destructed back in Standard 250.

She spent an entire rest period wandering through a Terran dictionary, wondering at all the words she'd never heard of—and this was her milk tongue! An hour was given to an adventure novel by an ancient Terran writer; her sides hurt from laughing when she finished, but she searched the shelves for more.

Hiking through the ship, she noticed that the weird effects of the drive seemed much less distracting at the ship's stern, where the cargo holds were. The bookroom wasn't too bad, once she adjusted. The control room was worst.

She filed that away to mention to Val Con.

The ship's labors ended and began again. At the end of three days, Miri was worried, visions of him lying rigid and trapped intruding between her and the words in the reader—but then she caught sight of him working very hard, doing exercises she was familiar with.

That's okay, then, she thought in relief, and continued on her way to the pool.

The ship was between labors, and Miri woke. Stretching, she realized that this wasn't what had awakened her; it was the crisp smell of breakfast hanging in the air, odors tantalizingly close to coffee and—*coffee?*

She sat up on the shelf—sleeping in the library had become a habit; it was too depressing to sleep all alone in one of the Clutch's big beds—and, weaving her hair into a single loose braid, she considered what her nose was telling her.

Coffee, she decided. She went to investigate.

Val Con was sitting crosslegged before a portable camp-stove in the center of the wide hallway, watching the entrance to the bookroom. A pan on the left burner held meat and pancakes; on the right steamed a ceramapot of dark, brown coffee.

"Good morning, cha'trez."

"Morning," she returned, staring at him from the doorway.

"You will join me for breakfast, I hope?" He waved a hand at the places set, camp fashion, with plates, cups, disposable napkins, and utensils.

"Is that *real* coffee?" she asked, coming closer.

"You tell me, my friend. The pack said something like 'Certified Brazilian,' I believe."

She grinned and pushed a cup at him. "Pour, dammit."

"Yes, Sergeant," he murmured, nodding at the pad he'd laid out for her to sit on.

She folded her legs and sat, studying his face. He turned, offering her the full cup, and lifted an eyebrow.

"Have you a problem, Miri Robertson?"

She took the cup. Gods, but real coffee smelled so good!

"You look—different," she told him.

"Ah." His shoulders dipped in the gesture she never quite understood. "I am sorry."

"I ain't." She sipped, closing her eyes to savor the taste and to buy herself time. Different, yes. Alive? His eyes were vividly green; his face in general was less haggard, less—prisoned.

She opened her eyes to find him watching her and smiled. Yes. It was as if his energy filled him joyfully now, rather than pushing him on past endurance.

"Where'd you get the goodies?" she asked, indicating the meal cooking on the small stove. "I thought we decided there wasn't any coffee."

"I was not—thinking properly," he explained, "when we looked before. Edger is nothing if not thorough, and so I looked for camp sets. He'd seen me use them when I stayed with the Clan." He grinned.

"There is approximately an eight years' supply of camp sets in the second storage compartment. Terran sets, so it seemed safe to assume there would be coffee."

She stared at him. "Not thinking properly? I'd like to know why not! You couldn't have had anything else on your mind."

He laughed as he turned the meat and the flapjacks.

She took another sip of coffee. "Val Con?"

"Yes."

She frowned slightly, watching his face. "How are you, my friend?"

"I am—well. Not very well. Nor even completely well. There was much—damage done, with little care taken. It was not expected that I would live quite so long." He shook his head. "I will have to work hard, to be certain that all heals rightly."

She hesitated. "I—needed to make sure you were okay, so I—spied—on you. That *slow* stuff you were doing—is that to make sure that all—heals rightly?"

He nodded. "It is called *L'apeleka*—a Clutch thing. It is—" He paused, eyes half-closed, then laughed softly, spreading his hands, palms upward. "The best I can do in Terran is that it is a way of—reaffirming oneself. Of celebrating proper thought."

"Oh." She blinked at him.

He laughed fully. "Forgive me, cha'trez, but Terran will not bend so far. I *do* know what *L'apeleka* is and I am certain that I could explain it to you, but you must tell me which you desire to learn first—Low Liaden or Clutch?"

She laughed, then sobered. "The Loop?"

"Exists." He looked at her closely. "The Loops are tools, Miri. They do not demand a course of action, only elucidate it."

She drank coffee. "But *you* ain't a tool."

His face hardened momentarily. "I think not." He turned his attention to the pan as she watched.

Funny, she thought, she felt warm, though she hadn't felt cold before. And she felt comforted. She wondered if she'd been sad without realizing it.

He divided the contents of the pan evenly between the two plates.

He did look well, she decided. Sure of himself, not just sure of what he could do.

Offering her a plate, Val Con tipped an eyebrow at her cup. "More coffee, cha'trez? It would be a shame to waste what is in the pot."

"Never happen." Laughing, she held it out for a refill. "Thanks, partner."

"So it runs that way?" He looked at her speculatively as he picked up his own plate. "I had thought the question not properly asked." He paused, watching her as she began to eat.

"And the other?" he asked softly.

She frowned, puzzled. "What other?"

"Ah, *that* question was not asked so well," he murmured, seemingly to himself. Picking up his fork, he began to eat.

Miri shook her head and returned to her breakfast, savoring tastes, smells, and silent comradeship.

Val Con ate his own meal with relish, his eyes on her. She had rested, he saw; the lines of strain that had been in her face since they'd met were gone, and she seemed easier within herself, as if she, too, had reaffirmed who she was. Her eyes, when they rested upon him, were unguarded. He hugged that small warmth to him and dared to hope.

In a short time, he set his plate aside and leaned back to watch her where she sat, her back against the wall and the cup cradled in her hands.

"Breakfast was fine." She smiled at him. "Thank you."

"You're welcome," he replied. "Miri?"

"Yo."

He shifted, and brought his gaze to meet hers. "Only if *you* wish it, Miri..."

She set the cup down, giving him her whole attention. "Okay."

"It would please me very much," he said, choosing each word with care, "to allow the—fact—of our marriage to endure."

She blinked. She blinked again and broke his gaze, looking down and groping for her cup.

Val Con held his breath.

"You got a family and stuff, doncha?" she asked, head bent. "They probably wouldn't be...overjoyed...about you marrying somebody who—somebody like me. 'Specially when you don't—" She swallowed, hard. "Partners are lovers, sometimes."

Slowly, he let his breath go. "There are," he told her softly, "several answers to be made. The first is that whom I wed is *my* choice, not the choice of the Clan." He paused, then dared to add, *"I* wish us to be wed."

Her shoulders twitched, but she did not look at him. After a moment, he continued. "It is unlikely that I will return to Liad, cha'trez."

Her eyes flicked to his, warm with pity. "You mind?"

"I mind," he admitted. "But I feel certain I would mind being dead much more." He smiled. "Understand that it is no great bargain I offer you: A short, skinny man with only the money in his pouch and a certain ability on the 'chora to recommend him—"

"So much?" She grinned. "Short and skinny?"

"Thus was I described to your friend Liz—"

She laughed, tossing off the rest of her coffee as he grinned. "Is Edger an honest man?"

"None more honest."

"And our—marriage—stands up to laws and stuff?"

He considered it. "I believe so. The post that Edger holds—T'carais—is somewhere between that of father, captain, priest, and mayor. If we are wed by custom—partnered as well, if you like—and it is certified and witnessed by the Clutch, there are few who would question it. The Clutch, like the mythical elephant, never forgets. Nor does it remember wrongly. If you will—if you truly desire it—then it is done."

She took a breath. "It's real?" she asked quietly. "Not something you're doing 'cause it's—expedient?"

He looked at her sharply, then smiled ruefully. "To the Clan of Middle River, the Spearmaker's Den, it is fact. It is something that I wish for completely: That you be my partner, that we be mated for life."

Miri picked up her cup and found it empty. "Is there more coffee?"

"I can make more if you wish."

"But?"

"But I would rather fill a cup with wine that we share."

She slid across the rock floor until she was next to him. "You have wine?"

"It is here," he said. "Though I should tell you that it is Green Nogalin. A large bottle of it."

Her brows rose. "That's the aphrodisiac? The one banned on about three-quarters of the Terran worlds?"

"So it is."

She shook her head. "And I thought Edger was an innocent." She paused. "Husband?"

Thank you, gods, he thought. "Yes, my wife?"

"Please open the wine."

He smiled and leaned close. "In a moment—"

Miri was on her feet, gun in hand, with the first siren shriek. Val Con was already far down the hall, strobe beams throwing his shadow crazily over the rock walls.

"The control room—quickly!"

They ran.

"What *is* it?" she demanded, braking to a halt just inside the door.

"Distress beacon." He was at the board, hands busy, head tipped up at the tank. "But I don't see—ah."

He upped the magnification and Miri saw it, too: a drifting bulk that could only be a ship. Keeping her eyes on it, she slid her gun back into its holster and went slowly toward the board.

Val Con moved his hand and began speaking in slow, distinct Trade. "This is Scout Commander Val Con yos'Phelium on Clutch vessel in tangential orbit. We hear your distress signal and will attempt a rescue. Reports required: damage and personnel." He touched the pink disk, listening.

Miri came up behind him. "You can't bring non-Clutch people onto this ship with its goofy drive! It'll make 'em crazy!"

He shook his head, frowning at the tank. "Isn't that better than being dead?"

She put her hands on his shoulders, her eyes on the ship drifting in the tank. "How come I gotta answer all the hard questions?"

Two things hit ship's comm as they dropped into normal space: the keening wail of a distress beacon and a clear, measured voice announcing name, location, and intention to rescue.

Tanser leapt out of his chair, swearing at the pilot. "Get me some magnification! Where're they coming from—*there!*"

A mid-sized asteroid floated to their starboard, oriented above them and the wreck. The pilot increased mag, as ordered, then did a doubletake and ran the screen as high as it would go.

Without a doubt, a smaller rock had separated from the larger, falling as if thrown toward the wreck.

Tanser grinned. "Hide us," he snapped.

"Huh?"

"Hide us! Hurry up, asshole! You know what's on that thing?"

The pilot was making rapid adjustments, nervously edging the ship into a flotilla of space junk. "No, what?"

"Them kids Hostro wants."

"How you figure that?" the pilot muttered, sweat dripping like icicles down his face as he matched speed with the junk and eased into the center of the drift.

"That's a Clutch ship, right?" Tanser asked, purely to draw out the revelation of his genius.

"Yeah," the pilot allowed.

"Well, Scout Commander Val Con yos'Phelium don't sound Clutch to me. Ten'll get you one the only people on that rockship out there is one little girl and her boyfriend. Real nice folks, they are, coming down to help out somebody in trouble." He settled back into his chair, sighing in self-satisfaction.

"So what're we gonna do, Borg?" the pilot asked, since the question seemed to be expected.

"We wait till they're on that wreck and then go get 'em." Tanser sighed again and permitted himself the luxury of a grin. "Caught like rats, Tommy. Gonna be so easy, it's almost a shame."

Jefferson sat by the bouncecomm, staring at it in frustration. It had stopped sending fifteen minutes before, and a cursory inspection of its innards had failed to provide him with a clue as to this malfunction. He slammed the lid down and went to the local unit to summon a comm-tech, on the bounce.

His fingers were shaking so badly, he had to punch the number twice.

CHAPTER TWENTY-TWO

Val Con matched speed and drift, fastened their pod to the entry port of the disabled vessel, and traded air.

The sensors, as near as Miri could tell, showed that the air in the other ship was good; no leaks were detected. Terrific. They were going to *have* to go inside. Because there might be survivors, too hurt or too scared to answer; or the board might be blown...Miri put a hand to her gun, making sure it was loose in the holster.

Val Con locked the board and turned to grin at her. "Ready?"

"Never readier," she lied. She didn't like it. Not at all. It smelled. It reeked.

He went first, rolling through the matched locks and into the unknown. There was a minute's silence before his voice drifted back to her. "All right, Miri."

She gulped air and rolled through, landing on her feet, gun out, in the hallway beyond. Illumination was provided by emergency dims, and gravity was a shade light. The only sound was the hum of the life-support system.

Val Con was moving silently down the hall. She saw with a certain amount of relief that his gun was out, as well. Following him reluctantly, she considered whether it was worthwhile mentioning that there was no one alive on this tub.

Robertson, she asked herself, very earnestly, you psychic?

No, Sarge, she replied.

Good, she approved. Now, get the lead out and cover your partner's butt.

The information that a half-hour's intensive research had provided on the Clutch was clarifying, but not encouraging.

Hostro's lawyer, when appealed to, gave him to understand that the word of a Clutch person in matters of contract was considered wholly binding. In the nine hundred Standards that Terrans had been dealing legally with the Clutch, the Clutch had never broken their word in any matter.

"I wouldn't worry about it, Justin," his lawyer told him comfortably. "The Clutch promises, the Clutch delivers. Never known to be an exception; no one's ever heard one lie..."

Justin Hostro thanked his man of business cordially and cut the connection, turning his attention to the files that the efficient Matthew had so rapidly obtained for him.

There was a great deal of speculation regarding the exact social structure of the Clutch—it was generally felt to be highly complex and extremely competitive. Justin Hostro scanned the data rapidly, searching for he knew not what.

Fact: At one time the warlike Yxtrang had considered the Clutch fair game. There were many documented attacks of Yxtrang upon Clutch vessels as late as eight hundred Standards before.

Then, the attacks ceased. It was observed to be the general rule that, given a Clutch vessel and an Yxtrang chancing across each other in normal space, no incident occurred. The Yxtrang passed on, as did the Clutch.

Justin Hostro had an uneasy feeling that he knew why this was so. And if the *Yxtrang* were afraid of the Clutch...

He closed the file and sat quite still, his hands folded precisely before him, his eyes regarding the scene just beyond the edge of his desk.

He was still lost in that regard when Matthew announced Edger and Watcher's return.

The only person left on the Terran ship was in no condition to be rescued. In fact, Miri thought dispassionately, about the only thing he *was* in condition for was colander duty. Whoever had shot him had been insanely thorough about it.

Val Con straightened from his examination of the body, shaking his head. "Yxtrang," he said. The word told a wealth of stories, none of them happy.

"How do you know?"

He waved a hand. "They use tiny pellets with fins on them to cut as they enter; their guns are bored for maximum spin..."

She sighed. "Think I'd learn not to ask you these questions." She spun slowly, checking out the storage hold in which they stood. "How'd they get in?"

"Matched speed and latched on." He shrugged. "It would be easy to force a storage hatch, since the mechanism is built not to withstand abuse—"

The ship shuddered with the impact of a locking magnet on the hull, and from the next hold came the anguished groan of machinery being forced against its will.

"Oh, *hell,*" Miri breathed.

Val Con was moving, swinging back toward the hallway. "Go!" he snapped. "Get back to the pod!"

She stared at him. Run? It was no good to run from Yxtrang.

He grabbed her arm, pivoted, and let her go with a push. "Go! Get the hell out of here!"

She ran, sensing him, swift and silent, at her right shoulder, and was absurdly relieved.

Suddenly she realized that Val Con was no longer with her.

Miri braked, cursing, and flattened her back against the wall, trying to see in both directions at once. Two feet downhall was a side corridor. She forced herself to think back: When exactly had he vanished?

It was impossible to know: He had been there, and then he had not. But he'd been gone *before* she'd passed that intersecting hallway, or so she thought.

From the holding section came the voices of men and the sound of boots against metal floors. Miri bit her lip. If she managed to top the best spurt of speed she'd ever had, she *might* reach the pod in time to figure out how to seal the latch against them.

Val Con's back there, damn his eyes! she cursed silently.

Miri unglued her back from the wall and moved cautiously down-corridor. She was four or five feet farther from the pod when the first shot was fired. She froze, listening to the sounds of confusion and voices yelling—*Terrans!*—and heard another sound that he could not have anticipated.

Several pairs of footsteps were still bearing down on her position.

Miri spun and dove for the cross-corridor.

Justin Hostro rose and bowed to Edger, then indicated a seat.

The T'carais inclined his head in response and remained on his feet. "The decision I am here for a simple one," he told the man. "I expect that you will be able to tell me what you have chosen in very few words. It is hardly worth the effort to sit, in such a case."

Hostro bent his own head and cleared his throat. "It is my decision, as an Elder of the Juntavas, to let your kin go with

their lives. A message to this effect has been relayed to those I
sent to search.

"I should, however, inform you that I am the most minor of
Elders of my Clan and cannot, therefore, speak for the more senior
Elders. It was their word that set me and my—immediate family—to
work on the apprehension of these members of your Clan. The—
eldest of our Elders is most anxious to obtain certain information from
Miri Robertson, and it is reasonable to expect that such inducements to
speech as he would employ would render her unlikely to live long.

"Thus, you should understand that, though I have agreed to let
your kin retain their knives, Miri Robertson is still considered an
outlaw by the eldest of our Elders. There is a price upon her head—
small, should she die in the capturing; larger, should those who trap
her be skilled enough to keep her alive. The man who is also your
kin is of no importance to the Eldest. But, if he is still with her
when she is taken his life will be forfeit."

Edger took several Standard minutes for consideration.

"I understand," he said finally. "It is enough for now that the
immediate threat posed by you and your close kin is removed. You
will, of course, provide me with the name and planet of the eldest
of your Elders, so that we may discuss the matter fully, for all the
families of your Clan."

Hostro licked his lips. Ruin. Ruin and most likely death. He
looked at that future and considered the other he had been offered;
then he took a breath and performed what was perhaps the only act
of heroism his life had encompassed.

"Of course," he told Edger. "I would be delighted to provide
you with an introduction to the eldest of our Elders."

They'd managed to cut Val Con off from the corridor. Four were
in the ransacked far hold—three Juntavas and himself.

One of the three became a bit ambitious in his aim and acquired a slug in the arm for his presumption, but that sort of thing
could not continue long. He *had* to get out. Soon. Sufficient time
had elapsed for Miri to have reached the pod and sealed it, though
she could not pilot it—a lapse in her education he intended to rectify
the moment current difficulties were resolved.

He cracked his gun, sighed, and reassembled it. He had to
move soon, even if nothing— Across the room, there was an

empty *click:* The man stationed near the door was temporarily out of ammunition.

Val Con moved.

He put his last two pellets into the man who had aspired to marksmanship, and lodged his throwing knife in the throat of his companion, who was so foolish as to rise above his cover to take aim. Reversing his gun, he used it as a club, smashing toward the shooting hand of the one survivor.

The man saw it coming and dodged—but lost his gun as it slid out of wet fingers. Val Con flipped the spent gun to his right hand and brought Edger's blade to his left; glittering and sharp and deadly, it flashed in toward the other's belly.

The man jumped back, rolling, and came up with a length of metal pipe in his hand.

Val Con slid to the left, but the Juntava was quick and swept out with the pipe, keeping him from the door.

Val Con dove forward, parrying with the gun—but the pipe shifted, snaking sideways and twisting, and the gun spun out of nerveless fingers as he danced clear, his face stinging where jagged metal had sliced it.

The Juntava sensed the advantage of his longer reach and swung the pipe again. Reaction threw Val Con's left hand up to ward off the blow, crystal blade in his grip.

And his opponent leapt back, swearing, his advantage negated: The knife had shorn away nearly a third of his weapon.

She could sit down here and pick them off all day long and far into the night.

As a tactician, Borg Tanser admired her for it. As force leader, he hated her for the three men dead at the mouth of her snug little hallway. There were other alternatives, of course. For example, they could just leave and evacuate the air from the wreck.

He considered the various angles to that and decided against. The bounty was higher—a lot higher—if she was delivered alive. If only he could come up with some way of luring her out of that damn cul-de-sac!

Suddenly Tanser froze, head snapping back toward the holding bays. The gunfire had stopped. He crept several feet down-corridor to be sure.

Silence. And no hail from the men he'd left to take out the boyfriend.

Dropping back to the mouth of the corridor, he spoke into the ear of his Second and moved off with rapid caution, gun at the ready.

The man screamed as the blade sheared through the muscle and tendons of his upper arm, but he managed an awkward spin that sent him out of range and bought him time to take his weapon into his other hand.

Val Con flipped his blade, catching it by the point. It was not a throwing knife, but when one had no choice...

The explosion and the pain were simultaneous—he was spun half-around with the force of the blast. He loosed the blade at the man who stood, gun in hand, in the doorway, before blackness claimed him. He never felt the second blow as the pipe cracked across his skull.

Morejant stood over the fallen boyfriend, pipe still at the ready, his arm bleeding badly. Tanser threw him a clamp from the kit on his belt.

"Where's Harris and Zell?"

"Dead." Morejant rasped, seeming loath to relinquish his guard over the figure on the floor. "Would've had me in another minute— sure glad you come along." He bent over the body, peering, then straightened and looked at Tanser.

"Boss, I think he's still breathing. You wanna finish 'im off?"

Tanser's attention was on the knife buried to the hilt in the steel wall two inches from his head. He levered it free and whistled softly: the crystal was unmarred, the edge unbroken. He thrust it in his belt.

"Boss?" Morejant repeated

"Naw." Tanser holstered his gun and came forward. Leaning over, he got a grip on the back of the boyfriend's collar and heaved him up to hang like a drowned kitten, blood dripping off the front of his shirt and pooling on the floor.

"Wrap yourself up," Tanser snapped at the staring Morejant, "and get a gun. We're gonna talk to the Sergeant."

They'd been hanging back for the last fifteen minutes—still there, but of out range. Every so often one of them would lob a shot inside, just to see if she was awake, she guessed. She didn't bother returning the favor.

The lull in activity had given Miri the opportunity to reload her gun, check remaining ammo, and think deeply on the inadvisability of disobeying a superior officer, not to mention straying one step from her partner's side when it looked like they were in for a hot time.

None of these thoughts were particularly comforting, nor were they useful. She banished them and shifted position; her attention was abruptly claimed by a movement at the mouth of the corridor.

Miri raised her gun, waiting for the man to get into range. But all he did was heave the bundle he carried in his arms forward, so that it struck the floor and rolled, well inside her range.

She sat frozen, gun still steady on the figure at the mouth, eyes on the man who lay too still, legs and arms every which way, graceless.

No, she thought. Oh, no, Val Con, you can't be...

"Sergeant?" boomed the sitting duck at the top of the hall.

She did not raise her eyes. "What the hell do you want?" she asked, her voice flat with hatred.

"I just wanted to tell you, Sergeant, that he ain't dead yet. We'll fix that, though, if I don't see your gun and your belt tossed up here within thirty-five seconds."

She licked her lips. "How do I know he ain't dead now? Take *your* word for it?"

"That's your gamble, Sergeant, not mine. You got another fifteen seconds."

Jamming the safety up, she snapped to her feet and hurled the gun with all her strength.

It hit a foot short and skidded to a stop against Tanser's left boot. A moment later, belt and pouch repeated the maneuver.

Tanser laughed. "Temper, temper. Now, you just walk on out here like a good girl—real slow. Don't want you to trip and get yourself shot 'cause somebody thought you were tryin' something fancy. We lost five men between you and the boyfriend, Sergeant. Proud of yourself?"

"Hey," Miri said, stepping carefully over Val Con's body. Blood was a darker stain on the dark shirt; there was no way to know if he was breathing. "Everybody's got an off day now and then."

CHAPTER TWENTY-THREE

Tanser himself formed part of the guard that took her across to the Juntavas ship. With his own hands he shoved her into the holding cell and set the lock.

Miri made a quick circuit of the cell: metal platform welded to the wall, sanitary facilities stark in one corner, a panel that looked like a menuboard. She approached this, asked it for water, and was surprised when it provided a pitcherful, chips of ice circling lazily within. She drank deeply.

Suddenly the door slid open, admitting a gaunt man with a wrap of healtape around his right forearm, dragging a limp, dark figure by its collar.

The man hauled his burden inside, apparently oblivious to the trail of red in its wake, and dumped it at Miri's feet.

"Sorry, Sarge, but we only got this one cell, so you gotta share. Wouldn't fret too much though," he confided, "'cause like as not the boyfriend'll bleed to death pretty soon and you'll have the place to yourself again."

If he had hoped for a show of emotion, he was disappointed. Frowning, his eyes fell on the still, dark bundle and he drew back, aiming a kick at undefended ribs.

Her foot intercepted his, bootheel clipping ankle neatly and painfully. Morejant nearly fell, then caught himself and spun back to find her between him and the man on the floor, death in her eyes.

Snarling, he turned away to leave.

"Hey, hero."

"What?" He turned back, hackles rising at the look on her face.

She waved at the boyfriend. "What about a medkit? Happens I ain't in favor of my partner bleeding to death."

"Then strangle him," Morejant advised her. "Only one we *gotta* keep alive is you. Why haul more weight than we need?"

She shifted position and he jumped, scuttling through the door and slamming the lock in place.

The tech cleared the malfunction inside of five minutes and went away with her fee in cash and a fifteen percent tip for a job well done.

No sooner had she gone than the bouncecomm chattered and whirred and lit up the green light that was Tanser's crew acknowledging receipt of the message.

Jefferson sighed and turned away, intent on soothing his frazzled nerves with a few swallows of local brew—and spun back, nerves fraying even more.

The bounce-comm chattered and rattled merrily, purple eye lit: Stand By For Message Incoming...

"Borg?"

"Yah?" Tanser looked up from his meal to find Tommy holding out a sheet of hardcopy.

"Message from Jeff," the pilot said. "Just come in. Thought it might be hot."

Tanser put down his fork and took the sheet. "Thanks."

A minute later, he swore loudly and pushed back from the table, leaving the dining hall at a determined half-run.

It was dark and cold and it hurt to breathe the air. It was bad air: he could feel the pain of it sliding in and out of his lungs like knives. He should stop; it was wrong to breathe such air. Yet another wrong added to a long list of them...

Drifting there in the cold and dark, it seemed that he moved away from the necessity of air, for the pain receded somewhat. Drifting still more, he perceived himself above a tunnel of even greater darkness than that in which he traveled. This new tunnel seemed to be lined with dark fur, promising warmth, and the diamond tips of the fur glittered and beckoned like stars.

Yes, he thought. I should go there, where there is warmth and stars and good, sweet air to breathe...

It seemed to him that he drifted nearer this place of warmth and stars, and he was content.

Suddenly a flare of living fire crossed the darkness and the moment was lost—he was drifting upward, toward lightening blackness and the pain that cut at him like crystalline knives...

Miri had done what she could with water and a makeshift bandage torn from her shirt. The pellet had entered and exited cleanly, barely nicking a lung. With a medkit, he would have mended without trouble in a couple of days. But with only water and cloth, he would die. There was no way to stop the slow, stubborn flow of blood.

Wearily, she rubbed a bloody hand across her cheek and used her damp scarf to dab at the gash across his face. Not a serious wound, though it would have scarred—she killed that thought instantly.

His brows twitched, and she froze as he passed a tongue across dry lips. "Who?"

"Miri."

"Not dead?" His lashes fluttered, as if he were struggling to lift their great weight.

"Not yet," she told him, somehow keeping her voice light and easy. Gently, she brushed the hair from his eyes. "You got a little beat up, though. Just lie there and rest, accazi? Don't try to talk. We'll talk later, after you rest."

He had won the battle with his lashes and was watching her face, his green eyes lucid. "Poor liar, Miri."

She sighed and shook her head. "Think I'd be better, wouldn't you? Guess I ain't practiced enough lately."

Something flickered across his face—a smile, perhaps; it was gone before she was certain. "Is there any water?"

She helped him drink from the second pitcher, the already-soaked bandage absorbing more than he swallowed, and eased him back. He captured her hand and wove their fingers clumsily together, then closed his eyes and lay still, so she thought he'd passed out.

"Where?"

She sighed. "Juntavas ship."

"Forgive me..."

"Only if you forgive me," she snapped. "I didn't go back to the pod. Useless damn thing to do. Can't pilot it."

"I know." He paused, and she saw she ghost of the ghost of a smile. "Miscalculation...."

She was wondering how to answer this when the lock jiggled. Rolling, she was on her feet between Val Con and the door when it slid open.

"How's the boyfriend, Sergeant?" Borg Tanser stepped cautiously into the room, medkit in one hand, pellet gun in the other.

"What's it to you?"

"Boss wants both of you alive," Tanser said. "New rules. Was just you. Seems Scout Commander Val Con yos'Phelium owns some stock now, too." He threw the box in a sharp underhand, and she caught it without a flinch.

"Well, whaddya waiting for, Sergeant?" He waved the gun. "Patch him up!"

The pilot blinked at the screen, swore, and upped mag. The big asteroid—the Clutch vessel—was behaving in a most peculiar manner, stuttering across the screen, phasing in, phasing out—in, out, in, out—going somewhere...

Gone.

Tommy rubbed his eyes and hit the inship, demanding strong black coffee, on the bounce.

Then he looked back at the screen. Gone, all right.

Sighing, he cleared the board and began to run check calibrations. It seemed like a good idea.

Jefferson gave a couple of minutes' frowning thought to the newest message from the boss before keying in the relay to Tanser, adding a rider that he should hang where he was until things were settled. It didn't seem like a good time to be out of touch with each other.

Shirts were provided, as was a pad and blanket for the bed, and the menuboard supplied Miri with a hot meal. Val Con had passed out sometime during her ministrations with the medkit and hadn't come round yet. She carried her second mug of coffee over and sat on the edge of the bed, watching him breathe.

His chest rose and fell with the rhythm of sleep; his breathing was no longer labored or shallow. The pulse that beat at the base of his throat was a little rickety, but hardly dangerous—nothing a day's rest wouldn't cure.

It had taken her over an hour to stop the bleeding from the pellet wounds, with her sweating and swearing, and Tanser holding the gun and snarling at her not to botch the job.

She'd had a go at patching the gash on his face. The pipe had just missed his eye, slicing diagonally across the high line of the right cheek. She'd done her best; the scar would be even, anyway, and it would fade in time from angry red to pale gold.

His lashes fluttered and his eyes were open, his wide mouth curving in a soft smile. He moved his hand to touch her knee.

"What are you thinking?"

She blinked. "That I love you," she said and dropped her hand over his. "Stupid damn thing, but what're you gonna do?"

"Accept it?" he guessed. Then he said more softly, "I may now tell you the same—that I love you—and you will believe me?"

"Yeah," she said, staring, "I guess so." She laughed. "Saving me from my lust to keep me for my love? Melodrama, Star Captain!"

"Scout Commander is sufficient," he murmured, shifting slightly. "How does one obtain dinner here?"

She finished her coffee and grinned at him. "One tells the nurse—that's me—that one is hungry. Then one is served something healthy. Like soup."

He sighed, closing his eyes. "In spite of this I feel I should inform you that I am very hungry."

Miri stood up. "Okay, pal, but remember: You asked for it!"

CHAPTER TWENTY-FOUR

Justin Hostro laid aside the three-page printout that was Borg Tanser's report and sat, his hands in a pyramid before him, his eyes on the gash in his desk.

Both were alive; though the man had taken some damage, it appeared that he would mend. So the letter of Edger's bargain was met. The problem now remained of how to exact punishment and yet make it appear that the hands of the Juntavas were clean. So might he yet come out of this with his life and his business intact.

An idea forming in his mind, he found the description of the wrecked yacht and reread it carefully. Then pushing back from his desk, he strolled to the comm unit by the far wall and punched in the code for Edger's rooms.

The shell-less one answered the call, bowed in recognition, and begged Hostro not to sever the connection while he went to fetch the T'carais. He vanished without waiting for an answer, leaving a garish abstract design on-screen for his caller's contemplation.

Hostro shuddered and turned his eyes to the Belansium planetscape above the comm. He was still absorbed in its study when Edger's voice roused him.

"Justin Hostro? You wished to speak with me?"

He bowed. "Indeed, sir. I am calling to inform you that your kin were overtaken by those of my family to whom I assigned this task. Happily, both are well, though presently not at liberty. I also wished to inform you of my intention to allow them to go free, returning their weapons and giving them a ship in which to continue their journey, since the ship they had been traveling in has, according to the pilot's report, gone into drive spontaneously and vanished."

There was a long pause. "I am pleased that you have given me these tidings, Justin Hostro," Edger said finally, "and would ask that you grant another request."

Hostro bowed. "If it is within my power. sir, certainly."

"I long to hear the voices of my sister and my brother. I would ask that you arrange to have them speak into a recording device before they are restored to liberty and that your kin bring this tape to me when they return."

Justin Hostro smiled. "Nothing could he easier, sir. It shall be done exactly as you have said."

Val Con and Miri sat on the floor under the menuboard.

"What do you suppose they're waiting for?" he asked, carefully balancing his glass of milk as he eased his back against the wall. "We've been hanging in normal space for days. If the two of us are so valuable, it seems Borg Tanser should waste no time taking us to his boss."

"I don't care if we never go anywhere," Miri told him. "Even if the view is monotonous. Better a little monotony than gettin' hauled up before the big boss. I don't think she likes me too much. Or he. And Justin Hostro don't like *either* of us. And that's who Tanser works for." She sipped her coffee. "Maybe we'll get time off for good behavior, huh?"

He raised an eyebrow. "I doubt that anyone who knows you would grant such a thing."

"You," she said with deep sadness, "are gonna be an *evil* old man."

"I certainly hope so…"

The door opened, and Borg Tanser strode into the room, gun ready, voicecorder over one shoulder. He dumped the 'corder beside Val Con, who looked up, one brow quirked.

"You know a turtle named Edger?" Tanser demanded. "Claims to be related to you."

"Yes."

"Good, 'cause Hostro's got a deal with the turtle. Includes giving you your weapons and lettin' you go. Seeing as how the rock you were on is gone, we're even gonna give you a ship. Sweet deal, huh?"

When neither of them answered, Tanser shook his head. "Turtle don't trust Hostro. Wants to hear your voices. Wants to hear how nice we been to you and how you're not hurt and how we're gonna let you go, all fair and square." He pointed at the 'corder.

"So you're gonna tell 'im that. Now. In Terran." He pointed his gun at Miri's head. "I said *now*, Commander!"

Both brows lifted and Val Con set the glass aside, pulled the 'corder onto his lap, and touched the GO button.

"I greet you, brother, and thank you for the lives of myself and the youngest of your sisters. I am to say to you these things, which are true: We are alive and have been well treated, having received food, a place to sleep, and medical aid. I regret that the ship of the Clan has continued its voyage without us. It was undamaged when it left us and should achieve its destination as planned, as it kept course without fail during the seven seasons of its labor." He glanced up, encountered Tanser's glare, and bent again to the device.

"I am also to say that we will be returned our knives and given a ship in which to continue our travels.

"My thanks to you, again, brother, for your care of two of your Clan who are foolish and hasty." He thumbed the OFF stud and looked at Tanser inquiringly.

"Your turn, Sergeant. Sweetness and light, remember."

Miri took the 'corder and punched it on. "Hi, Edger," she began in a singsong monotone completely unlike her usual manner of speaking. "Everything's fine. Wish you were here. Love to the family and see you soon." She banged the OFF switch and shoved the device at Tanser.

He took it by the strap, shaking his head in wonder. "Sergeant, it beats hell out of me how you ever lived this long." He waved the gun at them. "Okay, let's go."

"Go where?" Miri demanded.

"Didn't you just hear? We're givin' you a ship and turnin' you loose. Free citizens, see? The Juntavas keeps its word." He moved the gun again. "Move it."

Miri stood in the control room of the wrecked yacht, weaving her belt around her waist and watching the viewscreen. The Juntavas ship was just at the edge of her sight, dwindling rapidly until it disappeared

Sighing, she turned from the screen to where Val Con was lying on his back, fidgeting under the piloting board.

"They're gone," she told him.

He didn't answer, but continued his work. Miri sat on the floor to wait.

Presently, he emerged and sat up, the hair across his forehead damp with sweat.

"Well," she asked, "what's the bad news? We sit here for a couple days till we get bashed by low-flying junk? Or go on at sublight for Volmer?"

He gave her a tired grin. "And arrive as skeletons? The bad news could be worse, in fact. I can do some illegal things with power shunts and cross-currents and get up enough power for one modest Jump."

"One Jump?" She lifted her eyebrows.

"One *modest* Jump. We won't raise Volmer."

"Well," she said, bumping her elbow on the knife in her belt and frowning. "One Jump's better'n no Jumps. I guess. What do I do to help?"

The hunting had been good since the taking of the Terran yacht, and Commander Khaliiz was pleased. Now it was time to collect the prizes, to return home, to report, and to receive the payment of bounties and the accolades of success.

Commander Khaliiz issued his orders and the ship slid away into the underside of space. Perhaps, he thought, he would allow the new Adjutant the honor of bringing the Terran prize home.

Miri sighed and dragged a sleeve across her forehead, surveying the pile of junk she had assembled in the forward hold. Val Con was still in the control room, rearranging the innards of the ship's drive. Miri's task was to lighten the mass they had to move when the time came.

She sighed again as she remembered the location of another useless bit of mass and moved off in that direction.

The dead man weighed a lot, even in the light gravity, and it took her longer than she liked to move him up with the rest of the items to be spaced. Finally, she let him slip gently to the floor and stood, breathing hard, looking down at him, wondering who he might have been, and whether he had had a family.

Family meant something to some people. Like Val Con. And Edger. This man had been Terran, and Terrans did not form into clans. Still, she thought suddenly, turning the new idea around in her head, there might be somebody around who would want to know what had happened to him.

She bent and went through his pockets, removing papers, coins, a flat, flexible metal rectangle that looked as if it belonged in a computer, and a folder of holos featuring a woman and two little boys. Bundling it all together she dumped it in her pouch, then went in search of other junk to space.

Val Con was at the board, his hands moving in measured control as if he were playing the 'chora. Miri slid into the copilot's chair and watched the side of his face as he ran through his rituals and read the responses in the board's flickering lights.

After a time he leaned back and smiled at her.

"Everything that can be spaced is spaced," she told him, with a mock salute. "How's life in the clean world?"

He waved a hand at the board. "We have power. We have fuel. Where would you like to go?"

She tipped her head. "What're we near? What's a 'modest' Jump?" She shrugged her shoulders, half-smiling. *"Piloting for Dummies…"*

Frowning, he suddenly leaned forward and felt around on the short shelf under the pilot's board; he slid out of his chair and peered inside, pushing his arm way back.

"What?" she demanded.

"Coord book." He sat back on his heels and looked at her. "Miri, when you were gathering things together, did you come across a book, about so—" He shaped it in the air with quick golden fingers. "—probably bound in leather, containing many thin, metallic pages? It would have been in this room."

She shook her head. "Would've showed you something like that first, in case it was important."

He snapped to his feet and made a quick circuit of the room, checking behind and under every instrument panel and chair. Miri got up, pushed at the cushion in her chair looking for large lumps, but found none; she gave the pilot's chair the same treatment, then shook her head. Nothing.

She turned to say so and froze. Val Con was standing in the center of the room, staring at the screen. There was no particular expression on his face.

"Coord book's pretty important?" she ventured, coming to his side and laying a cautious hand on his arm.

He moved his eyes to her face. "Without coordinates, there is no Jump. Coordinates define direction, shape, location."

She considered the implications of his words. "Think Borg Tanser knows that?"

"Yes," he said grimly. "I do."

"Can't Jump without coords?" she persisted. "Take luck of the draw?"

He shook his head. "I could invent some coordinates, just to initiate a Jump, but the chances are very, very good that we'd leave drive to find ourselves inside a sun, or a planet, or an asteroid belt, or another ship, or—"

She laid her hand over his mouth. "Got it." She closed her eyes to think. Thin metallic pages? She had seen something, just recently. Not a book, but something...

"Like this?" She snapped open her pouch, pulled out the dead man's effects, and held out the metal rectangle.

Val Con took it, his eyes questioning.

"The guy in the hold," she explained. "I thought—maybe somebody might want to know what happened."

"Ah." He nodded. "We will tell his family, then." He turned his attention to the rectangle. "Why carry it with him?"

"Will it work?" she demanded.

He was on his way back to the board. "We will see what the computer thinks." Sliding into the pilot's chair, he inserted the page in a slot near the top of the board, flipped two switches, and hit a button.

Lights began to flicker and displays glowed to life. Miri settled back in the copilot's chair to watch.

"Perhaps a student?" Val Con murmured, more to himself than to her, his eyes on the readouts. "A smuggler?" He shook his head as the board flickered into stillness and the slot allowed the metal page to rise to convenient gripping height.

"Will it work?" she asked again, trying to keep the edge out of her voice.

He spun the chair to face her. "There is one set of coordinates within our range," he said slowly. "This particular page holds four. I am familiar with only one set—far out of range. It is for orbit around a planet called Pelaun, an inhabited world that has achieved the technical expertise necessary to establish electronic communication, transworld."

She blinked. "Spaceflight?"

"None."

"And the other coords? The one that's in our range?" She had a feeling she knew what the answer was going to be.

"They are not familiar to me," he said. "The only reason I recall the coords for Pelaun is because I was first Scout in-system."

"Well, I don't know as how I can think of anything *much* worse than being stuck for the rest of my life on some podunk world that thinks a planet-wide comm-net's a big deal."

He smiled slightly. "It's a bit less spectacular than a comm-net," he said gently. "Voice transmission only; no image. And the reception is horrible."

Miri stared at him, but he seemed to be serious. She shifted her eyes to the screen—and sat frozen for a long heartbeat while her mind scrambled to find words for what her eyes were seeing.

"Val Con?" her voice rasped out of her tight throat.

"Yes."

"Something worse," she told him. "There's Yxtrang, just Jumped in-system…"

CHAPTER TWENTY-FIVE

The Yxtrang pilot stared at the readout in disbelief, upped the magnification, and checked the readings once more, cold dread in his heart.

"Commander. Pilot requests permission to speak."

"Permission granted," Khaliiz said.

"The vessel which we captured on our last pass through this system is moving under power, Commander. The scans read the life forces of two creatures."

"Pilot's report heard and acknowledged. Stand by for orders. Second!"

"Commander."

"It was reported to me that none were left alive aboard yon vessel, Second. Discover the man who lied and bring him to me at once."

His Second saluted. "At once, Commander." He turned and marched from the bridge.

Khaliiz eyed the screen, perceived the ship-bounty slipping through his fingers, and was displeased.

"Pursue."

Val Con cursed very softly, then snapped back to the board, slapped the page into its slot, and demanded coords, position, speed, condition of power in the coils.

They were moving at about one-quarter the speed they could muster, locally. The Yxtrang were pouring on speed, moving to intercept.

"Could we leave now?" asked a small voice to his left.

He turned his head. Miri was sitting rigidly in the copilot's chair, her eyes frozen on the screen and the growing shape of the Yxtrang vessel. Her face was the color of milk; her freckles stood out vividly.

"We must wait until the power has reached sufficient level and the coordinates are locked into the board," he said, keeping his voice even. "We will leave in a few minutes."

"They'll *be* here in a few minutes." She bit her lip, hard, and managed to drag her eyes from the screen to his face. "Val Con, I'm *afraid* of Yxtrang."

He was aware of the tightness of the muscles in his own face, and did not try to give her a smile. "I am also afraid of Yxtrang," he said gently. His eyes flicked to the board, then to the screen. "Strap in."

"What're you gonna do?" She was watching him closely. Some of the color had returned to her face, but she was still stiff in every muscle.

"There is a game Terrans sometimes play," he murmured, dividing his attention between board and screen, his fingers busy with his own straps, "called 'chicken'...Strap in, cha'trez."

Moving like a manikin, she obeyed; she forced herself to lean back in the chair, her eyes on his profile.

He flipped a toggle. "I see you, Chrakec Yxtrang. Pass us by. We are unworthy to be your prey."

There was a pause for transmission, then a voice, harsh as broken glass, replied in Trade. "Unworthy? Thieves are always worthy game! That ship is ours, Liaden; we have won it once."

"Forgive us, Ckrakec Yxtrang, we are here by no fault of our own. We are not worthy of you. Pass by."

"Release my prize, Liaden, or I shall wrest it from you, and you will die."

Miri licked her lips, steadfastly refusing to look at the screen. Val Con's face was smooth and calm, his voice nearly gentle. "If I release your prize, I shall die in any case. Pass by, Hunter. There is only I, who am recently wounded."

"My scans show two, Liaden."

Miri closed her eyes. Val Con, measuring board against screen, eased the speed of the ship higher, toward the halfway point. "Only a woman, Ckrakec Yxtrang. What proof is that of your skill?"

There was a pause, during which Val Con slipped the speed up another notch and pressed the sequence that locked in the coords.

"Will it please you, when you are captured, Liaden, to watch me while I take my pleasure from your woman? Afterward, I shall blind you and give you as a toy to my crew."

"Alas, Ckrakec Yxtrang, these things would but cause me pain." Coils up! The Yxtrang were finally near enough, beginning the boarding maneuver, matching velocity, and direction...

"It would give you pain!" the Yxtrang cried. "All things give
Liadens pain! They are a soft race, born to be the prey of the strong.
In time, there will be no more Liadens. The cities of Liad will house
the children of Yxtrang."

"What then will you hunt, O Hunter?" He flipped a series of
toggles, leaned back in the pilot's chair, and held a hand out to Miri.

Slowly the ship began to spin.

There was a roar of laughter from the Yxtrang, horrible to hear.
"Very good, Liaden! Never shall it be said, after you are dead, that you
were an unworthy rabbit. A good maneuver. But not good enough."

In the screen, the Yxtrang ship began to spin as well, matching
velocity uncertainly.

Miri's hand was cold in his. He squeezed it, gave her a quick
smile, and released her, returning to the board.

He gave the ship more spin, and a touch more speed. The
Yxtrang moved to match both. Val Con added again to the spin,
but left the speed steady.

"Enough, Liaden! What do you hope to win? The ship is ours,
and we will act to keep it. Do you imagine I will grow tired of the
game and leave? Do you not know that even now I might fire upon
you and lay you open to the cold of space?"

"There is no bounty on ruined ships, Ckrakec Yxtrang, nor any
glory in reporting that a Liaden outwitted you. But," he said, sighing
deeply, "perhaps you are young and this your first hunt—"

There was a scream of rage over the comm, and the Yxtrang
ship edged closer. Val Con added more spin; ship's gravity was
increasing, and lifting his arm above the board the few inches required to manipulate the keys was an effort. His lungs were laboring
a little for air. He glanced over at Miri. She grinned raggedly.

"How much faster will you spin, Liaden? Until the gravity
crushes you?"

"If necessary. I am determined that you will collect no bounty
on this ship, Chrakec Yxtrang. It has become a matter of honor."
He increased the spin. He paused with his hand on the velocity lever.

"Speak not to me of honor, animal! We have toyed long enough.
We shall—"

Val Con shoved the velocity to the top, slammed on more spin,
hesitated, counting, eyes on the board—

Jump!

CHAPTER TWENTY-SIX

The blast hit like a tsunami, rocking the Yxtrang ship. Overloaded equipment sparked and smoked; crew members not firmly tied down joined other loose debris thrown against walls, floor, and ceiling.

The spin made it hard to stand, to move, to understand what had happened. For the moment, chaos held the ship in its grip and squeezed lungs tight, nerves tighter.

"Report! Report now!"

Reports began to trickle in. The pilot was dazed beyond sense, his Adjutant thrown against the wall...

The crew slowly pulled themselves together. Khaliiz took over the pilot's chair, read the impossible readings, and used emergency rockets to slow the spin. The Adjutant came to and began his work; he found whole compartments which refused to answer in the near darkness of the emergency lighting.

It became obvious that there was no such thing as a system: Individual processors still carried out their work, but the command computers were out, as were the backups.

Gravity came back to near normal as Khaliiz gained more and more control of his vessel. A technician managed to get one screen working, though Khaliiz was forced to rotate the ship to achieve a full 360-degree view capability.

"Commander, what happened?" ventured the Adjutant.

"Work! We speak of this later."

They hit normal space spinning. Hands flickered over an alarm-lit board, easing acceleration, killing spin, slowing all systems back to normal.

Val Con, shivering with reaction, drooped in the pilot's seat and turned his head, mouth curving in a smile. Then he gave a start.

Miri hung limp in the copilot's chair, held erect by the webbing, head lolling, face too white.

His fingers fumbled with the straps and he was out of the chair, kneeling before her to seek the fragile pulse in the throat. "Miri?" he whispered.

Her pulse was strong, her breathing deep. He closed his eyes in relief, then snapped to his feet and gathered her in his arms. He curled her on his lap, her head resting on his shoulder, and sat listening to her breathe and watching the unfamiliar pattern of light that was the system they were bound for.

After a time she stirred, muttering something unintelligible, and raised her head to stare into his face, her eyes slightly narrowed, as if she were looking into too bright a light.

"What'd you do?"

He lifted a brow. "When?"

She raised a hand to gesture vaguely, then allowed it to find a resting place on his chest. "With Yxtrang. Why'd they have to be so close? And the gravity—" She shuddered and his arms tightened momentarily.

"I *am* sorry," he said, "about the gravity. For the rest—" He grinned. "Allow me to give you your first lesson in piloting, which is this: Never, under any circumstances at all, take a ship into drive when there is another ship or mass closer than one thousandth of a light-second in any direction. It is a very dangerous thing to do. On the occasions when it *has* been done, one of two things occurred.

"Sometimes *both* objects go into hyperspace where it was planned only one would go. Neither comes out.

"The second possibility is that—if you are lucky, or foolhardy, or afraid—you will do everything perfectly for your ship and make the Jump without mishap." He sighed. "But the ship that remains behind is then immediately caught in a hysteresis energy effect proportional to the velocity and spin of the vessel that Jumped..."

Miri stared at him. "Poor Yxtrang," she said, her tone belying her words. "And we're okay? On course? Whatever that means."

He nodded. "The ship is intact and we are proceeding at moderate velocity toward an unfamiliar planetary system. We should reach scanning range in—" He glanced at the board. "—seven hours."

She sighed. "Time for a good, long sleep. Or something."

"Or something," he agreed, lifting a hand to trace the line of her cheek with a light fingertip.

She grinned, then her smile faded and she pulled away from his caress, using the hand that rested on his chest to emphasize her words.

"I want you to understand one thing, okay? No distress beacons. It goes off *five feet* from us, we ain't moving from this ship, accazi?"

"Yes, Miri," he murmured penitently, unable to control the twitch at the side of his mouth.

"Ah, you—" She leaned forward to kiss him.

The third planet had possibilities, he thought some while later. Too far out for decent scanning yet—not that this brute had anything like the instrumentation a Scout ship carried—but it definitely seemed the most likely of the five.

"They're all dead, ain't they?" said a voice at his elbow. "No stations, no traffic, no orbitals..." Staring at the screen, her face bleak, the glow of lovemaking gone out of her, she was shaking her head at the five little planets and their lovely yellow sun. "We're stuck in the back end of nowhere and we ain't never gettin' out." Her mouth twisted and she turned to look at him. "You think there's any people?"

He suddenly recalled the training she had not had. "Many people. At least on the third planet. See that silvery shimmer over the land mass that looks like a wine bottle?"

She squinted. "Yeah...What is it?"

"Smog." He smiled and took her hands in his. "Miri, listen: Where there is smog, there's technology. Where there's technology, there exists the means to build a transmitter. Where there's a signal, sooner or later, is a rescue." He lifted an eyebrow, winning a glimmer of her smile.

"You don't think Edger will let us stay missing, do you?" he asked. "He's bound to be along, in a decade or two..."

EPILOGUE

The Adjutant sat with the Engineer and the Commander, apart from the crew.

"Report," Khaliiz ordered.

The Engineer reported that things were not well. The Adjutant reported that a number of men were dead, more injured: the ship would be hard put to resist a determined boarding party. The Engineer, quaking, reported that it might not be possible to have full power drive for home.

Khaliiz thought.

"It is apparent," he said. "that the vessel we approached had been badly damaged in the previous battle. It exploded, giving up what energy was left in its drive cells."

He pointed at the Engineer. "You will make the reports read so, as you value the air you breathe!

"Who swore the ship empty, Adjutant?"

"Sir, it was my Second, Thrik."

"You will shoot him, personally. You will then record your demotion to Assistant Cook. This will be your lifegrade. You failed in your choice of assistants."

"Yes, sir. Thank you, sir," the Assistant Cook said.

"Get out!"

Khaliiz played idly with the cover of the destruct switch, though he had made his decision when he ordered the man shot. If he had meant to destroy the ship, he would have ordered the Second Adjutant to push the button. But he played with the cover, anyway, wondering if he'd been tricked—wondering if the little Liaden had blown himself up on purpose. Or if it had been an accident.

A distant boom claimed his attention, the echo ringing as an explosive gunblast will inside a ship.

It had been an accident, the Commander decided. For centuries, Liadens had lacked the courage to emulate the Yxtrang—lacked the honor to be truly worthy opponents. That could not change.

An accident.

CARPE DIEM

SECOND QUADRANT

Ramal Sector

The pilot stared at the readout in disbelief, upped the magnification, and checked the readings once more, cold dread in his heart.

"Commander. Pilot requests permission to speak."

"Permission granted," Khaliiz said.

"The vessel which we captured on our last pass through this system is moving under power, Commander. The scans read the life forces of two creatures."

"Pilot's report heard and acknowledged. Stand by for orders. Second!"

"Commander."

"It was reported to me that none were left alive aboard yon vessel, Second. Discover the man who lied and bring him to me at once."

His Second saluted. "At once, Commander." He turned and marched from the bridge.

Khaliiz eyed the screen, perceived the ship-bounty slipping through his fingers, and was displeased.

"Pursue."

Val Con cursed very softly, then snapped back to the board, slapped the page into its slot, and demanded data: coords, position, speed, and amount of power in the coils.

"Could we leave now?" asked a small voice to his left.

He turned his head. Miri was sitting rigidly in the copilot's chair, her eyes frozen on the screen and the growing shape of the Yxtrang vessel. Her freckles stood out vividly in a face the color of milk.

"We must wait until the power has reached sufficient level and the coordinates are locked into the board," he said, keeping his voice even. "We will leave in a few minutes."

"They'll *be* here in a few minutes." She bit her lip, hard, and managed to drag her eyes from the screen to his face. "Val Con, I'm *afraid* of Yxtrang."

Aware of the tightness of the muscles in his own face, he did not try to give her a smile. "I am also afraid of Yxtrang," he said gently. His eyes flicked to the board, then to the screen. "Strap in."

"What're you gonna do?" Miri was watching him closely, some of the color back in her face, but still stiff in every muscle.

"There is a game Terrans sometimes play," he murmured, dividing his attention between board and screen, fingers busy with his own straps, "called 'chicken'...Strap in, cha'trez."

He flipped a toggle. "I see you, Chrakec Yxtrang. Pass us by. We are unworthy to be your prey."

There was a transmission pause—or did it last a bit longer?— then a voice, harsh as broken glass, replied in Trade. "Unworthy? Thieves are always worthy game! That ship is ours, Liaden. We have won it once."

"Forgive us, Ckrakec Yxtrang, we are here by no fault of our own. We are not worthy of you. Pass by."

"Release my prize, Liaden, or I shall wrest it from you, and you will die."

Miri licked her lips, steadfastly refusing to look at the screen.

Val Con's face was smooth and calm, his voice nearly gentle. "If I release your prize, I shall die in any case. Pass by, Hunter. There is only I, who am recently wounded."

"My scans show two, Liaden."

Miri closed her eyes. Val Con, measuring board against screen, eased the speed of the ship higher, toward the halfway point.

"Only a woman, Ckrakec Yxtrang. What proof is that of your skill?"

There was a pause, during which Val Con slipped the speed up another notch and pressed the sequence that locked in the coords.

"Will it please you, when you are captured, Liaden, to watch me while I take my pleasure from your woman? Afterward, I shall blind you and give you as a toy to my crew."

"Alas, Ckrakec Yxtrang, these things would but cause me pain." Coils up! And the Yxtrang were finally near enough, beginning the boarding maneuver, matching velocity, and direction...

"It would give you pain!" the Yxtrang cried. "All things give Liadens pain! They are a soft race, born to be the prey of the strong. In time, there will be no more Liadens. The cities of Liad will house the children of Yxtrang."

Sharon Lee & Steve Miller

"What then will you hunt, O Hunter?" He flipped a series of toggles, leaned back in the pilot's chair, and held a hand out to Miri.

Slowly the ship began to spin.

There was a roar of laughter from the Yxtrang, horrible to hear. "Very good, Liaden. Never shall it be said, after you are dead, that you were an unworthy rabbit. A good maneuver. But not good enough."

In the screen, the Yxtrang ship began to spin as well, matching velocity uncertainly.

Miri's hand was cold in his. He squeezed it, gave her a quick smile, and released her, returning to the board.

More spin; a touch more acceleration. The Yxtrang moved to match both. Val Con added again to the spin but left the speed steady.

"Enough, Liaden! What do you hope to win? The ship is ours, and we will act to keep it. Do you imagine I will grow tired of the game and leave? Do you not know that even now I might fire upon you and lay you open to the cold of space?"

"There is no bounty on ruined ships, Ckrakec Yxtrang, nor any glory in reporting that a Liaden outwitted you. But," he said, sighing deeply, "perhaps you are young and this your first hunt—"

There was a scream of rage over the comm, and the Yxtrang ship edged closer. Val Con added more spin. Ship's gravity was increasing—lifting his arm above the board the few inches required to manipulate the keys was an effort. His lungs were laboring a little for air. He glanced over at Miri. She grinned raggedly at him.

"How much faster will you spin, Liaden? Until the gravity crushes you?"

"If necessary. I am determined that you will collect no bounty on this ship, Chrakec Yxtrang. It has become a matter of honor." More spin. He paused with his hand on the throttle.

"Speak not to me of honor, animal! We have toyed long enough. We shall—"

Val Con shoved the velocity to the top, slammed on more spin, hesitated, counting, eyes on the board—

Jump!

LUFKIT

Neefra's Tavern

The Terran creature's name was Jefferson, and it was sweating; it talked jerkily, swigging warm beer down its gullet, moving its big, rough hands aimlessly about, occasionally plucking at its companion's sleeve—and talking, always talking.

Much of what it said was of no value to the Liaden who stood beside it, delicately sipping at a glass of atrocious local wine; but Tyl Von sig'Alda was patient, by training if not by inclination, and the bits of useful information mixed in among the trash were jewels of very great price.

"Yxtrang," the creature was saying, fingering its empty mug in agitation. "Well, it had to be Yxtrang, didn't it? Stands to reason—the way the ship was cleaned out but not ruined. Coming back for it, Tanser said. Sure to come back for it. Yxtrang get a bounty for captured ships..." It faltered there, and its companion waved at the barkeeper for another beer. The creature took it absently, drank, and wiped its mouth with the back of a hand. It glanced furtively around the noisy bar and bent close enough for its listener to smell the beer on its breath, the stink of its sweat, and the reek of its fear. It was all sig'Alda could do not to recoil in disgust.

"Tanser knew it was Yxtrang," Jefferson whispered, voice rasping. *"Knew* it. And he left 'em there. Alive. Could've put a pellet into 'em—something quick and clean. But the turtle'd said let 'em go and the boss said okay..."

Horror seemingly choked it, and it pulled back, eyes glistening, showing a plentitude of white all around the irises. The one beside him sipped wine and murmured soothingly that of course the ways of the Clutch were mysterious, but that he had understood them not to involve themselves so much with the affairs of—men.

"This one did," Jefferson said fervently. "Claimed some kind of kinship with 'em both—brother and sister." It swigged beer.

"Crazy alien."

Most assuredly the victims were Val Con yos'Phelium and the female companion; though why an agent might be traveling with such a one was more than could be fathomed. Tyl Von sig'Alda assayed another sip of syrupy wine. The female…Headquarters had assumed a mischance during the journey home, assumed that the female had, perhaps, served for a time as camouflage. A sound enough theory.

Unless, sig'Alda thought, training was somehow broken? At once the Loop flickered to life, showing .999 against that possibility. He was aware of some dim, faraway feeling of relief. The Loop was the secret weapon of the Department of the Interior, an impartial mental computer implanted only in the best of its agents. Its guidance was essential to the Department's ascendancy over the enemies of Liad. It was an essential part of training. Training could not be broken.

Jefferson leaned close, breathing its beery breath into sig'Alda's face. "I have a son," it said hoarsely.

"Do you?" he murmured. And then, because the creature seemed to await a fuller response, he said, "I myself have a daughter."

It nodded its head in barbaric Terran agreement and withdrew slightly. "Then you know."

"Know?"

"Know what it's like," the creature explained, a trifle loudly, though not loud enough to signify within the overall clamor of the tavern. "Know what it's like to worry about 'em. My boy…And that turtle telling—bragging on himself, maybe. Maybe not even telling the truth. Who can tell what's truth to a turtle?"

Was that relevant, or more of the creature's ramblings? sig'Alda gave a mental shrug. Who could tell?

"But what did he say?" he inquired of Jefferson. "The turtle."

"Talking about how his clan or family or egg or whatever it is will hunt down the first and the last of a family, if you don't do what he says to do." Jefferson gulped the last of the beer and set the mug aside with a thump, black despair filling its half-crazed eyes. "And Tanser put 'em right in Yxtrang's path, after the turtle'd said let 'em go free. Gods."

There was a long moment's silence, while the Loop presented the chances of survival for Val Con yos'Phelium and his female, whomever and whatever she was, stranded in a ship marked for Yxtrang reclamation and deprived of coords and coils.

.001

So, then. He smiled at Jefferson. "Another beer, perhaps?"

"Naw…" The Terran was twitching, suddenly eager to be off, perhaps conscious all at once that it had been spilling secrets whole-sale into the ear of a stranger.

sig'Alda laid a gentle hand on its sleeve. "Tell me, did anyone check to see if the ship was still there? Even the Yxtrang might make an error from time to time."

The despairing eyes gazed back up at his face. "It was gone when we dropped back to look." It swallowed harshly. "Tanser laughed." Another painful working of the throat. "Tanser ain't got any kids."

It stood away from the bar abruptly and held out a horny hand. "Got to be going. Thanks for the beers."

sig'Alda placed his hand into the large one, forcing himself to bear the pressure and the up-and-down motion. "Perhaps we will meet again."

"Yeah," Jefferson said, not very convincingly. "Maybe." Its lips bent upward in a rictus that might have been meant as a smile. "G'night, now." And it turned and strode away, leaving Tyl Von sig'Alda staring into the depths of his sticky glass.

Jefferson went rapidly through side streets and back alleys, cursing his tongue and his need and the horrible, ever-present fear in his belly.

The man had been Liaden—and maybe the woman, too. Yxtrang and Liaden had been enemies, blood and bone, for longer than Terrans had been on the scene. Jefferson swallowed against the fear's abrupt nausea. Yxtrang would have special ways to treat a couple of representatives of their old, most-hated enemy…

Jefferson leaned against a convenient light post to get his breath and wait for the shaking to ease—but he only shook harder, grip-ping the post in misery and closing his eyes.

He never saw the slender shadow take aim in the empty street, never heard the gun's discreet, genteel cough or felt the pellet enter his ear and rend his brain.

The Terran crumpled slowly, as if falling into a swoon, and lay still in the puddle of light. Tyl Von sig'Alda slid his weapon away, glanced up and down the street, then walked carefully over to the carcass. He made short work of stripping the pouch and pockets of anything remotely valuable—it was to appear a mere murder for gain, as might happen to anyone walking alone in the dark back streets of Lufkit.

Jefferson had given much information freely; its continued existence had been a threat to sig'Alda himself. More, its elimination was a minor balance for the act of putting a Liaden—any Liaden—in the way of the Yxtrang. That the Liaden had been a member of his own Department and one of its best was a sad fact. Tanser's name had been duly noted; sig'Alda's report would mention it, and another bit of balance would no doubt follow.

sig'Alda stepped back, noting that the Loop gave him excellent chances of attaining the shuttle to Prime Station and the deck of *Raslain,* his passage away. Yet he hesitated, nagged by a consideration that was by rights none of his, he who was assigned to determine what had become of Val Con yos'Phelium, lost en route to his debriefing. And still there was the damned female...No. He would leave tonight, information pertinent to the mission having been gathered on Lufkit. His report to the commander would reflect Jefferson's certainty that yos'Phelium and the female had fallen to the Yxtrang bounty-crew, as well as the corroboration of the Loop. It was futile to spend time backtracking the female. He was not assigned to provide her a eulogy.

So thinking, he turned and faded into the shadows, leaving the street to the puddle of light and that which lay within it.

LIAD

Trealla Fantrol

"No! Absolutely not!"

"Shan…" Nova yos'Galan flung forward and caught her brother's sleeve in one slim hand. Head tipped back, she stared up into his face, seeing the ice forming in the silver eyes and the lines of Korval stubbornness tightening around the big mouth. "Shan, by the gods!"

He made the effort—he took a deeper breath, then another. "You tell me that the First Speaker wishes me to contract-wed. Why now? Why not last week or next week? Have you some sweet offer for the stupidest of the Clan? This is arbitrary beyond sense, sister!"

She recoiled from the anger in both his words and his face. "It is Val Con! I—I must consider what is proper. He has been missing all this while…"

"Is he truly missing? I know I haven't seen him for some time, but missing?"

Nova held up her hand, moved to the console, and touched several buttons, bringing the computer screen to life.

He moved closer as she scrolled the information there, finally settling on a spot.

"…the First Speaker's point is, however, valid insofar as it concerns the necessity of the Nadelm's education," she read. "I shall undertake to make myself available as soon as practicable following my thirtieth anniversary Name Day for instruction on the proper administration of a Clan from both the First Speaker and Korval's man of business. It is made extremely clear by the First Speaker, my sister, that I am expected to graduate to Delm very quickly."

Shan sensed the underlying impatience in those few words as clearly as he felt the tension singing in Nova.

"His *word,* from the last letter I had of him, nearly three Standards gone. His Name Day is more than a relumma past, and I have heard nothing! I must prepare, for the benefit of Korval. *yos'Galan must prepare, as well!*"

"Is he dead, then?"

His query was quite calm. Had she been less wrought up herself, she might have mistrusted such calmness. As it was, she gasped and stared up at him, dimly aware that somehow during the course of the interview the lines of melant'i had shifted so that it was no longer Korval's First Speaker, eldema-pernard'i, in conference with the Head of Line yos'Galan, but a younger sibling pleading with an elder.

"Dead?" she repeated, golden fingers snaking about each other in agitation. "How can I know? They answer no questions! The Scouts say he was placed on detached duty to the Department of the Interior these three years gone by. The Department of the Interior says he has been offered leave and refused it; that it is not their part to force a man to go where he would rather not. They refuse to relay the message that he come to his Clan, when next he is able..."

And that, Shan thought, was not as it should be. Even the Scouts, who had little patience with many things Liaden—even the Scouts, appealed to in need, had sent broadbeam across the stars that Scout Captain Val Con yos'Phelium was required immediately at home, on business of his Clan. So had Val Con come, too, in remarkably short time, shaky with too many Jumps made one after another, to stand and weep with the rest of them at his foster mother's bier.

"If he will not come to us—" Nova was saying distractedly, "If he is so angry with me, even now..."

And there was the nub of it, Shan knew. When last he had been home on leave, Val Con had quarreled with his sister, the First Speaker, over her insistence that he take himself a contract-bride and provide the Clan with his heir. That quarrel had been running for several years, with subtle variations as each jockeyed for position. There was very little real pressure that Nova as Korval-in-Trust could bring upon Korval Himself, whether he chose at the moment to take up the Ring and his Delmhood, or remain mere Second Speaker. However, the Second Speaker was bound to obey the First, as was any Clanmember, and the Clan demanded of each member a child, by universal Clan Law. A pretty problem of melant'i and ethics, to be sure, and one Shan was glad to contemplate from a distance. Obviously even Val Con had bowed to at least part of melant'i's necessity, as evidenced by that snappish letter. But still...

"That's hardly like him, denubia. Val Con's never held a grudge that long in all his life."

His attempted comfort backfired. Nova's violet eyes filled with tears, and her hands knotted convulsively.

"Then he is dead!"

"No." He bent to cup her face in his big brown hands. "Sister, listen to me: Has Anthora said he is dead?"

She blinked, gulped, and shook her head so the blond hair snared his wrists.

"Have you asked her?"

Another headshake, fine hairs clinging to his skin like grade-A silk, and he read the two terrors within her.

"Anthora is dramliza," he said patiently, beginning to pay out a Healer's line of comfort as pity overtook him. "She holds each of us in her mind like a flame, she told me once. Best to ask and know for certain."

Nova touched the tip of her tongue to her lips, hesitating.

"Ask," he urged, seeing with satisfaction that her agitation quieted under his weaving of comfort and gentle hope. "If this Department of the Interior flouts Clan tradition, then we will search ourselves. Korval has some resources, after all."

"Yes, of course," she murmured, moving her cheek against his palm in a most un-Novalike demonstration of affection. Shan cautiously lowered his level of input and pulled his hands away. She would do, he judged. Korval's First Speaker had a cool, level head. Even without his aid, she would have taken up her charge again very shortly and done all she perceived as necessary to keep the Clan in Trust for Korval's Own Self.

Shan shook his head slightly. He had briefly held the post Nova now filled and did not envy her the necessity of running a Clan composed of such diverse and strong-willed persons. *Dutiful Passage* was more to his taste, more in keeping with his abilities; yet the trading life had bored Nova to distraction.

He smiled down at her—the only one of the three yos'Galans who had inherited all their Terran mother's height. "Ask Anthora," he advised again. "And tell me what I can do to help us find our brother."

She returned his smile faintly, a bare upward curve of pale lips. "I will think upon it. In the meanwhile, do think upon what we discussed earlier…"

Anger flared, but he held it in check, unwilling to give her cause to fear the loss of another brother. "I will not contract-wed. I have done my duty, and the Clan has my daughter in its keeping. I have done more than my duty—I hear that the child Lazmeln got from me aspires to be a pilot. Leave it."

"If Val Con is dead—if he is eklykt'i—then yos'Galan must be ready to assume its position as Korval's First Line. You are Thodelm yos'Galan—head of our Line! *You* are A'nadelm, next to be Delm, if Val Con—"

"*If* Val Con!" The anger clawed loose for an instant before he enclosed it. "If Anthora claims our brother dead, I still demand to see the body: my right as kin, my right as cha'leket, my right as A'nadelm! You do not make me Korval so easily, sister. Nor do I contract-wed again, and so I do swear!"

Her face was stricken; he felt the grief roiling off her like bitter smoke and made his bow, utterly formal.

"With the First Speaker's permission," he said precisely, and left her before it was given.

LIAD

Solcintra

Shan reached Priscilla's house at first dark, when the fairy lights within the transparent walkway glowed under his boots like snowflakes. Taking the four steps to the town house's narrow vestibule in two strides, he laid his palm against the door. It slid open to admit him, and his heart clutched in wonder of it, even after so many years.

In the study, Priscilla lounged on pillows before a newly laid fire, papers in drifts around her, while Dablin, the resident cat, lay stretched in striped orange glory upon the scrubbed wood floor. His ears twitched at the sound of Shan's footsteps, but he did not deign to turn his head; the woman looked up, black eyes smiling, emotive grid a scintillation of joy/affection/caring/desire.

"Hello, love."

"You really should see to that door, Priscilla. Anyone might walk in."

She laughed softly as he crossed the room, open to and treasuring her joy, knowing that she read his emotions as clearly as he read hers—or did she read more clearly? Priscilla was not a mere Healer, after all; she was of the dramliz—a full-scale wizard, though on Sintia, the planet of her birth, the proper term was "witch."

"Have you eaten?" she asked, putting aside a sheaf of papers and extending a hand. "I can have Teyas bring you something."

He took her cool hand in his and, obedient to the gentle downward tug, settled to the pillows, chin propped on fist. She curled around to face him, cheek resting on a white arm. She was naked to the waist, as was her custom at home, and the platinum hoops in her ears gleamed in contrast to her short mop of thundercloud curls.

"I'm not hungry," he said, laying a hand over one breast; the nipple hardened against his palm, and he caught a flash of sheer lust from her. He looked up and smiled. "Hello Priscilla."

"Hello, Shan." One long finger traced the stark line of his cheek and lifted to follow the slant of a frost-colored eyebrow. "Nova made you angry."

"She has a very talent for it. Too like our father, poor child. Afraid she's driven Val Con away for once and all, or that he's gone and she must now command the Clan."

His father had been two years dead before Priscilla Mendoza had taken berth on the *Dutiful Passage*. However, she knew Nova and Val Con—Dablin, beginning the opening moves of his bathing ritual there before the fire, had been Val Con's gift to her.

Priscilla frowned. "Surely that's not like him? Has she contacted the Scouts? Left word for him to come home?"

Shan sighed and leaned back across the pillows, light eyes on the ceiling tiles. "She tried; but here's an oddity for you, Priscilla. The Scouts say Commander Val Con yos'Phelium hasn't been with them for more than three years, that he's on detached duty to something called the Department of the Interior. Ring any bells with you?"

She shook her head.

"Well, with me either, if it comes to that. Something to check on...At any rate, Nova calls this Department of the Interior, requests that a message be delivered to Commander yos'Phelium— kin-right, she tells them; his First Speaker requires him at Trealla Fantrol, on business of the Clan."

"The Department of the Interior is delighted to comply," Priscilla suggested when the silence had stretched a time.

Shan snorted. "The Department of the Interior informs Korval's First Speaker that Commander yos'Phelium is not at the moment available and adds that it is not Korval's lackey, to be delivering messages here and there around the galaxy. Nova points out that they are in violation of Clan Rule in that the commander has not returned home on leave in all the three years he has been with the Department. The Department replied that he has been offered leave several times and refused it; nor are they in the business of forcing a man to go where he would rather not."

"Nova hangs up in a fury," Priscilla murmured.

He laughed sharply. "Too true!"

"But what did she want you to do? Certainly the voice of Korval eldema-pernard'i carries more weight than that of Thodelm yos'Galan?"

"The First Speaker, in her wisdom, desires Thodelm yos'Galan to contract-wed."

Shock lanced through her, edged with astonishment, confusion, and the beginning of grief.

"Priscilla..." He reached for her, with both mind and hands, pulling her back down to lie beside him, her hand fisted on his chest despite the tide of comfort and love he poured out for her reading. "Priscilla, it will not happen! I will not allow it, and so I told her! My duty is done and—"

"If the First Speaker commands it, you'll have to. But why?" Anguish was added to the blare of other pains, and betrayal; she counted Nova among her friends. "Val Con's dead, is that it? The Department of the Interior—they lied to her. No, they said unavailable—truth. Of a kind. If Val Con's dead..." She raised herself up on her elbow and looked down on him with wide black eyes.

"You're Delm, aren't you? Korval Himself."

"I am *not* Delm, Priscilla. Strive for some sense! Scan me! Do I grieve for him—for my heart's own brother? Do I?"

"No."

He took a breath, feeling the warmth of her affection seeping into his bones like a draught of strong brandy. "Nova's duty as First Speaker is first to hold the Clan in trust for Val Con, who *is* Korval Himself. But the Clan exists even if Val Con doesn't, and a prudent Speaker must consider all contingencies, make plans for each—like captain and first mate, eh?" That drew a slight smile, though her eyes were tight on his face.

"Nova must consider the possibility of Val Con's death, as well as the chance that he's left the Clan," he went on. "But her guilt makes her favor the worst of all worlds above any other. With some reason—yos'Pheliums lately seem prone to leaving the Clan.

"There's Uncle Daav, for instance—Val Con's father—gone these twenty-five Standards and more. Nova forgets that he went for Balance, not anger. Not that it makes much difference, gone being gone. But you understand that the First Speaker must plan for yos'Galan to take its place as Korval's Prime Line, should Val Con's thirty-fifth birthday pass and he not, in fact, take up the Ring. She's simply beginning her strategy too early, and with too little information in hand. Korval must find its Nadelm, and the First Speaker must put the question to him plainly. That's all."

"How old is Val Con? Thirty?"

"Just turned," he agreed. "We've got five whole years to find him."

She did not say that a Scout might easily stay hidden for twelve times that long, or that the universe was wide. Instead she bent close, eyes locked on his, lips above his mouth by the breadth of one of Dablin's whiskers.

"You are my man," she said. It was not a command; it was a statement of her belief, open to his contradiction.

He lifted his hands and ran brown fingers roughly into her curls. "With all my heart."

The small gap closed, and she kissed him leisurely, then, yielding to his urgency, harder, hands at his shirt, at his belt; and they made love with body, heart, and mind, scattering pillows and papers every which way and boring Dablin to yawns.

Much later, when they both had had a glass or two and a bit to eat, and had gone upstairs to the bedroom and curled beneath the coverlet, she spoke into his ear. *"Do* you think Val Con's okay? Even if he's not dead, he could be—in trouble."

Shan laughed sleepily and pushed his face into the hollow of her neck. "Trust me, Priscilla. Wherever Val Con is at this moment, he has the best of everything possible."

ORBIT

Interdicted World I-2796-893-44

Miri rapped sharply on the wall at about the height of her shoulder and was rewarded with a solid metallic *thunk*. She sighed in equal parts of relief and frustration. The hallway had no hidden compartments, which meant that she would not have to deal with another bushel of amateur telescopes, or dolls, or jewels—but it also meant that there was nothing resembling a vegetable or vitamin anywhere on this tub, and she had, after all, a half-convalescent soldier on her hands.

One of the other hideys had yielded up a solitary platinum necklace, set with twelve matched emeralds. Val Con had handed it to her with a flourish and a smile. "For you—a hand-cut set."

"You keep it," Miri had told him. "Matches your eyes."

He had insisted, though, and now the thing was in her belt pouch, sharing space with a flawed sapphire, a matching ring and necklace, an enameled disk, a harmonica, and a couple of ration sticks. She would have traded the whole bunch for a handful of high-potency supplements.

"Damn it," she muttered, and settled her back against the cool wall, glaring at the pilfered elegance around her. Val Con had had a lot to say—for him, anyway—about the fineness of the yacht, pointing out the up-to-the-second water purification system, the lighted ceilings and side walls, and even the style and power of the coils they had blown to bits in that desperate Jump away from the Yxtrang.

The boarding crew had pretty well cleaned things out in the initial raid. The galley was bare—even the menuboard had been dismantled and removed. It was just plain, dumb luck that the Yxtrang had not been looking for secret compartments, or else she and Val Con would not even have had salmon and pretzels to eat.

What the hell are you doing here, anyway? she asked herself suddenly. Everything had happened so fast. Married. How in the name of anything holy had she wound up married?

"Damn Liaden tricked me," she told the empty hall. She laughed a little. Tricked three ways from yesterday—married and partnered to a Liaden; sister to an eight-foot, bottle-green Clutch-turtle with a name longer than she was; stranded on a coil-blown pleasure yacht around a world her new husband assured her was most likely Interdicted.

"Bored, were you, Robertson? Life not exciting enough with just the Juntavas after you?" She laughed again and shook her head, pushing away from the wall and starting back toward the bridge. Life...

The bridge was a racket of radio chatter and computer chimes in the midst of which a slender, dark-haired man sat quietly. Miri froze in the doorway, heart stuttering, eyes sharp on the stillness of him, remembering another time, not so many days before, when he had been that still and a deadly danger to them both.

Quietly she approached the pilot's board, noting with relief that his shoulders carried only the normal tensions of weariness and concentration—nothing of shock or the abnormal effort of attaining freedom.

Nonetheless, standing unheeded beside him and watching the absorption on his face as he extended a long-fingered hand to minutely adjust a dial, she felt dread stir and chill her, and impulsively put her hand on his wrist, interrupting the adjustment.

"Stop!" he snapped, glancing up quickly.

"Still here, huh, boss?" She pulled her hand away. "Time for a break."

"Later." He turned back toward the board and the senseless chatter coming up from the planet surface.

"I said *now,* spacer!" Her voice carried all the authority of a mercenary sergeant, and she braced herself for retaliation.

His eyes, brilliantly green, flicked to hers, his mouth straight in that look that meant he was going to have his way, come hell or high water—and suddenly he smiled, pushing the hair out of his eyes. "Cha'trez, forgive me. I was lost in the work, and only meant to say that I am attempting—"

"To put yourself in a bad spot," Miri interrupted. "I don't think you been outta that seat for ten hours. You gotta eat, you gotta walk around, you gotta rest—wasn't all that long ago the only things between you and the Last Walk were an autodoc and a scared merc."

There was a long pause during which green eyes measured gray. He was the first to sigh and drop his gaze.

"All right, Miri."

She looked at him suspiciously. "What's that mean?"

"It means that I will take a break now—walk a bit and join you for a meal." He grinned weakly and reached up to brush her cheek with light fingers. "I do tend toward singlemindedness occasionally, despite my family's best efforts." The grin broadened. "I would not have you think that I was brought up as poorly as that."

"Sure," she said uncertainly, sensing a joke of some kind. She pointed at the board. "You still doing the hunt-and-compare bit? 'Cause I can give a listen while you're off-duty."

"It would be of assistance," he said, standing and stretching to his full height. Miri grinned up at him, liking the slim, graceful body and the beardless golden face. She extended a hand to touch his right cheek, and he shifted to drop a kiss on her fingertips. "Soon," he said, and slipped silently away.

Shaking her head at the hammering of her heart, Miri dropped into the pilot's chair and picked up the earphones.

Dinner was prime-grade Milovian salmon, Boolean pretzel-bread, and water, consumed while seated cross-legged on the carpet amid the desolation that probably had been the private quarters of the yacht's owner.

Val Con ate his ration with neat efficiency, as if he were stoking his furnace with protein, Miri thought; as if taste and variety had nothing to do with the act of eating.

She ate more slowly, weary of the taste but forcing herself to finish every bit of the stuff, and finally she looked up to find Val Con watching her closely.

"This whole ship's a loony bin," she groused. "Triple-A prime salmon, telescopes, dolls, jewelry, secret compartments, and a coordinate page filled with Interdicted Worlds. How come?"

"The luxuries are bribes," Val Con said softly. "And the extra compartments are to hide them. Simple."

"Yeah?" She blinked. "Somebody's trading with Quarantined Worlds? But that's—"

"Illegal?" He shrugged. "It's only illegal when someone catches you."

"Hell of an attitude for a Scout."

He laughed. "Did I ever tell you about my grandmother?"

"Don't know when you would've had a chance. What about her?"

He smiled. "She was a smuggler."

"That a fact?" Miri said calmly. "What's the old lady doing now?"

"Forgive me," he murmured. "I should have said my many-times great-grandmother, Cantra yos'Phelium, co-founder of Clan Korval."

She grinned. "Not likely to go around embarrassing all the relatives then, is she?" Then she did a double-take. "Cantra, like the money?"

"Indeed," Val Con said around a sudden yawn. "Exactly Cantra, like the money."

"Better get some sleep, boss," she advised, hoping against all reason that he would forget about the blithering radio and the strings of signals to be overlaid and recorded.

"Not too bad an idea." He yawned again and without ado stretched out, putting his head on her lap.

"What the hell's wrong with you?"

"I'm tired, Miri."

She glared down at his shuttered face. "And you gotta put your head right there?"

One green eye opened. "Shall I put it on the floor?"

"Should you—I'll tell you what's wrong with you. You're spoiled."

The eye closed. "Undoubtedly."

"Rich kid from the good part of town; never had no trouble; never had to rough it; always a soft place to put your head…"

"Inarguably. Absolutely. Cantras and coaches. Satins and silks. Malchek and feeldophin."

She eyed him warily, noting without meaning to the long dark lashes and the firm, sweet mouth. "What's malchek and feeldophin?"

Both eyes opened wide, staring upside down into hers. "I don't know, Miri. But I'm certain they must be something."

"Think I'd learn." She sighed heavily and moved a hand to brush the hair away from his eyes. "I ain't good at sleeping sitting up, though."

"Ah. A compelling reason for me to put my head on the floor, I agree." He did so and opened his arms. "Come to bed, Miri."

Laughing, she stretched out beside him and put her head on his shoulder.

LIAD

Solcintra

The priority gong clanged, and Shan was up in an eruption of bed-clothes, slapping the stud before he was fully awake.

"yos'Galan," he snapped into the speaker, only then aware of Priscilla at his side.

"Tower here, Cap'n. Sorry to disturb you."

"That's quite all right, Rusty; I enjoy having my rest broken for crew maneuvers. I assume that you *are* doing a dry run and that there really *isn't* a priority message for me lying somewhere around the Tower?"

"Nosir—I mean, *yessir,* there's a message, all right, pin-beamed to you by name, priority wrap, balance in code. Hit about three minutes ago. But here's what's funny, Cap'n…"

"I knew there was a punch line! Don't disappoint me, Rusty."

"Yessir. We tagged the source of transmission as local—just north of Solcintra. Thought you'd want to know."

"We're in northern Solcintra…" Shan frowned. "You didn't by any chance send a priority message to me via the *Passage,* did you, Priscilla? There are more seemly ways to get my attention."

"The thought had occurred to me," she admitted, grinning.

"But action did not follow. Well, I doubt it's someone wanting to sell me a cloak." He touched a quick series of keys. "Transmit at will, Rusty—and thank you for your patience. It occurs to me that I'm becoming ill-tempered in my dotage."

Laughter burst from the comm as the receiver lit and beeped. "How long've we known each other?"

"Gods alone know. I recall the day they carried you on-ship, a babe in arms—"

"And you a gleam in Cap'n Er Thom's eye! Tower out."

"Good-bye, Tower." He shook his head and tapped keys—and the screen lit, displaying a bare line of gibberish, the word PRI-ORITY shrieking across the top margin. Shan sighed. "What day is it, Priscilla?"

"Banim Seconday."

"Ah, yes, and we're in the second relumma, year Trebloma..."
He keyed in the information, added his ship-code, and stepped back,
slipping an arm around her waist. Before them, the screen shimmered, null-words breaking, reforming, then becoming intelligible.

INFORMATION RECEIVED RE PROBLEM VIA GREENTREES.
COME HOME.

"My sister studies espionage. How refreshing." He sighed again
and gave Priscilla a slight squeeze before he withdrew his arm. "Adventures, Priscilla! Were you growing bored?"

"Not especially." She hesitated. "Shall I come with you, Captain?"

He reached to touch her cheek. "This is a Clan matter, beloved, not a ship matter; the first mate has no need to be with me.
However, I was to have seen Sennel this morning—if you would
do the kindness?"

He read her disappointment, a reawakening of the previous
night's uncertainties. "Fear not!" he cried with a gaiety his pattern did
not reflect. "I very much doubt that this is a clever plot to whisk me
away and marry me against my will to some lady from an outworld
Clan—"

She laughed in spite of herself as he went across to the dressing
room. He was out again in a handful of minutes, sealing the cuffs
of a wide-sleeved blue shirt.

"Only see how obedient I am! My father would have expired
of astonishment. First mate and captain are to meet with Delm
Intassi this afternoon to discuss a possible cargo. If for some reason
I cannot go, take Ken Rik with you and present my assurances to
Intassi that nothing less than my First Speaker's word would have
kept me from such an important appointment."

"Yes." She had flung the balcony door wide and was staring
down into the inner garden, her pattern overlaid with the hum that
signaled concentrated thought.

Shan stepped to her side and touched her shoulder. "Priscilla?"

She started just slightly, ebon eyes flashing to his face.

"Will you dine with me this evening? It seems we'd best talk
again about the maggot in Nova's head." He took her pale hand and
kept his eyes steady on hers. "I will marry no other lady, Priscilla. I
swear it to you."

Her eyes filled, even as his did. "Shan..."

"Yes?"

She took a hard breath, and then the words came in a rush. "Can't we declare ourselves lifemates? If we—act according to Liaden law...Nova can't insist you contract-wed if you're life-mated, can she?"

"No, of course not. But Thodelm yos'Galan owes allegiance to Korval. Since we have no Delm, I must ask the First Speaker's permission to a lifemating and—"

"The timing's bad."

"Dreadful might be more accurate." He glanced down at their linked hands, saw the Master Trader's amethyst gleaming against his brown skin, bracketed by her slim white fingers, and looked back to her face. "The last time we were in port I went to the First Speaker to ask her permission..."

Priscilla stiffened. "She refused?"

"I never asked. Already the time was bad. I'm a Trader, Priscilla! It's lunacy to deal at a known disadvantage!" The bedside clock chimed their usual hour of rising, and he shifted. "I should go."

"Yes." She loosed his hand and stepped back. "Give my love to your sisters."

"Always." He hesitated on the edge of a kiss, read in her a desire for reserve, and so merely bowed the bow of affection and esteem. "I'll see you soon, Priscilla."

"Walk the day in joy, my love."

LIAD

Trealla Fantrol

Shan sent the fast little groundcar through the curve at the top of the hill, slipped the stick, and spun into the drive with a purring uptake of speed. At the base of the first hill, he downshifted in deference to the possibilities of children, cats, and dogs and proceeded at a pace only another pilot might have called sedate.

Damn it, he thought, guiding the car through twists and turns he knew like the rhythm of his own heartbeat. It wasn't like Nova to indulge in espionage! That Department of the Interior had got her worried beyond sense.

Or worried in very good sense. The car slid beneath a flowered archway and continued down a straight road lined with fragrant colmeno bushes. Shan felt a finger of cold down his spine and shivered in the warm Liaden sunshine.

The car negotiated the final right turn, left turn, sharp right, and pulled into a space near the garage doors. Shan got out and slammed the door.

The south wing was quiet. Despite the lesson of past experience, it seemed as if Padi and Syl Vor might actually be with their tutors this morning—or engaged in quiet mayhem in another part of the house. Anthora's brand-new twins would be sleeping or gurgling in the nursery, charming those who had them in their care into the belief that *this* set of yos'Galans, at least, were as even-natured as they were sweet-tempered.

Nurses were so easy to fool. Shan shook his head and moved with lazy haste toward the main corridor, ears tracking the growing rumble of wheels across strellawood flooring. In contrast to nurses and tutors, Trealla Fantrol's butler was damn near impossible to fool.

They met at the intersection of corridors. The butler rotated the orange glass ball that served as his head and waved two of three arms in salute.

"Master Shan. Good day, sir. The First Speaker awaits you in the study." The voice, male and middle-aged, spoke Terran with the affected drawl of the upper classes and originated somewhere near the plate steel midsection.

"Jeeves," Shan said calmly. "Good day to you. Have you seen the children lately?"

"Miss Padi is in the garden with Mr. pel'Jonna, partaking of a botany lesson. Master Syl Vor and Ms. Gamkoda are engaged in geography, and Miss Shindi and Master Mik are having an early-morning nap."

"Dear me, what exemplary behavior! I believe they may be ill."

"On the contrary, sir, they enjoy their customary robust health. I believe, if I may say so, that this morning's quietude may be attributed to Miss Nova's promise that they would be allowed to visit you only if they behaved as became those of Korval."

"Ever more terrifying! But perhaps they don't yet have a firm grasp of family history."

"As you say, sir."

Shan grinned and turned right. "To my sister in the study, then! Be well, Jeeves."

"Be well, sir."

He went perhaps half a dozen paces before turning back. "Jeeves!"

"Sir?" The midsection rotated, and the orange ball lit in inquiry.

"Is Miss Anthora in the house? And Gordy?"

"Miss Anthora is with the First Speaker in the study. Your foster son has contracted an alliance of pleasure with Karae yo'Lanna and spent last evening in her company. Shall I contact Glavda Empri and inquire for him?"

"Ken Rik's granddaughter, is it? No, don't disturb the child; just ask him to call me at his earliest opportunity. The *Passage* will know where I am, if he doesn't find me here or at Pelthraza Street."

"Very good, sir." Jeeves rotated once more and wheeled off in pursuit of other imperatives. Shan grinned and headed for the study.

The door slid away and two heads turned toward him—one blond and one dark, violet eyes and silver. Anthora stood and came forward, small hands outstretched, welcome riding a warm wave between them.

"Shan-brother."

He ignored the hands and bent to hug her. "Hello, denubia. How's the contract-husband?"

She laughed, nose wrinkling. "Many days gone, thank the gods! But the twins are very good, don't you think?"

"Very good, indeed. I could have done no better."

That earned another laugh as a tug on his sleeve pulled him across the carpet to where Nova waited in cool uncertainty.

"Sister." He smiled and extended a hand, marking with what relief she took it. Not for the first time, he regretted that Nova's talent was one that gave her access only to the memories of those already dead, rather than to the living emotion all about her.

"Brother. Thank you for coming so promptly."

"The least I could do, when you'd gone to so much trouble and expense! Only why a pin-beam to the *Passage,* denubia, when a local call might have gotten you the same result?"

She looked coldly into his face, every inch the First Speaker of Liad's First Clan, her hand gripping his until he feared for the bones.

"Local calls can be too easily traced," she said. "Come see what we have." She waved to the comm on its corner of the wide desk.

"I've seen it," Anthora said to his hesitation, her emotive grid suddenly and suspiciously bland. "Would you care for some morning wine to help you read, brother?"

"Wine by all means—but not morning wine. A glass of the red, if you please." He glanced at Nova's face, but saw only waiting there while her pattern glimmered, chameleonlike, too changeable to read.

He slid into the desk chair and tipped the screen to the proper height. Amber letters spelled out words in High Liaden:

COMMUNICATION BEGINS

GREETINGS.

TO NOVA YOS'GALAN FIRST SPEAKER-IN-TRUST CLAN KORVAL, SHE WHO REMEMBERS, FIRST SISTER TO OUR SHARED BROTHER, VAL CON YOS'PHELIUM SCOUT, ARTIST OF THE EPHEMERAL, SLAYER OF THE ELDEST DRAGON, KNIFE CLAN OF MIDDLE RIVER'S SPRING SPAWN OF FARMER GREENTREES OF THE SPEARMAKER'S DEN, TOUGH GUY.

Shan blinked and leaned back in the chair, absently accepting the glass from Anthora's hand, wondering at the significance of the final two words being rendered in Terran.

KNOW THAT ON THE TWO HUNDREDTH AND FORTY-SECOND DAY
OF THIS STANDARD YEAR NUMBERED 1392 OUR BROTHER AND HIS
LIFEMATE, MIRI ROBERTSON MERCENARY SOLDIER, RETIRED, PER-
SONAL BODYGUARD, RETIRED, HAVE WEAPON WILL TRAVEL, DEPARTED
FROM LUFKIT PRIME STATION BY TESTIMONY OF HE WHO WATCHES
ON A SHIP OF THE CLAN, FLEEING NAMELESS ENEMIES.

KNOW FURTHER THAT ON THE TWO HUNDREDTH AND FORTY-
SIXTH DAY OF THIS STANDARD YEAR OUR BROTHER AND MY SISTER
HIS LIFEMATE FELL INTO THE HANDS OF CLAN JUNTAVAS OF THE
LINE WHICH LOOKS TO ELDER JUSTIN HOSTRO IN WHICH MISFORTUNE
OUR BROTHER TOOK INJURY FROM THE KIN OF ELDER HOSTRO

Dear gods, Shan thought. He damped his output, so that
Anthora would not be pummeled with his dread. He sipped wine
and touched the advance key.

NEGOTIATION WITH ELDER HOSTRO PROVED SATISFACTORY TO
THE POINT THAT OUR BROTHER'S INJURY WAS HEALED. IT WAS FUR-
THER NEGOTIATED THAT OUR KIN BE RETURNED THEIR KNIVES AND
GIVEN A SHIP ON WHICH TO CONTINUE THEIR JOURNEY, THE SHIP OF
THE CLAN HAVING RESUMED ITS LABOR DURING THE TIME THEY WERE
HELD BY CLAN JUNTAVAS. EVIDENCE INDICATING THAT THESE THINGS
WERE DONE PROVIDED BY JUSTIN HOSTRO AND FORTHCOMING TO
YOURSELF VIA HASTIEST COURIER AVAILABLE.

IT HAS COME TO MY ATTENTION THAT JUSTIN HOSTRO IS THE
MOST MINOR OF ELDERS WITHIN CLAN JUNTAVAS AND CANNOT GUAR-
ANTEE THE ACTIONS OF THE REMAINDER OF HIS CLAN. IN THIS CIR-
CUMSTANCE, I GO TO NEGOTIATE WITH THE ELDEST ELDER OF THE
JUNTAVAS ON THIS, THE TWO HUNDREDTH AND FIFTY-FIFTH DAY OF
STANDARD YEAR 1392. I UNDERTAKE THIS NEGOTIATION AS MIRI
ROBERTSON'S BROTHER AND T'CARAIS AND AS THE BROTHER OF OUR
SHARED BROTHER WHO TRAVELS AT HER SIDE.

KNOW AT LAST THAT OUR BROTHER'S STATED DESTINATION WAS
VOLMER DESIGNATION V-8735-927-3 AND THAT HE HAS NOT YET
ARRIVED AT THAT PORT THOUGH A SHIP OF THE CLANS OF MEN MUST
HAVE TAKEN HIM THERE BY THIS DAY. NOR HAS HE CONTACTED ME
AS I FEEL HE WOULD HAVE DONE WERE ALL WELL.

THAT JUSTIN HOSTRO MAY NOT HAVE BARGAINED IN GOOD FAITH

IS A MATTER I SHALL DISCUSS WITH THE MOST ELDER OF THE JUNTAVAS. THAT OUR BROTHER AND SISTER HAVE ATTAINED THAT STATE KNOW TO MEN AS "MISSING" IS INFORMATION I FELT THEIR REMAINING KIN MUST HAVE WITH UTMOST ALACRITY SO THAT A SEARCH MAY BE UNDERTAKEN WITH ALL HUMAN SPEEDINESS.

IN SHARED KINSHIP AND DUTY I SALUTE YOU. MAY SUCCESS MEET OUR MOST STRINGENT EFFORTS.

BEAMED THIS DAY 255 STANDARD YEAR 1392 BY:

TWELFTH SHELL FIFTH HATCHED KNIFE CLAN OF MIDDLE RIVER'S SPRING SPAWN OF FARMER GREENTREES OF THE SPEARMAKER'S DEN, THE EDGER.

COMMUNICATION ENDS

Shan leaned back and closed his eyes, thoughts tumbling. The first was that the message came from the old boy himself, Val Con's very brother Edger, in whom Shan had never quite believed, no matter how well told the tale. The second was that, of course, it would have to be checked, fraud being however dimly possible.

The third thought bestirred him to open his eyes and lean to the comm, touching keys, banishing Edger's message to memory as he opened a line to the *Passage.*

"Shan—" Nova began, her worry apparent.

He finished his query, hit SEND, and picked up his glass. "Annie, my own."

"Shan-brother?"

"Is Val Con alive, denubia? Progress report, please, as of this very moment, if possible."

"Alive?" She blinked at him. "Of course."

"Good. Wonderful, in fact." He stared at her over the rim of his glass. "Where?"

He sensed confusion; frustration quickly sublimated into thought. Anthora closed her eyes, casting this way and that, for all the worlds like a dog hunting a scent. Nova stirred and began to speak, but Shan held up a hand, his eyes on the youngest of them all.

"There!" she cried suddenly, finger pointing roofward and beyond, to what might be the Second Quadrant. She opened her eyes. "But a long way away, Shannie. I don't—when *you're* on Volmer you don't feel nearly so far away…"

"How far beyond Volmer?" He caught the edge of her frustration again and leaned forward. "Have I ever felt that distant? If you remember an approximate time, we can check the log on the *Passage*—"

But Anthora was shaking her head. "None of us has ever been that far—no. When Father—when Father was dying, at the very end—the day before he—he was that distant then…Oh, no!" Nova's pain broke over them, and Anthora flew forward to hug her and shake her. "He's *alive,* sister! *Physical* distance, not spiritual! I can't tell you how I know the difference—but there is one! And another difference—" She paused, looking to Shan, who nodded.

"There's a—an—echo—around Val Con. It's like—it's like how I sense Priscilla—not directly, you see—but through Shan…"

"His lifemate," Nova murmured, and suddenly spun. "Lifemate! Did you know of a lifemate? Who is she?"

Shan sipped wine. "I'd say she's a person with a sense of humor: 'Miri Robertson Mercenary Soldier, Retired, Personal Bodyguard, Retired, Have Weapon Will Travel'? Also a person to treat with a bit of respect. As for who else she is, as soon as the *Passage* gets through to Terran Census—aha! Right on cue!"

He touched the glowing purple stud and the screen filled with amber letters once more, this time forming Terran words.

"Well, let's see: Planet of origin: Surebleak…Date of Birth: Day 28, Standard Year 1365; Tag: mutated within acceptable limits. Parents: Katalina Tayzin; Chock Robertson. Job Fee paid: Half-bit; Day 116, Standard 1375, poor child…Outmigrated Day 4, Standard 1379…Reason for Migration: Job opportunity. And the job? Ah, here we are…" He hit ADVANCE and shook his head. "Apprentice soldier, Lizardi's Lunatics, Fendor. Angela Lizardi, Senior Commander. Poor, poor child."

"Mutated…" Nova was hanging over his shoulder, frowning at the screen.

"Within acceptable limits," Shan completed. "Now, on a backward, low-tech world like, shall we say, Surebleak, the phrase 'mutated within acceptable limits' can mean several things. But mostly it means 'half or full Liaden.'" He tapped the screen. "My guess is that Katalina Tayzin has gotten her name mangled into something more or less Terran-sounding. Chock Robertson seems rather definite."

"But who *is* she?" Nova demanded, running the advance down to blank screen.

"She's a soldier, sister!" Shan snapped. "Where have your wits gone begging? We'll run an employment check on her through the *Passage* if you like, to find where she went after being apprenticed to Lizardi's Lunatics—but you already know the most important thing about her."

Nova drew herself up and glared down at him. "Which is?"

"She's Korval's Own Lifemate," Shan said, and drank his wine.

ORBIT

Interdicted World I-2796-893-44

Flesh against flesh was warm, promoting drowsy comfort, though her exposed right flank was getting damn cold.

Unwilling yet to let go of the drowse, Miri nestled closer to Val Con's warmth, too comfortable even to care that a long lock of her hair was trapped under their combined weight and pulled at her temple. She smiled a little to herself.

Things had gotten pretty intense there, for a bit. It had started with her reaching to touch his right cheek—the one the Juntavas had cut—by way of saying "good night."

His eyes had opened wide; his fingers had lifted and traced the line of the scar. "It does not repel you?"

"Huh?" She blinked, then shook her head against his shoulder. "People get hurt in fights sometimes. Better a scar or two than something more fatal."

"Ah." Once more his fingers passed lightly across his own cheek; then they were at the lacings of her shirt, baring her breast and touching the faint white pucker where she had caught a near-spent pellet, way back on Contrast. Rolling with her so that he was half on top, he bent his head to kiss the scar.

Miri had had her share of scrapes—maybe more than her share of scars, what with her father…But Val Con, unlike one loobelli of a civilian she had slept with, did not ask where they were from, but just patiently and thoroughly sought each one out to kiss and caress until she had gotten a little intense, herself.

Now she snuggled even closer to his side, the steady beat of his heart filling her ears. He had even found the scars on her feet, from when she had kicked the grille out of the door and tried to walk away from the rehab center, her light house slippers hanging in bloody rags. She would have made it, too, except Liz had found her and made her swear to finish the therapy.

No sense, of course, she thought. Went to all that trouble to make sure Klamath didn't get me and almost let Cloud have me for nothing.

She stirred sharply, completely awake and almost breathless, as if she had suddenly found herself standing at the very edge of a sheer drop. Cloud. She had jammed so much of the stuff into her system by the time Liz had dragged her to rehab, she had barely remembered her own name.

And what if he asks you where you got them scars? she demanded of herself. You gonna tell him the truth, Robertson? Huh? Rich kid from Liad, hobnobs with the best people? Think he's gonna stand by words he said to some snip from Surebleak who was so addicted to Cloud it's a wonder she ever came away whole? Think it's gonna matter to him how long you been clean?

"Cha'trez?" His arms tightened, and he craned to see her, green eyes hazy and half asleep. "Is something wrong?"

She started, then reached up, touched his lips, and brushed her fingertips over the scar, aching at the beauty of him.

"You're on my hair," she said.

Miri woke alone, her head pillowed on Val Con's folded vest. She sighed, stretched deliberately, and was wide awake by the time the stretch was done. From the bridge she heard the radio's unceasing blather; she sighed again, rolled to her feet, and hurriedly pulled on her clothes before heading that way, his vest swinging in her hand.

Val Con stood, deep in thought. The bottle-shaped continent from the planet below had taken on three dimensions, overrunning the bridge: the neck of the bottle started in the companionway, and its bottom ran into the pilot's chair.

Miri shook her head in wonderment and leaned against the doorjamb to watch.

Duct tape from the repair box was rumpled into mountain ranges running north and south, gaps precisely cut out to allow river systems their courses. Spare instrument lamps dotted the map, some singly, others clustered. There were several pipe pieces in the map, each with a number written on the floor next to it.

Marking pens had also been used with art. The rivers had boundaries of blue, while some areas were enclosed by curly green lines and others simply outlined in brown. Three paper spaceships sat next to the three largest lamp-clusters; Val Con held another in his left hand. In his right was a ragged block of metal the Yxtrang had torn from somewhere.

Miri gazed at the arrangement thoughtfully. "If you bring your transport down 'round the oceanside of the blue lamps, you can take out the red ones before they know what hit 'em, then use their supplies to take the ship. Blue's gonna have to get involved to protect themselves, so you sit tight and let 'em bang their heads against your position for a bit, then mop up and go on a tiger hunt for green..."

He looked up, grinning and bright-eyed. "Are we invading, then, Sergeant?"

"Sure looks like a situation map to me, Commander."

Val Con stepped out of his construction, gently placing the fourth paper spaceship near one edge of the continent before moving to her. He kept the chink of metal in his hand.

"I don't doubt your invasion would work," he said, "but I am not a general, alas, and would hesitate to direct it."

"Don't blame you. Invasions are messy. Course, garrison duty's boring."

"And limited by supplies."

"Like us." She nodded at the map. "What's with the world view?"

He turned carefully to avoid stepping on a mountain range and pointed. "The lamps are towns, as lit when we pass over them at night. More lamps become a city—like here—and fewer are villages or less. So the blue is a large town or a small city, one with four transmissions from it."

"The pipes are transmission towers?"

He nodded. "The green is the largest city, and I suspect it has an airport of some consequence."

"And that?" She pointed at the metal block in his hand. "Where does that go?"

He hefted it, walked two graceful steps into the map, and very precisely placed it between the coastal mountains and a single red lamp, not far from where he had placed the paper spaceship. "There."

"Fine," Miri approved. "What is it?"

"Us."

She frowned at the map, letting the picture build in her mind. "The idea is to leave the ship in the mountains, then walk down that pass there—if it is a pass—and hope there's some way we can work things out to meet people *before* we go to town?"

He nodded. "It is the best course of action I can envision, given the limited data we have been able to gather." He sighed. "This is not a Scout ship." He seemed genuinely annoyed with the yacht for that shortcoming, and Miri grinned briefly before walking the perimeter and stepping in beside him.

"When do we land?"

"When the time is propitious," he murmured, idly adjusting the metal block with his foot.

"You figure the propitious time will he soon?" she persisted. "Reason I ask is we only got another two days of fish and maybe three of crackers, and then what we got is water."

"Ah," he said, shifting slightly to take another look at his creation before turning and smiling down into her eyes. "In that case, I would say that the most propitious time is immediately after lunch."

LIAD

Trealla Fantrol

Korval's man of business was closeted with the First Speaker, but before being whisked away he had managed one minor bit of magic and produced a credit history on Miri Robertson, Terran citizen. Shan slid the disk from the old gentleman's fingers with a smile. "Exactly what I was needing, sir. My thanks," he said, and carried it off.

Alone in his rooms, he fed the information to the computer and took a sip from his glass.

Apparently financial institutions did not consider mercenary soldiers good credit risks. There was a string of six "Applied. Credit Denied" before a surprising "Loan granted, Bank of Fendor, one-half cantra to Miri Robertson payable over a period of not more than four Standard Years at interest of 10.5%. Co-signator, Angela Lizardi. Collateral in form of Pension Fund 98-1077-45581 carried by Ilquith Securities. Transaction completed Day 353 Standard 1385."

Angela Lizardi again—apparently a commander who took active interest in her soldiers. And Miri Robertson pledges her pension for half a cantra cash, he thought. *I wonder why.*

The screen supplied no answer, but it did reflect an exemplary payment record, and then the notation "Balance paid in full, Day 4, Standard 1388."

She earned a bonus and killed the thing, Shan surmised, sipping wine. It was the best she could have done at ten point five. He touched a key and the credit file faded, to be replaced a heartbeat later by an employment history.

1379: APPRENTICE SOLDIER, LIZARDI'S LUNATICS.

The Lunatics had taken and fulfilled a series of contracts on a number of worlds: Eskelli, Porum, Contrast, Skittle, Klamath.

Shan froze. *Klamath?*

He had just extended a hand to request more information when the annunciator chimed.

"Come!"

The door whispered open behind him as he impatiently tapped keys.

"Klamath?" Anthora asked, leaning on his shoulder. "What's Klamath?"

"That is what we're trying to find out. We are, in fact, hoping my memory has finally deteriorated to the point that someone must be assigned to lead me about. Exercise your influence, sister, and see that it's Priscilla?"

She laughed. "As if I had any! And what use would you be to Priscilla without a memory?"

"The same use I'll be to her with impaired hearing. Do stop bellowing in my ear."

She stuck her tongue in it.

"That will do," he said. "Bring a chair over and sit nicely or leave."

"Yes, Shan-brother."

He glanced up as she moved away. "Tell me, denubia, did the contract-husband leave with all faculties intact? If yos'Galan owes for mental disability it would be best for me to settle it before the *Passage* leaves."

"I was very nice to him, Shannie. Truly I was." She dragged the chair into place and sat primly, hands folded in her lap. "Like this?"

"Precisely like that. Pretend you've had upbringing. Now if only the damned computer—Aha! Progress!"

The screen filled with amber letters, scrolling. Shan let it run, then slapped PAUSE and was silent for longer than it should have taken him to read the information there.

Anthora leaned back from her own perusal, frowning at his face and at his pattern, which had suddenly gone flat with pity.

"The world shook apart?" she asked tentatively. "It is horrible, Shannie, but why are we looking at it? I thought you were trying to find out about Val Con's lady."

"I am," he said expressionlessly, allowing the screen to continue a slow scroll. "She was there. Lizardi's Lunatics was one of the mercenary units hired to fight in the local civil war. A handful of people got off-planet before things went so unstable that rescue were hopeless. Countless people died, civilians and soldiers..." He touched PAUSE once more. "Survivors, Lizardi's Lunatics: Angela Lizardi, Senior Commander, Roth MacNealy, Brevet Lieutenant; Miri

Robertson, Sergeant; Scandal Arbuckle, Private; Lassiter K. Winfield, Private. *Five.* Gods, a full-staffed unit is nearly three hundred!"

"She has the luck," Anthora said gravely, and Shan felt the hairs rise on his neck.

"Does she?"

But his sister was frowning. "Isn't it odd? I always thought Val Con would chose a lady who was a musician, like he is."

"We don't know that she's not," Shan pointed out. "Though gods alone know what she might have to sing about."

Anthora turned wondering silver eyes on him. "She's alive."

"So she is." He tapped another series, recalling the employment history. "Let's see what else she's done with her life, then, shall we?"

Lizardi's Lunatics had been deactivated in 1384, and there was a two-year blank in Miri Robertson's record until she showed up again as sergeant with the Gyrfalks, under Senior Commander Suzuki Rialto and Junior Commander Jason Randolph Carmody. There followed another list of contracts accepted and fulfilled, interspersed with notations of the excellence of Sergeant Robertson's performance. In 1388 her rank was increased to sergeant master. In 1391 she resigned. Commanders Rialto and Carmody let the record show their sorrow at that decision and their willingness to take the sergeant back into the Gyrfalks at any time.

Some months later Miri Robertson was certified as bodyguard to a Sire Baldwin of Naome, and there the record ended, except for a muted chime indicating that auxiliary information was available.

Shan glanced at Anthora. "Well, sister? Do we press on?"

"By all means!" she cried, and wriggled a little to show the intensity of her interest.

Grinning, Shan touched the proper key. The auxiliary file clicked in and his grin faded.

In 1392, five Standard months after Miri Robertson had become Sire Baldwin's bodyguard, a party of Juntavas attacked the estate, killing many of the household staff. Of those listed missing and presumed escaped: Baldwin himself...and Miri Robertson.

The aux file faded, and Shan leaned back in his chair. "Well, sister? Does she still have the luck?"

"It seems so," Anthora said softly. "After all, she got from Naome to Lufkit, and then from Lufkit to Lufkit Prime Station and as far as wherever she and Val Con are now, and they're both alive." She tipped her head. "Doesn't that sound like the luck to you, Shannie?"

"Unfortunately," he said after a small pause. "it does." He sighed and rubbed the tip of his nose. "Does it occur to you that Clutch-turtles might well mistake relationships between humans? By Space, we don't even know that that damned message is from Edger!"

"Mr. dea'Gauss had a tracer put on the pin-beam," Anthora said. "Verification hasn't been made yet, but he feels there's small doubt that the message is genuine. And I *told* you, brother—I can see Val Con's lady through him, just like I see Priscilla through you!"

He turned to stare at her. "So you did." He touched keys, shut down the screen, reclaimed the disks, and slipped them safely away. "Which reminds me that I'm to dine with Priscilla this evening. Talk about a coil! If Val Con had his heart set on the woman, why couldn't he bring her home? And when did he have time to court and lifemate anyone? Unless..." He pushed away from the desk, stretching to his full six feet, reducing Anthora to a plump, precocious child.

"Unless?" she asked.

He bent to kiss her forehead. "A question for Jeeves on my way out, that's all. Please assure Nova that I'm at her command. We'll be dining at Ongit's before going back to Pelthraza Street. And tell Gordy I'll expect to see him here early tomorrow morning. He's loafed long enough."

"Oh, no," Anthora said earnestly. "He's been working very hard! Karea seems particularly pleased."

"I'm delighted for them both." He gave her a gentle shove toward the door. "I'm off to visit Syl Vor and Padi—then a quick word with Jeeves and away! Be a good child, now, and help your sister."

"All right, Shannie," said the most powerful wizard on Liad, and went docilely down the hall.

With some difficulty Jeeves was discovered crouched in a corner of the hearthroom, swaddled in cats, head-ball dim in what Val Con had used to call "sleep." Shan cleared his throat.

"Sir?" The ball glowed to gentle orange life.

"Please don't get up! I only need to ask you a question—you *are* available for questions, aren't you, Jeeves? It wouldn't concern me quite so much except that you're the brains to Trealla Fantrol, and if we were to have an intruder while you're napping with the cats I don't know what would happen."

"The intruders would be repelled, sir. I was not asleep, but merely offering comfort."

Shan rubbed the tip of his nose. "Comfort? I am to understand that the cats are distressed?"

"They miss Master Val Con, sir."

"They do." Shan considered the various and varicolored felines draped around Jeeves's metallic person. "I hesitate to mention this— but Pil Tor and Yodel have never *met* Master Val Con."

"Quite right, sir. But Merlin has told them all about him, so they feel his absence as keenly as the rest."

A grizzled gray tabby curled near the head-ball opened one yellow eye, as if daring a challenge to that explanation.

Shan swept a bow. "Never would I doubt you, sir."

The cat closed his eye, and the man swallowed a laugh. "Jeeves, if I might ask you to cast your mind back seven or eight Standards—possibly more: Has my brother ever mentioned the person Miri Robertson in your presence?"

There was silence. Shan bore it for nearly a minute.

"Jeeves?"

"Working, sir. I anticipate completion of the match in approximately—done. Master Val Con has never spoken of or to Miri Robertson in my presence." After a slight and unrobotic hesitation, Jeeves said, "Forgive me."

"There's nothing to forgive, old friend. I had a notion Val Con had been lifemated for a few years and had simply forgotten to let us know. Exactly the sort of thing that might slip one's mind, after all. It was dimly possible that he'd said something to you, however, the dangers of Scouts and soldiers being what they are."

"You speak in the context of a will."

"Exactly in the context of a will."

The orange ball flickered, and Merlin flicked a reproachful ear. "The will I have on file for Master Val Con has not been altered since Standard 1382. It does not mention Miri Robertson."

"And that," Shan said, "would seem to be that. Thank you, Jeeves, you've been very helpful. Do continue comforting the cats."

"The comfort is two-way, sir."

Shan sighed. "Are you distressed, Jeeves?"

"It is merely that I, too, miss Master Val Con."

"I see. Forgive me if this offends, but Val Con and I built you, which means—"

"I was Master Val Con's idea."

Shan blinked. "I beg your pardon?"

"I was Master Val Con's idea," Jeeves repeated, moving an arm to rub a restive tigerstripe. "You said so yourself, sir, several times during my construction."

"So I did." And a more cork-brained scheme, he added silently, may I never again be party to! "My thanks for calling that so my attention. Carry on."

"Thank you, sir. Good evening, sir."

Shan's footsteps faded down the hallway, and in a moment Jeeves noted the opening and closing of the door to the south patio. One of the younger cats, Yodel, mewed faintly and twitched in her sleep. Jeeves moved a hand to stroke her.

"There, there," he said. "There, there."

ORBIT

Interdicted World I-2796-893-44

The sound of the ship around them went from solid hum to pulsing throb as Miri slid into the copilot's seat. Val Con sat in the pilot's chair, hands moving with precision over the switches and keys and toggles as if he were playing the omnichora. All screens were up, showing different and changing views of the world below while the radio mumbled to itself. A number of the lights on the central board glowed red, a fact that Miri decided to ignore.

"No power left to shunt from the coils," Val Con murmured. "Altitude control jets low on fuel. Rocket thrust? Ah, well, rockets are only a luxury, after all..."

Miri considered the side of his face. "Is this dangerous?"

"Hmm? Strap in, please, cha'trez. We are approaching a mark." A slim finger touched a readout that was counting large blue numbers down from ten. Miri engaged the webbing as the numbers ran down. There was a sharp push and a heavy vibration as zero flashed. Val Con flipped a quick series of toggles, and the worst of the vibration faded.

"Is—this—dangerous?" Miri asked again, spacing the words and increasing the volume a tad, on the slim chance he hadn't heard her the first time.

His smile flickered, and he reached to take her hand. "Dangerous? We are descending with neither reserve rockets nor jet power to a planet without landing beacons, without an actual touchdown point chosen, and without being invited." The smile broadened. "A textbook exercise."

"Sure," Miri muttered. "And how many people get hurt when a textbook crashes?"

Val Con raised an eyebrow. "You doubt my skill?"

"Huh?" She was startled. "No, hey, look, boss, I ain't a pilot! I just gotta know if we're gonna get down—" She stopped because he was laughing, his hand warm around hers.

"Miri, I will contrive to bring us down as safely as possible, considering circumstances." He squeezed her fingers and let them go, turning back to his board. "As for whether we *will* get down, the answer is yes. We are no longer moving rapidly enough to maintain orbit."

She watched him go through another series of adjustments, then shook her head as he leaned back in the chair. "Tough Guy," she murmured.

He glanced over. "Yes."

"Tell the troops just enough to keep 'em honest, doncha?" she said, not sure if she felt admiration or frustration. "Got some guts—this stuff here." She waved a hand at the red-lit board. "Playing chicken with the Yxtrang...What were the chances of us getting out alive, when you pulled that hysteresis thing and we Jumped outta there?"

"Ah." He faced her seriously. "The pilot did not expect to reenter normal space."

"Thought we'd come apart in hyper," she translated and nodded to herself, thinking.

At the conclusion of thought, she reached over and patted his arm. "Good. Best choice there was. Yxtrang boarding party, against us two, even if we are hell on wheels..." She shook her head. "And I wouldn't want to have to shoot you. Heard that was the best thing to do for your partner, Yxtrang ever gets you cornered."

"There are sometimes," Val Con murmured, "other options."

"Yeah? How many Yxtrang you ever talk to in person?"

"One," he said promptly. "Though it is true that I took him unaware."

Miri blinked at him, then glanced at the ruddy board and at each of the screens in turn. "Remember to tell me about it," she managed at last. "Later."

"Yes, Miri," he said, sternly controlling his twitching lips, and turned back to the board.

The planet spun beneath them five times on the inbound spiral.

Miri watched the screens in fascination—she had never been on the flight deck of *anything* on a trip downworld before—and meticulously copied information Val Con read off to her: coordinates of major features, drainage patterns of important river basins, the direction and strength of atmospheric jet streams.

Her duties also included monitoring the radio, which still gave out its gabble of nonsense words and earsplitting music. But on the third pass over the continent south of their target something different came over the speaker.

Bringing the volume up, Miri heard the excited voices and the boom and thunder of heavy guns.

"Boss?" she asked quietly.

He glanced away from his board, frowning at the radio noise.

"Somebody's having a war," Miri said, and he sighed, hands and eyes already back to the business of piloting.

Miri kept with it, hearing the despair in the man's voice on the radio and counting the rhythms of the bursts and explosions until they were out of range. She found the station again on the next pass, but it was only playing music. And on the next pass they were inside the ion shield and could not hear anything at all.

The meager stars had given way to local dawn when Val Con finally brought the ship down. Miri found the switch from a ballistic trajectory to magnetic control unexpectedly harrowing: the deceleration reminded her all too vividly of their close call with the Yxtrang. The final lurch brought forth an involuntary burst of swearing, which she squelched in embarrassment, for by that time the ship was flying smoothly.

Val Con sealed the hatch behind them and slid the key into his pouch, shivering in the crystal air.

Miri tipped her head. "You cold?"

"Only a little," he murmured, lifting a brow. "Aren't you?"

She grinned, stretching tall on her toes. "Where I come from, Tough Guy, this is high summer." Then she, too, shivered as a random breeze ran through the ravine. "Course, when you get as old as me, your blood starts to thin out."

"So? I had no idea you were as old as that."

"You didn't ask; I didn't say." She frowned at the crouched ship, a pitted metal boulder among a tumble of rock. "Should we hide it better?"

"This should suffice. The country does not look well traveled, and from the air it will seem just another rock. We are only in difficulty if local technology proves to include long-range metal detection." He sighed. "We could send it into orbit, but there might be a way to repair…" His voice drifted off.

"So, for better or worse." She came closer and slid a small hand into his. *"Carpe diem,* and all like that." She grinned, and he smiled faintly, squeezing her hand as she looked around. "Well, where's this town of yours? I could sure use a cup of coffee."

"West," he said, and smiled at her confusion. *"That* way," he elaborated, pointing.

"Whyn't you say so? Though how you can tell up from down this soon after 'fall beats hell out of me." She shivered again in another eddy of breeze and wrinkled her nose. "Guess we better start walking."

"It would seem best," he agreed. He slipped away, moving like a shadow over the broken shale, Miri silent at his back.

An hour later they rested by a stream. Val Con knelt, cupped a hand into the rapid current—and turned his head as if he had heard the cry of protest she had stilled.

"Cha'trez, the water is good," he assured her. "Nor do I think the vegetables or grains will do us harm. The meat should also be edible. Whether all the nutritional needs of our bodies are met we must wait and see." He cupped his hand again and drank, then rose, sighing. "Had we been abandoned in a Scout ship instead of a smuggler's yacht we would have known these things with certainty before landing. As it is, we ride the luck."

Miri closed her eyes as he came to sit beside her. *"Carpe diem,"* she muttered, willing herself to relax.

"What is that?"

She opened her eyes to find him watching her. "What's what?"

"Carpe—diem? It does not sound Terran—and you have said it several times."

"Oh." She frowned. "Actually, it *is* Terran—at least, it's *from* Terra. Latin, I think the language was. Real old. I remember reading that two or three of the languages Terran derives from came from Latin, first." She paused, but he was watching her face with apparent interest.

"Time I was—sick—right after Klamath," she continued, "I got to read lots. Book I liked best was called *Dictionary of Phrase and Fable.* It was sort of a list of things that people had said or believed—and sometimes *still* said—and next to each one was an explanation of what it was really supposed to mean.

"*Carpe diem,* now—that's supposed to mean, 'seize the day,' enjoy yourself while you can. Seemed like good advice." She shook her head and smiled. "Great book. Sorry I had to give it back."

"How long were you able to spend with the book?" he asked gently. "After Klamath?"

"Hmm? Ah, not too long. Got busted up toward the end of things—my own damn fault. Got cocky." She shifted, breaking his gaze. "You want a sandwich before we get on?"

Both brows rose. "Salmon?"

"Got four," she told him earnestly.

"I think that I am not hungry, thank you." He came to his feet in one fluid motion and reached down to help her up, though he knew she could rise as easily as he, unaided.

"Besides," he said, pressing her hand warmly before letting her go. "I thought you wanted that cup of coffee."

The town sat in a three-sided bowl made of mountains, clustered in the center of a valley that was merely a widening of the pass they walked through. It was not a large town, which was good, and no one was yet abroad, though the sun had been up for several hours. In the near distance Val Con made out a field of some type of grain, while closer in—

Miri was not at his back.

He turned slowly and found her seated astride a fallen log, staring down into the protected little town, tension sharp in the lines of her face, in the set of her shoulders, and in the slender hands folded too still upon her knee.

He moved, deliberately scraping boot heel against stone. She started and looked at him.

"Mind if I rest a minute?" she asked, tension singing beneath the words.

"As long as you like." Silent again, he went to the log and sat behind her, putting his arms loosely around her waist, feeling her taut in every muscle. Laying his cheek against her hair, he exhaled gently. "What is it, cha'trez?"

"*I* was gonna ask *you.*" She flung her hands out with suppressed violence, directing his attention to the valley below. "What is it?"

He considered. Then, he said softly, "A town. Civilians. Not, it is true, a very large town—but sufficient for our present needs. A pattern such as this many times includes outlying farms or homes. If this place is true to that pattern, then that is very good for us. It may be possible for us to go to a single home and offer to trade labor for—language lessons."

She drew a deep breath. *"That's* a town?"

"Certainly it's a town," he said, keeping his voice matter-of-fact. "What else would it be?"

"The gods alone know. It's so small..." Her voice faded, significant of growing tension.

"So? Then perhaps we should take a few moments to study what we see." He raised an arm, pointing. "That large affair, there, with the many windows? That's probably a government building of some kind. It seems to have the proper hauteur about it."

She chuckled—a good sign—and it seemed that she relaxed, ever so slightly. "And that squatty one, with the railing around the front?"

"A trading post," he guessed. "Or a small store." He pointed again. "What do you make of the little blue one?"

"A barbershop? Or a bar?" She laughed a little, and the tension was definitely easing. "Both?"

"Perhaps—though I think it would be a bit crowded for either. And the metal objects—they do seem to be metal, do you think?—along the sides of the thoroughfare?"

"Cabs!" Miri announced with certainty, relaxing back into him. He moved his cheek away from her hair and slanted a glance at the side of her face. She was smiling slightly. Good.

"So? Then tell me about that one—you see? Over behind the little blue one—with the tower and the knob on the top?"

She was silent for a moment, then blinked and grinned. "A bordello."

"Do you really think so?" he murmured. "Perhaps we should go there first."

She laughed—a true laugh—her head against his shoulder, then abruptly sobered. "Val Con?"

"Yes?"

"You're a sneak."

He lifted a brow. "It is a common failing, I am told, among Liadens."

"That's what Terrans say." She frowned. "What do Liadens say?"

"Ah, well. Liadens…" He tightened his arms around her in a quick hug. "Liadens are very formal, you know. So it is likely that they would not say anything at all."

"Oh." She took a breath. "What do we do now?"

"I think we should take off our guns and put them in our pouches. In some places the possession of a weapon makes a person suspect, even, perhaps, a criminal. And I think we should each have another sandwich—so that we do not grow proud—" He echoed her laugh softly. "After we eat, we should go down into the valley and look for one of those outlying farms I spoke of, to see if we might not trade the labor of our strong young bodies for a roof and food and lessons in language."

"All that on a sandwich? Well, you're the boss."

"And when," he inquired, "will you be boss?"

"Next week." She stood, pulled a plastic-wrapped package out of her pouch, and handed it to him to unwrap while she stripped off the gun and holster and stowed them away.

VANDAR

Springbreeze Farm

"Borril! *Here,* Borril! Wind take the animal, where—ah *ha!* So there you are, sir! No skevitts this morning? Or did they all sit in the treetops and laugh at you? Ah, now, old thing..." She finished in a much sweeter tone, as the dog flung himself at her feet with a *whuff* and lay gazing up at her, worship in his beady yellow eyes.

She bent carefully, rubbed her knuckles briskly across his head ridges, and yanked on his pointy ears. Straightening, she sighed and eased her back, her eyes dwelling on the marker before her: "Jerrel Trelu, 1412-1475. Beloved zamir..."

Beloved zamir—what bosh! As if it had not just been Jerry and Estra, working the farm and raising the boy and doing what needed to be done, one thing at a time, side by side, him leaning on her, her leaning on him. Beloved husband, indeed!

A wind blew across the yard, straight down from Fornem's Gap, ice-toothed with winter, though it was barely fall. Zhena Trelu shivered and pulled her jacket close around her. "Wind gets colder every year," she muttered, and pulled herself up sharp. "Listen at you! Just the kind of poor-me you hate in Athna Brigsbee! Mooning the morning away like there wasn't any work to do!"

She snorted. There was always work to do. She bent creakily and gathered up the sweelims she had picked for the parlor—she liked a bit of color to rest her eyes on in the evening when she listened to the radio or read. "Let's go, Borril. Home!"

The wind sliced out of the gap again, but she refused to give it the satisfaction of a shiver. The signs all pointed to a bad winter. She sighed, her thoughts on the house she and Jerry had lived a lifetime in. The shutters needed mending; the chimney had to be cleaned and the tin inspected for corrosion—though what she could do about it if the whole roof was on the verge of falling in was more than she knew. It was a big, drafty old place, much too big for one old woman and her old dog. It had always been too big, really, even when there had been Jerrel and the boy and, later, the boy's zhena—and the dogs, of course. Always four or five dogs. Now there was only Borril, last of a tradition.

As if her thought had reached out and touched some chord within him, the dog suddenly bounded forward, giving tongue in mock ferocity, charging around the side of the house and out of sight.

"Borril!" she yelled, but any fool would know that that was useless. She picked up her pace and arrived at the corner of the house in time to hear Borril, in full stranger-at-the-gate alarm.

Across the barking cut a man's voice, speaking words Zhena Trelu understood to be foreign.

She rounded the corner and stopped in surprise.

Borril was between her and two strangers—barking and wagging his ridiculous puff of a tail. The taller of the two spoke again, sharply, and the barking subsided.

"Be quiet, dog!" Val Con snapped. "How dare you speak to us like that? Sit!"

Borril was confused. The tone was right, but the sounds were different than the sounds She used. He hesitated, then heard Her behind him and ran to Her side, relieved to be out of the situation.

"Borril, you bad dog! Sit!"

That was better. Borril sat, tail thumping on the ground.

"I *am* sorry," Zhena Trelu continued, trying not to stare. "Borril really is quite friendly. I hope he didn't frighten you."

Again, it was the taller who spoke, opening his hands and showing her empty palms. Zhena Trelu frowned. It did not take a genius to figure out that he did not understand what she was saying.

Sighing, she stepped forward. "*Stay,* Borril." As she moved, the two men came forward also, stopping when shock stopped her.

The shorter man was not a man at all. Not, that is, unless foreigners of whatever variety these were allowed a man the option of growing his hair long, braiding it, and wrapping it around his head liken vulgar copper crown. A woman, then, Zhena Trelu allowed. Or, more precisely, a girl. But dressed in such clothes!

Zhena Trelu was not a prude; she knew quite well what useful garments trousers were—especially working around the farm. But these...

First, they seemed to be made of leather—sleek, black leather. Second, they were skintight, hugging the girl's boy-flat belly and her—limbs—and neatly tucked into high black boots. The upper garment—a white shirt of some soft-looking fabric—was acceptable, though Zhena Trelu thought it might have been laced a little closer around that slender throat; and the loose leather vest was unexceptional. But what in the name of ice did a woman want to wear such a wide belt for? Unless it was to accentuate the impossible tininess of her waist?

"Am I *that* funny-looking?" Miri asked, and Zhena Trelu started, eyes going to her face.

No beauty, this one, with her face all sharp angles and freckles across the snubbed nose. The chin was square and willful, the full mouth incongruous. Her only claim to prettiness lay in a pair of very speaking gray eyes, at present resting with resigned irony on the other woman's face.

Zhena Trelu felt herself coloring. "I beg your pardon," she muttered. She moved her eyes from the girl to her companion— and found herself staring again.

Where the angles of the girl's face seemed all at odds with each other, the lines in her companion's face worked toward a cohesive whole. High cheeks curved smoothly to pointed chin; the nose was straight and not overlong; the mouth was generous and smiling, just a little. His hair was dark brown, chopped off blunt at the bottom of his ears, and one lock of it straggled across his forehead, over level dark brows and quite nearly into the startling green eyes. His skin was an odd golden color, except for the raw slash of a recent scar across his right cheek.

He was dressed in the same sort of clothes as the girl, the clinging leather and the wide belt keeping no secrets regarding his own thinness.

Zhena Trelu frowned. The girl's skin was pale, doubly so when compared to the man's rich complexion. And they both looked tired. Skinny, too—never mind the outlandish clothes—and foreigners to top it all, without even a word of the language.

The wind sliced across the open lawn; the girl shivered—and that decided it. If the child was sickening for something she needed to be out of the wind. What was her zamir thinking of, to have her out in the chilly autumn weather with no jacket on and that shirt laced up so loose? Zhena Trelu glared at him, and one of his eyebrows rose slightly as he tipped his head, rather like Borril trying to puzzle out one of the rambling monologues she addressed no him.

"Well," she told the young zhena sharply, "you might as well come on in. There's soup for dinner to warm you up, and you can have a rest before you get on." She turned and marched up to the house, treading carefully on the creaky porch steps.

Realizing that he was in danger of being left behind, Borril jumped up and galloped across the lawn, taking the three wooden steps in a bumbling leap. Zhena Trelu, fidgeting with the chancy catch on the wind door, grumbled at him.

"Borril, sit *down,* you lame-witted creature. *Borril!*" she raised her voice as he jumped, almost knocking her down.

"Borril." From her back, a steady voice spoke, firm with command. Woman and dog turned to look.

The slender zamir stood on the second step, bent slightly forward, one golden hand extended. "Borril!" he repeated firmly. "Sit."

Zhena Trelu watched in fascination as the dog waggled forward and thrust his blunt nose into the outstretched hand. "Sit," stated the owner of the hand again.

Borril sat.

The man reached out and tugged lightly on a pointy ear, turning his head as the girl came to his side.

"Borril?" she asked, extending a wary hand. The silly creature *whuffed* and pushed his head forward. In careful imitation of her companion, she tugged on an ear. Borril flung himself onto his side in ecstasy, rolling his eyes and sighing soulfully. The girl threw back her head and laughed.

Zhena Trelu turned back to the catch and pulled the door wide.

"Well, come on," she snapped when they just stood there, staring at her from the second step. "And don't pretend you're not hungry. Doesn't look like you've had a full meal between you since last harvest-time." Irritably, she transferred the sweelims to the hand holding open the door and waved at her hesitant guests with the other.

After a moment, the man moved, coming silently up the last step and crossing the porch into the hall; the girl trailed him by half a step, and Zhena Trelu bit back a sharp lesson on manners. Did the girl think the house was a den of iniquity, that she sent her man in ahead?

They're foreigners, Estra, she reminded herself as she led them down the ball. You're going to have to make allowances.

She dumped the flowers into the sink, turned the flame up under the soup pot, and looked back to find them standing side by side just inside the door, looking around as if neither one had ever seen a kitchen before.

"Soup'll be ready in a couple minutes," she said, and sighed at the girl's blink and the man's uncomprehending head-tip.

Feeling an utter fool, she tapped herself on the chest. "Zhena Trelu," she announced, trying to say each word clearly and pitching her voice a little louder than normal.

The man's face altered, losing years as he grinned. "Zhena Trelu," he said, matching her cadence.

So, it works, she congratulated herself. She pointed at him, tipping her head in imitation of Borril.

He moved his shoulders, lips parting for an answer.

"Tell the truth, Liaden," Miri muttered at his side.

His eyes snapped to her face, both brows up. Smiling in rueful resignation of what he found there, he turned back to the old woman and bowed very slightly, fingers over heart. "Val Con yos'Phelium, Clan Korval."

Zhena Trelu stared, trying to sort the sounds. Valconyos Fellum Can Corevahl? What kind of name—no, wait. Corevahl? He was a foreigner, after all, with wind only knew *what* kind of barbaric accent. She pointed. "Corvill?"

The level brows twitched together, and he frowned, green eyes intent. "Korval," he agreed warily, though still thumping harder on the last syllable than the first.

"Corvill." Zhena Trelu decided, and pointed at the girl, who grinned and shrugged.

"Miri."

"Meri?" Zhena Trelu asked, frowning.

"Miri," she corrected, refusing to look straight at Val Con, though a glance out of the corner of her eye showed him grinning widely.

"Meri," Zhena Trelu repeated, and brought her finger back to Val Con. "Corvill."

He inclined his head, murmured, "Zhena Trelu," and jerked his chin at the dog, curled on his rug next to the stove. "Borril."

"Well, that's fine. Now we're all introduced, and dinner's almost ready." The old woman went across to the stove, lifted the pot lid, and stirred the soup with a long wooden spoon. Going over to the cupboard. she pulled out three bowls and three plates, shoved them into the girl's hands, and waved at the table. "Set the table, Meri."

The girl turned hesitantly toward the table. From the depths of the cupboard, Zhena Trelu produced three glasses and three mismatched napkins, which she handed to the man. He took them without apparent confusion and headed for the table. Zhena Trelu nodded to herself and went back to the sink to rescue the languishing sweelims.

"Hello, Meri," Val Con murmured, setting the glasses by the bowls and plates she had laid out.

"Hello yourself, Corvill, my friend. Sounds like you rhyme with Borril. Speaking of which, what *is* Borril?" She looked up at him. "Besides ugly, I mean."

"Hmm?" He was considering the napkins—one each of white, green, and pink. "Borril is a dog, Miri—or, no," he corrected himself. "Borril is of the species that fills the watch-pet niche here." He smiled at her. "For all reasonable purposes, a dog."

"Oh." She looked at the napkins. "Who gets what color?"

"An excellent question. I was wondering the same." He placed them carefully in the center of the table. "We shall discover."

She grinned. "Clever. Something still missing though—oh." She turned and made her silent way across the kitchen to where the old woman was fussing with her flowers. "Zhena Trelu?"

Zhena Trelu started, nearly overturning the vase, and recovered with a breathless laugh. "Goodness, child, but you gave me a fright. What is it?"

Miri blinked at the unintelligible tirade, opened her mouth to ask for the missing items—and closed it again. The old lady wasn't going to understand any more than she was understood.

All right, Robertson, she directed herself. Use your brain—if you got one.

She looked about, then picked up the wooden spoon lying on the stove and showed it to Zhena Trelu. She turned and pointed at the table, beside which stood her partner, watching the proceedings with interest.

The old woman looked at the spoon, looked at the table, and then laughed. "Oh, is my memory going back on me! Silverware, is that it?" she asked the girl, who only smiled, uncomprehending.

Taking the spoon and putting it back where it belonged, Zhena Trelu went to the cupboard once more. *"Spoons,"* she said clearly. *"Knives. Forks."*

"Spoons." the girl repeated obediently as each set was placed in her hands. *"Knives. Forks."*

"That's right," Zhena Trelu said encouragingly. She made a sweeping motion with her hands, trying to indicate *all* the items the girl held. *"Silverware."*

Meri's brows pulled together in a frown. *"Silverware,* "she said, and the other woman smiled and went back to arranging flowers.

"Spoons," Miri told Val Con, shoving them into his hand. *"Knives. Forks."* She frowned. "That all seems simple enough. You savvy *silverware,* boss?"

"Perhaps *knives, spoons,* and *forks* are separate names and *silverware* is the name for all together?"

"Not too bad, for a bald-headed guess."

He laughed softly. "But that is what being a Scout is—guessing, and then waiting to see if your guess was correct."

"Yeah?" She looked unconvinced. "Ain't the way I heard it."

"Ah, *you* heard we were heroes, risking our lives among savage peoples, magically able to speak any language we hear and never misunderstanding custom or intent." Mischief glinted in the bright green eyes.

"Naw. Way I heard it, only things Scouts're good for is drinking up fancy liquor and tellin' tall tales 'bout the dragons they killed."

"Alas, I am found out..."

"Meri! Corvill! Bring your bowls over here now. Soup's hot."

Miri grinned at him. "That's us—wonder what we're supposed to do now?"

He glanced over his shoulder in time to see the old woman pull a ladle from its hook over the stove. "Bowls, I think," he murmured, and picked up two, moving toward the stove with a deliberately heavy step.

Miri blinked at the unaccustomed noise, then shrugged, picked up the remaining bowl, and followed.

Zhena Trelu smiled and ladled soup into the two bowls Corvill held ready. Then she filled Meri's bowl and touched the girl's shoulder. "Wait."

She opened yet another drawer, produced a half-loaf of bread, and held it out. Miri took it in her free hand and carried it to the table.

Zhena Trelu hesitated, nodded to herself, and went to the icebox, pulling out butter. Her hand hovered over the cheese for a moment before descending. Skinny as they were? How could there be a question?

Butter and cheese balanced in one hand, she hefted the milk pitcher with the other and pushed the door shut with her knee. At the table she poured milk for all before looking around for her seat.

They had left her the chair at the head of the table, she realized then: Jerrel's place. The two of them sat next to each other, in what in later years had come to be the boy's chair, and his wife's.

Zhena Trelu smiled, pleased to see that they had not touched their soup. Manners, then, foreign or no. She picked up her spoon and had a taste, and they followed suit. Certain that they understood they were free to go on without her, she laid her spoon down, pulled the bread toward her, and laboriously sawed off three ragged slices. Then she took the cheese out of its paper and hewed off a largish chunk for each of them, laying it on the plates next to their bread.

Her own slice she slid into the toaster, reminding herself to pay attention to it. There was something wrong with the contraption; lately it burned bread to cinders without ever giving warning that it was done.

She picked up her spoon again and addressed the soup, watching her guests but trying not to stare.

The boy was left-handed and ate seriously, giving his whole attention, apparently, to the meal.

Meri was right-handed and appeared distracted, darting quick bird-glances around the room. She picked up her bread and broke it in half, using it to soak up some broth while she said something to the boy, who laughed and reached for his glass, and then jerked his head up, staring at the toaster.

"Oh, wind take the thing!" Zhena Trelu cried, smacking the release. The toaster *chingged!* and discharged a scorched rectangular object that smoldered gently and dripped charred bits onto the tablecloth.

"Damn you," she muttered, mindful of her company, and pulled the plug vindictively. She sawed off another piece of bread and buttered it, sighing.

She offered her guests more of everything, but they either did not understand or were too shy to avail themselves of her hospitality. Zhena Trelu finished her milk, wiped her mouth carefully, and folded her hands in front of her, wondering what to do. The most reasonable course was so send them on their way; and, truth told, they did look more rested, though Meri's face was still paler than Corvill's.

Miri tipped her head, catching Val Con's eye. "Now what?"

"Now we pay for the meal," he murmured. He pulled the toaster toward him, turned it around, pushed down on the lever, and peered inside the bread slot. Miri watched him for a minute, then slipped out of her chair and gathered the dishes together.

As she carried them to the sink, she heard Zhena Trelu address one of her incomprehensible comments to "Corvill," and glanced over her shoulder.

The old woman had risen and was beckoning to Val Con, indicating that he should follow her. Picking up the toaster, he obeyed, throwing Miri a quick smile as he left the room.

She swallowed hard, slamming the lid on an unexpected need to run after him. Deliberately she turned to the sink and worked out the gimmick for the water, then puzzled out the soap and stood holding it in her hand.

Month ago you didn't know the man existed, she told herself sharply. Now you can't let him outta your sight?

Adjusting the water temperature, she began to lather the soap, carefully thinking of nothing. By the time Zhena Trelu returned alone, the glasses were washed and draining, and the girl was scrubbing diligently at a bowl.

VANDAR

Springbreeze Farm

What with one thing and another, it was only reasonable that they spend the night. Corvill fixed the toaster like a charm; it took him the better part of the afternoon, but Zhena Trelu was not critical. She could not have fixed it at all.

Meri had been set to dusting after the dishes were done, and Zhena Trelu went out to milk the cow. By the time she came back, Corvill was waiting to show her the repaired toaster, and she exclaimed over that for a bit, even toasting a celebratory piece for everybody and doling out the last of the poquit jam.

A startled glance at the clock about then told her it was time to start making supper, for which she drafted Meri's help, first directing Corvill's attention to the carpet sweeper.

After supper, she went out to give the scuppins their evening grain while Meri and Corvill did the dishes. On the way back to the house she stopped, shivering in the wind, to look up at the rock-toothed gash that was Fornem's Gap. It was fixing to rain tonight, for sure...

And who but a two-headed, heartless monster would send the pair of them on their way with night coming on and a cold rain due out of the gap before morning?

On the porch she paused again, listening to the soft sound of their voices, talking their foreign talk as if the weird word-sounds actually meant something. Shaking her head, she tramped back into the kitchen.

Meri was in the middle of a yawn, which she belatedly covered with a slender hand.

"Tired?" Zhena Trelu asked, and sighed at the girl's blank smile.

She reached out and firmly grasped one small hand. "Come with me."

Turning down the right-hand hallway, she marched the two of them up the main flight and turned left, past the upstairs parlor and the attic stairs to the boy's old room. Pushing the door open, she yanked on the light cord and finally released Meri's hand to point at the double-wide bed where Granic and his zhena had slept—the same bed the young zhena had died in, struggling to birth a child too big for her.

"You sleep there," she told Meri.

The girl moved soundlessly over the rag rug and scrubbed floorboards to sit on the edge of the bed. She smiled and raised her hand to cover another yawn, while Corvill waited quietly by the door.

"That's fine," Zhena Trelu said. "Good night, Meri." She nodded to the man. "Good night, Corvill."

"Good night, Zhena Trelu," she heard him say softly as she pulled the door shut behind her.

Val Con turned down the bed and undressed, folding his clothes onto the bench against the wall. Slipping under the covers, he took a deep breath, consciously relaxing, and let his eyes rest on Miri.

She undressed, letting her clothes lie where they fell, and went to the mirror across the room, unwrapping the braid from around her head. It seemed that she swayed slightly where she stood, but he was tired enough to believe it only a trick of his eyes.

"Come to bed, cha'trez."

She turned her head and gave him a faint smile. "You convinced me."

It took her too long to walk across the room—she was, indeed, swaying—and she sat on the edge of the bed with a *bump*. "Why'm I so tired?"

"Altitude, perhaps. Also, we have had to think very hard today—everything is strange, the words must be heard and remembered…" He shifted, pulling back the covers. "Miri, come to bed; you're cold."

"Nag, nag." But she slipped under the covers, her face beginning to relax as she closed her eyes—and tensing again as she snapped them open. "Light. Aah, the hell with it." She closed her eyes with finality.

The hell with it, he agreed silently, and closed his own eyes, letting the tide of weariness take him.

Someone shouted his name; there were rough hands on his shoulders, and he was fighting, and the voice cried his name again, and it seemed familiar, and he opened his eyes with a jerk, staring uncomprehending at the face suspended above him.

"It's Miri," she told him, breathlessly.

"Yes." He was shaking, he realized, even more bewildered. The room beyond Miri's shoulder was brightly lit, composed, empty of threat. He looked back into her eyes. "What happened?"

She let out a shaky breath. "You were having a nightmare. A bad dream." She released his shoulders and slid to one side, her cheek resting on her hand.

A bad dream? He cast his mind after—and found it immediately; he recognized it for what it was and knew he was shaking harder. The bedclothes were stifling, in spite of his chill. He pushed them away and began to get up.

"Val Con?"

He looked at her, and she saw the lines etched around his mouth and the shadow of fear in the green eyes. He was trembling so hard she could *see* it. She put out a hand and covered his, feeling the cold and the shaking.

"There's this old Terran cure for nightmares," she said, trying to keep her voice steady. "Goes like this: You have a bad dream, you tell somebody. Then you never have it again." She offered a smile, wondering if he heard her. "Works."

He took a slow, deep breath, then lay back down like a thing made of wood and pulled the cover back over him.

Miri moved closer, not touching but offering warmth, hoping to ease the trembling. She reached out to brush the hair from his eyes.

"Not a dream," he said, and his voice was as rigid as his body. "A memory. When I was put on—detached duty—from the Scouts to the Department of the Interior I—received my orders and went to fulfill them—immediately, as instructed. I entered the proper building and walked down the proper hallway—and every step I took down that hall it seemed there was something—crying out?— screaming—in me—telling me to run, to go far away, to on no account continue forward…"

"And did you?" she asked softly.

He made a sound, which she did not think was laughter. "Of course I did. What else would I have done? Disobeyed orders? The dishonor—the disgrace…Gone eklykt'i? My Clan…" He was holding himself so stiffly that she thought he would break.

"I continued down the corridor, fighting myself every step of the way—against every instinct I had otherwise. Against my hunch. The only time in my life I failed to heed a hunch…" He closed his eyes.

Miri shifted beside him, worriedly.

"I went down the hall," he said tonelessly, "through the proper door, handed my papers in, and commenced training as an Agent of Change. And they lied, gods, and made it seem truth and twisted what I saw and how I knew things and pushed and pulled inside my head until Val Con yos'Phelium was hardly more than a memory. And it hurt…" He took a breath that could not have filled his lungs—and suddenly the horrible control snapped and he was rolling toward her, his arms locking around her, his head burrowing into her shoulder.

"Ah, Miri," he cried, anguish twisting in his voice. "Miri, it *hurt…*"

And he burst into tears.

She held him until it subsided, stroking the dark hair, running her hands down his back, feeling the tension going, going—gone, finally, with the sudden last of the tears. She held him a little longer and sighed; his breathing told her he was asleep.

She shifted, trying to ease away, but his arms tightened, and he moved his head on her shoulder, muttering, so that she sighed, resigning herself to a cramped and sleepless night.

She woke to find him looking very seriously into her face.

"Morning," she said fuzzily. *"Is* it morning?"

"Early morning," he said softly. "I do not think Zhena Trelu is about yet."

"Good." She moved, meaning to give him a kiss—and stopped.

"What is wrong?" he asked.

She shrugged, glancing away from the brightness of his gaze. "I'm never sure whether you want me to kiss you or not."

"Ah, now that is very bad," he said. "A problem in communication. I suggest that the best course is for you to kiss me whenever you wish to do so. In this way you will eventually be able to ascertain when it is I most wish to be kissed."

"Yeah?" She grinned and swooped down, intending the veriest peck on the cheek, but he shifted his head and caught her lips with his. His fingers were as suddenly in her hair, loosing the braid, stroking lightly…

When the kiss was over, Miri lay trembling on his chest, looking at his face, all blurred with longing and lust and love. "Any more kisses like that," she said, hearing that her voice shook as well, "and I ain't guaranteeing the outcome."

He smiled gently, one eyebrow slipping up. "It's early."

She closed her eyes against the sight of him, against the sudden stab of—what?

Robertson, she pleaded with herself, don't go sappy on me. She felt his fingers, feather light and trembling, moving down her cheek, stroking the curve of her throat.

"Please, Miri," he said wistfully. "I would *like* another kiss."

Opening her eyes, she obliged him to the fullest extent possible.

LIAD

Solcintra Port

Yes, the middle-aged voice assured Cheever in uptown Terran, the First Speaker would be delighted to see Mr. McFarland as soon as he arrived. Should a car he dispatched from Trealla Fantrol, or did he have his own transportation?

"I got cab fare," Cheever growled, mistrusting the voice, the featureless grid from which it emanated, the packet in his inside vest pocket, and very nearly the turtle who had gotten him into this, except there was no sense to that. The turtle had dealt straight. Turtles always dealt straight.

"Very good, then, sir," the voice told him. "The First Speaker awaits your arrival." The connection stud went dark.

"Yeah, great," Cheever muttered as he stepped out of the booth into the noisy tide of Port traffic.

He was nearly to the city gate before he saw a cab and waved it frantically to a halt. The Liaden woman in the driver's slot slanted him a look he was not sure he liked as he settled in the passenger's seat.

"I want to go to Trealla Fantrol," he snapped in Trade.

"Ah."

Cheever glared at her. "You know how to get there, or doncha?"

"I know the way. The question becomes, 'Can you afford the fare?'"

He took a deep, frustrated breath. Damn Liaden was laughing at him. "You want your round-trip upfront, is that it? Name your choice: Unicredit, bits, or Liaden money, if you got change for a cantra."

She stared at him for a long moment, apparently oblivious to the confusion her motionless vehicle was causing among Port pedestrians. "*You* wish to go to Trealla Fantrol."

Cheever clamped his jaw and refused to look down at his worn leathers, though the shirtsleeve he saw from the corner of his eye was far from clean.

"Yeah, I do. This is a cab, ain't it? You can take me to Trealla Fantrol, right?"

"Indeed, this is a cab. As for taking you to Trealla Fantrol…" The shoulders rippled, conveying nothing. "It is a pleasant morning for a drive."

Abruptly the cab swerved into traffic, gained momentum, dashed down a side street, and, a moment later, sped through the main gates. Cheever sat back in the seat, swearing at shortened leg room, and stared out the window, thinking about his ship.

Solcintra went by in a blurring zigzag of tree-lined streets. The ground pilot knew her quadrant inside out, Cheever allowed grudgingly, then snapped upright in the short seat as they sailed through a second gate—this one old and stone and shrouded with purple blossoms—and were abruptly in open country.

"Hey!"

The cabbie turned her head, forward velocity unchecked.

"Where the hell we going?" Cheever yelled, staring in confusion at jade-green meadow on one side, trees on the other, and a twisty road running toward some kind of tower leaping up out of a stand of trees way on the far side of the valley.

"We are going to Trealla Fantrol. It is the destination you chose. I merely agreed to take you—as far as we are allowed to go."

There was an unmistakable note of malice in that last bit. Cheever silently cursed the Liaden race, this specimen in particular, and his own stupidity in mentioning that he had a cantra on him. She was going to take him to Trealla Fantrol, okay—the long way.

"Where I want to go's in Solcintra," he tried, keeping his voice reasonable.

"Then you do not wish to go to Trealla Fantrol."

"Oh." He frowned out the window, where the tower across the valley was taking on more details by the second. In fact, it did not look like a tower at all, but a tree, except who had ever heard of a tree that tall? He pointed at it. "That Trealla Fantrol?"

The cabbie laughed. "Indeed it is not. That is Jelaza Kazone. Perhaps you'd rather go there? Though I hear the Korval is not presently in residence."

"Trealla Fantrol," Cheever said firmly, "is where the First Speaker of Clan Korval lives. I *know* that."

"Do I dispute it? Look to your left hand and you will see the chimneys."

He found seven of them, crowning a tight cluster of trees, then lost sight of all as the cab plunged down a steep incline, dashed left into a sudden roadway, and proceeded at an abruptly conservative pace.

They had gone perhaps a quarter mile when she glanced at him once more. "It appears you are expected."

He looked back, laconic in the face of her surprise. "What makes you think so?"

"The last fare I had to Trealla Fantrol was stopped a cab's length inside the grounds." There was another ripple of thin shoulders. "One assumes that she was not expected."

They passed beneath an archway, and the perfume of the flowers was momentarily overpowering until driven away by a sharp, lemony scent from the bushes on both sides.

The bushes ended and the cab spun through a quick right turn, left turn, emerged into a sweeping elliptical drive, and stopped smoothly at the base of a stairway.

Cheever stared, hand curling into a fist on his thigh; the weight of the package in his pocket trebled, and he wished fervently that he had taken the time to buy a new shirt.

"Trealla Fantrol," the cabbie said. "I will take Unicredit."

He fumbled it out of his pouch and never even looked to see how much she charged him. The turtle had said it was urgent, that Cheever was to deliver the turtle's package to the First Speaker of Clan Korval at Trealla Fantrol, Solcintra, with all possible speed.

The cabbie shoved the card back into his slack fingers. "My thanks, Jump pilot. Fare you well."

He started, dropped the card back into his pouch, and took a deep breath as the cab door swung aside. "Thanks. Errr...maybe you better wait."

"A waste of my time. Trealla Fantrol expects you. It is unlikely you will be sent forth in a cab." The door slid closed, and the cab was moving, taking the rest of the ellipse in smooth acceleration before vanishing down the long drive.

Cheever squared his shoulders and went up the stairs.

He laid his palm against the center plate in the big wooden door and composed himself to wait. They were not going to like him, the people who lived here. He had a sinking feeling that they were going to like the turtle's message even less.

Beyond the door, there was a brief rumble. Then the door was pulled open from the inside, and the voice from the Port phone inquired, "Mr. McFarland?"

For an instant he wanted desperately to deny it, to run down the stairs and the long drive, back to the Port and the loaned ship. Wanted to ditch the package and forget he had ever said he would deliver it.

Wanted to back down on his guarantee to a Clutch-turtle?

"Yeah," he managed, if a little hoarsely.

"Do step inside, sir. I've been instructed to place you in the small salon. Please come with me."

He stepped into the velvet-dim hall, turned toward his host— and felt his jaw drop. The squat metal cylinder did not seem to notice; indeed, it may have been too busy closing the heavy door to pay any attention to Cheever's lapse of courtesy.

Door closed, the 'bot rotated on its axis and gestured with one of its three flexible arms. "Right this way, Mr. McFarland."

"Okay...Uh, didn't I talk to you on the phone?"

The orange ball balanced on top of the monstrosity flickered, and all three arms waved gently. "Quite right. I am the butler, sir; Jeeves. At, I might add, your service."

"Sure you are," Cheever said. He shook his head slightly. "We're going to the—small salon?"

"Exactly so. If you would be good enough to come with me, sir? It's just a step down the hall."

Jeeves's step was most people's hike, Cheever decided some minutes later. It took more time to cross the slippery marble foyer than it did to go through a normal Terran house, and he added a second or two to the trip by stopping to stare at the sweep of strellawood stairs.

"The grand staircase," Jeeves murmured as they moved on. "Each riser hand-carved with an episode from the Great Migration and other illustrious points of history. I'm told it's quite impressive."

"Uh...yeah. Yeah, it's real nice," Cheever said, and followed the 'bot down a side hall only a little less wide than the foyer.

There were wooden doors with crystal knobs set dead center; there were impossibly delicate lights glimmering here and there on the wood-paneled walls; there was more wood underfoot, resilient beneath his boots, muting the rumble of the 'bot's wheels. Cheever shook his head to clear it and nearly fell into his guide.

"Here we are, sir. I trust you'll find the aspect pleasant, what with the ethaldom in bloom. Lord yos'Galan will be with you shortly."

Three steps into the room, Cheever spun. *"Lord* yos'Galan!" But the 'bot was gone.

"I want to see *Lady* Nova yos'Galan," he told the empty room. "First Speaker of Clan Korval. The turtle *said* Lady Nova yos'Galan…" Hands tucked into belt, he prowled the perimeter of the room, wincing at the smudge his boot had left on the creamy carpet. Bookshelves filled to capacity—bound books mostly, which told how rich they were even if he had not had the evidence of the house, the grounds, and the grotesque, efficient robot. People who owned books at all owned book-tapes; Cheever's personal collection included several piloting manuals and the general concordance for the Traland Three Thousands, though of course he had done his own mods on *LucyBug…*

The door at his back clicked and creaked, and Cheever spun with pilot quickness, the weight of the package pulling his vest a little wide.

"Good morning!" an affable voice cried in Terran unsmirched by uptown twang or Liaden blurring. "Mr. McFarland, isn't it? I'm so very glad to meet you, sir!"

The man coming toward him was Terran-high, though an inch or two shorter than Cheever himself, and dressed in exquisitely clean trousers and a full-sleeved, claret-colored shirt that set off the white hair shockingly. Beneath the old man's hair was a young man's face: big nose, wide mouth curved in a grin, pale eyes warm under slanting, silver brows. He held out a large, square hand on which an amethyst ring gleamed.

"Shan yos'Galan at your service."

Cheever grinned and slapped his own hand around the one offered. "Cheever McFarland. Pleased to meet you."

"As I am to meet you—but I said that already, didn't I? Mustn't repeat myself. Has no one given you wine? My dear man…Our hospitality has been wanting, and you fresh from the Port. Very dusty sort of place, Solcintra Port. Don't you find it so?"

"Errr…" Cheever said as the big hand came to his shoulder and coaxed him toward a discreet onyx counter.

"Precisely," his host said. "Will you have some morning wine? Whiskey? Misravot? Brandy? We have an excellent jade and a passable white, but I confide in you, sir—the red excels them both."

Whiskey…Cheever could almost taste it. A whiskey would be real good. Regretfully, he shook his head. "You wouldn't maybe have some coffee?" He smiled a little sheepishly at the other man. "Been up for a while, see? 'Fraid the booze'd go straight to my head."

"We can't have that, can we? Jeeves," he said, apparently to the room at large. "Please bring Mr. McFarland some coffee."

Glass clinked against crystal as he poured himself a healthy swallow of red wine. "I can't help noticing the insignia on your vest. Bascomb Lines, isn't it?"

Cheever's hand went to his left breast, where the once-bright Sol System insignia had almost faded away. "Yeah…"

"Do you work for the line?" Shan asked, lifting his glass. "I've just recently concluded some business with Ms. Lillian Bascomb and Captain Barney Keller—do you know them?"

"Lillian—I know—knew Lillian real well. Barney an' me ran the board together on the big bruiser—he wasn't no captain then."

"A pilot of some skill! What's it like, piloting a big cruise ship? Exciting?"

Cheever shrugged. "It's okay. But I like a little ship—better handling, faster, put 'er in and out of someplace tight before anybody knows you been there. Can't do that kind of stuff with the big ones. Got to play it straight." He nodded. "Like running my own boat."

"Do you?" Shan murmured as the door swung open to reveal robot and tray. "Reprieved, sir! I hope you find the coffee to your liking. Jeeves, Mr. McFarland tells me he's been up for days and that only a cup of your finest will see him safely through the next hour. Cream, sir? Sweetening?"

"Just black, thanks." He took the steaming cup from the 'bot, stomach cramping as he remembered that the past days hadn't included too many meals, either.

"I'm amazed," Shan yos'Galan was saying, "to see you so quickly. We were warned to look for you only yesterday."

Cheever grimaced as he burned his tongue. "I left two days ago."

"Really? You must have been very far away."

"Farther than you think," Cheever told him with a glint of pride. "All the hell and gone in the Second Quad."

"Quite a trip," Shan murmured appreciatively. "And so quickly! No wonder you're tired. If you like, I can take your charge to my sister. I should have made her apologies to you sooner—my dreadful manners, sir, do bear with me! She was called to speak with our man of business. But I assure you that I am completely trustworthy to—"

Cheever set his cup on the bar with a *thckk*. "Turtle said to give the package to First Speaker Nova yos'Galan. Said I was to put it in her hands."

The light eyes quizzed him over the cup's fragile rim. "Commendable." He turned his head slightly. "Jeeves."

"Your lordship?"

"Please inform my sister that Mr. McFarland can deliver his package into no hands but her own. I trust her manners are equal to the task of excusing herself from Mr. dea'Gauss for half an hour."

"Certainly, sir." The 'bot wheeled out of the room, dragging the door shut behind it.

"She'll be by in a moment or two, and then we'll get you to bed, sir, never fear."

"Huh?" Cheever frankly stared. "Hey, look—I mean, that's really nice and all, Mr. yos'Galan, but you don't need to put me up. I'll snatch a couple hours at the Port while I'm waiting for clearance—it's a borrowed ship, see? Turtle's deal was he'd pay for repairs to *LucyBug* if I delivered this stuff for him. Came into the bar asking for the hottest pilot there. I said I was—not bragging; stupid to lie to a turtle—and the rest of 'em said yeah, that's right."

"I see. Very nice of the turtle. What was his name, by the way? My ghastly memory!"

"Edger, he said to call him. *Big* somebody. Voice like to crack your eardrums." Cheever picked up the cup and gulped down the contents. "Real character, ain't he?"

"So I've been told. But I really must insist that you guest with us, sir. It's the least we can do for the trouble you've gone to on our account! Do let me convince you!"

"No, listen, that's—"

"Shan?" The voice was soft, accented and thoroughly lovely.

And the person who came with it was slim and small and golden and perfect. The violet eyes were huge in an adorable pointed face, framed by spun-gold hair. Cheever frankly stared.

The diminutive goddess stared back, infinitesimal frown shadowing the smooth expanse between flawless brows.

Into the growing silence swept Shan yos'Galan. "Ah, there you are, sister! Allow me to present Mr. Cheever McFarland, who has something he must deliver only to you."

She bent in a bow so graceful that Cheever felt tears start to his eyes. "Cheever McFarland, I am happy to meet you."

"And I'm ha—happy—to meet you…" Some nearly paralyzed grain of sense stirred. "I've got something to deliver to Nova yos'Galan, First Speaker of Clan Korval."

"I am that person," she said softly. "You may unburden yourself."

His hand started toward the inside pocket, then checked. "I'm sorry, but see—since I don't know you and all. Edger said I was to ask you to tell me your name."

"My name." The frown line became more pronounced, and it was all Cheever could do not to go down on his knees and beg her not to tease herself about it; he would *give* her the damn package, if only…

"My name," she began, quite seriously, "is Nova yos'Galan First Speaker-in-Trust Clan Korval, She Who Remembers, First Sister to Val Con yos'Phelium Scout, Artist of the Ephemeral, Slayer of the Eldest Dragon, Knife Clan of Middle River's Spring Spawn of Farmer Greentrees of the Spearmaker's Den, Tough Guy."

It was music; it was angel-song. He could have listened to her voice for hours—days—years. It was inconceivable that he would ever tire of hearing…

"Uh—yeah," he stammered, reaching in at last and drawing the thing forth. "Here you go."

She took it gravely in small hands and bowed once more. "My thanks to you, Cheever McFarland, for the service you do Korval. Please allow Jeeves to show you to the guesting room."

"Yeah…" he said again, and managed a rough bow, mere parody of her smooth perfection. "I'll, umm, I'll see you later."

"We will speak again," she agreed.

He glanced back once as he followed the 'bot down the hall, and saw her hands already busy at the sealing tape.

LIAD

Trealla Fantrol

"Cut that out!" Gordy brushed the screen, diverting Lady Pounce's attack from the cursor to his hand. "Cut that out, too! Dumb cat."

She blinked angelic and slightly crossed blue eyes at him and tucked her paws neatly beneath her snowy chest.

Gordy sighed gustily. "If you want to stay up there, you stay just like that. No more killing the cursor, hear me? I've got to finish this check."

Lady Pounce slitted her eyes in amiable acquiescence and even purred a few notes, though Gordy did not believe a word of it. He turned his attention back to the gridwork of equations that represented the contents and balancing of the *Dutiful Passage's* holds. The grid had already been checked by Cargo Master yo'Lanna, who had generated it; by First Mate Mendoza; and by Captain yos'Galan. Scant chance Gordy would find an error missed by that seasoned team. Nor was there truly any reason for an associate trader to concern himself with administrative details, except that Shan insisted, explaining, with a sweep that drew all eyes to the Master Trader's amethyst on his hand, that there was enough knowledge in the wide universe that Gordy never need fear learning too much.

Immersed in checks and cross-checks, he did not hear the light step behind him, and he started badly at the sudden hail.

"Well met, young Gordon! How do you go on today?"

Gordy's fingers jammed home three keys at once, eliciting a peevish *beep* as he spun in the chair, blood mantling his cheeks. "Oh," he said quellingly. "Hi."

The slender, dark-haired gentleman performed a bow as exquisite as his clothing; to eyes unused to the nuances of such things, the movement was a confection of graceful delight. "Your enthusiasm does you credit. Indeed, the invariable warmth of your greetings has ever been numbered among my chiefest joys in our kinship."

Sure it has, Gordy thought. He came out of the chair slowly, towering over the other man like a mountain over a molehill, and solemnly bowed the bow between Clanmembers.

"Forgive me, kinsman," he said, the High Liaden words only slightly edged in Terran accent, "for the attention to my work that hid your approach and may have cloaked my greeting in less than cordiality. You must by this time in our association have the measure of my admiration for you."

"Oh, very good," Pat Rin murmured, dark eyes gleaming. "Quite nearly a hit, I believe. Well done, young Gordon."

Gordy ground his teeth, keeping face and voice smooth with an effort that became less with each trade deal he negotiated. "How may I serve you, sir?"

"I seek your foster father, child. Is he within the house? Or must I languish upon Lady Mendoza's doorstep for a sight of him, like all the rest of the world?"

Priscilla would have you arrested for vagrancy, Gordy thought savagely, while he politely inclined his head. "He was just up the hall, speaking to Jeeves."

Pat Rin sighed delicately and flicked a wholly imaginary speck of dust from a moss-green sleeve, rings glittering on shapely fingers. "Speaking to the robot? But Shan will speak to anything, won't he? I've noted it time and again."

"Shall I fetch him for you, sir? It would take but a—"

"Pat Rin! Well met, cousin, how do you go on?"

Gordy spun toward the door, face wreathed in disbelief.

Pat Rin laughed his soft, malicious laugh and performed another beautiful, sarcastic bow. "Kinsman. I am exceptionally well. How do you find yourself?"

"I leave that to Priscilla," Shan said, smiling vaguely and impartially on Gordy, Pat Rin, and Lady Pounce. "Morning isn't my best time, and if I had to spend half of it finding myself—well, you appreciate, cousin, I'd be in a fair way to getting nothing else done at all."

Pat Rin frowned at the rush of Terran but answered competently in the same tongue. "You see me here on your word. How may yos'Phelium serve yos'Galan?"

The silver eye sharpened. "yos'Phelium? Have you taken up Thodelm's melant'i?"

"Certainly not," Pat Rin said, dropping his eyes to watch the play of light among his rings. "But you see, cousin, we of Line yos'Phelium find ourselves without a lord these several years, so that we grow accustomed to coming to Korval's First Speaker for resolution of matters belonging more properly to the Line."

"A complaint, in fact."

"An observation. You are yourself Thodelm yos'Galan. Would you run to the First Speaker with every up and down of your close kin?"

Shan blinked, icicle-sharp eyes melting back to blandness. "Well, things are a bit confused these days, cousin, admit it. Korval has shrunk to a handful; the Nadelm fends the Ring from his finger; the lines of administration are crossed and recrossed a dozen times over." He smiled. "We muddle on."

"While Nadelm Korval remains missing, and the Clan does its least to discover him."

Shan said nothing.

Pat Rin shrugged and looked up from admiring his rings. "One hears rumors, as one goes about. All the world notes the continued absence of Val Con yos'Phelium. Many remark upon yos'Galan's complaisance. They recall that Korval passes the Ring from pilot to pilot. They recall that Shan yos'Galan wears the badge of a master pilot." He dropped his eyes again and concluded softly, "While Pat Rin yos'Phelium is no pilot at all, nor ever shall he be one."

The silence stretched. Gordy watched Shan's face, but saw only vagueness there.

"Rumor is a dangerous song to heed," Shan commented. "But none of this bears on my need to see you, cousin! I wonder about your trip."

Pat Rin actually blinked. "My trip?"

"Exactly! Weren't you planning a jaunt to Philomen soon, for a bit of rest from your labors?"

"Yes. My plans are firm, in fact."

"Fine, fine, excellent! You'll be wanting a pilot, I know, and it—"

"It happens that I employ an adequate pilot, kinsman. My thanks for your kind thought."

"Yes, but you see, we have at hand a more than adequate pilot—and you need not be out of pocket an additional tenth cantra! Korval will balance any difference between payscales." He raised his glass and sipped. "The man requires occupation, kinsman! Surely you wouldn't deny him work to pass the time away?"

Pat Rin considered him out of thoughtful dark eyes, and Shan bore the scrutiny patiently, seeing anew how much his cousin resembled Val Con: the same glossy dark hair, level brows, and firm mouth.

"So," Pat Rin murmured. "And what am I to do with my new pilot when we reach Philomen? Shoot him?"

"Well, certainly that's up to you," Shan said, "but I've no reason to expect his service will be as bad as that." He raised his glass. "The First Speaker strongly suggests that he enter your employ and remain there—oh, six Standard months should be more than sufficient."

The smaller man bowed. "Of course it must always be my most ardent wish to obey the First Speaker's word."

"Yes," Shan drawled. "I'd heard that."

Pat Rin laughed. "Rumor sings dangerous songs, as I have only recently been reminded. Understand that nothing would induce me to doubt you, but I yearn to hear the First Speaker's wishes from her very lips. Might she be available to speak with me?"

"I believe she's alone in the study. Shall I have Jeeves escort you?"

"Thank you, but I know the way." He bowed farewell. "Kinsman. I think I will not see you again before *Dutiful Passage* leaves us. Fare you well. You also, young Gordon." He was gone, mincing daintily in his fancy boots.

Gordy let his breath go in a explosive *pough!,* spun toward his foster father, and hesitated.

"Yes?"

"Is Pat Rin—in love—with Cousin Nova?"

Shan shook his head. "No...No, I don't think Pat Rin's in love with anyone."

"Except himself!"

Surprisingly, the response was another headshake. "Not at all."

Gordy flung out his hands, startling Lady Pounce into opening her eyes. "Then why's he *like* that?"

"Well," Shan said thoughtfully, swirling the dregs of his wine, "I suppose that, like most of us, he's not finished yet. Have you checked these equations?"

Gordy flushed. "I'll be done in fifteen minutes."

"Fine. I'll be back then. We'll be going up to the *Passage* tomorrow morning for the last checks; we've got departure scheduled for Solcintra sunrise, Treslan Seconday."

"I'll have to tell Karea good-bye..."

"Yes, of course." Shan sighed. "Finish your equations, Gordy." And he was abruptly gone, closing the door behind him.

Shan touched the PLAY key and leaned back, eyes closed, to listen again to Val Con's recorded message to Edger.

"I greet you, brother, and thank you for the lives of myself and the youngest of your sisters. I am to say to you these things, which are true: We are alive and have been well treated, having received food, a place to sleep, and medical aid. I regret that the ship of the Clan has continued its voyage without us. It was undamaged when it left us and should achieve its destination as planned, as it kept course without fail during the seven seasons of its labor."

There was a small pause, then Val Con finished, "I am also to say that we will be returned our knives and given a ship in which in continue our travels. My thanks to you again, brother, for your care of two of your Clan who are foolish and hasty."

A Korval ship had already been dispatched to the coordinates indicated in Val Con's message. Exact figures relating to the distance a ship of the Clutch would have traveled in "seven seasons of labor" had been included in the hodgepodge of information that made up the balance of Cheever McFarland's delivery. The possibility had to be covered, of course, but Shan felt no optimism that Korval's ship would find Val Con and his lifemate anywhere near those coords.

The tape hissed briefly, and then the other voice came in, bright, clear, singsonging its nonsense as if there was nothing in all the worlds to fear:

"Hi, Edger. Everything's fine. Wish you were here. Love to the family and see you soon."

The tape hummed, clicked, and rewound noisily before the machine shut off.

"I like her," Shan said to the dim and empty study. "But, gods, brother, the Juntavas?" The agreement between the intergalactic mob and Korval stretched back generations: You don't touch mine; I don't touch yours. Simple, effective, efficient. "Why didn't you tell them who you are? They would have dropped Korval Himself and his Lady like so many hot potatoes..."

Chilled, he considered an alternate scenario. Val Con reveals himself. The Juntavas, horrified beyond reason by their act, knowing a balancing of accounts with Korval would ruin both, simply cut two throats, leave two bodies drifting...

"Gods!" He snapped to his feet, covering the room in five long strides, to stare out at the twilit garden, where the fountain caught the sun's last rays, transmuting light to emeralds.

Memory provided a boy's high voice, half-pleading: "But there *isn't* a Delm Korval really, is there, Shan? Just a made-up person—it could as easily be you as me." And he heard his own voice, laughing in reply: "Oh, no! *You're* the Korval, denubia! I don't want to be Delm."

"But you *could* be, couldn't you?" the boy Val Con demanded in memory, and Shan turned cold in the present and whispered, "Only if you die, denubia." He shook himself, hard.

"They're alive," he whispered, willing his hands to unclench and bringing his heartbeat down with a Healer's stern discipline. "You have that on the best authority. Do strive for some sense, Shan."

And there were two to find now. Even if Val Con...His lifemate must be found and brought back to the Clan, for if they did not have a Delm, they might yet have a Delmae. Nova saw that, thank the gods. Korval ships Jumped in a dozen directions that long afternoon, seeking news, any news, of Val Con yos'Phelium or Miri Robertson. Lifemates will hold together, Shan told himself, staring at the shadows growing from the trees toward the house. Find one and we find both.

Sighing, he shook himself free of his thoughts and slipped away from the house of yos'Galan to go home at last to Priscilla.

VANDAR

Springbreeze Farm

She was never going to get it right.

The minute she thought she had command of a word it slipped away, unmoored by a dozen or more others. It was all she could do to remember the name of the dog, never mind the word for its species. And all morning Zhena Trelu had been in a waspish mood, yelling and pushing at her when she did not understand. Which was mostly.

After the third such incident, she had twisted away from the old woman's grasp and run, screen door slamming behind her.

Flinging herself to the ground beside the scruffy little flower patch that marked the edge of Zhena Trelu's property, Miri scrubbed her hands over her face and tried to calm her jangling nerves.

"This ain't like you, Robertson," she muttered. But that didn't help at all.

Her head hurt. She reached up and pulled the braid loose; unweaving it slowly, she ran shaking fingers through the crackling mass, mightily resisting the urge to yank it out in handfuls, and hunched over, staring at her hands and just breathing.

She found she was staring at her calloused trigger finger. What business did her hands have baking sweet things? Why should she have to sit and listen to endless repetitions of the names of the powders, granules, and dried leaves that went into food? She did not intend to be a bake-cook.

Worse was all that zhena-and-zamir stuff. Why should Miri be asked first whenever Zhena Trelu wanted Val Con to do something? Since when was he Miri's trooper? But no, there were rules, and one of them was that a zhena—wife? mistress? lady? lover?—could tell *her* zamir what to do, and he, perforce, would do it. What kind of partner was that?

They had figured out that Zhena Trelu owned the house and lived zamirless. They had gotten across that they were looking for a place to stay, and she had supplied some story for herself that Val Con was slowly getting down. But there! Barely a week had passed and Val Con could hold a conversation with the zhena while Miri's head hurt more and more...

She wanted to shoot, dammit—a little plinking would calm her down. But Val Con had not seemed to think too much of that and after some thought she could see why: They were guests here, wherever here was, and it just wouldn't be good form to fill somebody's sacred tree all full of pellet holes.

"Hello, Meri," he murmured from her side.

"My *name*," she gritted out, not lifting her head, "is Miri."

There was a small pause. "So it is."

She took one more deep breath and managed to raise her head and face him. "Sorry. Bad mood."

"I heard." He smiled slightly. "Zhena Trelu tells me you are a 'bad-tempered brat.' What is that, I wonder?"

She tried to smile back and was fairly certain that the effort was a failure. "Whatever it is, it ain't nice. I messed up something she was teaching me to bake. Told me to put in *pickles* and I put in *milk*. Or the other way around. *I* don't know..."

He frowned. "It must have been *milk* and not *pickles*. *Milk* is the white liquid we drink, isn't it?"

"I don't know. Told you I didn't know. Every time I think I know what something means, got it all lined up in my head with what it means in Terran, she hits me with forty-seven *more*—" She flung her hands out in exasperation. "I ain't never gonna catch up at this rate!"

"Cha'trez..." He tipped his head. "Why are you trying to match these words and Terran words? Surely that will only confuse matters. Perhaps if you waited until you have this language firmly before attempting to compile a lexicon, it would go better. For now, it might be best to simply learn the tongue, as you were taught in school."

"I didn't *go* to school!" she snapped, hearing the rising edge to her own voice.

Val Con frowned. "What?"

"I said," she repeated with awful clarity, "that I didn't go to school. Ever. In my whole life. Accazi?" Her head was throbbing; she bent her face down and jammed her fingers through her hair.

"No." His hands were on her wrists, insisting that she lower her hands. She allowed it, but kept her head bent, eyes on the ground, and heard him sigh.

"Miri, don't run from me. Please. I don't understand, and I would like you to explain."

"You don't understand?" She was on her feet, wrists yanked free—and he was up, too, hands loose, face wary and watchful.

"You don't *understand?* Ain't anything *to* understand—it's all real simple. On Surebleak, if you paid the school tax, you went to school. You didn't pay the tax, you didn't go to school. With me so far? My parents were broke—you *understand* broke, or do I gotta *explain* that, too? Real broke. Bad broke. So broke they could about come up with enough money every month to fool the landlord into thinking someday he'd collect the whole rent. And, while we're at it, there were rats—you *understand* rats?—and my mother was sick all the time and whenever we *did* get some money Robertson would come home, drink it all up or snort it all down, smack us both around—" She caught her breath, horrified to hear how close it sounded to a sob.

"So I didn't go to school," she finished tonelessly. "My mother taught me how to read; and when I joined Liz's unit she beat Trade and basic math into my head. Don't need a fancy education to get by in the Merc. Guess that's why I never learned the right way to learn a language. Doing the best I can. Sorry it ain't good enough."

Val Con was standing very still, eyes on her face, his own features holding such a scramble of expression that she sat down—hard—and clamped her jaw against the sudden surge of despair.

Now you've done it, you prize loobelli, she told herself, and swallowed hard, waiting for him to turn and go.

"Miri." He was on his knees before her, hand outstretched, but not touching.

"You understand now?" Her voice was a husky whisper; his face swam, unreadable, before her eyes.

"Yes." He moved his hand slowly, keeping it plainly in sight as if she were some wild thing he wished not to frighten, and gently stroked his fingers down the line of her jaw. "I am sorry, cha'trez. I was stupid."

The tears spilled over. "No, *I'm* stupid. Told you so."

"You did," he agreed. "And I wish you will soon stop feeling it is necessary to lie to me." He brushed as her wet cheeks with his fingers. "There is a great difference between education and intelligence, Miri. You are not stupid. Normally." He offered her the slightest of smiles. "And—normally—I am not stupid. But every-one makes mistakes, I am told."

Her lips twitched. "I heard that."

"Good." He sat back on his heels, eyes serious on her face. "Having now made our mistakes, let us consider what may best be done to rectify them." One brow slid up. "Does your head hurt very badly?"

She blinked. "Who said anything about my head hurting?"

"I still get a headache when I try to translate from one language to another," he said. "Speak to me in any tongue I know, and I will answer in that tongue. Ask me what a word in one language means in another, and it may take me hours to decide." He paused to push the hair out of his eyes. "Will you do something for me, cha'trez?"

"Do my best.

"That will suffice," he murmured, reminding her so forcefully of Edger that she laughed. He glanced at her from under his lashes before adding his own grin. "Are you comfortable here? Would you prefer to go inside?"

"I'm fine," she said hastily, visions of Zhena Trelu dancing in her aching head. She crossed her legs and tried to look alert. "What's the job?"

Val Con was rummaging in his pouch. "It is only to help me think more properly about the best way for you to learn this tongue..." His hand moved sharply, and her eyes followed the movement, seeing that he had flung several objects to the ground.

"Close your eyes!" he snapped, and she did, instantly. He slipped two fingers under her chin and raised her head until her closed eyes were directed to a point slightly over his head.

"Keep your eyes closed," he said more gently, "and tell me what you saw just now on the ground."

Her brows twitched. "Starting nearest you and moving east: credit card—metallic orange with three skinny blue stripes—cover-ing one corner is a wholebit. Then there's a flat white pebble the size of two bits together, a cantra-piece—obverse: the linked stars. Near-est me is the ship's key; there's a stylus next to that, then a short wire twisted like a corkscrew; a piece of paper with writing on it—don't know what language, but it looks like your hand—then back to the credit card." She paused, then nodded. "That's it."

There was a silence, lengthening.

After a time she said, almost hesitantly, "Val Con?"

"Yes."

"Can I open my eyes?"

"Yes."

She found him looking at her closely, the expression on his face a mix of amusement, wonder, and—anger? Before she could be sure, it was gone; he was lifting a brow and nodding downward.

She glanced at the jumbled arrangement and grinned, the ache in her head suddenly less acute. "Didn't miss one. Thought I'd be outta practice."

The second brow rose to join the first. "Dumb, Miri?"

"But there ain't anything to that!" she protested, genuinely startled. "It's a gag—a memory trick. Anybody can learn it—got nothing to do with brains."

"I see. A useful gag, eh?" He scooped the stuff up and dumped it haphazardly into his pouch. "How long can you retain it?"

"Depends. That batch'll probably fade out by the end of the day, unless you want me to remember it longer. Better tell me now if you do, though, 'cause I've gotta—" She moved her hands in one of her shapeless gestures. "It's kinda like putting a sticker on the memory, so I remember not to forget it."

"I see," he murmured again, apparently finding nothing the least confusing in this explanation. "Can you do the same with sounds? Put a tag on them so you do not forget?"

She shook her head. "It works better if I can see what I'm supposed to remember—either a picture, or a pattern, or written down." She bit her lip. "That's why I'm having so much trouble with this gibberish? 'Cause I can't tag sounds? Can't figure out how it looks?" She seemed inclined to blame herself severely.

Val Con shook his head, smiling. "Most people pay more attention to one set of—input—than the others. I, for instance, happen to key to sound. I rarely forget a piece of music I've heard, or a word. It seems a natural inclination: For some reason I decided that sounds were more important than anything else." His smile widened. "And so, when I became a cadet I suffered through hours of remedial work until I finally learned to tag a visual pattern and call it back."

He shifted, staring sightlessly at the scraggly grass between them. Miri waited, aware that she was tensing up again; she jumped half a foot when he moved his head to look at her.

Concern flickered over his face, and he leaned forward, grasping her arms lightly. "Cha'trez?" He moved his fingers, lightly massaging. "So *tense,* Miri. What is wrong?"

She shifted, not sure if she wanted to escape his touch. "Zhena Trelu—" she began.

"Will wait. She was upset when she spoke to me, and I think it might be good for her to have some quiet time, as well." He sat close to her on the grass and took her hand in his.

For some reason, that increased the tension. "Why're you doing that?" she snapped.

"It gives me joy to touch you," he said softly. "Shall I not?"

Yes, she wanted to yell, you should not! You should bloody well *go* if you're going and before things get any worse, or...

"I'm scared," she told him, finally identifying the emotion.

"It is not comfortable to be afraid," Val Con allowed gently. "Do you know what it is that frightens you? It may be something we can resolve."

She took a deep breath, fingers tightening around his. "I'm afraid of being stuck here—by myself."

"Ah." His eyes were troubled. "Will I abandon you, Miri?"

"How do I know what you'll do? Month ago I'd never clapped eyes on you. It'd make a hell of a lot more sense for you to get out on your own, though, wouldn't it? Be able to learn faster, move around more, settle in quicker, better. You're a Scout; I ain't nothing—"

"No...Miri." He lay a light finger across her lips. "I am not a Scout. Not now. Now I am a man who is trying—with the help of his partner and his friend—to insure that a long and joyful life will be possible together. A partner who," he added, mouth twisting slightly, "is afraid that he will run from her."

There did not seem to be anything to say to that, and the silence grew taut between them.

"Unless," Val Con murmured, "I am being sent away?"

She jerked as if he had slapped her. "No!"

"Good," he said, squeezing her fingers. "Because I am not certain that I would behave—with honor—in such a case." One brow slid up. "I would be lonely, too, do you think?" He sighed as he read the answer in her face. "Ah, *I* do not get lonely..."

Miri looked down at their entwined fingers, took a deep breath, and looked up. "Val Con?"

"Yes."

She took another breath. "I'm new at all this stuff. Not just the Scout-type things—*all* of it. Being partners. Being married. Never had a partner. Never wanted one." She tried a smile and caught the glimmer of his, answering. "Takes some getting used to," she concluded. "I'm sorry—"

But what she was sorry for was drowned in a bark of welcome as Borril hove into view. He was with them in a thrice, flopping to his side and *whuffing,* yellow eyes rolling in anticipation of a fine session of ear-pulling.

Miri and Val Con exchanged glances and began to laugh.

"Dog," Val Con said, yanking hard on a ridiculous ear, "I venture to say you were well indulged before we came here. But now that you have three pairs of hands to command, you've become insupportable…"

VANDAR

Springbreeze Farm

Val Con entered the room with unnatural scuffling to avoid startling the aging woman, and bowed when she looked up.

"Zhena Trelu?"

She smiled, relief washing her face. "Cory," she said, using the short form, as she had been doing since their second day with her. He had raised a brow at the first usage but had not protested, and Cory he had become.

"Did you find the child?" she asked him. "Is she all calmed down? I'm sorry I upset her—likely I was a bit sharp myself—but that girl has the wind's own temper with her!"

The man's brows pulled together slightly as he moved farther into the room. "Only noise," he said in his laborious Benish. "Like Borril. Sees something, maybe bad—makes noise. Maybe bad something goes away…" He perched on the arm of Jerry's reading chair, eyes intent.

Zhena Trelu sniffed. "Bad! Meri knows I'm not going to hurt her."

Cory moved his shoulders. "Here, things are not home. Miri is—" He sighed sharply, tipping his hands out toward her in a gesture she had come to know well the last five days.

"She's homesick, you mean. Misses her home." She drank down rest of her tea and set the cup aside. "Of course she is, poor child. I'll try to be more patient with her, Cory. You tell her that for me, will you?"

"Yes." But still he waited, watching her.

"What else? Are you hungry? I made you some sandwiches—they're on the kitchen table. You know where the milk is."

From the floor at her feet Borril gave vent to a heartrending groan. Cory laughed, then looked up again.

"Zhena Trelu. I ask—for Miri. Is there in your house—*these*…"

He swept a slender hand at the book-covered wall—Jerrel's books, mostly; dusty since his death. "For childs?"

"Children," she corrected, "Might have a few around from when Granic—my son—was a little boy. Why?"

"For Miri," he said. "To learn the words."

"Books to help her learn words?" she repeated. "But you're doing so well!"

"For Miri, Zhena Trelu," Cory told her for the third time.

She sighed. "You're a patient boy. All right, I'll look around and see if I still have any of Granic's old books."

He tipped his head. "Soon, Zhena Trelu?"

"Well, I—" She bridled, staring at him. He met her eyes calmly, his own a clear and bottomless green.

After a moment, Zhena Trelu sighed and pushed carefully out of her chair. "All right, Cory," she said, with a touch of acid. "Soon."

After supper, Zhena Trelu left the two of them to clean up and went to pursue Granic's old storybook collection through the attic, grumbling audibly as she went up the skinny stairs.

Miri ran water into the sink and started to wash while Val Con cleared the table. She turned her head to smile at him. "I feel better," she said, which was not quite a lie. She *did* feel better—a little. The headache was gone, which was a big plus; but she was still as jumpy as a Merc without kynak.

Val Con finished the glass he had been drying and set it aside. "After we are done with this, if you like, I can show you a way to make living here—easier, perhaps."

She looked at him doubtfully, not sure that she really needed to learn something *else* right now; and he tipped his head, catching her eyes on his.

"I promise not to give you a headache," he said solemnly. She gave a wan grin. "Okay," she said. "What the hell."

Brrrinngg!

Miri whirled, ready to charge, staring at the black box on the opposite wall. Until that moment it had always been silent.

It repeated its shrill noise, and Val Con had his hand on it; then he was lifting the top part away and bringing it to his ear.

"Zhena Trelu's house," he said carefully in Benish.

A pause filled with tiny crackles, then a woman's voice spoke, high-pitched in amazement. "What? Who is that? Where's Estra?"

Val Con sighed gently. "Zhena Trelu's house," he repeated clearly. "Cory. Attic."

There was another pause on the line, and he turned to look at Miri, standing tense by the sink. He wrinkled his nose, which made her laugh, and then the voice on the phone was spouting more questions.

"Cory? What are you doing there, Cory? Where are you from?" The amazement had been replaced by avaricious curiosity.

Gossip, Val Con thought darkly and withheld another sigh. "Work. Home. Who is *that?*"

"What!" the voice exclaimed, though it apparently did not expect to be answered, because it rushed right on. "This is Athna Brigsbee. You tell Estra that I'm on the phone and want to talk to her right away."

"Stay," he said, as if she were Borril, and let the receiver down to dangle by its cord. Leisurely he went down the long hallway, up the stairs, and to the thin attic stairway.

"Zhena Trelu?"

There was a thump and a rustle from above. "What?"

"Athna Brigsbee on the phone to talk to you right away."

"Wind take the woman!" Zhena Trelu grumped, and Val Con grinned. "Tell her to hold on, Cory. I'll be there soon."

"Yes." And he was gone, soundless, down the stairs and back to the kitchen.

"Hold on," he told Athna Brigsbee. "Zhena Trelu is here soon." He let the receiver back down without waiting for an answer, picked up his towel, and began drying the mountain of clean dishes Miri had produced.

By the time Zhena Trelu reached the dangling receiver, it was making indignant noises, which the two diligent workers at the sink seemed not to hear.

"Young man? Young man! Pick up this phone, young man! Just what do you think—"

"Hello, Athna," Zhena Trelu said, unable to resist a grin at Cory, who raised a brow and continued drying dishes.

"Estra? Well, thank goodness! I was terrified. That rude man...Who *is* he, Estra? I asked, of course..."

I just bet you did, Zhena Trelu thought. "Cory and his zhena are helping me out around the place. You know it's been threatening to fall down around my ears these last couple winters. Thought I'd get everything all lined up and then maybe sell it, come spring." She stopped, surprised at herself.

"Well, that's lovely for you, dear," Athna Brigsbee said. "I know how hard it's been for you to keep everything up since poor Jerrel passed on." Zhena Trelu gritted her teeth: Jerry and Athna had not been the best of friends.

"But *tell* me about them, Estra," the voice in her ear continued. "Where are they from? I asked Cory, but all he said was 'home.'" She gave a shrill little laugh.

Good for you, Cory, Zhena Trelu thought. "They don't speak Benish very well. They're refugees—survivors of that volcano and earthquake they had over in Porlint last year."

"But, Estra," Zhena Brigsbee protested, "when I talked about how we should all get together and *do* something about those poor people right after the disaster you were—well, I won't mince words. You were *cold*, Estra. And now to take *two* refugees into your house— and they don't even speak the language!"

There was a pause that Zhena Trelu spitefully refused to fill, then Athna took up her thread again, voice lowered. "Are you *sure* they're married, Estra? The stories I've heard! People taking refugees into their homes who turn out to be thieves, or murderers..."

"Meri and Cory aren't thieves," Zhena Trelu snapped. "And I sincerely doubt they're murderers. Just a young married couple that happened to need help the same time I needed help, so we're helping each other." She took a breath, trying to force the irritation down. "Athna, I really am going to have to go."

"Of course! But we *must* get together—say on Artas? I'll bring a nice scuppin salad and some brownies, and the four of us can have a lovely dinner and a nice talk—it's been such a long time, Estra! Well, I won't keep you any longer—I'll see you on Artas, for dinner. Take care of yourself, dear." The line went dead, leaving Zhena Trelu gasping in outrage.

Athna Brigsbee was coming to visit in two days? There was no stopping her, of course. That sharp nose smelled gossip, and she would not rest until the ferreted out every bit of information possible about Cory and Meri and then did her best to make that information known throughout Gylles and the neighboring county.

Zhena Trelu returned the receiver to its hook, turned toward the sink—and gasped as she saw the young couple as a stranger would see them.

Meri was putting away pans while Cory finished the drying, both dressed in the tight-fitting leather garments that were the only clothes they owned. As Zhena Trelu watched, Meri picked up the heavy iron skillet and bent to put it into the oven. The zhena tried to imagine the expression on Athna Brigsbee's face, were she presented with such a spectacle during her visit, and was almost tempted to allow the situation to continue.

"Meri," she said, shaking herself and moving toward the stove and the tea kettle. "Cory."

They turned to look at her, the girl drifting closer to the man's side, eyes great and gray in her thin face.

"Winter's coming," Zhena Trelu said, trying to talk slowly enough for Meri to understand, "and you're going to need warmer clothes. We'll go to town tomorrow and buy you something nice. Better clothes," she added, as she saw Cory's irrepressible eyebrow slide upward.

"Zhena Trelu," he murmured. "Buy is—" He tipped his hands out. "We not buy, maybe."

She frowned at him. "You don't have any money to buy clothes, is that it?" She shook her head, feigning irritation. "All the work you two have been doing around this place? Did you think you were working for nothing, Cory?"

"Dinner," Meri said unexpectedly. "Supper. Bed."

"For the little bit the pair of you eat," the older woman informed her with feeling, "I got the best end of *that* bargain. I owe you a few clothes—couple jackets, maybe. That should make us even for what you've done so far, all right?"

Meri looked at her husband, who moved his shoulders in that foreign gesture of his and bowed slightly. "Thank you, Zhena Trelu."

"You're welcome," she said, unaccountably touched.

Cory reached out and took the girl's hand, and the two of them slipped out of the kitchen, leaving only a soft "Good night" drifting behind them.

"Good night, children," Zhena Trelu said quietly, and turned to run water into the kettle.

"You should be as comfortable as possible," Val Con told Miri softly. "Later, you will be able to do this at any time, but to learn it is better to be at ease." He sat cross-legged in the middle of the double bed and smiled at her. "Perhaps you should unbraid your hair and take your boots off. Take off all of your clothes, if you will feel better so."

Miri grinned as she unbraided her hair. "I'd hate to tempt you like that."

"I," he said austerely, "am above such things. It is not for you to think that Scouts might be human."

She made the bow of student to teacher, hamming it, eyes very round. "Forgive me, Commander, I'll remember."

"Do so," he directed. Then he grinned. "I shall endeavor to keep my thoughts pure."

She shook her hair and combed rapid fingers through it, then sat on the wall-bench and yanked off her boots before shedding the rest of her clothes. "Now what?"

He patted the bed at his side. "Come lie down."

She lay on her back, eyes tight on his face, right hand fisted between her breasts.

"You are comfortable?" he asked. "Not cold? It is better if you put your arms at your sides and let your hands relax." He reached to brush the clinging copper threads from her cheeks; his fingers touched her lips lightly. "I promise you, cha'trez, this is a good thing—pretty and friendly—not at all frightening. Even I was able to learn it the first time."

She gave a gurgle of laughter and composed herself as he had suggested.

"Good," Val Con murmured, noting how tense her muscles still were. "Now I will tell you what will happen, then I will show you the way, and then I will ask that you repeat the process by yourself while I watch. All right?"

"Okay." Her eyes were on his, and he folded his hands on his knees, making no effort to break that link between them.

"The name of this technique," he said softly, "is 'The Rainbow.' It is a way of relaxing mind and body so that one may improve concentration and think—more rightly. People who are tense and confused make mistakes. And tension and confusion leach joy from life, which is a thing to be avoided. We should strive for more joy, not less—and that is what the Rainbow is for." He found his voice taking on the proper rhythm, found himself speaking the same words he had heard from Clonak ter'Meulen, all those years before.

"What you must do," he told Miri, "is picture the colors of the rainbow, one by one: red, orange, yellow, green, blue, purple, violet; and use the—key—of each color to relax more deeply. By the time you reach the end of the rainbow you will feel very nice indeed: warm and comfortable, perhaps a little as if you were floating. You will then walk down the stairway and through the door. That is what will happen." He lifted a brow. "Shall we continue?"

Miri was frowning "You're gonna hypnotize me?"

"No. I help you relax. Each person's Rainbow is unique. I may show you the way because of the superficial similarity of the color structure. But your Rainbow is *yours,* cha'trez. There is no danger. If you should become frightened or uncomfortable—or simply wish to go no further—you need only open your eyes. It is *your* will that commands, not mine."

"Got it." She closed her eyes, then opened them with a sigh. Her left hand had curled into a fist while he was talking, and she flexed it open before looking back at him with a ragged grin. "Well, let's give it a spin and see what comes up."

"All right." He smiled. "Close your eyes now, Miri, and breathe deeply. Try not to think of anything specific, but let the thoughts flutter by, unconsidered..." He closed his own eyes briefly, feeling for the proper rhythm and words. Wily old man, Clonak ter'Meulen, he thought; I wonder where you are now.

"Miri," he began gently. "Please visualize the color red. Hold it before your mind's eye. Tell me when you have it firm."

"Now," she said instantly.

"Good. Hold it; let it fill your head, pushing away all those little, half-formed thoughts. Let there be only red. There is only red. Warm, happy red, filling your thoughts entirely.

"Now," he said after a moment, "let the red flow down through your body, starting at the top of your head, warming and relaxing you—down through your face, your throat, your shoulders—warm, friendly, relaxing red..."

And so he took her through the Rainbow, slowly, gently, watching the tension ease out of her, her face soften, her breathing slow. He reminded her at yellow and again at purple, as Clonak had once reminded him, that she might open her eyes and return, should she so desire, but she did not choose that path.

"You are now concentrating on the color violet," he said softly. "The end of the Rainbow. How do you feel, cha'trez?"

"Nice," she murmured, voice slightly fuzzy. "Warm and kind of—cloudy-feeling. Safe." She smiled a little. "I'm glad we're closer here."

He tipped a brow at that but replied gently, "I am glad, also. Look about you now, Miri. Do you see the stairway?"

"Standing on the top stair," she told him, voice entirely unsurprised. "It goes down a way."

"Will it make you feel—unsafe—to walk down?"

"No," she said unhesitatingly. "Should I?"

"If *you* wish to, Miri."

"Okay." A slight pause, then she said, "Val Con?"

"Yes."

"There's a door."

"So?" he murmured. "What sort of door?"

"Old-time door—all shiny, dark-brown wood and a big brass knob. There's a keyhole as big as my fist."

"Why not go in? Or would you rather return now?"

"I'd rather go in," she said definitely. "But I don't have a key to fit this beast—"

"Perhaps in your pouch," he suggested softly.

"Naw, I don't have a key like—" Her brows twitched over closed eyes. "I'll be damned."

There was a longish pause before she said again, "Val Con?" Wonder and excitement filled her voice.

"Yes, cha'trez."

"It's a *library,*" she breathed. "You never *saw* so many books—tapes and bound—and a desk and a chair—big and soft—candles—little knickknack things and—uh-oh."

"What is wrong?" He expended the effort necessary to keep his voice smooth.

"I'm in trouble, boss—there's a Belansium planetscape in here."

He grinned. "I do not think you need worry. Does the room please you?"

"Please—it's *wonderful!* Is yours like this?"

"Everyone's room is different," he told her gently, firmly refusing to consider the shambles his own must be in, if it still existed at all. "I am happy that you are happy."

He paused, then decided on a departure from Clonak's technique. "Miri?"

"Yo."

"May I give you a gift?"

Her brows contracted slightly. "A gift? Why?"

He winced. "It gives me joy to do so," he said very gently. "Will you allow it?"

"Yes."

"Thank you," he said seriously. "Look on the seat of your chair. Do you see the book there? Not a large book—very thin, in fact. Bound, with paper pages..."

"Here it is!" After a moment she went on, hesitantly. "Val Con? It's—it's beautiful. You sure you want to give it to *me?*"

He extended a hand, stopping just short of touching her near-sleeping face. "I wish it," he said gently, "with all my heart." He paused. "Listen, now, and I will tell you about this book. You will see that each of the pages is blank, except for the first four, where I have written something for you."

"Yes."

"Good. The first page, that says 'Sleep,' does it not?"

"Yes," she agreed once more.

"And the next," he continued, "says 'Study;' the third, 'Relax;' and the fourth, 'Return.' Is that correct?"

"Exactly correct."

"Very good. Now, what you may do, whenever you come to your library, is look at this book and choose what you will do. If you choose to sleep, you need only open to that page, concentrate on the word there—and you will sleep. If you wish to allow your mind to review and integrate the day's affairs—or if you wish to work on a particular problem—you will open to the page marked 'Study,' concentrate on the word, and your mind will be ready to learn.

"If you find yourself growing tense, you might wish to go to your library and regard 'Relax.' And, if you wish to return to the world outside your room, you need only bring your attention to the fourth page, and you will awaken." He waited a moment to let it all sink in.

"Miri, please open your gift to the page on which I have written 'Return.' Concentrate on it..."

She took a sudden sharper breath, then her eyes flickered open, and she smiled at him, very gently.

He smiled back. "Hello, Miri."

"Hi." She stretched, catlike, her smile widening to a grin as she extended a hand and touched his scarred cheek. "You're beautiful."

He raised a brow. "I am happy that I please you," he murmured. "How do you feel?"

"Wonderful. This gimmick might not help me talk to Zhena Trelu, but if I feel this relaxed every time I go down and come back, we're up."

"But it will help you talk to Zhena Trelu. If you choose to do so, you may go to your library and concentrate on 'Study' and 'Sleep.' Then you will be able to assign your attention to sorting and making sense of all that has come to pass—today, for instance—while your body and your waking mind rest. Tomorrow you will then have access to all of today's data, not just a jumbled mess that you have no time to sort through."

"If you say so." Her brows twitched together in a frown. "Where'd you learn this gag?"

He unfolded his legs and stretched out beside her, head pillowed on an arm, eyes level with hers. "It is a Scout thing. A man named Clonak ter'Meulen taught me, when my uncle hired him to make Shan a master pilot."

"Your uncle hired a *Scout* to teach your cousin to pilot?"

"Oh, no—Shan had been a pilot for years! He merely required tutoring to attain his master's rank, and Uncle Er Thom would settle for no less. As for hiring a Scout..." He moved his shoulders. "Clonak desired passage; my uncle desired his son to have the best tutor available. So a bargain was struck."

"And he just taught you this Rainbow thing on the side?"

"Of his kindness. He had known my father, you see, and he was much taken with Shan and me. I achieved my third class that trip, under his training." He stroked her cheek lightly. "Will you do a thing for me now?"

"Do my best."

He smiled. "Will you go through the exercise again, while I watch? And when you achieve your library, would you assign your concentration to 'Sleep'? The past days have been very hard for you—I am sorry that I did not understand *how* hard, so that we could have resolved this sooner. And tomorrow we are to go to town and buy clothes, which may prove trying for us all..."

Miri laughed and laid her lips firmly against his; he felt her fingers in his hair, and a quickening of his own blood. When she leaned back, the laughter was still in her eyes. *"Sure* you want me to go to sleep?"

"Alas," he murmured, half smiling in regret and admiration.

"Slave driver." But she rolled onto her back and closed her eyes. In a little while, the rhythm of her breathing told him that she was asleep; and in an even shorter while, he followed her.

DUTIFUL PASSAGE

Liad Orbit

Priscilla took off her shirt and laid it neatly on the bed, then stretched with casual sensuality and bent to remove her boots. The soft belt with its cleverly worked silver buckle was next, followed by the dark blue trousers.

Unencumbered, she stretched again and crossed the first mate's quarters to the wide, cloth-covered chair. She curled into it like a cat, which reminded her of Dablin, so that she smiled for a moment before closing her eyes and beginning the discipline that erased all expression from her face.

The discipline progressed: breathing deepened; heartbeat slowed until it was a distant boom coming at long intervals, like an ocean beyond the hills; body temperature dropped four degrees. When she was satisfied that those functions had stabilized and would remain steady until the body itself failed of hunger or trauma, Priscilla withdrew her attention to her place of safety, admitted the prayer that would keep her whole on such a chancy venture, opened the door between her Self and that which was not her Self—and went forth.

Sounds, dazzling patterns, seductive perfumes: the *Passage* and all within it suddenly experienced with only the inner senses. There: Shan on the bridge. There: Lina in the common room. There: Gordy in the trader's room; Rusty at the comm; Ken Rik, Calypso, BillyJo, Vilt…Priscilla touched each, acknowledged all—and let them go.

The *Passage,* with its din of familiarity and love, dropped away, and she was alone in the noisy outside. She disallowed the clamor of strangers, brought up the template of the aura she sought, and focused on it, stretching awareness until her Self was barely more than a webbing of moth antennae, listening, quivering, straining far and farther…

It was at the point that Self was strained to the thinnest, when the thread that anchored her to the *Passage,* to the body, was at the limit of its elasticity, that she heard/sensed/saw it.

A glimmer, no more. A hint of familiarity; a bare taste of acerbic sweetness...

Awareness contracted as Self rushed toward the hint, unsubtle in desire; everything focused on the pattern growing in her senses, intent on contact, so that it was not until the last instant that she recognized the subpattern of one protected within deep meditation.

Aboard the *Passage* the body cried out, awareness and Self expanding toward dissolution as she struggled to absorb the psychic impact, scrambling even then for the shredding lifeline, clawing her way back, awareness a shivering knot of pain within the fire-shot network of Self—and plummeting into the body at last, heavy as a stone.

She cried out again as the pain ate along nerve and sinew, heartbeat stuttering, respiration a gasping mess, body soaked in sweat, and it was hot, hot, too hot—

Cool.

"Shan!" That cry was no less desperate, for all he was Healer and strong in his skill. "Shan, no!"

Cool enveloped her, leaching the heat and stifling the agony. She collapsed into it as if into his arms, and opened herself utterly, allowing him to cool even the memory of the pain, letting it vanish out of knowledge as heart rhythm steadied and breathing smoothed...She sighed and drifted, thinking of nothing.

"Priscilla."

It was with no common effort that she opened her eyes and looked into his face, vaguely surprised to find that she was indeed lying in his arms.

"No more, Priscilla." Face and voice were stern; exhausted witchsense brought her the echo of his terror. She thought about smiling, and perhaps she even did.

"I saw Val Con."

His pattern changed too subtly for her to read. "Where?"

She moved her head. "It doesn't work that way, love. There aren't any directions when you go—spirit-walking. He's alive...strong...Meditating—playing, perhaps. I should have remembered how the music rings around him when he plays...That's what got me in trouble. Rushing in before I looked close. Wooly-headed as Anthora."

"I don't recall that Anthora has ever put herself in quite so much danger in her checks on my brother—or on any of the rest of us. Understand me—no more. You will not endanger yourself searching for my renegade of a brother, who is, incidentally, quite capable of taking care of himself." His arms tightened fractionally, and she had no trouble reading the shift in his pattern that time. "I can't afford to lose you, Priscilla; have some sense."

There was no talking to him, not with the fright he had just had—she saw that clearly, exhausted as she was. She smiled once more and lifted a hand to his stark cheek. "Of course, dear," she murmured. And slept.

STARSHIP *CLARION*,
ALLIED TO CAPTAIN ROBERT CHEN-JACOBS
TAKING ORBIT ABOUT THE
WORLD NAMED KAGO

The trip had been hasty and wondrous; the captain of the Terran vessel in which Sheather and his T'carais traveled was a gracious individual with an understanding nearly as bright as that of Val Con yos'Phelium Scout. He was a treasure, was Captain Chen-Jacobs, and Sheather had lovingly subscribed him to memory, knowing already how much might be learned from those hasty persons of the Clans of Men.

Consider that his T'carais, known to men as Edger, claimed untold wisdoms acquired from his adopted brother, that same Val Con yos'Phelium Scout—and the T'carais had a memory both long and rich. Indeed, only see what Sheather himself had learned, through their last brief meeting with the brother of the T'carais and the lifemate of that brother. Another treasure entirely was Miri Robertson; and Sheather dwelled often upon the honed brightness of her, to his wider appreciation of what was.

"Four days from Lufkit to this place," Edger said beside him.

Sheather blinked solemnly. "The Clans of Men and the ways of those Clans are hasty indeed, brother. And yet I find myself— exhilarated—by their speediness, touched by the valiance of their striving."

"Do you so?" The T'carais considered him with care.

There was that in the voice of the T'carais which brought to mind vividly one's own position as a mere Seventh Shell; yet Sheather did not efface himself. "I find myself," he said instead, "looking at this action or another of an individual with the eyes of our new sister. It is a difficult endeavor, and one that I perhaps undertake imperfectly, yet I say to you, brother, that a certain—correctness—exists, though the view must be both hasty and imperfect." He foundered somewhat under the unwavering regard of his T'carais and the eldest of his brothers. "No doubt there is much thought yet required."

"No doubt," Edger responded calmly. "Honor me, brother, with your further thoughts upon this subject, when you have considered more widely."

"Certainly, brother."

"Your pardons, Most Wise." Captain Chen-Jacobs bowed deeply, and Sheather, seeing as his new sister might see, understood that the man was distressed.

His eldest brother, with what resources must be available to the one who was both T'carais and Edger for the Clan, had achieved the same understanding. "My pardon you do not need, for you have done us no harm," he assured the man in a booming voice. "But I perceive that you are uneasy and hope that ill news has not found you."

"Ill news?" The captain spread his hands, palms up, in a variation of the gesture favored by Val Con yos'Phelium Scout. "Who can tell? But you spoke of a pressing need to raise Shaltren when you boarded my ship, and I said that I would try to make arrangements for a connection from Kago."

Edger bent luminous eyes upon the man's face. "And have you not done so?"

"Wisdom, I have. But you spoke of haste, and I'm afraid the arrangements I've made are insufficient to your need."

Edger waited, eyes glowing.

"Understand, Wisdoms, that respectable ships do not ordinarily go to Shaltren. I have, in fact, located one. Its name is *Skeedaddle,* and the captain has said she will add you both to her passenger list."

"Thus far there is only amiable news, Robert Chen-Jacobs. Acquaint us with your trouble."

The man sighed heavily and shook his head, though what he denied was more than Sheather could find, even with the assistance of his sister's sight.

"My trouble is for you, Wisdoms. *Skeedaddle* and Captain Rolanni are willing to take you to Shaltren. But they do not leave for thirty days."

There was a silence, short for Clutch, long for a human. "It may be possible," Edger said, "to hire a ship and a pilot for the purpose of taking us to Shaltren. We shall investigate this possibility. For I confess to you, Robert Chen-Jacobs, that I am not entirely easy with human speediness and the rate at which events may sometimes take place. It is perhaps true that thirty days is too many to wait, in this instance." He turned his head. "What think you, young brother?"

Startled, Sheather blinked. "I?" He was aware of a conviction that thirty days was far, far too long and offered that information to his T'carais, adding diffidently, "It is what I perceive, brother, with the understanding I have of our sister's perception. The T'carais…"

But the T'carais, in a most unClutch-like manner, had turned back to Captain Chen-Jacobs. "My kinsman and I are grateful for your efforts, but I, too, feel that thirty days are too many to simply wait upon transportation, no matter how respectable. We shall find another way." He extended a three-fingered hand and inclined his head. "You have done well for us, Robert Chen-Jacobs. We are grateful."

The man hesitated fractionally before putting his hand into Edger's. "I'm sorry I couldn't be of more help. If there's anything else I can do…"

"You have done what was asked of you, and it may be yet that we shall utilize what you have wrought. But we must explore this other possibility. In the affairs of men, days are most often of the essence."

LIAD

Envolima City

Tyl Von sig'Alda sat in an office overlooking Envolima Spaceport, frowning at the screen before him. The bowl at his right hand had long since ceased to steam; the spicy scent cloyed, irritated for an instant, then was whisked away by the air-cleaning system.

Thirteen.

No other clan owned as many ships; indeed, Korval might be said to hoard the things. Tradeships, yachts, retired Scout ships, miners, intrasystem garbage scows—if it was a ship and came into Korval hands, there it remained until the care of men could no longer keep it spaceworthy. Never in the memory of the longest Rememberer had any of Korval loosed a vessel of their own will, excepting, perhaps, the very ship of the Migration.

Thirteen was a mote from such a fleet, yet even Korval could not afford to scatter ships like handfuls of seed throughout the galaxy.

That an exodus of thirteen ships occurred mere days after Korval-in-Trust's inquiry for Val Con yos'Phelium was—disturbing.

Of the five major tradeships, only *Dutiful Passage* remained about Liad; so it seemed half-breed yos'Galan was immune to whatever orders had sent lesser captains scrambling to file Change of Departures and ring their crews back from abruptly shortened leaves.

Well, and Korval ever moved to the necessities of its own madness, to Liad's gain, mostwise. Though of course that was never its primary object. Korval served the interests of Korval; it merely happened that its interest ranged widely. So widely that one Terran encyclopedia had labeled Korval "Liad's ruling House," likening its Delm to a king. And to individuals of mere Terran understanding that must seem to be the way of it.

Tyl Von sig'Alda touched the keypad, banishing the tale of ships. The next file was even less satisfactory, and frequent viewing had failed to sweeten the contents. Oh, it started well enough, with verification of Val Con yos'Phelium's most recent mission successfully completed: The Second Quadrant leader of the Terran Party, one Kelmont Jaeger, was dead, according to plan; precisely as ordered.

Well done, sig'Alda allowed, and sighed as the file scrolled on.

He was viewing now his own efforts at tracking the missing agent, looking, as he had countless times before, for that flaw in his reasoning; that glaring error in his conclusion that had led the commander to assign him this thrice-hopeless task. Even the verification of the Loop and the report he had given while under the drug had left the commander unmoved. Agent Tyl Von sig'Alda was assigned the project of ascertaining *without doubt* the whereabouts and condition of Val Con yos'Phelium.

Agents, as sig'Alda knew, were expendable. Yet the commander insisted on being certain that any unaccounted for had indeed been expended and neither captured nor subverted, though surely Loop and Option guarded against either...

sig'Alda sighed in sharp irritation. He had reached the point where it was a matter of retracing Val Con yos'Phelium's steps, thoughts, and conclusions. His office was cluttered with records of yos'Phelium's past missions—for his search, he had been granted ultimate clearance. He had requisitioned and attained yos'Phelium's Scout files; had listened to them over and over, until the man's quiet voice and precise phrasing seemed likely to haunt the few hours of sleep he allowed himself.

And still there was no clue.

Certain matters were obvious: both sanctioned escape routes had remained unused at mission end, and a ship lay empty at Lufkit Prime Station, doing nothing more than collecting berthing fees. Past missions illustrated yos'Phelium's resourcefulness: as had been the case in previous missions, alternatives to prepared and rehearsed situations had existed. This time the alternatives appeared to have failed, yet the data in hand were certainly too few to marshal as incontestable.

Further, he found that he was perforce made to study Korval itself. As much as the Department taught—and had demonstrated!— that the agent might safely be removed from the Clan to more ardently pursue Liad's own needs, it seemed clear from the records that an unquantified but significant portion of yos'Phelium's success was from the genes and mad genius of Clan Korval—which suddenly included the Department of the Interior among its ranging interests.

Thirteen ships sent forth from Korval. What did they know? He scrolled through the list again. As he watched, the screen shivered; then the list re-formed with yet another name appended: *Dutiful Passage*.

VANDAR

Springbreeze Farm and Environs

Val Con awoke chilly and discontented. Not only was Miri's head not on his shoulder, but body-sense told him that she was not even in bed, though he did detect some faint rustlings from across the room, which could just as easily be mice as his wife.

Irritably, he opened his eyes.

She was standing before the mirror across the room, fully clothed except for her belt, totally absorbed in arranging her hair. As he watched, she finished mooring the elaborate knot on the right side of her head and took her hands gingerly away. Satisfied that her hair was firmly anchored, she rummaged among the objects on the table below and came up with a slender, polished stick—the knife he had given her in Econsey, little more than a month earlier. The blade they had been wed by.

Miri flicked the knife open, closed, then thrust it through the center of the knot. She shook her head several times, hard, but hair and blade remained steadfast.

"Very nice," Val Con remarked. "Shall we be festive when we go to town, then?"

She grinned at him in the mirror. "Morning," she said, coming over to sit on the side of the bed. "I don't know 'bout festive, but I did notice Zhena Trelu don't wear a belt or a pouch. Which probably means we're not gonna be able to wear ours after we get these new clothes she's so hot for. An' I just wouldn't feel right without some kind of weapon—been a soldier too long, I guess." She shrugged.

He lifted an eyebrow. "Not too bad, for someone who is stupid."

"Bastard." But she was grinning, "Thought you told me Liadens were polite."

"Formality," he said, pausing to stretch, "must never be confused with courtesy." He rolled to his side, closer to her. "How are you this morning, cha'trez?"

"Really fine," she said seriously, and he read the truth of that in the clearness of her eyes and the looseness of the muscles in her face and body. "Rainbow's good to know," she added, and bent her head in self-conscious formality. "Thank you."

"You're welcome. I am only sorry that I did not realize sooner—I was not watching well..." *You could not have been watching at all,* he told himself bitterly, *to allow her to come to such a pass.*

But Miri had tipped her head, the line of a frown deepening between her brows. "You got other things to do, doncha? Can't always be watching me. An' I could've told you, couldn't I? Wasn't that I thought you wouldn't help; just didn't think there was anything you could do." She smiled apologetically. "Never been married before. Hard to get the hang of asking for help."

He put his hand over hers where it lay upon the bed. "We will learn together. I've never been married before, either."

"Yeah, you said that." She was still frowning. "Why not?"

"Scouts rarely take lifemates," he murmured. "One should enter into at least one contract-marriage—however, I did not choose to do so."

"But why not?" she persisted, watching him closely.

He rounded his eyes at her. "I was waiting for *you,* Miri." She laughed and squeezed his fingers. "Okay, you win..." she began, then her eyes fell on the sun-lit window and she leapt up. "Holy Panth, look at the time! I gotta feed those damn birds or Zhena Trelu'll fuse. Boss, start breakfast, okay? I'm *starved...*" And then she was at the door, hand on the knob.

"I am owed!" Val Con cried, surprising himself at least as much as her.

Miri spun. "Huh?"

He threw back the covers, slid out of bed, and began pulling on his clothes. "I am owed," he repeated. "I awaken and my wife is not at my side; I confess feelings of astonishing magnitude—and am disbelieved. I am ordered about. All this," he concluded, dragging his shirt over his head and glaring at her, "without so much as a kiss. I am deeply wronged."

"Oh." She came back across the room and stopped before him, studying his face. He was clowning—she had seen the glint of mischief in the green eyes—yet there seemed an undercurrent of serious intent in his attitude.

"So, how do I pay up?"

He gave it consideration. "I believe," he said, after a time, "that a kiss would do much toward balance."

"Right. Just so happens I've got a kiss on me. Is Terran currency okay?" She came closer, and his hands settled about her waist as she ran her hands up his arms to his shoulders and looked up into his bright eyes.

He smiled. "Terran currency is perfectly acceptable." He bent his head to collect.

Zhena Trelu followed the unaccustomed odor from the door of her bedroom to the kitchen and stopped, staring.

The biggest iron skillet was on the burner over a low flame, a generous handful of pungent bulbroot already starting to brown in the center. Cory was at the counter, grating cheese right from the block; several scuppin eggs, two sprigs of parslee, the milk pitcher, and a mixing bowl sat to hand, along with a knife and the remains of the bulbroot. The teapot was already steaming.

Meri, egg basket in hand, was on her way to the door; she turned, placed the basket on the floor, went to the stove, and poured out a cup of tea, which she took to the table, smiling.

"Good morning, Zhena Trelu," she said clearly. Then she was gone, the door banging behind her.

Cory looked up front his grating and grinned. "Good morning, Zhena Trelu."

"Good morning, yourself," she muttered, more than a little put out by all the activity. They were fixing a meal at *this* hour? Normally, they each had a cup of tea to start the day and then went about the chores until dinner. She sipped tea and frowned at the man's narrow back. "Cory?"

He turned, cheese in hand. "Yes, Zhena Trelu?"

"Why's Meri got her hair all done up like that? Looks—" It looked outlandish, is what it looked. Barbaric. "Different."

Cory moved his shoulders, smiling a little. "For town."

"For town? She doesn't have to fix her hair different for town. The braid will be fine."

One brow slid up. "It is for town, Zhena Trelu," he repeated. "Miri works hard."

And that, the old woman thought, taking another sip as he turned back to his cooking, would appear to be that. Well, and what business was it of hers if the two of them chose to go into town looking as if they had just escaped from the circus?

"It's just that," she told Cory's back, "this hairstyle doesn't make her look very pretty." And when one was as plain as Meri was in the first place, poor child...

Cory had turned around again, both eyebrows up. "Zhena Trelu? *Pretty* is?"

"Eh?" She set her cup down and pointed at the vase of sweelims on the table. "The flowers are pretty, Cory."

"Ah." He reached to the sink and showed her a pink-and-cream cup Granic's wife had made, a lovely thing, airy and smooth. "Pretty, this?"

"Yes," she agreed. "The cup's pretty. Very pretty."

He contemplated it for a moment before returning it with great care to the sink. Thoughtfully, he cracked eggs into the bowl, added milk, parslee, and grated cheese, then whipped it all together with a fork. After pouring the stuff into the skillet and adjusting the heat, he set the bowl in the sink and ran water into it.

"Borril," he asked over the water's noise, "is pretty?"

Zhena Trelu gave a crow of surprised laughter. "No. Cory, Borril is *not* pretty. Borril is—" But just then the outside door was pushed open and Meri marched in, carrying a basket containing three large eggs, the unlovely Borril at her heels.

"Pretty," Cory said, grinning at her.

Meri blinked incomprehension. "Pretty?"

He took the basket and put it on the counter, conducted her with ceremony to the table, and gestured to the flowers with a flourish. "Flowers are pretty," he said solemnly.

Meri bowed slightly to the sweelims. "Pretty flowers."

Hand under her elbow, Cory guided her back to the sink, where he held up the pink-and-cream cup. "The cup is *very* pretty."

She lifted a slender finger and ran it lightly down the glazed surface. "*Very* pretty."

Setting the cup down, he slid his arm around her waist and turned her to face the dog, which was curled up and yawning on the rug.

"Borril," he said, affecting to speak into her ear but talking loudly enough for Zhena Trelu to hear, "is *not* pretty."

Meri laughed.

Cory hugged her, then looked over her head at Zhena Trelu, who thought she knew what was coming.

"Miri is pretty."

Meri returned the hug and stepped back, raising a hand to his scarred cheek. *"Very* pretty, you," she said, and then she was at the pantry, tucking eggs away as Cory drifted back to the stove and poured tea.

Meri brought the cups to the table, but paused at the cupboard and glanced over her shoulder. "Zhena Trelu? You eat? Good eggs."

Zhena Trelu stopped on the edge of refusal. They might have a point, at that. Shopping was pretty tiring; it might be best to start off with a little something in the stomach.

"I'll have just a bit," she said, managing a sour smile. "Thank you very much."

Three plates were delivered to Cory at the stove. Meri pulled bread, jam, and butter from various keepsafes, brought them to the table, and returned flicker-quick—or so it seemed to the woman watching—with silverware and napkins. Pulling the bread to her, she cut off three quick, even slices and handed one to Zhena Trelu.

Cory and the plates arrived. He gave Zhena Trelu hers, put Meri's down at her place, and slid into his own seat. Accepting a piece of bread, he began to eat.

In a moment Meri had joined him, eating with every evidence of enjoyment.

Zhena Trelu picked up her fork and considered her plate. The eggs did not look like proper eggs at all—all scrambled up and smelling of cheese and spices. Gingerly, she took a smidgen and tasted it.

Odd, but not awful. She had another smidgen, and then a larger one—and suddenly discovered that her plate was empty.

A deep sigh brought her attention to Meri, who was sitting back in her chair, grinning, teacup cradled in her hands.

"Thank you," she said to Cory. *"Very* good eggs."

Zhena Trelu added her approval. "Yes, thank you, Cory. You're a good cook." A thought struck her. "Is that what you used to do to make money at home?"

There was a pause during which Cory leisurely finished his bread and butter and washed it down with a swallow of tea. Zhena Trelu had begun to despair of an answer when he tipped his head.

"I eat. I cook."

That was almost as bad as no answer, when she thought about it. But it did raise another point that had better get firmly settled before Athna Brigsbee started bullying and terrifying them with her questions. "Cory, where are you from?"

He rested his eyes on hers. "Home."

Zhena Trelu sighed. "Yes, Cory. But where *is* home?"

He gestured, waving a slender hand toward the east and little upward—the direction of Fornem's Gap.

Zhena Trelu sighed again. "All right, Cory, we'll do it this way. If someone asks you where you're from, you tell them 'Porlint.' We don't get many refugees up this way, but stranger things have happened, especially if you got yourselves turned around somehow and came through the gap."

Cory finished his tea and glanced at his wife. "Home is Porlint," he told her, and pointed a severe forefinger. "Where are you from?"

Meri blinked. "Porlint," she said meekly, then grinned. *"Cory."*

"Bad-tempered brat," he responded, but she only laughed and got up to clear the table.

The truck started up at the first hint from starter switch and key. Zhena Trelu nodded to herself in satisfaction and leaned across to open the passenger's door. Thin as the two of them were, she figured that they would all three be able to fit on the single bench seat.

The door swung wide, and Cory pulled himself into the cab. The girl followed immediately, standing poised on the ledge, gray eyes wary.

"If she's gotta move her arms to drive this thing, maybe you better not sit so close," she said seriously to Val Con. "If you don't mind, I can sit on your lap or something—give her room to operate." She grinned. "Thing looks as unsafe as this does, I don't wanna do anything 'bout adding to the other side's odds."

"You may be right," he murmured, taking note of various levers and foot pedals. "It is never wise to crowd the pilot." He shifted closer to the door, and Miri sat on his lap, settling sweetly in.

"No!" Zhena Trelu snapped.

Startled, Miri looked down into Val Con's eyes. "Wrongo, boss. *Now* what, do you think?"

"We shall attempt to ascertain." He turned his attention to the frowning old woman. "No?" he repeated in Benish. "Bad?"

Zhena Trelu stopped herself from making the first remark that occurred to her and reminded herself that they were foreigners, with wind-knew-what notions. For that matter, there had been her own son's zhena—stormy-tempered and wild to a fault, yet biddable enough with Granic and pathetically eager to do her best for him.

She sighed. "It's *good* that you children love each other. Very pretty. It's good to touch each other. But in town some people might not understand, if they saw Meri sitting there like a—well, never mind. When you're at home, you can touch each other and hug and that's *fine*. But when you're out with people—in town—you have to be *respectable*." She paused, wondering how much of her lecture was making sense to either of them. One of Cory's eyebrows was out of alignment with the other, but his eyes were serious on her face. Meri was watching her, too, the line of a frown just visible between her brows.

"Refugees already have a bad name," Zhena Trelu continued. "You don't want people in town maybe not hiring you when you go to get a job, because they think you don't know how to behave, now do you? Especially you, Cory: a zamir as trusted and responsible as you are—well, you have to always be sure to bring honor to your zhena, and not let her do things that will make people think poorly of her.

"So, Meri, you get up now and let Cory slide over here next to me...All right; sit down, Meri, and close the door."

Once everyone was settled to her satisfaction, she put the truck in gear and turned her full attention to driving.

Miri sighed and leaned carefully back into the seat—and discovered Val Con's arm already there. She nestled closer to his side, and the arm curved more tightly around her waist.

"Sneak," she muttered.

"But such a *nice* sneak. Did you receive the impression that we are rude, yet not fatally so? If there is need, perhaps we could yet hold each other's hand."

Miri raised her eyebrows. "In case I get scared, you mean."

"Or I."

She snorted.

Val Con looked at her. "What an extraordinary person I am," he murmured. "Never afraid, or lonely, or in need of laughter. Or a touch. I am quite overcome by my superiority."

She winced at the bitter note underlying the smooth voice, at the trouble shadowing his bright green eyes, and she recalled the urgency of his tears. Carefully she reached down to squeeze his fingers and summoned up a disrespectful grin.

"Yeah, well, I wouldn't be all that impressed. First of all, you gotta remember how hard it is to get a straight story out of you. Person could die of old age before she figures out the right question. You *manage* people—quiet about it—just don't treat 'no' like an answer. And the gods help whoever's there, you ever let that temper of yours off the leash." She gave him a thoughtful look. "Kinda like to be around to take notes, though—you sure got a way with words. Be useful, I ever wanna go back into the sergeant business."

He laughed, his arm tightening around her briefly. "I am chastised."

Then the truck swung uncertainly into a wider way, rattled over metal tracks, and raggedly negotiated a curve, coming upon an amazing structure: an open house in the middle of the road!

"A wooden tunnel?" Miri demanded.

"Hush," Val Con said.

And like Scout and soldier they watched the rest of the way to town, taking careful note of distance, direction, and terrain.

VANDAR

Gylles

Brillit's Emporium stood two stories tall in the very center of town, directly across from the many-windowed tower and just up the street from the little blue building. It faced an oval of sere vegetation set in the middle of the road—the so-called town green.

Zhena Trelu herded her charges across the street and up the steps to Brillit's front door, muttering under her breath as she saw Mrythis Wibecker come out of the glazing shop and stare at them. In less than ten breaths it would be all over town that Estra Trelu was here with her pet refugees. If there was one gossip in Gylles worse than Athna Brigsbee...

Corvill and Meri hesitated on the threshold, and Zhena Trelu gave each a firm push in the small of the back, propelling them into the dim, sawdusty interior.

"Ever look forward to a day," Miri murmured to Val Con, "when you won't get shoved around?"

Val Con's shoulders jerked, but he managed not to laugh.

Zhena Trelu took the lead, quick-marching them down aisles lined with gizmos and tantalizing gadgets which her charges would have liked to examine in more detail, to the foot of a wide stairway. She peered carefully in both directions before beginning the ascent, for all the worlds like a Merc expecting to see enemies bursting from the brush on either side.

Nothing of the sort happened, however, and she waved them ahead of her. Obeying the gesture, they climbed the stairs and waited while she made her more laborious way up and stood for a moment to catch her breath.

"All right, children; here we are. We'll get Cory settled first." And she marched off to the right, the pair of them trailing behind.

"She likes you best," Miri told her partner.

"Untrue," he returned. "She merely wishes to have me out of the way in order to spend more time with you."

"Estra! It's been a time, hasn't it? How are you?" The speaker was a plump, balding man a little taller than Zhena Trelu. He was wearing a gray jacket to match his gray trousers and a white shirt and a dark-blue neck-string. He was standing at the mouth of an aisle lined with racks of clothes.

Miri blinked. Clothes? And no valet in sight. How was one supposed to figure out which of all those clothes was the correct fit? Unless that was what that bald guy did. Gods, she thought. What a job.

Zhena Trelu was talking about them. "Porlum, this is Cory. Him and his zhena are doing some work around the place for me, and it looks like they'll be staying the winter. Thought it was high time for them to be having proper work clothes."

Porlum considered the man in the dark leather slacks and vest. A little under average height, but nothing to be unduly concerned with. The slenderness of his build might be more of a problem. Still, work clothes? He smiled at the smaller man, who did not return the courtesy, and nodded to Zhena Trelu. "I'm certain we'll come up with something suitable. Good, warm shirts and durable pants, of course. How many? And will you want him to have a set of—ah, dress clothes, also?"

Zhena Trelu frowned. "Three, four shirts, I think; couple of work pants—and a jacket, too, Porlum. Shoes..." She glanced at the high black boots on Cory's feet and sighed. "Work boots. I think we'll let the dress clothes go this time."

"As you say, Estra," the man agreed. "If zamir will come this way?"

"You go with Porlum, Cory," the old woman instructed. "He'll make sure you get the right things. Meri and I will meet you back here when we've gotten some things for her." She clamped her fingers around the girl's wrist and pulled her along.

Miri threw a glance over her shoulder in time to see Val Con disappearing down a clothes-lined aisle. As she watched, he ducked back to the end and waved, vanishing again immediately.

Grinning, Miri let herself be propelled farther into the store, to a place lined with clothes different from the clothes displayed in the area where they had left Val Con. A cadaverous woman with unlikely black hair, unlikelier red cheeks, and a thin, dissatisfied mouth looked at Miri, and her mouth turned sharply downward. She made no attempt to intercept Zhena Trelu, who peered about until Miri yanked on her sleeve and pointed.

"There you are, Salissa," Zhena Trelu said with a distinct lack of warmth. "This is Meri. She's been helping me out on the farm, and it's time she was getting some proper work clothes."

"I should think so!" Salissa sniffed. She turned to Miri. "Where did you come up with those—things—you're wearing? You look perfectly outlandish."

"Of course she looks outlandish," Zhena Trelu snapped. "She's a foreigner! *I* know she needs clothes—that's why we're here! Good, warm clothes, Salissa; the kind she can work in. And don't bother trying to talk to her much. She can't understand more than one word in ten."

She turned to Miri. "Meri, you go with Salissa, now. She'll find you some nice, warm clothes to work in. I'm going to buy some things for myself, and then I'll come back for you and we'll go find Cory."

With a sinking feeling in her stomach, Miri watched the old woman walk away, then squared her shoulders and turned around to glare at Salissa.

The small man had a mind of his own. He insisted on being shown the different grades of work shirts, subjecting each to close inspection, and finally deciding on the soft wool-and-julam blend—by far the warmest and most durable, in Porlum's opinion. Not that it was solicited.

The customer's stringent standards were also applied to trousers and work boots, though he deferred to Porlum in the matters of size and fit, as was proper, and allowed socks and a belt to be suggested.

In all particulars, however, was Cory's own taste followed—from the plain, rather than plaid, work shirts, to the tough black trousers. The jacket he chose was stuffed with hoyper feathers—a good, warm, well-crafted garment that because of its odd, greenish-gray color, had languished on the racks. The small man grinned when he saw it and pulled it on immediately.

Porlum studied the effect and nodded. The jacket fit well; the deep pockets and hood were just the thing for winter, and the off-color brought out the amazing green of the customer's eyes. He sighed. It was a pity Estra had not thought dress clothes required.

Cory was standing quite still, head tipped as if listening, then pointed at the pile on the counter—three shirts, a pair of pants, socks, and the peculiar clothing he had worn into the store. "I come back for this," he said, and was gone.

Val Con paused to consider the scene before him. Miri—dressed in something he was fairly certain Miri should never be dressed in— was having a disagreement with a black-haired woman. Zhena Trelu was standing to one side, apparently trying to resolve the situation by keeping Miri silent long enough for the other woman to prevail.

He walked forward.

"*Bad* is," Miri was telling the black-haired woman with a great deal of passion. "Not warm! Say Zhena Trelu *warm—*"

"With that hair and those freckles," the other woman cut in, "you'd better think about looking pretty! Isn't it worth being a little chilly, knowing you look pretty, instead of like a—a tomboy?"

"Now, Salissa," Zhena Trelu said. "She doesn't understand. And Meri, if you'll just let Salissa show you some more clothes—"

"No more clothes," Miri announced with decision. "Bad clothes. *My* clothes," she told Salissa clearly, "are pretty!"

"Those things you wore in here?" the saleswoman demanded. "Well, I suppose they are, if your idea of pretty is looking loose and—*hoydenish* and—"

"You will not," a quiet voice said, cutting across her rising tirade, "say those words to this zhena."

Salissa stared. A man was abruptly at the side of the red-haired woman, his green eyes resting blandly upon the saleswoman's face.

Those eyes regarded her for what felt like long minutes, before he spoke again. "You understand my words?"

She licked her lips. "Yes."

"Good," the man said, no particular inflection in his soft voice. He turned to the red-haired woman. "Cha'trez?"

Miri raised her hands in exasperation and looked down at herself. "Zhena Trelu say warm," she said, sticking to Benish. "Warm this not. Not pretty." She smiled a little. "Borril."

His lips twitched as he considered the garment. The bright yellow shirt was long-sleeved, to be sure, but made out of some flimsy material that would barely be adequate on the warmest day they had yet encountered on this world. The skirt was not quite as thin, but ruffled and furbelowed—impossible to work in.

He shook his head and turned to the old woman. "Zhena Trelu? Miri is—right? This is not warm. It is not pretty. There are clothes like Miri's clothes here?"

"I should say *not.*" Salissa sniffed with rather more assurance than she felt.

The green eyes flicked to her and ran—slowly and with deliberate insult—down her length and back to her face. He shrugged and turned back to Zhena Trelu. "There are other stores."

"What?" She gaped at him. "For wind's sake...Yes, there's another store. But this is the *best* store, Cory."

For a moment, she thought he would insist; then he moved his shoulders in that odd not-shrug of his and sighed.

"Zhena Trelu, you will—make sure Miri gets right clothes. Cha'trez, you want?"

She grinned and waved a slim hand at his new finery. "Warm. Work in..." She laid a hand on his chest, ostensibly to touch his shirt. "Soft."

He tipped an eyebrow at the old woman. "This is right? Not bad? *Respectable?*"

"There are women's clothes like the ones you're wearing. But, Cory, she ought to have at least one dress!"

His brows twitched together. "Dress? Dress clothes? No dress clothes."

Zhena Trelu sighed. "All right, Cory. Meri, come with me, dear...

But Miri tarried a moment longer to inspect his jacket. "Pretty," she admired, grinning at him. He grinned back.

"Meri!" called Zhena Trelu, and Miri laughed and ran off.

Having led the girl to the small section containing trousers and man-styled shirts for women, Zhena Trelu found that she had very little else to do. Miri's brief sojourn with Salissa had taught her the trick of the racks, and her quick eye had picked out the single recurring symbol on every item the saleswoman had chosen for her. She chose four shirts: pale blue, indigo, black-and-white check, and the palest of pale yellows.

Zhena Trelu approved those choices, allowing that they fit well enough, though there was a brief tussle over the snugness of the chosen trousers. That argument was put to rest when the girl tried on the pair Zhena Trelu thrust at her, buttoned them, and let go.

Effortlessly, they slid from waist to hip, where they hovered, apparently poised on the brink of further descent.

Zhena Trelu sighed and agreed that the others would have to do. When they left the dressing room, they found Cory leaning against the nearest end rack, holding something over one arm. When he saw Meri, he straightened, approving the light-blue shirt and indigo slacks with a grin.

"Very pretty." Stepping forward, he offered her a jacket that was the twin of his own, except that it was dark blue and several sizes smaller.

The girl's eyes widened, and she carefully put her armload of clothes on the floor. Cory helped her into the jacket as if she were a queen and the coat silk-lined fur instead of waterproof cotton stuffed with feathers. She pushed her hands deep into the pockets, fastened the front all the way to the throat, pulled the hood up to almost—but not quite—cover that outrageous hairdo, then ran her fingers over the sleeve and felt the thickness of the lining.

Cory took her by the shoulders and turned her to the mirror. She studied their reflection for a long time.

"Thank you for pretty—jacket?" she said, catching his eyes in the glass. She smiled a little. "Not Borril, us."

"Not Borril," he agreed, returning her smile, his fingers tightening slightly on her shoulders. "Very pretty us."

Then he loosed her and bent to pick up the abandoned clothing. Straightening, he smiled at the quiet old woman.

"Porlum will—make up—ticket? For all at once," he said, and went off without further ado, Meri at his side.

After a moment, Zhena Trelu followed.

They had just reached the sidewalk, Cory and Meri carrying between them the paper parcels containing their new clothes, as well as the cardboard box into which Porlum had carefully packed their foreign clothing, when disaster struck.

"Estra! Well, for goodness sake, if this isn't a surprise!" Athna Brigsbee cried, crossing the street with a wide smile on her face and her hand extended in welcome.

Resigning herself to the inevitable, Zhena Trelu forced a smile. "It's nice to see you, Athna," she managed, but so feebly that Cory, frowning, shot a look at her from under his lashes.

Characteristically, Athna Brigsbee did not notice. She seized Zhena Trelu's hand and wrung it until the bones protested before turning her voracious smile on the two slender figures standing patiently to one side.

"This must be Meri and Cory!" she surmised brightly, and Miri heard Val Con sigh. "Estra, the funniest thing! I just happened to run into Mrythis Wibecker a few moments ago in Jarvill's, and she said she'd seen you going into Brillit's with two *men!* She really should wear those glasses Dr. Lorm prescribed—but, my dear! so vain..." She turned her attention back to the refugees and their obviously new clothes.

"It's very kind of Zhena Trelu to buy you clothes," she said, speaking quite loudly. "You're both very grateful, aren't you? And you'll work twice as hard to pay for them."

"They've already earned their clothes," Zhena Trelu said firmly. "They work plenty hard already—I'm not sure I could bear up under it if they worked any harder." She turned to her charges. "Why don't you children go put the packages in the truck? No use carrying them with us to the library."

"Yes, Zhena Trelu," Cory said, and moved off at once. After a fractional pause, Meri followed.

"My dear," Athna said, not waiting until they were out of earshot. "What a very plain girl! And so surly! I know foreigners have all sorts of notions, but Estra, she can't be more than sixteen!"

Miri glanced at Val Con, noting the frown and the slight stiffness in his shoulders. "What's up?"

He glanced at her, lips relaxing into a faint smile. "That horrid woman..."

"Her?" She jerked her chin in the direction of the two old women. "Don't pay her no mind. All hot to hear the latest bad 'bout anybody. Ain't worth getting riled about. Waste of time." She slanted a look at him. "Like that dope of a woman in the store. Tough on her, weren't you? Took her down four pegs—counted 'em. Trouble is, she was only up three."

He grinned, then sobered. "She should not have spoken to you so." Pausing, he considered the street, judged it safe to cross to the truck, and stepped off the curb.

"Really," he continued. "She should not speak to anyone so. Perhaps I have taught her a lesson she will take to heart."

Miri studied the side of his face for a moment. "Gets hard, being treated like a complete know-nothing all the time, don't it?"

He reached up to yank on the truck's door handle and grinned at her, shoulders and face loose once more. "Indeed it does." The door did not open and he pulled again. "Locked."

Miri set her packages on the ground. "I'll get the key from Zhena Trelu," she began, but he shook his head.

"That should not be necessary." He reached into his pocket and pulled out a thin, flexible wire. Balancing on the foot-ledge, he played with wire and keyhole for a bare moment, then nodded and hauled down on the handle.

The door came open with a *pop.*

Grinning, he jumped to the ground, letting the door swing wide behind him, and began to put packages on the bench seat.

Miri shook her head at him. "Lazy."

When all the parcels were stowed, he slammed the door closed, solemnly checking to be sure the lock had caught. "For it would be very bad," he told Miri, offering her his hand, "if our new clothes were stolen by some desperate criminal."

She slid her hand into his. "What next? Back to Zhena Trelu and Badnews Berta?"

"Not just yet," he said, glancing around. "They seem deep in conversation—and I would like an opportunity to see what is here. Zhena Trelu rushes us about..."

"So, we go for a walk," she said, moving with him away from Brillit's and the two figures on the front walk. "How long you figure us for Zhena Trelu's, boss?"

He considered it. "I think we must stay the winter to balance the debt properly." He glanced at her. "Our work has not paid for these clothes, cha'trez."

"Didn't think it had," she said, untroubled. "We stay the winter and pay on our account. Then what?"

"It is also to be hoped that the winter will allow us opportunity to improve our command of Benish, as well as learn to read and write," Val Con continued. "Then we should be able to leave here and seek out a city, if that pleases you. It is generally true that cities offer a wider range of tasks to be performed for wages—whatever wages may consist of here. It may be that we already possess skills that will make it possible for us to be—independent."

"And not get shoved around." Miri sighed. "Sounds great. If I start slacking off on my lessons, you remind me it's so I don't need to be shoved any more, okay? I'll pick right up again."

He tipped his head. "Does it bother you so much? I do not think she means it ill."

She laughed softly. "Naw. It's just been a lot of years since anybody dared shove me. And now this old lady I could bust in half with one hand—" she stopped suddenly. "What in the name of bright blue chosemkis is *that?*"

They wandered over to the window containing the object in question, Val Con's brows pulled slightly together, Miri's eyes wide.

The thing was rectangular in shape and made of some shiny substance that appeared to be metal. The front was glassed in, giving a view of a multitude of coils, wires, and tubes. There were knobs on the top and sides, a piece of thin metal tubing extending from the back, and more knobs under the glass. The whole affair was garlanded with red, yellow, and blue streamers.

"I haven't the faintest notion," Val Con confessed. "A device of some kind, certainly. But what it may be meant to do—or not do..." he shrugged. "We can find the storekeeper and ask."

But that proved impossible. The shop door was locked, and a large piece of paper bearing hand-drawn symbols was attached to the inside of the window.

Miri sighed sharply. "We gotta learn how to read. This whole damn world's passing us by."

"In the fullness of time," he said, managing by some trick of his soft voice to evoke Edger's boom. "All things cannot happen at once."

The door to the next shop was open, and from it drifted music. *Real* music, Miri realized. The sound of someone actually playing an instrument, not the recorded music Zhena Trelu listened to on her radio every evening.

Val Con stopped, head tipped, face intent. Miri stood quietly at his side, watching him and listening to the sounds. It was nice, she decided; something like a guitar, but softer, unamplified.

The piece came to an end, and her partner sighed, very softly, and looked at her. "Miri..."

"Sure," she said, and squeezed his hand. "Let's go in. Why not?"

"And did you hear, Estra, about those horrid Bassilan rebels? Landed on the coast, not two hundred miles from here! Claiming sanctuary, just because our king had made some treaties with their barbaric Tomak years and years ago! Well, of course, the king said no, but do you believe it? The report is they're moving inland. They might even get to Gylles!"

"Poppycock," Zhena Trelu said, looking around uneasily. "The king's militia will have that bunch of troublemakers rounded up in wind's time. Just a bunch of common criminals, that's all they are. As if the king would stand for an invasion, even if Bentrill hasn't been to war since people stopped using bows and arrows and wearing hides."

"Well, perhaps you're right, dear," Zhena Brigsbee conceded sadly. "But, still, Estra, what if some got away!"

But Zhena Trelu was staring down Main Street, looking hard for two short, slender figures.

VANDAR

Gylles

Hakan Meltz looked up from his guitar and smiled at the two blurry figures in the doorway.

"Hi, there," he said in the casual way that was the despair of his father, the proprietor of the shop in which Hakan sat playing the guitar. His father did not allow guitar-playing in the store—except, of course, if one were demonstrating the instrument's properties to a potential buyer. Happily for Hakan, his father was currently in the capital, attending the king's assembly as alderman for the town of Gylles.

Hakan smiled again as the two figures moved farther into the shop and into the range of his shortsighted eyes.

The woman was toy-tiny, yet there was adult assurance about the set of her shoulders and the straightness with which the large gray eyes regarded him. She returned his smile with a thoroughly friendly grin, holding comfortably onto her companion's hand. The man lacked two inches of Hakan's height, twenty of his pounds, and all of his mustache. He wore his dark hair long for a man, and the line of a recent scar marred one smooth cheek. Smiling, he raised his free hand and indicated the instrument Hakan held.

"Very pretty," he said softly, the words accented in a way that tickled the other's ear. "It is?"

"This?" Hakan offered the instrument, and the shorter man slid his hand out of the woman's to take it. "It's a twelve-string guitar."

"Twelve-string guitar," the man murmured, turning it around and over. He righted it and tried a sweep across the strings with his long fingers, laughing softly at the discord he produced. He placed the fingers of his left hand carefully on the neck, tried another sweep, and nodded as if better satisfied. Working slowly, using a combination of strumming and plucking, he managed to pull a melody line out of the guitar while Hakan watched in growing puzzlement.

The guitar was strange to the man—that much seemed certain. But he worked with it as if he had once played something similar and knew what to expect of wood and gut.

The man came to himself with a start, glancing up with a smile of apology. "Forgive me," he said, handing the instrument back with obvious reluctance, fingers lingering on the neck. "It has been long," he said, as if to explain. "I am—"He frowned and moved his hands in what Hakan thought might be exasperation. "It is to be hungry," he concluded, head tipped as if he were unsure that he would be property understood.

But it there was one thing Hakan did understand it was the hunger for making music. "Lost your piece?" he asked, somehow certain that only catastrophe would have separated this individual from whatever it was he played. He put the guitar aside and stood, waving his hand to indicate the rows of musical instruments. "What's your specialty?" he began, feeling an impulse his father was certain to bewail rising within him. "Maybe we can work out a—"

From the back of the shop, the woman—forgotten in the music—called something out, emphasizing it with three musical keys pushed at random.

The man's brows shot up, and he looked at Hakan, eyes intensely green. "That?"

"Piano," Hakan told him. "You play *piano?*" But the man was already gone, heading toward the back of the store.

It was apparent that the man did play piano—or something so close to piano that it made little difference. He spent a few moments exploring the instrument, eyebrows lifting as he discovered foot pedals; running his fingers up and down the keyboard, he located true C, sharps, flats, and scales. Then his fingers moved, half-joking, it seemed to Hakan, and produced a tinkling little tune reminiscent of cool summer evenings playing hide-'n-seek.

His hands shifted, up-board and down, calling forth less childlike music. The woman leaning against the piano's side laughed softly and sang a line in a weird, chopping language, and the man grinned and moved his hands again, playing a clear intro riff.

The woman grinned at Hakan, straightened, and began to sing. He stood rock-still until the song was done, then dove across the room for his guitar.

It was thus that Kem Darnill found them some time later: Hakan painstakingly working out the melody; the piano correcting him now and then. Setting her books on the counter, she went quietly toward the threesome, trying not to disturb the music making.

The man at the piano looked up and smiled at her. "Hakan," he murmured.

"Hmm?" Hakan looked up, caught the other's nod, and turned his head.

"Kemmy!" He was on his feet, his smile a warmth she could feel. Sliding his hand into hers, he brought her forward.

"Kemmy, this is Cory and Miri. Cory plays piano, and Miri sings. Amazing stuff—you never heard anything like it. I've never heard anything like it, anyhow." He grinned at the pair on the piano bench. "This," he announced proudly, "is my fiancée, Kem."

Kem felt herself blush but managed a smile at the two strangers. Cory smiled and inclined his head in a formal little gesture; Miri grinned at her.

"Hi," Miri said. Her accent made Kem blink. Still, they seemed nice enough, and they were musicians...

"Oh, goodness!" she said suddenly, leaning forward. "Cory and Meri?"

"Cory," the man agreed, tipping his head.

"Miri," the woman said.

"Zhena Trelu's looking for both of you," Kem told them. "She's awful worried—thinks you've gotten lost or something." She hesitated, remembering that Zhena Trelu had said that they did not speak much Benish.

But the woman—Miri?—had turned to her companion with an expression of comic woe on her face. "Zhena Trelu!" she cried. *"Bad* us!" And she dropped her head against his arm, shoulders shaking.

Cory grinned and patted her gently on the back. Then he sighed and looked down at the piano, raising his hand and letting it fall to his knee.

"I don't get it," Hakan said, looking from Kem to his two new friends.

"They're staying with Zhena Trelu," Kem explained rapidly. "Helping her out around the farm. She brought them into town today to get winter clothes, and they wandered off— and that rattlepated Athna Brigsbee's out there calling them thieves and worse!"

"But that's great!" Hakan cried, turning to the other man. "Cory, listen to me—Zhena Trelu's got a piano! Real nice one—a hundred times better than this piece of junk," he added, with a fine disregard for the basic precepts of business.

Cory's brows pulled together, and he shook his head. "Zhena Trelu? No piano, Hakan."

Miri shifted at his side, murmuring something in a language that jarred on Kem's ears. Cory glanced at her and then at Hakan.

"There is a place—" He stopped, frowning, then sighed. Carefully he lifted his hands, wove the slim fingers together, and held the knot out to Hakan, one eyebrow up.

"Locked? A locked room, maybe?" Hakan looked at Kem, who could only shrug. "That makes sense. It was her zamir's piano, Cory. He had it set up in a room by itself. Could be she locked the room when he died—ought to let you play it, though. Regular sport, old Zhena Trelu. You just ask her about it, and I'm sure—"

"Hakan—" Cory was holding his hands out as if to stop Hakan's enthusiasm. "Too many words, Hakan."

"Ah, wind—I forgot." He turned back to Kem. "What were you supposed to do with them, once you found them?"

"They were supposed to be going to the library. Zhena Trelu went there, in case the two of them got ahead of schedule. I was supposed to take them to her, if I ran into them." She giggled. "I guess this qualifies as running into them."

"Well, then that's simple," Hakan decided, waving at the two foreigners. "Let's get ourselves down to the library. *I'll* ask Zhena Trelu for you, Cory."

"What about the store?" Kem demanded, vowing that nothing would prevent her from witnessing the expression on Athna Brigsbee's face when Zhena Trelu's charges were restored to her.

But Hakan was already turning the Open/Closed sign to the Closed side and pulling the key from his pocket.

"All for one," he said, waving them out the door with a flourish.

"And one for all," Kem said, laughing.

Hakan locked the door and turned up the street, slipping one hand into Kem's and the other into Miri's, as a child might. Hand-linked and laughing, the four of them began to run.

LIAD

. Trealla Fantrol

THAT INFORMATION IS RESTRICTED.

Nova had swept the screen clear and entered a second, more potent, ID before the cat lounging by the keyboard had time to blink.

There was perhaps a heartbeat of hesitation, then the response from Central Information:

THAT INFORMATION IS RESTRICTED.

Nova swore, though perhaps not as violently as she might have. "Restricted from the Council of Clans! Who dares it?"

Neither cat nor screen ventured an opinion, and after a moment of frowning thought, she reached for the keyboard once more.

Central took rather more time with the new request, but finally the letters began to appear, one by one, as if the computer itself was perplexed by the answer it had to give.

UNIVERSAL ACCESS OVERRIDE. REQUESTS REMANDED TO JAE'LABA STATION. ACCESS DENIED.

"So." Here at last, was the germ of something.

STATIONMAP, she demanded of Central. There was no hesitation at all. The screen flowered interconnecting lines, varicolored rhombi marking primary, secondary, and tertiary stations.

Nova paused, considering the flashing bit of purple that denoted the station at Jelaza Kazone. Korval's Own House, with Korval's own tricks up its sleeve, age upon age, Cantra to Daav...

"Not yet," she whispered, and touched QUERY.

JAE'LABA LOCATION?

In the upper left-hand corner a tertiary indicator glowed a brighter gold and began to pulse.

"As simple as that?" She was Liaden and mistrusted simplicity. She was of Korval and smelled a trap. And yet...

DETAIL, she commanded; and watched the indicator enlarge as another map grew about it, showing the familiar outline of Solcintra. A building took shape, enclosing the pulsing gold, and a legend appeared at the base of the screen.

SCOUT HEADQUARTERS.

"But Val Con's a Scout, after all," Anthora said reasonably a short time later.

"They denied him!" Nova cried, breaking the pattern of her pacing to face her sister. "Assigned to the Department of the Interior, they said! And information about the Department of the Interior is restricted—to my code and to the Council of Clans."

"Oh." Anthora bent to the desk, offering a finger for its occupant to sniff. "Good day, Lord Merlin."

Nova swallowed a sigh. She should have known better than to open such a discussion with Anthora, but Shan was gone with the *Passage,* and she was further robbed of Pat Rin's caustic intelligence...

"If a station is in a place," Anthora asked, rubbing Merlin's ears, "must it mean that it belongs to the owners of the place?"

Nova froze. "No. No, of course not. But—the Scouts..."

"Scouts are not gods," the wooly-headed baby of the family commented. "Val Con said Scouts spend a great deal of time mucking about in the mud and running afoul of custom." She looked up. "It's a simple thing to shunt information from one terminal to another. Even simpler to hide information an honest user would have no reason to look for, then dump what's hidden, with no one the wiser. A tertiary station? Who would trouble to invade something so unimportant? Who would think to look for tampering?"

The idea took simplicity and snarled it with a hundred knots, basing all on the honor of Liad's Scouts. It supposed an enemy more dangerous than an unrecorded organization disinclined to answer questions. Nova sat on the arm of a chair, staring at her sister with wondering violet eyes. The theory appealed, yes. It appealed mightily.

"The Scouts," Anthora continued, "have no reason to lie. Were our brother eklykt'i—were he even dead!—these things have come to those of Korval in the past, have they not? And the Scouts sent word, just as to any other."

"Truth." The melant'i of the Scouts was not in doubt. It was more possible to consider a new and secret enemy than to consider that the Scouts might have lied. "They say what they know. It worries me that they may not know all. It worries me more that this Department of the Interior has its eyes upon us while we are blind to them." She closed her eyes while Anthora bent to scratch Merlin under the chin, and for several minutes his purrs were the only sound heard in the room.

Then Nova snapped to her feet, brushed past sister and cat, and leaned to the keyboard.

"What do you, sister?"

"Whoever they are, they must have money. Mr. dea'Gauss may— Good day, Sor Dal. Has Mr. dea'Gauss leisure to speak?"

"I will ascertain, Eldema. One moment."

Somewhat less than a moment later the wait-signal cleared to show the old gentleman himself. He inclined his head respectfully. "Lady Nova."

"Mr. dea'Gauss. It's good of you to leave your work to speak to me." She followed the form with well-hidden impatience, mustering one of her thin smiles.

"I am always at Korval's service, your ladyship. How may I assist you?"

Gods, Nova thought. What can it portend that Mr. dea'Gauss becomes brusque? She moved a hand in acknowledgment of truth spoken and looked into the old dark eyes. "I desire information regarding the business we spoke of earlier, sir. Its funding and its expenditures. I desire this urgently."

The old eyes did not flicker. "Your ladyship is wise to check all contingencies before committing her resources. I shall see to it."

"My thanks to you, sir."

"Line dea'Gauss serves Korval," he said calmly. "Now as ever. With your ladyship's permission?"

"Of course."

The screen went blank.

"Mr. dea'Gauss is worried," Anthora said at her shoulder.

Nova glanced over. "You can read over comm lines?"

She looked surprised and thoughtful. "I don't think so...But I didn't need to, just now. It was obvious."

This from one who barely noticed rain from sun! Nova hesitated over a question and, Anthora-like, the other plucked it out of air and gave answer.

"Shannie told me to help you. Not," she added with a sniff, "that he had to. And before he left he said I must pay close attention to—things—and not be backward about speaking my thoughts. He said that there are often several ways to look at something, and I mustn't assume that because I've seen one or even two ways that you've seen the same ways. He said you need to see as much as possible, to keep Korval safe."

"Did he? I'm in debt for his concern."

"Don't be angry at Shannie, sister. He'll be searching, too, you know. And he has Priscilla with him. I taught her how to see Val Con." Her brow wrinkled slightly. "At least, she can't see him very clearly—and I'm not at all sure she sees him the same way I do. And it tires her, I think. But she has—a sense—of him. And of his lady. She'll be able to tell if the *Passage* comes near them."

"Will she?" Nova tried to catch her mental breath. It was often thus with Anthora, who took such abilities as easily as sight and hearing, even though the very language had to be bent and twisted in order for her to speak of them. "And can you—see—Val Con with his lady now? Are they well?"

Anthora nodded vigorously. "Val Con's more Val Con than he's been for—oh, a long time! And his lady is very bright."

She spoke with such clear approval that Nova found herself comforted a little.

"I'm going for a walk before Prime," Anthora said softly. "Come with me, do."

A walk? With Val Con yet missing, even though he was "more Val Con than he'd been"—and gods alone knew what that meant! Had he been ill? What was she thinking of, that supposed lifemate, that she was so careless of him?

"Sister..." Anthora slid her arms about Nova's waist in a wholly unexpected hug. "He is well. More—I believe him happy. We search; we do what we might, as well as we might. Val Con would never grudge you an hour's pleasure when there is nothing more for you to do."

Nova hugged back, cuddling the warmth of her sister's body against her. "Truth..." She stood away, summoning the second smile in an hour. "Let us go for a walk, then. The day does seem fair."

LIAD

Trealla Fantrol

The house was too empty.

Nova sighed. The information in front of her was important, or it would not be on her screen. Mr. dea'Gauss was not in the habit of bothering her with trifles. Yet the house was too empty: the children, by her own order, taken by their tutors to the Port for half a day's holiday; Anthora gone with the twins to visit Lady yo'Lanna...There was no one to claim her attention, no reason to make a decision immediately. The words on the screen not yet urgent enough to—

She blinked at the carpet, which was not blue enough by half, and what was that tiny screen doing *there* on the desk, when only that moment she had been looking at the large, amber colored—

"No!"

Nova pushed back at the Memory, half-sick with the effort to separate the room *she* knew from that other—long gone, changed, changed again—knowing even as she thought that it was useless if the time was come. Dismay rode briefly over loathing; dismay of the power that the past generations of Korval women had over her. Edger had addressed her as "She Who Remembers;" she wondered—and then was certain—if Val Con had explained her "talent" of reliving the memories of those long dead. Loathing rose again and she pushed at the Memory, hard.

The Memory expanded, the long-ago room taking on more and more substance, as the room *now* faded.

Nova recalled her own past with guilt, wondering which of her decisions or experiences might be forced on some unsuspecting child or unwelcoming grandmother—

Vertigo overtook her; she clutched at the table, then squared her shoulders and walked to the couch. She sat with unaccustomed heaviness, half expecting the thing to be nothing more than a Memory-phantom, substantial and actual to all but her body.

Carefully, striving to put bitterness and loathing and dismay all aside, she took a deep breath—and another, began the relaxing sequence the Healers had given her...

And it was there, as searing as her memory of the argument with Shan.

A Liaden youth, hair clipped tight in a style dating him hundreds of years in the past, was arguing. She knew him, ached to grant him his demand, yet denied him, nonetheless.

"Yes, Ker Lin, I did hear you. I believe *you* have not heard *me*. I am not speaking as your aunt in this. I am speaking as Delm!"

In the part of her mind shielded by the Healer's magic, Nova recalled the name, recalled a much older face from the portrait gallery at Jelaza Kazone—Ker Lin yos'Phelium, seven hundred and twelve years dead.

His face went rigid. "I hear the Delm," he said, courtesy thinly sheathing his anger. "I request the Delm listen once again."

What was this, after all? Ker Lin's Delm at that age must have been old Renoka yos'Phelium.

A flash of impatience was recalled, and a flare of almost feral love, before she gave him haughty leave. "You may speak. But you must offer more or different information, boy! I grow weary of hearing your 'musts!'"

Eyes. Gods and demons, what eyes the child had! Silver bright, shining, hypnotic—and the will!

"I have Seen that I shall join the Scouts in the spring," he said, with some fair semblance of calm. "I shall not wed until after my third mission."

"And I say you will do so now! I will see a yos'Phelium contract-wed into yo'—"

"Silence!" He gestured, and her voice choked in her throat; her bones rocked with the force of the command, and her blood chilled. She stood, moving as if against strong wind, found the energy needful to shake off his will, and glared down at him, the one of all of them who would be Delm...ah, yes, if he lived so long!

"Defend your actions!" she ordered, the High Tongue crackling with the force of her own will. "Defend, or be gone!"

His face lost some of its luster, it seemed, within a moment, to grow old and to fall away almost into the face of the child he had been, with tears at the corners of his eyes; then his eyes—only silver—were sad.

"If you will insist," he said, and she tried to tell herself it was merely halfling dignity she heard in his voice. "I have said that I have Seen what will happen, and I am taught not to foretell to others—"

"The melant'i of the situation, Ker Lin! We are alone: If you had done this in public, I would have had to send you away at once! I shall need to know."

Suddenly he looked defeated and small, and then, in an instant, he became a man.

"You will see a yos'Phelium contract-wed into yo'Hala," he said very quietly. "The child shall come to yos'Phelium, and the alliance thus formed will last for many, many years. I shall join the Scouts, and after my third mission I shall lifemate. Later I will be Delm."

Renoka bowed to that, believing all, because already she had believed half. "And in this present case, my wise? Who shall fulfill the contract with yo'Hala in your stead?"

"You, my aunt and Delm."

Blank astonishment was recalled, along with the beginning of a suspicion. "You know that Tan El yo'Lanna has my promise to wed him, when *Zipper* is next in port."

The eyes were silver ice; she thought she saw pity and knew, but would not allow herself to know. Selfishly she made him say it.

"Tell me, Ker Lin."

"Let be!" Pain roughened his voice, not command; but she was pitiless in her own pain.

"You are required!"

He bowed, then, very, very gently. "Aunt Renoka, forgive me." He paused, then looked at her straightly. *"Zipper's* drive failed in the outer arm. The cargo has been orbited, and news of its location will come to me when I am Delm." He paused and sighed. "The attempt to restart the drive was catastrophic. Dan Art yos'Galan alone has survived."

He bowed again, with all the love and care he could fit into the gesture, and left quietly.

"Let be!" Renoka cried out to the echoing room. "Let be!"

She called up flight schedules and requested docking information, angrily scrubbing at the tears that would neither stop nor take on urgency. The silver eyes—she sighed and cried the harder.

Alone in the house, Renoka looked over the blue carpet, waiting. After a while someone—not Ker Lin—came to tell her that Dan Art yos'Galan was rescued. She was already dressed in mourning when they arrived.

Nova opened her eyes and saw the proper furniture and the amber screen; she reached up and angrily scrubbed the tears from her face.

What had she touched? What had she done that demanded that Memory?

She glanced at the material on the screen: a list of proposed alliances and known wedding negotiations. With a clarity she mistrusted she heard Ker Lin's voice.

"Let be!"

She swept her hand across the controls savagely.

"Jeeves!" she yelled into the air. "Jeeves, bring me some tea!" The robot arrived in seconds, bulky engine to a train of three cats.

"Tea and company, I'm afraid, Miss Nova." Jeeves set the service down on the low table by the window, poured, and stepped back.

Nova bent down to pick up the middle cat, a sorry mop of varicolored stripes named Kifer. He began to purr and knead immediately, and Nova rubbed her face in his outrageously, wonderfully soft fur.

"Let them stay," she said to the robot. "I can use some company just now."

LIAD

Envolima City

Tyl Von sig'Alda sat in the quarters assigned him and frowned at the graph hung over the desk. Several specialists had provided the uniform opinion that the coils of the ruined ship where yos'Phelium and the female had been stranded might have been coaxed to provide one Jump, given an individual with the knowledge and the will. The computer took his opinions as fact and constructed a portrait of the Jump-sites so attainable.

Records rendered a portrait of Val Con yos'Phelium as a man of will and wide knowledge, from a Clan that valued ships and the lore of ships above all else. It was utterly conceivable that he had demanded and received of the tired coils one last effort, that he was already on some world or other, evading debriefing or striving valiantly to win home.

The female…He fingered the report recently acquired from several highly confidential sources. The female was negligible; a mere Terran mercenary, lacking education or any other discipline besides her skill at arms. True it was that she had survived the disaster of Klamath; also true was the fact that she had spent months afterward in rehabilitative therapy for the abuse of the substance Lethecronaxion—Cloud, as so many Terrans called it, kin to the drug utilized by the Department to induce its agents to complete recall.

The function of Cloud, however, was to inhibit memory. sig'Alda experienced shadowy revulsion. The female was a brute; a killer addicted to a drug that wiped her yesterdays from experience as quickly as she lived them. How came Val Con yos'Phelium to travel with such a one?

If she were a tool…He ran the odds, consciously adding pertinent factors from yos'Phelium's record and data gained during training.

.8

Well within the realm of possibility, then, that the female was but a convenient tool, held in check by her dependence upon the drug—and upon the supplier of the drug.

So then: The mission on Lufkit had gone well enough of itself, but something unknowable had gone amiss between its completion and the time Val Con yos'Phelium was to rendezvous with his transport home. Sometime after the completion of his mission and before the firefight between Lufkit police and members of the local chapter of Juntavas—substantiated in several popular newspapers from Lufkit—Val Con yos'Phelium had acquired the services of Miri Robertson, retired mercenary and former bodyguard.

Suppose that yos'Phelium had understood the situation to be worsening. Suppose further that he acknowledged sleep a physiological necessity. It would certainly be prudent, in a case where one expected disaster around every corner, to engage something to guard one's sleep. Chance had provided something well versed in guarding and competent with her weapons—and the solution had worked: Circumstances showed as much.

Provided with a solution that had answered so admirably in one instance—and perhaps yet unsure of what might await him—yos'Phelium takes the female with him aboard the Clutch ship. She is competent in her brutish way, and even loyal—he, of course, having taken care to provide himself with a supply of Lethecronaxion beforehand.

sig'Alda ran the odds once more.

.8

Well enough. The female was but a tool to yos'Phelium's hand—provided by chance, honed by necessity. He had been foolish to suspect anything else. What other use had a well-trained agent for a bitch Terran, after all?

Reasoning reconstructed to satisfactory tolerance, sig'Alda pulled the keyboard toward him, beginning to plot the coordinates of the planets on the graph that hung over the desk. Several of the worlds represented there were Interdicted. However, the duties of Scouts took them to many strange orbits, including those about Interdicted Worlds. Best he consider any reports the Scouts had on files regarding those particular Forbiddens before he made further plans.

VANDAR

Springbreeze Farm

Zhena Trelu left her boarders to clear up the supper dishes and made her way down the hall, key clenched tight in her hand, second thoughts buzzing in her head. The Meltz boy would be here soon, to tune Jerry's piano, just as she had said he could. Except now she was not so sure.

She paused at the door, looking from key to lock, telling herself hopefully that three years was a long time, telling herself that maybe the key did not work anymore, after all this time...

Undecided, she fidgeted with the key; then, with a sharp headshake, she clenched her fingers, her hand moving toward the pocket of her apron.

Behind her she heard a noise.

She jerked around—and there was Meri, gray eyes huge in her pointed face, one hand tentatively extended. "Zhena Trelu, please. Cory play yes."

It was said in the mildest possible tone, but the old woman clutched at the spark of resentment the words ignited, using that warmth to chase away the cold confusion.

"Why in wind should he?" she demanded, knowing it was unreasonable, but not caring. *Hers* was the loss, and how should that— that *child,* her husband standing healthy at her side, presume to judge..."You two are supposed to be working for me, not taking over my house! Telling me what to do. That's Jerry's piano! Nobody ever touched it but him. *Nobody.* And I should just hand it over to some—*foreigner* I first laid eyes on three weeks ago? Why? Like as not, the pair of you're only out to rob me—"

No!" The girl's voice cut passionately across the stream of nonsense. "Good Cory! *Patient* Cory! Works hard—fixes—helps. Helps you. Helps me. Who helps Cory?" She flung her hands out, and Zhena Trelu saw the shine of tears in the gray eyes. "Zhena Trelu. *Please.* Cory play yes."

And what good, the old woman thought suddenly, sanely, was a piano to a dead man? She closed her eyes, feeling suddenly close to tears herself. Jerrel Trelu had been a kind man; no one should go hungry for music in his zhena's house.

Slowly she opened her fingers around the key, turned back, and fumbled a moment with the lock before twisting the knob and pushing the door wide.

"Thank you, Zhena Trelu," Meri whispered behind her; but when she turned back, the girl was gone.

The piano was badly in need of tuning. Hakan worked carefully, Cory at his elbow, watching everything he did. On the doublechair to the right of the instrument, Miri and Kem had their heads together over a book. Kem's cool voice occasionally reached Hakan— she seemed to be teaching Miri the alphabet.

Zhena Trelu sat in the single chair on the other side of the lamp, ostensibly reading, but Cory, looking at her now and then from under long lashes, thought she had not turned a page since sitting down.

The tuning finally done, Hakan closed the case and waved Cory toward the keyboard, grinning. But the slighter man hesitated, then drifted soundlessly over to stand before the old woman and her book.

"Zhena Trelu," he said softly, and she looked up, frowning.

Slowly, with full pomp, he made her the bow of one who acknowledges an unpayable debt. "Thank you, Zhena Trelu. Very."

She sniffed. "Just don't you let me find you shirking your work and coming in here to play, hear me? Work comes first."

"Yes, Zhena Trelu." He smiled. "I will work."

She sniffed again, mindful of three pairs of young eyes on her. "Well, what're you waiting for? *You* were the one who wanted to play." She flicked her hand toward the piano. "So, *play.*"

He grinned and moved back to the instrument, slid onto the bench, and ran his fingers up and down the keys. Then he began to play, straightly and without flourish, the main line of the piece Hakan had been running through his guitar, three days past.

Hakan gave a shout and grabbed his guitar, taking up the weaving minor thread.

In the doublechair, Miri and Kem set aside the book to listen to the music. In the single chair, Zhena Trelu sat rapt.

In the manner of such things, one song led to another. At some point during the evening, wine was opened and poured; and, in the manner of *those* things, was found too soon to be gone. A little time later Zhena Trelu excused herself with a yawn and went upstairs to her bedroom, waving aside an offer of an escort from Kem and Meri.

Her departure brought Hakan to an awareness of the hour, and he and Kem bundled themselves together, eliciting promises from their new friends to come to supper on Marin evening and making arrangements for Hakan to pick them up.

When the taillights of Hakan's car had finally faded, Miri leaned back against Val Con with a sigh. "Boss, I think I'm drunk."

She heard him laugh softly and felt his fingers tighten where they rested on her shoulders. "I am afraid that I am also drunk, cha'trez."

"Couple of saps," she judged, turning around and grinning up at him. *"One* of us is supposed to stay sober to carry the other one home and get 'em in bed. Now what?"

He appeared to consider the problem while he laid his arm about her waist and drew her into the hallway. "I suppose," he said, locking the door with great care, "that we must then carry each other."

"Okay," Miri agreed, sliding her arm around his waist.

Leaning on each other, they gained their bedroom without mishap.

It was not yet dawn when Val Con drifted awake. He kept his eyes closed, feeling Miri pressed tightly against his side, her head on his shoulder, one arm flung across his chest. He was conscious first of a warm contentment; then he heard the song.

Though "heard" was not precisely the correct word; nor was "song." Cautiously, eyes still closed, he sought the song that was heard only within his head and found it, a thing of surpassing brightness and warmth, singing blithely to itself—and tasting strongly of hunch.

He regarded it for some time, remembering the old tales, knowing what it must be, joy building within him.

The gods make you a gift, he told himself gently.

And the part of him that was Korval replied: As it should be. The gods owe much.

Alive-and-well, sang the song-that-was-not-a-song from its joylit corner of his self. *Miri-alive. Miri-well.*

Fear surfaced for a moment as he recalled the man he now was. But then he recalled that his lifemate had shown no wizardly skills at all, so might not be able to hear him—and the fear was vanquished.

He moved a little in the predawn, curling around the woman beside him, burying his face in the cloud of her hair. Warm within, warm without, Val Con slid back into sleep.

VANDAR

Springbreeze Farm

Val Con sat at the piano, letting his fingers roam randomly over the keys. The sound of Zhena Trelu's radio reached him from down the hall, and somewhere close by Borril groaned and shifted. He wondered where Miri was and moved his attention for the briefest of instants to the song of her and its joyous message: *Alive-and-well, alive-and-well . . .*

Lips relaxing into a smile, Val Con turned his attention to the notes he played, ear snagging on a series of three that recalled the piece he and Hakan had been working on the previous night. Shaking his head, he ran lightly through the song, then returned to the beginning, playing in earnest.

Best you practice, he told himself with mock sternness. If Hakan succeeds in getting the two of us a job playing music, you must be ready and able.

He was unsure of the likelihood of such work, but Hakan hardly spoke of anything else. It seemed there was a fair of some type looming, and Hakan's heart was set upon the two of them playing in one of the exhibition halls. The wages, in Hakan's estimation, were barely less than a joke—in fact, he had suggested that Cory keep the whole sum himself, since Zhena Trelu did not see fit to provide either of her charges with pocketpaper. No, one was given to understand that the sole reason for playing—besides the playing itself—was the *exposure*. All the world, in Hakan's eyes, attended the Winterfair at Gylles.

A soundless something called him from his reflections, and he glanced up to see Miri hesitating in the doorway. He let his fingers slow on the keys and smiled at her. "Hello, Miri."

"Hi." Her answering smile was apologetic. "I didn't mean to bother you. Left my book."

"It's no bother," he said, watching her go gracefully across the room to the doublechair. She had taken to wearing her hair loose of late, which he found pleased him greatly. It seemed they both considered this world—this place—a sanctuary.

Miri had found her book and was turning to go.

"You might stay," he said, wishing she would. "Unless my playing will disturb you?"

She grinned. "Naw. Thought *I'd* bother *you.*"

"It's no bother," he repeated gently. "I would be pleased if you'd stay."

"Rather listen to you than Zhena Trelu's radio stories any day," she said, curling promptly into the doublechair and opening the book.

"High praise," he murmured, and grinned when she laughed. His fingers touched the keys, and he began to play once more.

He moved from song to song, working through the list of eleven that made up their scanty repertoire. The music had his whole attention, though now and then he heard a small sound as Miri turned a page.

The last of the eleven was a slippery thing requiring sharply curtailed ripples from the keyboard, as well as a jagged staircase of mismatched notes reaching toward an impossible crescendo. Such a line would have been bad enough on an omnichora, yet some demented creativity had thought it suitable for an instrument as clumsy as the piano...

Sighing at his failure yet again to realize the line's potential, he glanced up and saw Miri curled in the chair, head bent over her book, lamplight glittering over the red wealth of her hair.

Unbidden, his fingers moved on the keys, building a line like laughter, like something lovely and wild half-seen, poised to fly away. His other hand shifted and found the undercurrent of strength, of constancy and surprising courage. The two lines melded, became one, separated for a time, and rejoined, each making the other whole. His fingers found an end of it too soon, and he glanced up, aware that the volume of his playing had increased.

Miri was smiling. "That was pretty," she said. "What was it?"

He returned her smile. "You."

"Me?" Her disbelief was apparent.

"Certainly, you," he returned matter-of-factly. "Listen." He moved his hands again, picking out a limping, aged phrase, frail without fragility, predictable and obstinate.

"Zhena Trelu," he murmured, aware that Miri had left her chair and was drawing closer.

Shifting again, he played a bump-and-tumble bass line, and she immediately laughed and cried out, "Borril!"

"None other," he said, grinning, caught up in the game. Gods, it had been years since he had indulged in such foolery!

Fingers touched keys, and Miri stirred. "Kem."

"Correct again," he said, sliding down the bench to make room for her to sit beside him. Hands at the top of the scale, he ran through a chaos of high-pitched chords, sharps and flats mixed indiscriminately. "And Hakan, of course..."

She chuckled and sat on the edge of the bench, careful, it seemed, not to touch him.

He tipped his head and began a foghorn melody, running a not-quite-correct underline interspersed here and there with a hasty flutter of sound from the higher end of the board.

"Edger," Miri said, and he nodded.

Her ear was excellent: He ran through the short list of their mutual acquaintances, and she named each unfailingly, though one made her crow with laughter even as she protested, "Oh, no! Poor Jason!"

His hands shifted again, building a solidly balanced, stately topline, the undermelody as uncompromising as stone, except—did Miri detect the faintest hint of laughter? Of—informality? If it existed, it was a very ghost. Val Con's fingers had stopped, and the last note vibrated into stillness before she shook her head.

"Got me there. Don't think I know him."

"Her," he corrected. "My sister Nova."

"Pleasure, I'm sure," Miri said with a certain lack of enthusiasm. "Hope I never do anything to make her mad."

He laughed softly and began another line, this one gentle, relaxed, almost absurdly good-natured—until one heard the steel beneath the surface, sharp as any blade. "Shan," he murmured, then moved his hands once more.

The new tune was like a glitter of dark snowflakes seen briefly in the glare of a lightning bolt, like kittens giving each other chase upon waking. "Anthora," he said.

He sat back and inclined his head slightly. "Clan Korval," he told her. He reached to cover the keyboard.

Miri's hand on his sleeve stopped him. "Somebody missing, ain't there?"

He lifted an eyebrow.

"Val Con?" Miri asked. "Seems to me I heard he was Second Speaker."

"Ah, well," he said. "Val Con." His fingers dropped carelessly to the keys, playing a quick ripple of sound in the midrange that was merely an echo of his murmuring voice; then his hands lifted and brought the cover gently down into place.

"Oh," Miri said.

He turned to look at her and noticing the tension in the small muscles around her eyes. "Cha'trez? What is wrong?"

She frowned and moved her shoulders slightly, as if to shrug the problem away. "I—it's stupid, I guess. Just seems like you try to hide yourself from me, or something."

"Do I?" He turned on the bench to face her fully. "I am your friend. And your partner. And your lifemate. Do I not please you, Miri?"

"Please?" She looked surprised, then shifted sharply to sit astride the bench and looked him fully in the face. Her own was wide open, so that he knew the answer before she spoke it.

"I love you so much it hurts. So much I try not to think about it, 'cause I get scared." She clamped her jaw.

He extended a hand and stroked her cheek. "Such a large present, cha'trez, for someone you do not know." He tipped his head. "And you knew me well enough, did you not, to intercede with Zhena Trelu so I might have use of this piano?"

"How'd you know that?" She was regarding him with some suspicion. He stroked her cheek again, moving his fingers to trace the curve of her brows.

"Zhena Trelu told me; so I would know for certain how well I was loved." He ran his fingers down the line of her jaw. "You are so beautiful..." There was an ache of wonder in his voice.

She reached up to brush the hair from his eyes. "Val Con?" There was a pause while she searched his face and eyes; he felt as if she were searching his soul and held his breath, afraid. "You love me," she said finally and very softly, as if the discovery were a new one.

"Miri," he said suddenly, shifting into the most intimate of modes, nearly singing the Low Liaden words, "you are my wisdom and my laughter, the song of my heart, my home. Best-loved friend; wife and lover..."

She did not understand; the words meant nothing to her, though he saw her following the song of his voice. Almost sharply, he brought both hands up and ran his fingers into her hair, holding her so her eyes had to look into his. Consciously keeping his voice pitched for intimate speech, he reached for the hopelessly inadequate Terran words.

"I love you, Miri; you are my joy."

Releasing her, he sat back and was conscious of intense pleasure when she moved her hand to take his.

"Lifemates means what it says?" she asked, smiling at him just a little.

He raised a brow. "What else would it mean?"

"Just checking." She stood, pulling him with her. "Let's go to bed. Betcha it's after midnight…"

DUTIFUL PASSAGE

"Priscilla," Lina inquired with the straightforwardness of friendship, "is this wise?"

The other woman looked up from unbuckling her belt, her slim brows arched in surprise. "It's necessary," she said, and laid the belt smoothly aside.

Lina stifled a sigh. Believing in necessity, Priscilla would pursue her mad course, whether her friend consented to watch or no.

"Perhaps it might wait," she ventured, watching Priscilla slip her trousers off and fold them neatly atop her shirt, "until Shan is on the ship? He only trades until local dusk, Priscilla. Surely time is not of such—"

Lina had suspected all along that this enterprise had none of Shan yos'Galan's smile—which boded not so well for Lina Faaldom, if she had to seek him out to say "Old friend, your heart slipped away while I watched her; and the way of her going is such that a Healer may neither follow nor find…"

The bed shifted slightly as Priscilla lay down and smiled up at her friend. "I'm not in any danger, Lina. You'll be with me, after all."

The smaller woman laughed. "Yes, assuredly! The mouse shall guard the lion."

Priscilla nodded, quite serious. "Who better? You will watch closely and not rush into danger, as another lion might; and so keep yourself safe and able to assist." She smiled again, softly. "Wise Lina."

"Pah!" Lina banished flattery with a flick of a tiny hand. "Well, and if you must, you might as well—and quickly."

"Yes. You have the Words I gave you?"

"Of course." *Priscilla!* Lina was to cry, if there came a hint that things were not as they should be. *Priscilla, come home!* Heart-words, Priscilla had named them, saying that she would hear that phrase and return, no matter how far the distance.

The ways of the dramliz are wondrous, indeed, Lina thought, and clutched the heartwords tightly in memory.

Beside her, Priscilla's breathing had slowed and deepened, the pulse in her throat beating with alarming slowness. Healer-sense showed the pattern she recognized as Priscilla Mendoza pulled in upon itself, so dense it seemed that even outer eyes must see it.

And as she watched, that strangely dense pattern began to rise, until inner eyes placed it above the sleeping body; then even farther above, rising toward the cabin's ceiling, trailing behind it in a single thread no thicker than a strand of silk. Rising still, it faded through the ceiling and was lost to all Lina's sight.

The clamor of the galaxy was easier to ignore than it had been the last time. No sooner was the template in place than the aura it represented was found, flaring among the multitudes of lesser lights like a nova amid mere stars.

She approached slowly, mindful of the lesson that haste had taught her, traveling a time that could not be measured over a distance that seemed at once very great and no more than a roll from one side to another to embrace one who lay beside her.

Suddenly she was very close. Cautiously she opened a path from herself to him—and very nearly recoiled.

Temple training saved her from that error; her own necessity drew her close again, to examine what was there.

Protections. The boy she had known had encompassed no such walls and ramparts, though he had been adept enough at shielding himself. But even at that, with him awake, as he was now, and she with the need and the Aspect upon her, there should have been yet the small ways in, where one might enter and leave a seed-thought, to grow to suggestion and then into dream and so be absorbed into consciousness.

Disconcerted, she brought template against pattern, thinking that she had somehow erred in her urgency—but no. There could not be two such, matching, edge on edge, protected or wide open. And witch-sense brought her a bare hint of the passion that had previously overflowed him, burning still, but deep within, a bonfire at the heart of a citadel.

Val Con! She hurled his name, hoping for a crack in those protections, perhaps even a recognition.

He heard her, of that much was she certain, but the walls stood firm. Almost she turned to leave, defeated—and saw then, with witch-eyes, the bridge.

A sturdy structure, built with more honesty than skill, vanishing into the very heart of the tightly guarded place that Val Con yos'Phelium had inexplicably become and stretching away to—where?

Cautiously she followed the bridge back, marveling at its flexibility and strength, then found the source and marveled anew.

The pattern shone, life-passion licking through the gridwork even though consciousness was at the moment disengaged. Priscilla bent her attention closer and discovered the sleeper's core lightly locked behind doors while the rest remained open to any with eyes to see. She sensed a bit of lambent shine, which might indicate witch-sense; the bridge argued power, even as it showed an architect untrained. Had she been in her body, Priscilla might have smiled. She had found lifemate, and a fitting receptacle for her message.

Taking care not to disturb the other's slumber or cast the slightest quiver onto the bridge, Priscilla placed the thought-seed within the sleeping pattern and withdrew a little way to watch. Only when she was certain that neither the sleeping nor the wakeful had been disturbed by her action did she loose her hold upon the place and follow her mooring line home.

VANDAR

Springbreeze Farm

Val Con slipped out of bed and silently pulled on his clothes. He stood over Miri for a time, studying her face in the crisp moonlight, unaccountably delighted that the small, satisfied smile still lingered on her mouth. Gently he tucked the covers around her, fingertips barely brushing the tumble of copper silk, then turned and went like moonshadow across the room and out into the hall.

He paused briefly in the lower hall, decided against the piano, and continued on to the kitchen where Borril moaned but did not wake as the man took his jacket from its peg.

Just beyond the scuppin house he paused again, breath frosting on the air. Energy tingled through him, head-top to toe-tips: the excitement of making music coupled with the exuberance of making love, of being loved. He stretched high on his toes, arms flung out toward the meager stars. Tonight, tonight he could fly.

Or nearly so. On the verge of soaring, he brought his arms down and stood looking quietly at the sky, thinking of a ship.

Of his own will and heart, he had brought forbidden technology to an Interdicted World and left it, barely concealed, no more than three miles from habitation. Though it was coil-dead, ransacked—even the distress beacon dead—he should have sent it into orbit and oblivion the moment they had been safe on-world, rather than trying to reconcile Scout-conscience with bone-deep need.

He had no means to repair the ship, no excuse for the madness of keeping it by. It was only that it went hard against the heart to lose such a resource, even though reasoned thought showed it to be no use to him. From the very first—from Cantra forward—Korval had kept the ships that came to it. Thirty-one generations of yos'Pheliums had led Korval, gathering ships as they could, obeying Cantra's law. And to Val Con, of the Line Direct, seventh to bear the name—to Val Con yos'Phelium fell the task of sending a ship to certain death and acknowledging to his heart that he and his lifemate were stranded on a forbidden world, Clan-reft, and likely to eventually die here.

Homesickness swept through him, sudden and shocking: He recalled the library at Jelaza Kazone, the long row of identically bound Diaries. He remembered even more vividly Uncle Er Thom's office at Trealla Fantrol, his uncle seated at the desk, head bent over some work, fair hair gleaming in the scented firelight; remembered his own rooms, gray Merlin lounging on the window seat, blinking yellow eyes against the midmorning sun; Shan laughing and talking; Nova so solemn; Anthora; Padi; Pat Rin...

Out of the near-dawn he heard a sound, as if someone inexpressibly far away had cried his name. He spun, every sense straining; heard the echo die and nothing more.

After a time, he turned back toward the house, carrying home-memories like a dull ache behind his heart.

Miri woke as he opened the door; she grinned up at him and stretched with very evident enjoyment. "Morning."

"Good morning, cha'trez." He sat carefully on the edge of the bed and held out a mug. "Would you like some tea?"

"Why not?" She wriggled into a sitting position against the pillows and took the mug, the coverlet falling away from one slight breast. "Umm—nice," she said, sipping. "And thanks."

"You're welcome."

"Yeah. You're up early."

"A touch of performance exhilaration." He smiled. "Even with the exercise that followed I found I needed no more than a nap."

She laughed, shaking her head and hiding the breast behind a curtain of hair. "And here I thought I wore you out!" Her expression changed abruptly and she sipped her tea. "Had a dream, boss."

"So?" he murmured, watching her face closely from beneath long lashes. "Tell me."

"Funniest thing about it," she said slowly, "is that it was so real, like I knew the people. Like they were—family."

"Dreams are very odd," he offered when a moment had passed and she had not spoken further. "Perhaps these are people you have seen somewhere before, even in passing."

"Naw," she said hesitantly. Then, with complete surety, she repeated, "No. I'd remember a pair like this one, no matter how short a sight I'd had." She closed her eyes, brows drawn in concentration. "They were in a—it looked like a ship's bridge, but *big*—and they were standing together, shoulder to shoulder. She's a little taller than he is—black hair, all curly, black eyes, and pale—beautiful, boss; that's the only word for her. And him—white hair, but not old; light eyes; brown skin; big hands—holding a wineglass; wearing a purple ring...They said—" Her brows twitched, and he watched her breathlessly. *"Somebody* said, "We're looking for you. Help us." She sighed. "So damn *real.*"

"Priscilla," he breathed.

She opened her eyes. "Huh?"

"The people you described," he managed, fighting against hope and terror. "The white-haired man is my brother Shan; the woman is Priscilla Mendoza, who is—ah, she is first mate, say—on *Dutiful Passage,* which my brother captains."

There was silence between them for a moment, then a careful: "Val Con?"

"Yes."

"How'd your people get in my head?"

He hesitated, then reached out and took her hand. "Priscilla is of the dramliz—a wizard, Miri. I— Outside, I thought I heard someone call to me, but— Perhaps it was beyond her skill to leave a message in a waking mind, and so she chose the mind of my lifemate."

"Yeah, but how'd she know that, boss?"

He looked at her helplessly. "Miri, I am not dramliz. How would I know?"

"Right." She stroked his cheek, brushing the hair from his eyes. "It's okay, boss, honest." Her fingers trembled. "Why're we scared?"

"They are looking for us," he whispered. "They will put themselves in danger. The Department of the Interior—gods, my Clan..." And the ship was useless, useless...

"We must start for Liad today," she thought she heard him say. "Or we must warn them away."

Miri stared. Then, moving carefully against the miasma of fear and sorrow and guilt, she set the mug aside, threw her arms around him, and held tight.

SHALTREN

Cessilee

Grom Trogar stood before the starmap, absently fingering this gem and that: Shaltren's diamond, Talitha's niken, Foruner's topaz, Jelban's rosella. It was a magnificent map, with each one of the worlds that bowed to the might of the Juntavas—to the word of Grom Trogar—designated by a jewel produced by that world and tithed to the chairman.

He extended a broad forefinger to touch again the flashing blue-and-gold niken, then drew it back, frowning, as the receptionist's pretty voice came over the speaker.

"Mr. Chairman?"

"Yes?" he snapped.

"I'm sorry to bother you, sir," she said breathlessly. "But there are two, umm, *individuals* here to see you. They say their business is urgent. I—they don't have an appointment, sir, but they said they'd wait."

"Did they?" He considered the speaker stud, glowing bright red in the gloom of his office. "But we aren't that discourteous, are we? Please send these—individuals—in."

There was a pause and a half gasped "Yes, sir." Grom Trogar smiled as he strolled back to his desk.

Grom Trogar frowned at the two large individuals before him, even knowing that they, unlike most, could see his expression quite clearly in the dimness of his office. The knowledge titillated, adding a new dimension to a game long grown predictable.

"A Scout, Aged Ones?" he said. "Of Miri Robertson I am aware. I have urgent need to speak with her; less urgent need, I will admit, to see her dead. Though that will suffice."

"But of a Scout," he continued thoughtfully, "and the threat brought against this other member of your Clan—I am adrift in ignorance. I will investigate the matter thoroughly, and I promise you that it will go quite badly with Justin Hostro if he has failed to file a complete report."

"And the report Justin Hostro has already filed, Grom Trogar?" Edger rumbled politely. "Does it make mention of my kin in any way?"

"Merely that he had Miri Robertson in his hand, and that he allowed her to slip away. He begged forgiveness for his clumsiness and accepted the fine with good grace." He parted his lips in what passed for his smile. "Now I am shown the why of this uncharacteristic meekness. I am indebted, Aged Ones."

"Perhaps," the smaller of the two visitors suggested, "your indebtedness will allow you to call back your decree concerning our sister? She is young and very hasty, but it is in my heart that she has done nothing to warrant her name cried outlaw. Certainly she deserves no untimely death."

Trogar shrugged with a touch of impatience, and the larger visitor took up the discussion.

"It may very well be true that you are wronged in some smaller way, Grom Trogar. Name the offense, and let us as Elders decide upon the injury price."

The man sighed, deeply and regretfully. Really, the game was going quite well. "Aged Ones, I am sincerely grieved. But the truth is that there is no price that will buy my vengeance where Miri Robertson is concerned. She has slain many of my best fighters—individuals I will be hard-pressed to replace. My organization is left in a position of vulnerability—because of Miri Robertson.

"Further, she dared ally herself with Sire Baldwin, who was himself outlawed for crimes committed against m—the Juntavas. That she aided and abetted his escape from justice is inarguable. That she herself is privy to much of the information Baldwin stole from this organization must be a logical certainty. Information is a dangerous thing, Aged Ones. I cannot ignore the possibility that dangerous information is abroad, held in hands not fit to grasp it."

He sighed again. "Understand that I will do my utmost to see that this Scout goes unharmed, should he still be at her side when she is taken. And that is a great deal, Aged Ones. Surely you recall that the Scouts have been less than kind to my people over the years and years? Vagrants, they call us, and gypsies. They hound us from gatherplace to gatherplace, branding us thieves and jackals, hangers-on of Yxtrang, deadly danger to holy Liad. In the usual course of things, you must know that if he lay dying at my feet and I held in my hand the cup of water that would save him, I would upend the cup and laugh as he expired." He shook his head, too unfamiliar with the persons to whom he spoke to read the signs of outrage.

"But these are not ordinary times, Aged Ones," he went on. "Nor am I an ordinary man. I am Chairman of the Juntavas, and I have said to you that I am indebted. Here is how I shall pay: When Miri Robertson is taken, should the Scout still be with her, and if it is within the realm of what is possible, he shall go free. Of course, He Who Watches, who has been threatened by one in our employ, need fear nothing more from the Juntavas." He inclined his head.

"You have made a good bargain: When you entered, the lives of three were potentially forfeit. Now that we have spoken, you regain the lives of two." Grom Trogar rose from behind the steel-and-crystal desk and bowed briskly. "Be satisfied, Aged Ones. In your eyes Miri Robertson will soon be dead in any case—is it not so? What matter that I recover what is mine before she is gone? Good day."

"You are," the one called Edger said, "in error. The day has not thus far been good. I hold forth some hope, however, that it may improve. You have said much that is hurtful to me, as the brother of my brother and my sister. You have behaved in a manner—Elder to Elder—that I find distressing in the extreme. Even, Grom Trogar—were it not in the poorest possible taste—I would say that you have lied to me." He held up one large, three-fingered hand. "Understand that I have not said this. Only, did courtesy permit, that I would do so." He moved his head so that he might gaze at his kinsman, who stood at his right hand. "What think you, brother?"

"I think, T'carais," Sheather said with a certain hasty care, "that Elder Grom Trogar has perhaps spoken before all facts have been laid before him by the members of his Clan most conversant with the affair. This would perhaps lend his words a certain air of— glibness, T'carais—that might make one think he is lying. It is true that we have learned from our brother that humans break truth differently, so one may say what one does not believe and yet know it for a truth."

"There is," Edger conceded, "much in what you have said. Do you make recommendation as to our next step, brother? You would honor me by speaking what is in your heart."

Sheather inclined his head, considered for a moment the bright blade that was his sister, and spoke, finally, with some measure of *her* understanding of the way in which the worlds of Men turned. "T'carais, it comes to me that Grom Trogar knows not with whom he deals. A demonstration is perhaps in order, before we depart to allow him time to gather his facts and rethink the words he has said."

"I have heard," Edger said. He was still for a time, his luminous eyes on the man who stood so quietly behind the desk. Carefully he considered his brother's thought, perceiving its intent and origin. Even in its hastiness, he found it good.

"Grom Trogar," he said.

"Yes, Aged One? Is there a further service I might perform for you?"

"You have heard the words of my brother, Grom Trogar. I find myself in agreement with him. We shall school you, that you may not suffer by your ignorance of the worth of the Knife Clan of Middle River. Then we shall leave you for a time, that you might make inquiries and acquire facts. We will return to speak further with you in five Standard days. Now, attend me."

Edger closed his huge eyes briefly, opened them—and sang.

One note, held to the edge of endurance. Another. And a third.

The miraldine conference table shivered, acquired spiderwebs of cracks, then crumbled and fell in on itself, a glittering pile of rubble and dust.

Grom Trogar heard someone cursing fluently, disbelievingly, in the tongue of his youth; recognizing his own voice, he silenced it.

"Understand," Edger said, "that this is the simplest of the songs I might sing you, Grom Trogar. I chose it because its simplicity was sufficient for a demonstration, yet leaves more complex crystalline structures—as those which are part of your communication devices—unharmed. I am sorry that some of the gems in yon piece of artwork have also suffered." He motioned to his brother, Sheather, and inclined his head in the manner of Men, "Keep you well, Grom Trogar. We shall return in five days."

Moving with a quickness astonishing in persons so large, they crossed the room, striding over the crumbled table, and passed through the door. Grom Trogar saw his hand twitch toward the desk key that would forbid them exit, clenched it and let them go.

Slowly he moved to the shattered remains of the table, bent, and picked up a jagged blue shard. Holding it cupped, so that the sharp edges pricked his palm, he went over to the fabulous illustration of Juntavas might, in which each of one hundred and four worlds was marked by a flashing gem.

He was not really surprised to see that only thirty-one remained.

LIAD ORBIT

Scout Lieutenant Shadia Ne'Zame was unhappy.

"A whole blasted *year* on Liad," she grumbled to herself while the pilot part of her mind got on with the commonplaces of board calibration, vector analysis, coord check, and velocity match.

"I'm certain it's very nice that the Clan now has a fine healthy daughter to replace me, if and when my luck runs out," she continued, relishing the feel of the tantrum, "but I do think a year of my life is excessive. Stupid custom anyway, contract-marriage. Archaic. We have the technology; why not just have the Speakers negotiate among themselves for the genes and then grow the damn kids in jars? Let everyone else get on with things."

The board stuttered, then steadied: coords locked in. Her eyes flicked to the peripherals, anticipating the glow of the aqua go-stud indicating Tower's permission to depart.

Instead, the orange lit, concurrent with a muted chime.

Her right forefinger touched the connect. "Ne'Zame."

"Lieutenant Shadia? Delight of my night, were you going to leave without farewell? My heart is broken. Belike I'll die of it."

In spite of herself she grinned. "Clonak ter'Meulen, you hoary fraud."

"No one knows me like you, my sweet, my chernubia. My heart is at your feet, battered as it is. Care for my daughter, swear, do I die of your cruelty."

"Clonak, your daughter's older than I am!"

"Does that mean she needs no care? But I grow maudlin. No doubt I'll survive the damage, though I shall never altogether recover."

"I'm trembling in shame," she told him, though in fact it was repressed mirth. "Is there a purpose to this tying up of the airwaves and delay of my departure, or did you merely wish to chat?"

"Ah, the advantages of honored senility! But, yes, now that you bring it to mind, there was a reason for the call. When you complete your assignment, child, report to Auxiliary Headquarters on Nev'lorn and place yourself at the disposal of the commander there."

She sighed. "I suppose you have that in some sort of official form?"

"Transmission completed and locked to your filecomp. Will I see you again, Night's Delight?"

"How do I know? Are you going to be on Nev'lorn in a relumma?"

"For you, even Nev'lorn."

She laughed. "Farewell, Clonak. May your broken heart soon mend!"

"Farewell, Lieutenant Shadia. I doubt it. Clearance coming through—now. Jump at will, and the luck be with you!"

"And with you, old friend." She cut the connection, slapped the go-stud, and hit the sequence: *Jump!*

Leaning back in her chair, she blinked at the Jump-grayed screens and caught herself on the edge of a reminiscent chuckle.

An entire year on Liad, she thought, resuming her tirade. And then what? Return to the Scouts, ready—eager—to go out again; wanting nothing better than to fling myself out into the vast Uncharted, for the glory of Liad and a much-needed rest...

"Scout Lieutenant, First In, Shadia Ne'Zame," her orders had read, "upon return to active duty will, for the next three months Standard, occupy herself with observation of Interdicted Planets (list appended), tagging for pickup any and all flotsam of a possibly technological nature, listening and noting significant cultural advances or declines..."

"The *garbage run?*" she had demanded of the captain behind the desk.

He had shrugged elaborately. "Somebody has to do it." His comm had chimed then, and he had turned away, leaving Shadia to stew and finally walk away. Orders were orders, after all...

And now Clonak ter'Meulen and his sheer nonsense, with orders to report to Aux 'quarters when the garbage run was finished. Faint hint of some action there. Shadia allowed herself a smile and wondered if he would be on Nev'lorn, after all.

SHALTREN

Cessilee

"Aged Ones, I regret most deeply that I have found no cause to change my opinion." There was no artwork upon the walls here, and the conference table was of unadorned steel. Grom Trogar folded his hands upon the cold surface and met the eyes of the one called Edger.

"I see," that person boomed gravely. "And have you gathered further facts, Grom Trogar? Have you spoken with Justin Hostro, your kinsman, and demanded of him a fuller accounting?"

"I have all the information I require from Justin Hostro. I repeat that the decision of the Juntavas remains unchanged."

The words clashed upon Sheather's ears like crystal crying out under intolerable stress, and at his side, the T'carais sighed, most gently.

"In that wise, I, T'carais of the Knife Clan of Middle River, demand to be heard by the full council of Elders of Clan Juntavas. Satisfaction has not been gained; our talks describe circles, encompassing nothing. The lives of my sister and my brother, brief or long, are of far too much importance to hang upon your whim."

Grom Trogar smiled. "Aged One, you speak at this moment to the highest authority possible within the Juntavas. There is no Council of Elders: My voice speaks the final law." He spread his hands flat on the cold tabletop. "You have no recourse."

There was a pause, very brief, as Clutch measure such things.

"Grom Trogar," Edger said, and Sheather blinked in solemn amazement at the patience that the hastiest of their Clan could bring to bear, "it appears you consider us fools. Am I an eggling, to believe that a Clan which spans worlds has at its nexus one individual, whose solitary judgment—"

The intercom chimed overhead, and the receptionist's light, hasty voice skated above Edger's bass rumble. "Mr. Trogar? I am sorry to disturb you, sir, but the delegation from Stelubia has arrived."

"Thank you." Grom Trogar pushed back from the table and bowed with heartfelt irony to the two Clutch members, who were much worse than children. Oh, much worse than fools! "Aged Ones—indulge me. This business is quite urgent and will be but a matter of moments. Pray remain here, and we will continue our discussions when I return."

He was gone then, as if their permission were assured, the door opening and closing behind him with a snap.

The spirit of his sister rising in his heart, Sheather rose, went to the door, laid his hand against the mechanism, and then took it away. "Brother, the door is locked."

"Yes," the T'carais said, with great sadness. "I felt that it might be."

VANDAR

Springbreeze Farm

"What a beautiful morning!" Zhena Trelu exclaimed in surprise. The sun glittered, achingly bright, off the snow on the scuppin-house roof; the sky was cloudless and deeply blue; the iced shrubbery shivered in the very slightest of breezes. Such a day was a gift in midwinter.

Zhena Trelu pulled on a heavy sweater and a skirt instead of the trousers she usually wore around the house, combed her hair, and left the bedroom with a positive spring in her step, already compiling a list in her head.

Meri and Corvill were in the kitchen ahead of her, usual; Cory was seated in a chair, shoulders hunched, as his wife worked on his hair with comb and scissors.

"Sit up!" she said in Benish as Zhena Trelu went across to the stove for a cup of tea. "How can I see what to do when you hunch? I should cut your head off, yes?"

"My hair is fine," Cory protested weakly.

Meri snorted. "Very fine. So fine you don't see to play." She bent until her nose nearly touched his. "You look like Borril," she whispered loudly.

"No!" Cory recoiled in mock horror.

The girl stepped back, eyeing him consideringly. "No," she agreed finally. "Borril's much prettier." She came close again and put a small hand under his chin, coaxing his head up. "I promise it not hurt. I do it very fast."

Sighing, he allowed his head to be raised, though he screwed his eyes shut with exaggerated tightness. Grinning, Meri wielded comb and scissors, trimming the lock that fell across his forehead back to touch the straight brows. A few more deft snips took care of the ragged sides, though she left his hair long enough to cover his ears, to Zhena Trelu's dissatisfaction. It really ought to have been another two inches shorter; and a mustache would have been a great improvement.

Meri stepped back, nodded, and moved a hand to rumple his thick, shiny mop. "I think you live."

He opened his eyes and raised his hands to feel his new haircut. Meri leaned across the table and yanked the toaster toward him.

"Look!" she directed. "Honorable, I am. My word is good." Cory regarded his reflection in the toaster's side, then looked up with a grin. "Thank you, cha'trez. Not Borril now?"

"Very pretty now," she assured him, smiling, and moved across the room to put the scissors and comb away inside the dish closet. "Good morning, Zhena Trelu."

"Good morning, Meri." She sipped her tea, eyes on the beautiful, bright day outside the kitchen window. "Children," she said, "a day like this needs to be used. I'm going in to town to pick up some supplies, maybe stop at the library…There's some stuff it sure will be nice to have, when the weather turns serious." She brought her gaze back to the kitchen and the two young people before her. "Cory, I'm going to need you to carry things."

"Yes, Zhena Trelu," he murmured, setting the toaster carefully back in its accustomed place.

She sipped tea, knowing that her next words would disappoint Meri. The child did love books. But the truck had a limited amount of space, and the list in her head had grown to alarming proportions. Her shopping trip had begun to look like an all-day affair.

"Meri, dear, I'm afraid you'll have to stay home this time. There won't be enough room in the truck." Not looking at the girl, Zhena Trelu hurried on. "You tell Cory what you want from the library, all right? And if the two of you need anything else." She finished her tea and set the cup in the sink to be washed. "I'll be ready to leave in a couple minutes, Cory." She went off down the hall to get paper and pencil.

Miri looked at her husband. "She really does like you best."

"Not so," he replied, standing and stretching. "It is only the labor of my muscle-bound body she desires. *You* she perceives as intellectual." He bowed profoundly. "What will you have from the library, O sage?"

She grinned. "Oh, you know, whatever looks good—oops!" She brought fingers to her forehead. "Nearly forgot. You better take back the ones I got last time." She was already on her way out of the kitchen.

Grinning, he wandered over to the stove and poured himself a cup of tea. Miri's reading habits were amazing: science, gardening, murder mysteries, poetry—he had forgotten half the subjects covered by the last batch of books she had foraged. She had read each with serious concentration; gods alone knew how she managed to keep track of it all. His own tendency was to pick one or two subjects at a time and read through the levels available until he felt himself to have a clear fundamental understanding of the principles involved. Fiction had been a pleasure of his youth, sharply curtailed by school and then by duty.

He turned as she came back into the room, arms full of books, including the six he had borrowed. "You forgot!"

He sighed. "Forgive me, cha'trez. But *you* forget how very old I am—memory is the first to go, I am told."

She laughed, dumping the collection on the table, then turned and looked at him seriously. "You need gloves, boss. Tell Zhena Trelu so, okay? She wants you to fetch and carry, your hands oughta be warm."

"And you?" he asked. "I do not recall that you have gloves."

"I'll keep," she began. But Zhena Trelu was already calling down the hall for Cory to come along.

Sighing, he poured out the last of his tea and set the cup in the sink. He pulled his jacket from its peg and shrugged it on as he came back to Miri's side. Seriously he measured her fingers against his own before dropping a kiss on her palm.

"I will see what may be done," he said. "Keep well, cha'trez—and mind you protect Borril from strangers."

She laughed and hugged him as the truck's asthmatic horn wheezed peevishly at the back stairs. Val Con gathered up the books and dashed out the back door, letting it slam behind him.

Miri drifted to the window and watched the truck make its careful way down the drive and turn cautiously into the road. Borril groaned from his rug by the stove—the only sound in the house.

"Work to do, Robertson," she said against the silence. Then she smiled. Zhena Trelu was gone; there was no reason that the radio in the parlor should not be turned up as loud as possible.

Encouraged by that thought, she made her soundless way down the hall. Kneeling on the ottoman, she turned the control until it clicked and waited for the machine to warm up.

The announcer's voice gabbled into existence, and Miri strained her ears for the sense of it. Something about—Bassilans? and armies?

The professional whine of the newsman's voice, along with the crackle of static, defeated her. She twisted the numbered dial: Voices talking. Voices singing. Voices, voices—music. She stopped turning the dial and listened. Music, indeed, and of a variety that could claim kinship with the type of music Hakan made. Good enough, she decided, and upped the volume.

Then she was on her way back to the kitchen, rolling up her sleeves in anticipation of washing the dishes.

Zhena Trelu drove with precision unmarred by confidence. The last snow had been some days earlier, and the road was clear. There were, however, occasional patches of ice on the surface, and Zhena Trelu navigated the truck over each as if one wrong breath would buy them disaster.

Val Con considered the side of her face, decided that talking would only make her more nervous, and directed his attention to the day.

It *was* fine, though very cold, and he was briefly, intensely, grateful for the warmth of the clothing he wore. Liad was a warm place, after all, though he had been on worlds far chillier than Gylles in midwinter, and he found he preferred being warm to being cold.

The truck slowed; apparently Zhena Trelu was even more distrustful of the covered bridge than of the occasionally icy road. He hardly blamed her. The wooden structure rattled and groaned unnervingly, no matter what the season, seeming to threaten imminent collapse. But, once again, the truck made safe passage and, beyond the bridge, leapt ahead at nearly twenty-five miles an hour.

Val Con shifted on the seat squinting as a sunbeam, deflected by an icicle, stabbed into his eyes. On a rise to the right, a cluster of cows grazed the scant, winter grass; though they looked even less like the animals he had learned, as a child, to call "cows" than Borril looked like a dog.

Come home.

Startled, he considered the thought. Go home? But surely—

Home. The thought was insistent, strongly flavored with hunch. *Danger at home.*

The breath caught in his throat then, and he sent his awareness to touch the spot that still sang, untroubled: *Alive-and-well...*

And yet his hunch; always played, never in error: *Danger. Danger at home.*

Zhena Trelu turned the truck onto Main Street, and Val Con forced himself to breathe deeply, to consider both messages dispassionately. It was true that one could be in danger and yet be alive—be well.

The truck pulled to the curb, and Zhena Trelu turned off the switch and removed the keys.

"Zhena Trelu," he said quickly, almost breathlessly. "We must go home. Now."

She stared at him. "We just got here. There's a lot to do before we go home." Her face softened somewhat. "Meri's all right, Cory. Like as not, she's pleased to have the house to herself for the day."

"Meri is all right," he agreed, keeping his voice even and firm. "But there is danger at home, and she must not face it alone."

The old lady's face grew stern. "Poppycock," she decided, opening her door.

"Zhena Trelu," he began again, strongly tempted merely to take the keys from her.

"No!" she snapped, getting out of the truck and glaring at him from street level. "Now stop wasting my time, Cory. The faster we get everything done, the faster we'll be able to go home." She slammed the door.

Wincing at the sound, Val Con worked the handle on his side, slid to the ground, and closed the door gently. Turning left, he began to run.

"Cory!" Zhena Trelu yelled at his fleeing heck. "Corvill Robersun, come back here this instant!" But he gave no sign that he heard.

Zhena Trelu stood for a moment, bosom heaving, anger warring with worry. It was not really like him, she acknowledged, to just run off like that. Anger flared.

"What do you know what's like him or not?" she grumbled to herself. "Let him run all the way home. Teach him a lesson."

So saying, she turned her back on the truck and the man who was running away and marched across the street to Brillit's.

Tomat Meltz looked up when the entrance bell rang and frowned at the short, long-haired foreigner his son had taken up with.

"Hakan!" the little man called, with no regard at all for the proper way to behave in a place of business. "Hakan, are you here?"

"See here, young man," Zamir Meltz began in his best speech-before-Assembly voice.

"Cory?" Hakan appeared out of the back room like a conjuring trick, mustached face glowing. He held his hands out. "Cory, I was just trying to call—*we got the job!*"

"What?" The little man brushed this aside with a frown. "Just trying to call—who answered?"

"Huh?" Hakan blinked, joy diminishing visibly. "Nobody answered, Cory. You're here, aren't you?"

"Miri." It was nearly a whisper. "Miri is home alone." He looked up sharply and found his friend frowning at him in puzzlement.

"Hakan, please..." He extended a hand and grabbed the other's sleeve. "There—I feel that there is danger at home. Miri is alone. Hakan—drive me home."

The pause was less than a heartbeat. "Right. Let's go." Hakan dived back into the storeroom and reemerged seconds later, car keys in one hand, jacket in the other. The little man was already pulling the outside door open.

"Hakan!" Tomat Meltz snapped. "Just where do you think you're going? You're paid to help in this store, and the business day has just begun. If you think you can go running off on some—on some *skevitt chase*—"

"See you later, Dad," Hakan called as he charged through the door on his friend's heels. "I'm going to drive Cory home."

Tomat Meltz stood staring at the place where his son had been, then shook himself and walked carefully over to the door. He opened it to the roar of acceleration: Hakan was driving Cory home.

Zamir Meltz closed the door, walked back to the counter, and resumed his accounting. He was smiling, just a little.

SHALTREN

Cessilee

The Stelubia Delegation were not sufficiently impressed. Worse, they had apparently begun preliminary negotiations with that upstart of an O'Hand, who thought himself so safe in his rat's nest on Daphyd. Well, let him continue to think so yet a while; a lesson would shortly be forthcoming. But first Stelubia had to be secured.

Grom Trogar smiled and settled his dark glasses more firmly on his nose, aware of the comforting pressure of the weapon against his ribs, beneath his jacket.

"It is true," he acknowledged thoughtfully, "that the Juntavas has many detractors, all busily crying out that our power is failing, that even now we are ripe for the plucking. You will have noticed, I am certain, that the few attempts to pluck us have been checked, the ringleaders...punished." He smiled again, though none of the other six around the table joined him.

"It will perhaps be instructive for you to consider the individuals now held by the Juntavas, awaiting our disposal. I offer this instruction because it would sadden me, gentles, most deeply, if you were tricked into making a decision of alliance that might prove—painful—to all parties concerned."

He touched the appropriate disk on the panel before him, and the large screen to his left lit, showing the interior of the specially reinforced metal room with its metal table and chairs, in which was—

Nothing else at all.

Grow Trogar gaped. The proportions of the hole in the farther wall were quite modest, considering the size of the largest of the two escapees—a sharp-edged rectangle showing a glimpse of the hallway beyond. The steel sheet that had once been part of the wall had been pulled to one side and laid upon the floor, as if those who had cut it away had expended some care to insure that none would trip over it and injure themselves.

He was on his feet, moving through the door of his office and sweeping past the receptionist's desk. Tricked! They had tricked him! Well, it would be their last trick. A sad pity, indeed, that a being might reach the exalted age of eight or nine hundred Standards and yet be unable to recognize a man who will not be bested.

He did not have to go far to find them. At the main hall, he stopped, staring while the two of them sauntered forward, apparently intending to leave by the front entrance, as if they were not already dead.

Grom Trogar strode up to them, planted his legs wide, and glared, secure in the knowledge of the weapon that rode against his heart.

"Stupid reptiles!" he cried, oblivious to the six who had followed him out of his office; oblivious, as well, to the others summoned by the alarm system: security guards, unit managers, emergency personnel. "So you value your lives as little as that! You come onto my planet, into my city, dare to bargain with *me* for the lives of a Terran bitch and a Liaden Scout! You repudiate my judgment, question my power! You have greatly overstepped, Aged Ones. And now we shall see the price to be paid."

"Grom Trogar," the one called Edger rumbled, "you are obviously in a haste so great that it is harmful. You do not understand the meaning of the words you speak. We will allow you time to compose yourself and call together a Council of Elders, then we shall return to talk further. In reason and calmness—"

"Silence!" the man roared, riding his rage like a fire-crested wave. Was he a child to be so instructed? No! He was Grom Trogar, the ultimate voice of the mightiest network of power and wealth in all the galaxy!

"This ceases to be amusing, Aged One. Know that there is no Council of Elders to heed your ridiculous bargains, nor shall I create such a thing to placate you. Know also that the entire Juntavas shall be charged with hunting down Miri Robertson and your filthy, murdering Scout of a brother. And when they are found, I promise you that it will take them quite a long time to die. It will be amusing, I think, to have a Scout beg me for death. Almost as amusing as it will be to kill you, Aged One. This feud is between you and me—and you cannot win it."

Sheather shifted, perceived his brother's sign, and regained stillness, though there was something pricking him to attention that made his hand long for his blade…

"Grom Trogar," Edger repeated, "you are in harmful haste. Perhaps you are even ill. You cannot mean that you desire a personal feud between you and me. Consider yourself; consider what the blades of Middle River have already wrought within this place. A duel between us two is sheerest folly. Reconsider your words. We will return in some days and have calmer speech." He inclined his head and turned aside, meaning to detour around the man.

The weapon flared as Grom Trogar brought it from beneath his jacket; it hummed as he thumbed it to life and brought it up, aiming for the vulnerable spot, where neck met shoulder armor.

It is true that the members of the Clutch are often slow. But not *always* slow. Grom Trogar screamed once before his body understood that it was dead and slumped to the floor beside the evil, humming thing, his blood already pooling about it.

Edger turned to look long at his brother Sheather, then turned again to study the pitiful, soft man impaled upon the glowing crystal blade and the gun humming to itself in the growing pool of red.

Not a sound came from the humans all around.

"What say you, brother?" Edger asked gently.

Sheather bowed his head. "In defense of the T'carais I did strike. The weapon—the weapon, brother! It was no clean thing he sought, decided between two, with honor, with justice. Only to slay..." His sister's voice whispered in his heart; he stopped himself and raised his head to look into the eyes of his T'carais and his eldest brother. "If I have been in error, I do accept the penalty. Strike surely, brother!"

As T'carais, Edger made the sign of negation; as eldest brother, he added the sign of honored esteem. "Retrieve your blade. The blow was rightly dealt, in defense of T'carais and Clan." He raised his luminous eyes to the still-silent, watching humans.

"As for the weapon..." Edger sang a song consisting of seven notes, three of which human ears were not capable of hearing.

Grom Trogar's blood steamed where it pooled about the weapon as the power pack ruptured, leaked energy. There was a *flash!* of pinpoint light, a *snap!* of sound—and the weapon was molten metal, mixing with liquid red.

Finally, from the humans all about came a stir, a sound—a drawing close together and a drawing a little apart. One stepped forward to bow.

"I am called Sambra Reallen, Chairman Pro Tem," she said softly. "How may I serve you, Aged Ones?"

VANDAR

Springbreeze Farm

Hakan drove with the same casual intensity that characterized his guitar-playing. His eyes and hands worked together, and Val Con found that portion of himself which measured such things gauging the other man's reaction times.

They were approaching a patch of ice that had caused Zhena Trelu considerable anxiety on the way in, but Hakan did not even seem to notice that it was there. They were over and past it, with only the barest hint of instantly corrected skid.

Pilot material, this one, Val Con thought.

"Hakan," he said quietly. "I have said there is danger at home. Maybe it is not only danger for Miri; I do not know. It could be danger for you, too. I think that we should stop before..."

Hakan slowed the car, changed gears before they were fully out of the dipping curve, and accelerated again, shaking his head. "Not to worry. I said I'd take you home, didn't I? I'll help you, too. You say there's trouble, and I *believe* it—you've got such feeling about things." He glanced over, smiling. "I never had a chance to play with anybody who catches things so quickly—not just the notes, but the full spirit of the music. I think you live life that way, too. So I think you *know* that something's wrong."

Val Con frowned. "I have just said that I *don't* know," he reminded softly, but Hakan cut him off with a wave of his hand.

"Look, if Miri's hurt herself somehow, I had the medic course when I was in the militia. And I was in the volunteer fire department until the politics bored me out of it. I can help, whatever trouble."

"And will you take orders from me?" Val Con asked. "Will you do as I say, without talking, if there is a big danger?"

"You're the boss," Hakan said. Val Con clamped his mouth on a gasp. The other glanced at him. "You'd help me, wouldn't you? If it was Kem?"

"Yes..."

"Well, there you are," Hakan said.

Val Con rolled down the window in the door, letting the sharp air wash against his face, then reached out and touched that special place in his mind: *Alive-and-well.*

The covered bridge loomed—then quickly they were through it, boards rattling and car shaking, at a pace Zhena Trelu would have considered sheerest folly.

"You have been in the militia," Val Con murmured. "Have you been to war?"

"No. Hasn't been a war in these parts for a long, long time. I helped out after the explosion at the fireworks factory in Carnady, though. Folks said that was a lot like a war."

Val Con shifted, growing uneasier as the farm came closer. His mind was demanding reactions from him—*weapons, fight,* even *kill*—and he took a deep breath, consciously imposing calm while he took inventory. Edger's blade rode secure in his sleeve. He bent and slipped the throwing blade from the top of his work boot.

If Hakan noticed the knife, he said nothing.

"Do you have any weapons at all, Hakan?"

"You're really serious, huh? Yeah. I got a half-and-half there in the back, somewhere under everything."

Val Con turned in his seat, groping among guitar cases and sheet music.

A half-and-half, it turned out, was a large-bore weapon with a small-bore weapon overtop.

"It isn't much." Hakan's voice was unusually serious. "I've got a few shot shells, and there should be plenty of—"

"Explosives?" Val Con demanded, eyeing the shell meant for the larger bore.

Hakan choked a laugh. "No, *shot* shells—for birds and varmints at close range. The rifle has more range, but it's only for plinking, really...though I guess you could hurt somebody."

Val Con hefted it, understood the loading and firing. "Recoil?"

"Well, the shot..."

Stupid thing, Val Con thought. "Keep it for you," he said to Hakan.

They heard a sound: something uncommon over the sound of car and wind.

"Slow down," Val Con murmured, but Hakan had already done so.

The sound came again.

"Guns!" Hakan snapped, jamming the speed back on.

"Rapid-firing guns. Hakan, this may be very bad. You will listen, and you will do as I say. When we are close to the house. I will get out. If you see that I go no closer, or if I wave at you—go back to Gylles! Go back, but burn the bridge behind you. *Burn* it, Hakan, and tell the people that there is war here!"

They topped the last small hill, and Hakan cut the power to the engine, letting the car drift through the little clump of trees and into the farmyard.

Val Con finished loading the half-and-half, flipped the safety off, and laid it on the seat.

Four bodies in dirty uniforms lay in a group before the porch; two had been shot in the back.

Hakan gripped the gun, his good-natured face grim and a trifle pale. "Miri?"

"In the house, I think," Val Con said. He was gone in an instant, slipping noiselessly from the passenger seat and closing the door without a sound.

Hakan put the car in gear, let it drift back the few yards to the road, and pulled the keys out of the ignition. Guns clattered, shockingly close, and he froze, but the sound died away to nothing. Cautiously he opened the glovebox under the driver's seat and took out his militia cap.

The cap firmly on his head, it occurred to him to wonder if a militia corporal and a knife-wielding foreigner would be enough to stop an invasion force.

Then he thought what Cory must have thought: Miri's in there! Car keys in pocket, half-and-half held ready, the militia began to infiltrate.

Val Con stood invisibly in the shaded underbrush that Zhena Trelu called shrubbery, listening. From the house came the sound of voices speaking excitedly in an unknown language; nearer at hand was a whimpering noise. Blade in hand, he moved toward the smaller sound.

A bloody bundle of cloth—*No!* His eyes closed in protest, even as he reached for the glowing part within: *Alive-and-well, alive-and-well.* He let the song and the brightness have his attention for a full minute before putting it aside.

Viewed through calmer eyes, the bundle was fur, not cloth: Borril lay wedged between a thickly needled bush and the side of the house. His tail beat raggedly against the ground; his bloody head was propped against the wall.

Val Con fingered his throwing blade, keeping very still; he heard the voices of many men from inside the house and the sound of gunfire, close. Hesitantly, almost retching in revulsion, he reached into his own mind, located the switch he had never wanted to use again, and thought the Thought...

He receded from himself, fear burning away like fog as he gained the distance taught by the instructors of agents. His current mission was not some remotely patriotic killing of an anti-Liaden fanatic: his mission was to save Miri. He struggled mentally to open that walled-off portion of his mind, then nearly reeled as the programs ran his thoughts, stretching and erasing him...

> STATEMENT OF MISSION OBJECTIVE: Preserve Miri Robertson from attacking military forces and drive forces from base.
> LIMITATIONS: None
> MISSION PRIORITY: Ultimate
> ACCEPTABLE DAMAGE TO AGENT: Priority Override
> PAIN THRESHOLD: Disallow
> FULL AUTOMATIC: Yes
> ANALYSIS LOOP: Chance of Mission Success: .37
> GO: Go

In the initial training, each phase had taken hours to fulfill, then minutes, then seconds. Now it was simply the time it took to make the decision, to think the Thought: PRIORITY GOAL ACCEPTED.

He was more than pilot-fast, more than mercenary-accurate, more than berserker-deadly. He was again fully an Agent of Change. He blinked.

Dog and bush blurred just slightly out of focus; Val Con blinked again—yes. The creature before him had a good chance of survival, if it managed to live through the firefight. The wounds were not themselves mortal, though extended loss of blood could kill it. Alive or dead, it was not essential to the mission.

He slipped away, angling toward the house and the low window that looked out from the so-called formal dining room. Glass glittered in shards on the earth before him; the window frame itself was smashed and twisted. A soldier, his neck broken, lay just inside the room.

Analysis indicated that the kill had been made by Miri Robertson. Val Con went through the twisted frame; he heard a sound as his feet touched the floor; he spun and threw.

The guard moved before he died, making quite a bit of noise as blood welled into his throat.

"Kwtel?" a voice called from the next room.

Val Con ran to the body, pulled the clumsy sidearm from the dead grasp, found the safety switch, though he did not know if it was engaged or not, jerked the blade free, and spun to face the door.

"Kwtel?" the voice demanded again, louder and accompanied by the sound of several pairs of heavy boots moving across carpeted floors.

The first soldier's head came through the doorway.

Click!

That one, too, died by blade, but he fell before another, who was armed and began to fire instantly.

Val Con dove for the scant cover of the wooden dining table, yanked the safety to the proper notch and fired, shuddering with the recoil.

Screaming, the enemy dropped to the floor, hands at his face. Val Con fired again, and the noise stopped.

He damned himself briefly for poor shooting. Chance of Personal Survival showed as unknown for the action, seventy-five percent for the next minute. From the floor above came the sound of many feet, then a short burst of gunfire.

Retrieving his knife, he slipped down the hallway. The radio in the front parlor was playing, loud in the shocking stillness.

The kitchen was empty. He was turning to go when a familiar electrical *click* sent him diving across the room to snatch the receiver up before the bell sounded.

"Hello? This is Athna Brigsbee—"

"Shut up!" he snapped. "Emergency and danger! Send—"

"Cory? Will you tell me what's going on? I never, in—"

"Shut up, Brigsbee! Call army; call militia—enemy invasion!" As he spoke, the ugly sound of heavy automatic weapons began outside the house, answered by an odd *snap-snap-snap* barely louder than a pellet pistol.

"Invaders? Invaders! Oh, my word! Cory—where's Estra?"

"Estra okay, Miri missing. You call police—army. I go."

He let the phone down to dangle from its wire and, after momentary consideration, cut the outside wire.

From high in the house came four measured shots and, a moment later, three more.

Miri! Very faintly Val Con was aware of relief, then he was moving back toward the dining room.

The handgun held only three more shots, and he hefted one of the fallen long-arms. It was dirty, corroded in several spots, and had only seven rounds in the magazine. He thought he would be lucky if it worked at all; and the recoil might slow him.

A volley of shots sounded from upstairs, a high-pitched keening riding above: the Gyrfalks' battle cry!

More shots from upstairs; the rumble of booted feet, running; voices, shouting; pounding— Val Con was moving, taking the stairs three at a time, lugging the stupid weapons with him.

At the top of the stair was a crowd of soldiers, their backs toward him, watching the one who had apparently just broken in the attic door.

The heavy rifle was up and firing at the backs of heads—he managed three shots before the gun jammed, and he brought the pistol up to kill three more.

A shot was fired wildly from the left. Val Con dodged, cuffed the soldier heavily across the face with the spent pistol, and stepped to the next, knife out.

The confined space made it hard for the remaining soldiers to react. Behind, all they saw was smoke and the surging motions of someone demented.

One of the enemies dropped his weapon. Another followed suit, speaking sounds that might have meant surrender. Val Con found a soldier with a gun in his hand and killed him with a blade thrust. He looked for more, but saw only weak weaponless creatures, cowering before him.

From the attic came several more measured shots, then surrender sounds there, as well, and the Gyrfalks' keen.

Val Con lunged forward, snatched up a fallen weapon, and held it on the six survivors as he worked his way to the base of the attic stairs.

"Friend?" The word was in Terran, the voice husky and familiar.

Val Con hesitated, groping for a switch that slid from his mind-grip, and located an adequate response. "Cha'trez."

They heard another burst of gunfire outside. Hakan? Was Hakan there?

Down the attic stairs came a red-haired woman, pushing several unarmed enemies before her. She carried a well-oiled, wood-clad rifle; a stickknife of Liaden Scout issue was thrust through her belt.

She shoved her prisoners among his six and came to his side, looking worriedly into his face. "What took you so long?"

There was a sudden racket outside, punctuated by the sound of automatic guns.

"Guard them!" Val Con snapped, and rushed off, running silently down the stairs.

Miri stood very still, then looked at her prisoners and asked them very plainly, in Terran, *"Now* where's he gone to?"

Her tone must have sounded extremely threatening; they backed as a shivering group into Zhena Trelu's upstairs parlor, one of them tenderly helping the boy with the smashed nose and swollen eye.

Miri sat on the arm of the sewing chair, rifle ready across her knees. Her prisoners sat carefully on the floor and avoided looking at her.

"We won, I guess," she said, after a time and to no one in particular. "Hot damn."

LIAD

Dispassion. Control. Calculation. Success.

Tyl Von sig'Alda reviewed those concepts as he walked to the conference room. No hint of anything other than confidence escaped him; the occasional agent he passed registered no sign of doubt; the underlings and clerks averted their eyes, in the usual deference to an Agent of Change.

He had spent two days writing the report that outlined his reasoning, his deductions, the probabilities cited by his Loop, and his suggested course of action.

A bare quarter-shift after he had submitted it, he had received orders to attend the upcoming meeting. He had three days, then, to wait inside the deep complex, the underground control center that would one day be the command post for a galaxy. Three days to reconsider and to seek his own errors, while the Department moved deliberately on with the Plan.

The problem: the Terran female. The other problem: yos'Phelium himself.

The Loop flickered, indicating that he would reach the conference room within fifteen seconds of his targeted time.

He had been thorough, he assured himself; the report had been dispassionate. Calculating. Controlled.

Success...The door was before him.

Opening the door was proof enough of success.

The room was arranged for a working meeting: enough chairs but no more, an erasable board with supplies, and people waiting—for *him*. There was no interrupted conversation, no surprise.

The commander was there; his presence explained the careful scheduling of the meeting. The three others were his weapons master from first training, the shift biomed specialist, and the exotic pharmaceuticals specialist.

One chair remained empty. Tyl Von sig'Alda bowed to the room and sat down. Five chairs for the table with five equal sides—

an eloquent statement of the meeting's melant'i. All who sat there were met as experts, to teach and learn equally.

"Agent," the commander said gravely. "Your report has been read and analyzed. Additional factors beyond your prior scope of operation and information have been considered. We meet to synthesize an entirely appropriate response to the situation. The Department takes this matter to be of the utmost seriousness."

sig'Alda bowed his head in acknowledgment. Not merely important, but of the utmost seriousness…He touched the Loop; accessed the program allowing concentration on all levels.

"We concur in your assessment that yos'Phelium's genes and Clan environment have contributed to his success as an agent—and to the current uncertainties. Clan Korval tends toward maverick. That they are Liaden is more accident than intent. That they are a success cannot be denied. You have seen the files: They search for yos'Phelium even as we speak. More, Korval begins to meddle in our affairs—the First Speaker mentions us all too frequently in public conversations; subtle inquiries arise in strange places.

"We have considered eliminating the current leader, Nova yos'Galan. The house is tainted with Terran blood—" The commander paused and looked around the small table. "Actions reducing the leadership of Korval have occurred in the past. The timing of a new trimming must be weighed carefully. We do not, for example, know why they pursue their kin so ardently. Is it merely 'Clan business'? Is there a deeper plan? Do they intend to supplant us in controlling Liad's interests in space? Of all the Clans, only Korval might mount a respectable military threat against Liad without allies."

sig'Alda found the weight of the commander's eyes upon him alone.

"Understand that Val Con yos'Phelium's recruitment as an Agent was a five-year program requiring expenditure of several operatives, as well as much cost. His usefulness to the Department extends among many lines of action, not the least of which has been his extreme effectiveness in carrying out assignments on our behalf. That he leaves Korval in the hands of a half-blooded merchant family we intended, eventually, to exploit.

"Therefore, every contingency you mentioned in your report, and many others, have been analyzed. The possibility that Clan Korval

might attempt to reclaim yos'Phelium and secure him as Delm—
that alone—would make our search worthwhile. His knowledge
must not fall into half-blood hands. He must not be subverted to
use what he has learned from us—for the preservation of Liad!—
for the sole gain of Clan Korval. His abilities...Tyl Von sig'Alda,
this will be your most important assignment as an Agent of Change.
You will locate and return Agent yos'Phelium to us. If he is dead,
you will bring us a body, bones, witnesses."

The commander had named him! He nearly missed the bow
to the biomed specialist. That man began at once.

"The working model assumes you will locate yos'Phelium and
be required to secure him physically. To do so you must be aware
of certain factors." The man stood, grabbed up a point-writer, and
began marking on the message surface.

"Your information package contains complete graphs. The
overview is this: One, Korval seems purposefully aimed at achiev-
ing speed and accuracy of reflex in its members. Only a pilot may
become Delm; Delm's genes are those most likely to be passed on.

"Our tests show that, under normal circumstances, yos'Phelium's
response time is a measurable three to four percent faster than yours.
In certain high-stress situations tested during training his responses
were another two percent faster yet. You, of course, have continued to train and have a newer implementation of the Probability
Loop—we project that, effectively, you are his equal. Lack of vitamins, isolation, depression, injuries—your report indicates he received
combat damage—such factors suggest an advantage to you, should
he need to be reminded of his loyalties. We give you charts, as I
mentioned. Also—" The biomed man nodded across the table.

"At the commander's urging we have considered other possibilities," the pharmacist said, "and have developed a new design of
perceptual stimulants. These enhance the ability of the brain to process information received from the senses, thus increasing the ability
of the agent to respond rapidly and efficiently to outside stimuli."

She frowned severely at sig'Alda. "These stimulants are not to
be used during Jump; they should not be used at a rate of more than
six doses per Standard day. Note that only under extreme emergency conditions should you take three doses together. Take one if
you consider action likely, another if action is imminent or carries a
high risk factor.

"A muscle-tone enhancer will also be supplied: See me, it is an implant." With that, the pharmacist fell silent.

The commander spoke almost softly. "Your analysis of Val Con yos'Phelium's actions during recent events, Agent sig'Alda, is inconclusive in the extreme. We have gained no insight into the reasons or the circumstances contributing to yos'Phelium's use of the Terran mercenary. Others, however, have studied the mercenary with care."

sig'Alda felt the rebuke keenly, understanding that he might have followed his original urge to discover more.

The commander's pause was brief—enough to emphasize, not enough to require an answer. "Therapy records indicate a difficult case," he went on. "The Terran escaped from rehabilitative isolation several times during the course of treatment, and the doctor's final report reads merely: 'Subject no longer chemically dependent upon Lethecronaxion.' Our analysis of this phrasing indicates continued psychological dependence. This offers opportunity for manipulation."

The pharmacist touched a pocket and brought out several, small, plastic bags containing an ivory colored powder.

"This bag," she said, holding it out to him, "has a red dot on the seal. It is standard Lethecronaxion inasmuch as any drug of this kind is standard—of extremely high quality. Therapy records indicate the subject had a tendency to synergize this, ah, *Cloud,* with alcohol, thus becoming forgetful and intractable at once. The dose here is adequate for a large Terran male; the addict will be familiar with ingestion techniques."

sig'Alda was aware of uneasiness and touched the Loop for calm. Addicts...His dislike faded under the Loop exercise, and he once more gave the specialist full attention.

"This bag has a blue dot." She handed it to him. "It has the same overall weight, a double-strength dose of Cloud, and a time-release double dose of something you are well familiar with: MemStim."

sig'Alda smiled at the blue dot. Of course!

"Yes," the pharmacist said, apparently pleased with his approval. "Agents use MemStim while reporting to aid the exact recall of events. This particular mix also contains a disinhibitor and an experimental receptor flush-and-bind." The pharmacist dared a smile of her own. "I designed the packets several days ago. Tests on subjects of the approximate mass of the Terran show interesting effects.

"Initial effect is unremarkable to Lethecronaxion: all memory older than a few hours, and, later, memory older than a few minutes, becomes uncertain, clouded—hence the vernacular designation. At the time release, the flush was nearly instantaneous, throwing the subjects from complete cloud-effect to a deep MemStim state. The beauty of the flush-and-bind system is that it ties the MemStim to those receptors most affected by the Lethecronaxion. An addict—or, for that matter, anyone who takes MemStim—has trained receptor sites; in the case of a Cloud user, these sites are most likely to be triggers to painful memories, else why cloud them?" The pharmacist paused, glanced at the commander, and received a wave that indicated she should continue.

"Thus the subjects went from total repression of unwanted memories to a total and enhanced recall. Depending on the amount of alcohol and disinhibitor in their systems, subjects recalled their memories to the point of reexperience. Variously, subjects attempted suicide, became delirious, bit and clawed at themselves, or were otherwise incoherent for periods exceeding half a Standard day. I expect that when the receptor-stimulus time is reached—that is, when another fix is required—there will be another period of disorder."

sig'Alda placed the packets carefully into his belt. The Loop showed a ten-percent gain in Chance of Mission Success, stipulating the opportunity to introduce the mixed drugs to the Terran.

The commander bowed to the drug expert, then toward the weapons man, who began to speak.

"We've run an analysis on yos'Phelium's mission reports and compared it with known events in the recent unreported mission. We have the following guidelines and comparisons." He took a breath, fixed his eyes on a spot above sig'Alda's head, and began.

"First, we have uncovered a bias. The Department had been taking advantage of yos'Phelium's ability to operate close to his targets. This consideration figured in his last mission—terminating an upper-level Terran agent in a bombproofed building. A more carefully factored reading shows that Agent yos'Phelium has a tendency to use a knife or other bladed weapon far more frequently than would have been expected from his training. This affinity leaves him vulnerable to middistance pacification by projectile weapons. He has a good-to-excellent rating with pellet weapons, but Agent sig'Alda's rating is within the margin of error."

The weapons master deigned to meet sig'Alda's eyes. "You," he said calmly, "will take extra practice with a variety of weapons before leaving. You will be equal to yos'Phelium at his best. We have tapes of his practices, and a competition program will be constructed for your practice sessions." He paused and redirected his eyes to a point above sig'Alda's head. "Given Agent yos'Phelium's tendency toward bladed weapons, it is suggested that Agent sig'Alda wear flexi-mesh."

The commander bowed to the three experts. "Your reports are most useful."

The dismissal was clear, and they all rose. sig'Alda stood, as well, but at a glance from the commander he sat again as the experts left the room. Dispassion, control, he repeated to himself.

"Your desire to pursue your mission immediately is appreciated, sig'Alda," the commander said. "You will consider yourself to be on mission now; you will leave this building only to leave the planet under orders. I will now address a resource with which you cannot be familiar."

The commander stood, went to the door, and set the portal locks. Then glancing at a wrist device, he rotated in place.

sig'Alda felt confusion and astonishment. The commander was checking for a spy, here, within the heart of the Department?

The commander returned and sat, hand on table so that the wrist-warn could be seen clearly by both.

"You are among our most excellent agents," he said. "And the one we seek is also among our most excellent agents. Understand this completely and explicitly: Your mission is to find Val Con yos'Phelium and return with him. If he is dead you will provide explicit and complete proof. If you find him alive and he refuses, in spite of all your best persuasions, to return—then you will bring explicit and complete proof that he is dead. His head will do for proof; or several portions of his spinal column."

sig'Alda blinked.

"Yes. I give you precedence. Do you understand?"

"Yes." sig'Alda bowed. "yos'Phelium is to return, even if under extreme compulsion."

"Exactly. We must not, at this juncture in the Plan, allow any Clan an opportunity to question our goals or to subvert our information. Now— extreme compulsion takes several forms. Death is but one of them.

"You have heard it mentioned that your training came after yos'Phelium's. Certain safeguards available to you are not available to him. You, for example, may go into 'Hold'; keeping yourself and your mind closed to outside interference until brought back by a special command issued by myself. This avoids the possibility of interrogation. Earlier implementations were not as secure, nor were they self-activated.

"There is a set sequence of phrase and echo built into Agent yos'Phelium's Loop. When you present the beginning of the sequence, he will respond—he must. If you continue, he must continue. At the conclusion of this sequence, yos'Phelium will be as a tractable imbecile: He will follow orders without question."

The commander glanced at the wrist telltale, then back at the rapt sig'Alda. "You will be the third person to know this sequence. You will not, under any circumstances, divulge or discuss this with anyone but myself or my successor. Do you understand?"

"Yes, Commander."

"Good. Tyl Von sig'Alda clare try qwit—"

He blinked. The phrase had not quite made sense.

The commander was smiling. "All is well, Tyl Von. When the sequence is needed, it is yours by repeating yos'Phelium's name, and then 'clare try qwit glass fer.'"

The commander extended a hand. In it was a small blue pin in the shape of a Liaden glow-gull in full flight.

"You are my deputy, Tyl Von sig'Alda. You may not fail." The agent took the badge of trust and bowed, momentarily touching the commander's cold hand. There was nothing to say.

VANDAR

Hellin's Surcease

Val Con settled comfortably in the chair, leaned his head back, closed his eyes, and consciously discounted the sounds being made in other parts of the house by Hakan and his father. He checked heartbeat and respiration and found both within the tolerances for physical relaxation. The Loop was quiet—there was nothing, after all, to calculate, the mission being three days done—and his mind was clear. His status was that of an agent in excellent overall condition.

Deliberately, maintaining calm, he sought the switch level and the switch.

He noted resistance, a flicker that might have been Loop-phenomenon, and a slight acceleration of respiration.

Patiently, he brought his breathing back down and called the logic grid to prime consciousness:

The mission is done. There is no need for the agent to be on constant standby. The switch exists and has tested well in initial action. There is no reason to suspect that it will fail in another instance.

Resistance faded. Val Con achieved the switch level almost immediately and perceived the thing he had constructed within himself on Edger's ship, using the L'apeleka exercises Edger had taught him. He withdrew his whole attention to the switch level, concentrating only on the switch, then reached forth—

Heart rate spiked and he was half out of the chair, gripping the arm rests, gasping, eyes open but seeing inward, where the loop reported Chance of Mission Success at .03.

"Cory?"

He was fully out of the chair at that, spinning to face the intruder, heart stuttering back to normality, CMS fading from his inner eye.

Hakan was holding two mugs, steam gently curling from each. He held one out. "Want some tea?"

"Thank you." Val Con took the thing, slid back into his chair, and looked up at the younger man, seeing trouble in the soft blue eyes.

"Can I talk to you, Cory? About—about what happened."

The battle. Val Con inclined his head, and a measure of relief seemed to enter Hakan's face as he sat on the chair opposite. He stared into his mug.

"The newssheets say we're heroes," the musician said.

That was not new information; the four royal princes who had come over during the last three days to shake their hands had said the same thing, as had the commander of the militia mop-up squadron. Val Con waited.

Hakan looked up, mustache drooping, eyes as sharp as nearsightedness would allow. "Do you feel like a hero, Cory?"

Val Con sighed gently. "Hakan, how do I know?"

"Right," Hakan's gaze dropped to the mug again. "I feel rotten. I—" Then he looked up again, and it seemed that his eyes were filled with tears. "I killed three men. *Three.*" He turned to look at the window, voice dropping. "How many did you kill?"

Memory provided an exact tally. "More than three." Val Con sipped his tea. "You did well. Hakan, you did your duty. Besides the three dead, you wounded many and kept them from fighting. Remember that you were armed with only a gun for hunting—"

"That's it!" The other man's face was alight with passion. "That's it exactly! I felt like I was *hunting,* not...The one guy, he was—running through the brush, and I knew he was going to have to jump the stream and I just waited for him, Cory. Played him like he was a stag; and when he jumped, I—" His voice cracked, but his passion impelled him to finish. "He jumped and I killed him; and then I was on to the next guy—and I never felt anything, except that *that* was taken care of..."

A cool head in battle and the reactions of a pilot. Corrective surgery for the myopia and a bit of training, and he might well have been an adequate agent. Val Con sipped tea.

"You were in the militia. Did they tell you that you might need to kill in battle?" He paused. "You own a gun to hunt with. You say you have hunted and killed before."

"But not a *man,*" Hakan whispered. "I'd never killed a man before, Cory."

"Ah." Val Con considered the reddish depths of his tea. Why does he come to me? he wondered irritably. And he answered himself in the next breath: You were the Agent in Charge. To whom else would he go?

"It is—sad," he began slowly, eyes still turned down, "that men must be killed in battle. It would be better if no person ever—needed—to kill another person." He sighed, groping after concepts that should not be so tenuous, beliefs that had no strength of conviction, though he knew, somewhere very deep within himself, that he believed them with a passion that shadowed Hakan's grief. "The thing you did—the man who jumped and died. That man carried a—a big gun—a *heavy-automatic.* Is that right?"

"You saw him? Yeah, he was carrying a thalich gun. I used one once, in the militia. Thing can really tear up a target."

"So. Think about that man, with that gun, and one more man to guard his back—think about that man on Main Street in Gylles." He glanced up, saw that Hakan was looking vaguely ill, and pushed the point home. "One man, one gun—how many would *he* have killed? People who were unarmed, who were not soldiers, or—children, shopkeepers. Zhena Trelu. Kem."

He leaned forward and touched the other man's arm. Such a gesture seemed required. "You did well, Hakan. I can see no way in which you could have done better, after you decided to disobey me and stay."

Hakan actually grinned, though the expression was a little wobbly around the edges. "Well, what could I do? Miri was in there, and you go walking up to the house, just as cool—with a *knife,* for—I thought at least I could, you know, create a diversion. Keep the guys who were outside busy, so they didn't decide to go in the house. Give you and Miri a chance to get out alive."

"You achieved your goal. You lived through the battle. You have found abilities inside you that you did not know were there. All of this is good, Hakan."

Val Con shifted uncertainly. "You asked me—I have never met a hero. I don't know what a hero feels like. I think that it doesn't matter how *many* men you kill. I think that only animals kill without sadness, even when there is no choice except to kill. I think—you have not been playing your guitar, Hakan. When I have been—troubled—before, I found it was—good—to play music. To let the music help—sort out what has happened."

"Neither one of us has been playing," Hakan agreed. "Might be a good idea—" He made a determined effort, and the grin this time was much better. "There's still Winterfair to practice for, you know." He tipped his head. "My father's got a council meeting tonight. I'll invite Kem over for dinner, and we can practice after, okay?"

Practice? Music? Panic was noted; was contained. "All right…"

Hakan was looking at him sharply. "Maybe we could slide by and pick up Miri, too. Bet she's ready to go bats, being cooped up in a house with Zhena Trelu and Zhena Brigsbee."

Miri? Something else was added to the panic and quickly suppressed. "I don't think so, Hakan, thank you."

There was a pause, the expression on the younger man's face unreadable. "Well, okay, man. If you change your mind, though…"

"Thank you, Hakan."

THE WIDE UNIVERSE

The courier ship flashed into existence at the edge of the system, broadcasting on all frequencies, then skipping back into hyperspace on the third repetition of its message.

On Philomen, Cheever McFarland blinked at the radio and then at his employer. "Relative of yours?"

Pat Rin yos'Phelium turned a bland face toward him, brown eyes depthless and unreadable. "yos'Phelium is kin to yos'Phelium, certainly. You will have this matter here corrected in how soon a time?"

Cheever thought strenuously. "If I do it right, she'll be ready to go round midnight. But I can cut a few corners and get us out sooner."

Pat Rin raised elegant eyebrows. "I anticipate no need for haste, Pilot. Continue with your work." At the exit hatch he turned and bowed, very slightly. "Please."

The hatch cycled and he was gone.

Half a quadrant away, Shadia Ne'Zame snapped upright in the pilot's chair, slapped the tracer into action, got a line on the ship—and lost it as she vanished into Jump.

"Master Class piloting there, Shadia," she told herself, "which you could well emulate. Now, what's to do?"

She tapped the log for the recording, frowning.

Nev'lorn's quarters absorbed the message, even as two of the Guard dropped out of formation and shot after the courier. Halfway across the Access, the interloper faded, along with one Guard ship. The other executed a showy tumble and headed back to her post.

"Lost him," a cheerful young voice reported to Master Com. "But Cha Lor had him dead on."

Clonak ter'Meulen logged the response and replayed the courier ship's message. He was still frowning when his shiftmate came to relieve him.

"Broadbeam just caught, Cap'n." Rusty handed over a sheet of hardcopy with a slight forward tilt of his portly body. "Thought you'd want to see it."

"Bowing, Rusty? Lina must be teaching you manners."

"She tries, off and on." The other man was watching him closely, concern evident in face and pattern. Shan rustled the sheet and looked down.

ATTENTION ATTENTION ATTENTION. ALL JUNTAVAS EMPLOYEES, SUPPORTERS, DEPENDENTS, ALLIES SHALL FROM RECEIPT OF THIS MESSAGE FORWARD RENDER ASSISTANCE, AID, AND COMFORT TO SERGEANT MIRI ROBERTSON, CITIZEN OF TERRA, AND SCOUT COMMANDER VAL CON YOS'PHELIUM, CITIZEN OF LIAD; REDIVERTING, WHERE NECESSARY, YOUR OWN ACTIVITIES. REPEAT: AID AND COMFORT TO MIRI ROBERTSON AND/OR VAL CON YOS'PHELIUM IMPERATIVE, PRIORITY HIGHEST.

MESSAGE REPEATS...

"How lovely to have a Clutch Turtle with one's interest at heart," Shan murmured around the cold feeling in his stomach. He looked up and smiled into Rusty's worried eyes. "Pin-beam a copy to my sister if you please, Rusty."

"Yessir." He hesitated, then blurted, "Is everything okay?"

"Everything's okay," Shan said, as if he were comforting a child. "The Juntavas have taken my brother and his lady under their wing—which you must admit is far superior to having them hunt you from one corner of the galaxy to the other."

"Sure..." Hesitancy was plain in the round, uncomplicated face.

Shan gripped Rusty's arm. "Old friend. My brother has gotten himself into a bit of a scrape." He rattled the paper. "This appears to balance the matter."

"So everything's fine," the other summed up, hope glittering bright.

"Everything is fine," Shan said, and wondered, as he watched Rusty walk away, if that was a lie or the truth.

VANDAR

Hellin's Surcease

"But that's—" Kem turned around in the passenger's seat and stared at him. "Hakan, Cory and Miri are *married*. How can she be staying with Zhena Trelu and letting Cory stay with you?"

Hakan shrugged. "Militia captain split us up that way and told us to stay available. I don't think he realized they were married—and Cory just muttered something about her being safe now." He cast his mind back with an effort. "Don't think Miri liked it too much myself."

"I should think not." Kem eyed her fiancé worriedly, decided that talking about something was better than allowing him to lapse into another un-Hakanish silence, and put forward the idea that they might make a detour and pick Miri up before going home. "They'll *have* to talk to each other then."

"I asked Cory if I should swing over and get Miri. He said it wasn't a good time." Peering through the thickening snow, Hakan carefully slowed the car to turn into Berner's Lane. "Leave it alone, Kemmy," he said hesitantly. "Cory's pretty tense and I—it does things to you, being in a battle. He'll know what he needs to do— and what he doesn't."

"All right," Kem said softly as Hakan pulled into the drive and cut the motor. He sat for a moment, hands curled around the wheel, staring out at the blur of snow and gray sky.

"Kem?" he said. Then he turned rapidly, strong fingers closing lightly around her wrist. "Kemmy, I missed you."

"I missed you, too, Hakan." She hesitated, scandalized but certain that the time was right for telling truths. "I never want us to have to be apart again."

His face relaxed, his smile almost as bright as she remembered, and then he was serious again. "We've got a lot of things to talk about. But tonight—let's just be with each other tonight, all right?"

"All right. I'd like that." She smiled, and he cleared his throat awkwardly.

"Well...Let's go in and see what kind of mess Cory's made out of dinner."

Cory had made a work of art out of dinner, transforming everyday meat and vegetables into exotic viands, subtly spiced and astounding. Hakan contributed a bottle of wine from his father's fall pressing, and matters progressed as well as they could for a young lady with two virtually silent gentlemen as dinner companions.

Cory accepted compliments on his cooking with a slight smile and a formal bow of the head; he was predictably evasive about where he had learned the skill and fell silent the moment Kem ran out of questions.

Hakan loosened up a bit with the wine, and by the time the after-dinner fruit was eaten and the dishes were stacked neatly in the sink, he was very nearly the Hakan she knew. The phone call from Zamir Meltz informing his son and guest that he would be staying in Gylles that evening, rather than brave the growing snowstorm, seemed to restore him completely. He grinned at Kem. "Looks like you're snowed in too, honey. If you want to be."

"Hakan!" She jerked her head toward Cory, but the smaller man seemed absorbed in rinsing off the soup bowls.

Hakan's grin widened. "Hey, Cory—leave that stuff for tomorrow, man; we'll all three pitch in after breakfast. We got some practicing to do now! Winterfair's coming fast."

Cory turned, and Kem saw the worry on his scarred face. "Hakan—"

But Hakan had grabbed her hand and was hustling her down the hall to the parlor, whistling as he went.

Cory drifted soundlessly into the room as Hakan was tuning his guitar.

"Pull up a stool, my man, and get that keyboard smokin'."

"Hakan—" Cory began again, but he was interrupted by a quick staccato riff and a wide grin.

"What's the matter? Forget how to play?"

"No…"

"Well then, what're you waiting for?" The guitar went into a complicated arabesque of chords, and after a moment Cory went to the piano, slid onto the bench, and put the cover up.

He sat with his hands poised over the keyboard for so long that Kem thought he would refuse to play after all. Then, very carefully, as if he expected an explosion instead of music, he touched the keys and ran a soft set of scales.

From the guitar came the unmistakable intro riff to "Bylee's Beat." There was the slightest of hesitations before the piano took up its line.

Kem leaned back in her chair, eyes on the side of Hakan's face, preparing to lean back into the music. Hakan's frown and the protest of her own ears were simultaneous.

Disbelieving, she turned to stare at Cory. Notes were issuing obediently forth from the piano, correct and in proper time. Technically, Kem realized, the piece was probably perfect; even the crazy zigzag of sound that always made Cory shake his head was fully accomplished, without flaw.

But it was not *Cory's* music. There was no joy, no impetuosity, no subtle undertones. It was as if a music box were playing, rather than the musician she knew Cory to be.

Kem shifted in her chair, thought of going to the piano and making him stop, then paused and tipped her head as she caught some other sound there, under the sounds of piano and guitar.

Carefully, seeing that Hakan's frown had deepened, Kem got up to answer the door.

A very small person stood in the pool of yellow porch light, hood pulled back and red hair frosted with snow.

"Miri, for wind's sake! You're half frozen!" Kem caught her friend's arm and pulled her inside, peering toward the driveway as she did. She saw no car, no tire tracks. "How did you get here?"

"I walked," Miri said matter-of-factly.

Kem stared at her. "From Brigsbee's? In this? Miri—"

Miri shrugged. "I come to see Cory."

"Yes, but, love, you could have called us! Hakan would have come to get you. Give me that jacket—you're soaked! What in wind possessed you?"

"I come to see Cory," Miri repeated, and leaned forward to hug her. "Don't fuss, Kem! The walk is not long. And where I come from, it snows like this—oh, often!" She winced suddenly, her head turning toward the open parlor door.

"Hakan and Cory are practicing," Kem began weakly, but the other woman had spun back, gray eyes huge.

"He don't play like that!"

Kem moved her hands helplessly and noticed again the snow in her friend's hair. "Go in there by the fire," she ordered, glad of a problem she could solve. "I'll bring you some hot tea and whiskey. You'll be lucky not to get the very *brute* of a cold."

Miri smiled faintly and went toward the parlor, moving with a silent grace that rivaled Cory's own. Kem watched her for a moment, then headed down the hall to the kitchen.

Cory's hands went flat on the keys, ending soulless perfection in discord. Relieved, Hakan brought his palm against the strings and looked up.

His friend was staring at the door, with no particular expression on his face. Hakan turned to look.

Miri stood in the center of the double doorway, eyes only for the man at the piano. She stood there for a long moment; then she shifted, moved her eyes, and smiled warmly.

"Hakan." She came across to him with her small hands held out. "I don't get a chance to thank you for your help. Brave you were. Very a friend." She slid her hands into his and bent to kiss his cheek. "Thank you," she said again, straightening. Then she tipped her head, smile fading.

"Hakan, I come to see Cory. Talk, we must. It is your house, and I am sorry to—impose? This room, another room? With a door that closes? You can lend us that?"

"This room," he told her. "No imposition—that's what friends are for." He squinted at her to verify that the braid wrapped around her head *was* wet. "We better get you dry, though. You'll catch pneumonia or something."

"Kem brings tea, and the fire is good here. Soon I will dry. Thank you, Hakan, again. You are a good friend."

That was definitely a dismissal. Hakan rose and started for the door, guitar in hand. Grinning at Cory as he passed the piano, though the other did not seem to see, he almost bumped into Kem.

She set a large mug on the low table near the fire. "You drink every drop, now," she told Miri sternly. "We can't have you getting sick." She turned and went out, pulling the double doors firmly shut behind her.

Val Con had turned on the bench; he sat with his back to the piano. "Hello, Miri."

"Hi." She came to stand before him, noting with dread the blandness of his face and feeling stiff with more than cold.

"I ain't gonna keep you long," she said abruptly. "Just wanted to hear you say it, okay? So I *know.*"

He considered her warily. "Say it?"

"Yeah," she said harshly. "Say it. Figure it's pretty clear—you sending me off with the old ladies and then no word. Little surprised—didn't think that was your style. Thought you'd tell me straight. Something like 'Miri, go away.' She took a breath, eyes on his face. "That's what I came to hear."

Dismay was noted and overridden as the Loop flashed into existence, extrapolating a CMS of approximately .96, with the removal of the woman from the equation. His lips parted; they were dry, and he licked them.

Miri drifted a step closer, hands clearly in view, stance specifically nonthreatening.

"It's real simple," she said softly. "Like this: 'Miri, go away.'" There was a small silence before she leaned forward, her eyes holding his. "It ain't like I never heard it before."

Tension was building; he attended it briefly, found no specific source, and discounted it. He licked his lips again.

"Miri—" His voice choked out, tension increasing to a level that could not be ignored. He experienced a confusion of purpose; was unable to separate personal desire from the requirements of the mission.

The woman before him leaned closer. "That's a start. Two more to go."

"Why?" The word came out of the confusion, lashed with tension, so that it was nearly a shout.

"You want me to go away," she said. And then, very softly, she asked, "Don't you?"

Did he? What *did* he want? Surely nothing akin to what she supposed. Surely whatever he wanted was not a thing so deadly that the mere desiring of it should leave him sick and shaken. He cast his mind back, fighting the screaming tension. Once, certainly, he had wanted something...

"I want—" He heard his own voice from a singing distance. "I want to speak to my brother. Three years—four—and I sent him no word; never went home. Never dared go home—he would see! He would ask questions; he would probe and—endanger himself— Zerkam'ka...kinslayer..." His hands were cold, and he was shaking.

"Val Con."

She was holding his shoulders; he should not allow her to hold his shoulders. She was dangerous; she was Miri...

"Boss." Her fingers brushed the hair from his eyes and touched his cheek. "Your brother's safe, Val Con. You never went home."

"But I *wanted* to!" he cried. "Shan—" He reached out and cupped her face in icy, shaking hands. "You do the same—ask questions, put yourself in danger. Miri..." He took his hands away, seeing what must be done for her, as once he had done it for Shan. "Miri, run."

"No sense to it," she said with shocking calm. "You're real fast, boss. Catch me in a second." She touched his cheek again, then put both hands on his shoulders, fingers kneading. "Stiff as a board. You sleep since the fight?"

"A little..."

"Thought so. You and Hakan look like a couple zombies."

"Hakan told me he had never killed a man before," he said, not sure what it had to do with anything.

"Hell..." The small fingers continued their massage, soothing in a way that transcended the mere physical. "I tell you what, boss— they shouldn't let civilians have guns."

"And they should not let soldiers have agents," he said almost drowsily. "Miri—"

"I don't wanna hear 'run' outta you any more tonight, accazi? I don't know if you know it, but there's a *blizzard* going on out there. Already walked five miles in it—I sure ain't running nowhere in it."

One hand left his shoulder, cupped his chin, and lifted it until his eyes looked into hers. "Boss, what's going on?"

"I—" The Loop flashed, predicting disaster, an adrenaline surge snapped him toward his feet while something unnamed kept him nailed there, eyes looking into hers, trying to find words in Terran or Trade, words that would let her understand what had happened and the peril she was in. "I cannot—locate—the—the switch."

"Switch?" She frowned in incomprehension.

"Switch." He paused, groping after more proper words. Switch? Not precise. Key? No. Pattern of thinking? Closer, but Terran would mangle it beyond sense.

Gods, what a language! he thought savagely. It's impossible to explain anything in it!

He did not know he had spoken the thought aloud, until he heard her say, softly, "Yeah, but I don't think they did it that way on purpose, do you? Probably just the best anybody could come up with on the spur of the moment, and they thought they'd get back and sharpen it up later…" She looked closely into his eyes and moved her hand to stroke his cheek. "Can you give me just the broad outlines? We get you outta this jam, then I'll learn Low Liaden. Deal?"

Impossibly, he smiled—*truly* smiled. She saw his eyes light with joy as his mouth curved, and for just a moment she thought they had done it. Then the moment was gone and she was seeing him still, but through the other one—the agent one—as if she were seeing him through bars.

He closed his eyes, and she felt the effort he was making as if it were her own. She bit her lip and did not dare to move, barely dared to breathe, until he opened his eyes again.

"When we were on Edger's ship, I left you for a time to dance *L'apeleka* and relearn the—proper—way to think."

She nodded, watching with fascination as his hand rose—painfully slowly, fighting his own muscles all the way—and curved around hers where it rested on his shoulder. She squeezed his fingers and thought she felt a slight response.

"What I did then…" he said slowly. "Understand that I—gathered up all that was—that I felt was—wrong—and put it into one small…closet, Miri. A closet in my mind. I put a—a lock on the closet. Then I put the key in my pouch and pretended the closet did not exist." He paused and took a breath, his fingers exerting pressure on hers. "Another way: I had cornered the genie, so I found a bottle, shoved him inside, and firmly corked the mouth."

"And when the army attacked, the genie got loose."

"No," he said. "No. *I* opened the door—threw the switch. My choice. The lock was secure."

"Why?"

Why, indeed? He struggled for the memory itself, brushing aside datum she would scorn as meaningless.

"I was afraid," he achieved after several minutes. "I—you were in the house; there was danger. Many hostile people were between us, and I did not know what to do. I—*wanted* you to be safe, and I knew I would have to be—efficient and very quick. So I—" His fingers were gripping hers tightly, but if she was in pain she gave no sign. "I am not naturally good at killing people, Miri."

She blinked, then grinned. "Not the kind of thing folks usually apologize for." She paused. "So, you figured you'd go in, wipe out the enemy, shut off this switch thing, and everything'd be goomeky, right? 'Cept you can't find the bottle, and the genie's bigger'n you remembered."

"I—" Scout understanding signaled acceptance of the simile, and he inclined his head. "Something alike, yes."

"Hope it's close enough." She frowned. "You're caught up in this—ah, hell—this *master program* they imposed at spy school, and it won't let you find your gimmick for getting out. Pattern's a mess— you ain't sleeping—getting jumpier and more confused...Master program'd rather have you dead than have itself shut off again, boss." There was silence then. "You outsmarted it once with *L'apeleka*. Done any lately?"

"There is no room..."

"We'll find you room." She gnawed her lip, considering. "Okay, here's what: Lie down on the rug next to that fire, run through the Rainbow, and get inside your room. Once you're there, you can get yourself some rest, and I'll go rent the local gym."

"No..."

She went very still, eyes sharp. "No? Why not?"

"I—the militia captain was here to speak to me. His unit will be sweeping the gap, and he wanted whatever information I could give, since we so recently came that way." He hesitated. "They will find the ship, Miri. It is not so well hidden that a concerted search will miss it. I must go and send it away."

"That a fact."

"Yes." And it was, though not the fact he had intended—had *wanted*—to put forth.

"When were you planning on leaving?" Her voice was almost casual, belied only by the sharpness of her eyes.

"Tomorrow, after dawn. A single person can easily outmarch a unit. I would reach the ship in late morning, send it away, and be back with Hakan by evening."

"Simple," she agreed. "No need for you to go, though, boss. *L'apeleka's* more important. I'll get rid of the ship."

"You are not a pilot, Miri."

"Did I say I was? Shut up—I'm thinking."

Thought took no more than a dozen heartbeats; she squeezed his fingers gently. "I need to move around a little. You gonna be okay?"

"I will be okay."

She hesitated, staring into his eyes, then sighed and slipped away. At the sideboard she yanked drawers open and made a satisfied sound as she extracted a pencil and a sheaf of papers.

Kneeling next to the piano bench, she sketched with utter concentration for perhaps sixty seconds, then leaned back and pointed. "Here's what the board looked like when we left. You show me what it's gotta look like to lift."

He knelt, feeling the warmth of her body like a torch against his side, and considered what she had drawn.

The rendition was precise. Drawing a line beneath it, he sketched the pertinent instruments and the settings they had to achieve to engage the magnetics and initiate lift.

She studied it, frowning slightly, then nodded once. "Can do." Wadding the paper into a ball, she threw it into the heart of the fire. "Taken care of. Lie down on the rug and close your eyes."

"No."

"Now what?"

"Miri—" The unburdening came like a dam bursting; he sat suddenly on the worn rug and her face blurred before his tearing eyes. "On Edger's ship, when I was caught—'battleshock,' you said— but I was caught in the Rainbow. I needed to relax so badly; reached for the best way, the safest way...a Scout thing, Miri, I swear it to you! Made myself vulnerable and this other—arms proficiency program—imposed itself—trapped me...Nothing is safe—they teach you that. And it's true—the only truth they tell. Miri, I dare not..."

She moved, wrapping her arms around him, and he should have fought, but instead he bowed his head, pushing his face into the soft hollow of her neck, and heard her say, "All right...all right, kid. Val Con, Val Con, listen. Are you listening to me?"

Face against her flesh, he nodded.

"Good. Now you're gonna have to trust me, okay? I been at your back, ain't that true?"

"Yes."

"Okay. We're gonna get you down to your safe place—your room. I'll be with you every step of the way. You see anything scary, you sing out, and I'll get you out of it." Her arms tightened around him, fiercely. "Nobody's gonna trap you again, boss—an' you get my word on that one."

Her grip loosened; he was pushed gently away and found himself confronting a pair of very serious, gray eyes. "Lie down, Val Con. Please."

It might work. Something so very far away within him that he barely noted its input was screaming, clamoring, demanding that he do as she said; the Loops, for a wonder, were quiescent.

Slowly he gained his feet, approached the fire, and lay down on his back, arms loose at his sides. Miri, sitting beside him, grinned and saw the ghost of the ghost of his smile in return.

"Okay," she said, schooling her voice to that tone of friendly firmness she used in the most desperate battle situations. "Close your eyes and take a deep, deep breath." She took one herself, eyes only on his face.

"Now, visualize the color red..."

When they were at violet, the end of the Rainbow, she asked, "Do you see the stairway, Val Con?"

"Yes," he said softly. "The stairway is—still there."

"And are you okay?" she asked, hearing the slight hesitation. "Not frightened? Not threatened?"

"I am—well."

"Then do you choose to walk down the stairs?"

There was a small pause, then he said, "The door is also still in place." There was a hint of wonder in his voice.

"Will you open the door?" Miri asked. "Go inside?"

"In a moment..."

She drew a careful breath. "Val Con? Is something wrong? Maybe I can help you."

"Not—wrong. It is only that I have not been—inside—since...Miri," he said suddenly.

"Yo."

"Thank you—is it only 'thank you'? Nothing more? Cha'trez, thank you for loving me—for loving me so *well*."

"I ain't done yet," she said, managing to keep her voice pitched right. "But you're welcome. You going inside, or you gonna stand around on the landing all night?"

His lips curved in a smile. "Inside..." And there was silence. Miri sat, short nails scoring her palm, eyes glued to his face, teeth drilling into her lower lip so she would not shout and break the web.

"Miri?" It was a whisper. Then it came again, louder. "Miri!"

"Right here." And what to do if something *was* wrong? After all that bluff about not letting anything hurt him...

But the expression on his face was joy, and when he spoke again he nearly sang the words. "Miri, it's still here! Still whole. *They never got inside!*"

"You happy?" she asked inanely against the beat of her own rising joy, not quite understanding what was happening.

It almost seemed as if he would laugh. "Let us not overstate the case...A moment." There was a long silence. "I will sleep now," he said then, "and key myself to begin *L'apeleka* tomorrow. A large space, cha'trez, if you can. If not, I will dance outside."

"And put Hakan to all the trouble of explaining to the neighbors that you were okay yesterday and then just went bang off your head? I'll find you something with a roof over it. And don't worry about the ship. Good as in orbit already."

"Yes, Miri."

"Bastard." Grinning in spite of herself, she rose and stood looking down at him for a moment.

His chest rose and fell with the rhythm of deep relaxation, his body limp, his face looking years younger—a boy's face, fast asleep.

Cautiously she inspected the new pattern inside her head and was able, after several moments, to be satisfied. It was not nearly as screwy as it had been earlier in the day, when she had made the decision to hike over and talk to him, face to face. Maybe it'll work, Robertson, she thought, and went silently across the room and out the door, taking care that it was shut tightly behind her.

VANDAR

Hellin's Surcease

Hakan, looking up as Miri came into the kitchen, lay a muting palm on the strings and set the guitar aside.

"How's Cory?" he asked, voice almost soft.

"Better," she told him, dropping into the chair Kem pulled out for her. "I think better. He's—asleep."

"Good," Hakan murmured. He leaned forward slightly to peer into her face. "Porlint isn't a cold place, Miri. It's near the equator, so it hardly ever snows."

She blinked, then she bowed her head with a touch of Cory's formality. "Thank you, Hakan. I'll try to remember."

"That's all right." He eased back a little. "Do the two of you want to go back to Zhena Brigsbee's? I can drive you."

"Tomorrow," Kem amended softly.

Miri flickered forward and touched his hand, flashing a smile to the other woman. "Hakan, thank you again. But it would be better...Do you know a place—a big, empty place—Cory could use for five days—six? If you do, he should go there. Me, I need to be someplace else tomorrow, and then I go back to Zhena Brigsbee."

At Hakan's distinctly blank look, Miri bit her lip and tried again. "The battle is not easy for Cory—he only comes because I need him..."

"Cory was in Gylles! How did he know you needed him? Came running in to the store, asking me to take him home..."

She was aware of a strong desire for a slug of kynak, a quiet room, and a book; instead she took a deep mental breath. "You and Kem are together long enough, you will know when something is not right with the other one."

"That's right, honey," Kem said. "But why does Cory need a big, empty place? If he's depressed from the battle, wouldn't it be better for him to be with you?"

"Not until he—" She sighed, hearing the echo of Val Con's voice, snapping with frustration:...*You can't explain anything in it!* "He must—exercise so body and thoughts run together..."

She flung her hands out, silently damning the tears that were filling her eyes again. "Hakan, I don't explain so good, and I'm sorry—you and Cory have to fight, and it is my fault!"

"Your fault? A troop of Bassilan rebels walks in on you and it's your fault? Miri—"

"Honey, it *isn't* your fault—" Kem started, but Miri cut them both off.

"My fault! Because one of them kicks the door down, comes in, and points his rifle at me. Borril jumps, and the man hits him with the rifle; Borril jumps again, and I take the rifle away—shoot the man—and another man comes, so I shoot him—I am stupid, you see? I think they are bandits—maybe five, maybe six—the rifle, it is bad—rust, not oiled. I think I can stay and fight—"

"Stay and fight?" Hakan demanded. "Against six armed men?"

"Hakan, if there are six, already I take two—problem is not bad. But the third man—he doesn't come to find his friends. This one has a—a big gun—and I see him set it up and I see others behind him and I know I am stupid and there is no way to run. I have this bad rifle. I have my knife, but I am not Cory, who is good with knives. I am worried—Cory comes and he brings you—neither one a soldier! My fault, Hakan. I should have taken Borril and run away."

"Cory killed a lot of people, Miri—and I killed some, too."

"Three, Cory said." She frowned. "Hakan, why do you have a gun?"

"Huh?" He blinked. "I—well, it's a hunting gun, for—"

"Hunting? Why do you hunt? There are no stores? You don't make enough money to buy food?"

"Well, but—"

"You had no business shooting at those men with such a gun!" she cried. Catching the flare of pain on his face, she snapped forward to grab his shoulders. "Hakan, you were very brave—maybe you save my life. In battle, who can tell? You learn something now. You learn you can kill people. You learn how you feel about it." She leaned back, loosing his shoulders. "Maybe you should give away your gun."

"What about you?" His voice was husky, his expression still half aggrieved.

"Me? For a long time I am a soldier, Hakan. Soldiers don't break down doors and shoot people. Soldiers come, say they have taken the area, ask people to leave, and give escort, if the enemy is near." She shrugged. "People sometimes think bullets don't go through doors. Think their house won't burn—I don't know what people think." She shook her head. "You and Cory are not soldiers. You know how you feel. You hear how Cory played."

"Bad..."

"Like a machine," Kem added, and Miri nodded.

"This is why he needs a place—to be alone and to exercise. Please, Hakan—do you know? Kem? Anyplace, as long as no one goes there."

There was a long silence, and she despaired of their help. Then, Kem said softly, "Hakan? What about the barn?"

He considered the suggestion, his nearsighted gaze on nothing in particular. "Could work—it's sound, and we've still got the stove in there from when that crazy tourist was using the place as a studio." He nodded. "We'll do it. Cory can exercise in the barn till he grows a long, gray beard."

Relieved, Miri almost laughed. "Nothing takes that long. Tomorrow I show him where, then I do my errand and go back to Zhena Brigsbee." She looked at Kem. "If Zhena Trelu calls, you can—tell her something? I ask for a lot..."

Kem smiled. "I can cover you for a day, honey. Don't worry."

The tears came yet again, so she saw her friends through a sparkling kaleidoscope. "Thank you," she said, getting shakily to her feet. "Thank you both."

She was halfway across the kitchen when Hakan's voice stopped her.

"Miri?"

Now what? she wondered and turned back. "Hakan."

His expression was calmer, and he held Kem's hand as if he meant it, but his eyes were very puzzled. "Where are you really from, honey? In Porlint—"

"In Porlint," she interrupted tiredly, "little girls are not soldiers. I know, Hakan. Good night."

In a moment, the doorway was empty. They heard nothing for the short space it took her to walk the length of the hall, then only the sound of the parlor door, opening and closing behind her.

VANDAR

Fornem's Gap

"That looks like it, Robertson. Hit the timer and go."

Her hand hesitated over the last toggle, though, and she spun away from the board with a curse and took two steps before stopping to stare at Val Con's map all around her.

"Gods." Crossing her legs and sitting in the middle of it, she touched a duct-tape mountain, then picked up a paper spaceship. One world. One world to spend the rest of her life on, when she had once had her choice of hundreds...

"You're stuck, Robertson. Face facts and quit belly-achin'. I don't know what's got into you lately—turning into a damn watering can. You think it's tough here? What about Val Con? Grows up on Liad, goes for First-In Scout—been places; done things—got a family; misses his brother. Hear him kvetch?"

She sat for a little while longer, staring sightlessly at the map and thinking about Liz, about Jase and Suzuki and a dozen or so others. Thought about Skel—and there was no sense at all to that, because Skel was long dead and rotted on Klamath. If Klamath was still around.

"There's worse places, Robertson. Get moving."

Slowly she levered to her feet, moved to the board, and checked it one last time before setting the timer, sealing her jacket, and running for the exit.

She rolled out of the emergency hatch, spinning as she landed, then pitched the ship's key into the narrowing slit and skittered away in the knee-deep snow, heading for a downhill clump of scrub.

Ground, snow, and brush shivered; there was a grating, subaural scream, and Miri dove, twisting around to see—and the ship was already twenty feet up, heading straight into the cloud-cast sky.

She watched until it was nothing but a glint of hidden sunlight on scarred metal; watched until it was nothing at all. Watched until her eyes ached and she came to herself because the tears had frozen and were burning her cheeks.

She scrubbed them away with cold-reddened hands. Then, rigidly ignoring the gone feeling in her belly, she turned and marched back toward Gylles.

Body reported cold and darkness growing beyond closed eyes. The inner sentinel assigned to monitor outer conditions allowed the body to burn more calories, to generate more heat. The dark was of no account.

He danced: beat, breath, thought, movement, without division; only Self and the attributes of Self, thus named: Val Con yos'Phelium Scout, Artist of the Ephemeral, Slayer of the Eldest Dragon, Knife Clan of Middle River's Spring Spawn of Farmer Greentrees of the Spearmaker's Den, Tough Guy.

He had passed through the three most elementary Doors, taken the designated rest, and approached finally the fourth Door, *B'enelcaratak,* the Place of Celebrating Fragments.

He drew yet again upon his name and focused his celebration, his understanding, upon that special portion: Tough Guy.

There was a flare of bright warmth, perceived wholly, as name brought forth celebration of she who had named. He lived the joy, tears running unremarked from behind shielding lashes, and the dance changed to exultation of so sharp a blade, so bright a flame, so unlooked-for a lifemate—so beloved a friend.

The dance came back upon itself, joy constant, and he moved close to the Door, opened his understanding to the fragment of his name—and cried aloud, eyes opening to darkness, body shuddering, joy dissolved in an acid torrent of self-loathing.

He gained minimal control; he pushed his body to the stove in the corner and forced his hands to pick up wood and stack it in a pattern drawn of skill belonging to a man he once had been.

Hunching over the fire, he strove to warm his body while the coldness raging within filled his mouth with the taste of copper and his soul with despair.

"Miri." He put his hands toward the flames and spoke to her as if she stood there, in the shadow behind the stove. "This other— it is very strong, Miri—and I am not very strong at all. I tricked you—made you lifemate to a man who does not exist. Ah, gods…" His voice grew ragged with horror. "Gods, the things I have done!"

Being made over to somebody else's specs—that's dying, ain't it?

He froze, listening to her with memory's sharp ears.

Master program'd rather have you dead than have itself shut off again, boss.

How many tricks had they planted to turn himself against himself? To be sure that he would keep to the Department—or die rather than break free?

He had beaten them once—on Edger's ship. Had beaten them with one shard of certainty caught and held from the confusion of four years' divorce from his soul: They lied.

Of his own will, he had shattered the gain of that dance upon Edger's ship, but he held still that shard of truth. It was a beginning, though not the beginning he had thought to make. Humanlike, he had flung himself headlong into *L'apeleka* before all proper thought had been taken. He smiled ruefully at the darkness beyond the stove.

"The dance will be long," he said softly. "Cha'trez, do you wait for me..."

THE GARBAGE RUN

Pre-entry sounded. Shadia woke and cycled the pilot's chair to vertical, dragging the safety webbing into place with one smooth motion, eyes already sweeping the board. She registered the go-pattern, signaled pilot readiness, and brought up the screens, and the Scout ship phased gently into normal space.

Hanging in her forward screen was a midsize planet—one of three in the system, the only one habitable. Planet I-2796-893-44—Vandar, according to the locals—Interdicted and Off-Limits to Galactic Trade and Contact by Reason of Social Underdevelopment.

Sighing, she kicked in the log—and sighed again as the legend INITIATE DESIGNATED APPROACH scrolled across the bottom of the prime screen. More for something to do than because she doubted the ability of ship automatics, she slapped the board to manual and rolled smartly into the designated spiral.

"As if," she grumbled in Vimdiac, the tongue in which she most commonly talked to herself, "they have anything remotely strong enough to see me. Ah well, Shadia—consider it a bit of piloting practice, though the problem's hardly knotty. Hah! Getting a trifle overwise, are we? And just how precisely can you overlay the route, my braggart?"

For the next little while she busied herself with matching the designated approach point for point. In second aux screen, the blue of ship's approach ruthlessly overlaid the black route, while Shadia hummed in contented concentration.

"A cantra says you'll miss the pace at orbit entry; you were ever a— What by the children of Kamchek is *that?*"

It glinted in the light of the yellow sun as its orbit brought it from behind the world. Mid-orbit and holding. Shadia upped mag, directed the sensors, and very nearly snapped at the computer. The second aux screen showed ship's approach steady on the route.

A vessel, the computer reported, as if intuition had not told her that seconds earlier. Coil-dead, the sensors added, and the computer provided an image to aux three, delineating an orbit in strong decay. Life-form readings were uncompromisingly flat—not so much as a flea was alive on that ship, though sensors indicated a functioning support system.

Shadia punched Navcomp, remembered the board was on manual, and ran the calculation in her head, plotting the intersection of the route and the derelict. Velocity adjusted, sensors and scanners kicked to the top, the Scout ship moved in.

Her ship hung within seconds of the empty vessel. She had pulled the files: The ship was without Liaden reference marks, and the two numbers—a seven and an eleven connected by a dash, with the homeport apparently blotted out by a dab of paint—brought nothing up on the screen.

The damage the ship had endured was obvious: scars, scrapes, and bright metal-splashes, as if it had gone through a meteor swarm at speed with no screens. The longer she stared at it, the more she expected it to act as a ship should, to roll or orient, to acknowledge the presence of another ship.

The good news, if there was any, was the lack of major leaks. The spectroscope showed no untoward gas cloud, no signs that the ship had been opened to vacuum.

The bad news was the location, confirming again the need for the garbage run. Damn! The last time someone had found something around a proscribed world they had spent three years tracking everything down and filling out reports.

For a moment she considered forgetting that she had seen the thing, knowing full well that eventually her tapes would be audited and someone would spot it.

"Damn book!" she muttered. "Page 437, Paragraph 4: Report before boarding any suspicious or unauthorized vessel in a proscribed zone."

Unwillingly she punched up the coords for the nearest report bounce and powered up the emergency pin-beam. She hit the switch that would broadcast her sensor readings on the side band, all the while cursing her luck.

Some time later, she stood on the bridge of the derelict, frowning at the map on the floor. The yacht had fallen to Yxtrang—anyone with eyes could mark the signs—yet Yxtrang did not commonly take time from a raid to engage in meticulous cartography. Nor would one expect them, with an unprotected world at their feet, to delay even a heartbeat in the mapping of an expedition.

Shadia crouched, as if closer proximity would uncover rhyme— she did not expect reason—and finger-traced the familiar symbol for river.

Certainly Yxtrang, whatever their unknowable needs, would not use Liaden symbology on their map.

And certainly, she thought, eyeing the thing with new understanding, they would never map just so, as a Scout might map, taking time and infinite care, forcing hints of information from the yacht's pitiful scans and incorporating them into a body of fact that might be studied and known. The computer on such a vessel would never have had the capacity for the task, even assuming the ship had been undamaged at the time of mapping...

"Someone gone eklykt'i." Shadia sat back on her heels. Such things happened. Scouts tended to drop out of sight, to go native on some world they may have found and failed to report—or on any world that suited them better than stuffy, stifling Liad. It was not inconceivable that someone had found Vandar just to his taste.

She considered it, eyes on the map. The unknown Scout raises Vandar—leave for a moment the questions of why he might arrive in something as incongruous as a mere private yacht and in such ignorance of his world of choice that he must squander days in mapping and deciding. He arrives, we say, and in time descends to the planet surface, perhaps programming the yacht for an outbound course—or an inbound course, Shadia thought abruptly. Best to sink the thing in the sun and be done with it.

The empty yacht, then, is apprehended in its course by Yxtrang, who strip it and tag it for salvage.

"And leave it harmlessly in orbit around an inhabited world? Come now, Shadia!"

She sighed sharply and snapped to her feet. The facts were that a derelict yacht had no business about Vandar—never mind how it had gotten there. Her duty was clear, at least. Surface scans showed no disruptions such as an invading force of Yxtrang might engender, nor was she authorized to search out one gone eklykt'i. Speculation could be put aside for a later time. It would help fill the remaining hours of the garbage run.

She ran the hand sensors around, recording whatever details mere human eyes might miss. It was possible that she was stranding someone there—but that was their lookout, not hers. Besides, the way the orbit was canted, the ship was not good for much more than a few hundred days. Might as well finish the job properly.

Purposefully she turned to the board, flipped toggles, and initiated overrides, brows rising briefly as the Statcomp reported several mandatory energy governors missing entirely; she cycled the magnetics until the whine hurt her ears, fed all available energy, including life support, into one critical cell, and ran for the door.

She hit the pilot's chair and slapped toggles, not bothering with webbing, then jerked the Scout ship away in a dizzying roll, hands flashing over a board yellow-lit with warnings, building velocity at an alarming rate, blurring impossibly into Jump. Behind her, the derelict yacht exploded, raining daytime meteors onto the world below.

VANDAR

Springbreeze Farm

Dawn was three hours away when a shadow detached itself from the others clustered about the scuppin house and made its way soundlessly across the crusty snow to the base of the kitchen steps. At the top of the flight, the door swung open on newly oiled hinges, and a second shadow—shorter, more slender—leaned out, yellow light spilling from the room behind and gleaming off a wealth of copper hair.

"Morning," she said, as if she could see him plainly, though the light did not reach nearly so far. "You coming in or not?"

"Good morning," he murmured, drifting silently up the stairs. At the landing he paused and smiled and made his bow. "I would very much like to come in, please, Miri."

"Good thing." She grinned and slipped back into the room. "Breakfast's almost ready. Thought I'd have to give your half to the dog."

"Am I late?" he asked closing the door and unfastening his jacket. From the rug in the corner, Borril thumped his tail and gave a groan of welcome.

"Not late," Miri said from the stove. "I guess you're just right on time."

He grinned, hung his jacket on the peg between her blue one and Zhena Trelu's disreputable plaid, and bent to yank on Borril's ears. "Hello, dog. So you survived, did you? Quite the hero—the newssheets told your story most movingly."

Borril groaned loudly and dove sideways onto his head, rolling an ecstatic yellow eye.

Val Con laughed, reached out to grab the blunt snout, and gave a brisk shake. "Shameless creature. I've come home only to pull on your ridiculous ears, I suppose. Yes, I see the splint. Your own fault for breaking the leg in the first place. Surely you might have managed things better than that?"

The dog answered with another soulful groan, which squeezed off into a sigh as the man rose and moved toward the stove.

Miri glanced up and pointed a brisk finger at the cup steaming on the counter. "You walk all the way from Hakan's, boss?"

He curved cold hands gratefully about the teacup and bent his face into the fragrant steam. "It is quite lovely tonight—very clear. It is true there are not so many stars in this system, but I think tonight one might have counted each." He sipped carefully. "I was not so patient, alas."

"Could've stayed till morning," Miri said, doing efficient things with spatula and skillet while Val Con sniffed appreciatively. "Hakan would've brought you on his way into town."

He raised a brow. "But, you see, I wished to speak to my wife tonight, and I am very much afraid that Hakan was abed by the time my necessity had made itself known."

"There's the phone..."

Val Con laughed. "Inadequate." He went to the dish closet and pulled out silverware and napkins. "Would you like the plates over there?"

"Yeah..." she said, attention almost fully on the task at hand. Val Con divided knives, forks, spoons, and napkins—yellow for her, blue for him—carried the plates to the counter, and poured a second cup of tea. He took both cups to the table and returned to rummage in the icebox for bread and butter.

"Breakfast," Miri announced, bringing the plates to the table. "Hope you're hungry."

"Not quite ready to expire," he said, slipping into a chair and picking up the fork.

Miri grinned and attacked her own meal, surprised at her sudden hunger.

There was a sigh from her right; she glanced up to find him smiling at her. "It tastes wonderful, cha'trez; thank you. I was afraid I would have to eat my coat, you see."

She laughed and reached to pick up her cup, then shook her head at him. "Zhena Trelu thinks you run off. Wants me to call the cops and have you brought to justice."

"A rogue," he told his plate, with deep sorrow. "A man without honor." He glanced at her from under his lashes. "You did not believe this?"

She blinked. "No."

"Progress," he informed the plate, stabbing a forkful of breakfast. "Good."

The green eyes were back on her before she could frame a fitting reply. "Has Zhena Trelu brought you more clothes, cha'trez? The shirt is very nice."

She shook her head. "Funny thing—people from all over Bentrill have been sending us clothes, and books and—ah, hell, I don't even know what half the stuff is. Money. Lots of money, seems like. Zhena Trelu was trying to tell me how much we own right now, but I don't think I got it straight. Bunch of stuff for you piled up in the music room—" She slammed to a halt, catching the frozen look in his eyes.

"A bounty?" he asked quietly, fork forgotten in his hand. "For the soldiers we killed?"

Oh. Yxtrang took bounty; Liadens counted coup.

"I don't think it's a *bounty,*" she said carefully. "The way Kem explained it is people think we're heroes and are—grateful to us for stopping the army when we did. Would've been ugly, if they'd gotten into Gylles." She paused, biting her lip. "The stuff's for balance, I think, 'cause people feel like they owe the three of us something for doing them a favor."

"I see," he murmured, and returned his attention to breakfast.

She finished her own, savoring the taste, happy just to have him there, quiet and companionable. Tentatively she reached inside and touched the pattern-place in her head—and nearly dropped her fork.

The pattern shone. It glittered. It *scintillated.* She forced her inner eye to follow the interlockings and branching-aways—and felt the wholeness and the rightness and the warmth of it like joy in her own heart.

She drew a shaky breath, unaware that he was watching until he said her name.

"Yo." She withdrew from the pattern-place with a little wrench. "What are you thinking, Miri?"

"I—" She blinked. "Where's the genie, boss?"

"Ah." He leaned back in his chair, eyes on her face. "Subsumed, I think you would say; his powers taken and his vision destroyed."

"And it's not gonna happen again? You gotta fight again, you won't get stuck?" She shrugged, eyes bright. "Scariest thing I ever saw in my life, when that thing went haywire. I was looking right at it! One second, it's fine; next second, it's totally nuts."

"I am sorry," he said, "that you were frightened. And, no; I will not get trapped again. There is nothing left to be trapped within—only Val Con, the things he knows and the abilities he possesses."

She frowned. "The Loop?"

"Exists," he said calmly. "It is, after all, an ability I have—to observe and to render odds." He saw the shadow cross her face and leaned forward, hand outstretched. "Miri."

Slowly she slid her fingers into his. "Val Con?"

"Yes," he assured her, very gently. "Who else? Are you frightened, Miri? I—"

But she was shaking her head, eyes half closed as she touched the pattern inside her head. "Not scared. The pattern's—it's *right*. Not quite the same as it was—but it's okay."

He drew a breath, but she was suddenly wide-eyed and smiling as she squeezed his fingers. "Where'd you come up with the notion of genies, anyhow? Thought that was home-grown Terran stuff."

"So it is," he said, leaning back and releasing her hand. "But my foster mother was Terran, remember? And she told us stories. One had to do with a man who had found a bottle on a beach. He pulled out the cork and a genie emerged, bowing low and proclaiming indebtedness. He offered to perform three services, as balance for the debt."

"Sounds like the standard line," Miri agreed, watching his face. "Can't trust 'em, though. Genies are a very slippery bunch."

"So it seemed. But it must be said that the fellow who had found the bottle was not among the wisest of individuals." He picked up his teacup. "I was enraptured by the tale—it took strong hold of my mind, and I found myself considering how I might have managed the thing, were it to happen that a genie owed *me* three services." He smiled, eyes glinting in what she recognized as mischief.

"After much thought, I felt I had a plan which was foolproof. I was, after all, six years old—and very wise for my age. All that remained was to obtain a bottle containing a genie." He laughed a little and set his cup down. "So, I took myself to my uncle's wine cellar—"

"Oh, no," Miri breathed, eyes round.

"Oh, but yes," he assured her. "It was perhaps not *quite* wise of me to have chosen a time for this search when my uncle was at home. Though I still do not understand why he made such a fuss. It was not as if I had failed to recork the bottles that contained only wine..."

She was laughing, head tipped back on her slim neck. "And he let you live?"

"It was," he admitted, "a near thing."

Her shoulders jerked with more laughter, and she wiped at her cheeks with unsteady fingers. His eyes followed the motion, and feeling absurdly shy, she held her hand out to him.

He smiled gently at the silver snake curving about her finger, blue gem held firmly in its jaws. "I am happy that you choose to wear it again, cha'trez. Thank you."

She shrugged, dropping her eyes. "It was hard to wear it and work around here—afraid I was going to break it or lose it. King's carpenters, or whoever they were, did such a bang-up job of putting this place back together, there ain't nothing left to do but feed the scuppins." She glanced up, half smiling. "We're out of a job, boss."

"We shall find another, then." He lifted a brow. "What pattern?"

When she hesitated, he leaned forward, remembering old fears. "Does it hurt you, cha'trez?"

"Hurt?" She shook her head. "Naw, it's—nice. Mostly, it's nice," she corrected herself. "When you went all bats there during the battle, then it wasn't so nice, but it didn't hurt, even then. It was just—wrong." She bit her lip, looking at him worriedly. "Val Con, aren't you doing it? I was sure— It *feels* like you!"

Her shoulders were starting to tense, puzzlement giving way to alarm. He pushed his chair back, captured her hand, and coaxed her onto his lap. Straddling his knees, she looked into his eyes.

"Boss, it's *gotta* be you. I knew you were in trouble. Knew it! *Saw* it. Left you alone for three horrible days, like a certified pingdoogle, figurin' you'd pull out—"

"Miri. *Miri*—don't, cha'trez..." He ran light fingers down her face, trying to stroke away the lines of pain. "Please, Miri—it was not your failing."

She closed her eyes and drew a deep breath.

"Miri?"

"I'm okay." She opened her eyes to prove it, and Val Con smiled, very slightly.

"Good." He paused briefly. "Let us say that it is me," he began, feeling for the proper way to arrange the bulky Terran words.

"It truly does not distress you? I am happy if that is so. I was afraid that you would be able to—hear—and that it would hurt you."

"Why?" She frowned, eyes sharpening. "No, wait—you've got a pattern for me in your head? Does it hurt *you?*"

"Not a pattern," he said gently. "A song. I like it very much. It is—a comfort."

There was silence for a heartbeat or two. "Val Con?" she said then. "Yes."

"What is it? If you're not doing it, but it's you…" She shook her head. "I don't think I get it."

"I am trying, cha'trez—it is not so easy, in Terran." She shifted, and he smiled. "I am not blaming you, Miri. It is only that what I must explain is a Liaden thing. Did you speak Low Liaden, the name itself would tell you about the thing. In Terran, I must try to bend the words—though not so far, eh? Or they will be nonsense."

"Okay." She reached down and wove their fingers together, then looked up. "Go."

"Let us," he said, after a moment, "see if it will make sense this way: What you have in your head—what I have in mine—is a fragment of empathy. You, for me. I, for you. 'Alive-and-well,' my song seems to say. Also, I found tonight, it is directional. When I set out from Hakan's, I walked toward Zhena Brigsbee's house; then I thought to touch my song of you and found you had come back here." He smiled. "Perhaps that is why I was almost late for breakfast. How did you know I was coming?"

She shrugged, eyes on his. "I—ah, damn!—I felt you homing, I guess. Whatever that means." She frowned. "And I knew when you were in trouble."

"Yes. And I shall know if you are hurt, or in great distress. I think that, over time, one might become more skilled at reading the nuances." He sighed. "Not a good explanation, at all. Does it suffice you?"

"Gimme a century or two…Val Con?"

"Yes."

"Do all lifemates have this empathy thing? That's why you married me? 'Cause you could hear this song, or whatever?"

He shook his head "It is not a thing that is often given—" he began, silently damning the futility of trying to fully share the wonder. "And I have not been able to hear you for very long—certainly not before we came here. In the very old days I think that this was something more, that lifemates were, indeed, understood to be people who had become—joined. I—the tale goes that—again, in the old days, when such things were more common—those so joined became as—one person. Ah, that is wrong! That the thoughts flowed back and forth, one to the other, without need for words. That there was sharing—" He broke off, shaking his head sharply. "Cha'trez, I am very stupid."

"Naw, it's just a goofy idea. No sober Terran'd believe you." She thought for a moment. "This sharing stuff—that gonna happen to us?"

"I do not think so. After all, we are only ordinary people, not wizards in the full flush of our powers."

"Right." She sighed, stared intently at nothing, then grinned. "Guess I'll have to learn Low Liaden real soon."

"I would like that," he told her, holding her hand tightly. "Do you truly wish to learn?"

"Yes!" she said with unexpected passion, gray eyes blazing.

Breath suddenly caught in his throat, and his brows snapped together.

"What's up?"

"It is—a strange thing, Miri. I have only just thought." He smiled, though she was not sure of the expression in his eyes. "If I had not been recruited by the Department of the Interior, I would have had no cause to be on Lufkit at all, nor would I have walked down a certain alley at such a time..." And all my life, he thought, I would have awakened unwarm, not understanding that I missed the weight of a certain head upon my shoulder; grown ever more silent, unable to know that I listened for the sound of one voice laughing at my side. In the old days, it was told that one had been able to call, searching for the beloved one had yet to know...

"Now that's crazy, whatever language you say it in," Miri was snapping. "Better you'd stayed a Scout and been light-years away from Lufkit than had everybody and his first cousin messing around inside your head, hurting you—" She snapped it off, appalled again by the easy tears.

He bent forward to lay his lips against hers, meaning only to comfort her, but he felt the passion flare and stood, cradling her in his arms.

"What the hell do you think you're doing?" she demanded.

"Holding you." He was laughing softly. "Shall I put you down?"

"Naw. Just trying to remember the last time somebody picked me up and lived." She closed her eyes, apparently engaged in a mental tally. "Been awhile," she said presently. "I must have been ten or so."

"Not such awhile, then," he said. "Five or six years?"

"More like eighteen or nineteen." She snorted. "Soft-soaper."

He raised a brow, eyes traveling the short length of her. "So many?" he asked earnestly.

"At least so many."

He brought his gaze back to her face. "But—when shall you grow tall?"

She laughed. "Just as soon as you do. You gonna stand around and hold me all night?"

"There is merit to the suggestion," he allowed, "but I think instead that we should go to bed."

"You do, huh? I ain't tired."

"Good."

DUTIFUL PASSAGE

She went without anyone to guard her body, but the way was known and she had relearned caution. Time enough had passed for the seed to grow into consciousness. Time and past to have gone for an answer.

The familiar aura flared; she traveled the time required and knew that she need travel no farther.

Cautiously she opened an inner path and found herself again confronted with that bewildering array of defenses. Expanding the path, she discovered him at the core: asleep, at peace, shimmering slightly with the faint violet glow indicative of lust energetically expended.

There he lay, and there she saw him, and for all of that he was as unreachable as if she had never found him at all. Priscilla experienced a strong desire to grab his shoulders and shake him awake, demanding to know what under the smile of the Goddess had possessed him to build such a citadel around his soul. Had she been in body, she might even have done so.

As it was, she imposed Serenity upon herself and turned her attention to the bridge, stark and beautiful, and followed it to the scintillant pattern of the lifemate.

Once again that one was asleep, soul locked lightly behind a single portal. Priscilla allowed the shape and flavor of that barrier to grow before her inner eye and saw suddenly and with surety a large, wooden door, keyhole ornate with shining metal, wood gleaming with age and loving care.

She expended will, came close enough to try the latch—and paused to allow the landing to solidify about her.

The lifemate thought with extreme care, Priscilla understood suddenly, and formed her analogs with a firmness approaching physical solidity. A landing was necessary to accommodate the door, and a landing had thus been crafted; it would be discourteous to accost the door outside of context.

It was at the very instant that the landing came into itself, just a moment before she narrowed her attention to accommodate only the latch, that she perceived sitting on the floor just outside the door: a package.

Priscilla brought her concentration to bear, discerned the familiar yellow-and-black stripes of the Galactic Parcel Service, and found further a lading slip filled out in a round, clear hand:

For Priscilla Mendoza only.

Sign here: _____

Laughter almost destroyed concentration and sent her on her way home with neither package nor contact.

Sternly she embraced Serenity, then considered the analog minutely before signing her name, tearing the top slip away, and tucking it securely between handle and latch. She paused then and performed the action that, in body, would have been the laying of a hand in benediction upon the door.

"Goddess love you, sister."

Obedient to the other's necessity, she bent, picked up the package, and turned at last to go home.

ORBIT

Interdicted World I-2796-893-44

Tyl Von sig'Alda studied the planet below him with fanatic precision. He measured magnetic fields, tracked weather patterns, and located likely volcanic faults and tectonic features. He compared the star's light constant against Scout files, compared once again the computer model against the actuality, and knew within a tolerance even the commander must accept that he was very near his quarry at last.

His information so far was excellent; the Scout was to be commended for the accuracy of her report. The cloud of debris orbiting the third planet had proved to contain a high quantity of isotopes and alloys not yet discovered in nature.

There were identifiable fragments collected on the second day—a metallic screw of Terran standards and a ceramic nimlet used in adaptive purification systems were the first things recognized—and more on the third.

The Loop showed him a percentage verging on certainty that he had found the remains of Val Con yos'Phelium's escape vessel.

Satisfied, sig'Alda assigned to the computer the tedious task of backtracking the cloud to a common origin and turned his attention to radio transmissions.

He was not much disappointed when the study of transmission frequencies, strength, and patterns showed no obvious sign of a call for help from the world below. It was not to be expected that a former Scout would announce himself as an extraplanetary and demand entry to the most powerful transmitters on the planet.

Dutifully sig'Alda called up the first of the four "survival models" the Department had provided.

The first assumed that yos'Phelium wished to remove himself from the planet with the utmost speed and cared not into which hands he fell—Scout, agent, rogue, or trader. That reflected the "average survivor" model, and sig'Alda did not think such would be the case. Nevertheless, he had the computer check for the model: voice broadcasts in Trade, Liaden, or Terran in standard galactic frequencies; Trade-code broadcasts superimposed on planetary broadcasts; and sideband broadcasts using planetary frequencies in either code or voice.

The second—his own choice, based on exhaustive studies of the man—was the "informed survivor" model. It presumed discretion: one would not broadcast indiscriminately in galactic language from a planet under interdiction. Instead, any broadcast would be on Scout or Departmental frequencies, with a slight possibility that it might also be on a private Korval frequency. Code or timed bursts would be used to attract attention to the proper frequency, at which point the listener would respond, creating a dialog and an opportunity for a brief exchange in code or voice.

The third was the "intentional survivor" concept, and the key to it was that yos'Phelium had *chosen* this world in particular. He would be waiting, according to that model, for a message, or for a particular time or event—or he had chosen what the Scouts dignified as eklykt'i— to be among the Unreturned. In that circumstance he would need to be tracked and found and, perhaps, persuaded, which was not a task sig'Alda contemplated with any degree of eagerness.

The fourth was the "victim of circumstance" model, and sig'Alda gave it the least credence of all: the submodels had yos'Phelium dead or hopelessly wandering a savage world. sig'Alda grimaced. As likely *he* would wander about doing nothing as would yos'Phelium—even more likely, according to the Loop. After all, yos'Phelium had been a Scout commander, a man with a gift for evaluating worlds, for learning languages, and for prospering in alien environments.

The computer having provided a target continent—that with the heaviest overlaying of smog, to sig'Alda's sighing dismay—he went through the files obtained from Scout headquarters, found the appropriate language, and slid it into the sleep learner. In a few hours he would know the names of the mountains and seas, the right way to hold a cup of tea, and the political system as it was at last report.

Setting the computer to wake him if it discovered a match of any the four survival models, Tyl Von sig'Alda relaxed into trance began to learn.

A command of the local tongue failed to soothe his loathing for things not Liaden. The language reported by the Scouts was without subtlety. Unless one was of the elite, there was little to distinguish oneself from others; it was difficult to proclaim precedence or authority—and slightly more difficult for males than for females.

The society itself was bucolic. While one could insult others, it was not a culture where an accidental insult was likely to result in a blood feud or even a fistfight.

The Scouts had indicated that the rate of change was unspectacular, though they had warned that local technology was reaching the Suarez point, the point at which technological advance might become the focus of three or four generations of society, society itself becoming fragmented until the growth was assimilated.

The sleep tapes had also given him a look at the food, which was uniformly off-putting. He could look forward to the flesh of game animals in many areas, as well as fruits and vegetables that would be old by the time he ate them, the world's shipping systems being woefully underdeveloped.

sig'Alda sighed. The creatures there—aside from his quarry—were barely sentient, by any thinking person's standards. Their goals were limited by their backwardness, their vision shortsighted, by testimony of their language and culture—the whole world populated by faulty genes.

There were times when the Scouts, with their insistence on independence for such "developing" worlds, produced nothing but ugliness and waste. Were Liadens merely put in charge there the world would quickly become productive and useful. Once the Department was able to arrange things properly, such waste would be eliminated.

In the meantime, Tyl Von sig'Alda studied the files on local costume, confirmed that at least there was no need to change his skin tone or have the autodoc graft on a beard. He brightened at the thought that yos'Phelium would also not be changing—or hiding—his appearance much.

He studied also the computer grid, ran probability checks, and finally targeted his first search-site: a large, industrial city on the southern shore of the bottle-shaped continent. All he knew of yos'Phelium indicated that he would establish his headquarters in such a place, which was what pitiful vanguard of technology so backward a world could muster. From that point, yos'Phelium would have access to the world's most powerful transmitter; would have quick access to new innovations; would be able, if need be, to influence a group of locals to do his bidding and serve his ends. Also, the climate was somewhat warmer than the second-choice site, farther north.

Well satisfied with his choice, the Loop showing a CMS of .45 and a CPS of .76, Tyl Von sig'Alda prepared to invade Vandar.

DUTIFUL PASSAGE

"Good evening, Priscilla. Delightful to see you return."

She fumbled, found the mechanism, and opened her eyes. "Shan."

"How kind of you to recall. Perhaps after a moment you'll also recall that you promised to cease exposing yourself to this danger." His eyes were silver ice, his pattern a webwork of fury and terror.

"What in *hell* were you doing?" he snapped, terror rising even above anger.

What had she been doing? She struggled, squirming further into her body—and memory returned with a burst of half-hysterical laughter.

"Priscilla..." He was out of the chair, gripping her arms, shaking her where she lay on the bed. "Priscilla!"

"I was—Mother love her!—I had to pick up a package!" She grappled with the laughter, hiccuped into sense and stared up into his eyes. "I have a message from your brother."

Face and pattern went very still. "Indeed."

"Actually," she amended, slipping from between his hands and sitting cross-legged in the middle of the bed, "I have a package from your brother's lifemate. I assume it holds a message."

"But not from Val Con himself."

Impossible to read all the nuance there. She shook her head. "Val Con has—many protections. I tried twice—awake and asleep—and couldn't reach him. I—" She met his eyes squarely. "Some time ago, I went soul-walking and left a message with the lifemate: an image of you, an image of me, and the message, 'We are looking for you. Help us,' loaded with familiarity, family-caring." She paused, then added softly, "Lina kept watch over my body."

"Did she? What a gift it is to have friends."

She winced. "Shan—"

He waved a big hand and sat suddenly beside her on the bed. "Never mind. You'll have told Lina necessity existed, which it certainly does. For Korval." He looked at her, and the anger was gone completely, the terror fading fast. "Your melant'i is very difficult, Priscilla. Forgive me."

"Lifemates," she said, hearing the Seer-cadence echoing in the words, "are heart-known. He is my brother, too."

"A theory Nova would be just as happy not to entertain. But we are drifting from the subject of your package." He sighed, and she felt him working, shifting internal balances; wondering, she saw him sculpt intuitive understanding and shadowy theory into a clearly recognizable seed-thought.

Healers are not taught such things, she thought. She wondered, not for the first time, if years of close association had sharpened and altered both of their talents.

"Perhaps I can understand how you might leave a message with my brother's lady," Shan was saying, turning his construct over in his mind. "But I cannot for my heart see how she could have left you a package!"

Priscilla grinned. "You've had training, love; and she hasn't had any. She doesn't know it's impossible to leave packages in your mind for pickup." Laughter escaped again. "And she seems to have left it, and I seem to have brought it away—so I suppose it's not impossible, after all!"

"Brought it away..." He glanced around the room, eyebrows up. "You tell me you have this package with you."

"Oh, yes." She touched it within herself, reading the lading slip and seeing the angular slant of her own signature.

"Might I see it, Priscilla? Understand that I would never doubt you—"

"Of course." She laid her hand over his, then heard his sharp intake of breath as his inner eyes perceived it.

"Priscilla?"

"Yes?"

"It's dusty."

"It's been sitting on a landing for weeks, awaiting pickup; and she does tend to be extremely concrete in her thinking," Priscilla said with delight. "Entirely unschooled, but very strong-willed."

"Val Con's lifemate could hardly be anything but strong-willed, if she was to survive the mating," he murmured. "The tag says this is for you alone."

"We can open it together, if you like." She sensed his passionate agreement, opened the packet, and nearly laughed again.

Carefully, striving to recall exactly how physical hands would manage it, she unfolded the single sheet of yellow paper; she caught a wordless rush of something from Shan as the two flat-pix clipped to the top were uncovered.

The first showed a man, dark hair indifferently cut, the line of a scar slanting shockingly across one lean, golden cheek, green eyes lit with joy, wide mouth curved in pleasure. The entire image glowed bright, as if with some inner brilliance, and Priscilla felt her throat tighten with that reflected love.

The second picture was less sharp, less bright: merely a redhaired woman, freckles sprinkled across a small nose; gray eyes direct in a willful, intelligent face.

Priscilla heard Shan sigh, but was too enmeshed in her own perceptions to read the echo of his.

Deliberately she turned her attention to the body of the letter, finding again the round, painstakingly clear hand, apparently written in bright purple ink.

We're okay. Clan Korval in danger. Don't talk to Interior Department. Go to Edger if things get bad. Ship coil-blown—world restricted. Tell Shan: Access Grid seven-aught-three \Trimex:Veldrad. Repeat: Access Grid 703 \Trimex:Veldrad. Love to all.

Priscilla opened her eyes and saw Shan staring at her.

"Well," he said, and she was not fooled by the light note in his voice, "we seem to have done everything wrong! Not only has my sister had at least one delightful conversation with the Department of the Interior, but Edger has come to us! And there's no mention of the Juntavas, did you notice, Priscilla? As if that were no trouble at all."

He slipped his hand away from hers and rubbed the tip of his nose. "They're okay, she says—and Val Con looks worn to the bone. Got that scar in a brawl, I daresay—or a crash..." He sighed. "Access Grid 703, is it? Well, let us see."

But ship's comp, queried, took far too long to respond to the code, and when it did, the information was not satisfactory:

ADDRESS ON LIAD PRIME.

Shan sighed again and shook his head, and Priscilla felt his bone-deep worry as if it were her own. "It looks like we send it to Nova, my love," he said. "And await events. Gods, how I hate to await events!" He took her hand and smiled at her, wanly but with good intent.

"She looks quite sensible, doesn't she?"

Miri woke in the lightening gray of dawn, shifted up on one elbow, and lightly touched his scar.

He opened his eyes, mouth curving lazily into a smile. "Cha'trez…"

"Hi." She stroked the hair back from his face, then bent and kissed his forehead. "Letter's gone, boss."

"Ah." He reached up and pulled her back down beside him. "That is good, then."

LIAD

Trealla Fantrol

"Ready, Miss," Jeeves said from just behind her shoulder. But still she sat, her fingers poised above the keyboard, chewing her lip in most unNova-like hesitation.

It was not, she told herself firmly, the *way* they had gotten the message. After all, Korval had produced its share of dramliz over the generations, including her own sister, Anthora. It was rather, Nova thought suddenly, that she feared Access Grid 703 itself. Which was of course nonsense and not, in any case, to be allowed to come before duty and the best survival of the Clan.

Deliberately she opened a channel and fed in the address. "Instantaneous download, Jeeves," she murmured, though he had already reported ready. And she read:

OBJECTIVES AND GUIDANCE

THE AGENT WILL RECALL FROM TRAINING THAT ALLEGIANCE TO A SINGLE CLAN IS ADDICTION TO AN OUTDATED AND LIFE-THREAT-ENING PHILOSOPHY. FOR CENTURIES HAVE THE CLANS, EACH PURSU-ING THEIR OWN NECESSITY, STIFLED LIAD, ENTRAPPING INTELLI-GENT PERSONS IN A FALLACIOUS EMOTIONAL WEBWORK AND SO DENYING THE CHILDREN OF LIAD THEIR RIGHTFUL PLACE AMONG THE STARS.

THE FRUIT OF THIS NONSURVIVALIST WAY OF LIFE IS NOW CLEAR: TERRA SEEKS TO OVERPOWER AND ANNIHILATE US. WORKING FOR THEIR OWN PETTY INTERESTS, SEVERAL CLANS HAVE ALLOWED LIADEN BLOOD TO BECOME DILUTED AND HAVE GRANTED THESE HALF-BREEDS FULL RIGHTS. IT IS WELL-KNOWN THAT TERRA PROMOTES THOSE MATCHES, WHILE IT SEEKS TO BEST LIAD ON ALL OTHER FRONTS, AS WELL. IN VIEW OF THIS THREAT, IT IS THE PART OF THE INTELLIGENT PERSON TO FORSWEAR ALLEGIANCE TO CLAN AND, INSTEAD, TO ALLY HIMSELF WITH LIAD, THROUGH THIS DEPARTMENT.

IT IS THE PRIME OBJECTIVE OF THIS DEPARTMENT TO ESTABLISH THE SUPREMACY OF LIAD AND TRUE LIADENS. TO ACCOMPLISH THIS——

The image on the screen shivered, broke apart, and went blank.

"What!" Nova cried around the pain in her heart. She reached for the keys, noting the channel still wide open.

REPORT FOR DEBRIEFING.

"Yes, certainly," she muttered, and ran quick fingers over the board: RETURN FILE.

REPORT FOR DEBRIEFING, her correspondent insisted, and added an explanation: COMMANDER'S ORDERS.

RETURN FILE, Nova reiterated. "Jeeves! Disengage."

"Disengaged, Miss."

FILE WILL BE RETURNED AFTER DEBRIEFING. YOU WILL REPORT IMMEDIATELY. ACKNOWLEDGE.

MESSAGE ACKNOWLEDGED, Nova typed rapidly. REGRET CANNOT REPORT. APOLOGIES TO COMMANDER. FILE NOT REQUIRED THAT UR-GENTLY.

There was hesitation then, as if her correspondent perhaps knew Val Con well enough to recognize the authenticity of that reply. Nova glanced down, saw the open-channel light still glowing, and folded her hands in her lap.

REMAIN AT CURRENT LOCATION, the message came then. ESCORT WILL BE PROVIDED.

The channel light went dark.

NEV'LORN HEADQUARTERS

"Come now, Shadia," she muttered to herself in Vimdiac. "What can be hunting you in Auxiliary Headquarters?" The hairs at her nape refused to settle properly down, and she added jocularly, "Besides Clonak ter'Meulen, I mean."

No good. The part of her concerned with keeping her alive in conditions where she might well *be* hunted kept her hackles up, and against all sense she found herself scanning the dock as she crossed the strip and turned toward the duty desk.

Half a dozen steps was all it took to convince her. Too many techs in sight, or too few; eyes turned toward her that had no need to note her passage. Her mouth tasted of adrenaline, and she began to scan the strip in earnest, looking for a face that she recognized. Looking for a friend.

She saw him coming toward her, his lined face bemused and slightly simian, his light brown eyes bland; beneath his snub of a nose he wore a most unLiaden mustache.

She almost shouted to him, but the unease and the training stilled the urge. Whatever was wrong, it was to be survived. Survival hinged on ignoring them, on allowing them to think she thought nothing amiss—whoever, she added to herself wryly, *they* were.

She increased her pace then, as the plan took shape, and nearly ran the last little distance between them, hurtling straight into his arms. Raising her hands to his startled face, she sang out in the mode used between those most intimate, "Clonak, I am all joy to see you!"

Surprise flickered in the taffy eyes, then his arms tightened convincingly about her and he bent his head for her kiss. "Well, now, Night's Delight; and of course I am all joy to see you!"

He had caught the look in her eyes and knew that she had understood already that something was amiss. Quick, oh, very quick, Shadia! He released her on the thought, the warmth of the embrace fading instantly as his eyes caught the pattern he had been hoping against.

"And now, my dear, I'm afraid we must return momentarily to your ship." He placed a light hand on her back and felt the resistance melt immediately. Bright girl!

"And what a trip you've had, eh, Shadia? A chance to sleep, to pine away for—"

He chattered on, fitting in, "There, three on the left, two on the right," as if it were a part of the chatter. The pattern had coalesced into purpose: They were moving to cut Shadia and himself off from the ship!

"How bad?" she mumbled, looking brightly at him and matching his rapid walk.

"I need a liftoff, oh, fifteen seconds after we hit the ladder."

"We'll kill someone!"

"Give a five-second warning. If you prefer, I'll lift it!"

"'S'mine."

"Right," he said as they touched the edge of the hotpad.

The sound of rapid steps was heard, too close—breaking into a run as Shadia's hands touched the hatch.

Chonak caught the belt she flung at him, grabbed the first pistol that came to hand, and fired a flare into the hotpad.

Alarms screamed; he slammed the seal even as the ship's emergency blast warning gonged across the lift zone. His last sight of the base was of several people standing straight up, frozen, while others more knowledgeable ran and dove for cover.

"Now!"

He grabbed the seat as the blast warning ceased and nearly fell across it as lift began.

"Lose me that way," he muttered under his breath as he groped his way into the copilot's chair.

"Nine seconds," Shadia snapped.

"Oh. Good. Let's listen to the comm, eh?"

The comm was a nearly unintelligible mix of yelling, pleading, and demanding. Emergency channels crackled; within seconds there were reports of five injured, several seriously.

"Ne'Zame, report in! Do not orbit; repeat, do not orbit. Cut and return to base immediately!"

The ship was accelerating rapidly. Clonak felt crushed by the weight, but managed to get his hand to his lips in the age-old sign for silence.

Ground Control demanded action, and suddenly Orbital Control was getting into the act, too.

"What is it?" Shadia demanded finally, keeping the ship on manual.

"Department of the Interior. No way to warn you…" His breath came in gasps. It had been years, perhaps decades, since he had flown like this.

"Should I back off?" she asked, concern evident.

"Fly it!"

She flew it well. He watched her hands and eyes: She would do. She had the reactions.

"Prepare to Jump," he gasped.

"We're in atmosphere!"

"Just be ready. Anywhere. As soon as we're free—"

No wasted motion. Good. No panic. Better.

"Ne'Zame, orbit and standby for boarding. This is the Department of the Interior. Orbit and standby for boarding!"

Shadia threw a glance at him. Clonak smiled.

"Better?" she asked.

"Rainbow," he said succinctly. "Forgive me, child—there was no way to get to you sooner. It wasn't until I saw those techs—all out of position—that I *knew*. Department of the Interior—been getting into our records; detaching our people—set up Nev'lorn 'quarters to hold them at bay, and *damned* if they didn't follow us here! They must think we don't know it—they must think we're fools, Shadia…"

"Ne'Zame!" the comm snapped. "Orbit and open, or we'll board by force! Who authorized this unfiled flight—"

Clonak reached out and tapped the button.

"This is Clonak ter'Meulen," he said calmly. "*I* have authorized this unfiled flight. Administrative Override is in force."

"We do not recognize your authority, ter'Meulen. Ne'Zame has been detached to this Department! Orbit and open!"

Ship screens were full of ordinary traffic and, as the ship rose, they began to track the trajectories of the orbiting ships, the crawl of the suborbital transports, the— There was no sound. The lights were bright yellow.

Clonak glanced at Shadia, smiling.

She grimaced. "Intercept alert. My screen three."

"I had no doubt. Three ships on screen three. One of the warship class. What would have happened if you'd have been asleep?"

"I know, I know. I'm supposed to have that on audio, too, but it just gets so useless in the meteor…"

"Not to worry, my lovely. We need a Jump-ready status."

"Ready as I can be. We've still got too much pressure—"

"Right. Where's the moon? Ah. Let me give you the orbit." Shadia stared at him. "Without the comp?"

"Of course without the comp! They're reading every bit they can! They may be able to pick up our control codes."

Clonak forgot about the residual ache in his chest, forgot about the meaning of the three dots bearing down on their tiny scout craft, forgot about the people—the enemies?—dead or dying at the dock. Reading from the screen, he computed the orbit they were to achieve and began to dictate it, watching the course board with half an eye.

"Pressure's down." Shadia said, all business. "Can they make that reassignment stick? Will you get in trouble?"

He called out six more numbers before answering. "I'm already in trouble—and so are you. Department of the Interior's been sharking about for information on you ever since you made contact with the ship out on Vandar. Collected the beam report, I suppose. Your bad luck, Shadia."

"What comes of following the book. Damn!"

The ship shuddered; Shadia hit buttons and read numbers off to herself. "Laser carrying a charge beam. Close. What do we do?"

"Start to roll—just like you're going to orbit. When I say *now,* we Jump. Instantly."

"Clonak, that could kill us this close in!"

"They'll kill us, my dear. They will. Jump when I say."

She cleared a screen and watched the gravity wells of the moon and Nev'lorn and the minor blips of the other ships. "You got it."

The ship shuddered again; she switched to a backup board without hesitation. "Charged all hell out of my circuits!"

Alarms, both sound and light, came to life.

"They've fired. Rockets," she said quietly.

"Right."

Her hands went to buttons microseconds after the automatics had done the job: all shields up.

"What's going to happen to Nev'lorn?" she asked suddenly.

"It'll be empty within minutes, I suspect. Project Orange will go into effect, and with any luck at all the Department of the Interior will get a nasty—"

Flash!

Blinding light exploded inside the ship, sparks bouncing across the walls.

"Kill my ship, you clanless—" She stopped with her finger on the switch. "Liadens. Clonak, what should I do? They're Liadens! How can I return fire, even with this popgun?"

"Administrative Override, my dear. I order you—as Chief of Pilot Security—to react as occasion demands. You have one half-minute before we Jump."

Her hands flew over the board; the ship tumbled with the program, its self-defense rockets spewing suddenly, hopelessly, across space, toward the destroyer bearing rapidly down on it.

Flaaassshhh!

Again boards were blown; again she hit the circuit overrides.

There was another strike, and the ship protested—there was a high-pitched scream of air...

"Breached!" she cried.

"Now, Shadia."

Her hands continued their motion—a last firing in defense, in rebellion; they skipped in a single motion to the bright red button and slapped it, hard.

The enemy's charge hit as she hit the button—and the ship began to come apart as they jumped.

LIAD

Trealla Fantrol

The Memory was hard upon her, and Nova sought to relax into it as the Healers had taught her, trying to forget how much she hated her talent, how much she had always hated it—how helpless she was against the rising of its tide.

This Memory had belonged to one called Bindrea yos'Phelium. An ancient Memory—Trealla Fantrol had not yet been built when Bindrea was alive—but for all of that potent and quite impatient. Nova had had a brisk tussle at the outset for control of the landcar, managing to keep it in her hands only by driving much faster than she would have preferred, no matter what the emergency.

It was madness to go so quickly, no matter how well she knew the road. She shrugged to herself. All that she did was madness just now.

The children would be off-planet already, as well as Cousin Kareen yos'Phelium and Mr. dea'Gauss' heir. The old gentleman himself had refused evacuation.

"But the danger, sir!" Nova had protested, squandering moments of her own escape time.

"I am quite safe, Lady Nova," he had returned calmly. "Word has been left for the Accountant's Guild in my name, should anything untoward befall me."

"The Accountant's Guild?" she had demanded, while that minute and another slipped away.

"Exactly. It is to be hoped that the—persons—in question are canny enough to ask themselves what would happen should every accountant in Solcintra step away from their computers at once." He had smiled coolly. "Also, I have set inquiries about in the business of Korval. It is only proper that I be here to receive the answers."

"As you will, then, sir," she had said and cut the connection with scant courtesy, for the Memory crashed full-blown into consciousness then; time was suddenly far too short and even the use of a secured line was none too wise for so long a time.

Anthora had also refused to go, and time had fled so quickly that there was nothing left for Nova but to give a fierce hug, laying cheek against cheek, and go, leaving a sister—a member of the Line Direct—alone in the empty vault of their home.

Quite right, Bindrea's Memory interrupted. *Can't leave the Tree unguarded. Can't leave the Clan without representation. Might want to come back. Gods damn you, girl,* drive! *Is it your life you're saving or a game?*

Nova gunned the car, which seemed to pacify the Memory, then turned back again to her tally of madness.

Word had been sent to Shan and to Pat Rin; and to Shan had also gone a transcript of the Department of the Interior's Objectives. Nova shuddered. That Val Con owed those people duty— Val Con, who had been raised as a brother to his half-Terran cousins, who had called a Terran woman 'Mother,' who was a *Scout,* and who, by all reports received, had chosen to share his life with a woman who counted herself Terran.

Madness was everywhere, not the least of it having to do with the First Speaker of Clan Korval haring away from her Line House mere minutes ahead of those who must be deemed assassins—or worse.

The landcar swerved, took the curve into Jelaza Kazone's drive badly, straightened, then accelerated, seemingly straight for the Tree itself, which was impossibly tall and no comfort to her at all, though before it had always been so.

She roared into the front court and never slowed as Bindrea's Memory sent her charging toward a serviceway between two garages.

The serviceway ended before an outbuilding of the old style, built of rough-hewn red stone. Nova killed the car's power, fumbled with the door catch—and Bindrea was with her fully, moving her out of the car and sending her at a dead run across the thin court to the outbuilding's door.

It was Bindrea who slapped two locks—the first visible at shoulder height; the second invisible by her knee—and Bindrea who was relieved to see that the sleek little two-seater was still where she had left it.

It was Nova who slammed the hatch, fed power to the coils, cycled the magnetics, and began the test cycle. She called up the course computer and began to plot evasive maneuvers, drawing on what she knew of the planetary defense screen. Fingers moved so rapidly that it hardly mattered who controlled them; she locked the plan in; seeing a flicker of green light at the edge of vision, she frowned at the non-standard readout.

No worry, Bindrea's Memory assured her. *We're just interfacing with the world-net. Jelaza Kazone was the first defense base. We stayed tied in—unofficially—after they set it up permanently. That's the way it was when I was Delm. Any Delm who let that liaison lapse would've been a damn fool or worse. In my day, yos'Phelium didn't grow fools that benighted.*

The little ship reported ready, and Nova slapped the "Go" sequence, webbing in belatedly as her craft accelerated smoothly across the lawn and lifted effortlessly, its nose angled toward the blue-green sky of evening.

In Liad Defense Station Five, Pequi pel'Manda swore and hit RESET. Her screen wavered and solidified, showing static gray, and she punched up the auxilliary boards, swearing some more as the screen kept to gray—and then shimmered into normality. Across the top margin was the legend: POWER OUTAGE, MICROSTATION 392. SELF-CHECK POSITIVE. RESET.

Sighing, Pequi reset the board again and settled down to scan the small part of the planetary defense screen that was the responsibility of Station Five.

LIAD

Trealla Fantrol

Agent-in-Charge Rel Vad Yoltak laid his hand against the annunciator. The five additional agents making up the mission team scattered as ordered, and Yoltak imagined they might be laughing at him. For which he could not in justice blame them.

Six—two of them experienced off-planet agents—sent to bring away one man! It was laughable. That the Line House they were sent to for pickup showed none of the bustle and busyness of an inhabited house only lent spice to the joke.

He paused. The Loop suggested a 22 percent probability that he would meet resistance there: Abnormal conditions noted.

Yoltak put his hand against the bell again.

The door opened a crack, then swung abruptly wider, revealing a dark-haired woman with extraordinarily light blue eyes, unattractively full at breast and hip, and perhaps even a shade too tall. She was dressed in house-tunic and soft boots, and just behind her stood a towering monstrosity of a robot.

"Yes?" the woman said, smiling at him brightly. Her eyes moved after a heartbeat, scanning the guest yard, looking directly at each of the half-dozen of them, even yos'Rida crouching, well out of view, behind the armored car. The Loop could not read the meaning of that: Abnormal condition noted.

Rel Vad Yoltak bowed slightly. "We are here," he said in the mode of Command, "for Val Con yos'Phelium."

"Are you?" The light eyes widened innocently. "Then I regret to inform you, sir, that he has not been here for several relumma. Leave your name, do, and I shall deliver it to him when he returns."

Yoltak frowned; the tactical radio in his ear sounded a minute tone, informing him that all team hand weapons but his own were now armed.

"We have been reliably informed that Val Con yos'Phelium was here not more than an hour ago," he told the woman in the doorway imperiously. "We have urgent business with him regarding his duty to the Department of the Interior."

The smooth brow knit slightly, and the wide eyes became shadowed. "Department of the Interior?" she wondered, then shook her head, Terran-wise.

Yoltak ground his teeth. "You will," he informed her sharply, "surrender Val Con yos'Phelium to us, or we will enter and retrieve him."

"No," Anthora said softly. "No, I really don't think so, sir."

Behind him, one of the company shifted to lay her hand on the butt of the gun riding her hip—and cried out, snatching her hand away from metal suddenly grown too hot to touch.

The flash missed Yoltak by bare millimeters; his face still warmed to it. The Loop rendered odds approaching surety that the robot was armed: Abnormal condition noted.

"Weapons are not allowed to be drawn within the borders of Korval's valley," Anthora said quietly. "Please do remember it. The next reminder will not be as gentle."

Yoltak moved his right hand, intending to signal the charge—and found himself halted by an extraordinary pair of silver eyes.

"Rel Vad Yoltak," she said experimentally, though he had not told her his name. "How strange of you to think you might walk into this house at your will. I am quite sure that Line Yoltak does not at all look to Korval. I may be wrong, of course, but it seems to me that Yoltak belongs to Clan Simesta and takes guidance from Derani sel'Mindruyk, who is Delm."

"What if it does?" he snapped, still in the Command mode.

Anthora sighed. "Why only, if it does, then you are sadly lost, sir, and must make haste to Solcintra-city. You will be able to find a shuttle there, I am sure, to take you to Chonselta, which is your Clan's seat, if you have such need to enter a Clanhouse. *This* is Trealla Fantrol, yos'Galan's Line House, and the seat of Korval's First Speaker. You are—forgive me—neither welcome nor invited here."

"We are not concerned with Clans! I have said that we are here for Val Con yos'Phelium. We do not leave without him."

"And I, Anthora yos'Galan, have said that Val Con yos'Phelium has not been here for quite some time. Forgive me yet again that I send you forth unfulfilled." Steel glinted in the deep velvet voice, though the eyes remained as guileless as always. "You were allowed within our homeplace because it was not certain that you were a threat. Now that you have made threats, the house recognizes you as—undesirable." She glanced at the monster behind her. "Jeeves."

"Working, Miss Anthora. The representatives of the Department of the Interior have four minutes to gain the valley access road before Trealla Fantrol takes further action to protect itself."

Rel Vad Yoltak moved one step toward the half-breed bitch in the doorway—and found himself suddenly flung backward down the curving stairs, though no one had touched him! He snatched at his weapon, and the Loop countermanded the reaction so forcefully that his arm muscles spasmed. Exposed as he was, touching that gun could mean death: Abnormal condition noted.

"Three minutes and one-half," Anthora yos'Galan snapped as he came to his knees on the stairs. "I would move my folk with all due speed, were I you, Rel Vad Yoltak. Not," she added as an afterthought, "that it is my part to give a person of another Clan advice of any kind."

In the driveway, the car came suddenly to life, motor snarling. One of the agents lunged toward it, got into the driver's seat, and tried to kill the power. The car roared louder, bucking against the brake.

Yoltak's Loop gave the CMS as .15 and offered no information as to how their car's emergency remote had been subverted. Nowhere yet was there any sign of another human—only that woman with her icy, Terran-tainted manners and the monster, hand-built robot. The Loop indicated a .85 probability that yos'Phelium *had* been in the house, accessing Departmental files. The probability that he was *still* inside—and commanding this farce—went steadily down, though it remained well within the boundaries of what was possible.

Yoltak brought up his reserve of Loop energy and invested it in control of the Command mode.

"I *command* Val Con yos'Phelium to return to his superiors at the Department of the Interior!" With all that energy feeding it, the nuance should have been strong and nearly overpowering; instead Yoltak sounded like a schoolboy, even to his own ears.

A trace of some emotion flickered across the woman's face; his Loop read it as rage. She then seemed to peer into the far distance before returning her gaze to him.

"None of Korval is now under the dominion of the Department of the Interior," she said with a surety so sincere that his Loop read it as incontrovertible fact. "And you cannot shout hard enough or long enough to Command me. Time passes. Rapidly."

Her eyes sharpened, bright silver and scathingly intent.

"Run, Rel Vad Yoltak," she told him. "You are outmatched, your position weak, your numbers observed. Run! And do not come here again."

Yoltak gasped, his Loop flickering as if each word she spoke struck it directly, and saw that his Chance of Personal Survival was falling rapidly.

Heart stuttering, training fragmented and useless, Rel Vad Yoltak took her advice. The car was already moving as he flung himself into it. The Loop was unreadable in its gyrations, except for one recurring message: Abnormal condition noted.

VANDAR

Winterfair

Zhena Brigsbee was a hero.

The king said so, giving a pat little speech about her presence of mind during a national emergency. Then he waved at the colorless zhena standing at attention on his right, who obediently stepped forward and carefully pinned a gaudy bronze medal on Zhena Brigsbee's heroic bosom and stepped back while the older woman turned pink and fluttered and said, "your Majesty" and "Wind's sake" until one of the other people from the king's entourage guided her back to her seat.

Miri smothered a yawn. Borril was a hero, too, with a shiny medal attached to his new red collar. On the whole, she thought, the dog had behaved much better than Zhena B. Which just went to show that breeding did tell.

Zhena Trelu's name was called by the man with the list. She walked straight up the aisle to the king's chair with her fragile, nononsense stride and curtseyed briefly. Miri wrinkled her nose: Catch *her* performing any such shines in front of a roomful of people!

The king was much nicer to Zhena Trelu than he had been to Zhena Brigsbee, and Miri's opinion of him rose an erg or two. He did not give her any plastic clap-trap about how strong and upstanding she had been; just apologized, in a voice that sounded sincere, for letting her house get torn to shreds and hoped that the repair job was satisfactory. He did not wait for an answer to that but swept on, his voice taking on a note that somehow reminded Miri of Val Con in his snitzy mood, announcing that the house was thereby proclaimed a national monument, with Estra Trelu as its caretaker and administrator, which position she would hold for the rest of her life, drawing an annual salary of 5,892 speldron. The upkeep of house and furnishings was, of course, the responsibility of the Crown, as were the salaries and upkeep of the militia squad that was to be the all-hours, around-the-year guard.

The king gestured, and the colorless zhena stepped forward to offer Zhena Trelu a rolled tube of paper tied with a white ribbon. "Your charter," she said in a loud, colorless whisper.

The old woman stood still a moment, tube held between her palms. Then she said, firmly, "Thank you, your Majesty," made another of those stupid, dipping bows, and walked back to her seat.

Miri felt like applauding. Instead, she looked over at her partner, who smiled and squeezed her fingers.

"Nervous, Miri?" he asked in soft Benish.

She blinked. "What of?"

His shoulders jerked, and she opened her mouth to remind him that they had promised Kem that they would be dignified, which probably meant not laughing in public.

"Will Hakan Meltz please stand forward," the man with the list ordered. "Will Meri and Corvill Robersun stand forward."

Val Con squeezed her hand again and slid his fingers away as he stepped into the aisle. She followed, wondering at the size of the crowd that had turned out for the giving of medals and proclaiming of heroes. Val Con reached the edge of the cleared circle, paused until she gained his side, and they walked the rest of the way together.

Hakan was before the king's chair, bowing low and managing it more creditably than Miri would have expected. He straightened and was moved to one side by the colorless zhena, who motioned to Val Con.

The Liaden stepped forward, Miri right beside him, then stopped and bowed the bow between equals, graceful and brief.

Miri blinked—*equals?*—and reproduced the bow to an inch. Straightening, she saw the colorless zhena staring at her, seemingly about to speak, a bright blotch of color decorating each pale cheek. At a wave from the king, the woman swallowed her words and stepped back, her face still registering shock.

"For extraordinary service to the Kingdom of Bentrill," the king said in the more regal of his voices, "it is hereby declared that Hakan Meltz, Meri Robersun, and Corvill Robersun are Heroes of the Realm. As such they are entitled to and shall receive a sum of money equal to the present value of a quarterweight of hontoles.

"In addition to this, Meri and Corvill Robersun, natives of Porlint, are made by this decree Citizens of Bentrill." He stopped, brown eyes vague, apparently having forgotten the next part.

Good, Miri thought. No medals. I wonder what's a hontoles? She shot a quick glance at Hakan's face and noted the slightly glazed look around the blue eyes. Could be we're rich, she theorized. Whatever that means.

The king had remembered the rest of his lines.

"On behalf of the people of the nation of Bentrill, I wish to thank each of you for your valor and your courage in the thwarting of this danger to our realm. To this I add my personal gratitude and beg you to understand that my audience room is open to you at a moment's notice." He smiled vaguely and waved at the colorless zhena.

Hakan got his medal first—twice as large as Zhena Brigsbee's, or even Borril's—and made of bright gilt. He was also given a pouch, which crackled when he took it.

Val Con was next. The look Miri slanted sideways showed his face smooth and formal, his shoulders level. He stared past the woman pinning the medal to the front of his new white shirt and took the crinkly pouch without deigning to look down.

The zhena approached Miri with wariness not untouched with outrage. Resisting the temptation to stick her tongue out, Miri adopted Val Con's strategy instead. Fixing her eyes on a point just over the woman's shoulder, she failed to notice the affixing of the medal and acknowledged the pouch only by the finger-twitch necessary to keep it in hand.

The zhena stepped back to her place by the king's chair, and Miri sighed softly. *That* was over…

"Meri Robersun, Corvill Robersun: Raise your right hands," the list-keeper boomed.

What? But Val Con had already raised his hand to the height of shoulder, so she shifted her pouch to the other hand and did the same.

The king levered out of his chair and came forward, a plump, homely man with sad brown eyes and graying brown hair.

"With the power vested in me as sovereign of this State of Bentrill I do hereby give you the oath." He paused to raise his own hand, and when he spoke again, his voice was vibrantly clear.

"Do you, Meri Robersun, Corvill Robersun, swear to uphold the laws of this land, obey the king's lawgivers, respect the king's sovereignty, and fight, if called upon, to defend this country from invasion or rebellion?"

There was a short pause, then Val Con's voice replied quietly, "Yes."

The king's eyes moved.

"Yes," Miri assured him.

He smiled. "I do hereby declare you sworn citizens of Bentrill, having all rights and obligations pertaining thereto." He smiled again. "You may lower your hands. Come forward now."

They did, side by side and silent. The king extended his right hand and touched Miri on the right shoulder, then repeated the gesture for Val Con.

"My personal thanks, as well. This was not your country; you did not have to fight. You could as easily have run away and allowed the invasion force to proceed into Gylles. Bentrill is proud to add such people to her citizenry. If all goes as it should, neither you nor any other citizen of Bentrill will ever find it necessary to fight again. War is brutal and, thankfully, not common. But we must always be prepared." He smiled again, but this time it did not reach his eyes. "Thank you."

He turned and sat down. Val Con bowed, Miri bowed, and Hakan bowed, then they, too, returned to their seats.

DUTIFUL PASSAGE

He sat in the dimness of her quarters, screenglow liming stark cheek-bones and kissing frosty hair with gold.

Priscilla shivered, though the air was not cold. She shivered because the inner warmth she knew as Shan was gone and all her attempts to read him slid off a cool, mirroring shield—the Wall, he called it, behind which a Healer might retreat to rest and regroup. And to hide.

She could pull him out of it, of course—she was that strong. But it was not a thing that was done, to strip another of his protections and rout him from his safe place, simply because one was cold and alone and frightened in his absence.

"Shan?"

Nothing. He sat and stared at the screen and barely seemed to breathe.

Priscilla went quickly forward and laid her hand on his shoulder. "Shan."

He started, then caught himself and deliberately leaned back, head against her hip. "Good evening, Priscilla."

"What is it?" she demanded, desperately wanting to scan him, yet determined not to try it.

He waved a hand screenward. "A message from the First Speaker, to the point, as always."

She frowned at the amber letters. "Plan B? What does that mean?"

He sighed, and she felt the tightness of the shoulder muscles under her fingers.

"Plan B..." He paused, then continued, very carefully. "It means that the *Dutiful Passage* is from this moment forward acknowledged to be exclusively on the business of Clan Korval. It means that we unship our weapons and free ourselves of cargo. It means that other Korval ships, where possible, will take over parts of our route."

He shifted, then stilled. "It means that Korval is in deadly danger, that the First Speaker has evacuated the Clan from Liad; that the Nadelm may be untrustworthy; that my brother—*my brother!*" His voice broke, and he bowed his head, muscles bunching as Priscilla grabbed and shook.

"Shan, your brother is well!"

He craned his head to look into her face and raised a hand to her cheek. "Is he?"

"You know it." She stared at him, reading the anguish in his eyes and face. "We could both go," she offered tentatively, knowing that she was just strong enough to carry him so far, "and you could read him yourself. He might hear your thoughts more clearly than mine."

He gave a gasp of laughter. "And expose captain and first mate to unknown danger when we are poised on the edge of a war? Later, Priscilla—and send that we find them in body before."

"We will find them," she said, hearing a certain deepening of her voice.

Shan heard it, too. "A prophecy, Priscilla? We'll hope it's as true as the others you've given."

He leaned forward sharply, clearing the screen with a handsweep, spun in the chair, and stood, facing her. "Call an assembly of the crew for Second Hour; attendance mandatory; lattice-crew to attend via comm."

"Yes, Captain." She bowed obedience and respect.

He smiled then and shook his head, his Wall shimmering and resolidifying. "I love you, Priscilla."

DUTIFUL PASSAGE

They had shed cargo at Arsdred; more at Raggtown; still more at Wellsend, so they came into Krisko orbit lean and sleek, more like a cruiser in outline than a tradeship.

They had shed crew, as well. A few went because their Clan did not enjoy a sufficiently close relationship with Korval; others, because they were too important to Line and House to be put into the way of another Clan's danger. Most stayed—Terrans with shrugs for incomprehensible Liaden politics—though the captain had urged all to leave.

Priscilla had stayed, and Gordy, though Shan's urging in that quarter had approached actual commands; and she sighed now as she walked toward the captain's office. Shan himself had taught her the subtleties of melant'i, so she was alive to the knowledge that, while the captain might order her, Shan could not. And the captain would not order her gone: she was far too valuable a first mate. That did not, of course, mean that Shan had to like it.

She laid her hand upon the palm-plate, and his door slid open; he glanced up from his screen as she came into the room.

"Good day, Priscilla."

"Good day, Captain."

His mouth quirked, his pattern registering a certain wistfulness. "Still angry with me, love?"

She came forward and held out her hand—and nearly sagged in relief when he took it. "I thought you were angry with me."

"Only terrified for you," he said, and she read the truth of that deep within him. "It would seem to be my time to be terrified for those I hold dear." He pointed at the screen. "I have a pin-beam from Anthora."

"Is she well?" Priscilla asked, wondering at several new resonances within him, at a loss to ascribe them place or purpose in the matrix of the man she loved.

"Well?" Shan laughed shortly. "She reports repelling invaders from Trealla Fantrol's very door and begs my permission, as her Thodelm, to activate the primary defense screens—which she confesses she has already done. She also lets me know, most properly, that she and several of the cats plan to relocate to Jelaza Kazone for a time."

Priscilla sank to the arm of a chair, staring at him. "Anthora is still on Liad? But I thought—"

"That all were safely away? So did I. But my sister informs me that she has stayed to guard the Tree," he said with no little bitterness.

The Tree—the living symbol of Korval's greatness, hundreds of years old, a quarter-mile high and still growing. Priscilla forced her mind to work, to consider the use of symbology and the political advantage of leaving a caretaker in residence. Liadens had a long history of subtle politics, and she knew from her days in Temple the power of a long-held, potent symbol. She glanced up to find Shan watching her closely.

"Jelaza Kazone," she said slowly, feeling her way, "is the Delm's Own House—the original Clan House, you'd said. And Val Con once told me that the older parts are underground, so it's probably better fortified than Trealla Fantrol. If Anthora's purpose in remaining is to guard the tree, it makes good sense for her to be with it, at Jelaza Kazone."

"So she says," he replied dryly, and she caught a flare of something bright and hard and potent before it was skillfully leashed and subsumed within the rest of his pattern.

"In light of my sister's report of invaders with murderous intent," he said after a moment, "the captain has a task for the first mate."

She inclined her head and awaited the captain's instruction, dread coming seemingly from nowhere and lodging deep in her stomach.

"You will present the captain's compliments to Cargo Master yo'Lanna," Shan said softly, "and ask him to attend me here immediately. You will then yourself attach the four pods to be delivered at fifteen-oh-six, one to each of the prime articulation points, and lock them into place. Screen readout will indicate when the automatic system has meshed with the main computer. You will then return to me here."

"Weapons pods." She stared at him, the dread turning to fear. "The *Passage* has weapons, Shan—"

"It will now have its full complement." He shifted, avoiding her eyes, though he did not shield his inner self, for which she thanked the Goddess. "Anthora reports assassins calling at the front door, Priscilla. What would you have me do?"

He sighed sharply when she did not answer and raised his eyes to hers. "We are on the business of Clan Korval, as you heard me explain before the crew and privately. You see now what it means— what it can mean." He leaned forward, hand extended, light glittering off the Master Trader's ring. "We are at war, Priscilla! Or may be, soon. *Will* you go to safety?"

"Safety?" She shook her head, ignoring his hand. "The weapons—here. But you only just received Anthora's 'beam. You came here to load weapons."

"No." He sat back and rubbed the tip of his nose. "Priscilla, Korval is an old Clan and a wealthy one. We have warehouses everywhere. There are several weapons caches. It happens that Krisko houses one." He paused, then added, with a peculiar shimmer deep within his pattern, "By the luck."

"All right." She slid to her feet and bowed. "The first mate goes to fulfill the captain's orders."

She was two steps toward the door before he called her; she turned to find him standing before the desk, both hands held out to her.

"Paranoia, Priscilla—is that the right word? Korval…" He hesitated. "For centuries, since Cantra yos'Phelium brought the escape ship to Liad, the Delms of Korval have acted and implemented policy for *Korval alone*. We gather ships, for escape, for battle. We gather money, power, influence. Only a pilot may be Delm. We breed for pilots, Priscilla! To give the greatest chance of successful escape to the greatest number of Korval, should necessity arise. Renegades, even the most proper of us."

She came back to him, extending lines of comfort and love that went unacknowledged in his urgency to tell her.

"And you," he said, catching her hands and staring into her eyes. "Protect the Tree, you said, as if you had heard it from birth, as we did…" He shook his head. "Cantra yos'Phelium swore an oath to protect the Tree—Liad exists because a mad outlaw needed a safe place for a dead man's plant! Jelaza Kazone—Jela's Fulfillment! Generations dead and still Jela's damn Tree—" He dropped her hands and stepped back, outwardly calm, though she still read the tearing urgency within.

"Do you know what the captain's prime mandate is, should the ship be breached or need to be abandoned?" he asked.

"No." She projected calm, forcefully, swallowing amazement as he batted it aside as easily as a kitten batting away a ball.

"I'm to go to a certain safe place and remove the stasis box therein, taking it with me to safety. If it should happen that there is no room in the escape pod for the captain, he should hand over the stasis box to another and secure that person's oath to stand guard over the box until one of Korval should come and relieve him of it." Shan tipped his head. "Guess what's in the box, Priscilla."

She did not have to guess. "Seedlings."

"Seedlings." He nodded. "Every Korval ship has a stasis box; every captain has the same mandate. The *Passage,* as Korval's flag-ship, carries, in addition, several cans of seeds, as well as cloned genetic material, in the storage hold of each escape pod."

He reached forward and cupped her face in his big hands. "Priscilla, by the gods—by your own Goddess—go to safety. I beg you."

"I love you," she said, and saw the tears start to his eyes, just before he closed them and dropped his hands. She reached to touch his face. "Shan?"

The silver eyes opened, reflecting the exhaustion she read in his spirit. "Yes, Priscilla?"

"The captain gave me instructions. I—is it still required that I fulfill them?"

"Yes." He hesitated, then took her hand and looked closely into her eyes. "Understand that you are chosen, Priscilla, rather than Ken Rik—even though Line yo'Lanna and Clan Justus are both closely allied with us—because it is a more proper use of melant'i that one of Korval set the weapons in place and make us ready to meet necessity." He paused, and it was just possible to read his love through her own astonished joy. "With your permission, I will explain this to Ken Rik. I'll meet you in the cafeteria on the next hour, and we'll announce our lifemating to the crew."

She forced herself into Serenity and regarded him dispassion-ately. "This is for protection, of course."

"Of course," Shan said with a glimmer of his usual humor. "But don't, I pray you, Priscilla, ask me whether it's yours or mine."

Sharon Lee & Steve Miller   767

VANDAR

Winterfair

The chill in the air was not entirely due to the weather. Even Hakan felt it: the stares and glares, the change in conversational tone when they entered an area.

For the most part the huge room was busy. Lamps and candles were everywhere, illuminating people cheerfully working their way toward the exhibitions and competitions that would follow the fair's opening march. There was a darker corner at the back of the practice hall, toward which Cory seemed bent. As they circled, Hakan occasionally exchanged words with friends, and there was hesitation in the greetings, an awkwardness in the banter.

Hakan's burden of guitar cases and song books, no larger than Cory's, grew heavier as they got closer to the far corner. "Cory, it's pretty dim back here!"

"So much the better," the small man said with half a grin. "This way everyone will watch someone else and not steal the tunes we play."

Hakan frowned, then jerked his head about as someone rolled out a quick, bright riff of a song they had been practicing. "Yeah, I see what you mean. But—I feel like we're exiled back here!"

Cory carefully put down his load of cases and music.

"It may be better, Hakan," he said finally. "We are different from all these others. We are—what would you say?—the gust that breaks the branch. Everyone here knows who we are. I know only you; you know only a few."

Hakan felt his cheeks flush. "Do they really think that way?" he demanded. "Do they think the King's Court will choose us because of..."

"Hero," Cory said succinctly, and Hakan flushed deeper. "We play at a handicap, alone or together."

"It's not fair!" Hakan muttered, suddenly seeing a dozen faces turned in their direction, a hand pointing them out, a huddle of curious youngsters...

Crash!

There was mild laughter nearby as Cory slowly extricated himself from the bench he had fallen over.

Hakan rushed to his side. "Are you all right, man? You never trip!"

"Ah," Cory said mildly. "Do you mean I am not perfect?"

Hakan looked at hint sharply. "You've done this before, haven't you?"

"I've never been to a Winterfair, Hakan; how could I?"

"Damn it, Cory, you play more games than a fall breeze in the leaves! You've played before—in competition!"

Cory smiled, gave Hakan a brotherly pat on the wrist, and turned his back to open an instrument case. He spoke softly, nearly to himself. "Hakan, I know competition. I know I play well. Here? How do I know? In Gylles I only know how you play...and I enjoy working with your music. But now we are not so great—and now perhaps your friends will talk with you if you see them without me."

Hakan grinned. "You're really devious!"

Cory shrugged. "I hope you have the old strings I asked you to save. We should practice with them—for a while..."

Hakan laughed, opening his mandolette case. "Until they all break?"

"Exactly!" the smaller man said, pulling out a guitar. "Exactly."

The fairgrounds were a marvel to Miri. Tucked into a valley with a large hill sealing the windward side, the place was built entirely of timber. The permanent buildings and the many raised walkways were of wood, and over both the Avenue of Artists and the Parade were tall wooden frames supporting taut canvas to help keep out the snow and wind while still letting in light and air.

Some of the fair events took place away from the structures: the downhill sled races, the woodcutting championships, and the team sled-drags. Clearly, though, the focus was the fairgrounds and the wooden structures.

"Kem, this is like there is two Gylles! One for all the time, and one for the fair!"

Kem laughed. "Of course! The fair is something special—it brings in a lot of money each year, but you can't hold it in town. People come from all over the country! Look over there—that pole now, that's for..."

Without missing a step Miri noted its location, ignoring Kem's explanation of the obvious: a radio tower higher than the pennant poles.

"Why don't I see that before?" she asked, pausing to stare.

"They bring it in by train—the King's Voice goes to all the big events. There's even a chance that Hakan and Cory could be on radio all over Bentrill if they win the competition!"

"And the electric?" Miri demanded. "I see no wires!"

Kem looked at her in surprise. "I don't know—I think they use the train for the electric."

"Do they?" Miri said, and headed that way, purpose in her small stride. Kem gaped for a moment and then followed, hoping that her friend was not going to do anything rash.

Val Con and Miri said good night to Hakan quietly, careful not to wake Kem, who was asleep against his shoulder.

"Drive well, my friend," Val Con said, and Hakan grinned.

"No fear." His grin widened. "Oh, man, we were great!"

Val Con laughed gently. "Yes, Hakan. Drive carefully. Sleep well. Good night."

They stood on the porch and waved until the taillights were lost at the end of the drive, then slipped inside, moving down the dark hallway and up the steps in utter silence. Zhena Trelu had left the fair soon after Hakan and Cory had finished their first set, claiming exhaustion; it would be less than wise to wake her at this advanced hour of the night.

Miri lay down on the bed with a deep sigh. Val Con sat on the edge, eyes smiling.

"Did you have a good time, cha'trez?"

"Wonderful. This thing goes on for another week? I'll be spoiled for doing anything that looks like work!"

He was laughing. She snapped her fingers and twisted to sit up, digging into the deep pocket of her skirt.

"Almost forgot, boss. I got—" She hesitated, suddenly shy. "I got a present for you."

"A present? Will it explode, I wonder? Is that why you're sitting so far away?"

She grinned and slid closer, until her hip was against his, then offered him the blue plush box.

He took it in his long fingers, found the catch, and opened it. Miri, watching his face closely, saw his expression go from pleased expectation to smiling delight.

"A 'jiliata," he murmured, inclining his head to the silver dragon on its black cord. "I salute you." He looked up, green eyes glowing. "Lisamia keshoc, cha'trez."

She smiled and answered in her still-careful Low Liaden. "You are welcome, Val Con-husband. It gives me joy to give you joy."

He laughed and hugged her. "Spoken with the accent of Solcintra!" He offered the box. "Will you put it on?"

She slipped the necklace from its nesting place, ran the soft cord through her fingers, and slid it around his neck, twisting the intricate clasp shut. "There you go."

He raised his head, smiling, then lifted a brow at the look he surprised on her face. "Is there something wrong?"

"Not wrong." She touched his face, her hand fluttering from cheek to brow to lips. "Right." She grinned. "Punch drunk—fair drunk. Gods."

There was a small silence; her hand fell away, and she shifted a little, recalling a question from much earlier in the day. "We rich now, boss?"

He laughed lightly. "We have been rich for some time now, you and I. Today they merely gave us some money."

It was her turn to laugh; she squeezed his hand tightly. "We got you out of there kind of late—I meant to ask if they told you 'bout the station?"

"Station?" His brows furled. "The Winter Train?"

"Nah. The one they call the King's Voice. The radio station."

His eyes sharpened. "Ah! That is it! I thought the King's Voice was like the King's Eyes or—a representative of the king."

She shook her head. "Nope. It's a portable radio station, tower and all. Goes all 'round the country. Uses a generator in one of the trains."

"I must see it." It was almost hunger she felt coming through the pattern in her head. "I must see the transmitter!"

She nodded and fumbled in the pocket of her skirt. "Thought you would. Here we go: four passes, special deal for hero types. Had a time talking 'em loose. Thought Kem was gonna disown me."

Val Con hugged her tightly. "Miri, Miri. Things come to-gether! Soon we'll leave for Laxaco—the city where flying machines are ordinary and they have radio factories. We may be on our way home soon—or at least in contact."

"Promise me something," she said earnestly.

He moved back a bit. "What should I promise?"

"That we'll finish out this fair before you drag us away to the smog!"

He grinned. "Of course! We stay to the end of the party!"

She hugged him back then, for a long time.

VANDAR

Winterfair

The icy gray clouds flowed through Fornem's Gap, relentlessly driven by the stiff, oceanic breeze. Miri glared at them without result, while Val Con leaned against the front porch rail at her side, watching six of the king's honor guard march up the lane from their temporary camp. He sighed lightly at the two cars farther down the lane: sight-seers, looking over the battleground.

From the lane came a familiar roar, closely followed by Hakan's car, green and red fair-ribbons snapping smartly in the breeze. The driver's side window was down despite the cold, and Hakan's voice—but not his words—could be heard long before the car stopped.

"I said," he repeated breathlessly, "that we've got some bad news and some good news!"

"Bad news first," Miri said firmly as she opened the back door and started packing in the picnic lunch, picnic dinner, and snacks Zhena Trelu insisted on sending with them.

"Always," Val Con agreed.

"Right. The bad news is that Capstone Trio won't be coming in for the fair after all. They've all come down with pneumonia or something—the radio man called Kem's mother last night to tell her they'd need to come up with a replacement."

Miri shrugged. "Bad news like that beats the wind out of something serious!"

Hakan barely flushed. "Well, you haven't heard them, so you don't know—and I was going to get to meet them!"

Val Con finished stowing the extra blankets Zhena Trelu had sent and slid close to Hakan on the bench seat, keeping a wary eye on the large hot mug perched precariously next to the driver. "Then," he said, "you may tell us the good news."

"Right," Hakan said again. "The good news is that they've decided—the fair governors—to have a contest for the slot the Capstones would have been in. It'll be open to any trio!"

Miri snuggled in next to Val Con and slammed the door shut as the car began to accelerate.

Val Con stared straight ahead as Hakan shifted and looked at the two of them.

"Well?" he demanded.

"Well what?" Miri asked, then began shaking her head. "No. No. No chance. No way. I don't stand in front—"

Val Con was laughing, eyes straight ahead.

"Miri, I've heard you sing—you're terrific!" Hakan said. "We've got a great chance of winning. All we need to do is come up with a good name—already have a couple for you to think about—and practice today after the duo competition." He glanced at her face. "Look, you don't even have to sing all that much if—"

"No!" Miri exclaimed. In Terran, punctuated by an elbow in Val Con's side, she said, "Stop laughing, you devil!"

But Val Con continued to chuckle, ducking to let the argument bounce back and forth over his head, all the way to the fair.

Miri grumpily folded the newspapers under her arm as they left the practice room and headed for the competition hall. The problem was not listening to Val Con and Hakan practice. It was listening to the people around them, hearing the remarks—and collecting the papers. The two men were in a world only peripherally connected to Vandar, mumbling about song order and such like, oblivious to the points and the stares and the papers.

They were yesterday's papers, mostly, each with accounts of the battle, and four of the five, including the *King's Press,* featured photographs taken at the awards ceremony. The other paper had sketches that were barely recognizable—and which tipped her annoyance into anger, for the one of Val Con made the scar the most prominent feature on his face.

It was not snowing yet, which was some comfort, Miri thought. She shook her head. Somehow it had been settled that she would sing with them the next day, and she could not even blame the decision on Val Con, who had merely laughed throughout the whole argument. She still needed to come up with a name, though, having rejected out of hand Hakan's favorites: the Gap Trio, the Zhena Robersun Trio, and the Springbreeze Farm Trio.

"Wind'll take these things," she grumbled in Terran. "And I'm damned if I—"

Karooom!

"Wow! It's going to snow now!" Hakan cried. Then he stopped, abruptly realizing that his friends stood rooted in their tracks, heads craned skyward.

Miri's eyes were on one spot in the overcast; she moved her head ever so slightly, following the sound.

"What's the matter?" Hakan demanded, puzzled. "It's only thunder—"

"Hush!" Cory snapped.

Hakan listened, too. True, it had been a rather sudden bit of thunder; there was a distinct but distant rumble trailing away to the northeast and Fornem's Gap.

"That's funny," he said a moment later. "It sounds like the thunder there is echoing against the wind!"

Miri said something in the language she and Cory sometimes used between themselves. She said it three times, progressively louder, as if casting an incantation. "Sonic boom. Sonic boom. Sonic boom."

Cory answered in the same language, moved his shoulders in that foreign way of his, and finished with the same words.

"Sonic boom."

He sighed. "Do you always have this kind of thunder, Hakan? So isolated? No flash of lightning?"

"Well, we get thunder in snowstorms a few times a year— usually means it's going to be a big one. But I think I still hear that— you don't think it's a windtwist, do you? We haven't had one of those since I was a baby!"

"No, I think not, friend. Probably just a squall. I have heard this thunder once or twice—at home—and so has Miri, but we have heard nothing like it here."

The sound faded out; the conversations of the crowd around picked up, and in moments the isolated, far-rumbling thunder was stored away as a strange memory from the Winterfair.

"There!" Hakan said as they arrived at the competition hall. "It was the first cloud breaking its ice!"

He pointed to a gray curtain moving down the side of the mountain, obscuring all behind it.

"Just like Surebleak," Miri said in unenthusiastic Terran. "Except there's too many happy people around. And some idiot skypilot who don't know the local limits!"

"Cha'trez, we don't know that. After all, there is an active Benish aviation industry."

"Yeah? I'll tell you what. You prove that was homegrown or natural, and I'll take the next ten watch details we come up with!"

"Ah, but what if we are done with watches?"

She grinned. "Always wanna hedge your bet, doncha, Liaden?"

"Come on!" Hakan said, grabbing Cory's arm. "They're posting the competition order!"

Grinning, they made appropriate haste.

VANDAR

Winterfair

The snow pelted Miri as she wandered through the double-flapped cloth door, cold bit her nostrils, clearing them instantly of the scent of a thousand humans.

Hakan and Cory were scheduled after the next group. Miri grappled with the name once again, struggling to avoid "Hakan and Cory and Miri" or, as Hakan had also suggested, "Miri and Hakan and Cory." She sighed. Hakan's musical talent was balanced by inability to choose a name with a snap to it.

Despite the snow—or because of it—the fair outside the performance hall was lively. The sleds that had been sitting idly in the fields were in full use, ferrying families to and fro; the hill in the distance was masked by the white stuff. The braziers spotted here and there were well tended, and Miri moved slowly toward one, trying not to step on a child.

As a Merc, she had never had much to do with children; certainly she had never developed the amazing talent Val Con had demonstrated yesterday, of being able to talk and patiently answer questions. The man seemed to actually *like* kids!

Good thing, too, Miri thought, 'cause they were *every*where. One was at that very moment angling toward the brazier, followed by a shorter version, both with coats carelessly unfastened and hoods hanging down their backs. They stood in front of the fire and turned their faces into the snow, giggling, until the taller of the two spotted her beside them and smiled.

"Good fair, zhena."

"Good fair, zama," she answered, feeling her mouth curve into a smile. "Button your coats before you go sledding."

The smaller one gave a crow of laughter. "We *been* sledding," he told her. "*Now* we go eat!"

"Good choice," Miri said, and they laughed, waving as they moved away from the fire.

Miri moved down the snow-covered path, admiring the true whiteness of the snow, so unlike the gray precipitation of Surebleak.

Kids could be happy here—

She broke the thought off, ears straining against the muffling of the snow, against the soft whisper of flakes striking her coat.

It *was* there! From above the clouds came a thrumming, lurking noise, the sound of a modern craft, hovering.

Fair noise overwhelmed the sound, and for a moment she doubted herself. Then it came again—the kind of sound she had hoped and prayed and cursed for when Klamath had come apart around them, freezing them, frying them, killing them...She banished the memory and ran through the Rainbow's sequence so quickly that the colors blurred into a wheel before her mind's eye.

The thrumming sound came again—louder, it seemed—and she turned, resolved to run to Val Con, to bring him out to listen.

What for, Robertson? she asked herself derisively. What's he gonna do about it? Yell? You need a radio, quicktime.

Damn. A radio right here, and no way to send a message! There had to be a way...

A man came around the corner of the hall, shrouded in snow and blinded by it. She dodged, blinking up at the hugeness of him, and called out of happier memories, out of hope. "Jason? Edger?"

He stopped, taking shape out of the snow and smiling down at her. "Zhena?"

Miri laughed and apologized. "In the snow I mistake you for someone I know."

"Easy to do when the snow winds come!" he boomed good-naturedly. "Good fair!" He was gone then, leaving warmth behind amid the confusion.

A gong banged in the distance and was echoed by others—the new hour was starting. She rushed into the hall, a name for the trio on her lips.

Hakan and Val Con were still setting up. Miri moved to a front-row bench and instantly felt Val Con's gaze on her. She smiled, adding quick flutter of hand-talk—Old Trade—that said "Need to talk later." His wave and smile reassured her.

Val Con sat briefly at the piano before the introduction, testing it. He would be playing backup on the guitar in some of the songs, but in the others he would play melody while Hakan sang. A few touches of the instrument assured him; he nodded to someone off-stage, and a white-haired woman in fur boots walked to centerstage amid the stomping of feet and whistling from the audience.

"Next on the program is a new duo. Hakan, of course, is known to many of us; his partner Cory is a recent addition to our area, and we'll all get a chance to hear them right now!"

The music started instantly, and the audience chuckled as the emcee hurried off stage. Hakan waited until she had actually made the wings before he began to sing.

Miri relaxed. So far, no one had mentioned that Hakan and Cory were heroes. She sat back and listened extra hard, studying the music. The Snow Wind Trio was going to have to be damn good to get on the radio.

The applause died away, and Miri went toward the stage to join the small group at the bottom of the steps. She sighed. If the number of stage-side fans and the volume of applause meant anything, then Hakan and Cory were not the hit they had hoped to be.

Hakan stopped to talk with some friends, and Miri smiled wanly at her husband, surprised at the amount of joy in him.

He swung an arm around her waist and hugged her tight, laughing at raised eyebrows.

"So we are not traditional enough, we two?" he asked in Benish.

"Looks that way, boss," she replied in Terran.

He slanted a bright green glance at her face. "A problem, cha'trez?"

She shrugged and pulled him with her toward the back of the hall. They found seats on the aisle near the door-flaps and settled down just as the next group signaled that they were ready and the emcee came on stage.

"Problem or solution, I don't know," she said carefully. She turned to look him full in the face. "Someone's sitting upstairs, doing circles over the clouds. Not transport class. Say, an unbaffled ship or an out-and-out jet—can't tell with all this other noise. But doing a loiter."

"Ah," he said, and she clamped down hard on the need to ask him what "Ah" meant this time.

"Thing is," she said instead, "I know how to get their attention. If you want to."

Val Con raised an eyebrow, waiting.

"All we got to do," she said, as if she was not certain that he had already thought of it himself, "is get on the radio. This trio gig of Hakan's...If you and me can sing something in Terran or Liaden—a round, maybe—one part in Benish, one in Terran, one in Liaden." She saw his frown. "Know it's against the rules, boss, but I can't figure it otherwise. Unless you want to hijack the station!"

"Inefficient, hijacking a station. And you think your idiot sky-pilot will be listening?"

"What the hell do you think she's doing? Way it makes sense is they were doing the frequency scan, like you and me did, homed in on the radio like a beacon, and now they're circling, trying to decide if it's worth a stop."

He nodded. "You were wasted as a sergeant, Miri. You might have been a—"

"Hey! Cory! Miri! Somebody wants us to teach them our playing style!" Hakan called, arriving with two young women and a shy man in tow.

Val Con smiled vaguely at the group; Miri's smile contained a touch of frost.

"Hakan, it is to be flattered," she said more sharply than she had intended. "But us—we need to practice. We must be better!"

Hakan looked crestfallen, his exuberance lost in a mumble.

One of the young women bustled forward and nodded to Miri, as if to an equal. "I am Zhena Wrand. After you have practiced—and played—Hakan tells me you may compete tomorrow—after that, we will work with you! There is a new feel to what Hakan and Cory do. Not revolutionary, mind. But new, not as hide-bound. All these traditionals want nothing more than to hear exactly what they heard last year! You watch and see who wins—a traditional band! Next year, though, I—we—will be so good they can't ignore us!" With that she turned, lifted a hand to her friends, and stalked away.

Hakan stared after them strangely, then his eyes lighted as Kem arrived.

"Hakan and Cory—you did fine!" She smiled, tucking her hand into Hakan's.

"At least some people think so!" Hakan said, pointedly glancing at Miri.

Val Con began to say something, but Miri put her hand out, silencing him.

"Hakan?" she said very seriously. "Do you still want a trio?" His face actually paled. "Of course, Miri," he stammered. "I didn't mean—"

"Quiet," she ordered, and Val Con bent his head to hide his smile.

"If we have a trio, we do it right," Miri announced. "First, the name. The name should be 'Snow Wind Trio,' unless another—"

"No, that's good. Real good!" Hakan smiled at Kem, tightening his grip on her hand as Miri continued.

"Fine. We settle that much. Now." She pointed back and forth between Val Con and Hakan. "You two, you work good together. Me? I sing some. Mostly before I sing at parties, not on stage. And these is bests—the best groups in Bentrill! We have to be very, very and traditional—like that zhena said—or different! So different they can't compare. We don't have time to be all traditional. So—we practice being different!"

Miri turned to the other woman suddenly. "Listen, Kem, this fair—it might not be much fun for you. If we do good we can make a name—establish ourselves like Hakan wants to. But we need him to practice hard right now!"

Kem laughed, holding up a hand. "Miri, don't worry. Hakan is happiest when he's doing his music. If you and Cory can help make the music work—I couldn't ask for more."

She grabbed Miri's hand and gave it a squeeze. "I'll help, honey. I'll bring food, applaud, chase people away, whatever you need. All right?"

"All right." Miri looked at them all and smiled. "Zhena Trelu sends all this food. You help us eat it and we talk—then practice."

She led the way into the snow at such a determined pace that it took Val Con a moment to catch up and put his hand in hers.

VANDAR

Springbreeze Farm

Hell with it, Miri decided and tapped him on the shoulder. "Val Con?"

He stirred. "You are not asleep?"

"Nah. You ain't either."

"No. Adrenaline."

"Hmmph. Thought you could sleep anytime anywhere." She moved closer and slipped an arm loosely around his waist. "For that matter, thought I could, too. Tried to use the Rainbow, but I keep getting off track."

He backed into her, sighing. "I am not certain. My hunch is you are correct about this ship and its interest. But there are other matters, and the Loop—"

"What in the hell can that thing have to say about it?" she demanded. "If the Loop lets you see through clouds maybe it'd help."

He was silent for a moment before turning to face her.

"The Loop," he said with emphasis, "indicates that contacting a spaceship is beneficial only if we have plans to leave this planet. Have we such plans?"

She shifted irritably. "Why ask me?"

"We are lifemates, Miri," he said softly. "I ask to know. I ask because it is not so bad a place, really, and because life could be pleasant here. No Juntavas, no Department of the Interior..."

Trust him to see her second thoughts. She was silent for some time, trying to work it through.

"Well," she said eventually. "You got plans. Gotta keep an eye on that family of yours. Got stuff to say to your brother. Got stuff to say to Edger. And I might get bored of singing for my supper in a couple years..."

"Then we have such plans," he said. "In order to leave this world we should make earliest contact with a means of doing so— even the Juntavas or the Department. This is contraindicated if the ship belongs to Yxtrang; yet they would hardly wait, circling a single outpost, when there is a whole world to plunder. The chance of it being Yxtrang is something under one percent, by the way."

"What chance that it's Edger?" she asked hopefully.

"Less than ten percent—closer to nine."

"Mmmpf. Lots of percents left, huh? What's the odds mean, if you gotta use that thing?"

Val Con stroked her arm gently. "The odds are twenty-four percent that we have a Scout overhead; thirty percent chance that it is a smuggler, perhaps coming to see what has happened to his associates. There is a smaller chance that it is an accidental discovery, and the odds of it being the Juntavas are rather slim."

She shook her head in the dark. "You wanna boil it down for me? Long day, long night…"

"The largest chance," Val Con said, trying to phrase things as vaguely as possible yet give her the essential information, "is that it is someone directly looking for us—slightly better that it's the Department of the Interior than a Korval ship. The politics of either are hard to measure at this distance."

"Depending on what your brother decided to do with that computer code. Which I still don't know was a good idea."

"They had to be warned," he said mildly.

Miri snorted. "Tell me, then: All that Scout blood in your family—not to mention your grandma the smuggler—what's the chances of them coming into an Interdicted World, breaking the sound barrier and probably every aviation law on the books?"

Out of the darkness came a sigh. "Rhetorically? Not high."

"Look at the damn thing, Liaden. What's it say?"

He sighed again, then suddenly gave a low laugh. "It says that despite it all, it is only estimating. If it happens that an Yxtrang general wanted to have a holiday shoot, then all the Loop's numbers mean that, as unlikely as the event is, it could still happen."

"Great," Miri said. "Did I ever tell you about the time I needed to roll five sevens in a row to stay out of trouble?"

"Did you?"

"No. Rolled four."

"Ah—and then?"

"I had some trouble."

Val Con grinned in the dark. "Shall I ask more?"

"Later." She touched his cheek. "Basically what you're telling me is that if we're planning on going through with these shenanigans we're likely to have trouble. And if we don't, trouble might find us anyway."

"Will," he corrected, reaching out. He pulled her close and kissed her ear gently. "Cha'trez, let us talk the Rainbow together tonight. My hunch is that *we* are trouble; events flow roughly around us because we seize every opportunity."

"Carpe diem," she muttered, and laughed. "We seize the day. Sometimes, the day seizes back!"

He laughed with her and reached to touch the barely seen, much-beloved face. "True. Let us now seize a Rainbow. Red is the color of physical relaxation..."

Eventually they slept soundly.

MCGEE ORBIT

The message hit them as they hit orbit. His boss had been sitting in the co-pilot's seat since it had, staring at the screen and frowning. The couple of glances Cheever had been able to spare for the message board during the orbiting drill had not shown anything that seemed to warrant Pat Rin yos'Phelium's frown; a couple of lines of Liaden characters and a rendering of a dragon flying over a tree at the end of it all; like a seal.

"Right, then, Tower," he said into the mike. "Landing time acknowledged and recorded. Thanks." He checked the board once more, nodded, and leaned back in the chair, wondering what was going on.

"Pilot McFarland."

He straightened. "Yessir."

Pat Rin was still staring at the screen, one hand idly toying with the blue stone in his left ear. "I offer you the opportunity to leave my employ, Pilot—and at once."

Cheever goggled. "You're firing me?"

"Did I say it?" Pat Rin snapped. Abruptly he turned the chair around, so that Cheever could see his face. "Forgive me, Pilot," he said more carefully. "I am in every way satisfied with your service. I offer a letter of reference stating so, and a continuance of your pay until you may locate another employer."

"I'm doing the job, but you're gettin' rid of me," Cheever repeated, brow rumpled in perplexity. "Why?"

For a minute he thought the little dandy was going to go all high and holy on him, tell him to shut up and pack up.

But Pat Rin hesitated, then sighed. "Circumstances sometimes overtake one, Pilot. In my—business—one schools oneself to accept reversals and to use them to future advantage." Once again the slim fingers adjusted the blue earring. "Circumstances having thus overtaken me, I am constrained as an honorable man to offer an honorable man the means to avoid possible—unpleasantness—accruing to one in my employ."

Cheever chewed it over and finally had to shake his head. "Looks me like you're gonna need an extra gun, if these circumstances of yours're liable to turn ugly. Told your cousin Shan I'd keep an eye on you—part of the deal, see?" He thought some more, oblivious to the speculation in Pat Rin's eyes, and finally summed it up. "Might be he knew you were prone to circumstances, huh? Might he thought you'd be better off with some help this time out."

"It might be, Pilot," Pat Rin said gently. "Who am I to say?" He stared at the screen again for some minutes, then extended a languid hand and cleared it before looking back at the bigger man.

"You must understand," he said, "that there may be danger, or there may be none. At the present we will merely extend our itinerary and give over any plans of a return to Liad."

Cheever frowned. "For how long?"

Pat Rin adjusted the ear-stone a final time and stood with sensuous grace. He bowed ironically and smiled. "Why, Pilot, only until circumstances resolve themselves. Do wake me when we land." And he strolled off toward his cabin.

VANDAR

Winterfair

The key was the green light.

When the green light was lit, the broadcast was going out from the stage. When both red and green were on, it was going out from the microphone on the tables at the back of the hall. The yellow light meant that the hall was on standby.

Miri studied the competition rules while Val Con kibbitzed with the radio techs. He left the board with reluctance after a technician pointedly asked him not to touch, and climbed the steps onto the stage.

"No go?" Miri asked.

He moved his shoulders. "There is not much to be done from here at any rate—a relay board only. To subvert the system, I would need to be in the main shack." He grinned at her. "And we have already agreed that hijacking the station is not efficient."

"Probably just as well," she said. "Looks like that zhena up there—in the gray—decides what goes on the air." She shook her head. "Rules say they're gonna have each group play twice—two three-song sets. They'll do random drawings for play slots each time. That gives us a couple chances to catch the green light—you think Hakan'll be okay?"

Val Con sat on a bench and patted the spot beside him. "Hakan will be fine, Mini. He sees that you have done only proper things—the zhena has indicated what is required, and it shall be done. If he is not comfortable with our chances of winning he has not told me."

"What's the Loop say?"

He raised a brow. "Nothing. Lack of information."

"I don't mean about winning, damn it, I mean—"

"Miri, Miri...Both questions have the same answer. We cannot predict how the judging will go because there are different judges. We cannot predict who will be broadcast because we do not know what criteria the zhena in gray applies to her decisions."

"And if they put us on the air we don't know if anyone upstairs is still listening!"

"Exactly."

Miri grinned. "If it's Edger you can bet who'll be right down."

Val Con smiled and squeezed her hand. "I suspect even he would not be so hasty. Besides, Zhena Brigsbee would only say to Zhena Trelu, 'I told you there was something strange about those two...'"

Miri was sweating, but so were Val Con and Hakan. The first two songs had gone over well, and they had weathered the minor problem of having to use another song for their opening number—the one they had planned to play turned out to be the closing number of the preceding group.

So far they had followed Miri's direction to play for themselves rather than to fit custom. Val Con's piano solo had certainly scored some points in the first number, and Miri and Hakan's switched roles in the second—he singing the female side and she the male—had drawn attention again. Though whether the attention was good or bad was more than Miri could tell. Worse, the green light had yet to come on.

Hakan moved against the wave of applause to his microphone, grinning fit to split his face.

"Now," he said, then paused to catch his breath. "Now, the Snow Wind Trio is pleased to bring you something a little different. We'll sing a song you all know well—first the way Zhena Robersun learned it when she was young, then the way Zamir Robersun heard it as he traveled on his brother's ship, and finally as I learned it as child, here in Gylles. Here, then, is 'Leaf Dance.'"

The audience was silent. On the board across the room, the green light came on, and Miri gulped; hearing the introduction roll off Val Con's piano, she closed her eyes and broke in on the beat, concentrating on the words she had set to the Benish music. The original was a simpleminded, happy hymn to autumn, admirably suited for rounds. Out of some perverse sense of obligation to Hakan, innocently assisting in the shattering of galactic law, Miri had tried to stay as close as possible to the spirit of the original.

In what seemed like no time at all her part was over and Val Con took up his, the liquid sound of the Liaden words transforming the sweet little melody into something exotic and sensuous. Miri slid her hand into her pocket, wrapped her fingers around the

788   *Partners in Necessity*

absolutely forbidden harmonica nestled there, and quickly brought it to her mouth.

To Hakan it looked like magic: Miri's cupped hands were somehow producing an eerie, unexpected sound, playing haunting counterpoint to Cory's part of the round.

And then it was his turn to take a step closer to the mike and give the audience the song they had known all their lives, Miri's harmonica a faint, warm buzz beneath the familiar words.

He finished his verse, caught the signal from Cory, and kept the music coming, while Miri played the harmonica solo to the world, reminding the audience that as leaves dance, they die. The thought hooked her, calling up memories of friends, dancing and dead, recalling her to times when the harmonica had made the sounds the unit had dared not: the laughter, the curses, the sobs.

Coming back to herself, she let the improvisation flutter to an end. First Hakan and then Val Con let their music fade and stop. Miri whipped the harmonica across her mouth one last time, and bowed.

She bowed to a silence so absolute the wind could be heard against the door flaps. Then, in the silence, people began to stand, and for a heartstopping moment she thought they were going to storm the stage. Not knowing what else to do, she bowed again. Then she felt Val Con's hand in hers, felt him bowing with her, while the sight of him inside her head was a marvel of brightness and warmth.

The cheering started then, and lasted a long time.

The judges had not been as impressed by the performance as the audience had. The Snow Wind Trio was tied for second at the end of the first round; and that second was a long way in points from the first-place group, which was—as Zhena Wrand had insisted—as traditional as possible.

On the other hand, popular sentiment was clear: The Snow Wind Trio was a success. There was still a chance that they could gain more points in the second round, after the dinner break. In the meantime, they had been besieged as they walked through the hall.

Hakan stood with a list of offers in hand, reading them off one by one to Kem, Miri, and Val Con. "This one is for Laxaco's spring fest—three days at a club, one night in concert at the fest.

This one is for a tour. I don't think it's so good—it's mostly one-night stands at smaller clubs. This one's an offer of a year contract, four nights on, three nights off..."

"Hakan?" Miri asked finally.

"Miri?"

"Why don't we wait until after the fair to count the pennies? The wind doesn't finish blowing yet."

"But some of these people say they need to know tonight! Zhena Ovlia, for example—"

"Ought to learn something about manners," Kem said, and Miri gave a crow of approving laughter.

"No, wait," Hakan tried again. "I mean she's trying to get things moving in a hurry and if we can say yes tonight—"

"If we can say yes tonight," Val Con said softly, "we can say yes tomorrow. After our second set we see: Do we get on the radio again? Do we get the award? Are we second or third? All these add up. Tomorrow is time enough to see what we have. Let us be patient."

"You be patient for everybody," Miri told him. "Me, I'm going to see when we play tonight."

In a moment they were all on their feet.

The luck of the draw made them spectators for most of the evening: They were scheduled last, right after the leading group.

"Cha'trez, have you considered a short walk?" Val Con asked after the second group played.

Miri blinked at him. "What for?"

He laughed gently. "For your tension. You are concerned?"

"Yes, dammit, I'm concerned. You'd be, too, if you had any nerves. I never sang in front of a group as big as the one this morning, and it looks like the evening show's gonna be a sellout. Feel like I'll probably freeze up and forget the words, or fall flat my face, or—"

Val Con took her hand, offering comfort and assurance. "Miri, you will do fine. You always do well and more than well—and then belittle yourself, eh?"

He smiled at her and reached to touch her hair, oblivious to the shocked zhena sitting just behind. "You are very bright, cha'trez. I see you as you see me, remember? And this edge, this concern, is not bad to have. But further—"

"I feel like I'm ready to fight, and it's only people with guitars and words! Wish that damn idiot upstairs would *do* something, if he's still hanging around. And Hakan's so set on us going on tour and seeing the world, I feel like we gotta do it for him, so that he won't be disappointed." She took a deep breath, looked at him, and grinned. "Never pays to let a Merc think, you know? I'll be okay."

As he watched with his inner eye he saw a slight wavering of Miri's fires, a mistiness, and then she was brighter than ever, the melody of her absolutely true.

"We're playing for joy," she said slowly, shifting so that her shoulder touched his companionably. "Just like I said to Hakan."

"We are playing for joy," he agreed. "It is the best of all things to play for."

INTERDICTED WORLD
I-2796-893-44

It was a marvel the place did not take fire. The fairground was a maze of unsound wooden buildings, wooden walkways, wooden trade booths, and scattered mountains of chopped wood. And everywhere there was open flame—braziers, torches, cooking pits—tended by a half-witted barbarian or two, some clearly the worse for a jar or more of the atrocious local spirits.

More disturbing than the dangerous mix of fire and wood was the crowd itself. That this group of locals was as backward and ignorant as those in the south was expected; that the signs of disease and early aging were on many of them was not unexpected. Yet sig'Alda found the presence of so many infirmities distressing, so that he constantly reminded himself that his immunizations were current and that no disease known to modern medicine was capable of infecting him.

Out of the crowd bumbled a group of the local young, shouting and shrieking. One lost control of its balance and crashed heavily into sig'Alda, wrapping its arms around his legs in a clumsy attempt to save itself.

sig'Alda clenched himself into stillness and waited with what patience he could muster for the thing to sort itself out and be on its way. Instead, the cub tipped its face up, a vacuous smile on its fat face in loathsome parody of a proper and well-behaved Liaden child.

sig'Alda frowned. "Leave," he said curtly, and the round face puckered as it struggled with the meaning of the word.

"Laman?" An adult swooped out of the crowd and plucked the cub free, smiling to show a mouthful of crooked teeth. "I'm sorry, zamir, but you know what the young ones are!"

"Yes, certainly," sig'Alda said with scant courtesy, and moved on, counting wooden auditoriums until he came to the fourth on the left.

The music came up softly: "The Ballad of the RosaRing." They had schooled Hakan for an hour in his pronunciation of "Fly on by," the sum of his singing part. Val Con had a couple backup and fill-in lines, but primarily it was Miri's song to sing.

The audience, respectful, may have been expecting another set of rounds: what they got was the ballad, in Terran, of a pair of lovers separated forever when an experimental virus got loose on the RosaRing.

The translation they had given Hakan for the audience had the Ring a resource-rich island cursed with a strain of infectious madness—which to Miri's mind was as close as made no difference. The Ring virus had been deadly, the world it circled rich, and three rescue teams had been shot down by automatics before the fatcats had finally seen the stupid waste of it and quarantined the sector. The lover had been on the last rescue team. For Hakan—for the Winterfair—he escaped.

Miri sang the last "Fly on by," bowed low to hide her tears—which annoyed her—and lifted her head to the thundering crowd.

"Forget the words, Miri?" Val Con murmured at her side, and she laughed, breathlessly.

The crowd kept them at the front of the stage a moment more, then Miri unshipped her harmonica, ripped off a quick zipping sound with it, and the trio launched into the high-spirited Benish standard, "The Wind's Going My Way." The harmonica added a zest to the song Miri liked, and she dropped back to make room for the maneuver they had practiced.

Hakan dove for the piano, and passing Val Con the guitar, then Val Con was at the front lights, picking the tune rapidly with the harmonica's support. Some in the crowd laughed; there was even a sprinkling of premature applause, and, over on the side, the green light glowed steady.

They increased the speed of the song again, and once more, Miri watching for Val Con's signal. It came and they stopped, all together, bowing on the same instant.

The crowd stood, cheering and applauding and stamping their feet as the emcee stood uncertainly on the stage side, prepared to step up; but she stepped down instead as the cheering took up again.

"This never happens," Hakan whispered.

"No?" Miri said. She moved to the mike.

"Thank you! Thank you all!" she called, and the crowd grew quieter. "We are almost out of music now—" There was laughter as she paused to catch her breath. "But we know one more. Would you like to hear it?"

The audience roared assent, and Hakan stood transfixed.

"Zhena—" he began, but Cory was already back at the piano, and Miri was saying, "On the beat," with the hand-twitch that was the signal for "The Windmill Whirl." Hakan caught up his guitar and began to play.

DUTIFUL PASSAGE

"Be certain," Priscilla said for the third time, because that was the ritual—and because she distrusted his mood, all emotion bright and hard-edged and deliberate.

Shan folded his shirt neatly onto a chair and looked up at her, amusement flickering through eyes and pattern. "Come now, Priscilla, am I as faint-hearted as that?"

"You did say," she reminded him, "that it was madness for both captain and first mate to risk themselves when the Clan was in danger." She slid her trousers off and straightened, stern and lovely in her nakedness. "There *is* risk. One or both of us could die, if the Goddess frowns." She leaned forward, holding him with eyes alone. "Be *certain,* Shan."

"Well, I did say so," he agreed, sitting down to pull off his boots. "But that was before we had assassins at Trealla Fantrol, and the Clan spread to the Prime Points, and the *Passage* taking on weapons. All very well and good for Val Con to send a message telling us to stay out of trouble while he and his lady vacation. We're *in* trouble, damn him for a puppy!"

He unfastened his belt and sighed. "We need him, Priscilla. There's a reason why the Delm is chosen from yos'Phelium, and if the Ring falls into yos'Galan's keeping, we serve only as First Speaker-in-Trust, surrendering it with a sigh of relief the first moment duty allows."

He finished undressing, folded his trousers atop his shirt, and stood straight. "And now?"

"Now." She came across the room in a smooth glide and wrapped her arms around him, her breasts pushing into his chest as she kissed him deeply and thoroughly. When she was certain of his arousal, she stepped back, motioning to the bed. "Lie down."

Wordless for once, he obeyed, his eyes not moving from her face.

Priscilla nodded. "There is sometimes a danger, when you are soul-walking, of forgetting the pleasures and the pains of the body. Remember them, and cherish them all, so that when you come home, joy will ease your way back in."

She sat on the edge of the bed and touched his cheek very lightly, allowing him an instant to read all the tenderness and love she held for him, allowing herself the same instant to embrace the singing brightness of his regard for her. Firmly, then, she closed it off and composed herself to teach.

"You will enter trance," she instructed. "You will do this with all inner doors open and unguarded, with nothing at all left behind your Wall. You will remain in trance, awaiting my summons. It will be my responsibility to carry us both to your brother. It will be your responsibilities to keep your essence centered and balanced, and to be sure that you have left a connecting line between your soul and your body." She paused, considering him. "Can you do these things, Shan?"

"Yes."

"Be sure," she said, though nowhere in all the Teachings was a fourth asking of that question required. "Because, if you lose your lifeline or can't maintain your balance, I'm not strong enough to keep us both alive."

"I understand," he said. "I'm to stay in one piece and keep the way home clear. No matter what."

"No matter what," she agreed. "Even if something goes wrong. If I seem to fail, or you reach out and cannot find me—come back to your body!" She read his objection and repeated her order more gently. "Come back to your body, even if you think you're without me. Remember, my body is here, too. If I can, I will come back to it."

"And if you can't..." He closed his eyes, and she waited, listening to the hum of his thoughts, watching the interplay of needs and desires. At last he sighed and opened his eyes. "All right, Priscilla. May your Goddess have room in her heart to forgive me."

"She forgives everyone, my dear." She touched his bright hair. "Whenever you're ready."

Again he closed his eyes, and she watched him bring down his shields and his protections, extinguishing alarms—all with deft skill. He entered the trance quickly, his pattern thickening as he went into the second level, then thickening again, reinforcing itself and shining with the energy of his will. He achieved the final level, heartbeat slowing, breathing long and deep and leisurely, his pattern so solidly formed that it seemed to overlay and partly obscure his physical self.

Priscilla waited a bit longer, analyzing pattern and body. Only when she was satisfied that both were sound, that both trance and soul-shield were solid and unlikely to fail, did she lie down beside him and begin her own preparations.

INTERDICTED WORLD
I-2796-893-44

Tyl Von sig'Alda stood in the noisy, smelly hall, watching his prey on stage. He had seen the sketch in the primitive newssheet, of course, yet the actual sight of a Liaden gentleman with his face marred in such a way was nearly as unsettling as the noisome proximity of so many locals.

There was a small percent chance that yos'Phelium had seen him from the stage and, a smaller percent chance that the Terran bodyguard had, though the Loop noted the imprecision of attempting to calculate the reactions and alertness of a chronic user of Lethecronaxion. If yos'Phelium had seen him, completion of the mission could proceed rapidly. Events, however, would seem to wait upon a contretemp upon the stage.

The precise nature of the difficulty was not apparent. The Terran bitch was near incoherence—not unexpected in a drug-taking sycophant—and the local on stage also displayed attitudinal positions consistent with anger.

yos'Phelium had been standing quietly at the bodyguard's side. He now attempted to say something to the female local, which interrupted him with a brisk hand-wave and stepped to the front of the stage.

At the bulky microphone it spoke in a stilted, slurred version of the language sig'Alda had picked up through sleep-learning; he surmised that it was being formal in order to add legitimacy to the delivery of negative information.

"Our judges, zhena and zamir, families and friends, have asked you to do as they and disregard this performance of the Snow Wind Trio. In order to avoid disqualification the group will be required to play a set of the correct number of songs after the performance of the solo guitar semifinals because they overplayed in time and number—"

All around him the crowd roared disappointment and disapproval; the stands themselves shook. The female's announcements were overwhelmed for some moments—sig'Alda's Loop went into action, informing him that the likelihood of an actual riot was small.

sig'Alda brought his attention back to yos'Phelium, who had begun packing instruments in a businesslike fashion. The Terran was speaking urgently to the local male, all some distance from the female announcer at the microphone.

Carefully sig'Alda began to move against the crowd. yos'Phelium would have to descend the side steps from the stage. With fair fortune, sig'Alda would intercept him there, and they could depart this place and return to the calm dignity of Liad.

It appeared, however, that his thoughts of waylaying them at the stairs were echoed by dozens of locals. The slender walkway was crammed with jostling, shouting barbarians, making a smooth rendezvous with his compatriot impossible.

sig'Alda sat on a bench near the aisle, awaiting his moment, counting through an exercise designed to give patience in frustrating situations. That accomplished, he pondered variables.

He had not known that yos'Phelium was such an accomplished musician—his record had spoken of an *inclination* for the omnichora— yet the sounds of that last piece, though obviously of local origin, had been refined by the agent's contributions into something with merit. And the agent himself—sig'Alda made use of the Loop's recall mode to watch again the last moments of the performance— the agent himself had been unfettered and full of energy. The music had been played with passion by all.

The Loop came up suddenly, without bidding, even as sig'Alda found himself reciting the formula half out loud: "Dispassion, calculation, control, success—"

The probability was .82 that yos'Phelium's actions were inconsistent with those of an Agent on Duty. sig'Alda considered further. Lost without a ship on a barbarian world one might easily give up hope, attempt to throw oneself fully into a new and successful life...He shivered, half from the cold that had crept into the hall when the audience had begun to sift out the doors, and half from the thought of attempting to live at all long, depending solely on passion.

Consideration, of course, would have to be given to the possibility that the facial scar—and the Juntavas report of the incident had come from a drunken underling, after all—was the least portion of a grievous and partially disabling head injury. Mere proper Liaden medical attention might be all that would be required to return the agent properly to the fold.

Finally the trio was permitted to move, but so ringed with admiring locals that sig'Alda found his best tactic was to simply attach himself to the tail end of the throng and follow where it led. Eventually opportunity would arise.

As if the thought was the trigger, there was an unexpected event. The bodyguard was separating herself from the group! If he might intercept her, perhaps remove her from the equation, options would be clearer. He hesitated for a moment and saw the crowd close in again around yos'Phelium and the local musician.

With the Loop's approval, sig'Alda moved.

VANDAR

Winterfair

"Another set?" Miri asked rhetorically as they walked down the midway. "Is she nuts, or what?"

Val Con grinned and pushed the hair out of his eyes. "At least we have an hour or two to prepare—and to rest."

"Yeah, well, I don't know about you, but I'm strung so high, I wouldn't sleep if you whacked me over the head with a brick."

"Performance exhilaration," he murmured. "It means you sang with all your joy."

"I guess." She stopped, staring at the entrance to the hall, while the wind thrummed against the canvas stretched high above them. "Tell you what, boss. I'm going for a walk first; try to get this exhilaration thing buttoned up. Tell Hakan I'll be back in ten minutes, okay?"

"Okay," he said, squeezing her hand gently. He turned to go in and, vaguely uneasy, turned back in time to see her disappear into the tall crowd, heading toward the perimeter.

The Terran female had stopped, attention apparently engaged by the low-tech transmitting station and the landtrain that housed it. Tyl Von sig'Alda paused some distance back, closer than he liked to a smoky brazier, watching and considering.

The Loop counseled a direct approach and indicated a possibility as high as .99 that the Terran was currently drug-free. Certainly the performance he had just seen it deliver, though rude and barbaric, was inconsistent with an individual operating with Clouded faculties. sig'Alda stepped forward.

As he came to her side, she turned, eyes going wide. He bowed, not low, but enough to flatter and confuse.

"Good day," he said, speaking most gently in Terran. "You are Miri Robertson, are you not?"

Eyes and face had gone wary; stance suggested puzzlement and indecision. sig'Alda smiled, delighted to find her so very easy to read.

"Yeah," she said, her voice firm and fine. "Who're you?"

"A friend of your employer's," he said smoothly. "It has been noted that you have guarded with excellence, in circumstances both trying and unusual. Now that your duty is completed, and your employer going home, he sends me with this gift, indicative of his esteem." Sliding the little packet with its blue dot out, he saw the Terran's eyes widen, heard her breath catch, and saw the pale skin pale further as he pressed the thing into her hand.

"Cloud?" The fine voice rasped a little on the word, and sig'Alda inclined his head gravely.

"We have made a careful study of your preferences," he said, seeing how her fingers closed tight around the plastic envelope. "And when it came time for the gift to be chosen, I offered my knowledge of your tastes, so that the gift would be certain to please. I hope that you will allow yourself to be pleased and to look upon the gift with favor."

"Sure." The voice had flattened, and she stared at him out of sparkling gray eyes, eager, no doubt, to sample what she held so fiercely. "Thanks a lot."

"It is my pleasure to serve," he told her, and bowed once again. He left her still staring with those brilliant eyes, the little packet completely hidden in the clench of her hand.

VANDAR

Winterfair

The rehearsal hall was hot, and Val Con was sitting as far away from the corner fireplace as he could, restringing the mandolette and listening to Hakan chatter.

"We could," the younger man was saying, "just replay the set they disqualified—well, not the fourth song, but the first three. Except I hate to do that and take away the impact of that RosaRing ballad of Miri's." He shook his head in wonderment. "And she said she couldn't sing in front of a crowd! There wasn't a dry eye in the house, man—I'll bet you my share of the cash prize!"

"If we win the cash prize," Val Con murmured. "Perhaps we should do a new set, starting with the song that disqualified us."

"Something to that," Hakan said reflectively. Then he stood with a huge smile, opening his arms and hugging Kem, right there in front of everyone. Kem hugged back, steadfastly keeping her eyes away from the shocked faces, and Val Con shook his head to himself, remarking what a bad influence he and Miri had been on Hakan and his lady.

He picked up the last string, tied it, and threaded it, carefully turning the knob and—

The string snapped in his icy, clumsy hands, sweat beaded his forehead and panic blossomed in his belly. Heart stuttering, he dropped the mandolette, tears starting to fill his eyes.

"Cory?"

Val Con looked up with a barely stifled gasp as Hakan bent to his shoulder. "Are you all right, Cory?"

He took a deep breath, reviewed the Rainbow, and managed a shaky smile at his friends. "Nerves. I think, Hakan. I'll go outside and—get some air."

Hakan frowned uncertainly. "I'll come with you, if you want. You don't look so good, man."

"Miri—Miri will be coming soon." He came almost clumsily to his feet, snatched up his jacket, and went raggedly down the crowded room. Hakan looked at Kem, then bent to pick up the mandolette.

He leaned against the rough wooden wall and filled his lungs with knife-cold air. The violence of the panic had ebbed, leaving a clammy residue of despair in its wake. Val Con focused his attention inward, seeking the source of his feelings—and found it nearly at once.

It was emanating from the song that was Miri.

The terror this time was his own. Coldly he stepped away from it and turned his attention to determining her direction. The song tugged him north, and he went at a rapid walk, barely aware of the people he pushed past and sidestepped.

He turned the corner into a cross-street at a pace approaching a run, passing the infrequent fairgoers and the row of empty craft booths without seeing any of it, all attention fixed inward, where despair had solidified into something drear and nameless, and her song fragmented toward discord.

The man came out of nowhere, wrenching his attention outward with a touch on his sleeve and a murmured bit of the High Tongue.

"Good evening, galandaria. Where to, in such a haste?"

Val Con checked and danced back. The other checked, as well, and Val Con found himself looking at a slight man in a pilot's leather jacket, black-haired and black-eyed, face beardless and golden and curiously lacking in mobility.

"The commander sends greetings, Agent yos'Phelium." His voice was cultured and smooth, devoid of warmth.

Val Con raised a brow. "It must naturally gratify one to hear it," he murmured, "though I protest my unworthiness of such regard." He shifted slightly, testing the other man's reactions.

The man shifted in response, checking the foreshadowed charge, radiating self-confidence and control. "You mistake the matter," he said, "if you believe the commander allows even the least of us to fall from sight, uncounted and unsearched-for." He offered an arm imperiously. "Let us depart, Agent. The commander requires your report."

"My report..." Val Con frowned, counting the steps bearing down upon them, then spun and dodged away, putting a group of six fairgoers between them. Whirling back toward the top of the street, he found the nameless agent before him, poised for the throw. Val Con slammed to a halt, an empty craft booth to his left, the agent ready to leap in any direction he picked to run.

"So," the other said, pointing to the empty booth. "We will continue our discussion in there."

"No." Miri, where was Miri? He touched that portion of his being that reflected her—and pulled away, half-shuddering with her dread.

The inflexible face before him was shadowed by some unreadable emotion. "Will you die for so inconsequential a thing?"

Slowly, watching the man tightly, Val Con stepped back, muscles loose and half foolish, as in the *L'apeleka* stance named Awaiting. Cautiously, making no move that might be read as a threat, he opened the door, stepped into the booth, and retreated, though not nearly as far as the farther wall.

The agent came after him, sure-footed and assured as a tiger, and shut the door behind him.

"I will repeat my message," he said. "Agent Val Con yos'Phelium is ordered to Headquarters by the commander's own word, that he may be debriefed, recalibrated, and if necessary, retrained."

Val Con bowed, briefly and with irony. "As much as it grieves me to say so, I find that the commander's words leave me strangely unmoved. Pray carry my kindest regards with you when you go."

"So," the agent said again. His eyes closed, and the next breath he took was noticeably deeper than the one before; but Val Con was already moving to take advantage of that unexpected lapse. The agent opened his eyes, ducked, parried with a fist that came nowhere near connecting, whirled out of immediate danger, and cried out, fully in the mode of Command, "Val Con yos'Phelium clare try qwit—"

A string of no-words, meaningless in the necessity of battle: Val Con stumbled, twisted, and came barely erect, body half-sketching a *L'apeleka* phrase.

"Who secures Liad?" the agent demanded, and Val Con heard his own voice answer.

"The people of Liad."

"Who secures the people of Liad?" the agent persisted. The answer was not the one he would make: It came unbidden and uncontrolled. Even as he heard the words, he tried to shake them away, to form them into something else.

"The Department of the Interior secures the people of Liad," his voice said, while he hated the lie and his body continued, slowly, to move, developing more fully the phrase it had fallen into.

"Who secures the Department of the Interior?"

It was as if there were fog suddenly in the booth, or a shimmering veil between him and the agent. Through it, Val Con read the other's rising confidence and ground his teeth to keep his traitor voice silent.

"Who secures," the agent repeated, "the Department of the Interior?"

It was useless to fight. He grappled with his thoughts, trying to remember just what it was he must not allow, and heard himself murmur, through a mile of fog, "The commander secures the Department of the Interior."

His body continued of its own momentum; he paid it as little heed as the lessening distance between himself and the man who asked these tiresome, tiring questions.

"Who secures the commander?" his interrogator demanded.

"The agents," Val Con's voice told him. "The agents secure the commander."

The man before him smiled. "With what do the agents secure the commander?"

"With actions, and with blood."

"When the commander calls you to duty," the man demanded, the High Tongue knelling like a death-bell, "what do you say?"

Val Con's body twisted silently in the dance; he came to a point of fulcrum and smiled peacefully upon his questioner. *"Carpe diem."*

The words were like bright sun, burning away the fog. In the instant of answering, he recognized the *L'apeleka* dance named "Accepting the Lance;" recalled that the one giving ground before him was an enemy; recalled that there had been another answer to the last question, an answer that had made no sense. Miri had given him the proper answer—the true answer—and he had danced it into place in Hakan's barn...

"Val Con yos'Phelium," the agent cried. "try clare qwit—"

The cycle went faster that time: Again he was shackled; compelled to reply, mind slowly clouding while his body relentlessly repeated the pattern of "Accepting the Lance."

When the commander calls you to duty," the agent snarled, "what do you say?"

"Carpe diem!" Val Con cried; and the dance described acceptance

while the agent's hand flicked toward his pocket and Val Con loosened the throwing blade.

The knife struck the enemy high in the chest, close to the throat, and bounced away with a hollow *thunk* as the man brought his gun around.

Val Con dove and rolled in the narrow confines of the booth; he jackknifed and kicked the other's legs out from under him. The man used his fall to advantage, coming up on his knees, gun steady. As Val Con braced himself to leap, the Loop calculated the angle that would permit the greatest chance of nonfatal injury.

"Val Con?" The voice was in his very ear, instantly recognized, dearly loved, and absolutely impossible. Before him, the agent held his fire.

"Surrender and accompany me of your own will," he said. In his ear Shan's voice was worried, insistent: "Val Con!"

He lunged.

The agent fell badly, gun spinning out of his hand, head striking solidly into the thick wooden wall. The man was moving again, instantly, throwing himself over the weapon—but Val Con was already out the door and running.

Beyond the depot, half a mile closer to Gylles, Miri shuddered, stopped, and stiffened, head up, questing inside herself: Val Con's pattern was—*wrong.*

Even as she watched, the colors dimmed, and several major interlockings shuddered as if under insupportable strain. Directional sense wavered, failed for an instant—then the whole structure was back as it should be: bright and strong and sane.

She relaxed, then stiffened as the cycle began once more; watching the colors dim, she spun back, terror for him overcoming dread for herself and loathing of the plastic envelope in her pocket.

"Dammit, Val Con!"

He slammed around the side of a food hall, glued his back to the wooden support, and whispered, "Shan?"

"Where the devil are you?" demanded the voice in his ear—in his head—bringing with it a static crackle of concern/annoyance/determination/love.

"The Winterfair," he whispered, craning to catch sight of the enemy among the thronging midway. "Where are you?"

"The *Passage.* Give your coords, approximate local fix—"

"No!" Val Con cried. He shrank back, biting his lip. "Shan, you must not come here! There's appalling danger—"

"Plan B!" Shan's thought-voice overrode him. "Speak to me of danger, do!" Frustration, full anger, and not a little fear were added to the static pummeling him, and Val Con pushed hard against the wall, closing his eyes in an agony of emotion.

"Don't..." he whispered, though the snow wind tore the word from his lips. "Brother—beloved—I cannot go mad just today."

Abruptly the punishment ceased and was replaced before his knees began to buckle with a steadfast bone-warming glow. Val Con drew a hard breath against his brother's love and began to murmur again to the wind. "There is a man with a gun who will have me dead, and my lifemate is not with me. I've no time to argue points of melant'i with you! Stay clear—stay safe..."

"We need you." There was a wealth of emotion attending that, mercifully damped to shadow.

"The gunman has a ship," Val Con murmured. "Must have a ship! If the luck is willing, it is ours."

Warmth faded to coldness; the inner ear perceived an echoing vastness...

"Shan!"

Warmth solidified. "Here. Running close to the time—uses too much energy. Assume the ship—what then?"

"I'll take Miri to her people. Meet us—" In the midway crowd he glimpsed a familiar leather jacket on a man much shorter than average. The man checked, turned his head to the left, then to the right, and came confidently toward the corner of the food hall.

"Go!" Val Con cried to his brother, and—*pushed*—with his mind. Vastness roared, emptily; then Val Con was slipping silently down the wall, toward the dim back of the building.

Shan rolled and snapped to his feet, hand outstretched toward that last horrific vision: a man stalking purposefully toward him/Val Con, the outline of the gun clearly visible beneath his coat.

"He was right there, Priscilla! I saw him! Gods—" He spun back toward the bed, confounded by his familiar room aboard the *Passage*—and then hurled himself forward, horror filling him completely.

Priscilla was not breathing.

What by all the gods could have made the man bolt like that?

Miri leaned against a rack of skis, breathing hard and trying to track him. His pattern was steady at the moment and seemed rooted in one spot, a real relief after the crazy zigzagging and dodging he had been doing for the past ten minutes. She squared her shoulders and set out again, keeping her pace down to jog now that she was back among other pedestrians. All the hell clear across the fair. If that just wasn't like his wrong-headedness! Why hadn't he run *toward* her, if he was running from trouble? No sense to have—

She swallowed hard, remembering the envelope of Cloud in her pocket; remembering the Liaden who had given it to her. Gut feeling said that Val Con was running from the Liaden—except that didn't make sense at all. Nothing about the whole setup made sense, but it suddenly looked like a good idea to get to Val Con and face whatever was after him, back to back. After that—she squashed the thought. Ain't any "after that," Robertson, she told herself harshly. Get used to it.

Grief threatened to strangle her; instead, she put her attention back onto his pattern—and slammed to a halt, a cry caught in the knot of grief in her throat.

Someone pushed into her, cursing; she moved until she came up against a wall and put her hands against it, fingers digging into the wood, eyes staring straight ahead, seeing only within.

His pattern flickered, danced, expanded, distorted, all seen through a shroud of swirling flame and color. The flames drew in upon themselves briefly, then expanded and remained constant for a moment. The pattern seemed as if it were going to fade altogether— *did* fade...There was a touch, like a cold kiss upon her cheek...

And Val Con was gone.

"No..." It was a whimper, short nails scoring hardened wood. "No!" she cried again in a burst of anguish as she slammed her head against the wall and thrust her whole self into the void where his pattern had been a heartbeat before; she went through that space and out, so it seemed, to a place of flailing wind and burning ice-falls and a woman's voice crying out despairingly, as Miri reeled and went to her knees on the frozen ground.

Swallowing against nausea, steeled for silence and emptiness, she probed the place. And swallowed suddenly against joy.

He was back: whole, scintillant, sane. Alive.

"Alive," Miri whispered, she climbed to her feet, rubbing her forehead where she had hit it against the wall.

Shakily she got her bearings and, walking steadily, she set out to find him.

DUTIFUL PASSAGE

"Priscilla!"

Empty. A void where her mindsong should be—and the failing glow of the autonomic system.

Healer training took over, forcing the horror he felt out of consciousness, forcing his attention to the details that made up life. No breath; no heartbeat; autonomics fading to nothing even as he scanned...He needed a medic! But there was no time to call: Priscilla's body would be dead before Vilt could hope to get there from sickbay.

Terror lashed him, but was shunted aside as he lay his hand on her cooling breast; he grabbed and molded that terror in a way he had never been taught—and released it in a bolt of mind-searing energy.

He went to his knees with the shock of it; feeling the heart flutter beneath his hand, he began the sequence: press, release, press, release. The body caught the rhythm, lost it, caught weakly—and steadied. Breath began raggedly; the autonomic system glowed to full capacity. Shan withdrew his assistance, watching breathlessly as the body lived on without it.

He dragged himself to his feet, casting with Healer's senses for the thread that had anchored Priscilla to her body.

There was nothing—no strand, no echo of emotion. Priscilla was gone, as if she had never been.

Horror rose again, and he welcomed it, using the energy to cast his Seeking wider, touching over the patterns of all who remained within the *Passage,* searching for a hint, for a memory, for a chord that was Priscilla.

Lina's pattern held him longest, and then Gordy's—but Priscilla had not fled to her friend or to her foster son, and Shan sought further, opening himself as he had never done, reading as he knew he could not...

There! An echo, a glow of recall, a familiar, warm touch of comfort.

Following the hint, Shan encountered a scattering of human patterns, the random buzz that was the pattern of lower animals, the near-cogent hum of the norbears—the Pet Library, Priscilla's first refuge aboard the *Passage,* nearly eight Standards earlier. He narrowed his scan, searching minutely, and found her at last, hugged tight within the devoted, comforting pattern of Master Frodo, king of the norbears.

Recklessly Shan expended energy and found himself for a disorienting heartbeat not nearer the norbear and his beloved, but back in his body, slumped over Priscilla's, head pillowed on a breast that gently rose and fell, as if in sleep.

"No!" He wrenched himself away, and fled back toward the Pet Library, homing in on Master Frodo's pattern.

He extended a tendril of affection toward the tiny empath and received the usual happy greeting; but the creature's joy was somewhat mixed with puzzlement, so that he fed out, too, a line of comfort to the norbear before seeking Priscilla herself.

She was wrapped tightly behind an intense shield, reinforced at several points by the norbear's natural defenses.

Shan came as close as he dared, trying to recall exactly how he had bespoken Val Con, then once again expended energy and thought of calling her name. *Priscilla!*

The surface of her shield shimmered, a wisp of pattern escaping; then more slipped out, displaying recognition, quickly followed by dismay, fear, and love. He returned love, comfort, and security; he tried again to bespeak her, to urge her to leave Master Frodo's protections for his own, but she gave no sign that she heard.

Gently, infinitely patient, he kept sending love, comfort, and security, paying out a Healer's line of rescue, and finally he felt her first tenuous grip on the line strengthen and grow certain.

He ignored the strain and payed the line out, feeling her shed defenses, hesitate, and stand away from Master Frodo's shield, exposing the kernel of her being to the void.

Shan *reached* in some indefinable way, encircled his beloved, and shook them both loose of Master Frodo's influence.

He reentered his body with a suddenness that was agony, and Priscilla seemed to join him there for a moment before she fled, pouring across the physical link of their bodies until, with a shocking break, she left his awareness.

Vilt had come and gone, after administering vitamin shots and a very sound scolding for whatever it was that they had done to make each of them shed so much weight, so quickly. While he was scolding Shan, Priscilla had called Lina and asked her to go to Master Frodo with an extra ration of corn; then she had ordered two complete dinners to be delivered immediately to the captain's office.

The dinner itself was gone and Priscilla was sitting next to Shan on the couch, head resting on his shoulder as she thought about what he had told her. Finally she sighed and stirred, sitting up to look into his silver eyes.

"Shan?"

"Yes, Priscilla?"

"Why didn't you go to the Wizard's College in Solcintra?"

Surprise flickered. "Because I'm not a dramliza, Priscilla; I'm a Healer."

"Yes, but you see," she said, very gently, "Healers can't do the things you've been telling me *you've* done—that I know you've done, as I sit here in body before you! And no wizard that I know of—or witch, either—can speak directly, mind to mind."

He frowned. "Nonsense. You yourself left a dream with Val Con's lady—and she replied!"

"Yes, of course. But neither of us spoke *directly* to the other. Think how much easier it would have been, if that was a common sort of ability. Anthora might have spoken to Val Con months ago, relaying Nova's order to come home!"

He shifted uncomfortably, then finally grinned. "Well, what can my excuse be, except that neither Val Con nor I knew the thing was impossible, and so we had a very nice chat!" The grin faded. "More—he was receiving me as another Healer might: asked me to damp the emotional output. And I saw through his eyes!"

He straightened and grabbed her hand, his own eyes near-hypnotic in their intensity. "I saw a man with a gun come out of the crowd; saw him turn toward Val Con..." He slumped back. "Then we were cut loose."

"Where is he?" she asked, after the silence went beyond a dozen heartbeats.

Shan laughed sharply. "Refused to tell me! Stay away and stay safe, he said! No time to play melant'i games with me—by which I assume he means he speaks to me not as my brother, but as my future Delm! Hah! There's a change of song, Priscilla! And finally, just before he pushes us away and all but loses me my lifemate, he tells me to meet him. The man with the gun also has a spaceship, you see, so that all Val Con need do is murder him to be free to leave the planet at his leisure and go to Miri's people. Wherever that may be."

"Miri," Priscilla said. "It was Miri who cut us loose." She sighed and added, as the Goddess demanded truth to be told, "My fault."

"Your fault?" Shan blinked. "Miri shoves us out into the void, and it's your fault? Priscilla..."

"My fault," she repeated. "My pride. I was so sure I could keep you safe! And when you turned your attention to Val Con— you used energy at such a rate, I was frightened for you, for the link with the *Passage*. I gave you as much as I could, but it wasn't enough. You faded, and I nearly lost you, and I reached out, tapped the lifemate bridge between Val Con and Miri—there's so much energy there!" She paused, gripping his hand, the gem in his ring biting comfortably into her palm, and she gave thanks to the Goddess, who had tested her fully and allowed her to remain yet a time in the active universe.

"Miri felt the interference in the bridge," she told Shan. "I must have obscured her vision of Val Con—she must have thought him in great danger...dead. Think of the shock, when you are used to being in harmony with someone, when that person goes behind a wall and shuts you out..." She shook her head. "She's not trained— didn't know how to see me; didn't know how to seek. All she could do was thrust out with all the power of her will and try to reestablish her link with her lifemate."

"Casting us loose in the process," Shan finished, and sighed, "Formidable." He looked into her eyes. "But what you tell me indicates that you're not at fault—nor is Val Con, nor is Miri. The person who bears blame—for terrifying you; for all but killing you—is Shan yos'Galan, for his greed and the selfishness of his necessities."

"No—"

"Yes!" He touched her face and ran his fingers into her hair. "Priscilla, you must not allow me to endanger you! You see what I am—a man so lost to anything but his own desires that he may slay his lifemate!"

"Shan!" She drew herself up, hearing the resonance in her own voice. "That is untrue."

He started, stared at her face—Goddess alone knew what he saw there—then pushed forward, his arms going around her, his cheek against hers.

She held him, and he held her, for an unmeasured time; then she asked the question he must have been asking himself, over and over, since his conversation with his brother.

"Would Val Con kill a man for his ship?"

Shan stirred, sighing like a weary child. "yos'Pheliums have a peculiar passion for ships, Priscilla; family history is full of chancy deeds done for the sake of the things. Val Con?" He sat up and shook his head. "My brother tells a story of the time he had captured an Yxtrang—to talk with him, so he informed me, and have an open and equal exchange of views. He says that when they had finished their chat, he let the creature go, because there was no sense in killing him, though that argument has never stopped Yxtrang from killing as many non-Yxtrang as they chose."

He sighed again. "How do I know what he'll do, Priscilla? Would *you* let an Yxtrang go?"

VANDAR

Winterfair

The agent came forward, confidence in every stride; Val Con slid toward the back of the food hall, slipped around the corner, and ran, nearly knocking over a young couple lost in each other against the back wall.

Back on the midway, he became one more of a knot of fairgoers traveling in the general direction of the Winter Train. An agent *might* attempt a kill under such conditions; the Loop indicted that this particular agent had an overriding need for more discreet manners.

His thoughts ran in layers: one relieved by the stabilization of Miri's song; another, an amalgam of the Scout and the agent, concerned with weighing the likelihood of an attack, with being sure he left as little trail as possible, and with watching for signs of pursuit.

Another layer of thought wrestled with the puzzle of the agent's ship: was it on-world or in orbit? Was the agent alone, or did another wait with the vessel? How to find it? How to obtain the ship keys? It was unlikely that the man on his trail would voluntarily answer those questions, though coercion might be brought to bear. Val Con nearly sighed. It was possible to kill an agent, though difficult. But it was immeasurably more difficult to capture one.

"Plan B," Shan had said. What could have gone wrong? Was the Department openly attacking Korval? The Juntavas...He closed off that particular layer of thought. It merely distracted and brought unresolved emotions to the fore, when he needed all of his energy to preserve his life and that of his lifemate—and to gain that ship!

The crowd changed direction; he exchanged it for another, checking his song of her to make certain that Miri was still in the vicinity of the train.

The agent was good and knew that he was good; he was perhaps just a shade overconfident. The general speed with which he moved argued enhanced reactions—stimulants—which meant he would tire more quickly, over an extended period of time. Neither factor was significant in the short run. That he wore body armor indicated that he had studied Val Con as Val Con had studied his own targets in the past. Had he studied enough to know of the other blade—the blade Edger had given him? The possession of a weapon that could slip through body armor as easily as through water significantly altered the situation in Val Con's favor—and was negated by the burning necessity to keep the man alive long enough to learn about the ship.

The group he was traveling with turned off. He continued toward Miri at a somewhat quicker pace, the skin prickling at the back of his neck, while the Loop gave .99 surety that the agent was following behind.

sig'Alda identified the tread of the shoe, lost it, found it, and lost it again, which reminded him that he was chasing no mundane Terran politico but a trained agent.

An agent could not depend on luck. Already, though, he had been lucky in the extreme, for had the knife struck a bare two fingers higher, his body would even now be cooling in the dark shed. The speed! The anticipation! One moment to be beyond even the control of his own thoughts—and the next to conceive and execute that attack!

His chest hurt from the knife's strike; no doubt he was bruised. That such excellence should be lost to the Department! sig'Alda sighed in irritation. Regret of that had been the source of the second introduction of luck into his mission: that he should have had his target within sight and failed to neutralize him; that he should, instead, have offered the choice, already refused...Had yos'Phelium been carrying a gun, or even another knife, that mistake would have been fatal, too.

His quarry was ahead, sighted for a half second.

Ah, but it would not do to catch him too soon, would it? In the open light, with a crowd around?

sig'Alda slowed, allowing the other a more respectable lead. The Loop gave yos'Phelium a slight edge, if they fought hand to hand immediately. Barely considering the necessity and never doubting the wisdom of it, he took his third dose of accelerant.

Why was yos'Phelium running that way? Why not back toward the area containing the draft animals and vehicles, to escape to the larger countryside? Why—but wait. He had found the Terran in this general direction—at the base of the hill, by the transmitter; and he had originally found yos'Phelium rushing in that same direction. Now, given options, the man broke again for—

The transmitter. sig'Alda smiled. It fit one of the models perfectly. The songs had been a signal, deliberately timed, meant to be received by one who knew when and where to listen. The commander's words came back to him, saying that only Clan Korval might mount a military threat to the Department. Suppose the *Dutiful Passage,* large as a battleship, stood off-planet even now?

The Loop produced percentages that he did not like. That the songs had been deliberate signals—.97. That they had been prearranged and intended for a particular listener—.93. That they had reached their goal? No percentage.

Suppose they had not? Or that they *had,* and that his own advent had required a change in plans, which they were already radioing into space?

The Loop supported the hypothesis.

He ran, heedless of complaints, neglecting to follow Val Con yos'Phelium, now that he knew where he must be going. sig'Alda would be waiting at the transmitter when the traitor arrived.

Miri marked Val Con's progress. He was heading for the train on the far side of the depot, or for her, maybe—it was a little early to tell about details. He was not running a race anymore, which was good, and his pattern had steadied down after going through all those loopy changes.

As she trudged through the snow she wondered what *her* pattern looked like just then. Must be shot all to hell, what with the shock of that Liaden...

She squelched the thought, the packet of Cloud riding like a fifty-pound weight in her pocket.

Val Con had been running away from something, but she had seen nothing in his pattern that made her think he had killed anybody. That meant the skypilot was still at large, either walking toward her with Val Con, or maybe coming after him. Which meant— Ah, hell, Robertson, who you trying to kid? she demanded of herself. You don't know what it means. She saw the train, steam pouring from the boilers that fed the generators, and heard the occasional hiss of valves above the constant rumble of the huge belts.

What an arrangement they were. Some kind of cloth and rubber getup, looping between the big power takeoff reel, the generator, and the flywheel. Between them all, they fed the electric power from the generator to an enormous set of old-fashioned wet-chemical batteries on the railcar in front. The radio station drew its power from the storage batteries, which made sense: If the belt broke or the steam went down they would still have power enough to broadcast until the monster could be restarted.

Miri shook her head. Who would have thought that something so primitive could be so complicated?

One of the cars way in the back of the train was a studio, duplicating the setup in the music hall. There was no longer any need to invade that, since they had attracted the attention of someone with a ship. All according to plan.

She sniffed. *Carpe diem,* eh, Robertson? Now what?

Up the hill, limned by the reflected glow of the main fair lights, Miri saw someone going quickly toward the train.

She frowned and checked her pattern of Val Con. Then she faded carefully between the heavy couplings between two of the cars, watching the skypilot approach and taking a rapid inventory of her person, looking for something more potent than the skinny stick-knife and a handful of true-silver coins.

VANDAR

Winterfair

"Cory!"

Val Con continued hurriedly forward, ignoring the call.

"Cory!" The voice insisted, and out of the corner of his eye he saw a man moving clumsily to head him off. The man was tightly wrapped against the evening chill, and Val Con frowned, then caught the details of nose and chin: Hakan's father.

He waved and turned his steps slightly, as if to pass on by.

"Wait!" Zamir Meltz called, disastrously skidding on a patch of ice. He waved his arms, tottered, and muttered "Thank you," as Val Con caught his arm and held him upright.

"There you are, sir..." Val Con helped the older man to safer ground and stepped back, only to find his arm caught in a surprisingly strong grip.

"At least give me a chance to thank you—and to apologize."

Val Con sighed and forced himself to stay within the man's grasp. "I do not—"

Zamir Meltz smiled thinly. "I wish to thank you for your friendship and your partnership with Hakan. I've never seen him with so much energy, so many ideas! And I wish to apologize because the judges have done a stupid thing. They put rules before music— before art! I helped elect those judges, and I see I made bad choices." He bowed his head.

Val Con shifted, seeking Miri in his head. "Zamir, it is a difficult thing that happened. Miri is—distressed. She feels that she led the band wrongly when she called for that last song. That she played the mood of the crowd perfectly—that the performance itself was correct—is something you and I and Hakan know." He shifted again and, with relief, felt his arm loosed. "I am going now to Miri, to try to show her the difference between judges and art."

The elder Meltz smiled. "You have a good zhena there, young man—bold and full of life. You tell her I know she'll be sensible, and that I respect her art and herself, whether she plays to satisfy their rules or not!" He shook his head. "Next fair, there will be musicians instead of politicians as judges, as the breeze blows the leaves!" He nodded to Val Con and strode off, his spare shoulders square with purpose.

Val Con checked his sense of Miri once more, hearing a welcome change in her song as it smoothed back toward cohesiveness and became more and more the Miri he had come to treasure.

The melody went abruptly sharp in an echo of the extreme concentration that she had displayed during the Bassilan invasion. He took a quick fix on her location and quickened his pace to a jog, though his heart argued for more speed yet.

Carefully Val Con hurried, half searching behind for the agent, half searching ahead for his lifemate.

Equations flowed and altered as sig'Alda ran; certainties became questions. Assuming that the Terran had been near the transmitter— had been *stationed* near the transmitter—as part of a deliberate and prearranged plan, the chance that she had taken the drug was markedly less; though, of course, for an addict, such possibility was never entirely eliminated.

The Loop offered figures that were marginally in favor of her having used the Cloud, noting that she had had none prior to the performance. Cloud was potent; its lure to one sensitized was irresistible.

The light was uncertain, mostly derived from the glow of the fair behind him and a few lanterns and electric lights set about the train. The red-haired Terran was not where he had left her, and the multitude of tracks about made any attempt to discover her direction hopeless.

He glanced behind. There was no sign yet of yos'Phelium. sig'Alda sought further and found his quarry still within the limits of the fair light, speaking, it seemed, with a local.

The conversation ended abruptly, with the local walking back into the depths of the fair and yos'Phelium all but running, in sig'Alda's very direction.

sig'Alda smiled, admiring the clearness with which he could see that backlit runner. At this distance, it was still a chancy shot with a handgun, depending more on the luck that had saved him twice so far than any amount of skill he might bring to bear. But there was no hurry. yos'Phelium was coming to the transmitter. It remained only for Tyl Von sig'Alda to find an appropriate place to wait until his target ran within range.

VANDAR

Winterfair

Miri crouched behind the flatbed, watching the Liaden watch, fuming and trying to think.

Val Con had not killed the guy, though she was sure some of the craziness in his pattern had had to do with a conflict between them. Ergo, she thought, half grinning in self-derision. Ergo, Robertson, this monkey's more valuable alive then he is dead. Figure out why.

The answer was so simple, so pure, that it took her breath away. Spaceship. Damn and hell and blaze it all to cinders! She fingered the coins in her pocket, pulled out the stickknife and flipped it—open...shut—and sighed. The way she saw it, the patrol broke down into two separate options.

One: Keep an eye on the Liaden until Val Con arrived and gave her some kind of clue to what was going down. And two: If it looked like the target was moving out, stall him—without killing him.

Always draw the challenging watch, doncha, Robertson? she asked herself sardonically, remembering that Skel had always accused her of deliberately taking the storm shift, as if a body knew when trouble would break.

The Liaden she was watching moved, reaching into his fancy leather jacket and pulling out a gun. Miri craned around the corner of her protection, trying to sight along his line of vision, and nearly yelled.

Val Con was moving toward the train, backlit from the main fair—a target even a mediocre marksman could hardly miss. She checked his pattern and found it alive on several levels, encompassing that twist she associated with consciousness of danger. But he was running, all the same. And in another few moments he would be within range of the Liaden's gun.

All bets're off, Robertson, she told herself. She slid forward, knife out.

Her melody changed again. It was denser, more brilliant, and intensely alert, as if she had suddenly slipped into a role where intuition, reflex, and intent were inexpressibly more important than thought.

As if she were—hunting.

He broke into a run, flat out and danger be damned, as the Loop leapt to full life, elucidating .85 that she was stalking the agent; .35 that she would survive the first encounter by more than a minute; .20 that she would survive at all.

Miri, Miri, Miri! He flung his will out, trying to speak to her as Shan had spoken to him. *Miri, DON'T!*

There was no sign that she heard; her song reached a plateau, drew in upon itself, and formed into a lance.

Heart wailing, mind cold and certain, Val Con pulled on deep-buried reserves, feeling *L'apeleka* and override programs and desperation fueling the fresh burst of speed. Hunch prodded him into evasive action, and the next second he saw the flash; he heard one pellet snarl by his ear as another ripped the sleeve of his jacket.

The Middle River blade was loose in its special arm sheath, ready to slide into his hand in an instant. Before him—still so far away!—he saw the agent turn, gun rising; he saw Miri coming in, low and fast and mean, knife gleaming in her hand; saw the agent take the force of her charge on his gun arm; saw the downward slice and—

Saw the gun fly away.

The agent snapped into offensive, missed his setup as Miri dodged and ducked and slashed low, trying to cut his legs out front under him, and recovered enough to slap the knife away, arcing silver into the shadows.

Miri twisted and landed on her feet, countering the next attack—blindingly fast—with a move he had taught her. The agent was surprised to meet that familiar counter: he slowed minutely, slipped in the snow, and twisted as if to regain his balance, throat exposed and defenseless.

Val Con drew one last burst of speed from somewhere, not daring to scream and risk destroying her concentration, hoping against all knowledge that the agent's misstep had been real.

Miri lunged forward and took the bait.

The agent steadied, accepted her weight and momentum, bent, spun, and completed the kill with the sureness of a man thoroughly trained.

Miri went up and over his back, arching high into the air—a thin, red-haired doll in a blue hooded jacket—and smashed down onto the hard-packed snow.

She lay utterly still.

Val Con heard himself scream even as the blade came into his hand, saw the agent bend over to make certain of his work, then saw him start back, choking and gasping. Ship be damned and kin be damned and Liad and universe and life: the crystal blade caught and held the light as it came to ready, and Val Con jumped forward to close with the murderer of his wife.

The cannonball hit him just below the knees, pitching him into the snow while a banshee voice howled in his ear, "Stay away from him! It's Cloud—poison!"

He rolled and came to his feet; one glance showed him the agent snatching something that gleamed black metal out of the snow; saw Miri completing her own roll and diving toward him again, knocking him sideways.

Heard the cough of the pellet gun and felt Miri's body go stiff, and then slack, against him.

He was alive. No second shot had been made, either to be certain of the first kill or to set up the next. Val Con shifted Miri's weight, sighted through the splash of her hair across her face. The agent was standing perhaps three feet away, gun held ready, an expression of most unagentlike vacancy on his face.

Val Con brought his attention to his lifemate, discovering a feeble pulse in the thin wrist under his finger, and a patch of sticky wetness that seeped through, coat and shirt, to his skin, that could only be blood. *Her* blood.

Gently, reverently, he slipped from beneath her and came with slow fluidity to his feet and faced the agent, Middle River blade held in plain view, ready for the kill.

Gun steady, the agent looked at him out of wide, soft eyes, but he seemed inattentive. Val Con hesitated, then walked forward, extended a hand, and plucked the gun away. The man blinked but offered no resistance.

"I was to have shot someone," he said, the High Tongue registering wondering confusion. "I cannot properly recall...I was to have shot—*some*one..."

"And so you have!" Val Con snapped, his own voice taking on the cadence of authority. "Give me your kit!"

Dreamily the agent reached around his belt, unclipped something from beneath his jacket, and held it out.

Val Con snatched it out of his hand and spun back to the small huddled shape on the snow.

The wound was just above the right breast. His hands shook as he sealed the entry and exit holes and sprayed the dressings with antiseptic. Gods, gods—so close. And what he had to give her was rough first aid, though better than the rough-and-ready assistance a local medic might offer. For surety, for complete and quick healing, it was imperative to get her to an autodoc.

"Is she hurt badly?" the agent inquired from just behind his shoulder.

Val Con spun on one knee. "Badly enough," he managed with some semblance of sanity. He considered the agent's soft eyes, dreamy face, and careless stance. Cloud, Miri had said. Memory provided the relevant bit from the Lectures. "...*Lethecronaxion, street names: Cloud, Lethe, Now:* memory inhibitor; effects lasting from one to twelve hours; physical addiction, as well as psychological need of user to shield painful associations, make Lethecronaxion among the most deadly of the unregulated drugs."

Val Con sighed. "What is your name?"

The agent looked startled; covered it with a bow of introduction. "Tyl Von sig'Alda," he said most properly. "Clan Rugare."

"So." Val Con stared deep into the pupil-drowned eyes and saw nothing but guileless confusion. "Where is your ship?"

Confusion intensified. "My—ship, sir? I—Rugare is not a...I have no ship—of my own. I am a pilot-for-hire, if you have a ship but do not care to pilot yourself—"

Val Con cut him off, the High Tongue shaping the words into dismissal. "I see." Miri *had* to have assistance, and an autodoc was so far superior to a local hospital...

Gylles itself did not have a hospital, the nearest being in the next town, thirty miles southeast. Too far, mind and heart clamored, while his finger tracked the thready, ragged pulse. He looked again at the agent, trying to recall if there had been a way—*any* way—known to his instructors to bring an individual out of a Cloud-trance.

After a moment, he gave up. If the instructors of agents had the key to unlock a mind shrouded in Cloud, they had not shared it with Agent-in-Training Val Con yos'Phelium. There was, however, something else...

Slowly he came to his feet, careful to keep his body between Tyl Von sig'Alda, Clan Rugare, pilot-for-hire and Agent of Change, and Miri Robertson, lifemate, partner, lover, and friend. The dark, clouded eyes followed him, distant puzzlement plain on a face peculiarly vulnerable.

"Do you know me?" Val Con demanded.

The other signaled negation, half bowing. "Sir, I regret..."

"I am Val Con yos'Phelium." He watched for the flicker of recognition, hoping that the stimulants the man had taken were of the more powerful variety, and that the dose was sufficient to speed the Cloud through his system.

Nothing showed in face or eyes, then slowly something dawned. "Clan Korval?" he asked hesitantly.

"Exactly Clan Korval," Val Con snapped. "And this lady you have shot—in your passion to shoot *some*one—is my lifemate! How came you to do something so ill, man? And now you tell me you have no ship, when I know you must have, and are denying me the use of the 'doc out of murderous spite! Do you want my lifemate to *die?* Do you want the weight of my Balance to come down upon your head?" He leaned close and fancied he saw a glimmer of some returning sense deep in the dark, dark eyes. "Have you heard the tales of Korval's past Balances? They are true—every one!"

"Yes." The agent's voice held a note of actual ridicule. "Terrifying—the Balance dealt Plemia!"

Val Con smiled. "My brother is a merciful man," he said softly. "Do you think to find me so?"

The agent leapt forward and to the side, muscles coherent and alert. Val Con twisted and got a grip on him—then lost it as the man dropped, feinted, and came up with a palm-gun. Val Con froze, watching the eyes, which were changing yet again.

The gun was steady, the face firm and full of purpose. Val Con saw the finger tighten on the trigger—and he dove, tackling the man as Miri had tackled him.

The gun discharged into the air; the agent twisted, trying to lever himself to the top; Val Con countered, grabbed the wrist of the other's gun hand, and slammed it against the hard snow until the fingers opened and the tiny weapon spun away.

Again the agent tried to twist free, to gain the advantage. But Val Con willed himself a boulder—a dead weight to pin a struggling, hasty man—got his hands around the other's slender throat, and exerted pressure.

The agent froze.

Val Con kept the pressure constant, neither increasing nor decreasing, and let the silence grow for a moment while he felt the frenzied beating of the pulse beneath his fingers. Gods, how many stimulants had the man taken? Or had the Department merely issued their most potent because one of the commander's arcane calculations had rendered acceptable the odds that Tyl Von sig'Alda would achieve mission success before the accelerants wore out his heart? "Where is the ship?" he demanded.

The man beneath his hands was silent.

Val Con dared to raise himself and look into the other's face. The black eyes glittered with an inward-looking intensity bordering on madness; the face was flushed, the muscles painfully tight. Val Con felt hope flicker. This was a state he knew well: a deep MemStim frenzy. Carefully he took his hands away from the other's throat and sat next to him in the snow.

"Agent Tyl Von sig'Alda," he said, reaching into his memory for the commander's nightmare voice and speaking the High Tongue in the dialect of Ultimate Authority. "You will report as questioned. You will speak to answer questions. You will be silent when ordered. Is that understood?"

"Understood." The ravenous eyes looked upon him without recognition; sweat dewed his upper lip and forehead, and the pulse in his throat beat fast and ever harder.

Val Con willed himself into patience, making himself consider the proper questions and the proper order of asking.

"Timeframe," he said. "Directly before tracking the target to the Winterfair. You landed and secreted your vessel, correct?"

"Correct."

"Exact location, local longitude and latitude."

sig'Alda read the numbers unhesitatingly out of a mind that could not forget them.

Val Con touched his tongue to his lips. "What measures were

taken for concealment?"

"Ship's ambient field." The voice sounded a trifle breathless, as the heartbeat continued to accelerate.

"Detail other protections and solutions."

There were three, detailed entirely, while the voice grew faint and breath came in gasps.

Val Con looked at the man's face, locked as it was in his frenzy, then recalled it, in sharp counterpoint, clouded and confused. Tyl Von sig'Alda, Clan Rugare...

"Describe, briefly, makeup and known antidotes of accelerants ingested within the last one to three hours, as well as the drugs forced upon you by Miri Robertson."

"Lethecronaxion—no known antidote. MemStim—no known antidote. Accelerant—name unknown; antidote unknown; runs system in approximately three hours."

"Loop reading!" Val Con snapped.

"Chance of Mission Success: Point oh one. Chance of Personal Survival: Point oh three...falling— Point oh two, oh one! Chance of Mission Success: Zero!" Horror in the gasping voice. "Chance of Personal Survival—"

"No!" Val Con slapped the mad face before him, trying to pull him out of the trance. "Tyl Von, it lies!"

"Chance of Personal Survival..." The pulse was beyond repair, beyond belief that any heart could beat so and not rip itself to bits.

"Tyl Von sig'Alda, Clan Rugare!"

The man's body spasmed, his back arching as every muscle in his body locked, then slumped back in a bonelessness that had nothing to do with life, pulse and heartbeat gone forever.

After a time, Val Con reached out and closed the staring black eyes, then quickly and efficiently removed everything from the man's pockets, belt, and person. The leather pilot's jacket he left, despite the fact that it was not of Vandar and should not be found there.

"I will tell your Clan," he said, very softly.

He found the palm-gun and Miri's stickknife, slid them away with the other gun, went to Miri, and knelt at her side, laying his fingers against her throat.

She stirred, eyes flickering. "Skel?" she muttered. "Dammit, Skel..." Val Con waited, hovering over her, but the moment subsided before she came to true wakefulness.

Carefully, then, weary in bones and soul, he picked her up and began the long trudge back to the Winterfair, leaving Tyl Von sig'Alda alone and unburied on the hard, dark snow.

VANDAR

Winterfair

The walking was all there was; that and the slender body in his arms. He listened to her breathing, agonized that it was so shallow but joyous that it continued at all. Twice more she stirred and spoke to Skel, directing him once to put her down and go on alone: "s'an *order,* damn you..."

He spoke to her then, hardly heeding what he said, and it seemed that the sound of his voice calmed her. But for most of it, he walked, fighting the snow and a sort of leeching exhaustion, as if his strength were running out a drain rather than being efficiently expended.

It took, in fact, several heartbeats for him to recognize the lanky shape and concerned face before him. He frowned, studying the blondish hair, the bristly mustache, and the myopic blue eyes. "Hakan."

"Cory," the other said carefully. He gestured. "What happened, man?"

"I—" Val Con sighed. "Miri is hurt."

"Alive?"

"Alive," he agreed, feeling the sluggish beat of her heart and hearing the rasp of her breath.

"Right. You stay here and I'll get the fair med—"

"No!"

Hakan froze then frowned. "Cory—"

"She has had—aid. The fair doctor will not do more. I— Hakan, will you take us? It is wrong to ask..."

Understanding dawned in the nearsighted eyes. "Hospital's in Vale, Cory. Sure she can take the ride?"

"She can take the ride," Val Con said, "to the place we need to go."

"Right," Hakan said again. He glanced around, jerking his head at an alleyway between two wooden pavilions. "Shortcut to the parking lot."

"All right," Val Con said, and started walking once more.

Hakan did not speak again until they were clear of the buildings and had started across the field that had that morning been the site of the log-pulls.

"I can carry her, you know," he said, hesitantly. "Give you a rest."

Val Con blinked. Hakan to carry her? Nonkin, when there was her own lifemate to aid her? With an effort, he perceived the kindness of it and the concern for both that had prompted it, and noted his growing weakness. It was imperative that he conserve his strength for the tasks ahead, or Miri's lifemate would fail her at the last.

He smiled up at his friend and nodded. "Thank you."

"No problem." Hakan took his burden gently and set off across the field in a consciously smooth stride.

Val Con followed, fumbling among his store of *L'apeleka* dances. "The Spirit Demands" presented itself and he danced two steps as he walked, his mind encompassing the whole. His heartbeat increased, though not nearly to the level that Tyl Von sig'Alda's had; his breathing deepened; his body began to work with more accustomed efficiency, drawing on stored vitamins and other reserves.

"Thank you, brother," he whispered to the memory of Edger, and stretched his legs to catch up with Hakan.

"Turn right," he said sometime later. Miri was on the seat between them, her head on his knee, a scruffy lap rug tucked around her.

Hakan blinked. "Hospital's in Vale, Cory," he said with a sort of nervous patience. "That's left."

"We go right." Val Con reached into the High Tongue for the proper cadence of authority. Hakan frowned, his mouth straightening stubbornly—and, slowly, turned right.

"Thank you," Val Con said softly, but Hakan only drove on, silent.

Three times they passed spur roads going left, toward Vale and the hospital. Three times Hakan made as if to turn in that direction, and three times Val Con had his way.

The next time, he thought, seeing the determination in Hakan's face, in the set of his hands on the controls. He'll take the next road left, no matter what I say. He sighed to himself. Maddened with grief, I suppose, and don't know what I'm about.

"Skel?" Miri asked and shifted fretfully.

Val Con stroked her wild hair and touched her too-pale cheek. "Skel is not here, cha'trez. Rest now."

But she would not be soothed so easily; she moved her head on his knee and tried to toss the rug off. "Skel!" she insisted. "Damn weather. Damn weatherman. Take readings five times a day and what's the good? Weather ain't *got* a pattern down here, Brunner. World's comin' apart—the *land's* movin', Brunner—like walking on wax. Lost a squad this morning. The hill they were camped on just—fell down..." Her agitation was growing; Hakan glanced over and then back at the road as he touched the accelerator, his face tight with resolve.

Val Con captured the questing hand and held it tightly, one part of him trying to think how to calm her while another coldly and continually counted distance and direction. They must not overshoot the ship.

"Gonna have to ditch the machine, Brunner, you hear me? Unit's pinned—what's left. Told Liz I'd kill the gun—give 'em a chance to get out...What does 'galandaria' mean, anyway?"

"It means," Val Con said softly, stroking her cheek, willing her to be calm, "compatriot—countryman. Miri—it's Val Con, cha'trez—you must rest..."

She stilled abruptly. "Val Con?"

Had she come out of her memories then, back to the present? "Yes."

"Don't leave me, Val Con."

"No," he said, touching her lips lightly. "I won't leave you, Miri."

She sighed then, like a child assured that a dream-monster was well and truly slain, and slipped back into unconsciousness.

"Stop here," Val Con said, and sighed at Hakan's glare of stubborn denial.

"There's nothing here," the musician said flatly. "Just rocks and snow. Miri's *sick,* Cory—she needs a hospital, not a walk in the weather." He turned his eyes back to the road. "There's a turnoff about a half-mile up the road, get us to Vale in a little less than an hour."

"Hakan, stop the car."

The glare this time was less hard-edged, and the car actually did slow a bit.

"Miri is sick," Val Con said softly. "She needs the best medical care it is possible for her to have." He extended a hand. "Am I so mad with grief that I will murder my zhena?"

Hakan looked at him long and hard, then turned away and looked out at the crisp, starry night and the wild tumble of snow-covered rock. "Here?" he asked uncertainly.

"Actually," Val Con said, "approximately a quarter-mile back." He held his breath as the car slowed, stopped, and began to back up.

"Thank you, Hakan," he said softly. But the other only shook his head.

The ship itself was easy to find—merely a matter of following the line of half-filled footsteps back to their source. Val Con held up a hand as the turret beam lit. "Stay here a moment, Hakan," he said, and went on alone, clutching the multi-use key he had taken from Tyl Von sig'Alda's pockets.

The turret rotated, its beam seeking: Val Con twisted the thing in his hand, brought it to his mouth, and blew two sharp notes. After a pause, he added two more.

The turret stopped its rotation. Val Con pulled the portable beacon from his pocket, flashed a series of long-and-shorts at the beam, and sighed with relief when it simply went out.

"All right, Hakan," he called, and went to the ship's belly. He twisted the multikey, used it on the obvious hatch lock, then bent to find the hidden latch and disarm it.

The hatch slid open, silent in the silent night. The interior lights came up, touching the silver snow with gold.

Hakan stood holding Miri in his arms, mouth open. "An—airplane?" he asked doubtfully.

"Aircraft," Val Con corrected softly, and held out his arms. "I will take Miri, Hakan. Thank you for your aid."

"What?" The stubbornness was fully back in Hakan's face. "You have me drive you to an *aircraft* in the middle of nowhere, with Miri hurt and raving, and I'm supposed to just *leave* you here?" He shook his head. "No."

Val Con considered. Balance, after all, was owed. He bowed, very low. "As you wish. Come with me. Quickly."

The 'doc was behind a partition directly opposite the entrance to the control room. Val Con punched the emergency access, and the clear hatch cycled open. He had Hakan lay Miri on the pallet and then forgot him as he stripped off her coat and the bloodstained shirt, pulled off her boots, and peeled the skirt down. He scanned the board, relieved to find that the Department had thought enough of Tyl Von sig'Alda to supply his ship with a top-of-the-line autodoc, then cycled the hatch closed and watched the lights flicker as the 'doc cataloged Miri's injuries, taking blood samples, X rays, and brain scan. A chime sounded, and a line of characters appeared in the screen directly above the observation window.

GUNSHOT WOUND, HIGH RIGHT CHEST. NO FOREIGN BODIES NOTED WITHIN CHEST CAVITY. COMPLICATIONS: BLOOD LOSS, SHOCK, EXPOSURE. TRACES PSYCHOSTIMULATIVE DRUG DETECTED. PROJECTED REPAIR TIME: TWO HOURS FORTY-FIVE MINUTES.

The observation window opaqued. Val Con shuddered, knees sagging. It was going to be all right.

"Cory?" Hakan's voice was not doing well. Val Con straightened and turned to look at his friend.

Hakan's face was unnaturally pale, and he seemed to be trembling.

"Yes."

"Where's Miri?"

Val Con pointed. "In the—healing unit. This—" He touched the readout. "This says that she will be—repaired—in three hours." He smiled slightly. "She will still need to rest and regain her strength, but she will be out of danger."

Hakan frowned. "That machine is fixing Miri, right now?"

"Yes."

The musician nodded, glancing around, then squared his shoulders. "I've seen planes before, Cory—and this isn't a plane."

"No," Val Con said softly. "It's not."

"What is it, then?"

Val Con sighed. "An aircraft, say, Hakan—and now forget that you have seen it."

Hakan stared at him, and Val Con sighed again, moving out of the 'doc cubicle and crossing to the menuboard. "Would you like a cup of tea?"

"Tea?" Hakan shook his head, perhaps to clear it, and then sighed in his turn. "All right, Cory. Tea would be fine."

Val Con requested two—sweet for his guest, plain for himself—then took the cups out of the dispenser and handed one to Hakan. He sipped, astonished at how good the spicy Liaden tea was; then he saw his friend still staring about wild-eyed, and waved him toward the co-pilot's chair.

"Sit down, Hakan, and rest."

Hakan did, gingerly, and sipped his tea with caution. "Where did this come from?" he demanded.

Val Con looked at him levelly. "Out of the kitchen. You saw it."

"I saw you punch a couple buttons on that wall there, and then you handed me this!" The musician closed his eyes and seemed to be concentrating on taking deep breaths. Val Con wandered over to the pilot's station and sat down.

After a time, Hakan opened his eyes and looked at him, very calmly. "Where are you from, Cory?"

Val Con sighed. "Away."

"Not," Hakan insisted, "Porlint."

"No," Val Con agreed. "Not Porlint."

"Where, then?"

"No," Val Con said. "Hakan, I cannot tell you that. Ask me again, and I will lie to you—and I would rather not lie to my friend, to Miri's friend. I should not have brought you here. For anything less than Miri's life, I would not have brought you here." He smiled ruefully. "I have played a sorry joke on you, my friend—you have seen something that you cannot have seen. Not only that, but if you describe this ship—the kitchen, the medical machine—no one will believe you."

"Why not?"

Val Con moved his shoulders. "Can you go to a wall in any house in Gylles, push a few buttons, and get tea, hot and brewed to perfection? When you are hurt or ill, do you go to the doctor and have him slide you into a machine for an hour or two, until you feel better?"

Hakan shook his head.

"So, these things do not exist, do they? Cannot exist, I think Zhena Trelu would say."

Hakan closed his eyes.

Val Con sipped tea, cautiously allowing his body to relax; he ran the Rainbow very quickly and looked up to find Hakan's eyes on him.

"How long has this been here?"

"No more than a day," Val Con said softly. "And it will be gone before the start of another."

Sorrow shaded the mustached face. "You're leaving?"

"We don't belong here any more than this craft does, Hakan. It is an accident that we are here—a happy accident, as it turns out. We found friends and music—and anything that gains us so much is to be thanked."

Silence grew as they both drank their tea. Val Con shifted slightly, drawing the other man's attention back to him. "You should go, Hakan."

"Now? But, I mean, Miri—" He trailed off in confusion.

Val Con considered. "It is not safe to stop the healing once it is started, and Miri might not wake naturally for some hours after the machine releases her. She cannot say good-bye to you, Hakan, though I know she would wish to. I..." He shrugged. "Come back to this spot tomorrow," he said slowly, "and take away what is here." More regulations shattered by whim, he thought ruefully, reaching to touch the other's arm. "Be very careful, my friend."

Tears shone in the blue eyes as Hakan stood. "Kem's never going to forgive me for letting you two get away like this. She—we—love you both."

"And we love you." On some impulse he did not fully understand, Val Con extended a hand and touched one stubbled cheek very lightly, as if they were kin. "I see you, Hakan Meltz." He stood back. "Live in joy, you and Kem—and may all of your children love the music."

"Yeah..." Hakan followed Val Con to the hatch and stood looking out at the night.

"Can you find your way, Hakan? Should I walk with you back to the car?"

"I'll be all right," he said, pulling up his hood. "Just follow the footsteps out, like we did on the way in." He hesitated. "Good night, Cory."

"Good night, Hakan."

Val Con watched until he could no longer see Hakan's outline against the stars and snow, then he sealed the hatch and went back into the ship. The 'doc's timer showed one and a quarter hours still to go on Miri's treatment. Val Con set the ship's clock to wake him in an hour, then reclined in the pilot's chair and went to sleep.

VANDAR

Kosmorn Gore

ADDITIONAL TIME REQUIRED TO COMPLETE REPAIRS: TWENTY-FIVE
MINUTES.

Val Con touched the query button, frowning as the reason for
the additional time took shape on the screen.

BLOOD FILTERING AND RECALIBRATION OF NUTRIENT LEVELS
REQUIRED DUE TO STRONG ADVERSE REACTION TO INGESTION OF
PSYCHOSTIMULATIVE DRUG.

"Psychostimulative drug?" he repeated. Then, face clearing,
"Ah." The Cloud-and-MemStim mix she had flung into Tyl Von's
face; she must have inadvertently swallowed some of it herself. He
shook his head, keying in a request for the doc to send the makeup
of the drug to auxiliary screen three. How had Miri come to have
such a thing? he wondered, and shook his head again. He would
have to wait for her explanation.

He bent and picked up her clothes and shoved them into the
cleaning unit along with his own, adjusting the setting to "superclean" and "repair." The 'fresher also had a "superclean" setting. Val
Con chose it and stepped under the deluge.

The observation port had cleared, allowing a view of a slight, pale
body, a swirl of red hair, and a pair of languorous gray eyes. The
new scar was a smooth patch of pink above her small breast. Val
Con smiled and touched the release.

"Good morning, Miri."

"Hi." Her voice was husky, and she moved her head on the flat
pillow in a half-shake. "Think I don't know how to fall?"

He sighed. "I know that kill so well…"

"Yeah. Me, too." She grinned, a trifle lopsidedly. "Don't teach
your grandma to suck eggs, spacer."

"I would not dare."

She snorted. "Guess not, grandma you got. Feisty old toot, was she?"

"No more than the rest of us," he said softly, touching her face. "Are you hungry, Miri?"

"Could do with a snack." For the first time her eyes left his face and looked at the room beyond his shoulder. "Mind telling me where we are?"

"The agent's ship."

She frowned. "Just us?"

"Just us." He looked away, picking up a lock of copper hair and running it through his fingers, studying the process with intensity. "The agent—died. The Loop lied to him—as it did to me, on Edger's ship, you recall?" He looked back into her eyes.

"Yeah."

He sighed and shook his head. "He had taken stimulants and the—other drugs. The Loop added adrenaline in a massive dose, into a system already overloaded..."

"He had a heart attack," Miri said very quietly.

Val Con nodded. "Tyl Von sig'Alda," he murmured. "Clan Rugare."

She frowned. "You knew him?"

"No. He told me his name." He shook himself out of the memory. "What will you have to eat?"

"Whatever it is, I ain't eating it here," she said with an abrupt return of energy. "What kind of shape my clothes in?"

"The valet was adequate to the task," he told her. "A moment."

He returned almost immediately with her clothes, but she had already squirmed upright and sat with her legs dangling over the edge of the pallet. He shook his head and handed her the shirt, gritting his teeth against his need to help, trusting that she would ask his aid if it was required.

She finished up the buttons, sighed, and looked at the skirt. "Dump that thing over my head, willya?" He did, and she fastened it, then grabbed his arms and slid to her feet. "You didn't get hit, did you, boss?"

"No," he said softly. Then he began more urgently, "Miri, you must never—"

She held up a hand. "Don't say it, okay? Heard you screaming like death, coming up that hill. Ready to jump on him and hack him to pieces, was it?" She sighed and leaned against him, her arms going around his waist with unexpected strength. "Couple certifiables."

After a moment, she stood away from him. "Don't suppose there's any coffee."

"This is a Liaden ship," Val Con said, "so it is doubtful. We might check, however." He offered his arm.

She took it without hesitation, and together they went out into the main room.

There was no coffee, but the tea he ordered for her was nearly as good: dark and spicy and rich. She sipped her second cup half reclined in the copilot's chair, watching Val Con clean up the remains of their meal and wishing her brain would stop asking "Now what?"

He's gonna ask you about the Cloud, Robertson, she told herself. Whether that Tyl Von guy was lying to you or not. He's gonna ask. What're you gonna tell him?

Val Con came back to sit in the pilot's seat, carrying another cup of tea. He settled in and sipped, then lifted his eyes to her face.

Gods, she thought. Gods, please...

"Miri?" he said softly, and she swallowed a deep breath along with some more tea and met his eyes, level.

"Yo."

"Who is Skel?"

She shook her head in surprise. "Skel ain't nobody, boss. He died on Klamath." She took another breath. "Where'd you hear about Skel?"

"You were talking to him rather constantly at one point," Val Con said gently. "Ordering him to put you down and go on."

Miri closed her eyes and leaned her head against the rest. "Way it was supposed to go," she said tonelessly. "Liz's orders. Everybody for themselves, she said." Her voice took on a harsher cadence, as if words and tone were burned into memory forever. "If your partner falls and don't get up, run. If *I* fall—run. If you get hit and fall and it ain't fatal—get up, damn you, and *run!*"

"Miri..."

She opened her eyes, mouth tight with old pain. "'Nother unit—had us pinned with a heat-seek. Wasn't many of us by that time—twenty-five, twenty-six. Needed somebody to kill the gun, see? And I told Liz I'd do it." The eyes closed again, and she took a shuddering breath. "Made sense—I was smallest, fastest. Best choice. Liz saw it; said okay. Skel—he waited, after the gun blew. I took a hit on the way back, then the—the land moved—was movin' a lot, by then. Rocks fell—busted both my legs. Skel carried me. Got me to Liz before he got hit himself. Then *she* carried me, like she'd ordered us not to."

She sighed, her eyes opening to stare up at the ceiling. "Liz, Scandal, Mac, Win, me. Five. Klamath killed everybody else. Wasn't for the weatherman, we'd been dead, too."

She touched the chair's control and brought herself upright. "Never got a chance to thank him—Brunner, his name was. Ichliad Brunner. Don't know his Clan. Faked a report or something— never got the right of it—made the station send in shuttles—pulled off maybe five hundred, all told, before everything went to hell. Heard he got in trouble, later…"

"Miri…" He was standing over her, one hand half extended, pain and sorrow in his face. Her heart twisted in her chest, and she clenched her jaw against the wrenching need for him.

"You better hear the rest of it."

"Later." He touched her jaw, his fingers stroking the tight muscles.

"Now," she said, pulling her head back. His hand dropped to his side, wariness joining the other troubles in his face. Miri sighed. "Ain't much more."

"All right," he said softly, his eyes on hers. "Tell me the rest of it."

"Finished up in the hospital, got my legs back in shape. Wasn't sleeping so good—nightmares. Got to thinking about how every-body I knew was dead and how I *should've* been dead. Got to drink-ing too much kynak, but that just made the memories clearer, see? Tried a couple other things, trying to shake the memories—all the dead faces. Finally got hold of some Cloud. The memories went away. I could sleep and think and I wasn't so—sad—anymore." She sighed. "But the Cloud would wear off, and the memories would hurt worse than ever, 'cause you just put 'em on hold for a little while, you don't turn 'em off completely."

She broke his gaze and looked into the empty teacup, then looked back into his eyes. "I took a lot of Cloud."

There was silence. Val Con stood, apparently willing to hear even more. Miri sighed and forced herself to finish.

"Liz got me in a rehab program—took a long time, but I kicked it. Most people, with Cloud, they never made it back out." She gave a harsh bark of laughter. "My luck."

"Ah," he said.

"What in *hell* does that mean?" Tears, sudden and appalling, ran down her cheeks and dripped off her chin. She lifted a hand and scrubbed at them as Val Con came over and perched on the edge of the chair, facing her.

"It means," he said softly, "that, if I had been on Klamath, seen a world shake apart and my unit—my friends, my lovers, my family—die, I might wish to forget, also."

She shook her head. "That Tyl Von brought me a pack of Cloud, when I went out to calm down. Said it was from you, for doing my job so good."

"Must I say that he lied?" Val Con asked. He sighed. "The packet that he gave you was a mixture, Miri—half Cloud, half MemStim—a drug that is given agents when they report. It stimulates complete recall."

Her eyes widened. "No wonder he had a heart attack. From forgetting everything to remembering everything? It'd pull his brain apart!" She stopped. "Hell."

Val Con nodded. When several minutes had passed and she said no more, he touched her hand. "Have I now heard everything that I must hear this evening, Miri? For I think you should sleep so you may continue healing."

She stared at him. It's all right, Robertson, she told herself. It's really all right.

Peace, as shocking and unexpected as her tears, flooded in, and she leaned forward to hug him and put her cheek against his. "I think I ought to go to sleep and continue healing, too, now that you mention it. But if you want me to sleep anywhere but here, you're gonna have to carry me."

"That," Val Con said, "can be arranged."

VANDAR

Kosmorn Gore

Sunlight glittered off the snow-covered rocks, bringing tears to Kem's eyes as she followed Hakan. If the whole thing were not so wild—but, there. Miri hurt, and Hakan and Cory bringing her out here, and Cory putting her in a doctor machine…and cups of tea coming out of a wall and panels of lights in an aircraft that was like no aircraft possible.

Kem shook her head and squinted ahead, looking for the aircraft. Something as big as Hakan had described should certainly be visible in the bright sunshine.

Ahead of her, Hakan stopped, staring at an oblong depression in the snow. She came to his side and slid her hand into his.

"It's gone," he said, and looked at her, desolation in his eyes. "They're gone, Kemmy."

She looked at him helplessly, then looked back at the depression, squinted against the glare, and pointed. "What's that, Hakan?"

It turned out to be a flat wooden box, with a fitted, sliding top. When they slid the top back, a strong, spicy aroma was released, somewhat reminiscent of tea. Inside was a sheet of paper and a pouch.

"Dear Hakan and Kem," the note began, in Miri's slanting, rounded letters.

> *"We're sorry we have to leave before you can see us again. Please believe that I am much better and that I'm not going to die, probably for a long, long time, so pity Cory. In the box is also the money we got from the king for being heroes. There is different money in the place we're going to, so you use this. Please. Hakan, I'm sorry we couldn't finish the last set. You're a good musician and a good friend. Remember to always play for joy. Kem, I owe you so much! I'm sorry we put you and Hakan to such trouble. Thank you both for all your help. Tell Zhena Trelu we won't bother her anymore. We love you. Miri."*

There were several blank lines, then in a sharp, backhand script: *"Be well and be joyful, both of you. We'll miss you and think of you often, with love. May the music never stop for either of you. Cory."*

That was all. Kem blinked back tears and looked up from the letter to see Hakan pacing around the oblong indentation, peering carefully off in all directions. She went to him. "What is it?"

He pointed at the unmarked snow all around. "No running start," he said. "He lifted that *aircraft* of his straight up!"

She looked at his face, around at the snow, up at the sky, and back at his face, worriedly. "Is that possible, Hakan?"

He started to say something but instead shut his mouth and looked at her for a long, long time. Then he reached out and hugged her to him, pushing his face into her hair.

"No," he whispered. "No, it isn't."

Son of Authorial Denial

Liadens like to count things by the dozen. Steve holds that this has to do with the strong mercantile history of the race, in which—of course—lots of twelve would be the rule. Sharon's theory is perhaps best left undiscussed at this time.

Be that as it may, the appearance of *Partners In Necessity* marks a very special dozen for us, for twelve years ago this month—that is to say, in February, 1988—our first novel, a quirky little space opera called *Agent of Change*, made its appearance in bookstores.

Those of you who have been playing along at home know that *Agent* is, in fact, the second book in the Liaden series, following the action in *Conflict of Honors* by seven Standard years. That *Agent* was published first is our fault—we wrote it first, and sent it out into the world to woo an editor, a project that did not meet with... immediate...success.

While *Agent* was shopping for a publisher, we became interested in the character of Val Con's cousin and foster-brother, Shan, and started writing what we fondly believed would be a short story, as a background exploration. When next we looked up, we'd written a novel and had met not only Shan yos'Galan, but Priscilla Delacroix y Mendoza and all the rest of the varied crew of the *Dutiful Passage*.

Well, it was a book, so we dressed it up in its best manuscript style and mailed it off to the publisher currently considering *Agent*, who—surprise!—bought both and reasonably enough published them in the order received.

We're pleased that Stephe Pagel agreed to re-publish the books in "universe order"—*Conflict of Honors* first—and we're grateful that he has allowed a small scene that was excised by the previous editor to be re-inserted into the novel. Small though it is, it means a lot to us, and we're delighted to see the novel "whole" again.

Over the years, we've been distressed for those who, having read *Agent* and *Carpe Diem,* found all the tea in Solcintra insufficient to purchase a copy of *Conflict*. We've marveled at those others, who've become fans of the Liaden Universe on the basis of reading only *Carpe Diem*. It's extremely satisfying that the first three books are now equally available to everyone; free at last from the vagaries of regional distribution systems.

We're especially pleased, on this, our twelfth anniversary as novelists, to observe the stalwart friendships our characters have forged. We could wish them no better than the friends they have made for themselves.

Joy to all.

Sharon Lee and Steve Miller
August 1999

ABOUT THE AUTHORS

Sharon Lee and Steve Miller live in the rolling hills of Central Maine. Born and raised in Baltimore, Maryland, they met several times before taking the hint and formalizing the team in 1979. They removed to Maine with cats, books, and music following the completion of *Carpe Diem*, their third novel.

Their short fiction, written both jointly and singly, has appeared or will appear in numerous anthologies and magazines, including *Such a Pretty Face, Stars, Murder by Magic, Women of War, Absolute Magnitude, 3SF*, and several incarnations of *Amazing*.

Meisha Merlin Publishing has or will be publishing twelve novels cleverly disguised as ten books in Steve and Sharon's Liaden Universe®—*Partners in Necessity, Plan B, Pilots Choice, I Dare, Balance of Trade, Crystal Soldier, Crystal Dragon—The Tomorrow Log*, first of the Gem ser Edreth adventures, and the anthology *Low Port*, edited by Sharon and Steve. Sharon has also seen a mystery novel, *Barnburner*, published by Embiid in electronic and SRM Publisher, Ltd in paper.

I Dare, The Tomorrow Log, and *Balance of Trade* have been Locus magazine bestsellers. *Pilots Choice* (including novels *Local Custom* and *Scout's Progress*) was a finalist for the Pearl Award. *Local Custom* took second place in the 2002 Prism Awards for best futuristic romance, while *Scout's Progress* took first place. *Scout's Progress* has also won the *Romantic Times Bookclub* Reviewer's Choice Award for the best science fiction novel of 2002. In 2005, Balance of Trade received the Hal Clement Award for the best young adult science fiction novel of 2004.

Both Sharon and Steve have seen their non-fiction work and reviews published in a variety of newspapers and magazines. Steve was the founding curator of the University of Maryland's Kuhn Library Science Fiction Research Collection, and former Nebula Award juror. Sharon served the Science Fiction and Fantasy Writers of America, Inc. for five years, as executive director, vice president and president.

Sharon's interests include music, pine cone collecting, and seashores. Steve also enjoys music, plays chess, and collects cat whiskers. Both spend 'way too much time playing on the internet and have a web site at: www.korval.com.

More Liaden Universe® novels

Plan B
ISBN: 1-892065-00-2
Trade Edition: $14

Pilots Choice
ISBN: 1-892065-02-9
Trade Edition: $20

I Dare
ISBN: 1-892065-03-7
Trade Edition: $16

by Sharon Lee and Steve Miller

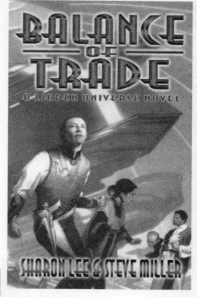

Balance of Trade
ISBN: 1-59222-020-7
Trade Edition: $16.95
ISBN: 1-59222-019-3
Hardcover Edition: $25

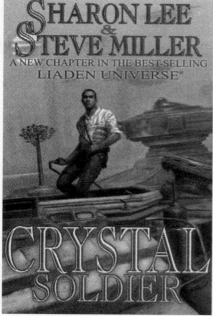

Crystal Soldier:
Book One of
the Great Migration
Duology
ISBN: 1-59222-084-3
Trade Edition: $16.95

Crystal Dragon:
Book Two of
the Great Migration Duology
ISBN: 1-59222-090-8
Trade Edition: $16.95
Feb. 2007

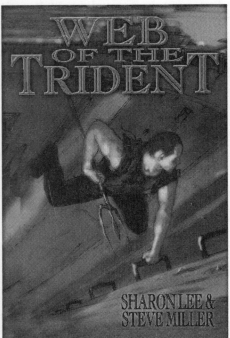